PRAISE FOR
JOHN LE CARRÉ

"No other contemporary novelist has more durably enjoyed [the] twin badges of being both well-read and well-regarded."
—Scott Turow

"They keep calling him a spy novelist, but of course he is much more; he is, indeed, one of a half-dozen best novelists now working in English."
—*Chicago Sun-Times*

"The finest imaginative social historian of the postwar years."
—*The Times Literary Supplement* (London)

"A master storyteller whose narratives purr by with the smooth whoosh of a Bentley . . . The most interesting English novelist alive for his discussion of the quest for absolutes in an ambiguous, secular age."
—*Time*

"Le Carré has no peer in selecting, sorting, and sifting states of mind from the murky world of espionage."
—*The Christian Science Monitor*

"John le Carré is one of our best living novelists."
—*New Statesman*

BOOKS BY JOHN LE CARRÉ

CALL FOR THE DEAD
A MURDER OF QUALITY
THE SPY WHO CAME IN FROM THE COLD
THE LOOKING GLASS WAR
A SMALL TOWN IN GERMANY
THE NAIVE AND SENTIMENTAL LOVER*
TINKER, TAILOR, SOLDIER, SPY*
THE HONOURABLE SCHOOLBOY*
SMILEY'S PEOPLE*
THE LITTLE DRUMMER GIRL*
A PERFECT SPY*
THE RUSSIA HOUSE*
THE SECRET PILGRIM
THE NIGHT MANAGER
OUR GAME
THE TAILOR OF PANAMA
SINGLE & SINGLE*

*AVAILABLE FROM POCKET BOOKS

For orders other than by individual consumers, Pocket Books grants a discount on the purchase of **10 or more** copies of single titles for special markets or premium use. For further details, please write to the Vice President of Special Markets, Pocket Books, 1230 Avenue of the Americas, 9th Floor, New York, NY 10020-1586.

For information on how individual consumers can place orders, please write to Mail Order Department, Simon & Schuster Inc., 100 Front Street, Riverside, NJ 08075.

JOHN
LE CARRÉ

THE RUSSIA
HOUSE

POCKET BOOKS

New York   London   Toronto   Sydney   Singapore

This book is a work of fiction. Names, characters, places, and incidents are
products of the author's imagination or are used fictitiously. Any resemblance to actual events or locales or persons, living or dead, is entirely
coincidental.

Grateful acknowledgement is made to the following for permission to
reprint previously published material

New Directions Publishing Corporation: Excerpt from "Dirge" by
Stevie Smith from *The Collected Poems of Stevie Smith*. Copyright © 1972 by
Stevie Smith. Reprinted by permission of New Directions Publishing
Corporation.

W. W. Norton & Co., Inc.: Brief excerpt from *Journal of a Solitude* by
May Sarton. Copyright © 1973 by May Sarton. Reprinted by permission of
W. W. Norton & Co., Inc.

Penguin Books Ltd.: Excerpt from "Nobel Prize" from *Selected Poems* by
Boris Pasternak, translated by Jon Stallworthy and Peter France (Allen
Lane, 1983). Copyright © 1983 by Peter France. Reprinted by permission
of Penguin Books Ltd., London.

POCKET BOOKS, a division of Simon & Schuster Inc.
1230 Avenue of the Americas, New York, NY 10020

Copyright © 1989 by David Cornwell

Published by arrangement with Alfred A. Knopf, Inc.

ISBN: 0-671-04279-3

First Pocket Books printing May 2000

10 9 8 7 6 5 4 3 2 1

POCKET and colophon are registered trademarks of
Simon & Schuster Inc.

Cover design by Tony Greco

Printed in the U.S.A.

For Bob Gottlieb,
a great editor and a long-suffering friend

Indeed, I think that people want peace so much that one of these days governments had better get out of their way and let them have it.

DWIGHT D. EISENHOWER

One must think like a hero to behave like a merely decent human being.

MAY SARTON

Foreword

Acknowledgements in novels can be as tedious as credits at the cinema, yet I am constantly touched by the willingness of busy people to give their time and wisdom to such a frivolous undertaking as mine, and I cannot miss this opportunity to thank them.

I recall with particular gratitude the help of Strobe Talbott, the illustrious Washington journalist, Sovietologist and writer on nuclear defence. If there are errors in this book, they are surely not his, and there would have been many more without him. Professor Lawrence Freedman, the author of several standard works on the modern conflict, also allowed me to sit at his feet, but must not be blamed for my simplicities.

Frank Gerrity, for many years an agent of the Federal Bureau of Investigation, introduced me to the mysteries of the lie detector, now sadly called the polygraph, and if my characters are not as complimentary about its powers as he is, the reader should blame them, not him.

I must also offer a disclaimer on behalf of John Roberts and his staff at the Great Britain—USSR Association, of which he is Director. It was he who accompanied me on my first visit to the USSR, opening all sorts of doors for me that might otherwise have stayed shut. But he knew nothing of my dark intent, neither did he probe. Of his staff, I may mention particularly Anne Vaughan.

My Soviet hosts at the Writers' Union showed a similar discretion, and a largeness of spirit that took me by surprise. Nobody who visits the Soviet Union in these extraordinary years, and is privileged to conduct the conversations that were granted me, can come away without an enduring love for its people and a sense of awe at the scale of the problems that face them. I hope that my Soviet friends will find reflected in this fable a little of the warmth that I felt in their company, and of the hopes we shared for a saner and more companionable future.

Jazz is a great unifier and I did not want for friends when it came to Barley's saxophone. Wally Fawkes, the celebrated cartoonist and jazz player, lent me his musician's ear, and John Calley his perfect pitch both in words and music. If such men would only run the world, I should have no more conflicts to write about.

1

In a broad Moscow street not two hundred yards from
the Leningrad station, on the upper floor of an ornate
and hideous hotel built by Stalin in the style known to
Muscovites as Empire During the Plague, the British
Council's first ever audio fair for the teaching of the
English language and the spread of British culture was
grinding to its excruciating end. The time was half past
five, the summer weather erratic. After fierce rain showers all day long, a false sunlight was blazing in the puddles and raising vapour from the pavements. Of the
passers-by, the younger ones wore jeans and sneakers, but
their elders were still huddled in their warms.

The room the Council had rented was not expensive
but neither was it appropriate to the occasion. I have seen
it. Not long ago, in Moscow on quite another mission, I
tiptoed up the great empty staircase and, with a diplomatic passport in my pocket, stood in the eternal dusk
that shrouds old ballrooms when they are asleep. With
its plump brown pillars and gilded mirrors, it was better
suited to the last hours of a sinking liner than the launch
of a great initiative. On the ceiling, snarling Russians in
proletarian caps shook their fists at Lenin. Their vigour
contrasted unhelpfully with the chipped green racks of

sound cassettes along the walls, featuring *Winnie-the-Pooh* and *Advanced Computer English in Three Hours*. The sackcloth sound-booths, locally procured and lacking many of their promised features, had the sadness of deck chairs on a rainy beach. The exhibitors' stands, crammed under the shadow of an overhanging gallery, seemed as blasphemous as betting shops in a tabernacle.

Nevertheless a fair of sorts had taken place. People had come, as Moscow people do, provided they have the documents and status to satisfy the hard-eyed boys in leather jackets at the door. Out of politeness. Out of curiosity. To talk to Westerners. Because it is there. And now on the fifth and final evening the great farewell cocktail party of exhibitors and invited guests was getting into its stride. A handful of the small *nomenklatura* of the Soviet cultural bureaucracy was gathering under the chandelier, the ladies in their beehive hairstyles and flowered frocks designed for slenderer frames, the gentlemen slimmed by the shiny French-tailored suits that signified access to the special clothing stores. Only their British hosts, in despondent shades of grey, observed the monotone of Socialist austerity. The hubbub rose, a brigade of pinafored governesses distributed the curling salami sandwiches and warm white wine. A senior British diplomat who was not quite the Ambassador shook the better hands and said he was delighted.

Only Niki Landau among them had withheld himself from the celebrations. He was stooped over the table in his empty stand, totting up his last orders and checking his dockets against expenses, for it was a maxim of Landau's never to go out and play until he had wrapped up his day's business.

And in the corner of his eye—an anxious blue blur was all that she amounted to—this Soviet woman he was deliberately ignoring. *Trouble,* he was thinking as he laboured. *Avoid.*

The air of festivity had not communicated itself to Landau, festive by temperament though he was. For one thing, he had a lifelong aversion to British officialdom, ever since his father had been forcibly returned to Poland. The British themselves, he told me later, he would hear no wrong of them. He was one of them by adoption and he had the poker-backed reverence of the convert. But the Foreign Office flunkies were another matter. And the loftier they were, and the more they twitched and smirked and raised their stupid eyebrows at him, the more he hated them and thought about his dad. For another thing, if he had been left to himself, he would never have come to the audio fair in the first place. He'd have been tucked up in Brighton with a nice new little friend he had, called Lydia, in a nice little private hotel he knew for taking little friends.

"Better to keep our powder dry till the Moscow book fair in September," Landau had advised his clients at their headquarters on the Western by-pass. "The Russkies love a book, you see, Bernard, but the audio market scares them and they aren't geared for it. Go in with the book fair, we'll clean up. Go in with the audio fair, we're dead."

But Landau's clients were young and rich and did not believe in death. "Niki boy," said Bernard, walking round behind him and putting a hand on his shoulder, which Landau didn't like, "in the world today, we've got to show the flag. We're patriots, see, Niki? Like you. That's why we're an offshore company. With the *glasnost* today, the Soviet Union, it's the Mount Everest of the recording business. And you're going to put us on the top, Niki. Because if you're not, we'll find somebody who will.

Somebody younger, Niki, right? Somebody with the drive and the class."

The drive Landau had still. But the class, as he himself was the first to tell you, the class, forget it. He was a card, that's what he liked to be. A pushy, short-arsed Polish card and proud of it. He was Old Nik the cheeky chappie of the Eastward-facing reps, capable, he liked to boast, of selling filthy pictures to a Georgian convent or hair tonic to a Roumanian billiard ball. He was Landau the undersized bedroom athlete, who wore raised heels to give his Slav body the English scale he admired, and ritzy suits that whistled "here I am." When Old Nik set up his stand, his travelling colleagues assured our unattributable enquirers, you could hear the tinkle of the handbell on his Polish vendor's barrow.

And little Landau shared the joke with them, he played their game. "Boys, I'm the Pole you wouldn't touch with a barge," he would declare proudly as he ordered up another round. Which was his way of getting them to laugh with him. Instead of at him. And then most likely, to demonstrate his point, he would whip a comb from his top pocket and drop into a crouch. And with the aid of a picture on the wall, or any other polished surface, he'd sweep back his too black hair in preparation for fresh conquest, using both his little hands to coax it into manliness. "Who's that comely one I'm looking at over there in the corner then?" he'd ask, in his godless blend of ghetto Polish and East End cockney. "Hullo there, sweetheart! Why are we suffering all alone tonight?" And once out of five times he'd score, which in Landau's book was an acceptable rate of return, always provided you kept asking.

But this evening Landau wasn't thinking of scoring or even asking. He was thinking that yet again he had worked his heart out all week for a pittance——or, as he put it more graphically to me, a tart's kiss. And that every fair these days, whether it was a book fair or an audio fair or any other kind of fair, took a little more out of him than he liked to admit to himself, just as every woman did. And gave him a fraction too little in return. And that tomorrow's plane back to London couldn't come too soon. And that if this Russian bird in blue didn't stop insinuating herself into his attention when he was trying to close his books and put on his party smile and join the jubilant throng, he would very likely say something to her in her own language that both of them would live to regret.

That she was Russian went without saying. Only a Russian woman would have a plastic perhaps-bag dangling from her arm in readiness for the chance purchase that is the triumph of everyday life, even if most perhaps-bags were of string. Only a Russian would be so nosy as to stand close enough to check a man's arithmetic. And only a Russian would preface her interruption with one of those fastidious grunts, which in a man always reminded Landau of his father doing up his shoe laces, and in a woman, Harry, bed.

"Excuse me, sir. Are you the gentleman from Abercrombie & Blair?" she asked.

"Not here, dear," said Landau without lifting his head. She had spoken English, so he had spoken English in return, which was the way he played it always.

"Mr. Barley?"

"Not Barley, dear. Landau."

"But this is Mr. Barley's stand."

"This is not Barley's stand. This is my stand. Abercrombie & Blair are next door."

Still without looking up, Landau jabbed his pencil-end

to the left, towards the empty stand on the other side of the partition, where a green-and-gold board proclaimed the ancient publishing house of Abercrombie & Blair of Norfolk Street, Strand.

"But that stand is empty. No one is there," the woman objected. "It was empty yesterday also."

"Correct. Right on," Landau retorted in a tone that was final enough for anybody. And he ostentatiously lowered himself further into his account book, waiting for the blue blur to remove itself. Which was rude of him, he knew, and her continuing presence made him feel ruder.

"But where is Scott Blair? Where is the man they call Barley? I must speak to him. It is very urgent."

Landau was by now hating the woman with unreasoning ferocity.

"*Mr.* Scott Blair," he began as he snapped up his head and stared at her full on, "more commonly known to his intimates as Barley, is *awol*, madam. That means absent without leave. His company booked a stand—yes. And Mr. Scott Blair is chairman, president, governor-general and for all I know lifetime dictator of that company. However, he did not occupy his stand—" But here, having caught her eye, he began to lose his footing. "Listen, dear, I happen to be trying to make a living here, right? I am not making it for Mr. Barley Scott Blair, love him as I may."

Then he stopped, as a chivalrous concern replaced his momentary anger. The woman was trembling. Not only with the hands that held her brown perhaps-bag but also at the neck, for her prim blue dress was finished with a collar of old lace and Landau could see how it shook against her skin and how her skin was actually whiter than the lace. Yet her mouth and jaw were set with determination and her expression commanded him.

"Please, sir, you must be very kind and help me," she said as if there were no choice.

Now Landau prided himself on knowing women. It was another of his irksome boasts but it was not without foundation. "Women, they're my hobby, my life's study and my consuming passion, Harry," he confided to me, and the conviction in his voice was as solemn as a Mason's pledge. He could no longer tell you how many he had had, but he was pleased to say that the figure ran into the hundreds and there was not one of them who had cause to regret the experience. "I play straight, I choose wisely, Harry," he assured me, tapping one side of his nose with his forefinger. "No cut wrists, no broken marriages, no harsh words afterwards." How true this was nobody would ever know, myself included, but there can be no doubt that the instincts that had guided him through his philanderings came rushing to his assistance as he formed his judgments about the woman.

She was earnest. She was intelligent. She was determined. She was scared, even though her dark eyes were lit with humour. And she had that rare quality which Landau in his flowery way liked to call the Class That Only Nature Can Bestow. In other words, she had quality as well as strength. And since in moments of crisis our thoughts do not run consecutively but rather sweep over us in waves of intuition and experience, he sensed all these things at once and was on terms with them by the time she spoke to him again.

"A Soviet friend of mine has written a creative and important work of literature," she said after taking a deep breath. "It is a novel. A great novel. Its message is important for all mankind."

She had dried up.

"A novel," Landau prompted. And then, for no reason

he could afterwards think of, "What's its title, dear?"

The strength in her, he decided, came neither from bravado nor insanity but from conviction.

"What's its message then, if it hasn't got a title?"

"It concerns actions before words. It rejects the gradualism of the *perestroika*. It demands action and rejects all cosmetic change."

"Nice," said Landau, impressed.

She spoke like my mother used to, Harry: chin up and straight into your face.

"In spite of *glasnost* and the supposed liberalism of the new guidelines, my friend's novel cannot yet be published in the Soviet Union," she continued. "Mr. Scott Blair has undertaken to publish it with discretion."

"Lady," said Landau kindly, his face now close to hers. "If your friend's novel is published by the great house of Abercrombie & Blair, believe me, you can be assured of total secrecy."

He said this partly as a joke he couldn't resist and partly because his instincts told him to take the stiffness out of their conversation and make it less conspicuous to anybody watching. And whether she understood the joke or not, the woman smiled also, a swift warm smile of self-encouragement that was like a victory over her fears.

"Then, Mr. Landau, if you love peace please take this manuscript with you back to England and give it immediately to Mr. Scott Blair. Only to Mr. Scott Blair. It is a gift of trust."

What happened next happened quickly, a street-corner transaction, willing seller to willing buyer. The first thing Landau did was look behind her, past her shoulder. He did that for his own preservation as well as hers. It was his experience that when the Russkies wanted to get up to a piece of mischief, they always had other people close by. But his end of the assembly room was empty, the area beneath the gallery where the stands were was dark and the party at the centre of the room was by now in full cry. The three boys in leather jackets at the front door were talking stodgily among themselves.

His survey completed, he read the girl's plastic name badge on her lapel, which was something he would normally have done earlier but her black-brown eyes had distracted him. Yekaterina Orlova, he read. And underneath, the word "October," given in both English and Russian, this being the name of one of Moscow's smaller State publishing houses specialising in translations of Soviet books for export, mainly to other Socialist countries, which I am afraid condemned it to a certain dowdiness.

Next he told her what to do, or perhaps he was already telling her by the time he read her badge. Landau was a street kid, up to all the tricks. The woman might be as brave as six lions and by the look of her probably was. But she was no conspirator. Therefore he took her unhesitatingly into his protection. And in doing so he spoke to her as he would to any woman who needed his basic counsel, such as where to find his hotel bedroom or what to tell her hubby when she got home.

"Got it with you then, have you, dear?" he asked, peering down at the perhaps-bag and smiling like a friend.

"Yes."

"In there, is it?"

"Yes."

"Then give me the whole bag normally," Landau said, talking her through her act. "That's the way. Now give me a friendly Russian kiss. The formal sort. Nice. You've brought me an official farewell gift on the last evening of the fair, you see. Something that will cement Anglo-Soviet relations and make me overweight on the flight home unless I dump it in the dustbin at the airport. Very normal transaction. I must have received half a dozen such gifts today already."

Part of this was spoken while he crouched with his back to her. For, reaching into the bag, he had already slipped out the brown-paper parcel that was inside it and was dropping it deftly into his briefcase, which was of the home filing variety, very compendious, with compartments that opened in a fan.

"Married, are we, Katya?"

No answer. Maybe she hadn't heard. Or she was too busy watching him.

"Is it your husband who's written the novel, then?" said Landau, undeterred by her silence.

"It is dangerous for you," she whispered. "You must believe in what you are doing. Then everything is clear."

As if he had not heard this warning at all, Landau selected, from a pile of samples that he had kept to give away tonight, a four-pack of the Royal Shakespeare Company's specially commissioned reading of *A Midsummer Night's Dream,* which he placed ostentatiously on the table and signed for her on the plastic casing with a felt-tip pen: "From Niki to Katya, Peace," and the date. Then he put the four-pack ceremoniously into the perhaps-bag for her, and gathered the handles of the bag together and pressed them into her hand, because she was becoming lifeless and he was worried she might break down or cease to function. Only then did he give her the reassurance that she seemed to be asking for, while he continued to hold her hand, which was cold, he told me, but nice.

"All of us have got to do something risky now and then, haven't we, dear?" Landau said lightly. "Going to adorn the party, are we?"

"No."

"Like a nice dinner out somewhere?"

"It is not convenient."

"You want me to take you to the door?"

"It doesn't matter."

"I think we've got to smile, dear," he said, still in English as he walked her across the room, chatting to her like the good salesman he had once again become.

Reaching the great landing, he shook her hand. "See you at the book fair, then? September. And thanks for warning me, okay? I'll bear it in mind. Still, the main thing is, we've got a deal. Which is always nice. Right?"

She took his hand and seemed to draw courage from it, for she smiled again and her smile was dazed but grateful, and almost irresistibly warm.

"My friend has made a great gesture," she explained as she pushed back an unruly lock of hair. "Please be sure that Mr. Barley is aware of this."

"I'll tell him. Don't you worry," said Landau jauntily.

He would have liked another smile just for himself, but she had lost interest in him. She was delving in her bag for her card, which he knew she had forgotten till this moment. "ORLOVA, Yekaterina Borisovna," it read, in Cyrillic one side and Roman the other, again with the name "October" in both renderings. She gave it to him, then walked stiffly down the pompous staircase, head up and one hand on the broad marble balustrade, the other hand trailing the perhaps-bag. The boys in leather jackets watched her all the way down to the hall. And Landau, while he popped the card into his top pocket with the half-dozen others he'd collected in the last two hours, saw them watch her and gave the boys a wink. And the boys after due reflection winked back at him, because this was the new season of openness when a pair of good Russian hips could be acknowledged for what they were, even to a foreigner.

For the fifty minutes of revelry that remained, Niki Landau threw his heart into the party. Sang and danced for a grim-faced Scottish librarian in pearls. Recited a witty political anecdote about Mrs. Thatcher for a pair of pale listeners from the State Copyright Agency, VAAP, till they suddenly emitted wild laughter. Buttered up three ladies from Progress Publishers and, in a series of nimble journeys to his briefcase, presented each with a memento of his stay, for Landau was a natural giver and remembered names and promises, just as he remembered so many other things, with the directness of an unencumbered mind. But all the while he kept the briefcase unobtrusively in view, and even before the guests had left, he was holding it in his spare hand while he made his farewells. And when he boarded the private bus that was waiting to take the reps back to their hotel, he sat with it on his knees while he joined in a tuneful unison of rugby songs, led as usual by Spikey Morgan.

"Ladies present now, boys," Landau warned and, standing up, commanded silence at the passages that he considered too broad. But even when he was playing the great conductor he contrived to keep a firm grip on the briefcase.

At the hotel entrance the usual gaggle of pimps, drug-pushers and currency dealers hung around and, together with their KGB minders, watched the group enter. But Landau saw nothing in their behaviour to concern him, whether over-watchful or over-casual. The crippled old warrior who guarded the passageway to the lifts demanded as usual to see his hotel pass, but when Landau, who had already presented him with a hundred Marlboros, asked him accusingly in Russian why he wasn't out flirting with his girlfriend tonight, he gave a rasping laugh and punched him on the shoulder in good-fellowship.

"If they're trying to frame me, I thought, they'd better be quick about it or the trail will be cold, Harry," he told me, taking the part of the opposition rather than his own. "When you frame, Harry, you've got to move in fast while the evidence is still planted on the victim," he explained, as if he had been framing people all his life.

"Bar of the National, nine o'clock then," Spikey Morgan said to him wearily when they had fought their way out at the fourth floor.

"Could be, could be not, Spikey," Landau replied. "I'm not quite myself, to be honest."

"Thank God for that," said Spikey through a yawn, and plodded off into his own dark corridor watched by the evil-eyed floor concierge in her horsebox.

Reaching his bedroom door Landau braced himself before putting the key into the lock. They'd do it now, he thought. Here and now would be the best time to snatch me and the manuscript.

But when he stepped inside, the room was empty and undisturbed and he felt foolish for having suspected it of being any different. Still alive, he thought, and set the briefcase on the bed.

Then he pulled the handkerchief-sized curtains as close as they would go, which was halfway, and hung the useless "Do Not Disturb" notice on the door, which he then locked. He emptied the pockets of his suit, including the pocket where he stored incoming business cards, pulled off his jacket and tie, his metal armbands, finally

his shirt. From the fridge he poured himself half an inch
of lemon vodka and took a sip. Landau was not a drinker
really, he explained to me, but when in Moscow he did
like a nice lemon vodka to end his day. Taking his glass to
the bathroom, he stood before the mirror and for a good
ten minutes anxiously examined the roots of his hair for
signs of white, touching out offending spots with the aid
of a new formula that was working wonders. Having
completed this labour to his satisfaction, he bound his
skull with an elaborate rubber turban like a bathing cap
and showered, while he sang "I am the very model of a
modern major-general" rather well. Then he towelled
himself, vigorously for the sake of his muscle-tone,
slipped into a bold flowered bathrobe and marched back
to the bedroom still singing.

And he did these things partly because he always did
them and needed the steadying familiarity of his own
routines, but partly also because he was proud of having
thrown caution to the winds for once and not found
twenty-five sound reasons for doing nothing, which these
days he might have done.

She was a lady, she was afraid, she needed help, Harry.
When did Niki Landau ever refuse a lady? And if he was
wrong about her, well then she'd made a crying fool of
him and he might as well pack up his toothbrush and
report himself at the front door of the Lubyanka for five
years' study of their excellent graffiti without the option.
Because he'd rather be made a fool of twenty times over
than turn away that woman without a reason. And so
saying, if only in his mind, for he was always alert to the
possibility of microphones, Landau drew her parcel from
the briefcase and with a certain shyness set to work unty-
ing the string but not cutting it, just the way he had
been taught by his sainted mother, whose photograph at

this moment nestled faithfully in his wallet. They've got the same glow, he thought in pleasant recognition as he worried patiently at the knot. It's the Slav skin. It's the Slav eyes, the smile. Two nice Slav girls together. The only difference was that Katya hadn't finished up in Treblinka.

The knot finally yielded. Landau coiled up the string and laid it on the bed. I have to know, you see, dear, he explained to the woman Yekaterina Borisovna in his mind. I don't want to pry, I'm not the nosy one, but if I've got to con my way through Moscow customs, I'd better know what I'm conning them out of, because it helps.

Delicately so as not to tear it, using both hands, Landau parted the brown paper. He did not see himself as any sort of a hero, or not yet. What was a danger to a Moscow beauty might not be a danger to him. He had grown up hard, it was true. The East End of London had been no rest cure for a ten-year-old Polish immigrant, and Landau had taken his share of split lips, broken noses, smashed knuckles and hunger. But if you had asked him now or at any time in the last thirty years what his definition of a hero was, he would have replied without a second's thought that a hero was the first man out of the back door when they started yelling for volunteers.

One thing he did know as he stared at the contents of that brown-paper parcel: he had the buzz on him. Why he had it was something he could sort out later when there weren't better things to do. But if dodgy work needed to be done tonight, Niki Landau was your man. Because when Niki has the buzz, Harry, no one buzzes better, as the girls all know.

The first thing he saw was the envelope. He registered the three notebooks underneath it and saw that the envelope and notebooks were joined with a thick elastic band, the kind he always saved but never found a use for. But it was the envelope that held him because it had her writing on it—a strict copybook kind of writing that confirmed his pure image of her. One square brown envelope, glued rather messily and addressed "Personal for Mr. Bartholomew Scott Blair, urgent."

Slipping it free of the elastic band, Landau held it to the light but it was opaque and revealed no shadow. He explored it with his finger and thumb. One sheet of thin paper inside, two at most. *Mr. Scott Blair has undertaken to publish it with discretion,* he remembered. *Mr. Landau, if you love peace . . . give it immediately to Mr. Scott Blair. Only to Mr. Scott Blair . . . it is a gift of trust.*

She trusts me too, he thought. He turned the envelope over. The back was blank.

And there being only so much that one may learn from a sealed brown envelope, and since Landau drew the line at reading Barley's or anybody else's personal mail, he opened his briefcase again and, having searched the stationery compartment, extracted from it a plain manila envelope of his own, with the words "From the desk of Mr. Nicholas P. Landau" inscribed tastefully on the flap. Then he popped the brown envelope inside the manila one and sealed it. Then he scribbled the name "Barley" on it and filed it in the compartment marked "Social," which contained such oddities as visiting cards that had been pressed on him by strangers and notes of odd commissions he had undertaken to perform for people—such as the publishing lady who needed refills for her Parker pen or the Ministry of Culture official who wanted a Snoopy T-shirt for his nephew or the lady from October who simply happened to be passing while he was wrapping up his stand.

And Landau did this because with the tradecraft that was instinctive in him, if totally untaught, he knew that his first job was to keep the envelope as far away as possible from the notebooks. If the notebooks were trouble, then he wanted nothing that would link them with the letter. And vice versa. And in this he was entirely right. Our most versatile and erudite trainers, dyed in all the oceans of our Service folklore, would not have told it to him one whit differently.

Only then did he take up the three notebooks and slip off the elastic band while he kept one ear cocked for footfalls in the corridor. Three grubby Russian notebooks, he reflected, selecting the top one and turning it slowly over. Bound in crudely illustrated board, the spine in fraying cloth. Two hundred and twenty-four pages of poor-quality, feint-ruled quarto, if Landau remembered correctly from the days when he peddled stationery, Soviet price around twenty kopeks retail from any good stationer, always provided that the delivery had arrived and that you were standing in the right queue on the right day.

Finally he opened the notebook and stared at the first page.

She's daft, he thought, fighting off his disgust.

She's in the hands of a nutter. Poor kid.

Meaningless scribblings, done by a lunatic with a mapping pen, in India ink at breakneck speed and furious angles. In the margins, sideways, longways. Diagonally across itself like a doctor's writing on the blink. Peppered with stupid exclamation marks and underlinings. Some of it Cyrillic, some English. "The Creator creates creators," he read in English. "To be. Not to be. To counter-be." Followed by a burst of stupid French about the warfare of folly and the folly of warfare, followed by a barbed-wire entanglement. Thank you very much, he thought, and flipped to another page, then another, both so dense with crazy writing you could hardly see the paper. "Having spent seventy years destroying the popular will, we cannot expect it suddenly to rise up and save us," he read. A quote? A night thought? There was no way to tell. References to writers, Russian, Latin and European. Talk of Nietzsche, Kafka and people he'd never heard of, let alone read. More talk of war, this time in English: "The old declare it, the young fight it, but today the babies and old people fight it too." He turned another page and came on nothing but a round brown stain. He lifted the notebook to his nose and sniffed. Booze, he thought with contempt. Stinks like a brewery. No wonder he's a mate of Barley Blair's. A double page devoted to a series of hysterical proclamations.

OUR GREATEST PROGRESS IS IN THE FIELD OF BACK-
    WARDNESS!
SOVIET PARALYSIS IS THE MOST PROGRESSIVE IN THE
    WORLD!
OUR BACKWARDNESS IS OUR GREATEST MILITARY SECRET!
IF WE DON'T KNOW OUR OWN INTENTIONS AND OUR
    OWN CAPACITIES, HOW CAN WE KNOW YOURS?
THE TRUE ENEMY IS OUR OWN INCOMPETENCE!

And on the next page, a poem, painstakingly copied from Lord knew where:

> He wires in and wires out,
> And leaves the people still in doubt
> Whether the snake that made the track
> Was going south or coming back.

Scrambling to his feet, Landau strode angrily to the window, which gave on to a glum courtyard full of uncollected rubbish.

"A blooming word-artist, Harry. That's what I thought he was. Some long-haired, drug-ridden, self-indulgent genius, and she's gone and thrown herself away on him same as they all do."

She was lucky there was no Moscow telephone directory or he'd have rung her up and told her what she'd got.

To stoke his anger, he took up the second book, licked his fingertip and whisked contemptuously through it page by page, which was how he came upon the drawings. Then everything went blank for him for a moment, like a flash of empty screen in the middle of a film, while he cursed himself for being an impetuous little Slav instead of a cool calm Englishman. Then he sat down on the bed again, but gently, as if there were someone resting in it, someone he had hurt with his premature condemnations.

For if Landau despised what too often passed for literature, his pleasure in technical matters was unconfined. Even when he didn't follow what he was looking at, he could relish a good page of mathematics all day long. And he knew at one glance, as he had known of the woman Katya, that what he was looking at here was quality. Not your ruled drawing, it was true. Light sketches but all the better for it. Drawn freehand without instruments by somebody who could think with a pencil. Tangents, parabolas, cones. And in between the drawings, businesslike descriptions that architects and engineers use, words like "aimpoint" and "captive carry" and "bias" and "gravity" and "trajectory." "Some in your English, Harry, and some in your Russian."

Though Harry is not my real name.

Yet when he began to compare the lettering of these beautifully written words in the second book with the rambling jungle in the first, he discovered to his astonishment certain unmistakable similarities. So that he had the sensation of looking at a kind of schizophrenic's diary with Dr. Jekyll writing one volume and Mr. Hyde the other.

He looked in the third notebook, which was as orderly and purposeful as the second but arranged like a kind of mathematical log with dates and numbers and formulae, and the word "error" repeating itself frequently, often underlined or lifted with an exclamation mark. Then suddenly Landau stared, and continued staring, and could not remove his eyes from what he was reading. The cosy obscurity of the writer's technical jargon had ended with a bang. So had his philosophical ramblings and elegant annotated drawings. The words came off the page with a blazoned clarity.

"The American strategists can sleep in peace. Their nightmares cannot be realised. The Soviet knight is dying inside his armour. He is a secondary power like you British. He can start a war but cannot continue one and cannot win one. Believe me."

Landau looked no further. A sense of respect, mingled with a strong instinct for self-preservation, advised him that he had disturbed the tomb enough. Taking up the elastic band, he put the three notebooks together and snapped it back over them. That's it, he thought. From here on I mind my business and do my duty. Which is to take the manuscript to my adopted England and give it immediately to Mr. Bartholomew *alias* Barley Scott Blair.

Barley Blair, he thought in amazement as he opened his wardrobe and hauled out the large aluminum hand-case where he kept his samples. Well, well. We often wondered whether we were nurturing a spy in our midst and now we know.

Landau's calm was absolute, he assured me. The Englishman had once more taken command of the Pole. "If Barley could do it, I could, Harry, that's what I said to myself." And it was what he said to me too, when for a short spell he appointed me his confessor. People do that to me sometimes. They sense the unrealised part of me and talk to it as if it were the reality.

Lifting the case on to the bed he snapped the locks and drew out two audio-visual kits that the Soviet officials had ordered him to remove from his display—one pictorial history of the twentieth century with spoken commentary, which they had arbitrarily ruled to be anti-Soviet, and one handbook of the human body with action photographs and a keep-fit exercise cassette, which, after gazing longingly at the pliant young goddess in the leotard, the officials had decided was pornographic.

The history kit was a glossy affair, built as a coffee-table book and containing a quantity of interior pockets for cassettes, parallel texts, progressive vocabulary cards and students' notes. Having emptied the pockets of their contents, Landau offered the notebooks to each in turn but found none large enough. He decided to convert two pockets into one. He fetched a pair of nail scissors from his sponge bag and set to work with steady hands, easing the steel staples out of the centre divide.

Barley Blair, he thought again as he inserted the point of the nail scissors. I should have guessed, if only because you were the one it couldn't possibly be. Mr. Bartholomew Scott Blair, surviving scion of Abercrombie & Blair—spy. The first staple had come loose. He gingerly extracted it. Barley Blair, who couldn't sell hay to a rich horse to save his dying mother on her birthday, we used to say: spy. He began prising the second staple. Whose principal claim to fame was that two years ago at the Belgrade book fair he had drunk Spikey Morgan under the table on straight vodkas, then played tenor sax with the band so beautifully that even the police were clapping. Spy. Gentleman spy. Well, here's a letter from your lady, as they say in the nursery rhyme.

Landau picked up the notebooks and offered them to the space he had prepared but it was still not big enough. He would have to make one pocket out of three.

Playing the drunk, thought Landau, his mind still on Barley. Playing the fool and fooling us. Burning up the last of your family money, running the old firm deeper into the ground. Oh yes. Except that somehow or another you always managed to find one of those smart City banking houses to bail you out in the nick of time, didn't you? And what about your chess-playing then? *That* should have been a clue, if Landau had only had eyes for it! How does a man who's drunk himself silly beat all comers at chess then, Harry—straight games—if he isn't a trained spy?

The three pockets had become one pocket, the notebooks fitted more or less inside, the printed indication above them still read "Student Notes."

"Notes," Landau explained in his mind to the inquisitive young customs officer at Sheremetyevo airport. "Notes, you see, son, like it says. Student's notes. That's why there's a pocket here for notes. And these notes that you are holding in your hand are the work of an actual student following the course. That's why they're here, son, do you see? They are *demonstration notes*. And the drawings here, they're to do with the—"

With socio-economic patterns, son. With demographic population shifts. With vital statistics that you Russkies can never get enough of, can you? Here, seen one of these? It's called a body book.

Which might or might not save Landau's hide, depending on how smart the boy was, and how much they knew, and how they felt about their wives that day.

But for the long night ahead of him, and for the dawn raid when they kicked the door down and burst in on him with drawn pistols and shouted, "All right, Landau, give us the notebooks!"—for that happy moment, the kit wouldn't do at all. "Notebooks, Officer? Notebooks? Oh, you mean that bunch of junk some loony Russian beauty pressed on me at the fair tonight. I think you'll probably find them in the rubbish basket, Officer, if the maid hasn't emptied it for once in her life."

For this contingency also, Landau now meticulously set the scene. Removing the notebooks from the pocket of the history kit, he placed them artistically in the wastepaper basket exactly as if he had flung them there in the rage he had felt when he had taken his first look. To keep them company, he tossed in his surplus trade literature and brochures, as well as a couple of useless farewell gifts he had received: the thin volume of yet another Russian poet, a tin-backed blotter. As a final touch, he added a pair of undarned socks that only your rich Westerner throws away.

Once again I must marvel, as later we all did, at Landau's untutored ingenuity.

Landau did not go out and play that night. He endured the familiar imprisonment of his Moscow hotel room. From his window he watched the long dusk turn to darkness and the dim lights of the city reluctantly brighten. He made himself tea in his little travelling kettle and ate a couple of fruit bars from his iron rations. He dwelt gratefully upon the most rewarding of his conquests. He smiled ruefully at others. He braced himself for pain and solitude and summoned up his hard childhood to help him. He went through the contents of his wallet and his briefcase and his pockets and took out everything that was particularly private to him which he would not wish to answer for across a bare table—a hot letter a little friend sent him years ago that could still revive his appetites, membership of a certain video-by-mail club that he belonged to. His first instinct was to "burn them like in the movies" but he was restrained by the sight of the smoke detectors in the ceiling, though he'd have laid any money they didn't work.

So he found a paper bag and, having torn up everything very small, he put the pieces in the bag, dropped the bag out of the window and saw it join the rubbish in the courtyard. Then he lay on the bed and watched the dark go by. Sometimes he felt brave, sometimes he was so scared that he had to drive his fingernails into his palms to hold himself together. Once he turned on the television set, hoping for nubile girl gymnasts, which he liked. But instead he got the Emperor himself telling his bemused children for the umpteenth time that the old order had no clothes. And when Spikey Morgan, half drunk at best, telephoned from the bar of the National, Landau kept him on the line for company till old Spikey fell asleep.

Only once, at his lowest point, did it cross Landau's mind to present himself at the British Embassy and seek the assistance of the diplomatic bag. His momentary weakness angered him. "Those flunkies?" he asked himself in scorn. "The ones who sent my dad back to Poland? I wouldn't trust them with a picture postcard of the Eiffel Tower, Harry."

Besides, that wasn't what she had asked him to do.

In the morning he dressed himself for his own execution, in his best suit, with the photograph of his mother inside his shirt.

And that is how I see Niki Landau still, whenever I dip into his file, or receive him for what we call a six-monthly top-up, which is when he likes to relive his hour of glory before signing yet another declaration of the Official Secrets Act. I see him stepping jauntily into the Moscow street with the metal suitcase in his hand, not knowing from Adam what's in it, but determined to risk his brave little neck for it anyway.

How he sees me, if he ever thinks of me, I dare not wonder. Hannah, whom I loved but failed, would have no doubt at all. "As another of those Englishmen with hope in their faces and none in their hearts," she would say, flushing with anger. For I am afraid she says whatever comes to her these days. Much of her old forbearance is gone.

2

The whole of Whitehall was agreed that no story should ever begin that way again. Indoctrinated ministers were furious about it. They set up a frightfully secret committee of enquiry to find out what went wrong, hear witnesses, name names, spare no blushes, point fingers, close gaps, prevent a recurrence, appoint me Chairman and draft a report. What conclusions our committee reached, if any, remains the loftiest secret of them all, particularly from those of us who sat on it. For the function of such committees, as we all well knew, is to talk earnestly until the dust has settled, and then ourselves return to dust. Which, like a disgruntled Cheshire cat, our committee duly did, leaving nothing behind us but our frightfully secret frown, a meaningless interim working paper, and a bunch of secret annexes in the Treasury archives.

It began, in the less sparing language of Ned and his colleagues at the Russia House, with an imperial cock-up, between the hours of five and eight-thirty on a warm Sunday evening, when one Nicholas P. Landau, travelling salesman and taxpayer in good standing, if of Polish origin, with nothing recorded against, presented himself at the doors of no fewer than four separate Whitehall ministries to plead an urgent interview with an officer of the

British Intelligence Branch, as he was pleased to call it, only to be ridiculed, fobbed off and in one instance physically manhandled. Though whether the two temporary doormen at the Defence Ministry went so far as to grab Landau by the collar and the seat of his pants, as he maintained they did, and frogmarch him to the door, or whether they merely assisted him back into the street, to use *their* words, is a point on which we were unable to achieve a consensus.

But why, our committee asked sternly, did the two doormen feel obliged to provide this assistance in the first place?

Mr. Landau refused to let us look inside his briefcase, sir. Yes, he offered to let us take charge of the briefcase while he waited, provided he kept charge of the key, sir. But that wasn't regulations. And yes, he shook it in our faces, patted it for us, tossed it about in his hands, apparently in order to demonstrate that there was nothing in it that any of us needed to be afraid of. But that wasn't regulations either. And when we tried with a minimum of force to relieve him of the said briefcase, this *gentleman*— as Landau in their testimony had belatedly become— resisted our efforts, sir, and shouted loudly in a foreign accent, causing a disturbance.

But what did he shout? we asked, distressed by the notion of anybody shouting in Whitehall on a Sunday.

Well, sir, so far as we were able to make him out, him in his emotional state, he shouted that this briefcase of his contained highly secret papers, sir. Which had been entrusted to him by a Russian, sir, in Moscow.

And him a rampageous little Pole, sir, they might have added. On a hot cricketing Sunday in London, sir, and us watching the replay of the Pakistanis against Botham in the back room.

Even at the Foreign Office, that freezing hearth of official British hospitality, where the despairing Landau presented himself as a last resort and with the greatest of reluctance, it was only by dint of high entreaty and some honest-to-God Slav tears that he fought his way to the rarefied ear of the Honourable Palmer Wellow, author of a discerning monograph on Liszt.

And if Landau had not used a new tactic, probably the Slav tears would not have helped. Because this time he placed the briefcase open on the counter so that the doorman, who was young but sceptical, could crane his pomaded head to the recently installed armoured glass and scowl down into it with his indolent eyes, and see for himself that it was only a bunch of dirty old notebooks in there and a brown envelope, not bombs.

"Come-back-Monday-ten-to-five," the doorman said through the wonderfully new electric speaker, as if announcing a Welsh railway station, and slumped back into the darkness of his box.

The gate stood ajar. Landau looked at the young man, and looked past him at the great portico built a hundred years earlier to daunt the unruly princes of the Raj. And the next thing anyone knew, he had picked up his briefcase and, defeating all the seemingly impenetrable defences set up to prevent exactly such an onslaught, was pelting hell-for-leather with it—"like a bloomin' Springbok, sir"—across the hallowed courtyard up the steps into the enormous hall. And he was in luck. Palmer Wellow, whatever else he was, belonged to the appeasement side of the Foreign Office. And it was Palmer's day on.

"Hullo, *hullo*," Palmer murmured as he descended the great steps and beheld the disordered figure of Landau panting between two stout guards. "Well you *are* in a muck. My name's Wellow. I'm a resident clerk here." He held his left fist to his shoulder as if he hated dogs. But his right hand was extended in greeting.

"I don't want a clerk," said Landau. "I want a high officer or nothing."

"Well, a clerk is *fairly* high," Palmer modestly assured him. "I expect you're put off by the language."

It was only right to record—and our committee did—that nobody could fault Palmer Wellow's performance thus far. He was droll but he was effective. He put no polished foot wrong. He led Landau to an interviewing room and sat him down, all attention. He ordered a cup of tea for him with sugar for his shock, and offered him a digestive biscuit. With a costly fountain pen given him by a friend, he wrote down Landau's name and address and those of the companies that hired his services. He wrote down the number of Landau's British passport and his date and place of birth, 1930 in Warsaw. He insisted with disarming truthfulness that he had no knowledge of intelligence matters, but undertook to pass on Landau's material to the "competent people," who would no doubt give it whatever attention it deserved. And because Landau once again insisted on it, he improvised a receipt for him on a sheet of Foreign Office blue draft, signed it and had the janitor add a date-and-time stamp. He told him that if there was anything further the authorities wished to discuss they would very probably get in touch with him, perhaps by means of the telephone.

Only then did Landau hesitatingly pass his scruffy package across the table and watch with lingering regret as Palmer's languid hand enfolded it.

"But why don't you simply give it to Mr. Scott Blair?" Palmer asked after he had studied the name on the envelope.

"I tried, for Christ's sake!" Landau burst out in fresh exasperation. "I told you. I rang him everywhere. I've rung him till I'm blue in the face, I tell you. He's not at his home, he's not at work, he's not at his club, he's not at anywhere," Landau protested, his English grammar slipping in despair. "From the airport I tried. All right, it's a Saturday."

"But it's Sunday," Palmer objected with a forgiving smile.

"So it was a Saturday yesterday, wasn't it! I try his firm. I get an electronic howl. I look in the phone book. There's one in Hammersmith. Not his initials but Scott Blair. I get an angry lady, tells me to go to hell. There's a rep I know, Archie Parr, does the West Country for him. I ask Archie: 'Archie, for Christ's sake, how do I get hold of Barley in a hurry?' 'He's skedaddled, Niki. Done one of his bunks. Hasn't been seen in the shop for weeks.' Enquiries, I try. London, the Home Counties. Not listed, not a Bartholomew. Well he wouldn't be, would he, not if he's a—"

"Not if he's a what?" said Palmer, intrigued.

"Look, he's vanished, right? He's vanished before. There could be reasons why he vanishes. Reasons that you don't know of because you're not meant to. Lives are at stake, could be. Not only his either. It's top urgent, she told me. And top secret. Now get on with it. Please."

The same evening, there being not much doing on the world front apart from a dreary crisis in the Gulf and a squalid television scandal about soldiers and money in Washington, Palmer took himself off to a rather good party in Montpelier Square that was being thrown by a group of his year from Cambridge—bachelors like himself, but fun. An account of this occasion, too, reached our committee's ears.

"Have any of you heard of a Somebody Scott Blair, by the by?" Wellow asked them at a late hour when his memory of Landau happened to have been revived by some bars of Chopin he was playing on the piano. "Wasn't there a Scott Blair who was up with us or something?" he asked again when he failed to get through the noise.

"Couple of years ahead of us. Trinity," came a fogged reply from across the room. "Read History. Jazz fiend. Wanted to blow his saxophone for a living. Old man wouldn't wear it. Barley Blair. Pissed as a rat from daybreak."

Palmer Wellow played a thunderous chord that stunned the garrulous company to silence. "I said, is he a poisonous spy?" he enunciated.

"The father? He's dead."

"The son, ass. Barley."

Like someone stepping from behind a curtain, his informant emerged from the crowd of young and less young men and stood before him, glass in hand. And Palmer to his pleasure recognised him as a dear chum from Trinity a hundred years ago.

"I really don't know whether Barley's a poisonous spy or not, I'm afraid," said Palmer's chum, with an asperity habitual to him, as the background babel rose to its former roar. "He's certainly a failure, if that's a qualification."

His curiosity whetted still further, Palmer returned to his spacious rooms at the Foreign Office and to Landau's envelope and notebooks, which he had entrusted to the janitor for safekeeping. And it is at this point that his actions, in the words of our interim working paper, took an unhelpful course. Or in the harsher words of Ned and his colleagues in the Russia House, this was where, in any civilised country, P. Wellow would have been strung by his thumbs from a high point in the city and left there in peace to reflect upon his attainments.

For what Palmer did was have a nice time with the notebooks. For two nights and one and a half days. Because he found them so amusing. He did not open the buff envelope—which was by now marked in Landau's handwriting "Extremely Private for the attention of Mr. B. Scott Blair or a top member of the Intelligence"— because like Landau he was of a school that felt it unbecoming to read other people's mail. In any case, it was glued at both ends, and Palmer was not a man to grapple with physical obstacles. But the notebook—with its crazed aphorisms and quotations, its exhaustive loathing of politicians and soldiery, its scatter-shot references to Pushkin the pure Renaissance man and to Kleist the pure suicide—held him fascinated.

He felt little sense of urgency, none of responsibility. He was a diplomat, not a Friend, as the spies were called. And Friends in Palmer's zoology were people without the intellectual horsepower to be what Palmer was. Indeed it was his outspoken resentment that the orthodox Foreign Office to which he belonged resembled more and more a cover organisation for the Friends' disgraceful activities. For Palmer too was a man of impressive erudition, if of a random kind. He had read Arabic and taken a First in Modern History. He had added Russian and Sanskrit in his spare time. He had everything but mathematics and common sense, which explains why he passed over the dreary pages of algebraic formulae, equations and diagrams that made up the other two notebooks, and in contrast to the writer's philosophical ramblings had a boringly disciplined appearance. And which also explains—though the committee had difficulty accepting such an explanation——why Palmer chose to ignore the Standing Order to Resident Clerks Relating to Defectors and Offers of Intelligence, whether solicited or otherwise, and to do his own thing.

"He makes the most frantic connections right across the board, Tig," he told a rather senior colleague in Research Department on the Tuesday, having decided that it was finally time to share his acquisition. "You simply must read him."

"But how do we know it's a he, Palms?"

Palmer just felt it, Tig. The vibes.

Palmer's senior colleague glanced at the first notebook, then at the second, then sat down and stared at the third. Then he looked at the drawings in the second book. Then his professional self took over in the emergency.

"I think I'd get this lot across to them fairly sharpish if I were you, Palms," he said. But on second thoughts he got it across to them himself, very sharpish indeed, having first telephoned Ned on the green line and told him to stand by.

Upon which, two days late, hell broke loose. At four o'clock on the Wednesday morning the lights on the top floor of Ned's stubby brick out-station in Victoria known as the Russia House were still burning brightly as the first bemused meeting of what later became the Bluebird team drew to a close. Five hours after that, having sat out two more meetings in the Service's headquarters in a grand new high-rise block on the Embankment, Ned was back at his desk, the files gathering around him as giddily as if the girls in Registry had decided to erect a street barricade.

"God may move in a mysterious way," Ned was heard to remark to his redheaded assistant, Brock, in a lull between deliveries, "but it's nothing to the way He picks his joes."

A joe in the parlance is a live source, and a live source in sane English is a spy. Was Ned referring to Landau when he spoke of joes? To Katya? To the unchristened writer of the notebooks? Or was his mind already fixed upon the vaporous outlines of that great British gentleman spy, Mr. Bartholomew Scott Blair? Brock did not know or care. He came from Glasgow but of Lithuanian parents, and abstract concepts made him angry.

As to myself, I had to wait another week before Ned decided with a proper reluctance that it was time to haul in old Palfrey. I've been old Palfrey since I can remember. To this day I have never understood what happened to my Christian names. "Where's old Palfrey?" they say. "Where's our tame legal eagle? Get the old lawbender in! Better chuck this one at Palfrey!"

I am quickly dealt with. You need not stumble on me long. Horatio Benedict dePalfrey are my names but you may forget the first two immediately, and somehow nobody has ever remembered the "de" at all. In the Service I am Harry, so quite often, being an obedient soul, I am Harry to myself. Alone in my poky little bachelor flat of an evening, I am quite inclined to call myself Harry while I cook my chop. Legal adviser to the illegals, that's me, and sometime junior partner to the extinct house of Mackie, Mackie & dePalfrey, Solicitors and Commissioners for Oaths, of Chancery Lane. But that was twenty years ago. For twenty years I have been your most humble secret servant, ready at any time to rob the scales of the same blind goddess whom my young heart was brought up to revere.

A palfrey, I am told, was neither a warhorse nor a hunter, but a saddle horse deemed suitable for ladies. Well, there's only one little lady who ever rode this Palfrey any distance, but she rode him nearly to his grave and her name was Hannah. And it was because of Hannah that I scurried for shelter inside the secret citadel where passion has no place, where the walls are so thick I cannot hear her beating fists or tearful voice imploring me to let her in and brave the scandal that so terrified a young solicitor at the threshold of a respectable career.

Hope in my face and nothing in my heart, she said. A wiser woman might have kept such observations to herself, it has always seemed to me. Sometimes the truth is by way of being a self-indulgence. "Then why do you pursue a hopeless case?" I would protest to her. "If the patient is dead, why keep trying to revive him?"

Because she was a woman, seemed to be the answer. Because she believed in the redemption of male souls. Because I had not paid enough for being inadequate.

But I have paid now, believe me.

It is because of Hannah that I walk the secret corridors to this day, calling my cowardice duty and my weakness sacrifice.

It is because of Hannah that I sit here late at night, in my grey box of an office with LEGAL on the door, files and tapes and films stacked around me like the case of Jarndyce v. Jarndyce without the pink string, while I draft our official whitewash of the operation we called the Bluebird and of its protagonist, Bartholomew, alias Barley, Scott Blair.

It is because of Hannah also that even while he scribbles at his exculpation, this old Palfrey now and then puts down his pen and lifts his head and dreams.

* * *

Niki Landau's recall to the British colours, if he had ever seriously abandoned them, took place exactly forty-eight hours after the notebooks hit Ned's desk. Ever since his miserable sojourn through Whitehall, Landau had been sick with anger and mortification. He hadn't gone to work, he hadn't bothered with his little flat in Golders Green which he normally buffed and pampered as if it were the lantern of his life. Not even Lydia could rouse him from his melancholy. I myself had hastily arranged the Home Office warrant to tap his phone. When she telephoned, we listened to him putting her off. And when she made a tragic appearance at his front door, our watchers reported that he let her stay for a cup of tea and then dismissed her.

"I don't know what I've done wrong but whatever it is, I'm sorry," they heard her remark sadly as she left.

She was hardly in the street before Ned rang. Afterwards, Landau shrewdly wondered to me whether that was a coincidence.

"Niki Landau?" Ned enquired in a voice you didn't feel like fooling with.

"I could be," said Landau, sitting up straight.

"My name's Ned. I think we have a mutual friend. No need to mention names. You kindly dropped a letter in for him the other day. Rather against the odds, I'm afraid. A package too."

Landau thrilled to the voice immediately. Capable and commanding. The voice of a good officer, not a cynic, Harry.

"Well, yes, I did," he said, but Ned was already talking again.

"I don't think we need to go into a lot of details over the telephone, but I do think you and I need to have a long chat and I think we need to shake your hand. Rather soon. When can we do that?"

"Whenever you say," said Landau. And had to stop himself from saying "sir."

"I always think now's a good time. How do you feel about that?"

"I feel a whole lot better, Ned," said Landau with a grin in his voice.

"I'm going to send a car for you. Won't be at all long, so perhaps you'd just stay where you are and wait for your front doorbell to ring. It's a green Rover, B registration. The driver's name is Sam. If you're worried, ask him to show you his card. If you're still worried, phone the number on it. Think you'll manage?"

"Our friend's all right, is he?" said Landau, unable to resist asking, but Ned had rung off.

The doorbell pealed a couple of minutes afterwards. They had the car waiting round the corner, thought Landau as he floated downstairs in a dream. This is it. I'm in the hands of the professionals. The house was in smart Belgravia, one of a terrace recently restored. Its newly painted white front glistened wholesomely at him in the evening sun. A palace of excellence, a shrine to the secret powers that rule our lives. A polished-brass sign on the pillared doorway said FOREIGN LIAISON STAFF. The door was already opening as Landau climbed the steps. And as the uniformed janitor closed it behind him Landau saw a slender, straight-built man in his early forties advance towards him through the sunbeams, first the trim silhouette, then the no-nonsense handsome healthy features, then the handshake: discreet but loyal as a naval salute.

"Well done, Niki. Come on in."

Good voices do not always belong to good faces, but Ned's did. As Landau followed him into the oval study, he felt he could say anything in the world to him and

Ned would still be on his side. Landau in fact saw a whole lot of things in Ned that he liked at once, which was Ned's Pied Piper gift: the careful charm, the restrained good looks, the power of quiet leadership and the "Come on in." Landau also sniffed the polyglot in him, for he was one himself. He had only to drop a Russian name or phrase for Ned to reach out for it and smile, and match it with a phrase of his own. He was one of us, Harry. If you had a secret, this was the man to tell it to, not that flunky in the Foreign Office.

But then Landau had not realised, until he began talking, how desperately he had been needing to confide. He opened his mouth, he was away. All he could do from then on was listen to himself in amazement, because he wasn't just talking about Katya and the notebooks, and why he had accepted them, and how he had hidden them, but about his whole life till now, his confusions about being a Slav, his love of Russia despite everything, and his feeling of being suspended between two cultures. Yet Ned did not lead him or check him in any way. He was a born listener. He hardly stirred except to write himself neat notes on bits of card, and if he interrupted, it was only to clear up a rare point of detail—the moment at Sheremetyevo, for example, when Landau was waved through to the departure lounge without a glance.

"Now did all your group receive that treatment or only you?"

"The lot of us. One nod, we were through."

"You didn't feel singled out in any way?"

"What for?"

"You didn't have the impression you might be getting a different kind of treatment from other people? A better one, for instance?"

"We went through like a bunch of sheep. A flock," Landau corrected himself. "We handed in our visas, that was it."

"Were other groups going through at the same rate, did you notice?"

"The Russkies didn't seem to be bothering at all. Maybe it was the summer Saturday. Maybe it was the *glasnost*. They pulled a few out to inspect and let the others through. I felt a fool, to be truthful. I didn't need to have taken the precautions that I did."

"You were no sort of fool. You did marvellously," said Ned, without a hint of patronising while he wrote again. "And on the plane, who did you sit next to, remember?"

"Spikey Morgan."

"Who else?"

"No one. I had the window."

"Which seat was that?"

Landau knew the seat number off pat. It was the one he prebooked whenever he could.

"Did you talk much on the flight?"

"Quite a lot, as a matter of fact."

"What about?"

"Women, mainly. Spikey's moved in with a pair of freewheelers in Notting Hill."

Ned gave a pleasant laugh. "And did you tell Spikey about the notebooks? In your relief, Niki? It would have been perfectly natural in the circumstances. To confide."

"I wouldn't dream of it, Ned. Not to a soul. I never did, I never will. I'm only telling you because he's vanished and you're official."

"How about Lydia?"

The offence to Landau's dignity momentarily outweighed his admiration of Ned, and even his surprise at Ned's familiarity with his affairs.

"My ladies, Ned, they know a little about me. They may even think they know more than they do," he replied. "But they do not share my secrets because they are not invited to."

Ned continued writing. And somehow the trim movement of the pen, coupled with the suggestion that he could have been indiscreet, provoked Landau into chancing his hand, because he had noticed already that every time he started to talk about Barley, a kind of freeze settled over Ned's quietly reassuring features.

"And Barley's really all right, is he? He hasn't had an accident or anything?"

Ned seemed not to hear. He took a fresh card and resumed his writing.

"I suppose Barley would have used the Embassy, wouldn't he?" said Landau. "Him being a professional. Barley. It's the chess that gives him away, if you want to know. He shouldn't play it, in my opinion. Not in public."

Then and only then did Ned's head rise slowly from the page. And Landau saw a stony expression in his face that was more frightening than his words. "We never mention names like that, Niki," said Ned very quietly. "Not even among ourselves. You couldn't know, so you've done nothing wrong. Just please don't do it again."

Then, seeing perhaps the effect that he had had on Landau, he got up and strolled to a satinwood sidetable and poured two glasses of sherry from a decanter and handed one to Landau. "And yes, he's all right," he said.

So they drank a silent toast to Barley, whose name Landau had by then sworn to himself ten times already would never again cross his lips.

"We don't want you to go to Gdansk next week," said Ned. "We've arranged a medical certificate and compensation for you. You're ill. Suspected ulcer. And stay away from work in the meantime, do you mind?"

"I'll do whatever you say," said Landau.

But before he left he signed a declaration of the Official Secrets Act while Ned benignly looked on. It's a weaselly document in legal terms, calculated to impress the signatory and no one else. But then the Act itself is scarcely a credit to its drafters either.

After that, Ned switched off the microphones and the hidden video cameras that the twelfth floor had insisted on because it was becoming that kind of operation.

And this far, Ned did everything alone, which was his good right as head of the Russia House. Fieldmen are nothing if not loners. He didn't even call in old Palfrey to read the riot act. Not yet.

If Landau had felt neglected until that afternoon, for the rest of the week he was swamped with attention. Early the next morning, Ned telephoned asking him with his customary courtesy to present himself to an address in Pimlico. It turned out to be a nineteen-thirties block of flats, with curved steel-framed windows painted green and an entrance that should have led to a cinema. In the presence of two men whom he did not introduce, Ned took Landau crisply through his story a second time, then threw him to the wolves.

The first to speak was a distraught, floating man with baby-pink cheeks and baby-clear eyes and a flaxen jacket to match his straggling flaxen hair. His voice floated too. "You said a blue dress, I think? My name's Walter," he added, as if himself startled by the news.

"I did, sir."

"You're sure?" he piped, rolling his head and peering crookedly at him from under his silken brow.

"Totally, sir. A blue dress with a brown perhaps-bag. Most perhaps-bags are made of string. Hers was brown plastic. 'Now, Niki,' I said to myself, 'today is not the day, but if you were ever thinking of having a tumble with this lady at a future date, which you might, you could always bring her a nice blue handbag from London to match her blue dress, couldn't you?' That's how I remember, you see. I have the connection in my head, sir."

And it is always an oddity of the tapes when I replay them that Landau called Walter "sir," while he never called Ned anything but Ned. But this was no great sign of respect in Landau so much as of a certain squeamishness that Walter inspired. After all, Landau was a ladies' man and Walter was quite the opposite.

"And the hair *black*, you say?" Walter sang, as if black hair strained credulity.

"Black, sir. Black and silky. Verging towards the raven. Definitely."

"Not dyed, you don't think?"

"I know the difference, sir," said Landau, touching his own head, for he wanted to give them everything by now, even the secret of his eternal youth.

"You said earlier she was Leningrad. Why did you say that?"

"The bearing, sir. I saw quality, I saw a Russian woman of Rome. That's how I think of her. Petersburg."

"But you didn't see Armenian? Or Georgian? Or Jewish, for example?"

Landau dwelt on the last suggestion but rejected it. "I'm Jewish myself, you see. I won't say it takes one to know one but I'll say I didn't go ting-a-ling inside."

A silence that could have been embarrassment seemed to encourage him to continue. "I think being Jewish is overdone, to be frank. If that's what you want to be, good luck I say. But if you don't need it, nobody should make you have it. Myself, I'm a Brit first, a Pole second and everything else comes afterwards. Never mind there's a lot would have it the other way round. That's their problem."

"Oh well said!" Walter cried energetically, flapping his fingers and giggling. "Oh that *does* put it in a nutshell. And you say her English was really rather good?"

"More than good, sir. Classic. A lesson to us all."

"Like a schoolteacher, you said."

"That was my impression," said Landau. "A teacher, a professor. I felt the learning. The intellect. The will."

"Could she not be an interpreter, you see?"

"Good interpreters efface themselves, in my opinion, sir. This lady projected herself."

"Oh well I say, that's rather a good answer," said Walter, shooting his pink cuffs. "And she was wearing a wedding ring. Well done."

"She certainly was, sir. A betrothal ring and a marriage ring. That's the first thing I look at after the usual, and in Russia it's not England, you have to look the wrong way round because the girls wear their wedding rings on the right hand. Single Russian women are a pest and divorce is off the peg. Give me a nice solid hubby and a couple of little ones for them to go home to any day. Then I might oblige."

"Let's ask you about that. You think she had children as well, do you, or not?"

"I am convinced of it, sir."

"Oh come, you can't be," Walter said peevishly, with a sudden downturn of the mouth. "You're not psychic, are you?"

"The hips, sir. The hips, the dignity even when she

was scared. She was not a Juno, she was not a sylph. She was a mother."

"Height?" Walter shrieked in a descant as his hairless eyebrows bucked upwards in alarm. "Can you do her height for us? Think of yourself. Measure her against you. Are you looking up or down?"

"Above the normal. I told you."

"Taller than you, then?"

"Yes."

"Five six? Five seven?"

"More like the second," said Landau sullenly.

"And her age again? You fumbled it before."

"If she's over thirty-five, she doesn't know it. A lovely skin, a fine form, a fine woman in her prime, especially the spirit, sir," Landau replied with a defeated grin, for while he might find Walter unsavoury in some way, he still had the Pole's weakness for eccentrics.

"It's a Sunday. Imagine she's English. Would you expect her to be going to church?"

"She'd definitely have given the problem a good going over," said Landau to his great surprise before he had time to think of an answer. "She might have said there was *no* God. She might have said there *was* a God. But she wouldn't have let it drift away from her like most of us. She'd have gone for it and come to a decision and done something about it if she thought she should."

Suddenly all Walter's quaint ways had resolved themselves into a long rubbery smile. "Oh you *are* good," he declared enviously. "Now do you know any science?" he continued as his voice again soared into the clouds.

"A bit. Kitchen science, really. What I pick up."

"Physics?"

"O-level, not more, sir. I used to sell the course books. I'm not sure I'd scrape through the exam, mind, even now. But they did enable me to improve myself, put it that way."

"What does telemetry mean?"

"Never heard of it."

"Not in English, not in Russian?"

"Not in any language, sir, I'm afraid. Telemetry has passed me by."

"How about CEP?"

"The what, sir?"

"Circular-error-probable. My goodness, he wrote enough about it, didn't he, in those funny notebooks that you brought us? Don't tell me CEP hasn't stuck in your mind."

"I didn't notice it. I skipped. That's all I did."

"Until you came to his point about the Soviet knight dying inside his armour. Where you stopped. Why?"

"I didn't come to it. I *happened* to come to it."

"All right, you happened to come to it. And you formed a view. Is that right? Of what the writer was telling us. What view?"

"Incompetence, I suppose. They're no good at it. The Russkies. They're duff."

"Duff at what?"

"The rockets. They make errors."

"What sort of errors?"

"All sorts. *Magnetic* errors. *Bias* errors, whatever those are. I don't know. That's your job, isn't it."

But Landau's defensive surliness only emphasised his virtue as a witness. For where he wished to shine and could not, his failure reassured them, as Walter's airy gesture of relief now testified.

"Well I think he's done terribly well," he declared as if Landau were nowhere within earshot, flinging up his hands again, this time in a theatrical gesture of conclusion. "He tells us what he remembers. He doesn't make things up to spin a better tale. You won't do that, will you, Niki?" he added anxiously, uncrossing his legs as if his crotch were nipping him.

"No, sir, you may rest assured."

"And you haven't? I mean, because sooner or later we'd find out. Then everything you've given us would lose its lustre."

"No, sir. It's the way I told it. No more, no less."

"I'm sure it is," said Walter to his colleagues in a tone of simple trust as he again sat back. "The hardest thing in our trade or anybody else's is to say 'I believe.' Niki's a natural source and rare as hen's teeth. If there were more of *him*, nobody would need *us*."

"This is Johnny," Ned explained, playing the aide-de-camp.

Johnny had wavy greying hair and a broad jaw and a file full of official-looking telegrams. With his gold watch-chain and tailored charcoal suit, he might have been a foreign barmaid's vision of an Englishman but he certainly wasn't Landau's.

"Niki, first we have to thank you, pal," Johnny said, in lazy East Coast American. We the larger beneficiaries, his munificent tone suggested. We the majority shareholders. I'm afraid Johnny is like that. A good officer, but unable to keep his American supremacy inside its box. I sometimes think that is the difference between American spies and our own. Americans, with their frank enjoyment of power and money, flaunt their luck. They lack the instinct to dissemble that comes so naturally to us British.

Anyway, Landau's hackles went up in a flash.

"Mind if I ask you a couple of questions?" Johnny said.

"If it's all right by Ned," said Landau.

"Of course it is," said Ned.

"So we're at the audio fair that night. Okay, pal?"

"Well, evening really, Johnny."

"You escort the woman Yekaterina Orlova across the room to the top of the staircase. Where the guards are. You say goodbye to her."

"She's holding my arm."

"She's holding your arm, great. In front of the guards. You watch her down the stairs. Do you also watch her into the street, pal?"

I had not heard Johnny use "pal" before, so I took it that he was trying to needle Landau somehow, a thing that Agency people learn from their in-house psychologists.

"Correct," Landau snapped.

"Right into the street? Pause and think," he suggested, with the attorney's false expansiveness.

"Into the street and out of my life."

Johnny waited till he was sure everyone was aware that he was waiting, and Landau more aware than anybody. "Niki, pal, we've had people stand at the top of that staircase in the last twenty-four hours. No one sees the street from the top of that staircase."

Landau's face darkened. Not in embarrassment. In anger. "I saw her walk down the stairs. I saw her cross the lobby to where the street is. She did not return. So unless somebody has moved the street in the last twenty-four hours, which I grant you under Stalin was always possible—"

"Let's go on, shall we?" said Ned.

"See anyone walk out after her?" Johnny asked, riding Landau a little harder.

"Down the stairs or into the street?"

"Both, pal. Both."

"No, I didn't. I didn't see her go into the street, did I, because you just told me I didn't. So why don't you answer the questions and I'll ask them?"

While Johnny sat idly back, Ned intervened. "Niki, some things have to be very carefully examined. There's a lot at stake and Johnny has his orders."

"I'm at stake too," said Landau. "My word's on the line and I don't like having it made a fool of by an American who's not even British."

Johnny had returned to the file. "Niki, will you please describe the security arrangements for the fair, as you yourself observed them?"

Landau took a tense breath. "Well then," he said, and started again. "We had these two young uniformed policemen hanging about the hotel lobby. Those are the boys who keep the lists of all the Russians who come and go, which is normal. Then upstairs inside the hall we had the nasties. Those are the plainclothes boys. The dawdlers, they call them, the *toptuny,*" he added for Johnny's enlightenment. "After a couple of days you know the *toptuny* by heart. They don't buy, they don't steal the exhibits or ask for freebies and there's always one of them with the butter-blond hair, don't ask me why. We had three boys and they didn't change all week. They were the ones who watched her go down the stairs."

"That everyone, pal?"

"As far as I know it is everyone but I'm waiting to be told I'm wrong."

"Were you not also aware of two ladies of indeterminate age, grey-haired persons who were also present every day of the fair, came early, left late, who also didn't buy, didn't enter negotiations with any of the standholders or exhibitors, or appear to have any legitimate purpose for attending the fair?"

"You're talking about Gert and Daisy, I suppose."

"Excuse me?"

"There was two old biddies from the Council of Libraries. They came for the beer. Their main pleasure was whipping brochures off the stands and cadging free handouts. We christened them Gert and Daisy after a certain British radio show popular in the war years and after."

"It did not occur to you that these ladies might also be performing a surveillance function?"

Ned's powerful hand was already out to restrain Landau but he was too late.

"Johnny," said Landau, boiling over. "This is Moscow, right? Moscow, Russia, *pal*. If I stopped to consider who had a surveillance function and who didn't, I wouldn't get out of bed in the morning and I wouldn't get into it at night. The birds in the trees are wired, for all I know."

Yet again Johnny was at his telegrams. "You say that Yekaterina Borisovna Orlova referred to the adjoining stand of Abercrombie & Blair as having been empty on the previous day, correct?"

"I do say so, yes."

"But you didn't see her the day before? Is that also correct?"

"It is."

"You also say that you have an eye for a pretty lady."

"I do, thank you, and may it long remain vigilant."

"Don't you think you should have noticed her then?"

"I do sometimes miss one," Landau confessed, colouring again. "If my back is turned, if I am bent over a desk or relieving myself in the toilet, it is possible my attention may flag for a moment."

But Johnny's nervelessness was acquiring its own authority. "You have relatives in Poland, do you not, Mr.

Landau?" The "pal" had evidently done its work, for listening to the tape I noticed he had dropped it.

"I do."

"Do you not have an elder sister highly placed in the Polish administration?"

"My sister works in the Polish Health Ministry as a hospital inspector. She is not highly placed and she is past retiring age."

"Have you at any time directly or indirectly been the witting target of pressure or blackmail by Communist-bloc agencies or third parties acting in their behalf?"

Landau turned to Ned. "A what target? My English isn't very good, I'm afraid."

"Conscious," said Ned with a warning smile. "Aware. Knowing."

"No I haven't," said Landau.

"In your travels to Eastern bloc countries, have you been intimate with women of those countries?"

"I've been to bed with some. I haven't been intimate."

Like a naughty schoolboy, Walter let out a squeak of choked laughter, lifting his shoulders to his neck and cupping his hand over his dreadful teeth. But Johnny soldiered doggedly on: "Mr. Landau, have you ever prior to this time had contacts with any intelligence agency of any hostile or friendly country anywhere?"

"Negative."

"Have you ever sold information to any person of whatever status or profession—newspaper, enquiry agency, police, military—for any purpose, however innocuous?"

"Negative."

"And you are not and never have been a member of a Communist party or any peace organisation or group sympathetic to its aims?"

"I'm a British subject," Landau retorted, thrusting out his little Polish jaw.

"And you have no idea, however vague, however mistily formed, of the overall message contained in the material you handled?"

"I didn't handle it. I passed it on."

"But you read it along the way."

"What I could, I read. Some. Then I gave up. As I told you."

"Why?"

"From a sense of decency, if you want to know. Something which I begin to suspect you are not troubled by."

But Johnny, far from blushing, was digging patiently in his file. He drew out an envelope and from the envelope a pack of postcard-sized photographs, which he dealt on to the table like playing-cards. Some were fuzzy, all were grainy. A few had foreground obstructions. They showed women coming down the steps of a bleak office building, some in groups, some singly. Some carried perhaps-bags, some had their heads down and carried nothing. And Landau remembered hearing that it was Moscow practice for ladies slipping out for lunchtime shopping to stuff whatever they needed into their pockets and leave their handbags lying on their desks in order to show the world they had only gone down the corridor.

"This one," said Landau suddenly, pointing with his forefinger.

Johnny played another of his courtroom tricks. He was really too intelligent for all this nonsense but that didn't stop him. He looked disappointed and mighty unbelieving. He looked as if he had caught Landau in a lie. The video film shows him overacting quite outrageously. "How can you be so damn sure, for God's sake? You never even *saw* her in an overcoat."

Landau is undismayed. "That's the lady. Katya," he says firmly. "I'd recognise her anywhere. Katya. She's done her hair up, but it's her. Katya. That's her bag too, plastic." He continues staring at the photograph. "And her wedding ring." For a moment he seems to forget he is not alone. "I'd do the same for her tomorrow," he says. "*And* the day after."

Which marked the satisfactory end to Johnny's hostile examination of the witness.

As the days progressed and one enigmatic interview followed another, never the same place twice, never the same people except for Ned, Landau had increasingly the feeling that things were advancing to a climax. In a sound laboratory behind Portland Place, they played him women's voices, Russians speaking Russian and Russians speaking English. But he didn't recognise Katya's. Another day, to his alarm, was devoted to money. Not theirs but Landau's. His bank statements—where the hell did they get them from? His tax returns, salary slips, savings, mortgage, endowment policy, worse than the Inland Revenue.

"Trust us, Niki," said Ned—but with such an honest, reassuring smile that Landau had the feeling that Ned had been out there fighting for him somehow, and that things were on the verge of coming right.

They're going to offer me a job, he thought on the Monday. They're going to turn me into a spy like Barley.

They're trying to put it right about my father twenty years after his death, he thought on the Tuesday.

Then on the Wednesday morning, Sam the driver pressed his doorbell for the last time and everything came clear.

"Where is it today then, Sam?" Landau asked him cheerfully. "The Bloody Tower?"

"Sing Sing," said Sam, and they had a good laugh.

But Sam delivered him not to the Tower and not to Sing Sing either, but to the side entrance of one of the very Whitehall ministries that Landau only eleven days earlier had attempted unsuccessfully to storm. The grey-eyed Brock guided him up a back staircase and disappeared. Landau entered a great room that looked on to the Thames. A row of men sat at a table facing him. To the left sat Walter with his tie set straight and his hair slicked down. To the right sat Ned. Both looked solemn. And between them, with his cuffed hands resting flat on the table and lines of refusal round his neat jaw, sat a younger, sharp-suited man whom Landau rightly assumed to be senior in rank to both of them, and who, as Landau later put it, looked as though he had stepped out of a different movie. He was sleek and tight-lipped and groomed for television. He was rich in more than money. He was forty and rising, but the worst thing about him was his innocence. He looked too young to be charged with adult crimes.

"My name's Clive," he said in an underpowered voice. "Come in, Landau. We've got a problem about what to do with you."

And beyond Clive—beyond all of them, in fact—Niki Landau as an afterthought saw me. Old Palfrey. And Ned saw him see me and Ned smiled and made a pleasant show of introducing us.

"Ah now, Niki, this is Harry," he said untruthfully.

Nobody else had earned a trade description till then but Ned provided one for me: "Harry's our in-house umpire, Niki. He makes sure everyone gets a fair deal."

"Nice," said Landau.

Which is where, in the history of the affair, I made my own modest entrance, as legal errand boy, as fixer and bit player, and pleaser, and finally as chronicler; now Rosencrantz, now Guildenstern, and just occasionally Palfrey.

And to take even more care of Landau there was Reg, who was big and ginger and reassuring. Reg led Landau to a dunce's chair at the centre of the room, then sat beside him on another. And Landau took to Reg at once, which was usual, for Reg was by trade a welfarer and his clients included defectors, grounded fieldmen and blown agents, and other men and women whose bonds to England might have worn a little thin if old Reg Wattle and his cosy wife Berenice had not been there to hold their hands.

"You've done a good job but we can't tell you why it's good, because that would be insecure," Clive continued in his arid voice when Landau was comfortably settled. "Even the little you know is too much. And we can't let you wander round Eastern Europe with our secrets in your head. It's too dangerous. For you and the people involved. So while you've performed a valuable service for us, you've also become a serious worry. If this were wartime, we could lock you up or shoot you or something. But it isn't, not officially."

Somewhere on his prudent little journey to power, Clive had taught himself to smile. It was an unfair weapon to use on friendly people, rather like silence on the telephone. But Clive knew nothing of unfairness because he knew nothing of its opposite. As to passion, it was what you used when you needed to persuade people.

"After all, you could point the finger at some very important people, couldn't you?" he continued so quietly that everyone kept still to hear him. "I know you wouldn't do that deliberately but when one's handcuffed to a radiator one doesn't have much choice. Not in the end."

And when Clive thought he had scared Landau just enough he glanced to me, and nodded to me, and watched me while I opened up the pompous leather folder I had brought with me and handed Landau the long document I had prepared, of which the purport was that Landau renounce in perpetuity all travel behind the Iron Curtain, that he never leave the country without first advising Reg so many days in advance, the details to be arranged between the two of them, and that Reg should look after Landau's passport in order to prevent mishaps. And that he accept irrevocably into his life the role of Reg or whomever the authorities should appoint in Reg's place as confidant, philosopher and discreet arbiter of his affairs of every kind——including the ticklish problem of how to handle the taxation on the cashier's cheque attached, drawn on the Fulham branch of a very boring British bank, in the sum of a hundred thousand pounds.

And that, in order that he be regularly scared by Authority, he should present himself every six months to the Service's Legal Adviser, Harry, for a top-up on the subject of Secrecy——to old Palfrey, Hannah's sometime lover, a man so bowed by life that he can be safely charged with keeping others upright. And that further to the above and pursuant to it and consequent upon it, the whole matter relating to a certain Russian woman and to her friend's literary manuscript, and to the contents of said manuscript——however much or little he may have understood their import——and to the part played by a certain British publisher, be as of this moment solemnly declared void, dead, inoperative and expunged, henceforth and for all time. Amen.

There was one copy and it would live in my safe till it was shredded or fell apart of old age. Landau read it twice while Reg read it over his shoulder. Then Landau disappeared into his own thoughts for a while without much regard for who was watching him or who was willing him to sign and cease to be a problem. Because Landau knew that in this instance he was the buyer, not the seller.

He saw himself standing at the window of his Moscow hotel room. He remembered how he had wished he could hang up his travellers' boots and settle to a less arduous life. And the amusing notion came to him that his Maker must have taken him at his word and fixed things accordingly, which to everyone's unease caused him to break out in a little burst of laughter.

"Well I hope old Johnny the Yank is footing the bill for this, Harry," he said.

But the joke did not receive the applause it deserved, since it happened to be true. So Landau took Reg's pen and signed, and handed me the document and watched me add my own signature as a witness, Horatio B. dePalfrey, which after twenty years has such a practised illegibility that if I had signed it Heinz's Tomato Sauce neither Landau nor anybody else could have told the difference, and put it back inside its leather coffin and patted down the lid. There was handshaking, mutual assurances were exchanged, and Clive murmured, "We're grateful to you, Niki," just like in the movie that Landau periodically convinced himself he was part of.

Then everybody shook Landau's hand yet again and, having watched him ride nobly into the sunset or more accurately walk jauntily off down the corridor chatting away at Reg Wattle, who was twice his size, they waited fretfully for the "take" on the intercepts for which I had already obtained the warrants under the infallible plea of intense American interest.

They tapped his office and home telephones, read his mail and fitted an electronic limpet to the rear axle of his beloved drop-head Triumph.

They followed him in his leisure hours and recruited a typist in his office to keep an eye on him as a "suspect foreigner" while he served out the last weeks of his notice.

They put potential lady-friends alongside him in the bars where he liked to do his hunting. Yet despite these cumbersome and needless precautions, dictated by that same intense American interest, they drew a blank. No hint of bragging or indiscretion reached their ears. Landau never complained, never boasted, never attempted to go public. He became, in fact, one of the few finished and perfectly happy short stories of the trade.

He was the perfect prologue. He never came back.

He never attempted to get in touch with Barley Scott Blair, the great British spy. He lived in awe of him for ever. Even for the grand opening of the video shop, when he would have loved more than anything in the world to bask in the presence of this real-life secret British hero, he never tried to stretch the rules. Perhaps it was satisfaction enough for him to know that, one night in Moscow when the old country had called on him, he too had behaved like the English gentleman he sometimes longed to be. Or perhaps the Pole in him was content to have cocked a snook at the Russian bear next door. Or perhaps it was the memory of Katya that kept him faithful, Katya the strong, the virtuous, Katya the brave and beautiful, who even in her own fear had taken care to warn him of the dangers to himself. "You must believe in what you are doing."

And Landau had believed. And Landau was proud as Punch that he had, as any of us should be.

Even his video shop flourished. It was a sensation. A little rich for some people's blood now and then, including that of the Golders Green police, with whom I had to have a friendly word. But for others pure balm.

Above all, we were able to love him, because he saw us as we wished to be seen, as the omniscient, capable and heroic custodians of our great nation's inner health. It was a view of us that Barley never quite seemed able to share—any more, I have to say, than Hannah could, though she only ever knew it from outside, as the place to which she could not follow me, as the shrine of ultimate compromise and therefore, in her unrelenting view, despair.

"They are definitely not the cure, Palfrey," she had told me only a few weeks before, when for some reason I was trying to extol the Service. "And they sound to *me* more likely to be the disease."

3

There is no such thing, we older hands like to say, as an intelligence operation that does not occasionally run to farce. The bigger the operation, the bigger the belly laughs, and it is a matter of Service history that the week-long manhunt for Bartholomew alias Barley Scott Blair generated enough frenzy and frustration to power a dozen secret networks. Orthodox young novices like Brock from the Russia House learned to hate Barley's life before they even found the man who led it.

After five days of chasing after him, they thought they knew everything about Barley except where he was. They knew his free-thinking parentage and his expensive education, both wasted, and the unedifying details of his marriages, all broken. They knew the café in Camden Town where he played his chess with any layabout spirit who happened to drift in. A regular gentleman, even if he was the guilty party, they told Wicklow, who was posing as a divorce agent. Under the usual tacky but effective pretexts, they had doorstepped a sister in Hove who despaired of him, tradesmen in Hampstead who were writing to him, a married daughter in Grantham who adored him and a grey-wolf son in the City who was so withdrawn he might have taken a vow of silence.

They had talked to members of a scratch jazz band for whom he had occasionally played saxophone, to the almoner at the hospital where he was enrolled as a visitor and to the vicar at the Kentish Town church where to everyone's amazement he sang tenor. "Such a lovely voice when he shows up," said the vicar indulgently. But when they tried, with old Palfrey's help again, to tap his phone to get more of this lovely voice, there was nothing to tap because he hadn't paid his bill.

They even found a trace on him in our own records. Or rather the Americans found it for them, which did not add to their enchantment. For it turned out that in the early sixties, when any Englishman who had the misfortune to possess a double-barrelled name was in danger of being recruited to the Secret Service, Barley's had been passed to New York for vetting under some partially observed bilateral security treaty. Furious, Brock checked again with Central Registry, who, after first denying all knowledge of Barley, dug up his card from a cut in the white index that was still waiting to be transferred to the computer. And from the white card, behold a white file containing the original vetting form and correspondence. Brock rushed into Ned's room as if he had found the clue to everything. Age, 22! Hobbies, theatre and music! Sports, nil! Reasons for considering him, a cousin named Lionel in the Life Guards!

The payoff alone was lacking. The recruiting officer had lunched Barley at the Athenaeum and stamped his file "No Further Action," taking the trouble to add the word "ever" in his own hand.

Nevertheless this quaint episode of more than twenty years ago had a certain oblique effect on their attitude towards him, just as they had puzzled uneasily for a while over the bizarre left-wing attachments of old Salisbury

Blair, his father. It undermined Barley's independence in their eyes. Not in Ned's, for Ned was made of stronger stuff. But in the others, Brock and the younger ones. It led them to feel they owned him somehow, if only as the unsuccessful aspirant to their mystique.

A further frustration was provided by Barley's disgraceful car, which the police found parked illegally in Lexham Gardens with the offside wing bashed in and the licence out of date and a half bottle of Scotch stuck in the glove compartment with a sheaf of love letters in Barley's hand. Neighbours had been complaining about it for weeks.

"Tow it, boot it, charge it or just crush it?" the obliging superintendent of traffic asked Ned over the phone.

"Forget it," Ned replied wearily. Nevertheless he and Brock hastened round there in the vain hope of a clue. The love letters turned out to have been written to a lady of the Gardens but she had given them back to him. She was the last person in the world, she assured them with a tragic air, to know where Barley was now.

It wasn't till the following Thursday, when Ned was patiently checking Barley's monthly bank statements, that he discovered among the overdrawn columns a quarterly standing order in favour of a property company in Lisbon, a hundred and something pounds to Real Somebody Limitada. He stared at it unbelievingly. He kept staring. Then he said a foul word where normally he never swore. Then he phoned Travel in a hurry and had them check old flightlists from Gatwick and Heathrow. When Travel phoned back, Ned swore again. They were home. Days of phone calls, interviews and banging on doors, the rules bent in all directions, watch lists, cables to friendly liaison services in half the capitals of the world, their vaunted Records Section humiliated in front of the Americans. Yet nobody they had spoken to and no researches had revealed the one crucial, indispensable, idiotic fact they needed to know: that ten years ago on a whim Barley Blair, having inherited a stray couple of thousand from a remote aunt, bought himself a scruffy pied-à-terre in Lisbon, where he was accustomed to take periodic rests from the burden of his many-sided soul. It could have been Cornwall, it could have been Provence or Timbuktu. But Lisbon by an accident had got him, down on the waterfront, next to a bit of rough parkland, and too near the fish market for a lot of people's sensitivities.

An embattled calm settled over the Russia House with this discovery and Brock's bony face took on a sallow fury.

"Who's our Brother Lisbon these days?" Ned asked him, light as a summer breeze once more.

Then he telephoned old Palfrey alias Harry and put him on permanent standby, which, as Hannah would have said, described my situation nicely.

Barley was sitting at the bar when Merridew walked in on him. He was perched on a stool and shooting his mouth off about human nature to a drink-sodden expatriate major of artillery named Graves: Major Arthur Winslow Graves, later whitelisted as a Barley contact, his only claim on history and he never knew it. Barley's long pliant back was arched away from the open door and the door led off the courtyard, so Merridew, who was a fat boy of thirty, was able to collect some much-needed breath before he made his pitch. He had been chasing Barley half the day, missing him everywhere and getting more furious with each rebuff:

At Barley's flat, not five minutes' walk from here,

where an Englishwoman with a common accent had told him through the letterbox to get stuffed.

At the British Library, where the lady librarian had reported that Barley had spent an afternoon browsing, by which she appeared to imply—though promptly denied it when directly asked—that he was in an alcoholic stupor.

And at a revolting Tudor tavern in Estoril, where Barley and friends had enjoyed a liquid supper under plastic muskets and noisily departed not half an hour before.

The hotel—it prefers to call itself a humble *pensão*— was an old convent, a place the English loved. To reach it Merridew had to scale a cobbled stairway overhung with vines and, having scaled it and taken a first cautious look, he had to hurry down it again in order to tell Brock to run, "and I mean really run," and telephone Ned from the café on the corner. Then scale it yet again, which was why he was feeling so puffed and even more than usually put-upon. Smells of cool sandstone and fresh-ground coffee mingled with the night plants. Merridew was impervious to them. He lacked breath. The sob of distant trams and the honking of boats provided the only background sounds to Barley's monologue. Merridew had no awareness of them.

"Blind children cannot *chew*, Gravey, my dear old charmer," Barley was explaining patiently while he rested the point of his spidery forefinger on the major's navel and his elbow on the bar beside an unfinished game of chess. "Fact of science, Gravey. Blind children have to be taught to bite. Come here. Close your eyes."

Tenderly taking hold of the major's head in both his hands, Barley guided it towards him, parted the unresisting jaws, and popped in a couple of cashews. "There's a lad. On the command champ, champ. Mind your tongue. Champ. Repeat."

Taking this as his cue Merridew hoisted his hail-fellow smile and ventured a step into the bar, where he was surprised by two life-sized carvings of mulatto ladies in court dress standing either side of him at the doorway. Colour of hair chestnut, colour of eyes green, he rehearsed, checking off Barley's points as if he were a horse. Height six foot nothing, clean-shaven, well-spoken, slender build, idiosyncratic dress. Idiosyncratic, my foot, thought tubby Merridew, still winded, while he examined Barley's linen bush-jacket, grey flannels and sandals. What do the fools in London expect him to wear on a hot night in Lisbon? Mink?

"Ah, excuse me," Merridew said pleasingly. "I'm actually *looking* for someone. I wonder if you can help me."

"Which proves, my dear old mother's arse," Barley resumed, when he had carefully restored the major to an upright position, "quoting the celebrated song, that notwithstanding the fact that the big juju man made us of meat, eating people is wrong."

"I say, do pardon me, but I rather think you're Mr. Bartholomew Scott Blair," said Merridew. "Yes? Correct?"

Keeping a grasp upon the major's lapel in order to avert a military disaster, Barley cautiously turned himself half-circle on his stool and looked Merridew over, beginning with his shoes and ending with his smile.

"My name's Merridew from the Embassy, you see. Only I'm the Commercial Second Secretary here. I'm frightfully sorry. We've received a rather pressing telegram for you over our link. We think you should pop round and read it straight away. Would you mind?"

Then unwisely Merridew permitted himself a mannerism peculiar to plump officials. He flung an arm out, cupped his hand and passed it officiously over the top of his head as if to confirm that his hair and his cover were still in their proper places. And this large gesture, performed by a fat man in a low room, seemed to raise fears in Barley that might otherwise have slumbered, for he became disconcertingly sober.

"Are you telling me somebody's dead, old boy?" he asked with a smile so tense it looked ready for the worst of jokes.

"Oh my dear sir. Don't be so Gothic, please. It's a commercial thing, not consular. Why else would it come over our link?" He tried a placatory giggle.

But Barley had not yielded. Not by an inch. He was still looking into the pit, wherever Merridew might choose to look himself. "So what the hell are we telling ourselves, actually?" he asked.

"Nothing," Merridew retorted, scared. "A pressing telegram. Don't take it so personally. Diplomatic wireless."

"Who's doing the pressing?"

"No one. I can't give you a précis in front of everyone. It's confidential. Our eyes only."

They forgot his spectacles, thought Merridew, while he returned Barley's stare. Round. Black-framed. Too small for his eyes. Slips them to the tip of his nose when he scowls at you. Gets you in his sights.

"Never knew an honest debt that couldn't wait till Monday," Barley declared, returning to the major. "Loosen your girdle, Mr. Merridew. Take a drink with the unwashed."

Merridew might not have been the slenderest of men or the tallest. But he had grip, he had cunning and like many fat men he had unexpected resources of indignation which he was able to turn on like a flood when they were needed.

"Look here, Scott Blair, your affairs are not my concern, I am glad to say. I am not a bailiff, I am not a common messenger. I am a diplomat and I have a certain standing. I've spent half the day traipsing round after you, I have a car and a clerk waiting outside and I have certain rights over my own life. I'm sorry."

Their duet might have continued indefinitely had not the major staged an unexpected revival. Jerking back his shoulders, he thrust his fists to the seams of his trousers and tucked his chin into a rictal grimace of respect. "Royal summons, Barley," he barked. "Embassy's the local Buck House. Invitation's a command. Mustn't insult Her Majesty."

"He's not Her Majesty," Barley objected patiently. "He isn't wearing a crown."

Merridew wondered whether he should summon Brock. He tried smiling winningly but Barley's attention had wandered to the alcove, where a vase of dried flowers hid an empty grate. He tried calling, "Okay? All set?" much as he might have called to a wife when she was keeping him waiting for a dinner party. But Barley's haggard gaze remained on the dead flowers. He seemed to see his whole life in them, every wrong turning and false step from there to here. Then just as Merridew was giving up hope, Barley began loading his junk into his bush-jacket pockets, ritualistically, as if setting off on a safari: his bent wallet, full of uncashed cheques and cancelled credit cards; his passport, mildewed with sweat and too much travel; the notebook and pencil he kept handy for penning gems of alcoholic wisdom to himself for contemplation when he was sober. And when he had done all this he dumped a large banknote on the bar like somebody who wouldn't be needing money for a long while.

"See the major into his cab, Manuel. That means help him down the steps and into the back seat and pay the driver in advance. When you've done that, you can keep the change. So long, Gravey. Thanks for the laughs."

Dew was falling. A young moon lay on its back among the moist stars. They descended the stairway, Merridew first, urging Barley to be sure and mind his step. The harbour was filled with roving lights. A black saloon with CD plates waited at the curbside. Brock lurked restively beside it in the darkness. A second unmarked car lay further back.

"Ah now, this is Eddie," said Merridew, making the introductions. "Eddie, I'm afraid we took our time. I trust you have made your phone call?"

"All done," said Brock.

"And everybody at home is happy, I trust, Eddie? The little ones all tucked up and so forth? You won't get flak from the missus?"

"It's all right," Brock growled in a tone that said shut up.

Barley sat in the front seat, his head pitched back on the rest, eyes closed. Merridew drove. Brock sat very still in the back. The second car pulled out slowly, in the way good watchers do.

"This the way you usually go to the Embassy?" Barley asked in his seeming doze.

"Ah now, the duty dog took the telegram to his house, you see," Merridew explained lavishly, as if responding to a particularly well-taken point. "I'm afraid that, come weekends, we have to batten down the Embassy against the Irish. Yes." He switched on the radio. A deep-throated woman began sobbing a succulent lament. "Fado," he declared. "I adore Fado. I think it's why I'm here. I'm sure it is. I'm sure I put Fado on my post request." He began conducting with his spare hand. "Fado," he explained.

"Are you the people who've been snooping round my daughter, asking her a lot of stupid questions?" Barley asked.

"Oh we're just commercial, I'm afraid," Merridew said, and kept conducting for all that he was worth. But inside himself he was by now gravely disturbed by Barley's want of innocence. Sooner them than me, he thought, feeling Barley's untamed gaze upon his right cheek. If this is what Head Office has to reckon with these days, God preserve me from a home posting.

They had rented the town house of a former member of the Service, a British banker with a second house in Cintra. Old Palfrey had clinched the deal for them. They wanted no official premises, nothing that could afterwards be held against them. Yet the sense of age and place had its own particular eloquence. A wrought-iron coaching lamp lit the vaulted entrance. The granite flagstones had been hacked to stop the horses slipping. Merridew rang the bell. Brock had closed in tight in case of accidents.

"Hullo. Come on in," said Ned pleasantly, opening the huge scrolled door.

"Well I'll be off, won't I," said Merridew. "Marvellous, terrific." Still burbling covering fire, he scampered back to his car before anyone could contradict him. And as he did so the second car cruised by like one good friend who has seen another to his doorstep on a dangerous night.

For a long moment, while Brock stood off observing them, Ned and Barley appraised one another as only Englishmen can who are of the same height and class and shape of head. And though Ned in appearance was the very archetype of quiet British self-command and balance, and in most ways therefore the exact reverse of Barley—and though Barley was loose-limbed and angular with a face that even in repose seemed determined to explore beyond the obvious—there was still enough of the other in each of them to permit a recognition. Through a closed door came the murmur of male voices, but Ned made as though he hadn't heard it. He led Barley down the passage to a library and said, "In here," while Brock stayed in the hall.

"How drunk are you?" Ned asked, lowering his voice and handing Barley a glass of iced water.

"Not," said Barley. "Who's hijacking me? What goes on?"

"My name's Ned. I'm about to move the goalposts. There's no telegram, no crisis in your affairs beyond the usual. No one's being hijacked. I'm from British Intelligence. So are the people waiting for you next door. You once applied to join us. Now's your chance to help."

A silence settled between them while Ned waited for Barley to respond. Ned was Barley's age exactly. For twenty-five years, in one guise or another, he had been revealing himself as a British secret agent to people he needed to obtain. But this was the first time that his client had failed to speak, blink, smile, step back or show the smallest sign of surprise.

"I don't know anything," said Barley.

"Maybe we want you to find something out."

"Find it out for yourselves."

"We can't. Not without you. That's why we're here."

Drifting over to the bookshelves, Barley tilted his head to one side and peered over the top of his round spectacles at the titles while he went on drinking his water.

"First you're commercial, now you're spies," he said.

"Why don't you have a word with the Ambassador?"

"He's a fool. I was at Cambridge with him." He took down a bound book and glanced at the frontispiece. "Crap," he pronounced with contempt. "Must buy them by the yard. Who owns this place?"

"The Ambassador will verify me. If you ask him whether he can manage golf on Thursday, he'll tell you not till five o'clock."

"I don't play golf," said Barley, taking down another volume. "I don't play anything actually. I've retired from all games."

"Except chess," Ned suggested, holding out the open telephone directory to him. With a shrug Barley dialled the number. Hearing the Ambassador he gave a raffish if rather puzzled smile. "Is that Tubby? Barley Blair, here. How about a spot of the golf on Thursday for your liver?"

An acid voice said it was engaged till five o'clock.

"Five won't do at all," Barley retorted. "We'll be playing in the dark at that rate—bugger's rung off," he complained, shaking the dead receiver. Then he saw Ned's hand on the telephone cradle.

"It isn't a joke, I'm afraid," said Ned. "It's actually very serious."

Lost once more in his own contemplations, Barley slowly replaced the receiver. "The line between actually very serious and actually very funny is actually very thin," he remarked.

"Well let's cross it, shall we?" said Ned.

The talk behind the door had ceased. Barley turned the handle and walked in. Ned followed. Brock stayed in the hall to guard the door. We had been listening to everything over the relay.

*   *   *

If Barley was curious as to what he would face in there, so were we. It's an odd game, turning a man's life inside out without meeting him. He entered slowly. He took a few paces into the room and stopped, his long arms dangling wide of his sides while Ned, halfway to the table, made the all-male introductions.

"This is Clive, this is Walter, and over here is Bob. This is Harry. Meet Barley, everyone."

Barley scarcely nodded as the names were spoken. He seemed to prefer the evidence of his eyes to anything he was being told.

The ornate furniture and the coppice of vulgar indoor plants interested him. So did an orange tree. He touched a fruit, caressed a leaf, then delicately sniffed his thumb and finger as if assuring himself that they were real. There was a passive anger about him that went ahead of finding out the cause. Anger at being woken, I thought. At being singled out and named—a thing that Hannah said I always feared the most.

I also remember thinking he was elegant. Not, God knows, by virtue of his shabby clothes. But in his gestures, in his faded chivalry. In his natural courtesy, even if he resisted it.

"You don't run to surnames, by any chance, do you?" Barley enquired when he had completed his inspection of the room.

"I'm afraid not," said Clive.

"Because a Mr. Rigby called on my daughter Anthea last week. Said he was a tax inspector. Some bilge about wanting to adjust an unfair assessment. Was he one of you clowns?"

"By the sound of him I should think he probably was," said Clive, with the arrogance of someone who can't be bothered to lie.

Barley looked at Clive, who had one of those English faces that seemed to have been embalmed while he was still a boy king, at his hard clever eyes with nothing behind them, at the ash beneath his skin. He turned to Walter, so round, wispy and amused, a teased-out Falstaff of the richer common rooms. And from Walter his gaze moved on to Bob, taking in the patrician scale of him, his greater age, his avuncular ease, the browns he wore instead of greys and blues. Bob was lounging with his legs stretched out, one arm flung proprietorially over a chair. Gold-framed half-glasses peeked from his handkerchief pocket. The soles of his cracked mahogany shoes were like flat-irons.

"Barley, I am the odd man out in this family," Bob announced comfortably in a rich Bostonian drawl. "I guess I am also the oldest and I don't want to be sitting here under a false flag. I am fifty-eight years old, God help me, I work for the Central Intelligence Agency, which as you probably know is based in Langley in the state of Virginia. I do have a surname but I will not insult you by offering you one because it surely would not be much like the real thing." He raised a liver-spotted hand in leisurely salute. "Proud to meet you, Barley. Let's have fun. Let's do some good."

Barley turned back to Ned. "Now that *is* jolly," he said, though with no detectable animus. "So where are we all off to? Nicaragua? Chile? Salvador? Iran? If you want a Third World leader assassinated, I'm your man."

"Don't rant," Clive drawled, though ranting was about the last thing Barley had been guilty of. "We're as bad as Bob's lot and we do the same things. We also have an Official Secrets Act, which they don't, and we expect you to sign it."

At which Clive nodded in my direction, causing

Barley to take proper if belated notice of my existence. I always try to sit a little apart on these occasions and I was doing so that night. Some residual fantasy, I suppose, about being an Officer of the Court. Barley looked at me and I was momentarily disconcerted by the animal straightness of his stare. It somehow did not fit our untidy portrait of him. And Barley, after running his eye over me and seeing I know not what, undertook a more detailed examination of the room.

It was plush and perhaps he thought Clive owned it. It would certainly have been Clive's taste, for Clive was only middle class in the sense that he was unaware there was a better taste. It had carved thrones and chintz sofas and electric candles on the walls. The team's table, which could have sat an entire Armistice ceremony, stood in a raised alcove lined with sprawling rubber-plants in Ali Baba jars.

"Why didn't you go to Moscow?" Clive asked without waiting any longer for Barley to settle. "You were expected. You rented a stand, booked your flight and your hotel. But you didn't show up and you haven't paid. You came to Lisbon with a woman instead. Why?"

"Would you rather I came here with a man?" Barley asked. "What's it got to do with you and the CIA whether I came here with a woman or a Muscovy duck?"

He pulled back a chair and sat down, more in protest than obedience.

Clive nodded to me and I did my routine number. I rose, I walked round the preposterous table and set the Official Secrets Act form in front of him. I drew an important pen from my waistcoat pocket and offered it to him with funereal gravity. But his eyes were fixed on a spot outside the room, which was a thing that tonight and in the months that followed I noticed in him often, his way of looking beyond the present company into some troubled private territory of his own; of bursting into noisy talk as a means of exorcising ghosts that no one else had seen; of snapping his fingers without cause, as if to say, "That's settled then," where, so far as anybody else knew, nothing had been proposed in the first place.

"Are you going to sign that thing?" said Clive.

"What do you do if I don't?" Barley asked.

"Nothing. Because I'm telling you now, formally and in front of witnesses, that this meeting and everything that passes between us is secret. Harry's a lawyer."

"I'm afraid that's true," I said.

Barley pushed the unsigned form away from him across the table. "And I'm telling you that if I feel the urge I'll paint it on the rooftops," he said with equal calm.

I resumed my place, taking my important pen with me.

"You seem to have made a pretty good mess of London too, before you left," Clive remarked as he returned the form to his folder. "Debts everywhere. No one knowing where you are. Trails of weeping mistresses. Are you trying to destroy yourself or what?"

"I inherited a romantic list," Barley said.

"What on earth does that mean?" said Clive, unabashed by his own ignorance. "Are we using a smart word for dirty books?"

"My grandfather made a corner in novels for the housemaid. In those days people had housemaids. My father called them 'Novels for the Masses' and continued the tradition."

Bob alone felt moved to offer solace. "God damn it, Barley," he cried, "what's so wrong with romantic literature? Better than some of the horse manure they put out.

My wife reads the stuff in bucketfuls. Never did *her* any harm."

"If you don't like the books you publish, why don't you change them?" Clive asked, who never read anything except Service files and the right-wing press.

"I have a Board," Barley replied wearily, as if to a tiresome child. "I have Trustees. I have family shareholders. I have aunts. They like the old safe lines. How-to's. Romances. Tie-ins. Birds of the British Empire." A glance at Bob. "Inside the CIA."

"Why didn't you go to the Moscow audio fair?" Clive repeated.

"The aunts cancelled the match."

"Will you explain that?"

"I thought I'd take the firm into audio cassettes. The family found out and thought I wouldn't. End of story."

"So you ran away," said Clive. "Is that what you normally do when somebody thwarts you? Perhaps you'd better tell us what this letter's about," he suggested and, without looking at Barley, slid it along the table to Ned.

Not the original. That was in Langley, being tested for everything from fingerprints to Legionnaires' disease by the unchallengeable forces of technology. A facsimile, prepared to Ned's meticulous instruction, down to the sealed brown envelope marked "Personal for Mr. Bartholomew Scott Blair, urgent," in Katya's hand, then slit with a paperknife to show it had been opened along the way. Clive handed it to Ned. Ned handed it to Barley. Walter scrabbled at his scalp with his paw and Bob looked on magnanimously like the nice guy who had donated the money. Barley shot a look in my direction, as if he had appointed himself my client. What do I do with this? he was asking with his glance. Do I read it or do I chuck it back at them? I remained, I hope, impassive. I didn't have clients any more. I had the Service.

"Read it slowly," Ned warned.

"Take all the time in the world, Barley," said Bob.

How often had we all of us not read the same letter during the last week? I wondered, watching Barley examine the envelope front and back, hold it away from him, hold it close, his round spectacles raised like goggles to his forehead. How many opinions had they not listened to and discarded? It was written in a train, six experts in Langley had pronounced. In bed, said three more in London. In the back of a car. In haste, in jest, in love, in terror. By a woman, by a man, they had said. The writer is left-handed, right-handed. Is someone whose script of origin is Cyrillic, is Roman, is both, is neither.

As a final twist of the comedy, they had even consulted old Palfrey. "Under our own copyright law the recipient owns the physical letter but the writer owns the copyright," I had told them. "I don't imagine anyone will take you through the Soviet courts." I couldn't tell whether they were worried or relieved by my opinion.

"Do you recognise the handwriting or not?" Clive asked Barley.

Poking his long fingers into the envelope, Barley finally fished out the letter—but disdainfully, as if still half expecting it to be a bill. Then paused. And removed his quaint round spectacles and laid them on the table. Then turned his chair and himself away from everyone. And as he began to read, his face buckled into a frown. He finished the first page then glanced at the end of the letter for the signature. He turned to the second page and read the rest of the letter clean through. Then he read the whole of it over again in one run from "My beloved Barley" to "Your loving K." After which he clutched the letter jealously into his lap with both hands and craned his trunk over it so that by design or accident his face was hidden from everyone and his forelock hung down like a hook and his private prayers stayed private to himself.

"She's potty," he pronounced into the blackness below him. "Certifiably, totally barmy. She wasn't even there."

Nobody asked, who's *she?* or where's *there?* Even Clive knew the value of a good silence.

"K short for Katya, short for Yekaterina, I take it," piped Walter after a further wait. "The patronymic is Borisovna." He was wearing a crooked bow tie, yellow, with a brown-and-orange motif.

"Don't know a K, don't know a Katya, don't know a Yekaterina," Barley said. "Borisovna ditto. Never screwed one, never flirted with one, never proposed to one, never even married one. Never *met* one, far as I remember. Yes, I did."

They waited, I waited; and we would have waited all night and there would not have been the creak of a chair or the clearing of a throat while Barley ransacked his memory for a Katya.

"Old cow in Aurora," Barley resumed. "Tried to flog me some art prints of Russian painters. I didn't bite. Aunts would have blown their corks."

"Aurora?" Clive asked, not knowing whether it was a city or a State agency.

"Publishers."

"Do you remember her other name?"

Barley shook his head, his face still out of sight. "Beard," he said. "Katya of the beard. Ninety in the shade."

Bob's rich voice had a stereophonic quality, and a knack of changing things simply by its reach. "Want to read it aloud, Barley?" he called with the hominess of an old scouting buddy. "Maybe reading it aloud will freshen up your memory. Want to try, Barley?"

Barley, Barley, everyone his friend except Clive, who never once, to my memory, called him anything but Blair.

"Yes, do that, will you. Read it aloud," said Clive, making an order of it, and Barley to my surprise seemed to think it a good idea. Sitting himself up with one joint-less movement of his back, he arranged his torso in such a way that both the letter and his face were in the light. Frowning as before, he started reading aloud in a tone of studied mystification.

"*My beloved Barley.*" He tilted the letter and began again. "*My beloved Barley, Do you remember a promise you made to me one night in Peredelkino as we lay on the verandah of our friends' dacha and recited to each other the poetry of a great Russian mystic who loved England? You swore to me that you would always prefer humanity to nations and that when the day came you would act like a decent human being.*"

He had stopped again.

"Is none of that true?" said Clive.

"I told you. I never *met* the hag!"

There was a force in Barley's denial that was not there before. He was shoving back something that was threatening him.

"*So now I am asking you to redeem your promise, though not in the way we might have imagined that night when we agreed to become lovers.* Total balls," he muttered. "Silly cow's got it all mixed up. *I ask you to show this book to English people who think as we do. Publish it for me, using the arguments you expressed with so much fire. Show it to your scientists and artists and intelligentsia and tell them it is the first stone of a great avalanche and they must throw the next stone for themselves. Tell them that with the new openness we can move together to destroy the destruction and castrate the monster we have created. Ask them which is more dangerous to mankind: to conform like a slave or resist like a man? Act like a decent human being, Barley. I love Herzen's England and you. Your loving K.* Who the hell is she? She's off her tree. They both are."

Leaving the letter on the table, Barley wandered off into the dark end of the room, softly cursing, hammering his right fist downward on to the air. "Hell's the woman up to?" he protested. "She's taken two completely different stories and twisted them together. Anyway, where's the book?" He had remembered us and was facing us again.

"The book is safe," said Clive, with a sideways glance at me.

"Where is it, please? It's mine."

"We rather thought it was her friend's," said Clive.

"I've been charged with it. You saw what he wrote. I'm his publisher. It's mine. You've no right to it."

He had landed with both feet in the very ground we wished him not to enter. But Clive was quick to distract him.

"*He?*" Clive repeated. "You mean Katya's a man? Why do you say *he?* You really are confusing us, you know. You're a confusing person, I suppose."

I had been expecting the outburst sooner. I had sensed already that Barley's submissiveness was a truce and not a victory, and that each time Clive reined him in he brought him nearer to revolt. So that when Barley sauntered up to the table, leaned across it and slackly raised his hands, palms forward, from his sides, in what might well have been a docile gesture of helplessness, I did not necessarily expect him to offer Clive a sweetly reasoned answer to his question. But not even I had reckoned with the scale of the detonation.

"You have no damned right!" Barley bellowed straight into Clive's face, smashing his palms on to the table so hard that my papers bounced up and down in front of me. Brock came rushing from the hall. Ned had to order him back. "That's *my* manuscript. Sent to me by *my* author. For *my* consideration in *my* good time. You have no right to steal it, read it or keep it. So give me the book and go home to your squalid island." He flung out an arm at Bob. "And take your Boston Brahmin with you."

"*Our* island," Clive reminded him. "The book, as you call it, is not a book at all and neither you nor we have any right to it," he continued frigidly and untruthfully. "I'm not interested in your precious publishing ethics. Nobody here is. All we know is, the manuscript in question contains military secrets about the Soviet Union that, assuming they are true, are vital to the defence of the West. To which hemisphere you also belong——I take it, thankfully. What would you do in our place? Ignore it? Throw it into the sea? Or try to find out how it came to be addressed to a derelict British publisher?"

"He wants it published! By me! Not hidden in your vaults!"

"Quite," said Clive with another glance at me.

"The manuscript has been officially impounded and classified as top secret," I said. "It's subject to the same restrictions as this meeting. But even more so." My old law tutor would have turned in his grave——not, I am afraid, for the first time. But it's always wonderful what a lawyer can achieve when nobody knows the law.

One minute and fourteen seconds was how long the silence lasted on the tape. Ned timed it with his stopwatch when he got back to the Russia House. He had been waiting for it, even relishing it, but he still began to fear that he had hit one of those maddening faults that always seem to happen with recorders at the crucial moment. But when he listened harder he caught the grumble of a distant car and a scrap of girl's laughter carrying to the window, because Barley by then had thrown the curtains open and was staring down into the square. For one minute and fourteen seconds, then, we watched Barley's strangely articulate back silhouetted against the Lisbon night. Then comes a most frightful crash like the shattering of several window panes at once, followed by an oil gush, and you would suppose that Barley had staged his long-delayed breakout, taking the ornamental Portuguese wall plates and curly flower vases with him. But the truth is, the whole rumpus is only the sound of Barley discovering the drinks table and dumping three cubes of ice into a crystal tumbler and pouring a decent measure of Scotch over them, all within a couple of inches' range of a microphone that Brock with his characteristic over-production had concealed in one of the richly carved compartments.

4

He had made a base camp at his own end of the room on a stiff school chair as far away from us as he could get. He perched on it sideways to us, stooped over his whisky glass, which he held in both hands, peering into it like a great thinker or at least a lonely one. He spoke not to us but to himself, emphatically and scathingly, not stirring except to take a sip from his glass or buck his head in affirmation of some private and usually abstracted point of narrative. He spoke in the mixture of pedantry and disbelief that people use to reconstruct a disastrous episode, such as a death or a traffic accident. So I was *here* and you were *there* and the other chap came from over *there*.

"It was last Moscow book fair. The Sunday. Not the Sunday before, the Sunday after," he said.

"September," Ned suggested, at which Barley rolled his head around and muttered "Thanks," as if genuinely grateful to be prodded. Then he wrinkled his nose and fussed his spectacles and began again.

"We were knackered," he said. "Most of the exhibitors had got out on the Friday. It was only a bunch of us who hung around. Those who had contracts to tidy up, or no particular reason to get back in a hurry."

He was a compelling man and he had centre stage. It was difficult not to attach to him a little, stuck out there on his own. It was difficult not to think, There but for the grace of God go I. And the more so since none of us knew where he was going.

"We got drunk on Saturday night and on the Sunday we all drove out to Peredelkino in Jumbo's car." Once again he seemed to have to remind himself that he had an audience. "Peredelkino is the Soviet writers' village," he said as if none of us had heard of it. "They get dachas there for as long as they behave themselves. Writers' Union runs it on a members-only basis—who gets a dacha, who writes best in prison, who doesn't write at all."

"Who's Jumbo?" said Ned—a rare interjection.

"Jumbo Oliphant. Peter Oliphant. Chairman of Lupus Books. Closet Scottish Fascist. Black-belt Freemason. Thinks he's got a special wavelength to the Sovs. Gold card." Remembering Bob, he tilted his head at him. "Not American Express, I'm afraid. A Moscow book fair gold card, dished out by the Russian organisers, saying what a big boy he is. Free car, free translator, free hotel, free caviar. Jumbo was born with a gold card in his mouth."

Bob grinned too broadly in order to show the joke was taken in good part. Yet he was a large-hearted man and Barley had spotted this. Barley, it occurred to me, was one of those people from whom good natures cannot hide, just as he could not disguise his own accessibility.

"So off we all went," Barley resumed, returning to his reverie. "Oliphant from Lupus, Emery from the Bodley Head. And some girl from Penguin, can't remember her name. Yes, I can. Magda. How the hell could I forget a Magda? And Blair from A. & B."

Riding like nabobs in Jumbo's stupid limo, said

Barley, tossing out short sentences like old clothes from his memory box. Ordinary car not good enough for our Jumbo, had to be a damn great Chaika with curtains in the bedroom, no brakes and a gorilla with bad breath for a driver. The plan was to take a look at Pasternak's dacha, which rumour had it was about to be declared a museum, though another rumour insisted that the bastards were about to pull it down. Maybe his grave as well. Jumbo Oliphant didn't know who Pasternak was at first but Magda murmured "Zhivago" and Jumbo had seen the film, said Barley. There was no earthly hurry, all they wanted was a bit of a walk and a peck of country air. But Jumbo's driver used the special lane reserved for official roadhogs in Chaikas, so they did the journey in about ten seconds flat instead of an hour, parked in a puddle and shlepped up to the cemetery still trembling with gratitude from the drive.

"Cemetery on a hillside among a lot of trees. Driver stays in the car. Raining. Not much, but he's worried about his awful suit." He paused, in contemplation of the driver. "Mad ape," he muttered.

But I had the feeling Barley was railing at himself and not the driver. I seemed to hear a whole self-accusing chorus in Barley, and I wondered whether the others were hearing it as well. He had people inside himself who really drove him mad.

Point was, Barley explained, that as luck would have it they had hit a day when the liberated masses were out in force. In the past, he said, whenever he'd been there, the place had been deserted. Just the fenced-in tombs and the creepy trees. But on that September Sunday with the unfamiliar smells of freedom in the air, there were about two hundred fans crammed round the grave and more by the time they left, all shapes and sizes. Grave was knee-deep in flowers, Barley said. Offerings pouring in all the time. People passing bouquets over the heads to get them on the heap.

Then the readings began. Little chap read poetry. Big girl read prose. Then a filthy little aeroplane flew so low overhead you couldn't hear a thing. Then it flew back the other way. Then back the same way.

"Wang, wang!" Barley yelled, his long wrist whipping back and forth through the air. "Wee-ah, wee-ah," he whined through his nose in disgust.

But the plane couldn't damp the enthusiasm of the crowd any more than the rain could. Someone began singing, the punters took up the refrain and it became a knees-up. Finally the plane pushed off, presumably because it was low on fuel. But that wasn't what you felt, said Barley. Not a bit. You felt the singing had shot the little swine out of the sky.

The singing grew stronger and deeper and more mystical. Barley knew three words of Russian and the others none. Didn't stop them joining in. Didn't stop the girl Magda from crying her eyes out. Or Jumbo Oliphant from swearing to God, through lumps in his throat, as they walked away down the hill that he was going to publish every word Pasternak had written, not just the film but the other stuff, so help me, and subsidise it out of his very own personal pocket as soon as he got back to his damask castle in the docklands.

"Jumbo has these hot flushes of enthusiasm," Barley explained with a disarming grin, returning to his audience, but principally to Ned. "Sometimes they don't die down for minutes on end." Then he paused and frowned again and pulled off his strange round spectacles that seemed to be more an infliction than a help, and peered at everybody in turn as if to remind himself of his situation.

They were still walking down the hill, he said, and still having a good cry when this same little Russian chap came darting up to them holding his cigarette to one side of his face like a candle, asking in English whether they were Americans.

Once again Clive was ahead of all of us. His head slowly lifted. There was a knife-edge to his managerial drawl. "Same? What same little Russian chap? We haven't had one."

Unpleasantly reminded of Clive's presence, Barley screwed up his face in a renewal of distaste. "He was the reader, for goodness' sake," he said. "Chap who'd read Pasternak's poetry at the graveside. He asked if we were American. I said no, thank God, British."

And I noticed, as I supposed we all did, that it was Barley himself, not Oliphant or Emery or the girl Magda, who had become the appointed spokesman of their group.

Barley had fallen into direct dialogue. He had the mynah bird's ear. He had a Russian accent for the little chap and a Scottish woof-woof voice for Oliphant. The mimicry slipped out of him as if he were unaware of it.

"You are writers?" the little chap asked, in Barley's voice for him.

"No, alas. Just publishers," said Barley, in his own.

"English publishers?"

"Here for the Moscow book fair. I run a corner shop called Abercrombie & Blair and this is the Chairman Himself of Lupus Books. Very rich bloke. Be a knight one day. Gold card and bar. Right, Jumbo?"

Oliphant protested that Barley was saying *far* too much. But the little chap wanted more.

"May I ask then what were you doing at Pasternak's grave?" said the little chap.

"Chance visit," Oliphant said, barging in again. "Total chance. We saw a crowd, we came up to see what was going on. Pure chance. Let's go."

But Barley had no intention of going. He was annoyed by Oliphant's manners, he said, and he wasn't going to stand by while a fat Scottish millionaire gave the brush-off to an undernourished Russian stranger.

"We're doing what everyone else here's doing," Barley replied. "We're paying our respects to a great writer. We liked your reading too. Very moving. Great stuff. Ace."

"You respect Boris Pasternak?" the little chap asked.

Oliphant again, the great civil rights activist, rendered by a gruff voice and a twisted jaw: "We have no position on the matter of Boris Pasternak or any other Soviet writer," he said. "We're here as guests. Solely as guests. We have no opinions on internal Soviet affairs."

"We think he's marvellous," Barley said. "World class. A star."

"But why?" asked the little chap, provoking the conflict.

Barley needed no urging. Never mind he wasn't totally convinced that Pasternak was the genius he was cracked up to be, he said. Never mind that, as a matter of fact, he thought Pasternak quite seriously overpraised. That was publisher's opinion, whereas this was war.

"We respect his talent and his art," Barley replied. "We respect his humanity. We respect his family and his culture. And tenthly or whatever it is, we respect his capacity to reach the hearts of the Russian people despite the fact that he had the daylights hounded out of him by a bunch of bureau-rats who are very probably the same little beasts who sent us that aeroplane."

"Can you quote him?" the little chap asked.

Barley had that kind of memory, he explained to us

awkwardly. "I gave him the first couplet of 'Nobel Prize.' I thought it was appropriate after that foul aeroplane."

"Give it to us now, please, will you?" said Clive, as if everything had to be checked.

Barley mumbled, and it crossed my mind that he might actually be a very shy man.

> "Like a beast in the pen, I'm cut off
> From my friends, freedom, the sun,
> But the hunters are gaining ground.
> I've nowhere else to run."

The little chap was frowning at the lighted end of his cigarette while he listened to this, said Barley, and for a moment he really did wonder whether they had walked into a provocation as Oliphant feared.

"If you respect Pasternak so much, why don't you come and meet some friends of mine?" the little chap suggested. "We are writers here. We have a dacha. We would be honoured to talk to distinguished British publishers."

Oliphant had only to hear the first half of this speech to develop a severe case of the bends, said Barley. Jumbo knew all about accepting invitations from strange Russians. He was an expert on it. He knew how they ensnared you, drugged you, compromised you with disgraceful photographs and obliged you to resign your directorships and give up your chances of a knighthood. He was also in the middle of an ambitious joint publishing deal through VAAP, and the last thing he needed was to be found in the company of undesirables. Oliphant boomed all this to Barley in a theatrical whisper that assumed the little stranger was deaf.

"Anyway," Oliphant ended triumphantly, "it's raining. What are we going to do about the car?"

Oliphant looked at his watch. The girl Magda looked at the ground. The bloke Emery looked at the girl Magda and thought there could be worse things to do on a Sunday afternoon in Moscow. But Barley, as he told it, took another look at the stranger and decided to like what he saw. He had no designs on the girl or on a knighthood. He had already decided he would rather be photographed in the raw with any number of Russian tarts than fully dressed on the arm of Jumbo Oliphant. So he waved them all off in Jumbo's limo and stayed behind with the stranger.

"Nezhdanov," Barley declared abruptly to the silent room, interrupting his own flow. "I've remembered the chap's name. Nezhdanov. Playwright. Ran one of these studio theatres, couldn't put on his own plays."

Walter spoke, his soaring voice shattering the momentary lull. "My dear boy, Vitaly Nezhdanov is a latterday *hero*. He has *three* one-acters opening in Moscow just five weeks from now, and everyone has the most exotic hopes for them. Not that he's a blind bit of good, but we're not allowed to say that because he's a dissident. Or was."

For the first time since I had set eyes on him, Barley's face took on a sublimely happy aspect, and at once I had the feeling that this was the real man, whom the clouds till now had hidden. "Oh, now that's really great," he said with the simple pleasure of someone able to enjoy another man's success. "Fantastic. That's just what Vitaly needed. Thanks for telling me," he said, looking a fraction of his age.

Then once again his face darkened over and he began drinking his whisky in little nips. "Well, there we all were," he murmured vaguely. "More the merrier. Meet my cousin. Have a sausage roll." But his eyes, I noticed, like his words, had acquired a remote quality, as if he were already looking forward to an ordeal.

I glanced along the table. Bob smiling. Bob would smile on his deathbed, but with an old scout's sincerity. Clive in profile, his face keen as an axe and about as profound. Walter never at rest. Walter with his clever head thrown back, twisting a hank of hair around his spongy forefinger while he smirked at the ornate ceiling, writhed and sweated. And Ned, the leader—capable, resourceful Ned—Ned the linguist and the warrior, the doer and the planner—sitting as he had sat from the beginning, to attention, waiting for the order to advance. Some people, I reflected, watching him, are cursed with too much loyalty, for a day could come when there was nothing left for them to serve.

Big, rambling house, Barley was reciting in the telegraphese he had resorted to. Edwardian clapboard, fretted verandahs, overgrown garden, birch forest. Rotting benches, charcoal fire, smell of a cricket ground on a rainy day, ivy. About thirty people, mostly men, sitting and standing around in the garden, cooking, drinking, ignoring the bad weather just like the English. Lousy old cars parked along the roadside, just like English cars used to be before Thatcher's pigs in clover took over the ship. Good faces, fluent voices, arty *nomenklatura*. Enter Nezhdanov leading Barley. No heads turn.

"Hostess was a poet," Barley said. "Tamara something. Dikey lady, white hair, jolly. Husband editor of one of the science magazines. Nezhdanov was his brother-in-law. Everyone was someone's brother-in-law. The lit. scene has clout over there. If you've got a voice and they let you use it, you've got a public."

In his arbitrary memory, Barley now split the occasion

into three parts. Lunch, which began around two-thirty when the rain stopped. Night, which followed immediately upon lunch. And what he called "the last bit," which was when whatever happened had happened, and which so far as any of us could ever fathom occurred in the blurred hours between about two and four when Barley, to use his own words, was drifting painlessly between nirvana and a near-terminal hangover.

Until lunch came along, Barley had pottered from group to group, he said——first with Nezhdanov, then alone, having a shmooze with whoever felt like talking to him.

"Shmooze?" Clive repeated suspiciously, as if he had learned of a new vice.

Bob hastened to interpret. "A chat, Clive," he explained in his friendly way. "A chat and a drink. Nothing sinister."

But when lunch was called, said Barley, they sat themselves at a trestle table with Barley up one end and Nezhdanov the other and bottles of Georgian white between them, and everyone talking their best English about whether truth was truth if it was not convenient to the great proletarian so-called Revolution, and whether we should revert to the spiritual values of our ancestors and whether the *perestroika* was having any positive effect on the lives of the common people, and how if you really wanted to know what was wrong with the Soviet Union the best way to find out was to try sending a refrigerator from Novosibirsk to Leningrad.

To my secret irritation, Clive again cut in. Like a man bored by irrelevances, he wanted names. Barley slapped his forehead with his palm, his hostility to Clive forgotten. Names, Clive, God. One chap a professor at Moscow State but I never caught his name, you see. Another chap in chemical procurement——that was Nezhdanov's half-brother, they called him the Apothecary. Somebody in the Soviet Academy of Sciences, Gregor, but I didn't get round to finding out what his name was, let alone his angle.

"Any women at the table?" Ned asked.

"Two, but no Katya," said Barley, and Ned like myself was visibly impressed by the pace of his perception.

"But there was *someone* else, wasn't there?" Ned suggested.

Barley leaned himself slowly backwards to drink. Then forward again as he planted the glass between his knees and stooped over it, nose down, inhaling its wisdom.

"Sure, sure, sure, there was someone else," he agreed. "There always is, isn't there?" he added enigmatically. "Not Katya. Someone else."

His voice had changed. From what to what I couldn't fathom. A shorter ring. A hint of regret or remorse. I waited as we all did. I think we all sensed even then that something extraordinary was appearing on the horizon.

"Thin bearded chap," Barley went on, staring into the gloom as if he were making him out at last. "Tall. Dark suit, black tie. Hollow face. Must be why he grew a beard. Sleeves too short. Black hair. Drunk."

"Did he have a name?" asked Ned.

Barley was still staring at the half-dark, describing what none of us could see.

"Goethe," he said at last. "Like the poet. They called him Goethe. Meet our distinguished writer Goethe. Could have been fifty, could have been eighteen. Thin as a boy. These dabs of colour on his cheeks, very high up. Beard."

Which, as Ned remarked later, when he was playing over the tape to the team, was operationally speaking the moment when the Bluebird spread his wings. It is not marked by any awesome silence or the intake of breath around the table. Instead, Barley chose this moment to be assailed by a sneezing fit, his first of many in our experience of him. It began as a series of single rounds, then accelerated to a grand salvo. Then it slowly petered out again while he beat his face with his handkerchief and cursed between convulsions.

"Bloody kennel cough," he explained apologetically.

"I was brilliant," Barley resumed. "Couldn't put a hoof wrong."

He had refilled his glass, this time with water. He was sipping from it in slow rhythmic movements like one of those plastic drinking birds that used to bob up and down between the miniatures on every gloomy English bar in the days before television sets replaced them.

"Mr. Wonderful, that was me. Star of stage and screen. Western, courteous and specious. That's why I go there, isn't it? Sovs are the only people daft enough to listen to my bullshit." His forelock dipped towards his glass again. "It's the way it happens there. You go for a walk in the countryside and end up arguing with a bunch of drunk poets about freedom versus responsibility. You take a leak in some filthy public loo, somebody leans over from the next stall and asks you whether there's life after death. Because you're a Westerner. So you know. And you tell them. And they remember. Nothing goes away."

He seemed to be in danger of ceasing to talk at all.

"Why don't you just tell us what happened and leave the reproaches to us?" Clive suggested, somehow implying that the reproaches were above Barley's station.

"I shone. That's what happened. A glib mind had a field day. Forget it."

But forgetting was the last thing anybody intended, as Bob's cheerful smile showed. "Barley, I think you are being too hard on yourself. Nobody should blame themselves for being entertaining, for Pete's sake. All you did was sing for your supper, by the sounds of it."

"What did you talk about?" said Clive, undeflected by Bob's goodheartedness.

Barley shrugged. "How to rebuild the Russian Empire between lunch and teatime. Peace, progress and *glasnost* by the bottleful. Instant disarmament without the option."

"Are these subjects you frequently enlarge upon?"

"When I'm in Russia, yes they are," Barley retorted, provoked again by Clive's tone, but never for long.

"May we know what you said?"

But Barley was not telling his story to Clive. He was telling it to himself and to the room and whoever was in it, to his fellow passengers, point for point, an inventory of his folly. "Disarmament was not a military matter and not a political one, I said. It was a matter of human will. We had to decide whether we wanted peace or war and prepare for it. Because what we prepared for was going to be what we got." He broke off. "It was top-of-my-head stuff," he explained, again selecting Ned. "Warmed-up arguments I'd read around the place."

As if he felt more explanation was required, he started again. "It so happened I was an expert that week. I'd thought the firm might commission a quick book. Some tout at the book fair wanted me to take UK rights in a book on *glasnost* and the crisis of peace. Essays by past and present hawks, reappraisals of strategy. Could real peace break out after all? They'd signed up some of the old American warhorses from the sixties and shown how a lot of them had turned full circle since they left office."

He was apologising and I wondered why. What was he preparing us for? Why did he feel he should lessen the shock in advance? Bob, who was no kind of fool, for all his candour, must have been asking himself the same question.

"Sounds a fine enough idea to me, Barley. *I* can see money in that. Might even take a piece of it myself," he added with a locker-room chuckle.

"So you had the patter," Clive said in his barbed undertone. "And you regurgitated it. Is that what you're telling us? I'm sure it isn't easy to reconstruct one's alcoholic flights of fancy but we'd be grateful if you'd do your best."

What had Clive studied, I wondered, if he ever had? Where? Who bore him, sired him? Where did the Service find these dead suburban souls with all their values, or lack of them, perfectly in place?

Yet Barley remained compliant in the face of this renewed onslaught. "I said I believed in Gorbachev," he said equably, giving himself a sip of water. "They mightn't, I did. I said the West's job was to find the other half of him, and the East's was to recognise the importance of the half they had. I said that if the Americans had ever bothered as much about disarmament as they had about putting some fool on the moon or pink stripes into toothpaste, we'd have had disarmament long ago. I said the West's great sin was to believe we could bankrupt the Soviet system by raising the bidding on the arms race, because that way were gambling with the fate of mankind. I said that by shaking our sabres the West had given the Soviet leaders the excuse to keep their gates locked and run a garrison state."

Walter let out a whinnying laugh and cupped his gappy teeth with his hairless hand. "Oh my Lord! So *we're* to blame for Russia's ills. Oh, I think that's *marvellously* rich! You don't think that by any chance they did it to themselves, for instance? Locked themselves up inside their own paranoia? No, he doesn't. I can see."

Undeterred, Barley resumed his confession. "Somebody asked me, didn't I think nuclear weapons had kept the peace for forty years? I said that was Jesuitical bollocks. Might as well say gunpowder had kept the peace between Waterloo and Sarajevo. Anyway, I said, what's peace? The bomb didn't stop Korea and it didn't stop Vietnam. It didn't stop anyone from pinching Czecho or blockading Berlin or building the Berlin Wall or going into Afghanistan. If that's peace, let's try it without the bomb. I said what was needed was not experiments in space but experiments in human nature. The superpowers should police the world together. I was flying."

"And did you *believe* any of this nonsense?" Clive asked.

Barley didn't seem to know. He seemed suddenly to regard himself as facile by definition, and became shamefaced. "Then we talked about jazz," he said. "Bix Beiderbecke, Louis Armstrong, Lester Young. I played some."

"You mean somebody had a *saxophone?*" Bob cried in spontaneous amusement. "What else did they have? Bass drums? A ten-piece band? Barley, I'm not believing this!"

I thought at first that Barley was walking out. He unwound himself and clambered to his feet. He peered round for the door, then headed apologetically towards it, so that Ned rose in alarm, afraid that Brock would get to him first. But Barley had halted halfway across the room where a low carved table stood. Stooping before it, he began lightly slapping his fingertips on the edge while he sang "pah-pah-paah, pah-pah-pah-pah," through his nose, to the simulated accompaniment of cymbals, wire brushes and drums.

Bob was already applauding, Walter too. So was I, and Ned was laughing. Clive alone found nothing to entertain him. Barley took a sobering pull from his glass and sat down again.

"Then they asked me what could be done," he said as if he'd never left his chair.

"Who did?" said Clive, with that maddening note of disbelief he had.

"One of the people at the table. What does it matter?"

"Let's assume everything matters," said Clive.

Barley was doing his Russian voice again, clogged and pressing. " 'All right, Barley. Given is all as you say. Who will conduct these experiments in human nature?' You will, I said. They were very surprised. Why us? I said because, when it came to radical change, the Sovs had it easier than the West. They had a small leadership and an intelligentsia with great traditional influence. In a Western democracy it was much harder to make yourself heard above the crowd. They were pleased by the paradox. So was I."

Not even this frontal assault upon the great democratic values could ruffle Bob's genial forbearance. "Well, Barley, that's a broadbrush judgment but I guess there's some truth in it at that."

"But did you suggest what should be *done?*" Clive insisted.

"I said there was only Utopia left. I said that what had looked like a pipe dream twenty years ago was today our only hope, whether we're talking disarmament or ecology or plain human survival. Gorbachev understood that, the West didn't want to. I said that Western intellectuals must find their voice. I said the West should be setting the example, not following it. It was everyone's duty to start the avalanche."

"So unilateral disarmament," said Clive, clamping his hands together in a knot. "Aldermaston, here we come. Well, well. Yes." Except that he didn't say "yes" so much as "ears," which was how he said yes when he meant no.

But Bob was impressed. "And all this eloquence just from reading around the subject a little?" he said. "Barley, I think that's extraordinary. Why, if I could absorb that way, I'd be a proud man."

Perhaps *too* extraordinary, he was also suggesting, but the implications evidently passed Barley by.

"And while you were saving us from our worst instincts, what was the man called Goethe doing?" asked Clive.

"Nothing. The others joined in. Goethe didn't."

"But he listened? Wide-eyed, I should imagine."

"We were redesigning the world by then. Yalta all over again. Everyone was talking at once. Except Goethe. He didn't eat, he didn't talk. I kept tossing ideas at him, simply because he wasn't joining in. All he did was grow paler and drink more. I gave him up."

And Goethe never spoke, Barley continued in the same tone of mystified self-recrimination. All through the afternoon not a dicky-bird, Barley said. Goethe would listen, he'd glare into some invisible crystal ball. He'd laugh, though not by any means when there was anything much to laugh about. Or he'd get up and cut a straightish line to the drinks table to fetch himself another vodka when everyone else was drinking wine, and come back with a tumbler of the stuff, which he knocked off in a couple of swigs whenever anyone proposed a fitting toast. But Goethe, he proposed no toasts at all, said Barley. He was one of those people who exert a moral influence by their silence, he said, so that you end up wondering whether they're dying of a secret illness or riding on some great accomplishment.

When Nezhdanov led the group indoors to listen to Count Basie on the stereo, Goethe tagged obediently along. It wasn't till late into the night, when Barley had given up all thought of him, that he finally heard Goethe speak.

Once again Ned permitted himself a rare question. "How did the others behave towards him?"

"They respected him. He was their mascot. 'Let's see what Goethe thinks.' He'd raise his glass and drink to them and we'd all laugh except Goethe."

"The women too?"

"Everyone. They deferred to him. Practically made way for him. The great Goethe, here he comes."

"And no one told you where he lived or worked?"

"They said he was on holiday from somewhere where drinking wasn't approved of. So it was a drinking holiday. They kept drinking to his drinking holiday. He was someone's brother. Tamara's, I don't know. Maybe cousin. I didn't catch it."

"Do you think they were protecting him?" said Clive.

Barley's pauses are like nobody else's, I thought. He has his own tenuous hold on present things. His mind leaves the room and you wait on tenterhooks to see whether it will come back.

"Yes," said Barley suddenly, sounding surprised by his own answer. "Yes, yes, they were protecting him. That's right. They were his supporters' club, of course they were."

"Protecting him from what?"

Another pause.

"Maybe from having to explain himself. I didn't think that at the time. But I think it now. Yes I do."

"And why should he not explain himself? Can you suggest a reason without inventing one?" asked Clive, determined apparently to hold Barley to the angry edge.

But Barley didn't rise. "I don't invent," he said, and I think we all knew that was true. He was gone again. "He was high-powered. You felt it in him," he said, returning.

"What does that mean?"

"The eloquent silence. All you hear at a hundred miles an hour is the ticking of the brain."

"But no one told you, 'He's a genius,' or whatever?"

"No one told me. No one needed to."

Barley glanced at Ned to find him nodding his understanding. A fieldman to his fingertips, if necessarily a grounded one, Ned had a way of popping up ahead of you when you thought he was still trying to catch you up.

Bob had another question. "Anyone take you by the elbow and explain to you just *why* Goethe had a drinking problem, Barley?"

Barley let out an unfettered laugh. His momentary freedoms were a little frightening. "You don't have to have a *reason* to drink in Russia, for Christ's sake! Name me a single Russian worth his salt who could face the problems of his country sober!"

He dropped into silence again, grimacing into the shadows. He wrinkled up his eyes and muttered an imprecation of some kind, I assumed against himself. Then snapped out of it. "Woke with a jolt round midnight." He laughed. " 'Christ. Where am I?' Lying in a deck chair on a verandah with a bloody blanket over me! Thought I was in the States at first. One of those New

England screened porches with panels of mosquito gauze and the garden beyond. Couldn't think how I'd got to America so fast after a pleasant lunch in Peredelkino. Then I remembered they'd stopped talking to me and I'd got bored. Nothing personal. They were drunk and they were tired of being drunk in a foreign language. So I'd settled on the verandah with a bottle of Scotch. Somebody had thrown a blanket over me to keep the dew off. The moon must have woken me, I thought. Big full moon. Bloodshot. Then I heard this chap talking to me. Very sombre. Immaculate English. Christ, I thought, new guests at this hour. 'Some things are necessary evils, Mr. Barley. Some things are more evil than necessary,' he says. He's quoting me from lunch. Part of my world-shaking lecture on peace. I don't know who I was quoting. Then I take a closer look around and I make out this nine-foot-tall bearded vulture hovering over me, clutching a bottle of vodka, hair flapping round his face in the breeze. Next thing I know he's crouching beside me with his knees up round his ears, filling up his glass. 'Hullo, Goethe,' I say. 'Why aren't you dead yet? Nice to see you about.' "

Whatever had set Barley free had put him back in prison again, for his face had once more clouded over.

"Then he gives me back another of my lunchtime pearls. 'All victims are equal. None are more equal than others.'

"I laugh. But not too much. I'm embarrassed, I suppose. Queasy. Feel I've been spied on. Chap sits there all through lunch, drunk, doesn't eat, doesn't say a word. All of a sudden ten hours later he's quoting me like a tape recorder. It's not comfortable.

" 'Who are you, Goethe?' I say. 'What do you do for a living when you're not drinking and listening?'

" 'I'm a moral outcast,' he says. 'I trade in defiled theories.'

" 'Always nice to meet a writer,' I say. 'What sort of stuff are you turning out these days?'

" 'Everything,' he says. 'History, comedy, lies, romances.' Then off he goes into some drivel he wrote about a lump of butter melting in the sun because it lacked a consistent point of view. Only thing was, he didn't talk like a writer. Too diffident. He was laughing at himself, and for all I knew he was laughing at me too. Not that he hadn't every right to, but that didn't make it any funnier."

Once more we waited, watching Barley's silhouette. Was the tension in us or in him? He took a sip from his glass. He rolled his head around and muttered something like "not well" or possibly "to hell" which neither his audience nor the microphones ever completely caught. We heard his chair crackle like wet firewood. On the tape it sounds like an armed attack.

"So then he says to me, 'Come on, Mr. Barley. You're a publisher. Aren't you going to ask me where I get my ideas from?' And I thought, That's not what publishers ask actually, old boy, but what the hell? 'Okay, Goethe,' I say. 'Where do you get your ideas from?'

" 'Mr. Barley. My ideas are obtained from—one'—he starts counting."

Barley too had spread his long fingers and was counting on them, using only the lightest Russian intonations. And once again I was struck by the delicacy of his musical memory, which he seemed to achieve less by repeating words than by retrieving them from some cursed echoing chamber where nothing ever faded from his hearing.

" 'My ideas are obtained from—one, the paper tablecloths of Berlin cafés in the nineteen-thirties.' Then he takes a heave of vodka and a great noisy snort of night air both at once. He creaks. Know what I mean? Those chaps with bubbling chests? 'Two,' he says, 'from the publications of my more gifted competitors. Three, from the obscene fantasies of generals and politicians of all nations. Four, from the liberated intellects of press-ganged Nazi scientists. Five, from the great Soviet people, whose every democratic wish is filtered upwards by means of consultation at all levels, then dumped in the Neva. And six, very occasionally from the mind of a distinguished Western intellectual who happens to drop into my life.' That's me, apparently, because he glues his eyes on me to see how I take it. Staring and staring like a precocious child. Transmitting these life-important signals. Then suddenly he changes and becomes suspicious. Russians do that. 'That was quite a performance you gave at lunch,' he says. 'How did you persuade Nezhdanov to invite you?' It's a sneer. Saying I don't believe you.

" 'I didn't persuade him,' I say. 'It was his idea. What are you trying to hang on me?'

" 'There is no ownership of ideas,' he says. 'You put it into his head. You are a clever fellow. Cunning work, I would say. Congratulations.'

"Then instead of sneering at me he's clutching on to my shoulders as if he's drowning. I don't know whether he's ill or he's lost his balance. I've got a nasty feeling he may want to be sick. I try to help him but I don't know how. He's hot as hell and sweating. His sweat's dripping on to me. Hair's all wet. These wild childish eyes. I'll loosen his collar, I think. Then I get his voice, shoved right down my ear, lips and hot breath all at once. I can't hear him at first, he's too near. I back away **but** he comes with me.

" 'I believe every word you said,' he whispers. 'You spoke into my heart. Promise me you are not a British spy and I'll make you a promise in return.'

"His words exactly," Barley said, as if he were ashamed of them. "He remembered every word I'd said. And I remember every word of his."

It was not the first time that Barley had spoken of memory as if it were an affliction, and perhaps that is why I found myself, as so often, thinking of Hannah.

"Poor Palfrey," she had taunted me in one of her cruel moods, studying her naked body in the mirror as she sipped her vodka and tonic and prepared to go back to her husband. "With a memory like yours, how will you ever forget a girl like me?"

Did Barley have that effect on everyone? I wondered—touch their central nerve unconsciously, send them rushing to their closest thoughts? Perhaps that was what he had done to Goethe too.

The passage that followed was never paraphrased, never condensed, never "reconstrued." For the initiated, either the unedited tape was played or else the transcript was offered in its entirety. For the uninitiated, it never existed. It was the crux of everything that followed and it was called with deliberate obfuscation "the Lisbon Approach." When the alchemists and theologians and end-users on both sides of the Atlantic had their turn, this was the passage they picked out and ran through their magic boxes to justify the preselected arguments that characterised their artful camps.

" 'Not a spy actually, Goethe, old boy. Not now, never have been, never will. May be your line of country, not mine. How about chess. Fond of chess? Let's talk about chess.'

"Doesn't seem to hear. 'And you are not an American? You are nobody's spy, not even ours?'

" 'Goethe, listen,' I say. 'I'm getting a bit jumpy, to be honest. I'm nobody's spy. I'm me. Let's either talk about chess or you try a different address, okay?' I thought that would shut him up, but it didn't. Knew all about chess, he said. In chess, one chap has a strategy, and if the other chap doesn't spot it or if he relaxes his watch, you win. In chess, the theory is the reality. But in life, in certain types of life, you can have a situation where a player has such grotesque fantasies about another one that he ends up by inventing the enemy he needs. Do I agree? Goethe, I agree totally. Then suddenly it's not chess any more and he's explaining himself the way Russians do when they're drunk. Why he's on the earth, for my ears only. Says he was born with two souls, just like Faust, which is why they call him Goethe. Says his mother was a painter but she painted what she saw, so naturally she wasn't allowed to exhibit or buy materials. Because anything we see is a State secret. Also if it's an illusion it's a State secret. Even if it doesn't work and never will, it's a State secret. And if it's a lie from top to bottom, then it's the hottest State secret of the lot. Says his father did twelve years in the camps and died of a surfeit of intellectual ability. Says the problem with his father was, he was a martyr. Victims are bad enough, saints are worse, he says, but martyrs are the living end. Do I agree?

"I agree. Don't know why I agree but I'm a polite soul and when a chap who is clutching my head tells me his father's done twelve years then died, I'm not about to quarrel with him even when I'm tight.

"I ask him his real name. Says he hasn't got one. His father took it with him. Says that in any decent society they shoot the ignorant, but in Russia it's the other way around, so they shot his father because, unlike his mother, he refused to die of a broken heart. Says he wants to make me this promise. Says he loves the English. The English are the moral leaders of Europe, the secret steadiers, the unifiers of the great European ideal. Says the English understand the relationship between words and action whereas in Russia nobody believes in action any more, so words have become a substitute, all the way up to the top, a substitute for the truth that nobody wants to hear because they can't change it, or they'll lose their jobs if they change it, or maybe they simply don't know *how* to change it. Says the Russians' misfortune is that they long to be European but their destiny is to become American, and that the Americans have poisoned the world with materialistic logic. If my neighbour has a car, I must have two cars. If my neighbour has a gun, I must have two guns. If my neighbour has a bomb, I must have a bigger bomb and more of them, never mind they can't reach their targets. So all I have to do is imagine my neighbour's gun and double it and I have the justification for whatever I want to manufacture. Do I agree?"

It is a miracle that nobody interrupted here, not even Walter. But he didn't, he held his tongue, as they all did. You don't even hear a chair creak before Barley goes on.

"So I agree. Yes, Goethe, I agree with you to the hilt. Anything's better than being asked whether I'm a British spy. Starts talking about the great nineteenth-century poet and mystic Piturin."

"Pecherin," says a high sharp voice. Walter has finally brimmed over.

"That's right. Pecherin," Barley agrees. "Vladimir Pecherin. Pecherin wanted to sacrifice himself for mankind, die on the cross with his mother at his feet. Have I heard of him? I haven't. Pecherin went to Ireland, became a monk, he says. But Goethe can't do that because he can't get a visa and anyway he doesn't like God. Pecherin liked God and didn't like science unless it took account of the human soul. I ask him how old he is. Goethe, not Pecherin. He looks about seven by now, going on a hundred. He says he's nearer to death than life. He says he's fifty but he's just been born."

Walter chimes in, but softly, like someone in church, not his usual squeak at all. "Why did you ask him his *age?* Of all the questions you could have asked? What on earth does it matter at that moment how many teeth he's got?"

"He's unsettling. Not a wrinkle on him till he scowled."

"And he said science. Not physics. Science?"

"Science. Then he starts reciting Pecherin. Translating as he goes. The Russian first, then the English. *How sweet it is to hate one's native land and avidly await its ruin . . . and in its ruin to discern the dawn of universal renaissance.* I may not have got it quite right but that's the gist. Pecherin understood that it was possible to love your country at the same time as hating its system, he says. Pecherin was nuts about England, just as Goethe is. England as the home of justice, truth and liberty. Pecherin showed there was nothing disloyal in betrayal provided you betrayed what you hated and fought for what you loved. Now supposing Pecherin had possessed great secrets about the Russian soul. What would he have done? Obvious. He'd have given them to the English.

"I'm wanting him out of my hair by now. I'm getting panicky. He's coming close again. Face against face. Wheezing and grinding like a steam engine. Heart breaking out of his chest. These big brown saucer eyes. 'What have you been drinking?' I said. 'Cortisone?'

" 'You know what else you said at lunch?' he says.

" 'Nothing,' I say. 'I wasn't there. It was two other blokes and they hit me first.' He's not hearing me again.

" 'You said, "Today one must think like a hero to behave like a merely decent human being." '

" 'That's not original,' I say. 'None of it is. It's stuff I picked up. It's not me. Now just forget everything I said and go back to your own people.' Doesn't listen. Grabs my arm. Hands like a girl's but they grip like iron. 'Promise me that if ever I find the courage to think like a hero, you will act like a merely decent human being.'

" 'Look,' I say. 'Leave this out and let's get something to eat. They've got some soup in there. I can smell it. You like soup? Soup?'

"He's not crying as far as I can tell but his face is absolutely soaked. Like a pain sweat all over this white skin. Hanging on to my wrist as if I were his priest. 'Promise me,' he says.

" 'But what am I supposed to be promising, for God's sake?'

" 'Promise you'll behave like a gentleman.'

" 'I'm not a gentleman. I'm a publisher.'

"Then he laughs. First time. Huge laughter with a sort of weird click in it. 'You cannot imagine how much confidence I derive from your rejection,' he says.

"That's where I stand up. Nice and easy, not to alarm him. While he goes on clutching me.

" 'I commit the sin of science every day,' he says. 'I turn plough-shares into swords. I mislead our masters. I mislead yours. I perpetuate the lie. I murder the humanity in myself every day. Listen to me.'

" 'Got to go now, Goethe, old lad. All those nice lady concierges at my hotel sitting up and worrying about me. Let me loose, will you, you're breaking my arm.'

"Hugs me. Pulls me right on to him. Makes me feel like a fat boy, he's so thin. Wet beard, wet hair, this burning heat.

" 'Promise,' he says.

"Squeezed it out of me. Fervour. Never saw anything like it. 'Promise! Promise!'

" 'All right,' I say. 'If you ever manage to be a hero, I'll be a decent human being. It's a deal. Okay? Now let me go, there's a good chap.'

" 'Promise,' he says.

" 'I promise,' I say, and shove him off me."

Walter is shouting. None of our preliminary warnings, no furious glares from Ned or Clive or myself, could switch him off any longer. "But did you *believe* him, Barley? Was he conning you? You're a sharp cookie underneath the flannel. What did you *feel?*"

Silence. And more silence. Then finally, "He was drunk. Maybe twice in my life I've been as drunk as he was. Call it three times. He'd been on the white stuff all day long and he was still drinking it like water. But he'd hit one of those clear spells. I believed him. He's not the kind of chap you don't believe."

Walter again, furious. "But *what* did you believe? What did you think he was talking to you about? What did you think he *did?* All this chatter about things not reaching their targets, lying to his masters and yours, chess that isn't chess but something else? You can *add,* can't you? Why didn't you come to us? I know why! You put your head in the sand. 'Don't know because don't *want* to know.' That's you."

And the next sound on the tape after that is Barley cursing himself again as he stomps round the room. "Damn, damn, damn," he whispers. On and on. Until, cutting through him, we hear Clive's voice. If it ever falls to Clive to order the destruction of the universe, I imagine him using this same deserted tone.

"I'm sorry but I'm afraid we're going to need your rather serious help," he says.

Ironically I believe Clive *was* sorry. He was a technology man, not at ease with live sources, a suburban espiocrat of the modern school. He believed that facts were the only kind of information and he despised whoever was not ruled by them. If he liked anything at all in life apart from his own advancement and his silver Mercedes car, which he refused to take out of the garage if it had so much as a scratch on it, then it was hardware and powerful Americans, in that order. For Clive to sparkle, the Bluebird should have been a broken code, a satellite or an Inter Agency committee. Then Barley need never have been born.

Whereas Ned was all the other way, and more at risk on account of it. He was by temperament and training an agent-runner and captain of men. Live sources were his element and, so far as he knew the word, his passion. He despised the in-fighting of intelligence politics and left all that happily to Clive, just as he left the analysis to Walter. In that sense he was the determined primitive, as people who deal in human nature have to be, while Clive, to whom human nature was one vast unsavoury quagmire, enjoyed the reputation of a modernist.

5

We had moved to the library where Ned and Barley had begun. Brock had set up a screen and projector. He had put chairs in a horseshoe with a special person in his mind for each chair, for Brock, like other violent minds, had an exaggerated appetite for menial labour. He had been listening to the interview over the relay and despite his sinister inklings about Barley a glow of excitement smouldered in his pale Baltic eyes. Barley, deep in thought, lounged in the front row between Bob and Clive, a privileged, if distracted, guest at a private screening. I watched his head in silhouette as Brock switched on the projector, first turned downward in contemplation, then sharply upward as the first frame struck the screen. Ned sat beside me. Not a word, but I could feel the disciplined intensity of his excitement. Twenty male faces flicked across our vision, most of them Soviet scientists who on a first hasty search around the Registries of London and Langley were deemed to have had possible access to the Bluebird information. Some were featured more than once: first with beards, then with their beards touched out. Others were shown when they were twenty years younger because that was all the archives had of them.

"Not among those present," Barley pronounced when

the parade was over, suddenly shoving his hand to his head as if he had been stung.

Bob just couldn't believe this. His incredulities were as charming as his credulities. "Not even a perhaps or a maybe, Barley? You sound pretty sure of yourself for a man who was drinking well when he made the original sighting. Jesus, *I've* been to parties where I couldn't remember my own name."

"Not a tickle, old boy," said Barley, and returned to his thoughts.

Now it was Katya's turn, though Barley couldn't know it. Bob advanced on her cautiously, a Langley professional showing us his footwork.

"Barley, these are some of the boys and girls around the Moscow publishing scene," he said over-casually as Brock ran up the first stills. "People you might have bumped into during your Russian travels, people at receptions, book fairs, people on the circuit. If you see anybody you know, holler."

"Bless us, that's Leonora!" Barley cut in with pleasure while Bob was still talking. On the screen a splendid burly woman with a backside like a football field was marching across a stretch of open tarmac. "Leni's top gun with SK," Barley added.

"SK?" Clive echoed as if he had unearthed a secret society.

"Soyuzkniga. SK order and distribute foreign books throughout the Soviet Union. Whether the books get there is another matter. Leni's a riot."

"Know her other name?"

"Zinovieva."

Confirmed, said Bob's smile to the knowing.

They showed him others and he picked the ones they knew he knew, but when they showed him the photograph of Katya that they had shown to Landau—Katya in her overcoat with her hair up, coming down the steps with her perhaps-bag—Barley muttered, "Pass," as he had to all the others he didn't know.

But Bob was delightfully upset. Bob said, "Hold her there, please," so unhappily that a babe in arms would have guessed that this picture had unrecognised significance.

So Brock held, as we all did: held our breath.

"Barley, the little lady here with the dark hair and big eyes in this picture is with the October Publishing Company, Moscow. Speaks a fine English, classical like yours and Goethe's. We understand she's a *redaktor*, commissioning and approving English-language translations of Soviet works. No bells?"

"No such luck," said Barley.

At which Clive handed him to me. With a tip of his head. Take him, Palfrey. Your witness. Scare him.

I do a special voice for my indoctrination sessions. It's supposed to instill the terror of the marriage vow and I hate it because it is the voice that Hannah hates. If my profession had a false white coat, this would be the moment where I administered the wicked injection. But that night as soon as I was alone with him, I chose a more protective tone and became a different and perhaps rejuvenated Palfrey, the one that Hannah used to swear could overcome. I addressed Barley not as I would some raw probationer but as a friend I was seeking to forewarn.

Here's the deal, I said, using the most non-legal jargon I could think of. Here's the noose we're putting round your neck. Take care. Consider.

Other people, I make them sit. I let Barley roam because I had seen that he was more at ease when he was able to pace and fidget and chuck his arms back in a luxurious

stretch. Empathy is a curse even when it is short-lived, and
not all the bad law in England can protect me from it.

And while I temporarily warmed to him I noticed a
number of things about him I had not registered in the
larger company. How his body leaned away from me, as if
he were guarding himself against his deep-rooted disposi-
tion to give himself to the first person who asked for him.
How his arms, despite their striving for self-discipline,
remained unruly, particularly at the elbows, which like
renegades seemed to be wanting to break free of whatever
uniform they were pressed into.

And I noticed my own frustration that I could still not
observe him closely enough, but cast round for other
glimpses of him in the gilded mirrors as he passed them.
Even to this day, I think of him as being a long way off.

And I noticed the pensiveness in him as he dipped in and
out of my homily, taking a point or two, then swinging
away from me in order to digest it, so that suddenly I was
facing a breadth of powerful back that was not to be reconciled with the unreconciled front.

And how, as he returned to me, his eyes lacked the sub-
servience that in other recipients of my wise words so often
sickened me. He was not daunted. He was not even
touched. His eyes disturbed me nonetheless, as they had
the first time they appraised me. They were too truthful,
too clear, too undefended. None of his milling gestures
could protect them. I felt that I or anyone else could have
waded into them and claimed possession of him, and the
feeling scared me as if it were a threat. It made me fear for
my own security.

I thought about his file. So many headlong crashes, acts
of seeming self-destruction, so little prudence. His frightful
school record. His efforts to earn himself a few laurels by
boxing, for which he ended up in the school sanatorium

with a broken jaw. His expulsion for being drunk while reading the Epistle at Sung Eucharist. "I was drunk from the night before, sir. It was not intentional." Flogged and expelled.

How convenient, I thought, for him and me, if I could have pointed to some great crime that haunted him, some act of cowardice or omission. But Ned had shown me his entire life, secret annexes and all, medical history, money, women, wives, children. And it was small stuff all the way. No big bang, no big crime. No big anything—which may have been the explanation of him. Was it for want of a greater sea that he had repeatedly wrecked himself against life's little rocks, challenging his Maker to come up with something bigger or stop bothering him? Would he be so headlong when faced with greater odds?

Then abruptly, before I am aware of it, our rôles are reversed. He is standing over me, peering down. The team is still waiting in the library and I hear sounds of their restlessness. The declaration form lies before me on the table. But it is me that he is reading, not the form.

"So have you any questions?" I ask up at him, conscious of his height. "Anything you want to know before you sign?" I am using my special voice after all, for self-protection.

He is at first puzzled, then amused. "Why? Have you got more answers you want to tell me?"

"It's an unfair business," I warn him sternly. "You've had a big secret thrust on you. You didn't ask for it but you can't unknow it. You know enough to hang a man and probably a woman. That places you in a certain category. It brings obligations you can't escape."

And, God help me, I think of Hannah again. He has woken the pain of her in me as if she were a brand-new wound.

He shrugs, brushing off the burden. "I don't know what I know," he says.

There is a thump on the door.

"The point is, they may want to tell you more," I say, softening again, trying to make him aware of my concern for him. "What you know already may be only the beginning of what they want you to find out."

He is signing. Without reading. He is a nightmare client. He could be signing his life away and he wouldn't know it and wouldn't care. They are knocking but I have still to add my name as witness.

"Thanks," he says.

"What for?"

I put away my pen. Got him, I think, in ice-cold triumph, just as Clive and the rest of them march in. A tricky customer but I signed him up.

But the other half of me is ashamed and mysteriously alarmed. I feel I have lit a fire inside our own camp, and there is no knowing how it will spread or who will put it out.

The only merit of the next act was that it was brief. I was sorry for Bob. He was never a sly man and he was certainly not a bigot. He was transparent, but that is not yet a crime, even in the secret world. He was more in Ned's stamp than Clive's, and nearer to the Service's way of doing things than to Langley's. There was a time when Langley had a lot of Bob's sort, and was the better for it.

"Barley, do you have any concept at all of the nature of the material that the source you call Goethe has so far provided? Of its overall message, shall we say?" Bob enquired awkwardly, putting up his broad smile.

Johnny had pitched the same sort of question at Landau, I remembered. And burned his fingers.

"How can I?" Barley replied. "I haven't set eyes on the stuff. You won't let me."

"Are you quite certain Goethe himself gave you no advance indication? No whispered word, author to publisher, of what he *might*—one day, if you both kept your promises—supply? Beyond what you have already accounted for in Peredelkino—the broad talk of weaponry and unreal enemies?"

"I've told you everything I remember," said Barley, shaking his head in confusion.

Also like Johnny before him, Bob began squinting at the brief he held below the table. But in Bob's case with genuine discomfort. "Barley, in the six visits you have made to the Soviet Union over the last seven years have you formed any connection, however briefly, with peaceniks, dissidents or other unofficial groups of that nature?"

"Is that a crime?"

Clive cut in. "Answer the question, will you?"

Amazingly, Barley obliged. Sometimes Clive was simply too small to reach him. "You meet all sorts, Bob. Jazz people, book people, intellectuals, journalists, artists—it's an impossible question. Sorry."

"Then can I turn it around a little and ask whether you are acquainted with any peace people back in England at all?"

"I've no idea."

"Barley, would you be aware that two members of a certain blues group you played with between 1977 and 1980 were involved with the Campaign for Nuclear Disarmament, as well as other peace outfits?"

Barley seemed puzzled but a little enchanted. "Really? Do they have names?"

"Would it amaze you if I said Maxi Burns and Bert Wunderley?"

To the amusement of everyone but Clive, Barley broke out in jolly laughter. "Oh my Lord! Forget the peace label, Bob. Maxi was a red-toothed Com. He'd have blown up the Houses of Parliament if he'd had a bomb. And Bert would have held his hand while he did it."

"I take it they were homosexual?" said Bob, with an old dog's smile.

"Gay as trivets," Barley agreed contentedly.

At which, with evident relief, Bob folded up his piece of paper and gave Clive a glance to say he'd finished, and Ned proposed to Barley that they take some air. Walter moved invitingly to the door and opened it. Ned must have wanted him as a foil, for Walter would never have dared otherwise. Barley hesitated a moment, then picked up a bottle of Scotch and a glass and dropped them one into each side pocket of his bush-jacket, in what I suspect was a gesture designed to shock us. Thus equipped he ambled after them, leaving the three of us alone without a word between us.

"Were those Russell Sheriton's questions you were shooting at him?" I asked Bob amiably enough.

"Russell's too bright for all that damn stuff these days, Harry," Bob replied with evident distaste. "Russell's come a long way."

Langley's power struggles were a mystery even to those who were involved in them, and certainly—however much we pretended otherwise—to our barons of the twelfth floor. But in the seethings and jockeyings, Sheriton's name had featured frequently as the man likely to come out at the top of the heap.

"So who authorised them?" I asked, still upon the questions. "Who drafted them, Bob?"

"Maybe Russell."

"You just said Russell was too bright!"

"Maybe he has to keep his boyars quiet," Bob said uncomfortably, lighting up his pipe and swinging out the match.

We settled down to wait on Ned.

The shade tree is in a public garden near the waterfront. I have stood under it and sat under it and watched the dawn rise over the harbour while the dew made teardrops on my grey raincoat. I have listened, without understanding, to an old mystic with a saintly face who likes to receive his disciples there, in that self-same spot by daylight. They are of all ages, and call him The Professor. The bench is built round its trunk and divided by iron arm-rests into seats. Barley sat at the centre with Ned and Walter either side of him. They had talked first in a sleepy sailors' tavern, then on a hilltop, Barley said, but Ned for some reason refuses to remember the hilltop. Now they had come back into the valley for their final place. Brock sat wakefully in the hired car keeping a view of them across the grass. From the warehouses on the other side of the road came a whine of cranes, a pumping of lorries and the yells of fishermen. It was five in the morning but the harbour is awake from three. The first clouds of dawn were shaping and breaking like the First Day.

"Choose somebody else," Barley said. He had said it before in several different ways. "I'm not your man."

"We didn't choose you," Ned said. "Goethe did. If we knew a way of getting back to him without you, we'd jump at it. He's taken a fix on you. Probably been waiting ten years for someone like you to turn up."

"He chose me because I wasn't a spy," said Barley. "Because I sang my bloody aria."

"And you won't be a spy now," said Ned. "You'll be a

publisher. His. All you'll be doing is collaborating with your author and with us at the same time. What's wrong with that?"

"You've got the draw, you've got the wits," said Walter. "No wonder you drink. You've been under-used for twenty years. Now's your chance to shine. You're lucky."

"I shone at Peredelkino. Every time I shine, the lights go out."

"You might even be solvent," said Ned. "Three weeks of preparation back in London while you're waiting for your visa, a jolly week in Moscow and you'll be off the hook for ever."

With the prudence that was innate in him, Ned had avoided the word "training."

Back comes Walter, a touch of the whip, a piece of flattery, both over the top, but Ned let him run. "Oh never mind the money, Barley's *far* too grand! It's one shot for your country and a lot of people never get the chance. They dream of it, they write in for it but it never comes their way. And afterwards, when you've done your bit, you can sit back and enjoy the benefits of being British, knowing you've earned them even if you sneer at them, which is your good right, something that has to be fought for like everything else."

And Ned had judged rightly. Barley laughed and told Walter "Come off it," or something of the kind.

"One shot for your author too, if you think about it," Ned cut in, with his plain man's talk. "You'll be saving his neck for him. If he's going to hand over State secrets, the least you can do for him is put him on to the competent people. You're a Harrow man, aren't you?" he added as if he had just remembered this. "Didn't I read somewhere you'd been educated at Harrow?"

"I just went to school there," Barley said and Walter let

out one of his hoots of laughter, in which Barley out of politeness joined.

"Why did you apply to us all those years ago? Do you remember what prompted you?" Ned asked. "Some sense of duty, was it?"

"I wanted to stay out of my father's firm. My tutor said teach at a prep school. My cousin Lionel said join the spies. You turned me down."

"Yes, well I'm afraid we can't do you the favour a second time," said Ned.

Like old companions the three men silently surveyed the waterfront. A chain of naval ships straddled the harbour mouth, their rigging drawn in necklaces of lights.

"Do you know, I've always dreamed there'd be one?" Walter sang suddenly, talking out to sea. "I'm a God man at heart, I'm sure I am. Or else a failed Marxist. I always believed that sooner or later their history had to throw one up. How much science have you got? None. You wouldn't. You're that generation—the last of the arts virgins. If I asked you what a rate of burn was, you'd probably think I was talking about baking a cake."

"Probably," Barley agreed, laughing again despite himself.

"CEP? Not a concept?"

"Don't like initials, I'm afraid."

"Circular-error-probable then. How's that?"

"Illiterate," Barley snapped, in one of his unpredictable fits of tetchiness.

"Recalibrate? Whom or what do I recalibrate, and what with?"

Barley didn't bother to reply.

"Very well, then. What's the Big Motherfucker, familiarly known in circles as the BMF? That won't offend your ear for English, will it? Nice Anglo-Saxon words?"

Barley shrugged.

"The BMF was the Soviet SS9 super rocket," Walter said. "It was wheeled out at a May Day parade in the dark years of the Cold War. Its dimensions were breathtaking and it was later credited with a notorious *footprint*. Also not a name to you? Footprint? Never mind, it will be. The footprint in this case was three huge holes in the Russian wastes that looked like the pattern of the Minuteman silo group with its command centre. The argument was whether they were made by independently targetable warheads, and could the Sovs therefore hit three American silos at once? Those who didn't want to believe they could called the footprints a fluke. Those who did upped the ante and said the warheads were for destroying cities not silos. The believers won the day and got themselves a green light for the ABM program. Never mind their theory was discredited three years later. They squeezed through. I'm losing you, I see."

"You never had me," Barley said.

"But he's a fast learner, of course he is," Walter assured Ned contentedly across Barley's body. "Publishers can get their minds halfway round anything."

"What's wrong with *finding out?*" Ned complained in the tone of a good man confused by smart talk. "That's what I never understand. We're not asking you to build the beastly rockets or push the button. We're asking you to help us improve our knowledge of the enemy. If you don't like the nuclear business, so much the better. And if the enemy turns out to be a friend where's the harm?"

"I thought the Cold War was supposed to be over," Barley said.

At which Ned, in what appeared to be genuine alarm, exclaimed, "Oh my dear Lord," under his breath.

But Walter showed no such restraint. Walter pretended to be indignant, and perhaps he was. He could be anything at any moment and often several things at once. "Cheap political theatricals and feigned friendships!" he snorted. "Here we are, locked into the biggest ideological face-off in history, and you tell me it's all over because a handful of statesmen find it convenient to hold hands in public and scrap a few obsolete toys. The evil empire's on its knees, oh yes! Their economy's a disaster, their ideology's up the spout and their backyard's blowing up in their faces. Just don't tell me that's a reason for unbuckling our guns, because I won't believe a word of you. It's a reason for spying the living daylights out of them twenty-five hours a day and kicking them in the balls every time they try to get off the floor. God *knows* who they won't think they are ten years from now!"

"I suppose you do realise that if you walk out on Goethe you'll be leaving him to the Americans?" said Ned, on a practical point of information. "Bob won't let him go, why should he? Don't be fooled by those old Yalie manners of his. How will you live with yourself *then?*"

"I don't want to live with myself," said Barley. "I can't think of anybody worse to live with."

A slate-coloured cloud slid across the red sunpath before shattering into fragments.

"It comes down to this," said Ned. "It's crude and un-English but I'll say it anyway. Do you want to be a passive or an active player in the defence of your country?"

Barley was still hunting for an answer when Walter supplied it for him, and with an air of finality that brooked no contradiction. "You're from a free society. You've got no choice," he said.

The din of the harbour rose with the advancing daylight. Barley slowly stood up and rubbed his back. He seemed to have a permanent patch of pain there, just above the waistband. Perhaps it accounted for his slope.

"Any decent Church would have burned you bastards at the stake long ago," he remarked wearily. He turned to Ned, peering down at him through his too-small spectacles. "I'm the wrong man," he warned him. "And you're a fool for using me."

"We're all the wrong men," said Ned. "We're dealing with wrong things."

Barley walked across the grass, beating his pockets for his keys. He entered a side street and vanished from their view as Brock went softly after him. The house was a wedge, narrow on the street, broad at the back. Barley unlocked the front door and closed it behind him. He pressed the time switch and began climbing the stairs, keeping an even pace because he had a long way to go.

She was a good woman and nothing was her fault. They were all good women. They were women with a mission to him, just as Hannah once had a mission to me—to save him, to straighten him out, to get his oh-so-many talents working in one direction, to help him make the fresh start that would get him clear of all the fresh starts he had made before. And Barley had encouraged her as he had encouraged all of them. He had stood beside them at the patient's bedside as if he were not himself the patient but a member of the healing team. "So what shall we do about this poor old chap that will get him up and functioning again?"

The only difference was, he had never believed in the remedy, any more than I had.

She lay face down, exhausted and possibly asleep. She had cleaned the flat. As prisoners clean cells and the bereaved tend tombs, she had scoured the surface of a world she couldn't alter. Other people might tell Barley he was too hard on himself. Women said it to him often. How he mustn't hold himself responsible for both halves of every relationship that collapsed on him. Barley knew better. He knew the distance between himself and everything. In those days he was still the unequalled expert on his own incurability.

He touched her shoulder but she didn't stir, so he knew she was awake.

"I had to go to the Embassy," he said. "People in London baying for my blood. I've got to go back and face the music or they'll take away my passport."

He fished a suitcase from under the bed and began filling it with the shirts she'd ironed for him.

"You said this time you weren't going back," she told him. "You'd served your English stretch, you said. You'd done your time."

"They've put me on the early flight. There's nothing I can do. There's a car coming for me in a few minutes." He went to the bathroom for his toothbrush and shaving gear. "They're throwing the whole book at me," he called. "There's nothing I can do."

"And I go back to my husband," she said.

"Stay here. Use the flat. Whatever. It'll only take a few weeks. Then it's done."

"If you just hadn't said all that stuff, we'd have been fine. I'd have been happy just having an affair. You should see your letters. Hear yourself."

Barley didn't look at her. He was stooped over his suitcase.

"Just don't do it to anyone else," she said.

That was as far as her calm could stretch. She began sobbing and was sobbing when he left, and she was still sobbing next morning when I pitched her some line and pushed a declaration form under her nose as I asked her how much he'd told her. Nothing. She blabbed out the whole story yet defended him to the death. Hannah would have done the same. Does it still, a surfeit of loyalty to this day, even though her illusions are destroyed.

Three weeks were all that Ned and his Russia House people had to knock Barley into shape. Three weekends, and fifteen days that didn't start till five when Barley slipped away from his office.

But Ned drove the job through as only Ned was able. Ned would have kept the trainers up all night and himself all night and day. And Barley, with the changefulness that was innate in him, swung and turned with every breeze, until he settled down and found a steady face and, as the day of his departure approached, a serious one as well. Often he seemed to embrace the entire ethic of our trade without demur. After all, he declared to Walter, was not seeming the only kind of being? Oh my *God,* yes! Walter cried, delighted—and not only in our trade! And was not the whole of man's identity a cover? Barley insisted: and was not the only world worth living in the secret one? Walter assured him that it was, and advised him to take up permanent residence there before prices rose.

Barley had loved Walter from the start, loved the fragility in him and, as I see it now, the transience. He seemed to know from the outset that he was holding the hand of a man who was on his way to the breaker's yard. At other times Barley's own face became as empty as the open grave. He would not have been Barley if he hadn't been a pendulum.

Most of all he took to the family atmosphere which Ned, with his instinct for the unanchored joe, assiduously tended—the chatty suppers, the sharing and being the star of the family, the games of chess with old Palfrey, whom Ned cunningly harnessed to Barley's wagon to redress the disturbingly ephemeral influence of Walter.

"Drop in whenever you're in the mood," Ned told me, with a friendly pat.

So I became Barley's old Harry.

Old Harry, give us a game of chess, damn you! Old Harry, why aren't you staying for supper? Old Harry, where's your bloody glass, man?

Ned invited Bob sparingly and Clive not at all. It was Ned's show, Ned's joe. And he had a shrewd eye for Barley's flashpoints.

For the safe house Ned had chosen a pretty Edwardian cottage in Knightsbridge, an area of London where Barley had no connection. Clive winced at the cost but the Americans were paying so his fastidiousness was misplaced. The house lay in a cul-de-sac not five minutes' walk from Harrods and I rented it in the name of the Ethical Research & Action Group, a charitable body I had registered years before and locked away for a rainy day. A cosy Service housekeeper named Miss Coad was placed in charge, and I duly swore her on to the Bluebird indoctrination list. The top-floor nursery was converted into a modest lecture room and, like the rest of the rooms, which were snug and well furnished, it was microphoned.

"This is your home from home for the duration," Ned told Barley as we showed him round. "Here's your bedroom when you need one, here's your key. Use the phone as much as you like but I'm afraid we'll be listening, so if it's private you'd do better from the box across the road."

For good measure, I had extended the Home Office warrant to cover the phone box too. Intense American interest.

Since Barley and I were not long sleepers, we played our chess when the others had turned in. He was an impulsive opponent and often a brilliant one, but there is a calculating streak in me that he never possessed and I was more attuned to his weaknesses than he to mine. After all, I had read his file. But I still remember games where he saw a whole campaign at a glance and with three or four moves and a bellow of amusement forced me to resign.

"Got you, Harry! Say you're sorry! Hang your head!"

But when we set them up again, I could feel the patience drain out of him. He would start to prowl and flick his hands around and let his mind take one of its journeys.

"Married, Harry?"

"Not so's you'd notice," I replied.

"Hell does that mean?"

"I have a wife in the country. I live in the town."

"Had her long?"

"Couple of lifetimes," I said carelessly, already wishing I had given him a different answer.

"Love her?"

"My dear chap!" But he was staring at me, wanting to know. "From a distance, I suppose. Yes," I added grudgingly.

"She love you back?"

"I assume so. It's some time since I asked her."

"Kiddywinks?"

"A boy. Man, I suppose."

"Ever see him?"

"A card at Christmas. Funerals and weddings. We're good enough friends in our way."

"What's he do?"

"He flirted with the law. Now he makes money."

"Is he happy?"

I was angry, which these days is unusual in me. Definitions of happiness and love were none of his damned business. He was a joe. It was my right to come close to him, not the other way around. But it was more unusual still that I should let my anger show. Yet I must have done, for I caught him gazing at me with concern, wondering no doubt whether he had accidentally touched upon some family tragedy. Then he coloured and swung away, looking for a distraction that would get us off the hook.

"He's not fighting it, sir, I'll put it that way," a Mr. Candyman, specialist in the latest thing in body microphones, told Ned. "I won't say he's a natural but he does listen and my goodness he does remember."

"He's a gentleman, Mr. Ned, which is what I like," said a lady watcher entrusted with teaching Barley the rudiments of streetcraft. "He's got the brains and he's got a sense of humour, which I often say is halfway to an eye." Later she confessed that she had declined his advances in accordance with Service rules, but that he had successfully introduced her to the work of Scott Fitzgerald.

"Whole thing's a load of hocus-pocus," Barley pronounced raucously at the end of a wearying session on the techniques of secret writing. But he clearly enjoyed it, all the same.

And as the day of reckoning drew nearer, his submissiveness became total. Even when I wheeled in the Service accountant, a dreary stick called Christopher, who had devoted five days to an awed inspection of the Abercrombie & Blair books, Barley showed none of the rebelliousness I had expected.

"But every last swine in publishing is broke, Chris old boy!" he protested, pacing the pretty drawing-room to the rhythms of his own humming, holding his whisky glass wide while he dipped at the knees for the long steps. "The big fellows like Jumbo eat the leaves and we gnaw the bark." A German voice: "You hef your methods, ve hef ours."

But neither Ned nor I gave a cuss about every last swine. Neither did Chris. We cared about the operation and were haunted by the nightmare that Barley might go bankrupt on us in the middle of it.

"But I don't *want* a bloody editor!" Barley cried, waving his longsuffering spectacles at us. "I can't *pay* a bloody editor. My sainted aunts in Ely will pop their *garters* if I hire a bloody editor!"

But I had already squared the sainted aunts. Over luncheon at Rules I had wooed and won the Lady Pandora Weir-Scott, better known to Barley as the Sacred Cow on account of her High Anglican beliefs. Posing as a Foreign Office Pontiff, I had explained to her in the greatest confidence that the house of Abercrombie & Blair was about to be the recipient of an under-the-counter Rockefeller grant to promote Anglo-Soviet cultural relations. But not a word, or the money would be whisked away and given to another deserving house.

"Well *I'm* a bloody sight more deserving than *anybody*," Lady Pandora averred, spreading her elbows wide to get the last scrap out of her lobster. "*You* try running Ammerford on thirty thousand a year."

Mischievously, I asked her whether I could safely approach her nephew.

"Not on your nelly. Leave him to me. He doesn't know money from muck and he can't lie for toffee."

The need to provide Barley with a minder seemed suddenly more pressing. "You advertised for him," Ned explained, brandishing a small ad from a recent edition of the cultural press in Barley's face. *Old Established British Publisher seeks qualified Russian reader for promotion to editor, 25–45, fiction and technical, curriculum vitae.*

And on the next afternoon Leonard Carl Wicklow presented himself for interview at the much mortgaged premises of Abercrombie & Blair of Norfolk Street, Strand.

"I have an angel for you, Mr. Barley," boomed Mrs. Dunbar's gin-soaked voice over the ancient intercom. "Shall I ask him to fly in?"

An angel in bicycle clips, a webbing kitbag slung across his chest. A high angelic brow, not a worry on it, blond angelic curls. Angelic blue eyes that knew no evil. An angelic nose, so mysteriously knocked off course that your first instinct on meeting him was to reach out and switch it straight again. Interview him as you would anybody, Ned had told Barley. Leonard Carl Wicklow, born Brighton 1964, honours graduate, School of Slavonic & East European Studies, University of London.

"Oh yes, you. Marvellous. Sit down," Barley grumbled. "Hell brings you to publishing? Lousy trade." He had lunched with one of his more strident lady novelists, and was still digesting the experience.

"Well it's been kind of an on-going thing of mine for years, actually, sir," said Wicklow, with a smile of angelic enthusiasm.

"Well if you do come to us you certainly won't *on-go*," Barley warned, bridling at this unprovoked assault on the English language. "You may *continue*. You may *endure*. You may even *prevail*. But you jolly well won't *on-go* while *I'm* in the driving seat."

"Don't know whether the bugger barks or purrs," he growled to Ned, the same evening back in Knightsbridge, as the three of us loped up the narrow stairs for our evening tryst with Walter.

"He does both rather well, actually," said Ned.

And Walter's seminars held Barley in their thrall, a sell-out every time. Barley loved anyone whose hold on life was tenuous, and Walter looked as if he were in danger of falling off the edge of the world each time he left his chair. They would talk tradecraft, they would talk nuclear theology, they would talk the horror story of Soviet science that the Bluebird, whoever he might be, was inescapably heir to. Walter was too good a tutor to reveal

what his subject was, and Barley was too interested to
enquire.

"*Control?*" Walter the ultimate hawk shouted at him
indignantly. "Can you honestly not distinguish between
control and *disarmament,* you ninny? Defuse world crisis, did
I hear? What *Guardian* bilge is that? Our leaders *adore* crisis. Our leaders *feast* on crisis. Our leaders spend their lives
quartering the globe in search of crisis to revive their flagging libidos!"

And Barley, far from taking offence, would crane forward in his chair, groan and clap and bay for more. He
would challenge Walter, leap to his feet and pound the
room shouting "*But*—hang on, damn you—*but!*" He had
the memory, he had the aptitude, as Walter had predicted.
And his scientific virginity yielded at the first assault, when
Walter delivered his introductory lecture on the balance of
terror, which he had contrived to turn into an inventory of
all the follies of mankind.

"There's no way out," he announced with satisfaction,
"and no amount of wishful dreaming will produce one. The
demon won't go back in its bottle, the face-off is for ever,
the embrace gets tighter and the toys cleverer with every
generation, and there's no such thing for either side as
enough security. Not for the main players, not for the nasty
little newcomers who each year run themselves up a suitcase bomb and join the club. We get tired of believing that,
because we're human. We may even con ourselves into
believing the threat has gone away. It never will. Never,
never, never."

"So who'll save us, Walt?" Barley asked. "You and
Nedsky?"

"Vanity, if anything will, which I doubt," Walter retorted.
"No leader wants to go down in history as the ass who
destroyed his country in an afternoon. And funk, I suppose.

Most of our gallant politicians do have a narcissistic objection to suicide, thank God."

"Otherwise no hope?"

"Not for man alone," said Walter contentedly, who more than once had seriously considered taking holy orders rather than the Service's.

"So what's Goethe trying to achieve?" Barley asked another time, with a hint of exasperation.

"Oh, save the world, I'm sure. We'd all like to do *that*."

"*How* save it? What's his message?"

"That's for you to find out, isn't it?"

"What's he told us so far? Why can't I know?"

"My dear boy, don't be so childish," Walter exclaimed petulantly, but Ned stepped quickly in.

"You know all you need to know," he said with a calming authority. "You're the messenger. It's what you're equipped to be, it's what he wants you to be. He's told us that a lot of things on the Soviet side don't work. He's painted a picture of failure at every level—inaccuracy, incompetence, mismanagement and, on top of that, falsified test results sent to Moscow. Perhaps it's true, perhaps he's made it up. Perhaps somebody made it up for him. It's a beguiling enough story as it stands."

"Do *we* think it's true?" Barley persisted stubbornly.

"You can't know."

"Why not?"

"Because under interrogation everybody talks. There are no heroes any more. You talk, I talk, Walter talks, Goethe talks, she talks. So if we tell you what we know about them, we risk compromising our capacity to spy on them. Do we know a particular secret about them? If the answer is no, then they know we lack the software, or the device, or the formula, or the super-secret ground station to find it out. But if the answer is yes, they'll take evasive action to make sure we can't go on watching and hearing them by that method."

Barley and I played chess.

"Do you reckon marriage only works from a distance then?" he asked me, resuming our earlier conversation as if we had never abandoned it.

"I'm quite sure love does," I replied with an exaggerated shudder, and quickly moved the subject to less intimate paths.

For his last evening, Miss Coad prepared a salmon trout and polished the silver plate. Bob was commanded, and produced a rare malt whisky and two bottles of Sancerre. But our festivities caught Barley in the same introspective mood, until Walter's spirited Final Sermon rescued him from the doldrums.

"The issue is *why*," Walter trilled suddenly, his cranky voice flying all over the room, while he helped himself to my glass of Sancerre. "That's what we're after. Not the substance, but the motive. *Why?* If we trust the motive, we trust the man. Then we trust his material. In the beginning was not the word, not the deed, not the silly serpent. In the beginning was *why?* Why did she pluck the apple? Was she bored? Was she inquisitive? Was she paid? Did Adam put her up to it? If not, who did? The Devil is every girl's cover story. Ignore him. Was she fronting for somebody? It's not enough to say, 'Because the apple is there.' That may do for Everest. It may even do for Paradise. But it won't do for Goethe and it won't do for us and it *certainly* won't do for our gallant American allies, will it, Bobby?"

And when we all burst out laughing he squeezed his eyes shut and raised his voice still higher.

"Or take the ravishing Katya! Why does Goethe pick on *her?* Why does he put *her* life at risk? And why does she let him? We don't know. But we must. We must know everything we can about her because in our profession the couriers are the message. If Goethe is genuine, the girl's head is on the block. That's a given. If he's not, what does that make her? Did she invent the stuff herself? Is she really in touch with him? Is she in touch with someone different and if so who?" He thrust a strengthless forefinger at Barley's face. "Then there's *you,* sir. Does Goethe think you're a spy or doesn't he? Did other people *tell* him you were a spy? Be a hamster. Store every nugget you can get. God bless you and all who sail in you."

I discreetly filled another glass and we drank. And I remember how in the deep quiet we distinctly heard the chimes of Big Ben floating up the river from Westminster.

It was not till early next morning when Barley's departure was only hours off that we granted him a limited sight of the documents he had so stridently demanded in Lisbon—Goethe's notebooks, re-created in facsimile by Langley under draconian conditions of secrecy, down to the thick Russian board backs and line-block drawings of jolly Soviet schoolkids on the covers.

Silently accepting them in both hands, Barley became pure publisher while the rest of us watched the transformation. He opened the first notebook, peered at the gutter, felt the weight and flipped to the back, seeming to work out how long it would take him to read it. He reached for the second, sliced it open at a random page and, seeing tightly written lines, pulled a face that as good as complained that the script was single-spaced and hand-written.

Then he ranged across all three notebooks at once, puzzling his way from illustration to text and text to literary effusion, while he kept his head stiffly backwards and to one side, as if determined to reserve his judgment.

But I noticed how, when he raised his eyes, they had lost

their sense of place, and appeared to be fixed on some far mountain of his own.

A routine search of Barley's Hampstead flat conducted by Ned and Brock after his departure revealed no hard clues to his state of mind. An old notebook in which he was accustomed to make his jottings was found amid the litter of his desk. The last entries looked recent. The most apt was probably a couplet he had culled from the later work of Stevie Smith.

> I am not so afraid of the dark night
> As the friends I do not know . . .

Ned conscientiously entered it on the file but refused to make anything of it. Name him a joe who didn't get butterflies in his stomach on the eve of his first run.

And on the back of an old bill tossed into the wastepaper basket Brock came on a quotation which he eventually traced to Roethke, and which for his own dark reasons he only mentioned weeks later.

> I learn by going where I have to go.

6

Katya woke sharply and, as she afterwards persuaded herself, with an immediate awareness that today was the day. She was an emancipated Soviet woman but superstition died hard in her.

"It was meant," she told herself later.

Through the threadbare curtains a white sun was appearing over the cement parade grounds of her north Moscow suburb. All round her the brick apartment blocks, decked with washing, rose like tattered pink giants into an empty sky.

It's Monday, she thought. I'm in my own bed. I'm free of the street after all. She was thinking of her dream.

Having woken she lay still a moment, patrolling her secret world and trying to shake her mind free of its bad thoughts. And when this didn't work she sprang from her bed and impulsively, as she did most things, ducked with practised deftness between the hanging clothes and crumbling bathroom fittings and showered herself.

She was a beautiful woman as Landau had observed. Her tall body was full but not plump, with a fine neat waist and strong legs. Her black hair was luxuriant and, when she was in a mood to neglect it, rampant. Her face was puckish but intelligent and seemed to animate everything around her. Whether clothed or naked she could make no gesture that did not have its grace.

When she had showered, she turned the taps as hard as they would go, then finished them off with a wallop of the wooden mallet that said, "Take that!" Humming to herself, she picked up the little mirror and strode back to her bedroom to dress. The street again: where was it? In Leningrad or Moscow? The shower had not washed her dream away.

Her bedroom was very small, the smallest of the three rooms that made up her tiny apartment, an alcove with a cupboard and a bed. But Katya was accustomed to these confinements and her swift movements as she brushed out her hair, twisted it and pinned it for the office, had a sensual, if haphazard, elegance. Indeed the apartment might have been a lot smaller had not Katya been entitled to an extra twenty metres for her work. Uncle Matvey was worth another nine; the twins and her own resourcefulness accounted for the rest. She had no quarrel with the apartment.

Maybe the street was in Kiev, she thought, recalling a recent visit there. No. The Kiev streets are wide but mine was narrow.

While she dressed, the block began to wake up and Katya gratefully counted off the rituals of the normal world. First through the adjoining wall came the Goglidzes' alarm clock sounding six-thirty, followed by their crazy borzoi howling to be let out. The poor Goglidzes, I must take them a gift, she thought. Last month Natasha had lost her mother and on Friday Otar's father had been rushed to hospital with a brain tumour. I'll give them some honey, she thought—and in the same instant found herself smiling a wry greeting to a former lover, a refusenik painter who against all the odds of Nature had contrived to keep a swarm of illegal bees on a rooftop behind the Arbat. He had treated her disgracefully, her friends assured her. But Katya always defended him in her mind. He was an artist, after all, perhaps a genius. He was a beautiful lover and between his rages he had made her laugh. Above all, she had loved him for achieving the impossible.

After the Goglidzes came the grizzling of the Volkhovs' baby daughter cutting her first teeth and a moment later through the floorboards the beat of their new Japanese stereo thumping out the latest American rock. How on earth could they afford such things, Katya wondered in another leap of empathy—Elizabeth always pregnant and Sasha on a hundred and sixty a month? After the Volkhovs came the unsmiling Karpovs, nothing but Radio Moscow for them. A week ago, the Karpovs' balcony had fallen down, killing a policeman and a dog. The wits in the block had wanted to get up a collection for the dog.

She became Katya the provider. On Mondays there was a chance of fresh chickens and vegetables brought privately from the country over the weekend. Her friend Tanya had a cousin who functioned informally as a dealer for smallholders. Phone Tanya.

Thinking this, she also thought about the concert tickets. She had taken her decision. As soon as she got to the office she would collect the two tickets for the Philharmonic which the editor Barzin had promised her as amends for his drunken advances at the May Day party. She had never even noticed his advances, but Barzin was always torturing himself about something, and who was she to stand in the way of his guilt—particularly if it took the form of concert tickets?

At lunchtime after shopping she would trade the tickets with the porter Morozov, who had pledged her twenty-four bars of imported soap wrapped in decorative paper. With the fancy soap she would buy the bolt of green check cloth of pure wool that the manager of the clothing shop was keeping locked in his storeroom for her. Katya resolutely refused to wonder why. This afternoon after the Hungarian reception she would hand the cloth to Olga Stanislavsky, who, in return for favours to be negotiated, would make two cowboy shirts on the East German sewing machine she had recently traded for her ancient family Singer, one for each twin in time for their birthday. And there might even be enough cloth left over to squeeze them both a private check-up from the dentist.

So goodbye concert. It was done.

The telephone was in the living room where her Uncle Matvey slept, a precious red one from Poland. Volodya had smuggled it from his factory and had the goodness not to take it with him when he made his final exit. Tiptoeing past the sleeping Matvey—and vouch-safing him a tender glance along the way, for Matvey had been her father's favourite brother—she carried the phone across the corridor on its long flex, set it on her bed and began dialling before she had decided whom to talk to first.

For twenty minutes she rang round her friends, trading gossip mostly about where things might be had, but some of it more intimate. Twice when she put the phone down, somebody rang her. The newest Czech film director was at Zoya's last night. Alexandra said he was devastating and today she would take her life in her hands and ring him up, but what could she use for a pretext? Katya racked her brains and came up with a suggestion. Three avant-garde sculptors, till now banned, were to hold their own exhibition at the Railway Workers' Union. Why not invite him to accompany her to the exhibition? Alexandra was delighted. Katya always had the best ideas.

Black-market beef could be bought every Thursday evening from the back of a refrigeration van on the road to Sheremetyevo, said Lyuba; ask for a Tartar named Jan, but don't let him near you! Cuban pineapples were on sale from a shop behind Kropotkin Street, said Olga; mention Dimitri and pay double what they ask.

Ringing off, Katya discovered she was being persecuted by the American book on disarmament that Nasayan had lent her, blue with Roman lettering. Nasayan was October's new non-fiction editor. Nobody liked him, nobody understood how he had got the job. But it was noted that he kept the key to the one copying machine, which placed him squarely in the murkier ranks of official-dom. Her bookshelves were in the corridor, crammed from floor to ceiling and overflowing. She hunted hard. The book was a Trojan horse. She wanted it out of her house, and Nasayan with it.

"Is somebody going to translate it then?" she had asked him sternly as he padded round her office, squinting at her letters, poking through her heap of unread manuscripts. "Is this why you wish me to read it?"

"I thought it was something that might interest you," he had replied. "You're a mother. A liberal, whatever that means. You got on your high horse over Chernobyl and the rivers and the Armenians. If you don't want to borrow it, don't."

Discovering his wretched book jammed between Hugh Walpole and Thomas Hardy, she wrapped it in newspaper, stuffed it in her perhaps-bag, then hung the bag on the front doorknob because, just as she remembered every-thing these days, so she forgot everything.

The doorknob that we bought together from the flea market! she thought with a surge of compassion. Volodya, my poor dear intolerable husband, reduced to nursing your historical nostalgia in a communal flat with five ill-smelling grass widowers like yourself!

Her telephoning over, she hastily watered her plants, then went to wake the twins. They were sleeping diagonally in their single bed. Standing over them, Katya gazed at them in awe, for a moment not brave enough to touch them. Then she smiled so that they would be sure to see her smile as they woke.

For an hour after that, she gave herself to them totally, which was how she planned each day. She cooked their *kasha,* peeled their oranges and sang daft songs with them, ending with the "Enthusiasts' March," their absolute favourite, which they growled in unison, chins on chests, like heroes of the Revolution——not knowing, though Katya knew and was repeatedly amused by it, that they were also singing the melody of a Nazi marching song. While they drank their tea she made their packed lunch, white bread for Sergey, black bread for Anna, a meat-cake inside for each of them. And after that she fastened Sergey's button-on collar and straightened Anna's red neckerchief and kissed them both before she brushed their hair because their school principal was a Pan-Slavist who preached that tidiness was an act of homage to the State.

And when she had done all this, she dropped into a crouch and gathered the twins into her arms, as she had each Monday for the last four weeks.

"So what do you do if Mummy doesn't come back one evening, if she's had to dash off to a conference or visit somebody who is ill?" she asked brightly.

"Telephone Daddy and tell him to come and stay with us," said Sergey, tugging himself free.

"And I look after Uncle Matvey," said Anna.

"And if Daddy is away too, what do you do then?"

They began giggling, Sergey because the notion unsettled him and Anna because she was thrilled by the prospect of disaster.

"Go to Auntie Olga's!" Anna cried. "Wind up Auntie Olga's clockwork canary! Make it sing!"

"And what is Auntie Olga's telephone number? Can you sing that too?"

They sang it, hooting with laughter, all three of them. The twins were still laughing as they clattered ahead of her down the stinking stairwell that served the adolescents as a love-nest and the alcoholics as a bar, and seemingly everybody except themselves as a lavatory. Stepping into the sunlight, they marched hand in hand with her across the park to school, Katya in the middle.

"And what is the objective purpose of your life today, Comrade?" Katya demanded of Sergey with mock ferocity as she straightened his collar once more.

"To serve the people and the Party with all my strength."

"And?"

"Not to let Vitaly Karpov pinch my lunch!"

More laughter as the twins ran away from her up the stone steps, Katya waving till they had disappeared.

In the metro she saw everything too brightly and from a distance. She noticed how glum the passengers were, as if she were not one of them herself; and how they all seemed to be reading Moscow newspapers, a sight that would have been unthinkable a year ago when newspapers were good for nothing but toilet paper and closing off draughts. On other days Katya might have read one too; or if not, a book or manuscript for work. But today, despite her efforts to rid herself of her stupid dream, she was living too many lives at once. She was cooking fish soup for her father to make up for some act of wilfulness. She was enduring a piano lesson at the elderly Tatyana Sergeyevna's and being rebuked for levity. She was running in the street, unable to wake. Or the street was running after her. Which was probably why she almost forgot to change trains.

Reaching her office, which was a half-heartedly modern affair of flaking wood and weeping concrete—more suited to a public swimming pool, she always thought, than to a State publishing house—she was surprised by the sight of workmen hammering and sawing in the entrance hall, and for a second she gave way to the disgusting notion that they were building a scaffold for her public execution.

"It's our *appropriation*," wheezed old Morozov, who always had to steal a word with her. "The money was allocated to us six years ago. Now some bureaucrat has consented to sign the order."

The lift was being repaired as usual. Lifts and churches, she thought, in Russia always under repair. She took the stairs, climbing swiftly without knowing what the hurry was, yelling cheerful good mornings at whoever needed one. Thinking afterwards about her haste, she wondered whether the ringing of her telephone had drawn her forward subconsciously, because as she entered her room there it was on her desk howling to be put out of its pain.

She grabbed the receiver and said "Da," out of breath, but evidently she spoke too soon, for the first thing she heard was a man's voice asking in English for Madame Orlova.

"This is Madame Orlova," she said, also in English.

"Madame Yekaterina Orlova?"

"Who is this, please?" she asked, smiling. "It is Lord Peter Wimsey perhaps? Who is this?"

One of my silly friends playing a joke. Lyuba's husband again, hoping for a date. Then her mouth dried.

"Ah well, you don't know me, I'm afraid. My name's Scott Blair. Barley Scott Blair from Abercrombie & Blair in London, publishers, over here on a business trip. I think we have a mutual friend in Niki Landau. Niki was very insistent I should give you a call. How do you do?"

"How do you do," Katya heard herself say, and felt a hot cloud come over her and a pain start at the centre of her stomach just below the rib cage. At the same moment Nasayan strolled in, hands in pockets and unshaven, which was his way of showing intellectual depth. Seeing her talking, he hunched his shoulders and stuck his ugly face at her in a resentful pout, willing her to get off the line.

"*Bonjour* to you, Katya Borisovna," he said sarcastically.

But the voice in the telephone was already talking again, pressing itself upon her. It was a strong voice so she assumed someone tall. It was confident so she assumed someone arrogant, the kind of Englishman who wears expensive suits, has no culture and walks with his hands behind his back.

"Look, I'll tell you why I'm calling," he was saying. "Apparently Niki promised to look out some old editions of Jane Austen for you with the original drawings, is that right?" He gave her no time to say whether it was right or wrong. "Only I've brought a couple over with me—rather nice ones, actually—and I wondered whether we could possibly arrange a handover at some mutually convenient point?"

Tired of glowering, Nasayan was picking through the papers in her in-tray after his usual habit.

"You are very kind," she said into the mouthpiece, using her dullest voice. She had closed her face, making it lifeless and official. That was for Nasayan. She had closed her mind. That was for herself.

"Niki's also sent you about a ton of Jackson's tea," the voice continued.

"A *ton?*" said Katya. "What are you talking about?"

"I didn't even know Jackson's were still in business, to be honest. They used to have a marvellous shop in Piccadilly a few doors down from Hatchard's. Anyway, I've got three different kinds of their tea sitting here in front of me—"

He had disappeared.

They have arrested him, she thought. He never rang. It's my dream again. God in Heaven, what do I do next?

"—Assam, Darjeeling and Orange Pekoe. What on earth's a pekoe? Sounds more like an exotic bird to me."

"I don't know. I suspect it will be a plant."

"I suspect you'll be right at that. Anyway, the question is, how can I give them to you? Can I bring them to you somewhere? Or can you drop in at the hotel and could we have a quick drink and a formal presentation?"

She was learning to appreciate his long-windedness. He was giving her time to steady herself. She pushed her fingers through her hair, discovering to her surprise that it was tidy.

"You have not told me which hotel you are staying at," she objected severely.

Nasayan's head jerked round to her in disapproval.

"Well, neither I did now. How ridiculous of me. I'm at the Odessa, know the Odessa? Just up the road from the old bath house? I've become quite fond of it. Always ask for it, don't always get it. My daytimes are rather taken up with meetings—always the way when one's over on a flying visit—but evenings are relatively free at the moment, if that's any good to you. I mean how about tonight—no time like the present—would tonight be any good for you?"

Nasayan was lighting one of his filthy cigarettes, though the whole office knew she hated smoking. Having lit it, he hoisted it in the air and sucked from it with his woman's lips. She grimaced at him but he ignored her.

"That is actually quite convenient," Katya said in her most military manner. "Tonight I have to attend an official reception in your district. It is for an important delegation from Hungary," she added, not sure whom she was meaning to impress. "We have been looking forward to it for many weeks."

"Great. Marvellous. Suggest a time. Six? Eight? What suits you best?"

"The reception is at six o'clock. I shall come at perhaps eight-fifteen."

"Perhaps-eight-fifteen it is. You got the name, did you? Scott Blair. Scott like the Antarctic, Blair like a trumpet. I'm tall and seedy, about two hundred years old, with spectacles I can't see through. But Niki tells me you're the Soviet answer to the Venus de Milo so I expect I'll recognise you anyway."

"That is most ridiculous!" she exclaimed, laughing despite herself.

"I'll be hanging around the lobby looking out for you, but why don't I give you my room telephone number just in case. Got a pencil?"

As she rang off, the contrary passions that had been gathering in her burst their banks and she turned on Nasayan with flashing eyes.

"Grigory Tigranovich. Whatever your position here, you have no right to haunt my room like this, inspect my correspondence and listen to my telephone conversations. Here is your book. If you have something to say to me, say it later."

Then she scooped up a sheaf of translator's manuscript on the achievements of Cuban agricultural cooperatives and with cold hands began leafing through the pages, pre-

tending to count them. A full hour passed before she telephoned Nasayan.

"You must forgive my anger," she said. "A close friend of
mine died at the weekend. I was not myself."

By lunchtime she had changed her plans. Morozov
could wait for his tickets, the shopkeeper for his bars of
fancy soap, Olga Stanislavsky for her cloth. She walked, she
took a bus, not a cab. She walked again, crossing one courtyard after another until she found the down-at-heel block-
house she was looking for and the alley that ran beside it.
"This is how you get hold of me when you need me," he
had said. "The janitor is a friend of mine. He will not even
know who made the sign."

You have to believe in what you are doing, she reminded
herself.

I do. I absolutely do.

She had the picture postcard in her hand, a Rembrandt
from the Hermitage in Leningrad. "Love to you all," her
message read, signed "Alina," and a heart.

She had found the street. She was standing in it. It was
the street of her bad dream. She pressed the bell, three
rings, then shoved the card under the door.

A perfect Moscow morning, alight and beckoning, the
air alpine, a day to forgive all sins. The telephone call
behind him, Barley stepped out of his hotel and, standing
on the warm pavement, loosened his wrists and shoulders
and rolled his head round his collar while he turned his
mind outward and let the city drown his fears with its
conflicting smells and voices. The stink of Russian petrol,
tobacco, cheap scent and river water—hullo! Two more
days here I shan't know I'm smelling you. The sporadic
cavalry charges of the commuter cars—hullo! The belch-
ing brown lorries thundering through the pot-holes in

pursuit. The eerie emptiness between. The limousines with their blackened windows, the unmarked buildings splitting before their time—are you a block of offices, a barracks or a school? The dough-faced boys smoking in the doorways, waiting. The chauffeurs, reading newspapers in their parked cars, waiting. The unspeaking group of solemn men in hats, staring at a closed door, waiting.

Why did it always draw me? he wondered, contemplating his life in the past tense, which had recently become his habit. Why did I keep coming back here? He was feeling high and bright, he couldn't help it. He was not used to fear.

Because of their making do, he decided. Because they can rough it better than we can. Because of their love of anarchy and their terror of chaos, and the tension in between.

Because God always found excuses not to come here.

Because of their universal ignorance, and the brilliance that bursts through it. Because of their sense of humour, as good as ours and better.

Because they are the last great frontier in an over-discovered world. Because they try so hard to be like us and start from so far back.

Because of the huge heart beating inside the huge shambles. Because the shambles is my own.

I shall come at perhaps-eight-fifteen, she had said. What had he heard in her voice? Guardedness? Guarding whom? Herself? Him? Me? In our profession, the couriers are the message.

Look outwards, Barley told himself. Outwards is the only place to be.

From the metro a group of teenage girls in cotton frocks and boys in denim jackets trotted purposefully to work or instruction, their glum expressions switching to laughter at

a word. Spotting the foreigner they studied him with cool
glances—his rounded, pop-eye spectacles, his shabby
handmade shoes, his old imperialist suit. In Moscow, if
nowhere else, Barley Blair observed the bourgeois propri-
eties of dress.

Joining the stream he let it carry him, not caring which
way he went. By contrast with his determinedly contented mood the early food queues had a restless and
unsettled look. The grim-suited labour heroes and war
veterans, their breastplates of medals jingling in the sunlight as they waded through the crowds, had an air of
being late for wherever they were marching. Even their
sloth seemed to have an air of protest. In the new climate,
doing nothing was itself an act of opposition. Because by
doing nothing we change nothing. And by changing
nothing we hang on to what we understand, even if it is
the bars of our own jail.

I shall come at perhaps-eight-fifteen.

Reaching the wide river Barley again dawdled. On the
far bank the fairytale domes of the Kremlin lifted into a
cloudless heaven. A Jerusalem with its tongue pulled out,
he thought. So many towers, scarcely a bell. So many
churches, barely a spoken prayer.

Hearing a voice close beside him he swung round too
sharply and discovered an old couple in their best clothes
asking him the way to somewhere. But Barley of the perfect memory had few words of Russian. It was a music he
had listened to often without summoning the nerve to penetrate its mysteries.

He laughed and made an apologetic face. "Don't speak
it, old boy. I'm an imperialist hyena. English!"

The old man grasped his wrist in friendship.

In every foreign city he had ever been, strangers asked
him the way to places he didn't know in languages he

didn't understand. Only in Moscow did they bless him for his ignorance.

He retraced his steps, pausing at unswept windows, pretending to examine what they offered. Painted wooden dolls. Who for? Dusty tins of fruit, or were they fish? Battered packets hanging from red string, contents a mystery, perhaps pekoes. Jars of pickled medical samples, lit by ten-watt bulbs. He was approaching his hotel again. A drunk-eyed peasant woman pushed a bunch of dying tulips at him, wrapped in newspaper.

"Awfully kind of you," he cried and, rummaging through his pockets, found among the junk a rouble note.

A green Lada was parked outside the hotel entrance, the radiator smashed. A hand-inked card in the windscreen said VAAP. The driver was leaning over the bonnet detaching the wiper blades as a precaution against theft.

"Scott Blair?" Barley asked him. "You looking for me?" The driver paid him not the slightest attention but continued with his work. "Blair?" said Barley. "Scott?"

"Those for me, dear?" Wicklow enquired, coming up behind him. "You're fine," he added quietly. "Clean as a whistle."

Wicklow will watch your back for you, Ned had said. Wicklow, if anybody, will know whether you're being followed. Wicklow and who else? Barley wondered. Last night, as soon as they had checked in to the hotel, Wicklow had vanished until after midnight, and as Barley had put himself to bed he had seen him from his window, standing in the street talking to two young men in jeans.

They got into the car. Barley tossed the tulips on to the back ledge. Wicklow sat in the front seat chatting cheerily to the driver in his perfect Russian. The driver let out a great bellow of laughter. Wicklow laughed too.

"Want to share it?" Barley asked.

Wicklow was already doing so. "I asked him whether he'd like to drive the Queen when she came here on her State visit. There's a saying here. If you steal, steal a million. If you screw, screw a queen."

Barley lowered his window and tapped out a tune on the sill. Life was a romp till perhaps-eight-fifteen.

"Barley! Welcome to Barbary, my dear chap. For God's sake, man, don't shake hands with me across the threshold, we have enough troubles as it is! You look positively healthy," Alik Zapadny complained in alarm when they had time to examine each other. "Why have you no hangover, may I ask? Are you in love, Barley? Are you divorced again? What have you been up to that you require to confess to me?"

Zapadny's drawn face examined him with desperate intelligence, the shadows of confinement stamped for ever in his hollowed cheeks. When Barley had first known him, Zapadny had been a dubious translator in disgrace working under other names. Now he was a dubious hero of the Reconstruction, dressed in a larger man's white collar and black suit.

"I've heard the Voice, Alik," Barley explained, with a rush of the old fondness as he slipped him a bunch of back-numbers of the *Times* wrapped in brown paper. "In bed with a good book every night at ten. Meet Len Wicklow, our Russian specialist. Knows more about you than you do, don't we, Leonard Carl?"

"Well, thank God somebody does!" Zapadny protested, careful not to acknowledge the gift. "We are becoming so unsure of ourselves these days, now that our great Russian mystery is being held up to public view. How much do you know about your new boss, by the way, Mr. Wicklow? Have you heard, for instance, how he undertook the re-education of the Soviet Union single-handed? Oh yes. He had a charming vision of a hundred million under-educated Soviet workers longing to improve themselves in their leisure. He was going to sell them a great range of titles about how to teach themselves Greek and trigonometry and basic housekeeping. We had to explain to him that the Soviet man-in-the-street regards himself as finite and in his leisure hours he is drunk. Do you know what we bought from him instead to keep him happy? A golf book! You would not imagine how many of our worthy citizens are fascinated by your capitalist golf." And in haste, still a dangerous joke—"Not that we have any capitalists *here*. Oh my God, no."

They sat ten strong at a yellow table under an icon of Lenin made in wood veneers. Zapadny was the speaker, the others were listeners and smokers. Not one of them, so far as Barley knew, was competent to sign a contract or approve a deal.

"Now, Barley, what is this total nonsense you are putting about that you have come here in order to buy Soviet books, please?" Zapadny demanded by way of opening courtesies, lifting his hooped eyebrows and placing the tips of his fingers together like Sherlock Holmes. "You British *never* buy our books. You make us buy yours instead. Besides, you are broke, or so our friends from London tell us. A. & B. are living off God's good air and Scotch whisky, they say. Personally I consider that an excellent diet. But why have you come? I think you only wanted an excuse to visit us again."

Time was passing. The yellow table floated in the sunbeams. A pall of cigarette smoke floated over it. Black-and-white images of Katya in photographic form came and went in Barley's mind. The Devil is every girl's cover story. They drank tea out of pretty Leningrad cups. Zapadny was delivering his standard caveat against trying to make deals directly with Soviet publishers, selecting Wicklow as his audience: the day-and-night war between VAAP and the rest of the world was evidently raging well. Two pale men wandered in to listen and wandered out again. Wicklow was earning favour by handing round blue Gauloises.

"We've had an injection of capital, Alik," Barley heard himself explaining from a long way off. "Times have changed. Russia's top of the pops these days. I've only got to tell the money boys I'm building up a Russian list and they come rushing after me as fast as their short fat legs will carry them."

"But, Barley, these *boys,* as you call them, can grow into *men* very quickly," Zapadny, the great sophisticate, warned to a fresh burst of docile laughter. "Particularly when they are wishing to be repaid, I would say."

"It's the way I described it in my telex, Alik. Maybe you haven't had time to read it," said Barley, showing a little muscle. "If things work out as we plan, A. & B. will be launching a brand-new imprint devoted entirely to things Russian within the year. Fiction, nonfiction, poetry, juveniles, the sciences. We've got a new line in popular medicine, all paperback. The subjects travel, so do the reputations of the authors. We'd like real Soviet doctors and scientists to contribute. We don't want sheep farming in Outer Mongolia or fish farming in the Arctic Circle but if you have sensible subjects you want to suggest we're here to listen and buy. We'll announce our list at the next Moscow book fair, and if things go well we'll bring out our first six titles next spring."

"And have you, forgive me, a sales force these days, Barley, or are you relying on divine intervention as before?" Zapadny enquired with his showy delicacy.

Resisting the temptation to tell Zapadny to watch his

manners, Barley struggled on. "We're negotiating a distribution deal with several major publishers and we'll make an announcement soon. Except for fiction. For the fiction we'll use our own expanded team," he said, unable to remember for the life of him why they had settled on this bizarre arrangement or indeed whether they had.

"Fiction is still the A. & B. flagship, sir," Wicklow explained devoutly, helping Barley out.

"Fiction should *always* be one's flagship," Zapadny corrected him. "I would say that the novel is the greatest of all marathons. That is only my personal opinion, naturally. It is the highest form of art. Higher than poetry, higher than the short story. But please don't quote me."

"Well, it is for us literary superpowers, sir, put it that way," said Wicklow smarmily.

Very gratified, Zapadny turned to Barley. "On fiction, we should like in this special case to provide our own translator and take a further five percent royalty on the translation," he said.

"No problem," Barley said genially in his sleep. "These days, that's the kind of money A. & B. puts under the plate."

But to Barley's amazement Wicklow briskly intervened: "Excuse me, sir, that means a double royalty. I don't think we can swallow that and live. You must have misheard what Mr. Zapadny was saying."

"He's right," said Barley, sitting up sharply. "How the hell can we afford another five percent?"

Feeling like a conjuror who is proceeding to his next bogus act, Barley fished a folder from his briefcase and scattered half a dozen copies of a glossy prospectus at the sunbeams. "Our American connection is described on page two," he announced. "Potomac Boston is our partner in the project, A. & B. to buy full English-language rights in any

Soviet work, and sell off North America to Potomac. They
have a sister company in Toronto, so we'll throw in Canada.
Right, Wickers?"

"Yes, sir."

How the hell did Wicklow learn all this junk so quickly?
Barley thought.

Zapadny was still studying the prospectus, turning one
stiff, immaculate page after another. "Did *you* print this
shit, Barley?" he enquired politely.

"Potomac did," said Barley.

"But the Potomac River is so far from the city of
Boston," Zapadny objected, airing his knowledge of
American geography for the few who shared it. "Unless
they have recently moved it, it is in Washington. What
mutual attraction can they have, I ask myself, the city of
Boston and this river? Are we speaking of an *old* company,
Barley, or a *new* one?"

"New in the field. Old in business. They're merchants,
ex-Washington now in Boston. Venture capital. Diversified
portfolio. Film production, carparks, slot machines, call-
girls and cocaine. All the usual. Publishing's just one of
their sidelines."

But in his mind's ear as the laughter rose it was Ned
who was doing the talking. "Congratulations, Barley. Bob
here has come up with a wealthy Boston chum who's willing to take you on as a partner. All you have to do is spend
his money."

And Bob, with his flat-iron feet and tweedy jacket, smiling the buyer's smile.

Eleven-thirty. Eight hours and forty-five minutes until
perhaps-eight-fifteen.

"The driver wants to know what to expect when he
meets the Queen," Wicklow was yelling enthusiastically

over the back of his seat. "It's really getting to him. Does she take bribes? Does she have people executed for small offences? How does it feel to live in a country ruled by two fierce women?"

"Tell him it's exhausting but we're equal to it," Barley said with a huge yawn.

And having refreshed himself with a nip from his flask he leaned back in the cushions and woke to find himself following Wicklow down a prison corridor. Except that instead of the cries of the incarcerated, it was the whistle of a tea kettle that he heard and the clicking of an abacus echoing through the gloom. A moment later, Wicklow and Barley are standing in the offices of a British railway company, vintage 1935. Flyblown light bulbs and defunct electric fans dangle from the cast-iron rafters. Amazons in headscarves preside over antiquated Cyrillic typewriters large as ovens. Ledgers cram the dusty shelves. Stacks of shoe boxes stuffed with buff folders rise from the floorboards to the sills.

"Barley! Jesus! Welcome to Prometheus Unbound! They tell me you got some money finally. Who gave it you?" yells a middle-aged figure in Fidel Castro battle gear leaping at them through the clutter. "We deal direct, okay? To hell with those arseholes in VAAP?"

"Yuri, marvellous to see you! Meet Len Wicklow, our Russian-speaking editor."

"You a spy?"

"Only in my spare time, sir."

"Jesus! Nice chap! Reminds me of my kid brother."

They are in Madison Avenue. Venetian blinds, wall charts and armchairs. Yuri is fat, exuberant and Jewish. Barley has brought him a bottle of Black Label and tights for his beautiful new wife. Tossing away the whisky cap, Yuri insists on pouring tots into the teacups. They enter the

Russian ether. Talk of Bulgakov, Platonov, Akhmatova. Will Solzhenitsyn be permitted? Will Brodsky? Talk of a ragtag list of contemporary British writers who have arbitrarily found official favour and therefore fame in Russia. Barley has not heard of some, loathes others. Gusts of laughter, toasts, news of English friends, death to the arseholes in VAAP. Russia is changing by the hour, has Barley heard? Did he see that piece in *Moscow News* last Thursday about the neo-Fascist crazies in Pamyat, with their way-out nationalism and their anti-Semitism and their anti-everyone except themselves? And how about that piece in *Ogonyok* about Sigmund Freud? And *Novy Mir*'s stand on Nabokov? Editors, designers, translators proliferate in the usual amazing numbers, but no Katyas. Everyone is drunk, even those who have declined the alcohol. A great writer named Misha is presented and seated where his audience can watch him.

"Misha hasn't been to prison yet," Yuri explains apologetically, to huge laughter. "But maybe if he's lucky, they'll send him before it's too late, so that he can get published in the West!"

They talk the latest Soviet masterpieces of fiction. Yuri has chosen a mere eight from his own list—every one of them a sure bestseller, Barley. Publish them and you will be able to open a Swiss bank account for me. A hunt for plastic carrier bags before Wicklow takes charge of the carbon copies of eight unpublishable manuscripts, for this is a world in which the photocopier and electric typewriter are still the forbidden instruments of sedition.

They talk theatre and Afghanistan. Soon we shall all meet in London! Yuri cries, like a mad gambler staking all. "I send you my son, okay? Will you send me yours? Listen, we exchange hostages and that way nobody bombs each other!"

Everyone falls silent when Barley speaks, and stays silent for Misha the great writer. Wicklow translates while Yuri and three others object to Wicklow's translation. Misha objects to the objections. The downturn has begun.

Somebody demands to know why Britain is still run by the Fascist Conservative Party. Why doesn't the proletariat kick the bastards out? Barley offers something unoriginal about democracy being the worst of systems except for the others. No one laughs. Perhaps they have heard it, perhaps they don't like it. In the wake of the whisky it is time to get out while the smiles are still fading. How can the English preach human rights, somebody sullenly demands, when they are enslaving the Irish and the Scots? Why do you support the disgusting government in South Africa? yells a ninety-year-old blonde in a ball-dress. I don't, says Barley. I truly don't.

"Listen," says Yuri, at the door. "Stay away from that bastard Zapadny, okay? I don't say he's KGB. All I say is, he needed some damn good friends to get him back into circulation. You're a nice fellow. Know what I mean?"

They have already embraced many times.

"Yuri," says Barley. "My old mother brought me up to believe that all of you were KGB."

"Me too?"

"You specially. She said you were the worst."

"I love you. Hear me? Send me your son. What's his name?"

One-thirty and they are an hour late for their next step along the hard road to perhaps-eight-fifteen.

Dark timber, splendid food, respectful menials, the atmosphere of a baronial hunting lodge. They are sitting at the long table below the balcony in the Writers' Union, Alik Zapadny once again presiding. Several promising

young writers of sixty stroll over, listen and stroll away
again, taking their great thoughts with them. Zapadny
points out those recently released from prison and those
who he hopes will soon replace them. Literary bureaucrats
pull up chairs and practise their English. Wicklow inter-
prets, Barley sparkles, all on fruit juice and the residue of
Black Label. The world is going to be a better place, Barley
assures Zapadny, as if he were an expert on the world.

Rashly he quotes Zinoviev. "When will it all end? When
people stop queuing for the Tomb?"—a reference to Lenin's
mausoleum.

The applause this time is not so deafening.

At two o'clock in conformity with the new drinking
laws and in the nick of time, the waiter brings a carafe of
wine, and Zapadny in Barley's honour extracts a bottle of
pepper vodka from his worm-eaten briefcase.

"Did Yuri tell you I was KGB?" he asks mournfully.

"Of course he didn't," says Barley stoutly.

"Please do not regard yourself as singled out. He tells it
to all Westerners. As a matter of fact, I sometimes worry a
little bit about Yuri. He's a nice fellow but everyone knows
he is a lousy publisher, so how does a Jew like him get his
position? His little boy was christened at Zagorsk last
week. How do you explain this?"

"It's not my problem, Alik. Live and let live. Finito." And
aside: "Wickers, get me out of here, I'm getting sober."

By six, after two more enormously eloquent meetings,
and having miraculously succeeded in declining half a
dozen invitations for the evening, Barley is back in his hotel
room, fighting with the shower to sober up while Wicklow
shouts cheerful publishing talk at him through the door for
the benefit of the microphones. For Wicklow has Ned's
orders to stay with Barley till the last moment in case he
gets stage fright or fluffs his lines.

7

The Odessa Hotel in that third year of the Great Soviet Reconstruction was not the jewel of Moscow's rugged tourist trade but it was not the worst piece either. It was dilapidated, it was down-at-heel, it was selective in its favours. Tied to the rouble rather than to the dollar, it lacked such refinements as foreign-currency bars and groups of travel-weary Minnesotans appealing tearfully for their missing luggage. It was so ill-lit that the brass lamps and blackamoors and galleried dining room recalled the bad old past at the point of its collapse rather than the Socialist phoenix rising from the ashes. And when you stepped from the juddering lift and braved the frown of your floor concierge, crouching in her box surrounded by blackened room-keys and mossy telephones, you were quite likely to have the sensation of being returned to the vilest institutions of your youth.

But then the Reconstruction was not yet a visual medium. It was strictly in the audio stage.

Nevertheless, for those who looked for it, the Odessa in those days had soul, and with luck has it still. The good ladies of reception keep a kindly heart behind their iron stares; the porters have been known to wink you to the lift without demanding to see your hotel pass for the fifth time

in one day. The restaurant manager, given the right
encouragement, will usher you graciously to your alcove
and likes a good face in return. And in the evenings
between six and nine the lobby becomes an impromptu
pageant of the hundred nations of the Empire. Smartly
dressed administrators from Tashkent, flaxen school-
teachers from Estonia, fiery-eyed Party functionaries from
Turkmenia and Georgia, factory managers from Kiev,
naval engineers from Archangel—not to mention Cubans,
Afghans, Poles, Roumanians and a platoon of dowdily arrogant East Germans—pour out of their airport charabancs
and descend from the sunlight of the street into the quelling
darkness of the lobby in order to pay their homage to Rome
and shift their luggage in metric stages towards the tribune.

And Barley, himself a reluctant emissary though from a
different empire, that evening took his place among them.

First he sat, only to have an old lady thump him on the
shoulder and demand his seat. Then he hovered in an
alcove near the lift until he risked being walled in by a ram-
part of cardboard suitcases and brown parcels. Finally he
removed himself to the protection of a central pillar and
there he remained, apologising to everyone, watching the
glass door turn off and on and shuffling out of everybody's
light, then into it again, while he brandished Jane Austen's
Emma at his chest and in his other hand a lurid carrier bag
from Heathrow airport.

It was a good thing that Katya arrived to save him.

There was no secret to their meeting, nothing secretive
in their behaviour. Each caught the other's eyes at the same
instant, while Katya was still being buffeted through the
door. Barley threw up an arm, waving Jane Austen.

"Hullo, it's me. Blair. Jolly good!" he yelled.

Katya vanished and reappeared victorious. Did she hear
him? She smiled anyway and lifted her eyes to Heaven in

mute show, making excuses for her lateness. She shoved back a lock of black hair and Barley saw Landau's wedding and betrothal rings.

"You should have seen me trying to get away," she was signalling across the heads. Or: "Couldn't get a cab for love nor money."

"Doesn't matter a bit," Barley was signalling back.

Then she cut him dead while she scowled and rummaged in her handbag for her identity card to show to the plainclothes boy, whose agreeable job that night was to challenge all attractive ladies entering the hotel. It was a red card that she produced so Barley divined the Writers' Union.

Then Barley himself was distracted while he tried in his passable, if clotted, French to explain to a tall Palestinian that no, he was afraid he was *not* a member of the Peace Group, old boy, and alas *not* the manager of the hotel either, and he doubted very much whether there was one.

Wicklow, who had observed these events from halfway up the staircase, reported later that he had never seen an overt encounter better done.

As actors Barley and Katya were dressed for different plays: Katya for high drama in her blue dress and old lace collar that had so taken Landau's fancy; and Barley for low English comedy in a pinstripe suit of his father's that was too short for him in the sleeve, and a pair of very scuffed buckskin boots by Ducker's of Oxford that only a collector of bygones could have regarded as still splendid.

When they met they surprised each other. After all, they were still strangers, closer to the forces that had brought them here than to one another. Discarding the impulse to give her a formal peck on the cheek, Barley found himself instead puzzling over her eyes, which were not only very dark and full of light at the same time but heavily fringed, so that he couldn't help wondering whether she was endowed with a double set of eyelashes.

And since Barley on his side wore that indefinably foolish expression which overcomes certain Englishmen in the presence of beautiful women, it was Katya's suspicion that her first instinct on the telephone had been right and he was haughty.

Meanwhile they were standing close enough to feel the warmth of each other's bodies and for Barley to smell her make-up. The babel of foreign languages continued round them.

"You are Mr. Barley, I think," she told him breathlessly and laid a hand along his forearm, for she had a way of touching people as if seeking to assure herself that they were real.

"Yes indeed, the same, hullo, well done, and you're Katya Orlova, Niki's friend. Wonderful you could make it. Masterpiece of timing. How are you?"

Photographs don't lie but they don't tell the truth either, Barley was thinking, watching her breast rise and fall with her breathing. They don't catch the glow of a girl who looks as though she's just witnessed a miracle and you're the person she's chosen to tell first.

The restless crowd in the lobby brought him to his senses. No two people, however purposefully united, could have survived for long exchanging pleasantries in the centre of that turmoil.

"Tell you what," he said, as if he had had a bright idea on the spur of the moment. "Why don't I buy you a bun? Niki was determined I should make a fuss of you. You met each other at that fair, he tells me. What a character. Heart of gold," he continued cheerfully as he led her towards the staircase and a sign that read BUFFET. "Salt of the earth. A pain in the neck as well, of course, but who isn't?"

"Oh Mr. Landau is a *very* kind man," she said, speaking much as Barley was for the benefit of an unidentified audience, but sounding very persuasive nevertheless.

"And reliable," Barley called approvingly as they gained the first-floor landing. Now Barley too was for some reason out of breath. "Ask Niki to do a thing, he does it. In his own way, it's true. But he does it and keeps his thoughts to himself. I always think that's a sign of a good friend, don't you?"

"I would say that without discretion there can be no friendship," she replied as if quoting from a marriage book. "True friendship must be based on mutual trust."

And Barley while responding warmly to such profundity could not fail to recognise the similarity of her cadences to those of Goethe.

In a curtained area stood a thirty-foot food counter with a single tray of sugar biscuits on it. Behind it three bulky ladies in white uniforms and helmets of transparent plastic had mounted guard over a regimental samovar while they argued among themselves.

"Sound judge of a book too, in his own way, old Niki," Barley observed, stretching out the topic as they took up their places before the rope barrier. "*Bête intellectuelle*, as the French say. Tea, please, ladies. Marvellous."

The ladies went on haranguing each other. Katya stared at them with no expression on her face. Suddenly to Barley's astonishment she drew out her red pass and snarled—there was no other word for it—with the result that one of them detached herself from her companions long enough to yank two cups from a rack and slap them viciously on two saucers as if she were breech-loading an old rifle. Still furious, she filled a huge kettle. And having with further signs of rage unearthed a modern box of matches, she turned up a gas ring and dumped the kettle on it before returning to her comrades.

"Care for a biscuit?" Barley asked. *"Foie gras?"*

"Thank you. I ate cake already at the reception."

"Oh my God. Good cake?"

"It was not very interesting."

"But nice Hungarians?"

"The speeches were not significant. I would say they were banal. I blame our Soviet side for this. We are not sufficiently relaxed with foreigners even when they are from Socialist countries."

Both for a moment had run out of lines. Barley was remembering a girl he had known at university, a general's daughter with skin like rose petals who lived only for the rights of animals until she hurriedly married a groom from the local hunt. Katya was staring gloomily into the further end of the room where a dozen stand-up tables were placed in strict lines. At one of them stood Leonard Wicklow sharing a joke with a young man his own age. At another an elderly *Rittmeister* in riding boots was drinking lemonade with a girl in jeans and throwing out his arms as if to describe his lost estates.

"Can't think why I didn't offer you dinner," Barley said, meeting her eyes again with the feeling of falling straight into them. "One doesn't want to be too forward, I suppose. Not unless one can get away with it."

"It would not have been convenient," she replied, frowning.

The kettle began chugging but the war-hardened women of the buffet kept their backs to it.

"Always so difficult, performing on the telephone, don't you think?" Barley said, for small talk. "Addressing oneself to a sort of plastic flower, I mean, instead of a human face. Hate the beastly thing personally, don't you?"

"Hate what, please?"

"The telephone. Talking at a distance." The kettle began

spitting on the gas. "You get the silliest ideas about people when you can't see them."

Jump, he told himself. *Now.*

"I was saying the very same thing to a publishing friend of mine only the other day," he went on, at the same jolly, conversational level. "We were discussing a new novel someone sent me. I'd shown it to him, strictly confidentially, and he was absolutely knocked out by it. Said it was the best thing he'd seen for years. Dynamite, in fact." Her eyes fixed on his own and they were scaringly direct. "But so *odd* not to have any sort of picture of the writer," he continued airily. "I don't even know the chap's name. Let alone where he gets all his information from, learnt his craft and so forth. Know what I mean? Like hearing a bit of music and not being sure whether it's Brahms or Cole Porter."

She was frowning. She had drawn in her lips and seemed to be moistening them inside her mouth. "I do not regard such personal questions as appropriate to an artist. Some writers can work only in obscurity. Talent is talent. It does not require explanations."

"Well I wasn't talking so much about explanations, you see, as about authenticity," Barley explained. A path of down followed the line of her cheekbone but unlike the hair on her head it was gold. "I mean, *you* know publishing. If a fellow's written a novel about the hill tribes of Northern Burma, for instance, one's entitled to ask whether he's ever been south of Minsk. Specially if it's a really important novel, which this one is. A potential world-beater, according to my chum. In a case like that, I reckon you're entitled to insist that the writer should stand up and declare his qualifications."

Bolder than the others, the senior lady was pouring boiling water into the samovar. A second was unlocking the regimental cash box. A third was scooping rations of tea into a handscale. Searching in his pockets Barley came up with a three-rouble note. At the sight of it the woman at the cash box broke into a despairing tirade.

"I expect she wants change," Barley said stupidly. "Don't we all?"

Then he saw that Katya had put thirty kopeks on the counter and that she had two very small dimples when she smiled. He took the books and bag. She followed him with the teacups on a tray. But as they reached their table she addressed him with an expression of challenge.

"If an author is obliged to prove that he is saying the truth, so also is his publisher," she said.

"Oh, I'm for honesty on all sides. The more people put their cards on the table, the better off we'll *all* be."

"I am informed that the author was inspired by a Russian poet."

"Pecherin," Barley replied. "Looked him up. Born 1807 in Dymerka, province of Kiev."

Her lips were near the brim of her cup, her eyes down. And though he had plenty of other things on his mind, Barley noticed that her right ear, protruding from her hair, had become transparent in the evening light from the window.

"The author was also inspired by certain opinions of an Englishman concerning world peace," she said with the utmost severity.

"Do you think he would like to meet that Englishman again?"

"This can be established. It is not known."

"Well the Englishman would like to meet *him*," said Barley. "They've got an awful lot to say to each other. Where do you live?"

"With my children."

"Where are your children?"

A pause while Barley again had the uncomfortable sensation of having offended against some unfamiliar ethic.

"We live close to the Aeroport metro station. There is no airport there any more. There are apartments. How long are you staying in Moscow, please, Mr. Barley?"

"A week. Any address for your apartment?"

"It is not convenient. You are staying all the time here at the Hotel Odessa?"

"Unless they chuck me out. What does your husband do?"

"It is not important."

"Is he in publishing?"

"No."

"Is he a writer?"

"No."

"So what is he? A composer? A frontier guard? A cook? How does he maintain you in the style to which you are accustomed?"

He had made her laugh again, which seemed to please her as much as it did him. "He was manager of a timber concern," she said.

"What's he manager of now?"

"His factory prefabricates houses for rural areas. We are divorced, like everyone else in Moscow."

"What are the kids? Boys? Girls? How old?"

And that put an end to laughter. For a moment he thought she would walk out on him. Her head lifted, her face closed and an angry fire filled her eyes. "I have a boy and a girl. They are twins, eight years old. It is not relevant."

"You speak beautiful English. Better than I do. It's like well water."

"Thank you, I have a natural comprehension of foreign languages."

"It's better than that. It's unearthly. It's as if English had stopped at Jane Austen. Where did you learn it?"

"In Leningrad. I was at school there. English is also my passion."

"Where were you at university?"

"Also in Leningrad."

"When did you come to Moscow?"

"When I married."

"How did you meet him?"

"My husband and I knew each other from childhood. While we were at school, we attended summer camps together."

"Did you catch fish?"

"Also rabbits," she said as her smile came back again to light the whole room. "Volodya is a Siberian boy. He knows how to sleep in the snow, skin a rabbit and catch fish through the ice. At the time I married him I was in retreat from intellectual values. I thought the most important thing a man could know was how to skin a rabbit."

"I was *really* wondering how you met the author," Barley explained.

He watched her wrestle with her indecision, noticing how readily her eyes reflected her changing emotions, now coming to him, now retreating. Until he lost her altogether as she stooped below the level of the table, pushed away her flying hair and picked up her handbag. "Please thank Mr. Landau for the books and the tea," she said. "I shall thank him myself next time he comes to Moscow."

"Don't go. Please. I need your advice." He lowered his voice and it was suddenly very serious. "I need your instructions about what to do with that crazy manuscript. I can't fly solo. Who wrote it? Who's Goethe?"

"Unfortunately I have to return to my children."

"Isn't somebody looking after them?"

"Naturally."

"Ring up. Say you're running late. Say you've met a fascinating man who wants to talk literature to you all night. We've hardly met. I need time. I've got masses of questions for you."

Gathering up the volumes of Jane Austen she started towards the door. And like a persistent salesman Barley stumbled at her side.

"Please," he said. "Look. I'm a lousy English publisher with about ten thousand enormously serious things to discuss with a beautiful Russian woman. I don't bite, I don't lie. Have dinner with me."

"It is not convenient."

"Is another night convenient? What do I do? Burn joss? Put a candle in my window? You're what I came here for. Help me to help you."

His appeal had confused her.

"Can I have your home number?" he insisted.

"It is not convenient," she muttered.

They were descending the wide staircase. Glancing at the sea of heads Barley saw Wicklow and his friend among them. He grasped Katya's arm, not fiercely but nevertheless causing her to stand still.

"When?" he said.

He was still holding her arm at the bicep, just above the inside of the elbow where it was firmest and most full.

"Perhaps I shall call you late tonight," she replied, relenting.

"Not perhaps."

"I shall call you."

Remaining on the stair he watched her approach the edge of the crowd, then seem to take a breath before spreading her arms and barging her way to the door. He was sweating. A damp shawl hung over his back and shoul-

ders. He wanted a drink. Above all he wanted to get rid of
the microphone harness. He wanted to smash it into very
small pieces and trample on them and send them registered
and personal to Ned.

Wicklow, with his crooked nose, was skipping up the
stairs at him, grinning like a thief and talking some bilge
about a Soviet biography of Bernard Shaw.

She walked quickly, looking for a taxi but needing
movement. Clouds had gathered and there were no stars,
just the wide streets and the glow of arc-lights from
Petrovka. She needed distance from him and from herself. A panic born not of fear but of a violent aversion was
threatening to seize hold of her. He should not have
mentioned the twins. He had no right to knock down the
paper walls between one life and another. He should not
pester her with bureaucratic questions. She had trusted
him: why did he not trust her?

She turned a corner and kept walking. He is a typical
imperialist, false, importunate and untrusting. A taxi
passed, not heeding her. A second slowed down long
enough to hear her call her destination, then sped away in
search of a more lucrative assignment—to ferry whores, to
carry furniture, to deliver black-market vegetables, meat
and vodka, to work the tourist traps. The rain was beginning, big drops, well aimed.

His humour, so ill-placed. His inquisitions, so impertinent. I shall never go near him again. She should take the
metro but dreaded the confinement. Attractive, naturally,
as many Englishmen are. That graceful clumsiness. He was
witty and without doubt sensitive. She had not expected
him to come so close. Or perhaps it was she who went too
close to him.

She kept walking, steadying herself, looking for a taxi.

The rain fell harder. She pulled a folding umbrella from her bag and opened it. East German, a present from a short-lived lover she had not been proud of. Reaching a cross-roads, she was about to step into the street when a boy in a blue Lada pulled up beside her. She had not hailed him.

"How's business, sister?"

Was he a taxi, was he a freebooter? She jumped in and gave her destination. The boy started to argue. The rain was thundering on the car roof.

"It's urgent," she said, and handed him two three-rouble notes. "It's urgent," she repeated and glanced at her watch, at the same time wondering whether glancing at watches was something people did when they were in a hurry to get to hospital.

The boy seemed to have taken her cause to heart. He was driving and talking at breakneck speed while the rain poured through his open window. His sick mother in Novgorod had fainted while picking apples from a ladder and woken up with both legs in plaster, he said. The wind-screen was a torrent of gushing water. He had not stopped to attach the wipers.

"How is she now?" Katya asked, tying a scarf round her hair. A woman in a hurry to get to hospital does not exchange small talk about the plight of others, she thought.

The boy hauled the car to a halt. She saw the gates. The sky was calm again, the night warm and sweet-smelling. She wondered whether it had rained at all.

"Here," said the boy, holding out her three-rouble notes. "Next time, okay? What's your name? You like fresh fruit, coffee, vodka?"

"Keep it," she snapped, and pushed the money back at him.

The gates stood open, leading to what could have been

an office block with a few lights dimly burning. A flight of stone steps, half-buried in mud and rubbish, rose to an overhead walkway. The walkway led across a sliproad. Looking down, Katya saw parked ambulances, their blue lights lazily rotating, drivers and attendants smoking in a group. At their feet lay a woman on a stretcher, her smashed face wrenched to one side as if to escape a second blow.

He took care of me, she thought as her mind returned to Barley for a moment.

She hurried towards the grey block that rose ahead of her. A clinic designed by Dante and built by Franz Kafka, she remembered. The staff go there to steal medicines and sell them on the black market; the doctors are all moonlighting to feed their families, she remembered. A place for the lowlife and riffraff of our empire, for the luckless proletariat with neither the influence nor connections of the few. The voice in her head had a rhythm that marched with her as she strode confidently through the double doors. A woman snapped at her, and Katya, rather than show her card, handed her a rouble. The lobby echoed like a swimming pool. Behind a marble counter, more women ignored everyone except one another. An old man in blue uniform sat dozing in a chair, his open eyes staring at a defunct television set. She strode past him and entered a corridor lined with patients' beds. Last time there had been no beds in the corridor. Perhaps they cleared them out to make room for someone important. An exhausted trainee was giving blood to an old woman, assisted by a nurse in open overalls and jeans. Nobody groaned, nobody complained. Nobody asked why they must die in a corridor. An illuminated sign gave the first letters of the word "Emergency." She followed it. Look as though you own the place, he had advised her the first time. And it had worked. It still did.

The waiting-room was a discarded lecture hall lit like a night ward. On the platform, a matron with a saintly face sat at the head of a line of applicants as long as a retreating army. In the auditorium, the wretched of the earth growled and whispered in the twilight, nursed their children. Men with half-dressed injuries lay on benches. Drunks lolled and swore. The air stank of antiseptic, wine and old blood.

Ten minutes to wait. Yet again she found her mind slipping back to Barley. His straight familiar eyes, his air of hopeless valour. Why would I not give him my home telephone number? His hand on her arm as if it had been there for ever. "You're what I came here for." Selecting a broken bench near the rear door marked "Lavatories," she sat and peered ahead of her. You can die there and nobody will ask your name, he had said. There is the door, there is the alcove for the cloakroom, she rehearsed. Then there are the lavatories. The telephone is in the cloakroom but it is never used because nobody knows it is there. Nobody can get through to the hospital on the open line, but this line was put in for a bigwig doctor who wanted to keep in touch with his private patients and his mistress, until he got himself transferred. Some idiot installed it out of sight behind a pillar. It's been there ever since.

How do you know about such places? she had asked him. This entrance, this wing, this telephone, sit down and wait. How do you know?

I walk, he had replied, and she had had a vision of him striding the Moscow streets without sleep, food or herself, walking. I am the wandering Gentile, he had told her. I walk to keep company with my mind, I drink to hide from it. When I walk, you are beside me; I can see your face at my shoulder.

He will walk until he falls, she thought. And I shall follow him.

On the bench beside her a peasant woman in a saffron headscarf had begun to pray in Ukrainian. She was holding a small icon in both hands and bowing her head over it, deeper each time, till she was prodding her hairless forehead with the tin frame. Her eyes grew bright and as they closed, Katya saw tears come out from between the lids. In the blink of a star I shall look like you, she thought.

She remembered how he had told her about visiting a mortuary in Siberia, a factory for the dead, situated in one of the phantom cities where he worked. How the corpses came out of a chute and were passed around a carousel, male and female mixed, to be hosed and labelled and stripped of their gold by the old women of the night. Death is a secret like any other, he had told her; a secret is something that is revealed to one person at a time.

Why do you always try to educate me to the meaning of death? she had demanded of him, sickened. Because you have taught me how to live, he had replied.

The telephone is the safest in Russia, he had said. Even our lunatics in the security *Organs* would not think of tapping the unused telephone of an emergency hospital.

She remembered their last meeting in Moscow, in the deepest part of winter. He had picked up a slow train at a backwater station, a place with no name in the centre of nowhere. He had bought no ticket and travelled hard class, pushing ten roubles into the conductor's palm like everybody else. Our gallant competent *Organs* are so bourgeois these days they no longer know how to mix with the workers, he had said. She pictured him a waif in his thick underclothes, lying in semi-darkness on the top berth reserved for luggage, listening to the smokers' coughing and the grumble of the drunks, suffocating from the stink of humanity and the leaky water-heater while he stared at the appalling things he knew and never spoke of. What kind of

hell must that be, she wondered, to be tormented by your
own creations? To know that the absolute best you can do
in your career is the absolute worst for mankind?

She saw herself waiting for him to arrive, bivouacked
among the thousands of other waiting-wounded at the
Kazansky railway station under the foul fluorescent
lights. The train is delayed, is cancelled, is derailed, said
the rumours. Heavy snowfalls all the way to Moscow. The
train is arriving, it never started, I need never have bothered to tell so many lies. The station staff had poured
formaldehyde into the lavatories and the whole concourse
stank of it. She was wearing Volodya's fur hat because it
hid more of her face. Her mohair scarf covered her chin,
her sheepskin coat the rest of her. She had never known
such desire for anyone. It was a heat and a hunger at once
inside the fur.

When he stepped off the train and walked towards her
through the slush, her body was stiff and embarrassed like
a boy's. As she stood beside him in the crowded metro, she
nearly screamed in the silence as he pressed against her.
She had borrowed Alexandra's apartment. Alexandra had
gone to the Ukraine with her husband. She unlocked the
front door and made him go ahead. Sometimes he seemed
not to know where he was or, after all her planning, not to
care. Sometimes she was scared to touch him, he was too
frail. But not today. Today she ran at him, grasped him
with all her force, gathering him to her without skill or
tenderness, punishing him for her months and nights of
fruitless longing.

But he? He embraced her as her father used to, keeping
his waist clear of her and his shoulders firm. And as she
pulled away from him she knew that the time was past
when he could bury his torment in her body.

You are the only religion I have, he whispered, kissing

her brow with closed lips. Listen to me, Katya, while I tell you what I have decided to do.

The peasant woman was kneeling on the floor, loving her icon, pressing it to her breast and lips. Katya had to climb over her to reach the gangway. A pale young man in a leather jacket had sat himself at the end of the bench. He had one arm tucked into his shirt, so she supposed it was his wrist that was broken. His head had fallen forward and as she squeezed past him she noticed that his nose was broken too, though healed.

The alcove was in darkness. A broken light bulb dangled uselessly. A massive wooden counter barred her way to the cloakroom. She tried to lift the flap but it was too heavy so she wriggled under it. She was standing among empty coat-racks and hangers and uncollected hats. The pillar was a metre across. A handwritten sign said NO CHANGE GIVEN and she read it by the light of an opening and closing door. The telephone was in its usual place on the other side, but when she placed herself before it she could hardly see it in the dark.

She stared at it, willing it to ring. Her panic was over. She was strong again. Where are you? she wondered. In one of your postal numbers, one of your blurs on the map? In Kazakhstan? In the Middle Volga? In the Urals? He visited all of them, she knew. In the old days she had been able to tell by his complexion when he had been working outdoors. At other times he looked as though he had been underground for months. Where are you with your dreadful guilt? she wondered. Where are you with your terrifying decision? In a dark place like this? In a small-town telegraph office that is open round the clock? She imagined him arrested, the way she sometimes dreamed of him, trussed and white in a hut, tied to a wooden horse, scarcely bucking any more as they went on beating him. The phone was ringing. She lifted the receiver and heard a flat voice.

"This is Pyotr," he said, which was their code to protect each other—if I am in their hands, and they force me to call you, I shall tell them a different name so that you can hide.

"And this is Alina," she replied, amazed that she could speak at all. After that she didn't care. He's alive. He hasn't been arrested. They are not beating him. They have not tied him to a wooden horse. She felt lazy and bored. He was alive, he was speaking to her. Facts, no emotion, his voice at first remote and only half familiar. Backwards and forwards, only facts. Do this. He said this. I said this. Tell him I thank him for coming to Moscow. Tell him he is behaving like a reasonable human being. I am well. How are you?

She rang off, too weak to talk any more. She returned to the lecture hall and sat on a bench with the rest of them, reaching for breath, knowing nobody would care.

The boy in the leather jacket was still lounging on the bench. She noticed his bent nose again, perfect yet off-true. She remembered Barley again and was grateful for his existence.

He lay on his bed in his shirt-sleeves. His bedroom was an airless box hacked from a grand bedchamber and filled with the water-chorus of every Russian hotel, the snuffle of the taps, the trickle of the cistern from the tiny bathroom, the gulping of the huge black radiator, the groan of the refrigerator as it flung itself upon a fresh cycle of convulsions. He was sipping whisky from a toothmug, pretending to read by the useless bedlight. The telephone lay at his elbow, and beside the telephone lay his notebook for messages and great thoughts. Phones can be alive whether or not they're on their cradles, Ned had warned him. Not this one, it isn't, thought Barley. This one's dead as a dodo till she rings. He was reading wonderful García Márquez but the print was like barbed wire to him; he kept stumbling and having to go back.

A car went by in the street, then a pedestrian. Then it was the turn of the rain, cracking like tired shot against the window panes. Without a scream or a laugh or a cry of anger, Moscow had returned herself to the great spaces.

He remembered her eyes. What did they see in me? A relic, he decided. Dressed in my father's suit. A lousy actor concealed by his own performance, and behind the grease-paint nothing. She was looking for the conviction in me and saw instead the moral bankruptcy of my English class and time. She was looking for future hope and finding vestiges of a finished history. She was looking for connection and saw the notice on me saying RESERVED. So she took one look at me and ran.

Reserved for whom? For what great day or passion have I reserved myself?

He tried to imagine her body. With a face like that, who needs a body anyway?

He drank. She's courage. She's trouble. He drank again. Katya, if that's who you are, I am reserved for you.

If.

He wondered what else there was to know of her. Nothing except the truth. There had been an epoch, long forgotten, when he had mistaken beauty for intelligence, but Katya was so obviously intelligent there could be no problem this time of confusing the two qualities. There had been another epoch, God help him, when he had mistaken beauty for virtue. But in Katya he had sensed such iridescent virtue that if she were to pop her head round the door at this moment and tell him she had just murdered her children, he would instantly find six ways of assuring her she was not to blame.

If.

He took another pull of Scotch and with a jolt remembered Andy.

Andy Macready, trumpeter, lying in hospital with his head cut off. Thyroid, said his missus vaguely. When they'd first discovered it, Andy didn't want the surgery. He'd prefer to take the long swim and not come back, he said, so they got drunk together and planned the trip to Capri, one last great meal, a gallon of red and the long swim to nowhere through the filthy Mediterranean. But when the thyroid really got to him Andy discovered he preferred life to death, so he voted for the surgery instead. And they cut his head off his body, all but the vertebrae, and kept him going on tubes. So Andy was alive still, with nothing to live for and nothing to die of, cursing that he hadn't done the swim in time, and trying to find a meaning for himself that death wouldn't take away.

Phone Andy's missus, he thought. Ask her how her old man is. He peered at his watch, calculating what time it was in the real or unreal world of Mrs. Macready. His hand started for the phone but didn't pick it up in case it rang.

He thought of his daughter Anthea. Good old Ant.

He thought of his son Hal in the City. Sorry I screwed it up for you, Hal, but you've still got a bit of time left to get it right.

He thought of his flat in Lisbon and the girl crying her heart out, and he wondered with a shudder what had become of her. He thought of his other women, but his guilts weren't quite up to their usual, so he wondered about that too. He thought of Katya again and realised he had been thinking of her all the time.

A tap at the door. She has come to me. She is wearing a simple housecoat and is naked underneath. Barley, she whispers, darling. Will you still love me afterwards?

She does nothing of the kind. She has no precedent and no sequel. She is not part of the familiar, well-thumbed series.

It was Wicklow, his guardian angel, checking on his ward.

"Come on in, Wickers. Care for a spot?"

Wicklow raised his eyebrows, asking has she phoned? He was wearing a leather jacket and there were drops of rain on it. Barley shook his head. Wicklow poured himself a glass of mineral water.

"I've been running through some of the books they pushed at us today, sir," he said, in the fancy tone they both adopted for the microphones. "I wondered whether you'd like an update on some of the non-fiction titles."

"Wickers, date me up," said Barley hospitably, stretching himself on the bed again while Wicklow took the chair.

"Well there is just *one* of their submissions I'd like to share with you, sir. It's that fitness handbook on dieting and exercises. I think we might consider it for one of our co-production splashes. I wondered whether we could sign one of their top illustrators and raise the Russian impact level."

"Raise it. Sky's the limit."

"Well I'll have to ask Yuri first."

"Ask him."

Hiatus. Let's run that through again, thought Barley.

"Oh, by the way, sir. You were asking why so many Russians use the word 'convenient.' "

"Well now, so I was," said Barley, who had been asking nothing of the kind.

"The word they're thinking of is *udobno*. It means convenient but it also means proper, which must be a bit confusing sometimes. I mean it's one thing not to be convenient. It's another not to be proper."

"It is indeed," Barley agreed after long thought while he sipped his Scotch.

Then he must have dozed because the next thing he knew he was sitting bolt upright with the receiver to his ear and Wicklow standing over him. This was Russia, so she didn't say her name.

"Come round," he said.

"I am sorry to call so late. Do I disturb you?"

"Of course you do. All the time. That was a great cup of tea. Wish it could have lasted longer. Where are you?"

"You invited me for dinner tomorrow night, I think."

He was reaching for his notebook. Wicklow held it ready.

"Lunch, tea, dinner, all three of them," he said. "Where do I send the glass coach?" He scribbled down an address. "What's your home telephone number, by the way, in case I get lost or you do?" She gave him that too, reluctantly, a departure from principle, but she gave it all the same. Wicklow watched him write it all down, then softly left the room as they continued talking.

You never know, Barley thought, steadying his mind with another long pull of Scotch when he had rung off. With beautiful, intelligent, virtuous women, you simply never know where they stand. Is she pining for me, or am I a face in her crowd?

Then suddenly the Moscow fear hit him at gale force. It sprang out at him when he was least expecting it, after he had fought it off all day. The muffled terrors of the city burst thundering upon his ears and after them the piping voice of Walter.

"Is she really in touch with him? Did she invent the stuff herself? Is she in touch with someone different, and if so who?"

8

The Russia House

Then he could have done, because the interesting, he knew he was doing it because... with the... Fair public... and will have something... ... This was Russia... to do... to...

Come out of, to end...

"I mustn't even... to be," he... "I think I..."

Of course you can, at the club. Now, was a great way of it.

"With... could have fisted... When... or your..."

"Are you... g... his you don't. Which... have taking...

In the situation room in the basement of the Russia House the atmosphere was of a tense and permanent night air-raid. Ned sat at his command desk before a bank of telephones. Sometimes one winked and he spoke into it in terse monosyllables. Two female assistants softly put round the telegrams and cleared the out-trays. Two illuminated post-office clocks, one London time, one Moscow time, shone like twin moons from the end wall. In Moscow it was midnight. In London nine. Ned scarcely looked up as his head janitor unlocked the door to me.

It was the earliest I had been able to get away. I had spent the morning at the Treasury solicitors' and the afternoon with the lawyers from Cheltenham. Supper was helping to entertain a delegation of espiocrats from Sweden before they were packed off to the obligatory musical.

Walter and Bob were bowed over a Moscow street map. Brock was on the internal telephone to the cypher room. Ned was immersed in what seemed to be a lengthy inventory. He waved me to a chair and shoved a batch of incoming signals at me, scribbled messages from the front.

0954 hrs Barley has successfully telephoned Katya at October. They have made an appointment for 2015 at the Odessa tonight. More.

1320 hrs irregulars have followed Katya to number 14 so-and-so street. She posted a letter at what appears to be an empty house. Photographs to follow soonest by bag. More.

2018 hrs Katya has arrived at the Odessa Hotel. Barley and Katya are talking in the canteen. Wicklow and one irregular observing. More.

2105 hrs Katya departs Odessa. Summary of conversation to follow. Tapes to follow soonest by bag. More.

2200 hrs interim. Katya has promised to telephone Barley tonight. More.

2250 hrs Katya followed to the so-and-so hospital. Wicklow and one irregular covering. More.

2325 hrs Katya receives phone call on disused hospital telephone. Speaks three minutes twenty seconds. More.

And now suddenly, no more.

Spying is normality taken to extremes. Spying is waiting.

"Is Clive Without India receiving tonight?" Ned asked, as if my presence had reminded him of something.

I replied that Clive would be in his suite all evening. He had been locked up in the American Embassy all day, and he had told me he proposed to be on call.

I had a car so we drove to Head Office together.

"Have you seen this bloody document?" Ned asked me, tapping the folder on his lap.

"Which bloody document is that?"

"The Bluebird distribution list. Bluebird readers and their satraps."

I was cautiously non-committal. Ned's bad temper in mid-operation was legendary. The light on the door of Clive's office was green, meaning come in if you dare. The brass plate said "Deputy" in lettering to outshine the Royal Mint.

"What the devil's happened to the need-to-know, Clive?" Ned asked him, waving the distribution list as soon as we were in the presence. "We give Langley one batch of highly sensitive, unsourced material and overnight they've recruited more cooks than broth. I mean what is this? Hollywood? We've got a live joe out there. We've got a defector in place we've never met."

Clive toured the gold carpet. He had a habit when he was arguing with Ned of turning his whole body at once, like a playing-card. He did so now.

"So you think the Bluebird readership list too long?" he enquired in the tone of one taking evidence.

"Yes, and so should you. And so should Russell Sheriton. Who the devil are the Pentagon Scientific Liaison Board? What's the White House Academic Advisory Team when it's at home?"

"You would prefer me to take a high line and insist Bluebird be confined to their Inter-Agency Committee? Principals only, no staff, no aides? Is that what you are telling me?"

"If you think you can get the toothpaste back in the tube, yes."

Clive affected to consider this on its merits. But I knew, and so did Ned, that Clive considered nothing on its merits. He considered who was in favour of something and who was against it. Then he considered who was the better ally.

"Firstly, not a single one of those elevated gentlemen I have mentioned is capable of making head or tail of the Bluebird material without expert guidance," Clive resumed in his bloodless voice. "Either we let them flounder in ignorance or we admit their appendages and accept the price. The same goes for their Defense Intelligence team, their Navy, Army, Air Force and White House evaluators."

"Is this Russell Sheriton speaking or you?" Ned demanded.

"How can we tell them not to call in their scientific panels when we offer them immensely complex material in the same breath?" Clive persisted, neatly letting Ned's question pass him by. "If Bluebird's genuine, they're going to need all the help they can get."

"*If,*" Ned echoed, flaring. "*If* he's genuine. My God, Clive, you're worse than they are. There are two hundred and forty people on that list and every one of them has a wife, a mistress and fifteen best friends."

"And *secondly,*" Clive went on, when we had forgotten there had been a firstly, "it's not *our* intelligence to dispose of. It's Langley's." He had swung on me before Ned could get in his reply. "Palfrey. Confirm. Under our sharing treaty with the Americans, is it not the case that we give Langley first rights on all strategic material?"

"In strategic matters our dependence on Langley is total," I conceded. "They give us what they want us to know. In return we are obliged to give them whatever we find out. It isn't often much but that's the deal."

Clive listened carefully to this and approved it. His coldness had an unaccustomed ferocity and I wondered why. If he had possessed a conscience, I would have said it was uneasy. What had he been doing at the Embassy all day? What had he given away to whom for what?

"It is a common misapprehension of this Service," Clive continued, talking straight at Ned now, "that we and the Americans are in the same boat. We're not. Not when it comes to strategy. We haven't a defence analyst in the country who is capable of holding a candle to his American counterpart on matters of strategy. Where strategy is concerned, we are a tiny, ignorant British coracle and they are the *Queen Elizabeth*. It is not our place to tell them how to run their ship."

We were still marvelling at the vigour of this declaration
when Clive's hot line began ringing and he went for it
greedily, for he always loved answering his hot line in front
of his subordinates. He was unlucky. It was Brock calling
for Ned.

Katya had just phoned Barley at the Odessa and they
had agreed a meeting for tomorrow evening, said Brock.
Moscow station required Ned's urgent approval of their
operational proposals for the encounter. Ned left at once.

"What are you brewing with the Americans?" I asked
Clive, but he didn't bother with me.

All next day I spent talking to my Swedes. In the Russia
House, life was scarcely more enlivening. Spying is waiting.
Around four I slipped back to my room and telephoned
Hannah. Sometimes I do that. By four she is back from the
Cancer Institute where she works part time, and her husband never comes home before seven. She told me how her
day had gone. I scarcely listened. I gave her some story
about my son, Alan, who was in deep water with a nurse up
in Birmingham, a nice enough girl but really not Alan's
class.

"I may ring you later," she said.

Sometimes she said that, but she never rang.

Barley walked at Katya's side and he could hear her
footsteps like a tighter echo of his own. The flaking mansions of Dickensian Moscow were bathed in stale twilight. The first courtyard was gloomy, the second dark.
Cats stared at them from the rubbish. Two long-haired
boys who might have been students were playing tennis
across a row of packing cases. A third leaned against the
wall. A door stood ahead of them, daubed with graffiti
and a red crescent moon. "Watch for the red marks,"
Wicklow had advised. She was pale and he wondered if

he was pale too, because it would be a living miracle if he wasn't. Some men will never be heroes, some heroes will never be men, he thought, with urgent acknowledgements to Joseph Conrad. And Barley Blair, he'll never be either. He grabbed the doorhandle and yanked it. She kept her distance. She was wearing a headscarf and a raincoat. The handle turned but the door wouldn't budge. He shoved it with both hands, then shoved harder. The tennis players yelled at him in Russian. He stopped dead, feeling fire on his back.

"They say you should please kick it," Katya said, and to his amazement he saw that she was smiling.

"If you can smile now," he said, "how do you look when you're happy?"

But he must have said it to himself because she didn't answer. He kicked it and it gave, the grit beneath it screaming. The boys laughed and went back to their game. He stepped into the black and she followed him. He pressed a switch but no light came. The door slammed shut behind them and when he groped for the handle he couldn't find it. They stood in deep darkness, smelling cats and onions and cooking oil and listening to bits of music and argument from other people's lives. He struck a match. Three steps appeared, then half a bicycle, then the entrance to a filthy lift. Then his fingers burned. You go to the fourth floor, Wicklow had said. Watch for the red marks. How the devil do I watch for red marks in the dark? God answered him with a pale light from the floor above.

"Where are we, please?" she asked politely.

"It's a friend of mine," he said. "A painter."

He pulled back the lift door, then the grille. He said "Please" but she was already past him, standing in the lift and looking upward, willing it to rise.

"He's away for a few days. It's just somewhere to talk," he said.

He noticed her eyelashes again, the moisture in her eyes. He wanted to console her but she wasn't sad enough.

"He's a painter," he said again, as if that legitimised a friend.

"Official?"

"No. I don't think so. I don't know."

Why hadn't Wicklow told him which kind of bloody painter the man was supposed to be?

He was about to press the button when a small girl in tortoiseshell spectacles hopped in after them hugging a plastic bear. She called a greeting and Katya's face lit up as she greeted her in return. The lift juddered upwards, the buttons popping like cap pistols at each floor. At the third the child politely said goodbye, and Barley and Katya said goodbye in unison. At the fourth the lift bumped to a halt as if it had hit the ceiling and perhaps it had. He shoved her ashore and leapt after her. A passage opened before them, filled with the stench of baby, perhaps a lot of babies. At the end of it, on what seemed to be a blank wall, a red arrow directed them left. They came on a narrow wooden staircase leading upwards. On the bottom step Wicklow crouched like a leprechaun reading a weighty book by the aid of a mechanic's light. He did not lift his head as they climbed past him but Barley saw Katya stare at him all the same.

"What's the matter? Seen a ghost?" he asked her.

Could she hear him? Could he hear himself? Had he spoken? They were in a long attic. Chinks of sky pierced the tiles, bats' mess smeared the rafters. A path of scaffolders' boards had been laid over the joists. Barley took her hand. Her palm was broad and strong and dry. Its nakedness against his own was like the gift of her entire body.

He advanced cautiously, smelling turpentine and linseed and hearing the tapping of an unexpected wind. He squeezed between a pair of iron cisterns and saw a life-sized paper sea-gull in full flight strung from a beam, turning on its thread. He pulled her after him. Beyond it, fixed to a shower-rail, hung a striped curtain. If there's no sea-gull there's no meeting, Wicklow had said. No sea-gull means abort. That's my epitaph, thought Barley. "There was no sea-gull, so he aborted." He swept the curtain aside and entered a painter's studio, once more drawing her after him. At its centre stood an easel and a model's upholstered box. An aged Chesterfield rested on its stuffing. It's a one-time facility, Wicklow had said. So am I, Wickers, so am I. A homemade skylight was cut into the slope of the roof. A red mark was daubed on its frame. Russians don't trust walls, Wicklow had explained, she'll talk better in the open air.

The skylight opened, to the consternation of a colony of doves and sparrows. He nodded her through first, noticing the easy flow of her long body as she stooped. He clambered after her, barking his spine and saying "Damn" exactly as he knew he would. They were standing between two gables in a leaded valley only wide enough for their feet. The pulse of traffic rose from streets they couldn't see. She was facing him and close. Let's live up here, he thought. Your eyes, me, the sky. He was rubbing his back, screwing up his eyes against the pain.

"You are hurt?"

"Just a fractured spine."

"Who is that man on the stairs?" she said.

"He works for me. He's my editor. He's keeping a look-out while we talk."

"He was at the hospital last night."

"What hospital?"

"Last night after seeing you, I was obliged to visit a certain hospital."

"Are you ill? Why did you go to hospital?" Barley asked, no longer rubbing his back.

"It is not important. He was there. He appeared to have a broken arm."

"He can't have been there," Barley said, not believing himself. "He was with me the whole evening after you left. We had a discussion about Russian books."

He saw the suspicion slowly leave her eyes. "I am tired. You must excuse me."

"Let me tell you what I've worked out, then you can tell me it's no good. We talk, then I take you out to dinner. If the People's custodians were listening to our call last night they'll expect that anyway. The studio belongs to a painter friend of mine, a jazz nut like me. I never told you his name because I couldn't remember it and perhaps I never knew it. I thought we could bring him a drink and look at his pictures but he didn't appear. We went on to dinner, talked literature and world peace. Despite my reputation I did not make a pass at you. I was too much in awe of your beauty. How's that?"

"It is convenient."

Dropping into a crouch, he produced a half bottle of Scotch and unscrewed the cap. "Do you drink this stuff?"

"No."

"Me neither." He hoped she would settle beside him but she remained standing. He poured a tot into the cap and set the bottle at his feet.

"What's his name?" he said. "The author's. Goethe. Who is he?"

"It is not important."

"What's his unit? Firm? Postbox number? Ministry? Laboratory? Where's he working? We haven't time to fool around."

"I don't know."

"Where's he stationed? You won't tell me that either, will you?"

"In many places. It depends where he is working."

"How did you meet him?"

"I don't know. I don't know what I may tell you."

"What did he tell you to tell me?"

She faltered, as if he had caught her out. She frowned. "Whatever is necessary. I should trust you. He was generous. It is his nature."

"So what's holding you up?" Nothing. "Why do you think I'm here?" Nothing. "Do you think I enjoy playing cops-and-robbers in Moscow?"

"I don't know."

"Why did you send me the book if you don't trust me?"

"It was for him that I sent it. I did not select you. He did," she replied moodily.

"Where is he now? At the hospital? How do you speak to him?" He looked up at her, waiting for her answer. "Why don't you just start talking and see how it goes?" he suggested. "Who he is, who you are. What he does for a living."

"I don't know."

"Who was in the woodshed at 3 a.m. on the night of the crime." More nothing. "Tell me why you've dragged me into this. You started this. I didn't. Katya? It's me. I'm Barley Blair. I do jokes, I do bird noises, I drink. I'm a friend."

He loved her grave silences while she stared at him. He loved her listening with her eyes and the sense of recovered companionship each time she spoke.

"There has been no crime," she said. "He is my friend. His name and occupation are unimportant."

Barley took a sip while he thought about this. "So is this

what you usually do for friends? Smuggle their illicit manuscripts to the West for them?" She thinks with her eyes as well, he thought. "Did he happen to mention to you what his manuscript was about?"

"Naturally. He would not endanger me without my consent."

He caught the protectiveness in her voice and resented it. "What did he tell you was in it?" he asked.

"The manuscript describes my country's involvement in the preparation of anti-humanitarian weapons of mass destruction over many years. It paints a portrait of corruption and incompetence in all fields of the defence-industrial complex. Also of criminal mismanagement and ethical shortcomings."

"That's quite a mouthful. Do you know any details beyond that?"

"I am not acquainted with military matters."

"So he's a soldier."

"No."

"So what is he?"

Silence.

"But you approve of that? Passing that stuff out to the West?"

"He is not passing it to the West or to any bloc. He respects the British but that is not important. His gesture will ensure true openness among scientists of all nations. It will help to destroy the arms race." She had still to come to him. She was speaking flatly as if she had learned her lines by heart. "He believes there is no time left. We must destroy the abuse of science and the political systems responsible for it. When he speaks philosophy, he speaks English," she added.

And you listen, he thought. With your eyes. In English. While you wonder whether you can trust me.

"Is he a scientist?" he asked.

"Yes. He is a scientist."

"I hate them all. What branch? Is he a physicist?"

"Perhaps. I don't know."

"His information comes from across the board. Accuracy, aim-points, command and control, rocket motors. Is he one man? Who gives him the material? How does he know so much?"

"I don't know. He is one man. That is obvious. I do not have so many friends. He is not a group. Perhaps he also supervises the work of others. I don't know."

"Is he high up? A big boss? Is he working here in Moscow? Is he a headquarters man? What is he?"

She shook her head at each question. "He does not work in Moscow. Otherwise I have not asked him and he does not tell me."

"Does he test things?"

"I don't know. He goes to many places. All over the Soviet Union. Sometimes he has been in the sun, sometimes he has been very cold, sometimes both. I don't know."

"Has he ever mentioned his unit?"

"No."

"Box numbers? The names of his bosses? The name of a colleague or subordinate?"

"He is not interested to tell me such things."

And he believed her. While he was with her, he would believe that north was south and babies grew on jacaranda trees.

She was watching him, waiting for his next question.

"Does he understand the consequences of publishing this stuff?" he asked. "To himself, I mean? Does he know what he's playing with?"

"He says that there are times when our actions must

come first and we must consider consequences only when they occur." She seemed to expect him to say something but he was learning to slow down. "If we see one goal clearly we may advance one step. If we contemplate all goals at once we shall not advance at all."

"How about you? Has he thought about the consequences to you at all if any of this comes to light?"

"He is reconciled."

"Are you?"

"Naturally. It was my decision also. Why else would I support him?"

"And the children?" he asked.

"It is for them and for their generation," she said with a resolution bordering on anger.

"What about the consequences to Mother Russia?"

"We regard the destruction of Russia as preferable to the destruction of all mankind. The greatest burden is the past. For all nations, not only Russia. We regard ourselves as the executioners of the past. He says that if we cannot execute our past, how shall we construct our future? We shall not build a new world until we have got rid of the mentalities of the old. In order to express truth we must also be prepared to be the apostles of negation. He quotes Turgenev. A nihilist is a person who does not take anything for granted, however much that principle is revered."

"And you?"

"I am not a nihilist. I am a humanist. If it is given to us to play a part for the future, we must play it."

He was searching her voice for a hint of doubt. He found none. She was tone perfect.

"How long's he been talking like this? Always? Or is it only recent?"

"He has always been idealistic. That is his nature. He has always been extremely critical in a constructive sense.

There was a time when he was able to convince himself that the weapons of annihilation were so terrible they would have the effect of abolishing war. He believed they would produce an alteration in the mind of the military establishments. He was persuaded by the paradox that the greatest weapons contained within them the greatest capacity for peace. He was in this regard an enthusiast of American strategic opinions."

She was starting towards him. He could feel it in her, the stirring of a need. She was waking and approaching him. Under the Moscow sky, she was shedding her mistrust after too much loneliness and deprival.

"So what changed him?"

"He has experienced for many years the incompetence and arrogance of our military and bureaucratic organisations. He has seen how it drags on the feet of progress. That is his expression. He is inspired by the *perestroika* and by the prospect of world peace. But he is not Utopian, he is not passive. He knows that nothing will come of its own accord. He knows that our people are deluded and lack collective power. The new revolution must be imposed from above. By intellectuals. By artists. By administrators. By scientists. He wishes to make his own irreversible contribution in accordance with the exhortations of our leadership. He quotes a Russian saying: 'If the ice is thin, one must walk fast.' He says we have lived too long in an era we no longer need. Progress can only be achieved when the era is finished."

"And you agree?"

"Yes and so do you!" Heat, now. Fire in her eyes. An English too perfect, learned in the cloister, from permitted classics of the past. "He says that he heard you criticise your own country in similar terms!"

"Does he have any small thoughts?" Barley asked. "I mean, does he like the movies? What car does he drive?"

She had turned away from him and he had the side view of her face cut against the empty sky. He took another nip of Scotch.

"You said he might be a physicist," he reminded her.

"He was trained as a physicist. I believe he has also qualified in aspects of engineering. In the field in which he works, I believe that the distinctions are not always closely observed."

"Where was he trained?"

"Already at school he was regarded as a prodigy. At fourteen he won a Mathematics Olympiad. His success was printed in the Leningrad newspapers. He went to the Litmo, afterwards to post-graduate studies at the University. He is extremely brilliant."

"When I was at school those were the people I hated," said Barley, but to his alarm she scowled.

"But you did not hate Goethe. You inspired him. He often quotes his friend Scott Blair. 'If there is to be hope, we must all betray our countries.' Did you really say this?"

"What's a Litmo?" said Barley.

"Litmo is the Leningrad Institute for Mechanical and Optical Science. From university he was sent to Novosibirsk to study at the scientific city of Akademgorodok. He made candidate of sciences, doctor of sciences. He made everything."

He wanted to press her about the everything, but he was scared of rushing her so he let her speak about herself instead. "So how did you get mixed up with him?"

"When I was a child."

"How old was the child?"

He felt her reticence collect again and then dissolve as if she had to remind herself she was in safe company—or in company so unsafe that to be further compromised made little difference.

"I was a great intellectual of sixteen," she said, with a grave smile.

"How old was the prodigy?"

"Thirty."

"What year are we talking about?"

"Nineteen sixty-eight. He was still an idealist for peace. He said they would never send in the tanks. 'The Czechs are our friends,' he said. 'They are like the Serbs and the Bulgarians. If it were Warsaw, perhaps they would send in the tanks. But against our Czechs, never, never.' "

She had turned her whole back to him. She was too many women at once. She had her back to him and was talking to the sky, yet she was drawing him into her life and appointing him her confidant.

It was August in Leningrad, she said, she was sixteen and studying French and German in her last year at school. She was a star pupil and a peace-dreamer and a revolutionary of the most romantic kind. She was on the brink of womanhood and thought herself mature. She was speaking of herself with irony. She had read Erich Fromm and Ortega y Gasset and Kafka and seen *Dr. Strangelove.* She regarded Sakharov as right in his thinking but wrong in his method. She was concerned about the Russian Jews but shared her father's view that they had brought their troubles on themselves. Her father was Professor of Humanities at the University, and her school was for sons and daughters of the Leningrad *nomenklatura.* It was August, 1968, but Katya and her friends were still able to live in political hope. Barley tried to remember whether he had ever lived in political hope and decided it was unlikely. She was talking as if nothing would ever stop her talking again. He wished he could hold her hand again as he had held it on the stairs. He wished he could hold any part of her but best of all her face, and kiss her instead of listening to her love story.

"We believed that East and West were drawing closer together," she said. "When the American students demonstrated against Vietnam, we were proud of them and regarded them as our comrades. When the students of Paris rioted, we wished we could be beside them at the barricades, wearing their nice French clothes."

She turned and smiled at him again over her shoulder. A horned moon had appeared above the stars at her left side and Barley had some vague literary memory that it boded bad luck. A flock of gulls had settled on a roof across the street. I'll never leave you, he thought.

"There was a man in our courtyard who had been absent for nine years," she was saying. "One morning he was back, pretending he had never been away. My father invited him to dinner and played him music all evening. I had never consciously met anyone who had been freshly persecuted so I naturally hoped that he would talk of the horrors of the camps. But all he wished to do was listen to Shostakovich. I did not understand in those days that some suffering cannot be described. From Czechoslovakia we heard of extraordinary reforms. We believed that these reforms would soon come to the Soviet Union and that we would have hard currency and be free to travel."

"Where was your mother?"

"Dead."

"How did she die?"

"Of tuberculosis. She was already ill when I was born. On the twentieth of August there was a closed showing of a Godard film at the Club of Scientists." Her voice had become strict against herself. "The invitations were for two persons. My father, after making enquiries about the moral content of the film, was reluctant to take me but I insisted. In the end he decided I should accompany him for the sake of my French studies. Do you know the Club of Scientists in Leningrad?"

"I can't say I do," he said, leaning back.

"Have you seen *À Bout de Souffle?*"

"I starred in it," he said, and she broke out laughing while he sipped his Scotch.

"Then you will remember that it is a very tense film. Yes?"

"Yes."

"It was the most powerful film I had ever seen. Everyone was greatly impressed by it, but for me it was a thunderbolt. The Club of Scientists is on the embankment of the river Neva. It is full of old glory, with marble staircases and very low sofas which are difficult to sit on in a tight skirt." She was sideways to him again, her head forward. "There is a beautiful winter-garden and a room like a mosque with heavy curtains and rich carpets. My father loved me very much but he was concerned for me and he was strict. When the film was over we moved to a dining room with wood panels. It was beautiful. We sat at long tables and that was where I met Yakov. My father introduced us. 'Here is a new genius from the world of physics,' he said. My father had the fault of sometimes being sarcastic with young men. Also Yakov was beautiful. I had heard something about him but nobody had told me how vulnerable he was, more like an artist than a scientist. I asked him what he was doing and he replied that he had returned to Leningrad to recover his innocence. I laughed and for a girl of sixteen produced an impressive response. I said I found it strange that a scientist of all people should be seeking innocence. He explained that in Akademgorodok he had shown too much brilliance in certain fields and had made himself too attractive to the military. It appears that in matters of physics the distinction between peaceful and military research is often very small. Now they were offering him everything—privileges, money to make his researches—but he was still refusing them because he wished to preserve his energies for peaceful means. This made them angry because they customarily recruit the cream of our scientists and do not expect refusal. So he had returned to his old university in order to recover his innocence. He proposed initially to study theoretical physics and was looking for influential people to support him, but they were reluctant because of his attitude. He had no permit to reside in Leningrad. He spoke very freely, as our scientists may. Also he was full of enthusiasm for the Gorodok. He spoke of the foreigners who in those days passed through, the brilliant young Americans from Stanford and MIT, also the English. He described the painters who were forbidden in Moscow but permitted to exhibit in the Gorodok. The seminars, the intensity of life, the free exchanges of ideas—and, as I was sure, of love. 'In what other country but Russia would Richter and Rostropovich come and play their music specially for the scientists, Okudzhava sing and Voznesensky read his poems! This is the world that we scientists must build for others!' He made jokes and I laughed like a mature woman. He was very witty in those days but also vulnerable, as he is today. There is a part of him that refuses to grow up. It is the artist in him, but it is the perfectionist also. Already in those days he was an outspoken critic of the incompetence of the authorities. He said there were so many eggs and sausages in the Gorodok supermarket that the shoppers poured out by bus from Novosibirsk and emptied the shelves by ten in the morning. Why could not the eggs make the journey instead of the people? This would be much better! Nobody collected the rubbish, he said, and the electricity kept cutting off. Sometimes the rubbish was knee-deep in the streets. And they call it a sci-

entific Paradise! I made another precocious comment.
'That's the trouble with Paradise,' I said. 'There is nobody
to collect the rubbish.' Everyone was very amused. I was a
success. He described the old guard trying to come to grips
with the ideas of the new men and going away shaking
their heads like peasants who have seen a tractor for the
first time. Never mind, he said. Progress will prevail. He
said that the armoured train of the Revolution which Stalin
had derailed was at last in motion again and the next stop
would be Mars. That was when my father interrupted with
one of his cynical opinions. He was finding Yakov too vocif-
erous. 'But, Yakov Yefremovich,' he said, 'was not Mars the
god of war?' Immediately Yakov became reflective. I had
not imagined a man could change so quickly, one minute
bold, the next so lonely and distressed. I blamed my father.
I was furious with him. Yakov tried to recover but my
father had thrown him into despair. Did Yakov talk to you
about his father?"

She was sitting across the valley from him, propped
against the opposing slope of the rooftiles, her long legs
stretched before her, her dress drawn tightly over her body.
The sky was darkening behind her, the moon and stars
were growing.

"He told me his father died of an overdose of intelligence," Barley replied.

"He took part in a camp uprising. He was in despair.
Yakov did not know of his father's death for many years.
One day an old man came to Yakov's house and said he had
shot Yakov's father. He had been a guard at the camp and
was ordered to take part in the execution of the rebels.
They were shot down in dozens by machine guns near the
Vorkuta railway terminal. The guard was weeping. Yakov
was only fourteen at the time but he gave the old man his
forgiveness and some vodka."

I can't do this, Barley thought. I'm not equal to these dimensions.

"What year was his father shot?" he asked. Be a hamster. It's about the only thing you're fit for.

"I think it was the spring of 1952. While Yakov remained silent, everybody at the table began to talk vehemently about Czechoslovakia," she continued in her perfect archaeological English. "Some said the ruling gang would send in the tanks. My father was sure of it. Some said they would be justified in doing so. My father said they would do it whether they were justified or not. The red Czars would do exactly as they pleased, he said, just as the white Czars had done. The system would win because the system always won and the system was our curse. This was my father's conviction as it later became Yakov's. But Yakov was at that time still determined to believe in the Revolution. He wished his own father's death to have been worthwhile. He listened intently to what my father had to say but then he became aggressive. 'They will never send in the tanks!' he said. 'The Revolution will survive!' He beat the table with his fist. You have seen his hands? Like a pianist's, so white and thin? He had been drinking. So had my father and my father also became angry. He wished to be left in peace with his pessimism. As a distinguished humanist, he did not like to be contradicted by a young scientist whom he regarded as an upstart. Perhaps also my father was jealous, because while they quarrelled, I fell completely in love with Yakov."

Barley took another sip of Scotch.

"You don't find that shocking?" she demanded indignantly as her smile leapt back to her face. "A girl of sixteen, for an experienced man of thirty?"

Barley wasn't feeling very quick-witted, but she seemed

to need his reassurance. "I'm speechless but on the whole I'd say they were both very lucky," he said.

"When the reception ended I asked my father for three roubles to go to the Café Sever to eat ice-cream with my companions. There were several daughters of academics at the reception, some were my school comrades. We made a group and I invited Yakov to join us. On the way I asked him where he lived and he told me: in the street of Professor Popov. He asked me, 'Who was Popov?' I laughed. Everyone knows who Popov is, I said. Popov was the great Russian inventor of radio who transmitted a signal even before Marconi, I told him. Yakov was not so sure. 'Perhaps Popov never existed,' he replied. 'Perhaps the Party invented him in order to satisfy our Russian obsession with being the first to invent everything.' From this I knew that he was still struggling with doubts about what they would do concerning Czechoslovakia."

Feeling anything but wise, Barley gave a wise nod.

"I asked him whether his apartment was a communal or a separate one. He said it was a room which he shared with an old acquaintance from the Litmo who was working in a special night laboratory, so they seldom met. I said, 'Then show me where you live. I wish to know that you are comfortable.' He was my first lover," she said simply. "He was extremely delicate, as I had expected him to be, but also passionate."

"Bravo," said Barley so softly that perhaps she didn't hear.

"I stayed with him three hours and took the last metro home. My father was waiting up for me and I talked to him like a stranger visiting his house. I did not sleep. Next day I heard the news in English on the BBC. The tanks had gone into Prague. My father, who had predicted this, was in despair. But I was not concerned for my father. Instead of going to school I went back to look for Yakov. His room-

mate told me I would find him at the Saigon, which was
the informal name of a cafeteria on the Nevsky Prospekt, a
place for poets and drug-pedlars and speculators, not professors' daughters. He was drinking coffee but he was
drunk. He had been drinking vodka since he heard the
news. 'Your father is right,' he said. 'The system will always
win. We talk freedom but we are oppressors.' Three
months later he had returned to Novosibirsk. He was bitter with himself but he still went. 'It is a choice between
dying of obscurity or dying of compromise,' he said. 'Since
that is a choice between death and death, we may as well
choose the more comfortable alternative.' "

"Where did that leave you?" Barley asked.

"I was ashamed of him. I told him that he was my ideal
and that he had disappointed me. I had been reading the
novels of Stendhal, so I addressed him like a great French
heroine. Nevertheless I believed that he had taken an
immoral decision. He had talked one thing and done the
opposite. In the Soviet Union, I told him, too many people
do this. I told him I would never speak to him again until
he had corrected his immoral choice. I reminded him of E.
M. Forster, whom we both admired. I told him that he
must connect. That his thoughts and actions must be one.
Naturally I soon relented and for a while we resumed our
relationship, but it was no longer romantic and when he
took up his new work we corresponded without warmth. I
was ashamed for him. Perhaps also for myself."

"And so you married Volodya," Barley said.

"That is correct."

"And you kept Yakov going on the side?" he suggested,
as if it were the most normal thing in the world.

She was blushing and scowling at once. "For a while, it
is true, Yakov and I maintained a clandestine relationship.
Not often, but sometimes. He said we were a novel that

had not been finished. Each of us was looking to the other to complete his destiny. He was correct, but I had not realised the strength of his influence over me or of mine over him. I thought that if we met more we might become free of each other. When I realised this was not the case I ceased to see him. I loved him but I refused to see him. Also I was pregnant from Volodya."

"When did you get together again?"

"After the last Moscow book fair. You were his catalyst. He had been on vacation and drinking very heavily. He had written many internal papers and registered many official complaints. None of them had made any impression on the system, though I think he had succeeded in annoying the authorities. Now you had spoken into his heart. You had put his thoughts into words at a crucial moment in his life, and you had related words to actions, which Yakov does not find easy. The next day, he telephoned me at my office, using a pretext. He had borrowed the apartment of a friend. My relationship with Volodya was by then disintegrating, although we were still living together because Volodya had to wait for an apartment. While we sat in the room of Yakov's friend, he spoke very much about you. You had made everything come clear for him. That was his phrase to me. 'The Englishman has given me the solution. From now on, there is only action, there is only sacrifice,' he said. 'Words are the curse of our Russian society. They are a substitute for deeds.' Yakov knew that I had contact with Western publishers, so he told me to look for your name among our lists of foreign visitors. He set to work at once to prepare a manuscript. I should give it to you. He was drinking a great deal. I was scared for him. 'How can you write if you are drunk?' He replied that he drank to survive."

Barley took another nip of whisky. "Did you tell Volodya about Yakov?"

"No."

"Did Volodya find out?"

"No."

"So who does know?"

It seemed she had been asking herself the same question, for she replied with great promptness.

"Yakov tells his friends nothing. This I know. If I am the one who borrows the apartment, I say only that it is for a private matter. In Russia we have secrecy and we have loneliness, but we have no word for privacy."

"What about your girlfriends? Not a hint to them?"

"We are not angels. If I ask them for certain favours, they make certain assumptions. Sometimes it is I who provide the favours. That is all."

"And nobody helped Yakov compile his manuscript?"

"No."

"None of his drinking friends?"

"No."

"How can you be certain?"

"Because I am certain that in his thoughts he is completely alone."

"Are you happy with him?"

"Please?"

"Do you like him—as well as love him? Does he make you laugh?"

"I believe that Yakov is a great and vulnerable man who cannot survive without me. To be a perfectionist is to be a child. It is also to be impractical. I believe that without me he would break."

"Do you think he's broken now?"

"Yakov would say, which one is sane? The one who plans the extermination of mankind, or the one who takes steps to prevent it?"

"How about the one who does both?"

She didn't reply. He was provoking her and she knew it. He was jealous, wanting to erode the edges of her faith.

"Is he married?" he asked.

An angry look swept across her face. "I do not believe he is married but it is not important."

"Has he got kids?"

"These are ridiculous questions."

"It's a pretty ridiculous situation."

"He says that human beings are the only creatures to make victims of their children. He is determined to provide no victims."

Except yours, Barley thought: but he managed not to say it.

"So, you followed his career with interest," he suggested roughly, returning to the question of Goethe's access.

"From a distance, and without detail."

"And all that time you didn't know what work he did? Is that what you're saying?"

"What I knew, I deduced only from our discussions of ethical problems. 'How much of mankind should we exterminate in order to preserve mankind? How can we talk of a struggle for peace when we plan only terrible wars? How can we speak of selective targets when we have not the accuracy to hit them?' When we discuss these matters, I am naturally aware of his involvement. When he tells me that the greatest danger to mankind is not the reality of Soviet power but the illusion of it, I do not question him. I encourage him. I urge him to be consistent and if necessary brave. But I do not question him."

"Rogov? He never mentioned a Rogov? Professor Arkady Rogov?"

"I told you. He does not discuss his colleagues."

"Who said Rogov was a colleague?"

"I assumed this from your questions," she retorted hotly and yet again he believed her.

"How do you communicate with him?" he asked, recovering his gentler tone.

"It is not important. When a certain friend of his receives a certain message, he informs Yakov and Yakov telephones me."

"Does the certain friend know who the certain message is from?"

"He has no reason. He knows it is a woman. That is all."

"Is Yakov afraid?"

"Since he talks so much about courage, I assume he is afraid. He quotes Nietzsche. 'The ultimate goodness is not to be afraid.' He quotes Pasternak. 'The root of beauty—' "

"Are you?" he interrupted.

She stared away from him. In the houses across the streets, home lights were appearing in the windows.

"I must think not of my children but of *all* children," she said, and he noticed two tears lying neglected on her cheeks. He took another pull of whisky and hummed a few bars of Basie. When he looked again, the tears had gone.

"He talks about the great lie," she said, as if she had just remembered.

"What great lie?"

"Everything is part of the same great lie, down to the smallest spare part of the least significant weapon. Even the results that are sent to Moscow are subject to the great lie."

"Results? What results? Results of what?"

"I don't know."

"Of testing?"

She seemed to have forgotten her denial. "I believe, of testing. I believe he is saying that the results of testing are deliberately distorted in order to satisfy the orders of the generals and the official production requirements of the bureaucrats. Perhaps it is he personally who distorts them. He is very complicated. Sometimes he talks about his many privileges of which he has become ashamed."

The shopping list, Walter had called it. With a deadened sense of duty, Barley crossed off the last items. "Has he mentioned particular projects?"

"No."

"Has he mentioned being involved in command systems? How the field commander is controlled?"

"No."

"Has he ever told you what steps are taken to prevent mistaken launches?"

"No."

"Has he ever suggested he might be engaged in data processing?"

She was tired. "No."

"Does he get promoted now and then? Medals? Big parties as he moves up the ladder?"

"He does not speak of promotion except that it is all corrupt. I told you already that maybe he has been too loud in his criticisms of the system. I do not know."

She had withdrawn from him. Her face was out of sight behind the curtain of her hair.

"You will do best to ask him all further questions for yourself," she said, in the tone of someone packing up to leave. "He wishes you to meet him in Leningrad on Friday. He is attending an important conference at one of the military scientific institutions."

First the sky swayed, then Barley became aware of the evening chill. It had closed over him like an icy cloud, though the sky was dark and clear and the new moon, when it finally kept still, shed a warming glow.

"He has proposed three places and three times," she continued in the same flat tone. "You will please keep each appointment until he is successful. He will keep one of them if he can. He sends you his greetings and his thanks. He loves you."

She dictated three addresses and watched him while he wrote them in his diary, using his apology for a code. Then she waited while he had a sneezing fit, watching him as he heaved and cursed his Maker.

They dined like exhausted lovers in a cellar with an old grey dog and a gypsy who sang blues to a guitar. Who owned the place, who allowed it to exist or why, were mysteries Barley had never troubled to solve. All he knew was that in some previous incarnation, at some forgotten book fair, he had arrived here drunk with a group of crazy Polish publishers and played "Bless This House" on someone's saxophone.

They talked stiffly, and as they talked the gap between them widened until it seemed to Barley to engulf the totality of his insignificance. He gazed at her and felt that he had nothing to offer her that she did not have tenfold. In the ordinary way, he would have made a passionate declaration of love to her. A lunge into absolutes would have been essential to his need to break the tension of a new relationship. But in Katya's presence he could find no absolutes to put opposite her own. He saw his life as a series of useless resurrections, one failure supplanted by another. He was appalled to think that he belonged to a society that existed only in materialism and gave so little thought to its great themes. But he could tell her none of this. To tell her anything was to assail the image that she had of him, and he had nothing to offer in its place.

They discussed books and he watched her slipping away from him. Her face became distracted, her voice prosaic. He went after her, he sang and danced, but she had gone. She was making the same flat statements he had been listening to all day long while he had been waiting to meet her. In a minute, he thought, I'll be telling her about Potomac Boston and explaining how the river and the city are not joined. And God help him, he was doing just that.

It was not till eleven o'clock, when the management put the lights out and he walked her down the lifeless street to the metro station, that it dawned on him against all sane reckoning that he might have made an impression upon her that in some modest way compared with the impression she had made on him. She had taken his arm. Her fingers lay along the inside of his forearm and she had fallen into a wide stride in order to keep pace with him. The white mouth of the elevator shafts stood open to receive her. The chandeliers twinkled above them like inverted Christmas trees as he took her in the formal Russian embrace: left cheek, right cheek, left cheek and goodnight.

"Mr. Blair, sir! Thought I spotted you! Quite a coincidence! Come aboard, we'll run you home!"

Barley climbed in and Wicklow with his acrobat's agility spirited himself into the back seat where he set to work to dislodge the recorder from the small of Barley's back.

They drove him to the Odessa and dropped him. They had work to do. The lobby was like an airport terminal in thick fog. In every sofa and armchair, unofficial guests who had paid the going rate slumbered in the gloom. Barley peered benignly round them, wrinkling his nose. Some wore jumpsuits. Others were more formally dressed.

"Snoot, anybody?" he called, quite loud. No response. "Anyone care for a glass of *whisky* at all?" he enquired, fishing his bottle, still two-thirds full, from the poacher's pocket of his raincoat. He gave himself a long pull by way of example, then passed the bottle along the line.

And that was how Wicklow found him two hours later—in the lobby, squatted companionably among a group of grateful night souls, enjoying a last one before turning in.

9

"Who on earth are Clive's new Americans?" I murmured to Ned as we assembled like early worshippers round Brock's tape recorder in the situation room.

The London clock said six. Victoria Street had not yet begun its morning growl. The squeaking of the spool sounded like a chorus of starlings as Brock wound the tape in place. It had arrived by courier half an hour ago, having travelled overland by bag to Helsinki, then by special plane to Northolt. If Ned had been willing to listen to the technological tempters, we could have avoided the whole costly process, for the Langley wizards were swearing by a new device that transmitted spoken word securely. But Ned was Ned and he preferred his own tried methods.

He sat at his desk and was putting his signature to a document which he was shielding with his hand. He folded the paper, put it in its envelope and sealed the flap before handing it to tall Emma, one of his assistants. By then I had given up expecting a reply, so that his vehemence startled me.

"They're bloody carpetbaggers," he snapped.

"From Langley?"

"God knows. Security."

"Whose?" I insisted.

He shook his head, too furious to answer. Was it the document he had just signed that was annoying him, or the presence of the American interlopers? There were two of them. Johnny from their London station was escorting them. They wore navy blazers and short hair, and they had a Mormon cleanliness that I found slightly revolting. Clive stood between them, but Bob had sat himself demonstratively at the far end of the room with Walter, who looked wretched—I supposed at first because of the hour. Even Johnny seemed discomfited by their presence, and so immediately was I. These dull, unfamiliar faces had no place at the heart of our operation, and at such a crucial moment. They were like a gathering of mourners in advance of an anticipated death. But whose? I looked again at Walter, and my anxieties were compounded.

I looked again at the new Americans, so slight, so trim, so characterless. Security, Ned had said. Yet why? And why *now?*

Why did they look at everyone except Walter? Why did Walter look at everyone except them? And why did Bob sit apart from them, and Johnny go on staring at his hands? I was grateful to have my thoughts interrupted. We heard the boom of footsteps on wood stairs. Brock had started the recorder. We heard clunks and Barley's oath as he barked his back on the window frame. Then the shuffling of feet again as they clambered on to the rooftop.

It's a séance, I thought as their first words reached us. Barley and Katya are addressing us from the great beyond. The immobile strangers with their executioners' faces were forgotten.

Ned was the only one of us with earphones. They made a difference, I later discovered when I tried them. You hear the Moscow doves shuffling on the gable and the rapid breathing inside Katya's voice. You hear the beating of your own joe's heart through the body mikes.

Brock played the whole rooftop scene before Ned ordered a break. Only our new Americans seemed unaffected. Their brown glances brushed each one of us but settled nowhere. Walter was blushing.

Brock played the dinner scene and still no one stirred: not a sigh or a creak or a handclap, not even when he stopped the spool and wound it back.

Ned pulled off his earphones.

"Yakov Yefremovich, last name unknown, physicist, aged thirty in 1968, ergo born 1938," he announced as he grabbed a pink trace request from the pile before him and scribbled on it. "Walter, offers?"

Walter had to gather himself. He seemed distraught, and his voice had none of its usual flightiness. "Yefrem, Soviet scientist, other names unknown, father of Yakov Yefremovich q.v., shot in Vorkuta after an uprising in the spring of '52," he declared without looking at his pad. "There can't be *that* many scientific Yefrems who were executed for an overdose of intelligence, even in dear Stalin's day," he added rather pathetically.

It was absurd, but I fancied I saw tears in his eyes. Perhaps someone really *has* died, I thought, glancing once more at our two Mormons.

"Johnny?" said Ned, writing.

"Ned, we think we'll take Boris, other names unknown, widower, Professor of Humanities, Leningrad University, late sixties, one daughter Yekaterina," said Johnny, still to his hands.

Ned seized another trace form, filled it in and tossed it into his out-tray like money he was pleased to throw away.

"Palfrey. Want to play?"

"Put me down for the Leningrad newspapers, will you

please, Ned?" I said as airily as I could, given that the
Mormons had turned their brown gaze full upon me. "I'd
like runners, starters and winners of the Mathematics
Olympiad of 1952," I said amid laughter. "And for safety's
sake perhaps you'd throw in '51 and '53 as well. And shall
we add his academic medals, please, somewhere along the
line? 'He made candidate of sciences, he made doctor of sciences. He made everything,' she said. Can we have that,
please? Thank you."

When all the bids were in, Ned glared around for Emma
to take the trace forms down to Registry. But that wasn't
good enough for Walter, who was suddenly determined to
be counted—for, leaping to his feet, he marched fussily to
Ned's desk, all five foot nothing of him, his little wrists flying out in front of him.

"I shall do *all* the ferreting myself," he announced in far
too grand a tone, as he grabbed the pink bundle to his
breast. "This war is *far* too important to be left to our blue-
rinse generals of Registry, irresistible though they may be."

And I remember noticing how our Mormons watched
him all the way to the door, then watched each other as we
listened to his merry little heels prinking down the corridor.
And I do not think I am speaking with hindsight when I
tell you that my blood ran chill for Walter, without my having the smallest idea why.

"A breath of country air," Ned told me on the internal
telephone an hour later when I was barely back at my
desk at Head Office. "Tell Clive I need you."

"Then you'd better go, hadn't you?" said Clive, still clos-
eted with his Mormons.

We had borrowed a fast Ford from the car pool. As Ned
drove, he brushed aside my few attempts at conversation
and handed me the file to read instead. We entered the

Berkshire countryside but he still didn't talk. And when Brock rang on the carphone to give him some elliptical confirmation he required, he merely grunted, "Then tell him," and returned to his brooding.

We were forty miles from London, on the foulest planet of man's discovery. We were in the slums of modern science, where the grass is always nicely cut. The ancient gateposts were mastered by eroded sandstone lions. A polite man in a brown sports jacket opened Ned's door. His colleague poked a detector underneath the chassis. Politely, they patted us both down.

"Taking the briefcase, are we, gentlemen?"

"Yes," said Ned.

"Care to open it, sir?"

"No."

"Dip it in the box, can we, gentlemen? We're not talking unexposed film, I presume, sir?"

"Please," I said. "Dip it in the box."

We watched while they lowered the briefcase into what looked like a green coal bin, and took it out again.

"Thank you," I said, taking it back.

"It's my pleasure, sir. Not at all, I'm sure."

The blue van said FOLLOW ME. An Alsatian dog frowned at us from its barred rear window. The gates opened electronically and beyond them lay mounds of clipped grass like mass graves grown over. Olive downs stretched towards the sunset. A mushroom-shaped cloud would have looked entirely natural. We entered parkland. A pair of buzzards wheeled in the cloudless sky. High wire fenced off the hay fields. Smokeless brick buildings nestled in artful hollows. A noticeboard urged protective clothing in Zones D to K. A skull and crossbones said "You Have Been Warned." The van ahead of us was moving at a funeral's pace. We lumbered round a

bend and saw empty tennis courts and aluminium towers. Lanes of coloured pipe jogged beside us, guiding us
to a cluster of green sheds. At their centre, on a hilltop,
stood the last vestige of the pre-nuclear age: a Berkshire
cottage of brick and flint with "Administrator" stencilled
on the gate. A burly man came tripping down the crazy-
paving path to greet us. He wore a blazer of British racing green and a tie with gold squash rackets on it, and a
handkerchief shoved into his cuff.

"You're from the Firm. Well done. I'm O'Mara. Which
of you is who? I've told him to kick his heels in the lab till
we whistle for him."

"Good," said Ned.

O'Mara had grey-blond hair and an offhand regimental
voice cracked by alcohol. His neck was puffy and his athlete's fingers were stained mahogany with nicotine.
"O'Mara keeps the long-haired scientists in line," Ned had
told me in one of our rare exchanges during the drive. "He's
half personnel, half security, all shit."

The drawing-room had the air of being tended by
Napoleonic prisoners of war. Even the bricks of the fireplace had been polished and the plaster lines between them
picked out in loving white. We sat in rose-patterned armchairs drinking gin and tonic, lots of ice. Horse-brasses
twinkled from the glistening black beams.

"Just come back from the States," O'Mara recalled, as if
accounting for our recent separation. He raised his glass
and ducked his mouth to it, meeting it halfway. "You fellows go there a lot?"

"Occasionally," said Ned.

"Now and then," I said. "When duty calls."

"We send quite a few of our chaps out there on loan,
actually. Oklahoma. Nevada. Utah. Most of them like it
pretty well. A few get the heebie-jeebies, run for home."

He drank and took a moment to swallow. "Visited their weapons laboratory at Livermore, out in California. Nice enough place. Decent guest house. Money galore. Asked us to attend a seminar on death. Bloody macabre if you think about it, but the shrinks seemed to believe it would do everybody good and the wines were extraordinary. I suppose if you're planning to consign large chunks of humanity to the flames you might as well know how it works." He drank again, all the time in the world. The hilltop at that hour was a very quiet place. "Surprising how many people hadn't given the subject much thought. Specially the young. The older ones were a bit more squeamish. They could remember the age of innocence, if it ever existed. You're a prompt fatality if you die straight off, and a soft one if you do it the slow way. I never realised. Gives a new meaning to the value of being at the centre of things, I suppose. Still, we're into the fourth generation now. Dulls the pangs. You chaps golfers?"

"No," said Ned.

"I'm afraid not," I said. "I used to take lessons but they somehow never made much difference."

"Marvellous courses but they made us hire bloody Noddy carts. Wouldn't be seen dead in the things over here." He drank again, the same slow ritual. "Wintle's an oddball," he explained when he had swallowed. "They're all oddballs but Wintle's got odder balls than most. He's done Socialism, he's done Jesus. Now he's into contemplation and Tai Chi. Married, thank God. Grammar school but talks proper. Three years to go."

"How much have you told him?" Ned asked.

"They always think they're under suspicion. I've told him he isn't, and I've told him to keep his stupid mouth shut when it's over."

"And do you think he will?" I asked.

O'Mara shook his head. "Don't know how to, most of 'em, however hard we boot 'em."

There was a knock at the door and Wintle came in, an eternal student of fifty-seven. He was tall but crooked, with a curly grey head that shot off at an angle, and an air of brilliance almost extinguished. He wore a sleeveless Fair Isle pullover, Oxford bags and moccasins. He sat with his knees together and held his sherry glass away from him like a chemical retort he wasn't sure of.

Ned turned professional. His tantrums were set aside. "We're in the business of tracking Soviet scientists," he said, managing to make himself sound dull. "Watching the snakes and ladders of their defence establishment. Nothing very sexy, I'm afraid."

"So you're Intelligence," said Wintle. "I thought as much, though I didn't say anything."

It occurred to me that he was a very lonely man.

"Mind your own fucking business what they are," O'Mara advised him perfectly pleasantly. "They're English and they've got a job to do, same as you."

Ned fished a couple of typed sheets from a folder and handed them to Wintle, who put down his glass to take them. His hands had a way of finishing knuckles down and fingers curled, like a man begging to be freed.

"We're trying to maximalise some of our neglected old material," Ned said, falling into a jargon he would otherwise have eschewed. "This is an account of your debriefing when you returned from a visit to Akademgorodok in August, 1963. Do you remember a Major Vauxhall? It's not exactly a literary masterpiece but you mention the names of two or three Soviet scientists we'd be grateful to catch up with, if they're still around and you remember them."

As if to protect himself from a gas attack, Wintle pulled on a pair of extraordinarily ugly steel-framed spectacles.

"As *I* recall that debriefing, *Major* Vauxhall gave me his *word* of honour that everything I said was *entirely* voluntary and confidential," he declared with a didactic jerkiness. "I am therefore *very* surprised to see my name *and* my words lying about in open Ministerial archives a full twenty-five *years* after the event."

"Well it's the nearest you'll ever get to immortality, sport, so I should shut up and enjoy it," O'Mara advised.

I interposed myself like somebody separating belligerents in a family row. If Wintle could just expand a little on the interviewer's rather bald account, I suggested. Maybe flesh out one or two of the Soviet scientists whose names are listed on the final page, and perhaps throw in some account of the Cambridge team while he was about it? If he wouldn't mind answering just one or two questions which might tilt the scales?

" 'Team' is *not* a word I would use in this context, thank you," Wintle retorted, pouncing on the word like some bony predator. "Not on the British side anyway. *Team* suggests common purpose. We were a Cambridge *group,* yes. A *team,* no. Some went for the ride, some went for the self-aggrandisement. I refer particularly to Professor Callow, who had a *highly* exaggerated opinion of his work on accelerators, since refuted." His Birmingham accent had escaped from its confinement. "A very small minority *indeed* had ideological motives. They happened to believe in science without borders. A free exchange of knowledge for the common benefit of mankind."

"Wankers," O'Mara explained to us helpfully.

"We'd the French there, Americans galore, the Swedes, Dutch, even one or two Germans," Wintle continued, oblivious to O'Mara's gibe. "All of them had hope, in my opinion, and the Russians had it in bucketfuls. It was us British who were dragging our feet. We still are."

O'Mara groaned and took a restorative pull of gin. But Ned's good smile, even if a little battered, encouraged Wintle to run on.

"It was the height of the Khrushchev era, as you will doubtless recall. Kennedy this side, Khrushchev that side. A golden age was beckoning, said some. People in those days talked about Khrushchev very much as they talk of Gorbachev now, I'm sure. Though I do have to say that, in my opinion, our enthusiasm *then* was more genuine and spontaneous than the so-called enthusiasm *now*."

O'Mara yawned and fixed his pouchy gaze disconcertingly upon myself.

"*We* told them whatever *we* knew. *They* did the same," Wintle was saying as his voice gathered assurance. "*We* read *our* papers. *They* read *theirs*. Callow didn't cut any ice, I'm bound to say. They rumbled *him* in no time. But we'd Panson on cybernetics and *he* flew the flag all right, and we had me. *My* modest lecture was quite a success, though I do say it myself. I haven't heard applause like it since, to be frank. I wouldn't be surprised if they still talk about it over there. The barricades came down so fast you could *literally* hear them crashing in the lecture hall. 'Flow, not demarcation.' That was our slogan. 'Flow' wasn't the word for it either, not if you saw the vodka that was drunk at the late-night parties. *Or* the girls there. *Or* heard the chat. The KGB was listening, of course. We knew *all* about that. We'd had the pep talk before we left, though several objected to it. Not me, I'm a patriot. But there wasn't a blind thing that any of them could do, not *their* KGB and not *ours*." He had evidently hit a favourite theme for he straightened himself to deliver a prepared speech. "I'd like to add here that *their* KGB is greatly misjudged, in my opinion. I have it on *good* authority that the Soviet KGB has very *frequently* sheltered some of the most tolerant elements of the Soviet intelligentsia."

"Jesus—well don't tell me ours hasn't," O'Mara said.

"Furthermore I've no doubt whatever that the Soviet authorities very *rightly* argued that in any trade-off of scientific knowledge with the West, the Soviet Union had more to *gain* than *lose*." Wintle's slanted head was switching from one to another of us like a railway signal, and his upturned hand was resting on his thigh in anguish. "They had the culture too. None of your arts-sciences divide for *them,* thank you. They had the Renaissance dream of rounded man, still do have. I'm not much of a one for culture myself. I don't have the time. But it was all there for those who had the *interest.* And reasonably charged too, I understand. Some of the events were complimentary."

Wintle needed to blow his nose. And to blow his nose Wintle needed first to spread his handkerchief on his knee, then poke it into operational mode with his febrile fingertips. Ned seized upon the natural break.

"Well now, I wonder whether we could take a look at one or two of those Soviet scientists whose names you kindly gave to Major Vauxhall," he suggested, taking the sheaf of papers I was holding out to him.

We had arrived at the moment we had come for. Of the four of us in the room, I suspected, only Wintle was unaware of this, for O'Mara's yellowed eyes had lifted to Ned's face and he was studying him with a dyspeptic shrewdness.

Ned led with his discards, as I would have done. He had marked them for himself in green. Two were known to be dead, a third was in disgrace. He was testing Wintle's memory, rehearsing him for the real thing when it came. Sergey? said Wintle. My goodness yes, Sergey! But what was his other name then? Popov? Popovich? That's right,

Protopopov! Sergey Protopopov, engineer specialising in fuels!

Ned coaxed him patiently along, three names, a fourth, guiding his memory, exercising it: "Well now, just think about him a second before you say no again. Really no? Okay. Let's try Savelyev."

"Come again?"

Wintle's memory, I noticed, had the Englishman's embarrassment with Russian surnames. It preferred first names that it could anglicise.

"Savelyev," Ned repeated. Again I caught O'Mara's eye upon him. Ned peered at the report in his hand, perhaps a mite too carelessly. "That's it. Savelyev." He spelt it. " 'Young, idealistic, talkative, called himself a humanitarian. Working on particles, brought up in Leningrad.' Those were your words, according to Major Vauxhall all those lifetimes ago. Anything more I might add? You didn't keep up with him, for instance? Savelyev?"

Wintle was smiling in marvel. "Was that his name, then? Savelyev? Well I'm blowed. There you are. I'd forgotten. To me he's still Yakov, you see."

"Fine. Yakov Savelyev. Remember his patronymic?"

Wintle shook his head, still smiling.

"Anything to add to your original description?"

We had to wait. Wintle had a different sense of time from ours. And to judge by his smirk, a different sense of humour.

"Very sensitive fellow, Yakov was. Wouldn't dare ask his questions in the plenum. Had to hang back and pluck your sleeve when it was over. 'Excuse me, sir, but what do you think of so-and-so?' Good questions, mind. A very cultural man too, they say, in his way. I'm told he cut quite a dash at some of the poetry readings. And the art shows."

Wintle's voice trailed off and I feared he was about to

fabricate, which is a thing people do often when they have run out of information but want to keep their ascendancy. But to my relief he was merely retrieving memories from his store—or rather milking them out of the ether with his upright fingers.

"Always going from one group to another, Yakov was," he said, with the same irritating smile of superiority. "Standing himself at the edge of a discussion, very earnest. Perching on the edge of a chair. There was some mystery about his father, I never knew what. They say he was a scientist too, but executed. Well a lot were, weren't they, scientists. They killed them off like fruit flies, I've read about it. If they didn't kill them, they kept them in prison. Tupolev, Petliakov, Korolev—some of their greatest stars of aircraft technology designed their best stuff in prison. Ramzin invented a new boiler for heat engines in prison. Their first rocketry research unit was set up in prison. Korolev ran it."

"Bloody well done, old boy," said O'Mara, bored again.

"Gave me this piece of rock," Wintle continued.

And I saw his hand, upward on his knee again, opening and closing round the imaginary gift.

"*Rock?*" said Ned. "Yakov gave it to you? Do you mean music? No, you mean a geological sample of some kind."

"When we Westerners left Akadem," Wintle resumed, as if launching himself and us upon an entirely new story, "we *stripped* ourselves of our possessions. *Literally.* If you'd seen our group on that last day, you would *not* have believed it. We'd our Russian hosts crying *their eyes* out, hugging and embracing, flowers on the buses, even Callow was having a weep if you can believe it. And us Westerners unloading everything we had: books, papers, pens, watches, razors, toothpaste, even our *toothbrushes.* Gramophone records if we'd brought them. Spare underclothes, ties, shoes, shirts, socks, everything except the minimum we needed for our decency to fly home in. We didn't *agree* to do it. We hadn't even *discussed* it. It happened *spontaneously.* There was some did more, of course. Particularly the Americans, being impulsive. I heard of one fellow offering a marriage of convenience to a girl who was desperate to get out. I didn't do that. I wouldn't. I'm a patriot."

"But you gave some of your goodies to Yakov," Ned suggested, while he affected to write painstakingly in a diary.

"I started to, yes. It's a bit like feeding birds in the park, handing out your treasures is. You pick the one who's not getting his share and you try to fatten him up. Besides, I'd taken to young Yakov, you couldn't help it, him being so soulful."

The hand had frozen round the empty shape, the fingertips striving to unite. The other hand had risen to his brow and taken hold of a sizable pinch of flesh.

" 'Here you are, Yakov,' I said. 'Don't be slow in coming forward. You're too shy for your own health, you are.' I'd an electric shaver in those days. Plus batteries, transformer, all in a nice carrying case. But he didn't seem to be that comfortable with them. He put them aside sort of thing, and kept shuffling about. Then I realised he was trying to give something to *me*. It was this rock, wrapped in newspaper. They'd no fancy wrapping, naturally. 'It's a piece of my country,' he says. 'To thank you for your lecture,' he says. He wanted me to love the good in it always, however bad it might sometimes seem from outside. Spoke a beautiful English, mind, better than half of *us*. I was a bit embarrassed, frankly, if you want to know. I kept that piece of old rock for very many years. Then my wife threw it out during one of her spring-cleans. I thought of writing to him sometimes, I never did. He was arrogant, mind, in his way. Well a lot of them were. I dare say *we* were in *our* way, too. We all thought science could rule the world. Well I suppose it does now, though not in the way it was meant to, I'm sure."

"Did he write to you?" said Ned.

Wintle wondered about this for a long time. "You can never tell, can you? You never know what's been stopped in the post. Or who by."

From the briefcase I passed Ned the bunch of photographs. Ned passed them to Wintle while O'Mara watched. Wintle leafed through them and suddenly let out a cry.

"That's him! Yakov! The man who gave me the rock." He thrust the pictures back at Ned. "Look for yourself! Look at those eyes! *Then* tell me he's not a dreamer!"

Extracted from the Leningrad evening paper dated 5th January 1954 and reconstituted by Photographic Section, Yakov Yefremovich Savelyev as a teenaged genius.

There were other names, and Ned took Wintle laboriously through each one of them, laying false trails, brushing over his tracks until he was satisfied that in Wintle's mind at least Savelyev meant no more than the rest.

"Clever of you to hide your trump in the middle of your hand," O'Mara remarked as, glass in hand, he walked us down the drive to the car. "Last time I heard of Savelyev he was running their testing range in darkest Kazakhstan, dreaming up ways to read their own telemetry without everyone reading it over their shoulder. What's he up to now? Selling the shop?"

It is not often I take pleasure in my work but our meeting and the place had sickened me, and O'Mara had sickened me more than both. It is not often that I seize someone by the arm either, and have to recoil, and loosen my grip.

"I take it you have signed the Official Secrets Act?" I asked him quietly enough.

"Practically wrote the bloody thing," O'Mara retorted, very surprised.

"Then you will know that all knowledge that comes to you officially and all speculation based upon that knowledge are the perpetual property of the Crown." Another legal distortion, but never mind. I released him. "So if you like your job here, and you are hoping for promotion, and if you are looking forward to your pension, I suggest you never think of this meeting again or of any name associated with it. Thank you so much for the gin. Goodbye."

On the journey back, with the identification of Bluebird confirmed and phoned ahead of us in word code to the Russia House, Ned remained withdrawn. Yet when we reached Victoria Street he was suddenly determined not to let me go. "You stick around," he ordered me, and guided me ahead of him down the basement steps.

At first glance the scene in the situation room was one of purest joy. The centerpiece was Walter, poised like an artist before a whiteboard as big as he was, drawing up the details of Savelyev's life in coloured crayons. If he had been wearing a broad-brimmed hat and smock, he could not have looked more rakish. Only at second glance did I recall my eerie apprehensions of that morning.

Around him—which meant behind him, for the whiteboard was propped against the wall beneath the clocks—stood Brock and Bob, and Jack our cypher clerk, and Ned's girl Emma, and a senior girl called Pat who was one of the mainstays of Soviet Registry. They held glasses of champagne and each of them in his different way was smiling, though Bob's smile was more like a grimace of pain suppressed.

"A lonely decider," Walter declaimed rhapsodically. He

froze a moment as he heard us, but did not turn his head. "A fifty-year-old achiever shaking his mid-life bars, looking at mortality and a wasted life. Well, aren't we all?"

He stood back. Then skipped forward again and chalked in a date. Then took a swig of champagne. And I sensed something ghoulish and scaring about him, like make-up on the dying.

"Living at their secret centre all his adult life," he continued gaily. "But keeping his mouth shut. Taking his own decisions, all by himself in the dark, bless him. Getting his own back on history if it kills him, which it probably will." Another date, and the word OLYMPIAD. "He's the vintage year. Any younger, he'd be brainwashed. Any older, he'd be looking for an old fart's sinecure."

He drank, his back still turned to us. I glanced at Bob for enlightenment but he was looking studiously at the floor. I glanced at Ned. His eyes were on Walter but his face was expressionless. I glanced at Walter again and saw that his breath was coming to him in defiant gasps.

"I invented him, I'm sure I did," Walter puffed, seemingly oblivious to the dismay around him. "I've been predicting him for years." He wrote the words FATHER EXECUTED. "Even after they'd drafted him, the poor lamb tried so *hard* to be good. He wasn't sneaky. He wasn't resentful. He had his doubts but, as scientists go, he was a good soldier. Until one day—*bingo!* He wakes up and discovers it's all a load of junk and he's wasted his genius on a bunch of incompetent gangsters and brought the world to the edge of ruin into the bargain." He was writing in fierce strokes while the sweat ran over his temples: WORKING UNDER ROGOV AT 109 TESTING SITE KAZAKHSTAN. "He doesn't know it but he's joined the great Russian male menopausal revolution of the eighties. He's had all the lies, he's had Stalin, the Khrushchev chink of light and the long dark of

Brezhnev. But he's still got one last shot in him, one last menopausal chance to print himself on the world. And the new buzz-words are ringing in his ears: revolution from above, openness, peace, change, courage, reconstruction. He's even being *encouraged* to revolt."

He was writing faster than ever, shortwinded or not: TELEMETRY, ACCURACY. "Where will they land?" he was asking rhetorically between gasps. "How close will how many get to how many targets when? What's the expansion and temperature of the skin? What's gravity up to? Crucial questions and the Bluebird knows the answers. He knows because he's in charge of making the missiles talk while they go along—without the Americans hearing, which is his skill. Because he's contrived the encryption systems that dodge the American super-listeners in Turkey and mainland China. He sees all the answers in clear, before Brother Rogov fudges them for his lords and masters in Moscow. Which, according to the Bluebird, is Rogov's specialty. 'Professor Arkady Rogov is an arse-licking toady,' he tells us in notebook two. A fair judgment. That's what Arkady Rogov is. A verifiable, fully paid-up, spineless, arse-licking toady, meeting his norms and earning his medals and his privileges. Who does that remind us of? No one. Certainly not our own dear Clive. So Bluebird blows his lid. He confesses his agony to Katya and Katya says, 'Don't just whimper, do something.' And by golly, he does it. He gives us every bloody thing he can lay his hands on. The Crown Jewels doubled and re-doubled. Encryptions decrypted. Telemetry *en clair*. Retrospective code-breaks to help us check it out. The unbuggered, head-on truth, before it gets repainted for Moscow consumption. All right, he's potty. Who isn't, who's any good?" He took a last swig from his glass, and I saw that the centre of his face was a crimson mass of pain and embarrassment and indignation. "Life's a botch," he explained as he shoved the glass into my hand.

The next I knew, he had slipped past us up the stairs and we heard the steel doors successively opening and slamming shut, one after another, till he had reached the street.

"Walter was a liability," Clive explained to me tersely next morning when I bearded him. "To us, he was merely eccentric, perhaps. But to others——" It was the nearest I had ever known him come to acknowledging the existence of sex. He quickly censored himself. "I've given Walter to Training Section," he continued, with a return to his most frigid manner. "He raised too many eyebrows on the other side."

He meant on the other side of the Atlantic.

So Walter, wonderful Walter, disappeared and I was right——we never saw the Mormons again and Clive never once referred to them. Were they mere messengers from Langley, or had they formed their verdict and exacted their punishment? Were they from Langley at all, or from one of the mushrooming groups of initials that Ned had so objected to when he complained to Clive about the Bluebird distribution list? Or were they Ned's greatest of all pet hates——tame psychiatrists?

Whatever they were, the effect of them was felt all through the Russia House, and Walter's absence yawned at us like a shell-hole made by our best ally's guns. Bob felt it and was ashamed. Even hard-faced Johnny remained ill at ease.

"I'll want you nearer to the operation," Ned told me.

It seemed a wretched consolation for Walter's disappearance.

"You're on edge again," said Hannah as we walked.

It was lunchtime. Her office was close to Regent's Park. Sometimes on warm days we would share a sandwich together. Sometimes we even did a bit of zoo. Sometimes she gave the Cancer Institute a rest and we ended up in bed.

I asked after her husband, Derek. He was one of the few subjects we had in common. Had Derek lost his temper again? Had he beaten her up? Sometimes, in the days when we had been full-time lovers, I used to think it was Derek who held us together. But today she didn't want to talk about Derek. She wanted to know why I was on edge.

"They sacked a man I rather liked," I said. "Well, not sacked, but threw him on the rubbish heap."

"What did he do wrong?"

"Nothing at all. They just decided to see him in a different light."

"Why?"

"Because it suited them. They withdrew their tolerance of him in order to satisfy certain requirements."

She thought about this. "You mean that convention got the better of them," she suggested. Like you, she was saying. Like us.

Why do I keep coming back to her, I wondered. To visit the scene of the crime? To seek, for the thousandth time, her absolution? Or do I visit her as we visit our old schools, trying to understand what happened to our youth?

Hannah is still a beautiful woman, which is a consolation. The greying and the broadening have yet to come. When I catch her face backlit, and glimpse her valiant, vulnerable smile, I see her as I saw her twenty years ago, and tell myself I have not ruined her after all. "She's all right. Look at her. She's smiling and undamaged. It's Derek, not you, who kicks her around."

But I am never sure. Never sure at all.

The Union Jack that had so enraged the dictator Stalin when he observed it from the battlements of the

Kremlin dangled dispiritedly from its mast in the British Embassy forecourt. The cream-coloured palace behind it resembled an old wedding cake waiting to be cut, the river lay docile as the morning downpour flailed its oily back. At the iron gates two Russian policemen studied Barley's passport while the rain smeared the ink. The younger copied out his name. The elder dubiously compared his harrowed features with his photograph. Barley was wearing a drenched brown mackintosh. His hair was plastered to his scalp. He looked a little shorter than his usual height.

"Well, *honestly* what a day!" cried the well-bred girl in a pleated tartan skirt, waiting in the lobby. "Hullo, I'm Felicity. You *are* who I think you are, aren't you? A jolly wet Scott Blair? The Economic Counsellor *is* expecting you."

"I thought the Economic people were in the other building."

"Oh, that's Commercial. They're *quite* different."

Barley followed her swinging tail up the ancestral staircase. As always when he entered a British mission, a sense of dislocation overtook him, but this morning it was absolute. The tuneless whistling came from his local paper boy in Hampstead. The huffing and bumping of the floor polisher was the Co-op milk van. It was eight in the morning, and official Britain was not yet officially awake. The Economic Counsellor was a stubby Scotsman with silver hair. His name was Craig.

"Mr. Blair, sir! How do you do? Sit you down! Do you take the tea or the coffee? They both taste the same, I'm afraid, but we're working on it. Gradually, but we'll get there."

Seizing Barley's mackintosh, he impaled it on a Ministry of Works coat-tree. Above the desk a framed photograph showed the Queen in riding habit. A notice beside her warned that speech in this room was not secure. Felicity brought tea and Garibaldi biscuits. Craig talked vigorously, as if he couldn't wait to get rid of his news. His red face was shiny from shaving.

"Oh and I hear you've been having the most *fantastic* runaround from those brigands in VAAP! Have they been making any sense at all? Are you getting anywhere, or are they just giving you the usual Moscow flannel? It's all *makework* here, you see. Seldom but seldom is anything actually transacted. The profit motive, somewhat like diligence, is unknown to them. It's all Brownie points and scratching one another's you-know-whats. The impossible combination, I always say, of incurable idleness harnessed to unattainable visions. The Ambassador used my very phrase in a despatch recently. No credit given, none asked. How do they ever come to grips, I ask you, with an economy built upon sloth, tribalism and hidden unemployment? Answer, they don't! When will they ever break free? What will happen if they do? Answer, God alone knows. I'm seeing the bookworld here as a microcosm for their entire dilemma, follow me?"

He roared on until he seemed to decide that Barley and the microphones had had their fill. "Well, I've surely relished our little conversation here this morning. You've given me much food for thought, I don't mind telling you. There's a great danger in our business of getting cut off from the source here. Will you allow me to pass you around a little now? Our Chancery people will never forgive me if I don't."

With a nod of command, he led the way along a passage to a metal door with an evil eyehole in it. The door opened as they reached it and closed as Barley stepped inside.

Craig is your link, Ned had said. He's hell on earth but he'll take you to your leader.

* * *

Barley's first impression was that he was in a darkened ward, his next that the ward was a sauna, for the only light came from a corner of the floor and there was a smell of resin. Then he decided that the sauna was suspended, for he detected a rocking underfoot.

Seating himself gingerly on a bridge chair, he discerned two figures behind a table. Above the first hung a curling poster of a Beefeater defending London Bridge. Above the second, Lake Windermere languished under a British Rail sunset.

"Bravo, Barley," exclaimed a sturdy English voice, not unlike Ned's, from below the Beefeater. "My name's Paddy, short for Patrick, and this gent is Cy. He's American."

"Hi, Barley," said Cy.

"We're just the local messenger boys here," Paddy explained. "We're rather limited in what we can do, naturally. Our main job is to supply the camels and hot meals. Ned sends his very special greetings. So does Clive. If they weren't so sullied they'd have come over and done their nail-biting with us. Hazard of the profession. Comes to us all, I'm afraid."

As he spoke, the poor light released him. He was shaggy but lithe, with the craggy brows and faraway eyes of an explorer. Cy was sleek and urban and younger by a dozen years. Their four hands lay on a street map of Leningrad. Paddy's shirtcuffs were frayed. Cy's were drip dry.

"I'm to ask you whether you want to go on, by the by," Paddy said, as if that were a rather good joke. "If you want to bail out that's your good right and no hard feelings. Want to bail out? What do you say?"

"Zapadny will kill me," Barley muttered.

"Why's that?"

"I'm his guest. He's footing my bill, fixing my program." Lifting his hand to his forehead, he scrubbed at it as a way of reviving communication with his brain. "What do I tell him? I can't just up-sticks, bye-bye, I'm off to Leningrad. He'd think I was loony."

"But you *are* saying Leningrad, not London?" Paddy persisted kindly enough.

"I haven't got a visa. I've got Moscow. I haven't got Leningrad."

"But assuming."

Another lengthy delay.

"I need to talk to him," Barley said, as if that were an explanation.

"To Zapadny?"

"Goethe. Got to talk to him."

Dragging the back of his right wrist across his mouth in one of his habitual gestures, Barley looked at it as if expecting blood. "I won't lie to him," he muttered.

"There's no question of your lying to him. Ned wants a partnership, not a deception."

"That goes for us too," said Cy.

"I won't be sly with him. I'll talk to him straight or not at all."

"Ned wouldn't wish it any other way," said Paddy. "We want to give him everything he needs."

"Us too," said Cy.

"Potomac Boston, Incorporated, Barley, your new American trading partner," Paddy proposed in a fresh voice, glancing at a paper before him. "The head of their publishing operation is a Mr. Henziger, is that right?"

"J.P.," Barley said.

"Ever met him?"

Barley shook his head and winced. "Name on the contract," he said.

"That the nearest you've got to him?"

"We've spoken on the phone a couple of times. Ned

thought we ought to be heard on the transatlantic line. Cover."

"But you've no mental portrait of him otherwise?" Paddy persisted, in the way he had of forcing clear replies even if it made a pedant of him. "He's not a drawn character for you in some way?"

"He's a name with money and offices in Boston and he's a voice on the phone. That's all he's ever been."

"And in your conversations with local third parties— with Zapadny, say—J. P. Henziger has not featured as some kind of horror figure? You haven't given him a false beard or a wooden leg or a lurid sexlife? Nothing one might have to take into account if one were making him flesh, as it were?"

Barley considered the question but seemed to lose hold of it.

"No?" asked Paddy.

"No," Barley said, and again unwisely shook his head.

"So a situation that might have arisen is this," said Paddy. "Mr. J. P. Henziger of Potomac Boston, young, dynamic, pushy, is presently to be found on holiday in Europe with his wife. It's the season. They are at this moment, let us say, at the Marski Hotel in Helsinki. Know the Marski?"

"I've had a drink there," Barley said, as if he were ashamed of it.

"And in this impulsive American way they have, the Henzigers have taken it into their heads to make a lightning trip to Leningrad. Over to you, I think, Cy."

Cy unlocked his smile and obliged. He had a sharp face when it came alive and an intelligent, if snappish, way of talking.

"The Henzigers take a three-day guided tour, Barley. Visas at the Finnish border, the guide, the bus, the whole nine yards. They're straightforward people, decent. This is Russia and it's their first time. *Glasnost* is news back home in Boston. He has money invested in you. Knowing you are in Moscow spending it, he requires you to drop everything, hurry to Leningrad, carry his bags for him and report progress. That's normal practice, typical of a young tycoon. You see a problem? Some way it doesn't play for you?"

Barley's head was clearing and his vision with it.

"No. It plays. I can make it work if you can."

"First thing this morning UK time, J.P. calls your London office from the Marski, gets your machine," Cy continued. "J.P. does not talk to machines. An hour from now he telexes you care of Zapadny at VAAP, copy to Craig here at the British Embassy, Moscow, requesting you to meet with him this Friday at the Hotel Evropeiskaya, alias the Europe, Leningrad, which is where his tour-group is staying. Zapadny will wriggle, maybe raise a cry of pain. But since you are spending J.P.'s cash it's our prediction Zapadny will have no choice but to bow to market forces. Figure?"

"Yes," said Barley.

Paddy took back the story. "If he's got any sense he'll help you get your visas changed. If he sulks, Wicklow can whisk them across to OVIR and they'll change them while he waits. You wouldn't make too much of it to Zapadny, in our view. You wouldn't grovel or apologise, not to Zapadny. You'd make a virtue of it. Tell him that's how life is lived these days in the fast lane."

"J. P. Henziger is family," Cy said. "He's a fine officer. So's his wife."

He stopped abruptly.

Like an umpire who has spotted a foul, Barley had flung out an arm and was pointing it at Paddy's chest.

"Hang on, you two! Hold your water. Half a mo! What use will *either* of them be, however *fine* they are, if they're riding round Leningrad locked in a bloody tour-bus all day?"

Paddy took only a moment to recover from this unexpected onslaught. "You tell him, Cy," he said.

"Barley, on their arrival at the Hotel Europe Thursday evening Mrs. Henziger will contract a severe dose of Leningrad tummy. J.P. will have no taste for sightseeing while his lovely lady is laid low with the runs. He'll dig in with her at the hotel. No problem."

Paddy set the lamp and power-pack next to the map of Leningrad. Katya's three addresses were ringed in red.

It was late afternoon before Barley telephoned her, about the time when he reckoned she would be locking away her paperclips. He had taken a nap and followed it with a couple of Scotches to bring himself up to par. But when he started talking he discovered that his voice was too high, and he had to bring it down.

"Ah. Hullo! You got home all right," he said, sounding like someone he'd never met. "Train didn't turn into a pumpkin or anything?"

"Thank you, it was not a problem."

"Great. Well, I just rang to find out, really. Yes. Say thank you for a marvellous evening. Mmhmh. And goodbye for the time being."

"Thank you also. It was productive."

"Hoped we might have had another chance to meet, you see. Trouble is, I've got to go to Leningrad. Some stupid bit of business has cropped up and made me change my plans."

A prolonged silence. "Then you must sit down," she said.

Barley wondered which of them had gone mad. "Why?"

"It is our custom, when we are preparing for a long journey, first to sit down. You are sitting now?"

He could hear the happiness in her voice and it made him happy too.

"I'm lying down, actually. Will that do?"

"I have not heard of it. You are supposed to sit on your luggage or a bench, sigh a little and then cross yourself. But I expect that lying down will have the same effect."

"It does."

"Will you come back to Moscow from Leningrad?"

"Well, not on this trip. I think we'll fly straight back to school."

"School?"

"England. Stupid expression of mine."

"What does it denote?"

"Obligations. Immaturity. Ignorance. The usual English vices."

"You have many obligations?"

"Suitcases of 'em. But I'm learning to sort them out. I actually said no yesterday and astonished everybody."

"Why do you have to say no? Why not say yes? Perhaps they would be even more astonished."

"Yes, well that was the trouble with last night, wasn't it? I never got round to talking about myself. We talked about you, the great poets down the ages, Mr. Gorbachev, publishing. But we left out the main topic. Me. I'll have to make a special trip just to come and bore you."

"I am sure you will not bore me."

"Is there anything I can bring you?"

"Please?"

"Next time I come. Any special wishes? An electric toothbrush? Paper curlers? More Jane Austen?"

A long delicious pause.

"I wish you a good journey, Barley," she said.

The last lunch with Zapadny was a wake without a corpse. They sat fourteen, all men, the only guests in the enormous upstairs restaurant of an unfinished new hotel.

Waiters brought food and vanished to the distant outskirts. Zapadny had to send scouts to find them. There was no drink and precious little conversation unless Barley and Zapadny contrived it between them. There was canned music of the fifties. There was a lot of hammering.

"But we have arranged a great party for you, Barley," Zapadny protested. "Vassily is bringing his drums, Viktor will lend you his saxophone, a friend of mine who makes his own moonshine has promised us six bottles, there will be some mad painters and writers. It has all the makings of a most disreputable evening and you have the weekend to recover. Tell your American Potomac bastard to go to hell. We do not like you so serious."

"Our tycoons are your bureaucrats, Alik. We ignore them at our peril. So do you."

Zapadny's smile was neither warm nor forgiving. "We even thought you might have lost your heart a little to one of our celebrated Moscow beauties. Can't the delicious Katya persuade you to stay?"

"Who's Katya?" Barley heard himself reply while he was still wondering why the ceiling hadn't fallen in.

A buzz of eager amusement rose from around the table.

"This is Moscow, Barley," Zapadny reminded him, very pleased with himself. "Nothing happens without something happening. The intelligentsia is small, we are all broke and local telephone calls are free. You cannot dine with Katya Orlova in an intimate and rather crazy restaurant without at least fifteen of us being advised of it next morning."

"It was strictly business," Barley said.

"Then why didn't you take Mr. Wicklow along with you?"

"He's much too young," said Barley, and scored another peal of Russian merriment.

* * *

The night sleeper to Leningrad leaves Moscow at a few minutes before midnight, traditionally so that Russia's numberless bureaucrats may claim a second day's subsistence for the journey. The compartment had four berths, and Wicklow and Barley had the lower pair until a heavyweight blond lady insisted Barley exchange places with her. The fourth berth was occupied by a quiet man of apparent means who spoke elegant English and carried an air of private grief about him. First he wore a lawyer's dark suit, then he wore wildly striped pyjamas that would have graced a clown, but his mood did not brighten with his costume. There was more business when the blond lady refused to take off even her hat until the three men had removed themselves to the corridor. Harmony was restored when she called them back and, clad in a pink tracksuit with pompoms on the shoulders, fed them homemade pastries in gratitude for their gallantry. And when Barley produced whisky she was so impressed she made them eat her sausage too, insisting they drink the health of Mrs. Thatcher more than once.

"Where do you come from?" the sad man asked Barley across the divide as they settled for the night.

"London," said Barley.

"London in England. Not from the moon, not from the stars, but London in England," the sad man confirmed and, unlike Barley, soon appeared to fall asleep. But a couple of hours later as they pulled into a station, he resumed their conversation. "Do you know where we are now?" he asked without bothering to establish whether Barley was awake.

"I don't think I do."

"If Anna Karenina were travelling with us tonight and had her wits about her, this would be the place where she would abandon the unsatisfactory Vronsky."

"Marvellous," said Barley, quite mystified. His whisky was gone but the sad man had Georgian brandy.

"It was a swamp before, it is a swamp today," the sad man said. "If you are studying the Russian disease, you must live in the Russian swamp."

He was talking about Leningrad.

10

A low cottonwool sky hung over the imported palaces, making them dreary in their fancy dress. Summer music played in the parks but the summer clung behind the clouds, leaving a chalky Nordic mist to trick and tremble on the Venetian waterways. Barley walked and, as always when he was in Leningrad, he had the sensation of walking through other cities, now Prague, now Vienna, now a bit of Paris or a corner of Regent's Park. No other city that he knew hid its shame behind so many sweet façades or asked such terrible questions with its smile. Who worshipped in these locked, unreal churches? And whose God? How many bodies had choked these graceful canals or floated frozen to the sea? Where else on earth has so much barbarism built itself such pretty monuments? Even the people in the street, so slow-spoken, decorous, reserved, seemed joined to one another by their monstrous dissembling. And Barley, as he loitered and gazed like any tourist—and like any spy counted off the minutes—Barley felt himself a part of their duplicity.

He had shaken hands with an American tycoon who was not a tycoon, and commiserated with him about his sick wife who was not sick and probably not his wife.

He had instructed a subordinate who was not his subordinate to give succour in an emergency that did not exist.

He was on his way to keep a rendezvous with an author who was not an author but was seeking martyrdom in a city where martyrdom could be had free across the counter, whether or not you happened to stand in line for it.

He was scared numb and had a hangover for the fourth day running.

He was a citizen of Leningrad at last.

Finding himself in the Nevsky Prospekt he realised he was looking for the cafeteria called informally the Saigon, a place for poets, drug-pedlars and speculators, not professors' daughters. "Your father is right," he heard her say. "The system will always win."

He had his own street map, courtesy of Paddy— German, with a multi-lingual text. From Cy he had a copy of *Crime and Punishment,* a battered Penguin paperback in a translation to drive him to despair. He had put them both in a plastic carrier bag. Wicklow had insisted. Not just any bag but this bag, advertising some beastly American cigarette and recognisable at five hundred metres. Now his only mission in life was to trail Raskolnikov on his fateful journey to murder the old lady, which was why he was searching for a courtyard leading off the Griboyedev Canal. Iron gates opened to it, a spreading tree gave it shade. He wandered in it slowly, peering at his Penguin book, then guardedly at the grimy windows as if expecting the old pawnbroker's blood to come seeping down the yellowing paintwork. Only occasionally did he allow his gaze to stray into that unfocussed middle distance which is the preserve of the English upper classes, and which comprises such extraneous objects as passers-by, or those not passing by but doing nothing; or the gate that led to Plekhanova Street which only very local people knew of, said Paddy, such as scientists who in their youth had studied at the

Litmo around the corner, but who, so far as Barley could see from his casual searching of the approaches, showed no sign of returning.

He was out of breath. A bubble of nausea like an air-pocket filled his lower chest. He reached the gate and opened it. He passed through an entrance hall. He climbed the short flight of steps to the street. He glanced both ways and made another show of comparing his findings while Wicklow's hated microphone harness sawed his back. He turned round and sauntered back through the courtyard and under the spreading tree until he was once more along-side the canal. He sat on a bench and unfolded the street map. Ten minutes, Paddy had said, handing him a scratched sports-watch in place of his unreliable heirloom. Five before, five after, then abort.

"You are lost?" asked a pale man who looked too old to be a tout. He was wearing Italian racing-driver glasses and Nike sneakers. His Russian English had an American accent.

"I'm always lost, old boy, thank you," said Barley politely. "It's the way I like it."

"You want to sell me something? Cigarettes? Scotch? Fountain pen? You want to trade drugs or currency or something like this?"

"Thanks, but I'm very nice as I am," Barley replied, relieved to hear himself speaking normally. "If you'd just move out of the sun a little, I'll be even nicer."

"You want to meet an international group of people including girls? I can show you the real Russia nobody ever gets to see."

"Old boy, to be perfectly honest, I don't believe you'd know the real Russia if it got up and bit you in the balls," said Barley, returning to his map. The man drifted away.

On Fridays even the great scientists will be doing what

everyone else is doing, Paddy had said. They'll be closing
down the week and getting drunk. They'll have had their
three-day knees-up, they'll have shown each other their
achievements and traded their researches. Their Leningrad
hosts will be feeding them a lavish lunch but leaving them
time to get at the shops before they return to their postbox
numbers. That will be your friend's first chance to slip away
from the group if he's going to.

My friend. *My* Raskolnikov friend. Not *his* friend. Mine.
In case I come unstuck.

One rendezvous down and two to go.

Barley stood up, rubbed his back and with time to waste
continued his literary tour of Leningrad. Recrossing the
Nevsky Prospekt, he gazed at the weathered faces of the
shoppers and in a rush of empathy prayed to be assumed
into their ranks: "I'm one of you! I share your confusions!
Accept me! Hide me! Ignore me!" He steadied himself.
Look round. Look foolish. Gawp.

Behind him stood the Kazan Cathedral. Ahead of him
rose the House of Books, where as a good publisher Barley
now lingered, squinting into the windows and upwards at
the stubby tower with its vile globe. But he did not stay for
long in case he was recognised by somebody from one of
the editorial offices upstairs. He entered Zhelyabova Street
and approached one of the great department stores of
Leningrad, with its wartime English fashions in the window and fur hats out of season. He placed himself conspic-
uously at the main entrance, hooking the carrier bag over
his middle finger and unfolding his map for refuge.

Not here, he thought. For Christ's sake, not here. Give
us a decent privacy, Goethe, please. Not here.

"If he selects the shop, he's reckoning on a very public
meeting," Paddy had said. "He's got to fling up his arms
and shout, 'Scott Blair, can it be you?'"

For the next ten minutes Barley thought of nothing. He stared at the map, lifted his head and stared at buildings. He stared at girls, and in Leningrad that summer's day the girls were staring back. But their alertness did not reassure him and he ducked back into his map. Sweat was running like marbles over his rib cage. He had a fantasy that the microphones would short-circuit. Twice he cleared his throat because he feared he wouldn't be able to speak. But when he tried to moisten his lips he discovered that his tongue had withered.

The ten minutes were up but he waited another two because he owed them: to himself, to Katya, to Goethe. He folded the map, not making the right folds, but then he had never managed that anyway. He stuffed the map into the gaudy plastic bag. He rejoined the crowds and discovered that after all he could walk like everybody else, no sudden lurches, no bone-cracking falls headlong to the pavement.

He strolled back down the Nevsky towards the Anichkov Bridge, looking for the No. 7 trolleybus to Smolny for his third and final appearance before the assembled spies of Leningrad.

Two boys in jeans stood ahead of him in the queue. Three babushkas stood behind him. The trolleybus arrived and the boys leapt in. Barley followed them aboard. The two boys chatted noisily. An old man stood up in order to let one of the babushkas sit. We're a good crowd in here, Barley thought in another lurch of dependence upon those he was deceiving; let's stay together all day and enjoy each other. A small boy was frowning into his face, asking him something. On an inspiration, Barley pulled back his sleeve and showed him Paddy's steel wristwatch. The boy studied it and gave a hiss of rage. The trolleybus clanged to a halt.

He's funked it, thought Barley in relief as he entered the

park. The sun broke clear of the clouds. He's chickened and who can blame him?

But by then he had spotted him. Goethe, precisely as advertised. Goethe, the great lover and thinker, seated on the third bench to your left as you enter the gravel path, a nihilist who takes no principle for granted.

Goethe. Reading his newspaper. Sober and half his original size, dressed in a black suit certainly, but looking like his smaller, older brother. Barley's heart sank, then leapt, at the sight of such sheer ordinariness. The shadow of the great poet was extinct. Lines of age marked the once-smooth face. The mercurial had no place in this clerkish, bearded Russian taking his midday air on a park bench.

But Goethe nonetheless, and seated amid a cluster of warring Russian shrines: not a pistol shot from the fiery statues of Marx, Engels and Lenin, who forced their bronze scowls on him from strangely separated plinths; not a musket shot from the sacred Room 67, where Lenin had set up his revolutionary headquarters in a boarding school for the better class of Petersburg girl; not a funeral march from Rastrelli's blue baroque cathedral built to ease the declining years of an empress; not a blindfold walk from the Leningrad Party Headquarters with its oversize policemen glowering at the liberated masses.

Smola means tar, Barley recalled stupidly in this continuing moment of monstrous normality. In Smolny, Peter the Great stored his tar for the first Russian navy.

Those nearest to Goethe were as normal as the man himself. The day might have started dull but the new sunlight had worked miracles and the good citizens were stripping off as if a common urge had seized them. Boys bare to the waist, girls like thrownaway flowers, hulking women in satin brassières lay sprawled at Goethe's feet, playing radios, munching sandwiches and discussing whatever it was that made them grimace, ponder and laugh in swift succession.

A chip path ran close to the bench. Barley launched himself upon it studying the *Informationen* at the back of the folded map. In the field, Ned had said, in a session devoted to the macabre etiquette of tradecraft, the source is the star and the star decides whether to make the meeting or abort.

Fifty yards separated Barley from his star but the path joined them like a ruled line. Was he walking too fast or too slowly? One moment he was pressing up against the couple in front of him, the next he was being shoved aside from behind. If he ignores you, wait five minutes then try a second pass, Paddy had said. Squinting over his map, Barley saw Goethe's face lift as if he had scented his approach. He saw the whiteness of his cheeks and the unlit hollows of his eyes; then the whiteness of the newspaper as he folded it together like a camper's blanket. He saw that there was something angular and not quite reconciled about his movements, so that he resembled in Barley's racing mind a figure of over-orderly clockwork in a Swiss town: now I will lift my white face, now I strike twelve with my white flag, now I stand up and march away. The newspaper folded, Goethe put it in his pocket and gave a pedagogic glance at his wristwatch. Then with the same mechanical air of being someone else's invention, he took his place in the army of pedestrians and loped among them towards the river.

Now Barley's pace was set, for it was Goethe's. His quarry was following the path towards a row of parked cars. Eyes and brain clear, Barley walked after him and, reaching the cars, saw him standing against the fast-flowing Neva, his jacket puffed out by the river breeze. A pleasure steamer passed but the passengers gave no sign of pleasure. A coaling boat hobbled by, dappled in red lead, and the filthy smoke from its funnel was beautiful in the dancing river light. Goethe leaned over the balustrade and peered down at the current as if calculating its speed. Barley headed towards him, slurring his feet while he orientated himself from his map with increasing diligence. Even when he heard himself addressed, in the immaculate English that had woken him on the verandah in Peredelkino, he did not immediately respond.

"Sir? Excuse me, sir. I think we are acquainted."

But Barley at first refused to hear. The voice was too nervous, too tentative. He went on frowning at his *Informationen*. Must be another tout, he was saying to himself. Another of those drug-pedlars or pimps.

"Sir?" Goethe repeated, as if he himself were now unsure.

Only now, won over by the stranger's insistence, did Barley reluctantly raise his head.

"I think you are Mr. Scott Blair, sir, the distinguished publisher from England."

At which Barley finally persuaded himself to recognise the man addressing him, first with doubt, then unfeigned but muted pleasure as he thrust out his hand.

"Well, I'm damned," he said quietly. "Good God. The great Goethe, as I live and breathe. We met at that disgraceful literary party. We were the only two people sober. How are you?"

"Oh, I am *very* well," Goethe said as his strained voice gathered courage. But his hand when Barley shook it was slippery with sweat. "I do not know how I could be better at this moment. Welcome to Leningrad, Mr. Barley. What a pity I have an appointment this afternoon. You can walk a little? We can exchange ideas?" His voice barely fell. "It is safest to keep moving," he explained.

He had grasped Barley's arm and was propelling him swiftly along the embankment. His urgency had driven every tactical thought from Barley's mind. Barley glanced at the bobbing figure beside him, at the pallor of his racked cheeks, the tracks of pain or fear or worry that ran down them. He saw the hunted eyes flicking nervously at every passing face. And his only instinct was to protect him: for Goethe's own sake and for Katya's.

"If we could walk for half an hour, we would see the battleship *Aurora*, which fired the blank shot to launch the Revolution. But the next revolution shall begin with a few gentle phrases of Bach. It is time. Do you agree?"

"And no conductor," said Barley, with a grin.

"Or maybe some of that jazz you play so beautifully. Yes, yes! I have it! You shall announce our revolution by playing Lester Young on the saxophone. You have read the new Rybakov novel? Twenty years suppressed and therefore a great Russian masterpiece? It is a rape of time, I think."

"It hasn't appeared in English yet."

"You have read mine?" The thin hand had tightened on his arm. The pressed-in voice had fallen to a murmur.

"What I could understand of it, yes."

"What do you think?"

"It's brave."

"No more than that?"

"It's sensational. What I could understand of it. Great."

"We recognised each other that night. It was magic. You know our Russian saying 'One fisherman always sees another from afar'? We are fishermen. We shall feed the thousands with our truth."

"Maybe we will at that," said Barley doubtfully, and felt the gaunt head swing round to him. "I have to discuss it with you a bit, Goethe. We've got one or two problems."

"That's why you have come. I too. Thank you for coming to Leningrad. When will you publish? It must be soon. The writers here, they wait three, five years for publication even if they are not Rybakov. I can't do that. Russia has no time. Neither have I."

A line of tugs drew by, a two-man scull flicked cheekily in their wake. Two lovers were embracing at the parapet. And in the shadow of the cathedral a young woman stood rocking a pram while she read from the book she was holding in her spare hand.

"When I didn't show up at the Moscow audio fair, Katya gave your manuscript to a colleague of mine," Barley said cautiously.

"I know. She had to take a chance."

"What you don't know is that the colleague couldn't find me when he got back to England. So he gave it to the authorities. People of discretion. Experts."

Goethe turned sharply to Barley in alarm and the shadow of dismay spread swiftly over his fraught features. "I do not *like* experts," he said. "They are our jailers. I despise experts more than anyone on earth."

"You're one yourself, aren't you?"

"Therefore I know! Experts are addicts. They solve nothing! They are servants of whatever system hires them. They perpetuate it. When we are tortured, we shall be tortured by experts. When we are hanged, experts will hang us. Did you not read what I wrote? When the world is destroyed, it will be destroyed not by its madmen but by the sanity of its experts and the superior ignorance of its bureaucrats. You have betrayed me."

"Nobody's betrayed you," Barley said angrily. "The manuscript went astray, that's all. Our bureaucrats are not your bureaucrats. They've read it, they admire it, but they need to know more about you. They can't believe the message unless they can believe the source."

"But do they want to publish it?"

"First of all they need to reassure themselves you're not a trick, and their best way to do that is to talk to you."

Goethe was striding too fast, taking Barley with him. He was staring out ahead of him. Sweat was running down his temples.

"I'm an arts man, Goethe," Barley said breathlessly to his averted face. "All I know about physics is *Beowulf,* girls and warm beer. I'm out of my depth. So's Katya. If you want to go this road, go it with the experts and leave us out. That's what I came to tell you."

They crossed a path and struck out across another segment of lawn. A group of schoolchildren broke ranks to let them through.

"You came to tell me that you refuse to publish me?"

"How *can* I publish you?" Barley retorted, in turn fired by Goethe's desperation. "Even if we could knock the material into shape, what about Katya? She's your courier, remember? She's passed Soviet defence secrets to a foreign power. That's not exactly a laugh a minute over here. If they ever find out about the two of you, she'll be dead the day the first copy hits the stands. What sort of part is that for a publisher to play? Do you think I'm going to sit in London and press the button on the two of you here?"

Goethe was panting, but his eyes had ceased to scan the crowds and were turned to Barley.

"Listen to me," Barley pleaded. "Just hold on a minute. I understand. I really think I understand. You had a talent and it was put to unfair uses. You know all the ways the system stinks and you want to wash your soul. But you're not Christ and you're not Pecherin. You're out of court. If you want to kill yourself, that's your business. But you'll kill her too. And if you don't care who you kill, why should you care who you save?"

They were heading for a picnic place with chairs and tables cut from logs. They sat side by side and Barley spread his map. They bent over it, pretending to examine it together. Goethe was still measuring Barley's words, matching them against his purposes.

"There is only *now*," he explained finally, his voice not above a murmur. "There is no other dimension but *now*. In the past we have done everything badly for the sake of the future. Now we must do everything right for the sake of the present. To lose time is to lose everything. Our Russian history does not give us second chances. When we leap across an abyss, she does not give us the opportunity for a second step. And when we fail she gives us what we deserve: another Stalin, another Brezhnev, another purge, another ice age of terrified monotony. If the present momentum continues, I shall have been in the vanguard. If it stops or goes back, I shall be another statistic of our post-Revolutionary history."

"So will Katya," Barley said.

Goethe's finger, unable to stay still, was travelling across the map. He glanced round him, then continued. "We are in Leningrad, Barley, the cradle of our great Revolution. Nobody triumphs here without sacrifice. You said we needed an experiment in human nature. Why are you so shocked when I put your words into practice?"

"You got me wrong that day. I'm not the man you took me for. I'm the original useless mouth. You just met me when the wind was in the right direction."

With a frightening control Goethe opened his hands and spread them palms downward on the map. "You do not need to remind me that man is not equal to his rhetoric," he said. "Our new people talk about openness, disarmament, peace. So let them have their openness. And their disarmament. And their peace. Let us call their bluff and give them what they ask. And make sure that this time they cannot put the clock back." He was standing, no longer able to bear the confinement of the table.

Barley stood beside him. "Goethe, for God's sake. Take it easy."

"To the devil with easy! It is easy that kills!" He began striding again. "We do not break the curse of secrecy by passing our secrets from hand to hand like thieves! I have lived a great lie! And you tell me to keep it secret! How did the lie survive? By secrecy. How did our great vision crumble to this dreadful mess? By secrecy. How do you keep your own people ignorant of the insanity of your war plans? By secrecy. By keeping out the light. Show my work to your spies if that's what you must do. But publish me as well. That is what you promised and I shall believe your promise. I have dropped a notebook containing further chapters into your carrier bag. No doubt it answers many of the questions the idiots wish to put to me."

The breeze of the river washed over Barley's heated face as they strode along. Glancing at Goethe's glistening features, he fancied he glimpsed traces of the hurt innocence that seemed to be the source of his outrage.

"I shall wish a book jacket that is only letters," he announced. "No drawing, please, no sensational design. You heard me?"

"We haven't even got a title," Barley objected.

"You will please use my own name as the author. No evasions, no pseudonyms. To use a pseudonym is to invent another secret."

"I don't even *know* your name."

"They will know it. After what Katya told you, and with the new chapters, they will have no problem. Keep correct accounts. Every six months, please send the money to a deserving cause. Nobody shall say I did this for my own profit."

Through the approaching trees the strains of martial music vied with the clatter of invisible trams.

"Goethe," said Barley.

"What is the matter? Are you afraid?"

"Come to England. They'll smuggle you out. They're smart. Then you can tell the world everything you want. We'll rent the Albert Hall for you. Put you on television, radio—you name it. And when it's over, they'll give you a passport and money and you can live happily ever after in Australia."

They had stopped again. Had Goethe heard? Had he understood? Still nothing stirred behind his unblinking stare. His eyes were fixed on Barley as if he were a distant spot upon a vast horizon.

"I am not a defector, Barley. I am a Russian, and my future is here, even if it is a short one. Will you publish me or not? I need to know."

Buying time, Barley reached into his jacket pocket and pulled out Cy's worn paperback. "I'm to give you this," he said. "A memento of our meeting. Their questions are bound into the text, together with an address in Finland you can write to and a phone number in Moscow with instructions on what to say when you call. If you'll do business with them direct, they've got all sorts of clever toys they can give you to make communication easier." He placed the paperback in Goethe's open hand and it remained there.

"Will you publish me? Yes or no."

"How do they get hold of you? They have to know."

"Tell them I can be reached through my publisher."

"Take Katya out of the equation. Stay with the spies and keep away from her."

Goethe's gaze had descended to Barley's suit and remained there, as if the sight of it troubled him. His sad smile was like a last holiday.

"You are wearing grey today, Barley. My father was sent to prison by grey men. He was shot by an old man who wore a grey uniform. It is the grey men who have ruined my beautiful profession. Take care or they will ruin yours too. Will you publish me or must I start again in my search for a decent human being?"

For a while Barley could not answer. His mechanisms of evasion had run out.

"If I can get control of the material, and find a way through it to a book, I'll publish you," he replied.

"I asked you, yes or no."

Promise him anything he asks within reason, Paddy had said. But what was reason? "All right," he replied. "Yes."

Goethe handed Barley back the book and Barley in a daze returned it to his pocket. They embraced and Barley smelt sweat and stale tobacco smoke and felt again the desperate strength of their farewell in Peredelkino. As abruptly as Goethe had seized him, so he now released him and with another nervous glance round him set off quickly towards the trolleybus stop. And as Barley watched him he noticed how the old couple from the outdoor café was watching his departure too, standing in the shadow of the dark blue trees.

Barley sneezed, then started sneezing seriously. Then really sneezed. He walked back into the park, his face buried in his handkerchief while he shook his shoulders and sneezed and shook again.

"Why, *Scott!*" J. P. Henziger exclaimed, with the over-bright enthusiasm of a busy man kept waiting, as he snatched back the door on the largest bedroom in the

Hotel Europe. "Scott, this is a day when we discover who our friends are. Come in, please. What kept you? Say hullo to Maisie."

He was mid-forties, muscular and prehensile, but he had the kind of ugly friendly face that Barley would normally have warmed to instantly. He wore an elephant hair round one wrist and a gold-link bracelet round the other. Half-moons of sweat blackened his denim armpits. Wicklow appeared behind him and quickly closed the door.

Twin beds, draped in olive counterpanes, commanded the centre of the room. In one of them languished Mrs. Henziger, a thirty-five-year-old kitten without her make-up, her combed-out tresses spread tragically over her freckled shoulders. A man in a black suit hovered uneasily at her side. He wore liver-coloured spectacles. A medical practitioner's case lay open on the bed. Henziger continued vamping for the microphones.

"Scott, I want you to meet Dr. Pete Bernstorf from the U.S. Consulate General here in Leningrad, a fine physician. We are indebted to him. Maisie is improving fast. We are indebted to Mr. Wicklow also. Leonard fixed the hotel, the tour people, the pharmacy. How was your day?"

"One bloody long laugh," Barley blurted, and for a moment the script threatened to go badly wrong.

Barley tossed the carrier bag on to the bed and with it the rejected paperback book from his jacket pocket. With shaking hands he pulled off his jacket, tore the microphone harness out of his shirt and flung it after the bag and the book. He reached behind him into his waistband and, brushing aside Wicklow's offer of assistance, extracted the grey recording box from the small of his back and threw that on the bed as well, so that Maisie let out a stifled "shit" and moved her legs quickly to one side. Marching to the washbasin, he emptied his whisky flask into a toothmug,

hugging one arm across his chest as if he had been shot.
Then he drank and went on drinking, oblivious to the perfect drill unfolding round him.

Henziger, light as a cat for all his bulk, grabbed the carrier bag, picked out the notebook and shoved it at
Bernstorf, who spirited it into his medical case among the
phials and instruments, where it mysteriously disappeared.
Henziger passed him the paperback, which also vanished.
Wicklow swept up the recorder and harness. They too went
into the case, which Bernstorf snapped shut while he issued
departing instructions to the patient: no solids for forty-
eight hours, Mrs. Henziger, tea, a piece of brown bread if
you must, make sure you complete the course of antibiotics
whether or not you feel better. He had not finished before
Henziger chimed in.

"And, Doctor, if ever you are in Boston, and you need
anything, because I mean *anything*, here's my card and
here's my promise and here's . . ."

Toothmug in hand, Barley remained facing the washbasin, glowering in the mirror as the Good Samaritan's case
made its journey to the door.

Of all his nights in Russia and, come to think of it, of
all his nights anywhere in the world, this was Barley's
worst.

Henziger had heard that a cooperative restaurant had
just opened in Leningrad, cooperative being the new codeword for private. Wicklow had tracked it down and
reported it full, but rejection for Henziger was challenge.
By dint of heavy telephoning and heavier tipping, an extra
table was laid for them, three feet from the worst and nois-
iest gypsy opera Barley ever hoped to hear.

And there they now sat, celebrating Mrs. Henziger's
miraculous recovery. The mewing of the singers was ampli-

fied by electronic bullhorns. There was no remission between numbers.

And all round them sat the Russia that the slumbering puritan in Barley had long hated but never seen: the not-so-secret czars of capitalism, the industrial parvenus and conspicuous consumers, the Party fat-cats and racketeers, their jewelled women reeking of Western perfumes and Russian deodorant, the waiters doting on the richest tables. The singers' frightful voices rose, the music rose to drown them, the voices rose again and Henziger's voice rose above them all.

"Scott, I want you to know something," he bellowed to Barley, leaning excitedly across the table. "This little country is on the move. I smell hope here, I smell change, I smell commerce. And we in Potomac are buying ourselves a piece of it. I'm proud." But his voice had been taken away from him by the band. "Proud," his lips repeated soundlessly to a million gypsy decibels.

And the trouble was, Henziger was a nice fellow and Maisie was a sport, which made it worse. As the agony dragged on, Barley entered the blessed state of deafness. Inside the cacophony he discovered his own safe room. From its arrow-slit windows his secret self stared into the white Leningrad night. Where have you gone, Goethe? he asked. Who stands in for her when she isn't there? Who darns your black socks and cooks your washed-out soup for you while you drag her by the hair along your noble altruistic path to self-destruction?

Somehow without his being aware of it they must have returned to the hotel, for he woke to discover himself propped on Wicklow's arm among the Finnish alcoholics stumbling shamefacedly round the lobby.

"Great party," he told anyone who would hear him. "Splendid band. Thank you for coming to Leningrad."

But as Wicklow patiently hauled him up to bed the undrunk part of Barley glanced over his shoulder, down the wide staircase. And in the darkness near the entrance, he saw Katya, seated with her legs crossed, her perhaps-bag on her lap. She was wearing a pinched black jacket. A white silk scarf was knotted under her chin, and her face was pressed towards him with that tense smile she had, sad and hopeful, open to love.

But as his gaze cleared he saw her say something saucy out of the corner of her mouth to the porter, and he realised she was just another Leningrad tart looking for a trick.

And next day, to the fanfare of the most discreet of British trumpets, our hero came home.

Ned wanted no display, no Americans and certainly no Clive, but he was determined on a gesture, so we drove to Gatwick and, having posted Brock at the Arrivals barrier with a card saying "Potomac," we installed ourselves in a hospitality lounge that the Service shared uneasily with the Foreign Office amid endless argument about who had drunk the gin.

We waited, the plane was delayed. Clive phoned from Grosvenor Square to ask "Has he arrived, Palfrey?" as if he half expected him to stay in Russia.

Another half-hour passed before Clive phoned again and this time Ned himself took the call. He had scarcely slammed the phone down before the door opened and Wicklow slipped in grinning like a choirboy but contriving at the same time to shoot his eyes in warning.

Seconds after him, enter Barley looking like his own surveillance photographs, except that he was white-faced. "Buggers cheered!" he blurted before Brock had got the door shut. "That prissy captain with his Surrey vowels! I'll kill the swine."

While Barley stormed on, Wicklow discreetly explained the cause of his distress. Their charter flight out of Leningrad had been occupied by a delegation of young British traders whom Barley had arbitrarily branded yuppies of the vilest sort, which by the sound of them they were. Several were drunk by the time they boarded, the rest were quick to catch up. They had not been more than a few minutes in the air when the captain, who in Barley's view was the provocateur of the incident, announced that the plane had left Soviet airspace. A roar went up while the air hostesses scampered up and down the aisle doling out champagne. Then they all broke into "Rule, Britannia!"

"Give me Aeroflot every time," Barley raged at the assembled faces. "I'm going to write to the airline. I'm going to——"

"You're going to do nothing of the kind," Ned kindly interrupted him. "You're going to let us make an enormous fuss of you. You can have your tantrum later."

As he said this, he went on shaking Barley's hand until Barley eventually smiled.

"Where's Walt?" he asked, peering round.

"I'm afraid he's off on a job," said Ned, but Barley had already lost interest. His hand trembled violently as he drank and he wept a bit, which Ned assured me was par for the course for joes coming back from the field.

11

The pattern of the next three days, like the wreck of a smashed aeroplane, was afterwards minutely examined for technical faults, though few were found.

After his outburst at the airport Barley entered the bright stage, smiling a lot to himself on the car journey, greeting familiar landmarks with his habitual shy affection. He also had a sneezing fit.

As soon as we reached the Knightsbridge house, where Ned was determined Barley should spend the night before returning to his flat, he dumped his luggage in the hall, flung his arms round Miss Coad and, declaring his undying love for her, presented her with a splendid lynx-fur hat which neither Wicklow nor anyone else could afterwards remember him buying.

At this point I removed myself. Clive had commanded me to the twelfth floor for what he termed "a crucial discussion," though it turned out that what he really wanted was to tap me. Was Scott Blair nervous? Was he above himself? How was he, Palfrey? Johnny was there, listening but scarcely speaking. Bob, he said, had been recalled to Langley for consultations. I told them what I had seen, no less, certainly no more. Both were puzzled by Barley's tears.

"You mean he said he was going back?" said Clive.

The same night Ned dined with Barley alone. This was not yet the debriefing. It was the coming down. The tapes reveal Barley in staccato mood and his voice a key higher than usual. By the time I joined them for coffee he was talking about Goethe but with artificial objectivity.

Goethe had aged, had lost his bounce.

Goethe was really shot up.

Goethe seemed to have stopped drinking. He was getting his highs elsewhere. "You should have seen his hands, Harry, shaking over that map."

You should have seen yours, I thought, when you were drinking champagne at the airport.

He referred to Katya only once that evening, also in a deliberately unemotional way. I think he was determined we should know that he had no feelings that were not ours to control. That was not deviousness on Barley's part. With the exception of what we had taught him, he was incapable of it. It was his fear of where his feelings might end up if they were no longer anchored to us.

Katya was more scared for her kids than she was for herself, he said, again with studied detachment. He supposed most mothers were. On the other hand her children were the cyphers for the world she wished to save. So in a sense what she was doing was a kind of absolute version of mother love, don't you agree, Nedsky?

Ned agreed. Nothing harder than to experiment with one's own children, Barley, he said.

But a marvellous girl, Barley insisted, now in patronising mode. A bit too hell-bent for Barley's personal taste these days, but if you liked your women to have the moral fibre of Joan of Arc, then Katya was for you. And she was beautiful. No question. A bit too haywire to be classical, if we knew what he meant, but undeniably striking.

We couldn't tell him we had been admiring photographs of her for the last week, so we took his word for it.

At eleven, complaining of the time difference, Barley flopped. We stood in the hall watching him haul himself upstairs to bed.

"Anyway it was good stuff, was it?" he asked as he clung to the banister and grinned down at us through his little round spectacles. "The new notebook he gave us. You've looked at it."

"The boffins are burning the midnight oil over it at this moment," Ned replied. He could hardly say they were fighting over it like cats and dogs.

"Experts are addicts," Barley said, with another grin.

But he remained on the half-landing swaying, while he seemed to search for an appropriate exit line.

"Somebody ought to do a bit of work on those body microphones, Nedsky. Bloody saddle-sores all over my back. The next bloke you send had better have a thicker hide. Where's Uncle Bob, by the by?"

"He sends love," said Ned. "Business is brisk at the moment. He hopes to catch up with you soon."

"Is he out hunting with Walt?"

"If I knew I wouldn't tell you," said Ned, and we all laughed.

That night, I remember, I received a particularly irrelevant phone call from Margaret, my wife, about a parking ticket she had picked up in Basingstoke—in her view, unfairly.

"It was *my* space, I had put my indicator out when this bloody little man in a brand-new Jaguar, a white one, with slicked black hair—"

Unwisely I laughed, and suggested to her that Jaguars with slicked black hair had no special dispensation at parking meters. Humour was never Margaret's strong point.

The next morning, the Sunday, Clive again required my attendance, first to pump me about the previous night, then to hear me "talk turkey" with Johnny on such esoteric matters as whether Barley could legally be styled an employee of our Service and, if so, whether by taking our shilling he had renounced certain rights—his right to legal representation in the event of a dispute with us, for instance. I was Delphic, which annoyed them, but basically I said the answer was yes. Yes, he had renounced those rights. Or more exactly, yes, we could gull him into thinking he had, whether he had in law or not.

Johnny, if I have not mentioned it already, had graduated from Harvard Law School, so for once it was not necessary for Langley to send us a chorus of legal advisers.

In the afternoon, Barley being restless and the day sunny, we drove to Maidenhead and walked the towpath beside the Thames. By the time we returned, I suppose you could say Barley had been debriefed: for what with no questions coming down to us from our analysts, and his operational encounters already covered by technical means, there was really very little left to debrief him about.

Was Barley affected by our worries? We were as jolly as we could be, but I couldn't help wondering whether the atmosphere of menacing stagnation was getting through to him. Or perhaps his feelings were such a maelstrom of confusion and anticlimax that he merely lumped us in with them.

On the Sunday night we ate supper together in Knightsbridge and Barley was so mild-mannered and reposed that Ned decided—as I would have done—that it was safe to send him back to Hampstead.

His flat was in a Victorian block off East Heath Road and the static surveillance post was situated directly below it, manned by a bright young Service couple. The rightful tenants had been temporarily resettled elsewhere. Around eleven the couple reported that Barley was in his flat alone but prowling. They could hear but not see him. Ned had drawn the line at video. He was doing a lot of talking to himself, they said, and when he opened his mail, curses and groans came over the monitors.

Ned was unbothered. He had read Barley's mail already and knew it contained no horrors beyond the usual.

Around 1 a.m., Barley rang his daughter Anthea in Grantham.

"What's an ig?"

"An Eskimo house without a loo. How was Moscow?"

"What do you get if you cross the Atlantic with the *Titanic?*"

"About halfway. How was Moscow?"

"What do you get if you cross a sheep with a kangaroo?"

"I asked you how Moscow was."

"A woolly jumper. How's your boring husband?"

"Asleep, trying to be. What became of the cream bun you took to Lisbon?"

"Rained off."

"I thought she was permanent."

"She is. I'm not."

Barley next telephoned two women, the first a former wife over whom he had retained visiting rights, the second not previously listed. Neither could oblige him at such short notice, not least because they were in bed with their men.

At one-forty the couple reported that Barley's bedroom lights were out. Ned gratefully went to sleep, but I was already in my little flat and sleep was the last thing in my mind. Memories of Hannah were teeming through my head, mixed with images of Barley in the Knightsbridge house. I remembered his falsely casual way of talking about Katya and her children and I kept comparing it with my own repeated denials of my love for Hannah, back in the days when it endangered me. *Hannah looks a bit down in the mouth,* some innocent would remark every five minutes of my day. *Is that husband of hers leading her a dance or what?* And I'd smile. *I gather he likes to knock her around a bit,* I'd say, with exactly that same superior tone of detachment that I had heard in Barley, while the cancerous secret fires inside me ate away my heart.

Next morning Barley went to his office to resume work, but it was agreed that he would drop by the Knightsbridge house on his way home from work in case there were points to clear up. This was not quite the loose arrangement that it sounds, for Ned by now was locked in a serious shoot-out with the twelfth floor, and it was likely that by evening he would either have to give ground or face a full-scale battle with the mandarins.

But by then Barley had disappeared.

According to Brock's watchers, Barley left his office in Norfolk Street a little earlier than expected, at four-forty-three, carrying his saxophone in its case. Wicklow, who was in Abercrombie & Blair's back office typing up an account of the Moscow trip, was unaware of his departure. But a pair of Brock's boys in jeans followed Barley west down the Strand and, when he changed his mind, crossed with him into Soho where he went to earth in an afternoon watering-hole frequented by publishers and agents. He spent twenty minutes there, emerged still carrying his saxophone and looking perfectly steady. He hailed a cab, and one of the boys was close enough to hear him give the address of the safe house. The same boy bleeped Brock, who called Ned in Knightsbridge to say "Stand by, your guest is on his way." I was elsewhere, fighting other wars.

Thus far nobody was to blame, except that neither of the boys thought to take the cab's number, an oversight that later cost them dear. It was rush hour. A trip between the Strand and Knightsbridge could take an age. It was not till seven-thirty that Ned gave up waiting and, worried but not yet alarmed, returned to the Russia House.

At nine when nobody had any sensible suggestions Ned reluctantly declared an in-house alert, which by definition excluded the Americans. As usual, Ned was operational cool. Perhaps subconsciously he had steeled himself for such a crisis, for Brock later commented that he slipped into a prepared routine. He did not inform Clive, but as he explained to me later, telling Clive in the present poisoned atmosphere was as good as sending a singing telegram to Langley.

Ned drove himself first to Bloomsbury where the Service listeners owned a run of cellars under Russell Square. He used a car from the pool and must have driven like the wind. The head duty listener was Mary, a compulsive eater of forty, rose-faced and spinsterish. Her only known loves were unattainable voices. Ned handed her a list of Barley's contacts, compiled by the departed Walter from intercepts and watch reports. Could Mary cover them immediately? Like now?

Mary damn well could not. "Stretching regulations is one thing, Ned. A dozen illegal taps is completely another, can't you even *see?*"

Ned might have argued that the extra numbers were covered by the existing Home Office warrant but he didn't bother. He phoned me in Pimlico just as I was uncorking the bottle of Burgundy with which I proposed to console myself after a dirty day. It's a rather awful little flat and I had the window open to get out the smell of frying. I remember closing the window while we talked.

Phone warrants are in theory signed by the Home Secretary or in his absence by his Minister. But there is a trick to this, for he has provided the Legal Adviser with a delegated authority to be used only in emergency and accounted for in writing within twenty-four hours. I scribbled out my authority, signed it, turned off the gas—I was still boiling the Brussels sprouts—clambered into a cab and twenty minutes later handed the authority to Mary. Within the hour the telephones of Barley's twelve contacts were covered.

What was I thinking as I did all this? Did I think Barley had done away with himself? No, I did not. His concerns were for the living. The last thing he wished to do was leave them to their fate.

But I considered the possibility that he had broken ranks, and I suppose my worst fantasy was of Barley loudly clapping as the Aeroflot pilot announced that his plane had re-entered Soviet airspace.

In the meantime, on Ned's orders, Brock had persuaded the police to put out an emergency call for any metropolitan cab-driver who had picked up a tall man with a saxophone on the corner of Old Compton Street at five-thirty, destination Knightsbridge but probably changed en route. Yes, a tenor saxophone—a baritone sax was twice the size. By ten they had their man. The cab had started out for Knightsbridge but at Trafalgar Square Barley had indeed changed his mind and asked to be driven to Harley Street. The fare came to three pounds. Barley gave the driver a fiver and told him to keep the change.

By a small miracle of quick thinking, assisted by the late Walter's records, Ned made the connection—Andrew George Macready, alias Andy, former jazz trumpeter and listed Barley contact, had been admitted to the Sisters of Mercy Hospice, Harley Street, three weeks ago, see scrawled letter intercept in pencil, Mrs. Macready to Hampstead, serial 47A, and Walter's lapidary comment on the minute sheet: *Macready is Barley's guru on mortality.*

I still remember how I clung to the grab handle of Ned's car with both hands. We arrived at the hospice to be told Macready was under sedation. Barley had sat with him for an hour and they had managed to exchange a few words. The night matron, who had just come on duty, had taken Barley a cup of tea, no milk or sugar. Barley had topped it up with whisky from a flask. He had offered the matron a dram but she declined. He asked her whether he might "play old Andy a couple of his favourite numbers." He played softly for ten minutes exactly, which was what she had allowed him. Several of the nuns had gathered in the corridor to listen, and one of them recognised the tune as Basie's "Blue and Sentimental." He left his phone number and a cheque for a hundred pounds "for the croupier" on a brass collection plate at the door. The matron had told him he could come back whenever he wanted.

"You're not police, are you?" she asked me unhappily as we made for the door.

"Good Lord, no. Why ever should we be?"

She shook her head and would not answer, but I thought I knew what she had seen in him. A man in flight, hiding from his own actions.

Using the car telephone as we sped back to the Russia House, Ned ordered Brock to list all clubs, concert halls and pubs in the London area where jazz was being played tonight. He should distribute as many watchers as he could muster over these events.

For good measure I added the lawyer's ten cents' worth. In no circumstance was Brock or any watcher physically to restrain Barley or close with him. Whatever other rights

Barley might have waived, he had not waived his right to defend himself and he was a powerful man.

We were settling for a long wait when Mary the head listener rang, this time all sweetness and oil. "Ned, I think you ought to get round here a tiny bit fastish. Some of your eggs have hatched."

We tear back to Russell Square, Ned leaning the car against the curves at sixty miles an hour.

In her cellar lair Mary received us with the doting smile she reserved for moments of disaster. A favourite girl called Pepsi stood beside her, dressed in green overalls. A tape recorder turned on the desk.

"Who the hell's *that* at this hour?" a stentorian voice demanded and I recognised immediately Barley's formidable Aunt Pandora, the Sacred Cow whom I had entertained to lunch. Hiatus while coins were fed into the machine. Followed by Barley's courteous voice.

"I'm rather afraid I've had it, Pan. I'm kissing the firm goodbye."

"Don't talk cock," Aunt Pandora retorted. "Some fool girl's been getting at you again."

"I'm serious, Pan. This time it's for real. I had to tell you."

"You're *always* serious. That's why you're such a fraud pretending to be frivolous."

"I'm going to talk to Guy in the morning." Guy Solomons, family solicitor, listed Barley contact. "Wicklow, the new man, can take it over. He's a tough little runt and he's a fast learner."

"Did you trace the phone box?" Ned asked Mary as Barley rang off.

"No time," said Mary proudly.

From the tape we heard the renewed ring of a phone. Barley again. "Reggie? I'm having a blow tonight. Come and play."

Mary handed us a piece of card on which she had written, *Canon Reginald Cowan, drummer and clerk in holy orders.*

"Can't," said Reggie. "Bloody Confirmation class."

"Ditch them," said Barley.

"Can't. Buggers are here with me now."

"We need you, Reggie. Old Andy's dying."

"So are we all. All the bloody time."

As the tape was ending, Brock came through on a live call from the Russia House asking for Ned urgently. His watchers had reported that Barley had looked in on his Soho drinking club an hour ago, drunk five whiskies then moved on to the Noah's Arch at King's Cross.

"Noah's *Arch?* You mean Ark."

"Arch. It's an arch under the railway line. Noah's an eight-foot West Indian. Barley's joined the band."

"Alone?"

"So far."

"What sort of place?"

"Diner and boozer. Sixty tables, stage, brick walls, whores, the usual."

Brock thought all pretty girls were whores.

"How full?" said Ned.

"Two-thirds and rising."

"What's he playing?"

" 'Lover Man,' Duke Ellington."

"How many exits?"

"One."

"Put together one team of three men and park them at a table near the door. If he leaves, straddle him but don't touch him. Call Resources and tell them I want Ben Lugg to get his cab over to the Noah's Arch immediately and wait with his flag down. He'll know what to do." Lugg was the Service's tame cabby. "Are there any public phones in the club?"

"Two."

"Have them occupied till I get there. Has he seen you?"

"No."

"Don't let him. What's across the road?"

"A launderette."

"Is it open?"

"No."

"Wait for me in front of it." He swung round on Mary, who was still smiling. "There are two phones at the Noah's Arch, King's Cross," he said, speaking very slowly. "Have them faulted *now*. If the management's got its own line, have that faulted too. *Now*. I don't care how short-staffed the engineers are, fault them *now*. If there are phone boxes in the street outside, fault the lot. *Now*."

We abandoned the Service car and hailed a cab. Brock was waiting as ordered in the doorway of the launderette. Ben Lugg was parked at the curbside. Tickets were five ninety-five at the door. Ned led me past the watchers' table without a glance and shoved his way to the front.

Nobody was dancing. The band's front line was taking a break. Barley was standing centre stage in front of a gold chair, playing with the gentle backing of the double bass and drums. A brick arch made a sound chamber over him. He was still wearing his publishing suit and seemed to have forgotten to remove his jacket. Rotating coloured lights wandered over him, occasionally closing on his face which was running sweat. His expression was nerveless and remote. He was holding the long notes and I knew they were a requiem for Andy and for whoever else was occupying his beleaguered mind. A couple of girls had sat themselves in the band seats and were staring at him with unblinking eyes. A line of beers was also awaiting his attention. Beside him stood the immense Noah with his arms folded across his chest, listening with

his head down. The piece ended. Deliberately and tenderly, as if he were dressing a friend's wound, Barley
cleaned out his sax and laid it to rest in its case. Noah did
not allow applause but there was a scuffling noise while
everyone snapped their fingers and there were calls of
"encore" but Barley didn't bother with them. He drained
a couple of the beers, gave a wave round and picked his
way delicately through the crowd to the door. We went
after him and as we stepped into the street Ben Lugg
drew alongside with his flag up.

"Mo's," Barley ordered as he flopped into the back seat.
He had another flask of Scotch from somewhere and was
unscrewing the cap. "Hullo, Harry. How's love at a distance?"

"Great, thanks. I recommend it."

"Where on earth's Mo's?" Ned asked as he settled beside
him and I parked myself on the jump seat.

"Tufnell Park. Underneath the Falmouth Arms."

"Good sound?" Ned asked.

"The best."

But it was not Barley's false cheerfulness that alarmed
me. It was the remoteness of him, the deadness of his eyes,
the way he kept himself confined inside the fastness of his
English courtesy.

Mo was a blonde in her fifties and she spent a long time
kissing Barley before she would let us sit at her table.
Barley played blues and Mo wanted him to stay, I think for
the night, but Barley could stay nowhere long, so we went
to a music pizza house in Islington where he played another
solo and Ben Lugg came in with us to have a cup of tea and
a listen. Ben was a boxer in his day and still talked about
the fight game. From Islington we crossed the river to the
Elephant to hear a black group playing soul in a bus
garage. It was four-fifteen but Barley was showing no sign

of sleep; he preferred to sit with the group drinking spiked cocoa out of pint-sized china mugs. When we at last gentled him towards Ben's cab, the two girls from Noah's reappeared from nowhere and sat themselves either side of him in the back seat.

"Now then, you girls," said Ben while Ned and I waited on the pavement. "Hop it."

"Stay where you are, I should," Barley advised them.

"It's not your cab, dears. It's this bloke's"—indicating Ned—"now piss off, like good girls."

Barley swung his fist at Ben's head, which was adorned with a black Homburg hat. Ben blocked the blow like a man waving away a cobweb, and in the same movement drew Barley carefully out of the cab and handed him over to Ned, who took him equally carefully in an armlock.

Still in his Homburg, Ben disappeared into the back of the cab and came out with a girl in each hand.

"Why don't we all get a bit of fresh air?" Ned suggested while Ben gave the girls a tenner each to get lost.

"Good idea," said Barley.

So we crossed the river in slow procession, with Brock's watchers bringing up the rear and Ben Lugg's cab crawling along behind us. A dirty brown dawn was rising over dockland.

"Sorry about that," said Barley after a while. "No harm done, is there, Nedsky?"

"None that I know of," said Ned.

"Be alert," Barley advised. "Your Country Needs Lerts. Right, Nedsky? Just felt like making a spot of music," he explained to me. "You a musical man, Harry? Chum of mine used to play to his girl over the phone. Only piano, mind, not sax, but he said it did the trick. You could try it out on your missus."

"We're leaving for America tomorrow," said Ned.

Barley took the news conversationally. "Nice for you. Nice time of year. Country looking at its best, I'd say."

"It's nice for you too, actually," said Ned. "We thought we'd take you along."

"Casual, is it?" Barley asked. "Or better pack a dinner jacket to be on the safe side?"

12

We flew to the island in a small plane, arriving at dusk. The small plane belonged to a grand American corporation. Nobody said who owned the island. It was narrow and wooded, its middle sagged into the sea and its ends were propped up by conical peaks, so that my impression from the air was of a Bedouin tent collapsing into the Atlantic. I put it at two miles long. We saw the New England mansion and its grounds at one end, and the tiny white dock at the other, though I learned later that the mansion was called a summer house because nobody went there in winter. It had been built at the turn of the century by a rich Bostonian, in the days when such people called themselves rusticators. We felt the wings rock and smelt salt sea through the rattling cabin windows. We saw sunspots flicking over the waves like searchlights at a tattoo, and cormorants warring in the wind. We saw a light-beacon on the mainland to the west. We had been following the coast of Maine for fifty-eight minutes by my watch. The trees came up either side of us, the sky vanished, and suddenly we were bouncing and swinging along a grass avenue with Randy and his boys waiting with a jeep at the end of it. Randy was wholesome as only privileged Americans can be. He wore a wind-cheater and a tie. I felt I knew his mother.

"I'm your host here, gentlemen, for as long as you elect to stay, and welcome to our island." He shook Barley's hand first. They must have shown him photographs. "Mr. Brown, sir, this is a real honour. Ned? Harry?"

"Jolly nice of you," said Barley.

The pine trees, as we wound down the hillside, stood black against the sea. The boys followed in a second car.

"You gentlemen fly British? Mrs. Thatcher really got a hold of that line!" said Randy.

"Time she went down with the ship," Barley growled.

Randy laughed as if laughing were something he'd learned on the course. Brown was Barley's workname for the trip. Even his passport, which Ned carried, said that he was Brown.

We bumped across a causeway to the gatehouse. The gates opened and closed behind us. We were on our own headland. At the top of it stood the mansion lit by arc-lights hidden in the bushes. Lawns and wind-burned shrubs fell away from it to either side. The posts of a broken jetty stepped precariously out to sea. Randy parked the jeep and, taking Barley's luggage, led us along an illuminated path between hydrangeas to a boat-house. On our crossing to Boston, Barley had dozed and drunk and groaned at the film. On our small plane he had frowned at the New England landscape as if its beauty troubled him. But once we landed he seemed to re-enter his own world.

"Mr. Brown, sir, my orders are to accommodate you in the bridal suite," said Randy.

"Can't think of anywhere nicer, old boy," said Barley politely.

"You really *say* that, Mr. Brown: *old boy?*"

Randy ushered us through a stone-flagged hall to a captain's cabin. The style was designer homestead. A reproduction brass bed stood in a corner, a reproduction scrub-wood writing desk at the window. Doubtful ship's fittings hung on the walls. In the alcove where the all-American kitchen was, Barley identified the refrigerator, pulled it open and peered hopefully inside.

"Mr. Brown likes a bottle of Scotch in his room of an evening, Randy. If you've such a thing in your locker he'd be grateful."

The summer house was a museum of golden childhoods. In the porch, honey-coloured croquet mallets lay propped against a dusty goat-cart laden with lobster buoys gathered from the beach. There were smells of beeswax and leather. In the hall, portraits of young men and women in broad hats hung beside primitive paintings of whalers. We followed Randy up a wide polished staircase, Barley trailing behind us. On each landing, arched windows bordered with stained glass made jewelled gateways to the sea. We entered a corridor of blue bedrooms. The largest was reserved for Clive. From our balconies we could look down the gardens to the boat-house and across the sea to the mainland. The dusk was turning to dark.

In a white-raftered dining room, a Langley vestal managed not to look at us while she served Maine lobster and white wine.

While we ate, Randy explained the rules of the house. "No fraternising with the staff, please, gentlemen, just a good morning and hullo. Anything needs saying to them, best let me say it for you. The guards are for your convenience and safety, gentlemen, but we would like you to remain within the confines of the property. Please. Thank you."

Dinner and speeches over, Randy took Ned to the communications room and I walked Barley back to the boat-house. A fierce wind was ripping over the gardens. As we passed in and out of the light-cones Barley seemed to be smiling into it recklessly. Boys with handsets watched us pass.

"How about chess?" I asked him as we reached his door.

I wished I could see his face more clearly but I had lost it, just as I had lost his mood. I felt a pat on the arm as he wished me goodnight. His door opened and closed again, but not before I had glimpsed the spectral figure of a sentry standing not two yards from us in the darkness.

"A wise lawyer, a fine officer," Russell Sheriton advised me next morning in a reverential murmur, knowing I was neither, as his strong, soft palms enveloped my hand. "One of the true greats. Harry, how are you doing?"

Little had changed in him since his tour of duty in London: the rings beneath the eyes a little doggier, a little sadder, the blue suit a size or two larger, the same white-shirted paunch. The same mortician's aftershave, six years on, anointed the Agency's newest head of Soviet operations.

A group of his young men stood respectfully apart from him, clutching their travel bags and looking like stranded passengers at an airport. Clive and Bob were mounted either side of him like cohorts. Bob looked older by ten years. A chastened smile had replaced his old-world self-assurance. He greeted us too effusively, as if he had been warned to stay away from us.

The Island Conference, as it euphemistically became known, was about to begin.

There is an underlying pleasantness to the events of the next days, an air of good men going about their business, which I am in danger of forgetting as I recall the rest.

It is the hardest point for me to make, yet I owe it to Barley to try, for he never took against our hosts—he never blamed them for anything that happened to him, then or later. He could grumble about Americans in general, but no sooner had he met them individually than he spoke of them as decent fellows all. There was not a man among them he wouldn't have been happy to swap a drink with any evening at the local, if we'd had one. And of course Barley always saw the force of any argument that was directed against him, just as he was always vastly impressed by other people's industry.

And my goodness, were they industrious! If numbers, money and sheer endeavour alone could have produced intelligence, the Agency would have had it by the cartload—except that, alas, the human head is not a cart, and there is such a thing as unintelligence as well.

And how deeply they yearned to be loved!—and Barley warmed immediately to their need. Even as they tore into him, they needed to be loved. And by Barley, too! Just as to this day they need to be loved for all their staged putsches, destabilisations and wild adventures against The Enemy Out There.

Yet it was this very mystery of good hearts turned inside out that gave our week its underlying terror.

Years ago I talked to a man who had been flogged, an English mercenary who was doing us a few favours in Africa and needed paying off. What he remembered most was not the lash but the orange juice they gave him afterwards. He remembers being helped back to his hut, he remembers being laid face down on the straw. But what he really remembers is the glass of fresh orange juice that a warder set at his head, then crouched beside him, waiting patiently, till he was strong enough to drink some. Yet it was this same warder who had flogged him.

We too had our glasses of orange juice. And we had our decent warders, even if they were disguised behind headsets and a surface animosity that quickly melted before Barley's warmth. Within a day of our arrival, the same guards with whom we were forbidden to fraternise were tiptoeing at any odd moment in and out of Barley's boat-house, stealing a Coke or a Scotch from him before slipping back to their posts. They sensed he was that kind of man. And as Americans they were fascinated by his celebrity.

There was one old hand called Edgar, an ex-Marine, who gave him quite a run for his money at chess. Barley, I learned later, got his name and address out of him, against every known canon of the trade, so that they could play a contest by post "when all this is over."

Not only warders either. In Sheriton's chorus of young men, as in Sheriton himself, there was a moderation that was like an even beat of sanity against the hysterical highs and lows of those whom Sheriton himself dubbed collectively the egomaniacs.

But that, I suppose, is the tragedy of great nations. So much talent bursting to be used, so much goodness longing to come out. Yet all so miserably spoken for that sometimes we could scarcely believe it was America speaking to us at all.

But it was. The lash was real.

The interrogations took place in the billiards room. The wooden floor had been painted dark red for dancing and the billiards table replaced by a ring of chairs. But an ivory scorer and a row of initialled cue-cases still lined the wall, and the long downlight made a pool at the centre where Barley was obliged to sit. Ned fetched him from the boat-house.

"Mr. Brown, sir, I am proud to shake your hand and I have just decided that my name for the duration of our relationship is Haggarty," Sheriton declared. "I took one look at you, I felt Irish. Don't ask me why." He was leading Barley at a good pace across the room. "Most of all, I wish to congratulate you. You have all the virtues: memory, observation, British grit, saxophone."

This in one hypnotic flow while Barley grinned sheepishly and allowed himself to be settled in the place of honour.

But Ned already sat stiffly, arms folded across his chest, and Clive, though he was of the circle, had managed to paint himself out of the picture. He sat among Sheriton's young men and had pushed his chair back till they hid him.

Sheriton remained standing before Barley and was talking down at him, even when his words said he was addressing someone else. "Clive, would you permit me to bombard Mr. Brown with some impertinent questions? Ned, will you tell Mr. Brown, please, that he is in the United States of America and that if he doesn't care to answer anything he needn't, because his silence will be taken as clear evidence of his guilt?"

"Mr. Brown can look after himself," Barley said—but still grinning, still not quite believing in the tension.

"He can? That's great, Mr. Brown! Because for the next couple of days that's exactly what we hope you'll do!"

Sheriton went to the sideboard and poured himself some coffee and came back with it. His voice struck the calmer note of common sense. "Mr. Brown, we are buying a Picasso, okay? Everybody round this room is buying the same Picasso. Blue, saignant, well-done, what the fuck? There are about three people in the world who understand it. But when you get to the bottom line there's one question counts. Did Picasso paint it, or did J. P. Shmuck, Jr., of South Bend, Indiana, or Omsk, Russia, paste it together in his potato barn? Because remember this." He was prodding his own soft chest and holding his coffee cup in his spare hand. "No resale. This is not London. This is Washington. And for Washington, intelligence has to be useful, and that means it has to be used, not contemplated in Socratic detachment." He lowered his voice in reverent commiseration. "And you're the guy who's selling it to us, Mr. Brown. Like it or not, you personally are the nearest we shall get to the source until the day we persuade the man you call Goethe to change his ways and work to us direct. If we ever do. Doubtful. Very, very doubtful."

Sheriton took a turn and moved to the edge of the ring. "You are the linchpin, Mr. Brown. You are *the man.* You are *it.* But how much of *it,* are you? A little of it? Some of it? Or all of it? Do you write the script, act, produce and direct? Or are you the bit part you say you are, the innocent bystander we all have yet to meet?"

Sheriton sighed, as if it were a little hard on a man of his tender sensitivities. "Mr. Brown, do you have a regular girl these days, or are you screwing the backlist?"

Ned was halfway to his feet but Barley had already answered. Yet his voice was not abrasive, even now, it was not hostile. It was as if he were unwilling to disturb the good atmosphere all of us were enjoying.

"Well now, how about you, sunshine? Does Mrs. Haggarty oblige or are we reduced to the habits of our youth?"

Sheriton was not even interested.

"Mr. Brown, we are buying *your* Picasso, not mine. Washington doesn't like its assets cruising the singles bars. We have to play this very frank, very honest. No English reticence, no old-school persiflage. We've fallen for that horse manure before and we will never, *never* fall for it again."

This, I thought, for Bob, whose head was once again turned downward to his hands.

"Mr. Brown is not cruising the singles bars," Ned cut in hotly. "And it's not his material. It's Goethe's. I don't see that his private life has the least to do with it."

Keep your thoughts to yourself, Clive had told me. His eyes repeated the message to Ned now.

"Oh, Ned, come on now, come *on!*" Sheriton protested. "The way Washington is these days, you have to be married and born again before you can get on a fucking bus. What takes you to Russia every five minutes, Mr. Brown? Are you buying property there?"

Barley was grinning, but no longer so pleasantly. Sheriton was getting to him, which was exactly what Sheriton intended.

"As a matter of fact, old boy, it's a rôle I rather inherited. My old father always preferred the Soviet Union to the United States, and went to a lot of trouble publishing their books. He was a Fabian. A kind of New Dealer. If he'd been one of your people he'd have been blacklisted."

"He'd have been framed, fried and immortalised. I read his record. It's awful. Tell us more about him, Mr. Brown. What did he bequeath to you that you inherited?"

"What the devil's that to anyone?" said Ned.

He was right. The matter of Barley's eccentric father had been aired and dismissed as irrelevant by the twelfth floor long ago. But not apparently by the Agency. Or not any more.

"And in the thirties, as you no doubt also know then," Barley continued in his calmer tone, "he started up a Russian Book Club. It didn't last long but he had a go. And in the war when he could get the paper he'd publish pro-Soviet propaganda, most of it glorifying Stalin."

"And after the war what did he do then? Go help them build the Berlin Wall on weekends?"

"He had hopes, then he packed them in," Barley replied

after reflection. The contemplative part of him had regained the upper hand. "He could have forgiven the Russians most things, but not the Terror, not the camps and not the deportations. It broke his heart."

"Would his heart have been broken if the Sovs had used less muscular methods?"

"I don't expect so. I think he'd have died a happy man."

Sheriton wiped his palms on his handkerchief and like an over-weight Oliver Twist carried his coffee cup in both hands back to the refreshments table, where he unscrewed the thermos jug and peered mournfully inside before pouring himself a fresh cup.

"Acorns," he complained. "They gather acorns and press them and make coffee out of them. That's what they do out here." There was an empty chair beside Bob. Sheriton lowered himself into it and sighed. "Mr. Brown, will you let me spell it out for you a little? There is no longer the space in life to take each humble member of the human family on his merits, okay? So everybody who is anybody has a record. Here's yours. Your father was a Communist sympathiser, latterly disenchanted. In the eight years since he died you have made no fewer than six visits to the Soviet Union. You have sold the Sovs precisely four very lousy books from your own list and published precisely three of theirs. Two awful modern novels which didn't do a damn thing, a piece of crap about acupuncture which did eighteen copies in the trade edition. You're on the verge of bankruptcy yet we calculate your outlay for these trips at twelve thousand pounds and your revenue at nineteen hundred. You're divorced, freestyle and British public school. You drink like you're watering the desert single-handed and you pick jazz friends with records that make Benedict Arnold look like Shirley Temple. Seen from Washington, you're rampant. Seen from here, you're very nice, but how will I explain this to the next Congressional sub-committee of Bible-belt knuckle-draggers who take it into their heads to pillory Goethe's material because it endangers Fortress America?"

"Why does it do that?" said Barley.

I think we were all surprised by his calm. Sheriton certainly was. He was looking at Barley over his shoulder until then, affecting a slightly pitiful stance as he explained his dilemma. Now he straightened up, and faced Barley full on with an alert and quizzical directness.

"Pardon me, Mr. Brown?"

"Why does Goethe's material scare them? If the Russians can't shoot straight, Fortress America should be jumping for joy."

"Oh we are, Mr. Brown, we are. We're ecstatic. Never mind that the entire American military might is invested in the belief that the Soviet hardware is accurate as hell. Never mind that a perception of Soviet accuracy is *all* in this game. That with accuracy, you can sneak up on your enemy while he's out playing golf, take out his ICBMs unawares and leave him unable to respond in kind. Whereas without accuracy, you'd damn well better not try it, because that's when your enemy turns right around and takes out your twenty favourite towns. Never mind that zillions of taxpayers' dollars and whole junk-yards of political rhetoric have been lavished on the fond nightmare of a Soviet first strike and the American window of vulnerability. Never mind that even today the idea of Soviet supremacy in the matter of ICBMs is the main argument in favour of Star Wars, and the principal strategic fun-game at Washington cocktail parties." To my astonishment, Sheriton abruptly changed voices and broke into the accents of a Deep South hillbilly. "Time we blew those mothers apart before they do the same to us, Mr. Brown. This li'l ole planet just ain't big enough for two super-powers, Mr. Brown. Which one do *you* favour, Mr. Brown, when poo-ush comes to sheu-uve?"

Then he waited, while his pouchy face resumed its contemplation of life's many injustices.

"And I *believe* in Goethe," he went on in a startled voice. "I am on record as buying Goethe outright from the day he stepped out of the closet. Retail. Goethe for my money is a source whose time has come. And do you know what that tells me? It tells me that I also have to believe in Mr. Brown here and that Mr. Brown needs to be very candid with me or I'm dead." He cupped a paw reverently over his left breast. "I believe in Mr. Brown, I believe in Goethe, I believe in the material. And I'm scared shitless."

Some people change their minds, I was thinking. Some people have a change of heart. But it takes Russell Sheriton to announce that he has seen the light on the road to Damascus. Ned was staring at him in disbelief. Clive had chosen to admire the cue-cases. But Sheriton remained pouting at his coffee, reflecting on his bad luck. Of his young men, one had his chin in his hand while he studied the toe-cap of his Harvard shoe. Another was peering at the sea through the window as if the truth might rather lie out there.

But nobody was looking at Barley, nobody seemed to have the nerve. He was sitting still and looking young. We had told him a little, but nothing like this. Least of all had we told him that the Bluebird material had set the industrial-military factions at one another's throats and raised roars of outrage from some of Washington's most sleazy lobbies.

Old Palfrey spoke for the first time. As I did so, I had a sense of performing in the theatre of the absurd. It was as if the real world were slipping out from under our feet.

"What Haggarty is asking you is this," I said. "Will you voluntarily submit to questioning by the Americans so that they can take a view of the source once and for all? You can say no. It's your choice. Is that right, Clive?"

Clive didn't like me for that but he gave his reluctant assent before once more ducking below the horizon.

The faces round the ring had turned to Barley like flowers in the sun.

"What do you say?" I asked him.

For a while he said nothing. He stretched, he drew the back of his wrist across his mouth, he looked vaguely embarrassed. He shrugged. He looked towards Ned but could not find his eye, so he looked back at me, rather foolishly. What was he thinking, if anything? That to say "no" would be to cut him off from Goethe for good? From Katya? Had he even got that far in his mind? To this day I have no idea. He grinned, apparently in embarrassment.

"What do *you* think, Harry? In for a penny? What does my mouthpiece say?"

"It's more a question of what the client says," I answered glossily, smiling back at him.

"We'll never know if we don't give it a try, will we?"

"I suppose we never will," I said.

Which seems to be the nearest he ever came to saying, "I'll do it."

"Yale has these secret societies, you see, Harry," Bob was explaining to me. "Why, the place is shot through with them. If you've heard of Skull and Bones, Scroll and Key, you've still only heard the tip of the iceberg. And these societies, they emphasise the team. Harvard now— why, Harvard goes all the other way and puts its money on individual brilliance. So the Agency, when it's fishing for recruits in those waters, has a way of picking its team players from Yale and its high flyers from Harvard. I won't go so far as to say that every Harvard man is a

prima donna or every Yale man gives blind obedience to
the cause. But that's the broad tradition. Are you a Yale
man, Mr. Quinn?"

"West Point," said Quinn.

It was evening and the first delegation had just flown in.
We sat in the same room with the same red floor under the
same billiards light, waiting for Barley. Quinn sat at the
head and Todd and Larry sat to either side of him. Todd and
Larry were Quinn's people. They were clean-limbed and
pretty and, for a man of my age, ludicrously youthful.

"Quinn's from way up there," Sheriton had told us.
"Quinn talks to Defense, he talks to the corporations, he
talks to God."

"But who hires him?" Ned had asked.

Sheriton seemed genuinely puzzled by the question. He
smiled as if pardoning a solecism in a foreigner.

"Well now, Ned, I guess we all do," he said.

Quinn was six foot one, wide-shouldered and big-eared.
He wore his suit like body armour. There were no medals
on it, no badges of rank. His rank was in his stubborn jaw
and shaded empty eyes, and in the smile of enraged inferi-
ority that overcame him in the presence of civilians.

Ned entered first, then came Barley. Nobody stood up.
From his deliberately humble place in the centre of the
American row, Sheriton meekly made the introductions.

Quinn likes them plain, he had warned us. Tell your
man not to be too damn clever. Sheriton was following his
own advice.

It was right that Larry should open the questioning
because Larry was the outgoing one. Todd was virginal and
withdrawn, but Larry wore an overlarge wedding ring and
had the colourful tie and did the laughing for them both.

"Mr. Brown, sir, we have to think this thing through
from the point of view of your detractors," he explained

with elaborate insincerity. "In our business, there's unveri-
fied intelligence and there's verified intelligence. We'd like
to verify your intelligence. That's our job and that's what
we're paid for. Please don't take any hint of suspicion personally, Mr. Brown. Analysis is a science apart. We have to
respect its laws."

"We have to imagine it's an organised put-together,"
Todd blurted belligerently from Larry's side. *"Smoke."*

Amusement, until Larry laughingly explained to Barley
that he was not being offered a cigarette: "smoke" was the
trade word for deception.

"Mr. Brown, sir, whose idea was it, please, to go out to
Peredelkino that day after the book fair?" asked Larry.

"Mine, probably."

"Are you sure of that, sir?"

"We were drunk when we made the plan, but I'm pretty
sure it was me who proposed it."

"You drink quite a lot, don't you, Mr. Brown?" said
Larry.

Quinn's enormous hands had settled round a pencil as if
they proposed to strangle it.

"Fair amount."

"Does drinking make you forget things, sir?"

"Sometimes."

"And sometimes not. After all, we have long verbatims
between you and Goethe when you were both totally ine-
briated. Had you ever been to Peredelkino before that day,
sir?"

"Yes."

"Often?"

"Two or three times. Maybe four."

"Did you visit with friends out there?"

"I visited friends, yes," said Barley, instinctively bridling
at the American usage.

"Soviet friends?"

"Of course."

Larry paused long enough to make Soviet friends sound like a confession.

"Care to identify these friends, please, sir, names?"

Barley identified the friends. A writer. A woman poet. A literary bureaucrat. Larry wrote them down, moving his pencil slowly for effect. Smiling as he wrote, while Quinn's shadowed eyes continued glowering at Barley on fixed lines down the table.

"On the day of your trip then, Mr. Brown," Larry resumed, "on this Day One, as we may call it, did it not occur to you to press a few doorbells of your old acquaintance, see who was around, sir, say hullo?" Larry asked.

Barley didn't seem to know whether it had occurred to him or not. He shrugged and performed his habitual trick of pulling the back of his hand across his mouth, the perfect untruthful witness.

"Didn't want to saddle them with Jumbo, I suppose. Too many of us to cope with. Didn't occur to me really."

"Sure," said Larry.

Three excuses, I noted unhappily. Three where one would have been enough. I glanced at Ned and knew he was thinking the same. Sheriton was busy not thinking at all. Bob was busy being Sheriton's man. Todd was murmuring in Quinn's ear.

"So was it also *your* idea to visit Pasternak's tomb, Mr. Brown, sir?" Larry enquired, as if it were an idea anyone could be proud of having had.

"Grave," Barley corrected him testily. "Yes, it was. Shouldn't think the others knew it was there till I told them."

"And Pasternak's dacha too, I believe." Larry consulted his notes. " 'If the bastards hadn't pulled it down.' " He made *bastards* sound particularly dirty.

"That's right, his dacha too."

"But you didn't visit the Pasternak dacha, am I right? You didn't even establish whether the dacha still existed. The Pasternak dacha disappeared totally from the agenda."

"It was raining," Barley said.

"But you did have a car. And a driver, Mr. Brown. Even if he was malodorous."

Larry smiled again and opened his mouth just wide enough to let the point of his tongue caress his upper lip. Then he closed it and allowed a further pause for uncomfortable thoughts.

"So *you* mustered the party, Mr. Brown, and *you* identified the aims of the journey," Larry resumed in a tone of whimsical regret. "You rode point, you led the group up the hill to the tomb. Grave, forgive me. It was you personally, no one else, that Mr. Nezhdanov spoke to as you all came down the hill. He asked if you were American. You said, '*No, thank God, British.*' "

No laughter, not even a smile from Larry himself. Quinn looked as though he were concealing an abdominal wound with difficulty.

"It was you too, Mr. Brown, who quite by chance were able to quote the poet, speak out for the company during a discussion of his merits, and almost *by magic* to detach yourself from your companions and find yourself seated next to the man we call Goethe during lunch. 'Meet our distinguished writer Goethe.' Mr. Brown, we have a field report from London regarding the girl Magda from Penguin Books. We understand it was obtained unobtrusively, in non-suspicious social circumstances, by a non-American third party. Magda had the impression you wished to handle the Nezhdanov interview on your own. Can you explain that, please?"

Barley had disappeared again. Not from the room but

from my understanding. He had left suspicion to the dreamers and entered his own realms of reality. It was Ned not Barley who, unable to contain himself in the face of this admission of Agency skulduggery, produced the desired outburst.

"Well, she's not going to tell your informant she was panting to tuck her boyfriend into bed for the afternoon, is she?"

But again that single answer might have done the trick if Barley had not capped it with his own. "Maybe I *did* pack them off," he conceded in a remote but friendly enough voice. "After a week of book fair any reasonable soul has had enough of publishers to last him a lifetime."

Larry's smile had a doubtful slant. "Well hell," he said, and shook his pretty head before handing over his witness to Todd.

But not yet, because Quinn was speaking. Not to Barley, not to Sheriton, not even to Clive. Not really to anyone. But he was speaking all the same. The captive little mouth was writhing like a hooked eel.

"This man been fluttered?"

"Sir, we have protocol problems," Larry explained, with a glance at me.

At first I honestly did not understand. Larry had to explain.

"What we used to call a lie detector, sir. A polygraph. Known in the business as a flutterer. I don't think you have them over there."

"We do in certain cases," said Clive hospitably from beside me before I had a chance to answer. "Where you insist on it, we bend towards you and apply it. They're coming in."

Only then did the troubled, inward Todd take over. Todd was not prolix; he was at first bite not anything. But

I had met counsel like Todd before: men who make a crusade of their charmlessness and learn to use their verbal clumsiness as a bludgeon.

"Describe your relationship with Niki Landau, Mr. Brown."

"I haven't one," Barley said. "We've been pronounced strangers till Doomsday. I had to sign a paper saying I'd never speak to him. Ask Harry."

"Prior to that arrangement, please?"

"We had the odd jar together."

"The odd what?"

"Jar. Drink. Scotch. He's a nice chap."

"But not socially your class, surely? He did not go to Harrow and Cambridge, I take it?"

"What difference does that make?"

"Do you disapprove of the British social structure, Mr. Brown?"

"One of the crying pities of the modern world, it always seemed to me, old boy."

" 'He's a nice chap.' That means you like him?"

"He's an irritating little sod but I liked him, yes. Still do."

"You never did deals with him? Any deal?"

"He worked for other houses. I was my own boss. What deals could we do?"

"Ever *buy* anything from him?"

"Why should I?"

"I would like to know, please, what you and Niki Landau transacted together on the occasions when you were alone, often in Communist capital cities."

"He boasted about his conquests. He liked good music. Classical stuff."

"He ever discuss his *sister* with you? His *sister* still in Poland?"

"No."

"He ever express his resentment to you regarding the alleged ill-treatment of his father by the British authorities?"

"No."

"When was your last intimate conversation with Niki Landau, please?"

Barley finally allowed himself to betray a certain irritation. "You make us sound like a pair of queens," he complained.

Quinn's face did not flicker. Perhaps he had made that deduction already.

"The question was *when*, Mr. Brown," said Todd, in a tone suggesting that his patience was being stretched.

"Frankfurt, I suppose. Last year. Couple of belts in the Hessischer Hof."

"That the Frankfurt book fair?"

"One doesn't go to Frankfurt for fun, old boy."

"No dialogue with Landau since?"

"Don't recall one."

"Nothing at the London book fair this spring?"

Barley appeared to rack his brains. "Oh my hat. Stella. You're right."

"I beg your pardon?"

"Niki had spotted a girl who used to work for me. Stella. Decided he fancied her. He fancied everybody, really. By way of being a stoat. Wanted me to introduce them."

"And you did?"

"Tried to."

"You pimped for him. That the term?"

"That's right, old boy."

"What transpired, please?"

"I asked her for a drink at the Roebuck round the corner, six o'clock. Niki turned up, she didn't."

"So you were left alone with Landau? One on one?"

"That's right. One to one."

"What did you talk about?"

"Stella, I suppose. The weather. Might have been anything."

"Mr. Brown, do you have anything very much to do with past or former Soviet citizens in the United Kingdom?"

"Cultural Attaché, now and then. When he can be bothered to answer, which isn't often. If a Sov writer comes over and the Embassy gives a binge for him, I'll probably go along."

"We understand you like to play chess at a certain café in the area of Camden Town, London."

"So?"

"Is this not a café frequented by Russian exiles, Mr. Brown?"

Barley raised his voice but otherwise held steady. "So I know Leo. Leo likes to lead from weakness. I know Josef. Josef charges at anything that moves. I don't go to bed with them and I don't trade secrets with them."

"You do have a very selective memory, though, don't you, Mr. Brown? Considering the extraordinarily detailed accounts you give of other episodes and persons?"

Still Barley did not flare, which made his reply all the more devastating. For a moment, indeed, it seemed he would not even answer; the tolerance that was now so deeply seated in him seemed to tell him not to bother.

"I remember what's important to me, old boy. If I haven't got a dirty enough mind to match yours, that's your bloody business."

Todd coloured. And went on colouring. Larry's smile widened till it nearly split his face. Quinn had put on a sentry's scowl. Clive had not heard a thing.

But Ned was pink with pleasure and even Russell Sheriton, sunk in a crocodile's sleep, seemed to be remembering, among so many disappointments, something vaguely beautiful.

The same evening as I was taking a walk along the beach, I came on Barley and two of his guards, out of sight of the mansion, skimming flat stones to see who could get the most bounces.

"Got you! Got you!" he was shouting, leaning back and flinging his arms at the clouds.

"The mullahs are smelling heresy," Sheriton declared over dinner, regaling us with the latest state of play. Barley had pleaded a headache and asked for an omelette in the boat-house. "Most of these guys came to town on a Margin of Safety ticket. That means raise military spending and develop any new system however crazy that will bring peace and prosperity to the arms industry for the next fifty years. If they're not sleeping with the manufacturers, they're sure as hell eating with them. The Bluebird is telling them a very bad story."

"And if it's the truth?" I asked.

Sheriton sadly helped himself to another piece of pecan pie. "The truth? The Sovs can't play? They're cost-cutting at every corner and the buffoons in Moscow don't know one half of the bad news because the buffoons in the field cheat on them so they can earn their gold watches and free caviar? You think *that's* the truth?" He took a huge mouthful but it didn't alter the shape of his face. "You think that certain unpleasant *comparisons* aren't made?" He poured himself some coffee. "You know what's the worst thing for our democratically elected neanderthals? The total worst? It's the implications against *us*. Moribund on the Sov side means moribund *our* side. The mullahs hate that. So do the manufacturers." He shook his head in disapproval. "To hear the Sovs can't do solid fuel from shit, their rocket motors suck instead of blow? Their early-warning errors worse than ours? Their heavies can't even get out of the kennel? That our intelligence estimates are ludicrously exaggerated? The mullahs get terrible vibes from these things." He reflected on the inconstancy of mullahs. "How do you peddle the arms race when the only asshole you have to race against is yourself? Bluebird is life-threatening intelligence. A lot of highly paid favourite sons are in serious danger of having their rice-bowls broken, all on account of Bluebird. You want truth, that's it."

"So why stick your neck out?" I objected. "If it's not a popular ticket, why run on it?"

And suddenly I didn't know where to put myself.

It isn't often that old Palfrey stops a conversation, causes every head to swing round at him in amazement. And I certainly hadn't meant to this time. Yet Ned and Bob and Clive were staring at me as if I had taken leave of my senses, and Sheriton's young men—we had two of them, if I remember rightly—independently put down their forks and began independently wiping their fingers on their napkins.

Only Sheriton didn't seem to have heard. He had decided that a little cheese wouldn't hurt him after all. He had pulled the trolley to him, and was morosely examining the display. But none of us imagined that cheese was uppermost in his mind, and it was clear to me that he was buying time while he wondered whether to reply and how.

"Harry," he began carefully, addressing not me but a piece of Danish blue. "Harry, I swear to God. You have before you a man committed to peace and brotherly love. By this I mean that my primary ambition is to knock so much shit out of the Pentagon firebreathers that they will never again tell the President of the United States that twenty rabbits make a tiger, or that every fucking sardine fisherman three miles out of port is a Soviet nuclear submarine in drag. I also wish to hear no more bullshit about digging little holes in the ground and surviving nuclear war. I am a glasnostic, Harry. I have made certain discoveries about myself. I was born a glasnostic, my parents are old glasnostics from way back. For me, glasnosticism is a way of life. I want my children to live. Quote me and enjoy me."

"I didn't know you had any children," said Ned.

"Figurative," said Sheriton.

But Sheriton, if you pulled away the wrapping, was telling us a truthful version of his new self. Ned sensed it, I sensed it. And if Clive didn't, that was only because he had deliberately abbreviated his perceptions. It was a truth that lay not so much in his words, which as often as not were designed to obscure his feelings rather than express them, but in a new and irrepressible humility that had entered his manner since his cut-throat days in London. At the age of fifty, after quarter of a century as a Cold War brawler, Russell Sheriton, to use Walter's expression, was shaking his mid-life bars. It had never occurred to me that I could like him, but that evening I began to.

"Brady's bright," Sheriton warned us with a yawn as we turned in. "Brady can hear the grass growing."

And Brady, parse him how you would, was bright as boot-buttons.

You spotted it in his clever face and in the nerveless immobility of his courteous body. His ancient sports coat was older than he was, and as he came into the room you knew he took pleasure in being unspectacular. His young assistant wore a sports coat too and, like his master, had a classy dowdiness.

"Looks like you've done a fine thing, Barley," Brady said cheerfully in his Southern lilt, setting his briefcase on the table. "Anybody say thank you along the way? I'm Brady and I'm too damned old to fool around with funny names. This is Skelton. *Thank you*."

The billiards room again but without Quinn's table and upright chairs. Instead, we lounged gratefully in deep cushions. A storm was brewing. Randy's vestals had closed the shutters and put on lights. As the wind rose, the mansion began clinking like restless bottles on a shelf. Brady unpopped his briefcase, a gem from the days when they knew how to make them. Like the university professor he occasionally was, he wore a polka-dot blue tie.

"Barley, did I read somewhere, or am I dreaming, you once played sax in the great Ray Noble's band?"

"Beardless boy in those days, Brady."

"Wasn't Ray just the sweetest man you ever knew? Didn't he make the best sound ever?" Brady asked as only Southerners can.

"Ray was a prince." Barley hummed a few bars from "Cherokee."

"Too bad about his politics," Brady said, smiling. "We all tried to talk him out of that nonsense, but Ray would go his way. Ever play chess with him?"

"Yes I did, as a matter of fact."

"Who won?"

"Me, I think. Not sure. Yes, me."

Brady smiled. "So did I."

Skelton smiled too.

They talked London and which part of Hampstead Barley lived in: "Barley, I just love that area. Hampstead is my idea of civilization." They talked the bands Barley had played. "My God, don't tell me *he's* still around! At his age I wouldn't even buy unripe bananas!" They talked British politics and Brady just *had* to know what it was that Barley thought so wrong with Mrs. T.

Barley appeared to have to think about that, and at first came up with no suggestions. Perhaps he had caught Ned's warning eye.

"Hell, Barley, it's not *her* fault she hasn't any worthwhile opponents, is it?"

"Woman's a bloody Red," Barley growled, to the secret alarm of the British side.

Brady didn't laugh, just raised his eyebrows and waited, as we all did.

"Elective dictatorship," Barley continued, quietly gathering steam. "God bless the corporation and bugger the individual."

He seemed to be about to enlarge on this thesis, then to our relief changed his mind and let it rest.

Nevertheless it was a light enough beginning, and after ten minutes Barley must have been feeling pretty much at ease. Until in his languid way Brady came to "this present thing you've gotten yourself into, Barley," and proposed that Barley should go over the turf again in his own words, "but homing in on that historic eye-to-eye you two fellows had in Leningrad."

Barley did as Brady wanted, and though I like to think I listened quite as sharply as Brady, I heard nothing in Barley's narrative that seemed to me contradictory or particularly revealing beyond what was already on the record.

And at first blush Brady didn't seem to hear anything surprising either, for when Barley had finished, Brady gave him a reassuring smile and said, "Well now, thank you, Barley," in a voice of apparent approval. His slender fingers poked among his papers. "Worst thing about spying, I always say, is the hanging around. Must be like being a fighter pilot," he said, selecting a page and peering at it.

"One minute sitting home eating your chicken dinner, next minute frightening the hell out of yourself at eight hundred miles an hour. Then it's back home in time to wash the dishes." He had apparently found what he was looking for. "Is that how it felt to you, Barley, stuck out there in Muscovy without a prayer?"

"A bit."

"Hanging around waiting for Katya? Hanging around waiting for Goethe? You seemed to do quite some hanging around after you and Goethe had finished your little pow-wow, didn't you?"

Perching his spectacles on the tip of his nose, Brady was studying the paper before passing it to Skelton. I knew the pause was contrived but it scared me all the same, and I think it scared Ned for he glanced at Sheriton, then anxiously back to Barley. "According to our field reports, you and Goethe broke up around fourteen thirty-three Leningrad time. Seen the picture? Show it to him, Skelton."

All of us had seen it. All but Barley. It portrayed the two men in the gardens of the Smolny after they had said goodbye. Goethe had turned away. Barley's hands were still held out to him from their farewell embrace. The electronic timeprint in the top left corner said fourteen thirty-three and twenty seconds.

"Remember your last words to him?" Brady asked, with an air of sweet reminiscence.

"I said I'd publish him."

"Remember *his* last words to *you?*"

"He wanted to know whether he should look for another decent human being."

"One hell of a goodbye," Brady remarked comfortably while Barley continued to look at the photograph, and Brady and Skelton looked at Barley. "What did you do then, Barley?"

"Went back to the Europe. Handed over his stuff."

"What route did you take? Remember?"

"Same way I got there. Trolleybus into town, then walked a bit."

"Have to wait long for the trolleybus?" Brady asked, while his Southern accent became, to my ear at least, more of a mocking-bird than a regional digression.

"Not that I remember."

"How long?"

"Five minutes. Maybe longer."

I could not remember one occasion until now when Barley had pleaded an imperfect memory.

"Many people in line?"

"Not many. A few. I didn't count."

"The trolleybus runs every ten minutes. The ride into town takes another ten. The walk to the Europe, at your pace, ten. Our people have timed it all ways up. Ten's the outside. But according to Mr. and Mrs. Henziger, you didn't show up in their hotel room till fifteen fifty-five. That leaves us with quite a tidy hole, Barley. Like a hole in time. Mind telling me how we're going to fill it? I don't expect you went on a drinking spree, did you? You were carrying some pretty valuable merchandise. I'd have thought you wanted to unload it pretty quick."

Barley was becoming wary and Brady must have seen that he was, for his hospitable Southern smile was offering a new kind of encouragement, the kind that said "come clean."

As to Ned, he was sitting stock still with both feet flat on the ground, and his straight gaze was fixed on Barley's troubled face.

Only Clive and Sheriton seemed to have pledged themselves to display no emotions at all.

"What were you doing, Barley?" Brady said.

"I mooched," said Barley, not lying at all well.

"Carrying Goethe's notebook? The notebook he had *entrusted* to you with his life? Mooched? You picked a damned odd afternoon to mooch for fifty minutes, Barley. Where d'you go?"

"I wandered back along the river. Where we'd been. Paddy had told me to take my time. Not to rush back to the hotel but to go at a leisurely speed."

"That's true," Ned murmured. "Those were my instructions via Moscow station."

"For fifty minutes?" Brady persisted, ignoring Ned's intervention.

"I don't know how long it was. I wasn't looking at my watch. If you take time, you take time."

"And it didn't cross your mind that with a tape and a power-pack in your pants, and a notebook full of potentially priceless intelligence material in your carrier bag, the shortest distance between two points might *just* be a straight line?"

Barley was getting dangerously angry but the danger was to himself as Ned's expression, and I fear my own, could have warned him.

"Look, you're not listening, are you?" he said rudely. "I told you. Paddy told me to take time. They trained me that way in London, on our stupid little runs. Take time. Never hurry if you're carrying something. Better to make the conscious effort to go slowly."

Yet again, brave Ned did his best. "That's what he was taught," he said.

But he was watching Barley as he spoke.

Brady was also watching Barley. "So you mooched *away* from the trolleybus stop, *towards* the Communist Party Headquarters in the Smolny Institute——not to mention the Komsomol and a couple of other Party shrines——*carrying*

Goethe's notebook—in your bag? Why did you do that, Barley? Fellows in the field do some damned strange things, you don't have to tell *me* that, but this strikes me as plain suicidal."

"I was obeying orders, blast you, Brady! I was taking my time! How often do I have to tell you?"

But even as he flared it occurred to me that Barley was caught not so much in a lie as in a dilemma. There was too much honesty in his appeal, too much loneliness in his assailed eyes. And Brady to his credit seemed to understand this too, for he showed no sign of triumph at Barley's distress, preferring to befriend him rather than to goad.

"You see, Barley, a lot of people around here would attach a heap of suspicion to a gap like that," Brady said. "They would have a picture of you sitting in somebody's office or car while that somebody photographed Goethe's notebook or gave you orders. Did you do any of that? I guess now's the time to say so if you did. There's never going to be a good time, but this is about as good as we're likely to get."

"No."

"No, you won't tell?"

"That's not what happened."

"Well, something happened. Do you remember what was in your mind while you mooched?"

"Goethe. Publishing him. Bringing down the temple if he had to."

"What temple's that, exactly? Can we get away from the metaphysical a little?"

"Katya. The children. Taking them with him if he gets caught. I don't know who has the right to do that. I can't work it out."

"So you mooched and tried to work it out."

Maybe Barley did mooch, maybe he didn't. He had clammed up.

"Wouldn't it have been more normal to hand over the notebook first and try to work out the ethics afterwards? I'm surprised you were able to think clearly with that damn thing burning a hole in your carrier bag. I'm not suggesting we're any of us very logical in these situations, but even by the laws of *un*logic, I would feel you had put yourself in a damned uncomfortable situation. I think you did something. I think you think so too."

"I bought a hat."

"What kind of hat?"

"A fur hat. A woman's hat."

"Who for?"

"Miss Coad."

"That a girlfriend?"

"She's the housekeeper at the safe house in Knightsbridge," Ned cut in before Barley could reply.

"Where'd you buy it?"

"On the way between the tram stop and the hotel. I don't know where. A shop."

"That all?"

"Just a hat. One hat."

"How long did that take you?"

"I had to queue."

"How long did it take?"

"I don't know."

"What else did you do?"

"Nothing. I bought a hat."

"You're lying, Barley. Not gravely, but you are undoubtedly lying. What else did you do?"

"I phoned her."

"Miss Coad?"

"Katya."

"Where from?"

"A post office."

"Which one?"

Ned had put a hand across his forehead as if to shield his eyes from the sun. But the storm had taken hold, and outside the window both sea and sky were black.

"Don't know. Big place. Phone cabins under a sort of iron balcony."

"You called her at her office or at her home?"

"Office. It was office hours. Her office."

"Why don't we hear you do that on the body tapes?"

"I switched them off."

"What was the purpose of the call?"

"I wanted to make sure she was all right."

"How did you go about that?"

"I said hullo. She said hullo. I said I was in Leningrad, I'd met my contact, business was going along fine. Anyone listening would think I was talking about Henziger. Katya would know I was talking about Goethe."

"Makes pretty good sense to me," said Brady with a forgiving smile.

"I said, so goodbye again till the Moscow book fair and take care. She said she would. Take care, I mean. Goodbye."

"Anything else?"

"I told her to destroy the Jane Austens I'd given her. I said they were the wrong edition. I'd bring her some new ones."

"Why'd you do that?"

"The Jane Austens had questions for Goethe printed into the text. They were duplicates of the questions in the paperback he wouldn't take from me. In case she got to him and I didn't. They were a danger to her. Since he wasn't going to answer them anyway, I didn't want them lying around her house."

Nothing stirred in the room. Just the sea wind making the shutters crack, and puffing in the eaves.

"How long did your call with Katya take, Barley?"

"I don't know."

"How much money did it cost you?"

"I don't know. I paid at the desk. Two roubles something. I talked a lot about the book fair. So did she. I wanted to listen to her."

This time it was Brady's turn to keep quiet.

"I had a feeling that as long as I was talking, life was normal. She was all right."

Brady took a while, then against all our expectation closed the show: "So, small talk," he suggested as he began to pack his wares into his grandfather's attaché case.

"That's it," Barley agreed. "Small talk. Chit chat."

"As between acquaintances," Brady suggested, popping the case shut. "Thank you, Barley. I admire you."

We sat in the huge drawing room, Brady at our centre, Barley gone.

"Drop him down a hole, Clive," Brady advised, in a voice still steeped in courtesy. "He's flakey, he's a liability and he thinks too damn much. Bluebird is making waves you would not believe. The fiefdoms are up in arms, the Air generals are in spasm, Defense says he's a charter to give away the store, the Pentagon's accusing the Agency of promoting bogus goods. Your only hope is throw this man out and put in a professional, one of ours."

"Bluebird won't deal with a professional," said Ned, and I heard the fury simmering in his voice and knew it was about to boil over.

Skelton too had a suggestion. It was the first time I had heard him speak, and I had to crane my head to catch his cultured college voice.

"Fuck Bluebird," he said. "Bluebird's got no business calling the shots. He's a traitor and a guilt-driven crazy and who knows what else he is besides? Hold his feet to the fire. Tell him if he stops producing we'll sell him to his own people and the girl with him."

"If Goethe's a good boy, he gets the jackpot, I'll see to it," Brady promised. "A million's no problem. Ten million's better. If you frighten him enough and pay him enough, maybe the neanderthals will believe he's on the level. Russell, give my love. Clive, it's been a pleasure. Harry. Ned."

With Skelton at his side he started to move towards the door.

But Ned wasn't saying goodbye. He didn't raise his voice or bang the table but neither did he hold back the dark glow in his eyes or the edge of outrage in his words.

"Brady!"

"Something on your mind, Ned?"

"Bluebird won't be bullied. Not by them, not by you. Blackmail may look nice in the planning room but it won't play on the ground. Listen to the tapes if you don't believe me. Bluebird's in search of martyrdom. You don't threaten martyrs."

"So what do I do with them, Ned?"

"Did Barley lie to you?"

"Not unduly."

"He's straight. It's a straight case. Do you remember straight? While you're thinking round corners, Bluebird's going straight for goal. And he's chosen Barley as his running mate. Barley's the only chance we have."

"He's in love with the girl," said Brady. "He's complicated. He's a liability."

"He's in love with hundreds of girls. He proposes to

every girl he meets. That's who he is. It's not Barley who thinks too much. It's your people."

Brady was interested. Not in his own conviction, if he had any, but in Ned's.

"I've done all kinds," Ned went on. "So have you. Some cases are never straight, even when they're over. This one was straight from the first day, and if anyone is shoving it off course, we are."

I had never heard him speak with so much fervour. Neither had Sheriton, for he was transfixed, and perhaps it was for this reason that Clive felt obliged to interpose himself with a fanfare of civil servants' exit music. "Yes, well I think we have ample food for thought here, Brady. Russell, we must talk this through. Perhaps there's a middle way. I rather think there may be. Why don't we take soundings? Kick it around a little. Run over it one more time."

But nobody had left. Brady, for all Clive's ushering platitudes, had remained exactly where he was, and I observed a raw kindliness in his features that was like the real man beneath the mask.

"Nobody hired us for our brotherly love, Ned. That's just not what they put us spooks on earth for. We knew that when we signed up." He smiled. "Guess if plain decency was the name of the game, you'd be running the show in place of Deputy Clive here."

Clive was not pleased by this suggestion, but it did not prevent him from escorting Brady to his jeep.

For a moment I thought I was alone with Ned and Sheriton, until I saw Randy our host framed in the doorway, wearing an expression of star-struck disbelief. "Was that *the* Brady?" he asked breathlessly. "The Brady who did like *everything?*"

"It was Greta Garbo," Sheriton said. "Go away, Randy. Please."

*   *   *

I should play you more of that steadying music while Sheriton's young men take Barley back again, and walk with him on the beach and joke with him and produce the street map of Leningrad for him, and painstakingly log the very shop where Miss Coad's lynx hat was bought, and how he paid for it and where the receipt might have got to if there ever was one, and whether Barley had declared the hat to customs at Gatwick, and the very post office where he must have made his telephone call.

I should describe to you the spare hours Ned and I spent sitting around Barley's boat-house in the evenings, hunting for ways to shake him from his introspections and finding none.

For Barley's journey away from us—I felt it even then—had not flagged from the moment when he first agreed to be interrogated.

Then comes the morning following—a real sparkler, as they call it there; I think it must have been the Thursday—when the little plane from Logan airport brought us Merv and Stanley in time for their favourite breakfast of pancakes and bacon and pure maple syrup.

Randy's kitchen was well acquainted with their tastes.

They were bearish, kindly men of the soil, with pumice-stone faces and big hands, and they arrived looking like a vaudeville duo, wearing dark trilby hats and humping a salesman's suitcase which they kept close to them while they ate and later set down gingerly on the red-painted floor of the billiards room.

Their profession had made their faces dull, but they were the type our own Service likes best—straightforward, loyal, uncomplicated foot-soldiers with a job to do and kids to feed, who loved their country without making a to-do of it.

Merv's hair was cropped to a moleskin fuzz. Stanley had bandy legs and wore some sort of loyal badge.

"You can be Jesus Christ, Mr. Brown. You can be a fifteen-hundred-a-month typist," Sheriton had said as we stood around in Barley's boat-house in a state of shifty supplication. "It's voodoo, it's alchemy, it's the Ouija board, it's reading fucking tea-leaves. And if you don't go through with it, you're dead."

Clive spoke next. Clive could find reasons for anything. "If he's nothing to hide, why should he be bothered?" he said. "It's their version of the Official Secrets Act."

"What does Ned say?" Barley asked.

Not Nedsky any more. Ned.

There was a defeat in Ned's reply that I shall never forget, and in his eyes as well. Brady's interrogation of Barley had shaken his faith in himself, and even in his joe.

"It's your choice," he said lamely. And as if to himself, "A pretty disgusting one too, if you ask me."

Barley turned to me, exactly as he had done before, when I had first asked him whether he would submit to the American questioning. "Harry? What do I do?"

Why did he insist on my opinion? It was unfair. I expect I looked as uncomfortable as Ned. I certainly felt so, though I managed a light-hearted shrug. "Either humour them and go along with it or tell them to go to hell. It's up to you," I replied, much as I had on the first occasion.

Thus the eternal lawyer.

Barley's stillness again. His indecision slowly giving way to resignation. His separation from us as he stares through the window at the sea. "Well, let's hope they don't catch me telling the truth," he says.

He stands up and flips his wrists around, loosening his shoulders, while the rest of us like so many butlers confirm among ourselves by furtive looks and nods that our master has said yes.

At their work Merv and Stanley had the respectful nimbleness of executioners. Either they had brought the chair with them or the island kept one for them as a permanency, an upright wooden throne with a scalloped arm-rest on the left side. Merv set it handy for the electric socket while Stanley spoke to Barley like a grandfather.

"Mr. Brown, sir, this is not a situation where you should expect hostility. It is our wish you should not be troubled by a relationship with your examiners. The examiner is not adversarial, he is an impartial functionary, it's the machine that does the work. Kindly remove your jacket, no need to roll back your sleeves, sir, or unbutton your shirt, thank you. Very easy now, please, nice and relaxed."

Meanwhile with the greatest delicacy Merv slipped a doctor's blood-pressure cuff over Barley's left bicep until it was flush with the artery inside his elbow. Then he inflated the cuff until the dial said fifty milligrams while Stanley, with the devotion of a boxing second, fitted a one-inch-diameter rubberised tube round Barley's chest, careful to avoid the nipples so that it didn't chafe. Then Stanley fitted a second tube across Barley's abdomen while Merv slipped a double finger stall over the two central fingers of Barley's left hand, with an electrode inside it to pick up the sweat glands and the galvanised skin response and the changes of skin temperature over which the subject, provided he has a conscience, has no control—or so preach the converted, for I had had it all explained to me by Stanley beforehand, much as a concerned relative will inform himself in advance about the details of a loved one's surgical operation. Some polygraphers, Harry, they liked an extra band around the head like an encephalograph. Not Stanley. Some polygraphers, Harry, they liked to shout and rage at the subject. Not Stanley. Stanley reckoned that a lot of people got disturbed by an accusatory question, whether or not they were guilty.

"Mr. Brown, sir, we ask you to make no movement, fast or slow," Merv was saying. "If you do make such a movement we are liable to get a violent disturbance in the pattern which will necessitate further testing and a repetition of the questions. Thank you. First we like to establish a norm. By norm we mean a level of voice, a level of physical response—imagine a seismograph, you are the earth, you provide the disturbance. Thank you, sir. Answer to be 'yes' or 'no' only, please, always answer truthfully. We break off after every eight questions, that will be to loosen the pressure cuff in order to prevent discomfort. While the cuff is loosened we shall engage in normal conversation, but no humour, please, no undue excitation of any kind. Is your name Brown?"

"No."

"Do you have a different name from the one you are using?"

"Yes."

"Are you British born, Mr. Brown?"

"Yes."

"Did you fly here, Mr. Brown?"

"Yes."

"Did you come here by boat, Mr. Brown?"

"No."

"Have you truthfully answered my questions so far, Mr. Brown?"

"Yes."

"Do you intend to answer my questions truthfully throughout the remainder of this test, Mr. Brown?"

"Yes."

"Thank you," said Merv, with a gentle smile, while Stanley released the air from the cuff. "Those are what we call the non-relevant questions. Married?"

"Not at the moment."

"Kids?"

"Two, actually."

"Boys or girls?"

"One of each."

"Wise man. Alrighty?" He began pumping up the cuff again. "Now we go relevant. Easy now. That's nice. That's very nice."

In the open suitcase, the four spectral wire claws described their four mauve skylines across the graph paper while the four black needles nodded inside their dials. Merv had taken up a sheaf of questions and settled himself at a small table at Barley's side. Not even Russell Sheriton had been allowed to know the questions the faceless desk inquisitors in Langley had selected. No casual tampering by Barley's terrestrial co-habitants was to be allowed to breathe upon the mystic powers of the box.

Merv spoke tonelessly. Merv, I was sure, prided himself upon the impartiality of his voice. He was the March of Time. He was Houston Control.

"I am knowingly engaged in a conspiracy to supply untrue information to the intelligence services of Britain and the United States of America. Yes, I am so engaged. No, I am not so engaged."

"No."

"My motive is to promote peace between nations. Yes or no?"

"No."

"I am operating in collusion with Soviet Intelligence."

"No."

"I am proud of my mission on behalf of world Communism."

"No."

"I am operating in collusion with Niki Landau."

"No."

"Niki Landau is my lover."

"No."

"Was my lover."

"No."

"I am homosexual."

"No."

A break while Stanley once more eased the pressure. "How's it feeling, Mr. Brown? Not too much pain?"

"Never enough, old boy. I thrive on it."

But we didn't look at him in these breaks, I noticed. We looked at the floor or at our hands, or at the beckoning wind-bent trees outside the window. It was Stanley's turn. A cosier tone, but the same mechanical flatness.

"I am operating in collusion with the woman Katya Orlova and her lover."

"No."

"The man I call Goethe is known to me as a plant of Soviet Intelligence."

"No."

"The material he has passed to me has been prepared by Soviet Intelligence."

"No."

"I am the victim of sexual entrapment."

"No."

"I am being blackmailed."

"No."

"I am being coerced."

"Yes."

"By the Soviets?"

"No."

"I am being threatened with financial ruin if I do not collaborate with the Soviets."

"No."

Another break. Round Three. Merv's turn.

"I lied when I said I had telephoned Katya Orlova from Leningrad."

"No."

"From Leningrad I called my Soviet Control and told him of my discussion with Goethe."

"No."

"I am the lover of Katya Orlova."

"No."

"I have been the lover of Katya Orlova at some time."

"No."

"I am being blackmailed regarding my relationship with Katya Orlova."

"No."

"I have told the truth so far throughout this interview."

"Yes."

"I am an enemy of the United States of America."

"No."

"My aim is to undermine the military preparedness of the United States of America."

"Do you mind running that one by me again, old boy?"

"Hold it," said Merv, and Stanley at the suitcase held it, while Merv made a pencilled annotation on the graph paper. "Don't break the rhythm, please, Mr. Brown. We have people do that on purpose when they want to shake off a bad question."

Round Four and Stanley's turn again. The questions droned on and it was clear they would not stop until they had reached the nadir of their vulgarity. Barley's "no"s had acquired a deadened rhythm and a mocking passivity. He remained sitting exactly as they had placed him. I had never seen him so still for so long.

They broke again but Barley no longer relaxed between rounds. His stillness was becoming unbearable. His chin was lifted, his eyes were closed and he appeared to be smiling, God alone knew what about. Sometimes his "no" fell before the end of a sentence. Sometimes he waited so long that the two men paused and looked up, the one from his dials and the other from his papers, and they seemed to me to have the torturer's anxiety that they might have taxed their man too hard. Till the "no" finally fell again, neither louder nor quieter, a letter delayed in the mail.

Where does he get his stoicism from? No, no, to everything. Why does he sit there like a man preparing himself for the indignities of age, meekly mouthing "no"? What does this meekness mean, *no, yes, no, no,* till lunchtime, when they take him off the machine?

But in another part of my head, I think I knew the answer, even if I could not yet put it into words: his reality had moved elsewhere.

Spying is waiting.

We waited three days, and you may still count the hours in my grey hairs. We had split on lines of seniority: Sheriton to go with Bob and Clive to Langley; Ned to stay on the island with his joe, Palfrey to remain with them on standby, though what I was standing by for was a mystery to me. I hated the island by then and I suspected that Ned and Barley did too, though I could get no nearer to Ned than I could to Barley. He had become remote and for the time being humourless. Something had happened to his pride.

So we waited. And played distracted chess, seldom finishing a game. And listened to Randy talk about his yacht. And listened for the telephone. And to the screaming of the birds and the pulse of the sea.

It was a mad time, and the vagaries of the isolated place with its fuming skies and storms and patches of idyllic beauty made it madder. A "dungeon fog," as Randy called it, enveloped us and with it a mindless fear that we would never leave the island. The fog cleared but we were still there. The shared intimacy should have drawn us closer, but both men had withdrawn to their kingdoms, Ned to his room and Barley to the outdoors. With the rain whipping over the island like grapeshot I would peer through the streaming window and glimpse him pounding over the cliff in his oilskins, picking up his knees as if wrestling with uncomfortable shoes—or once, playing solitary cricket on the beach with Edgar the guard, a piece of driftwood and a tennis ball. In sunny spells he sported an old blue sailing cap which he had unearthed from a sea-chest in his room. He wore it with a grim face, eyes upon unconquered colonies. One day Edgar appeared with an old yellow dog he had unearthed from somewhere and they made it run back and forth between them. On another day there was a regatta off the mainland and a shoal of white yachts clustered in a ring like tiny teeth. Barley stood watching them interminably, seemingly delighted by the carnival, while Edgar stood off watching Barley.

He's thinking of his Hannah, I thought. He's waiting for life to provide him with the moment of choice. It did not occur to me till much later that some people do not take their decisions in quite that way.

My last image of the island has the convenient distortions of a dream. I had spoken to Clive only twice on the telephone, which for him was virtually a blackout. Once he wished to know "how your friends are bearing up" and I gathered from Ned that he had already asked him the same question. And once he needed to hear about the arrangements I had made for Barley's compensation, including the subsidies to his company, and whether the monies would come from our own funds or in the form of a supplementary estimate. I had a few notes with me and was able to enlighten him.

It is midday and *The New York Times* and *Washington Post* have just arrived on the table in the sunroom. I am stooped over them when I hear Randy yelling at the guards to get Ned to the telephone. As I turn, I see Ned himself entering from the garden side and striding across the hall to the communications room. I glance beyond him, up to the first-floor landing, and I see Barley, a motionless silhouette. There are some old bookcases up there, and that morning he has persuaded Randy to unlock them so that he can browse. It is the landing with the semi-circular window, the one that looks over the hydrangeas to the sea.

He is standing with his back turned and a book hanging from one long hand, and he is staring at the Atlantic. His feet are apart, his spare hand is raised, as it often is, to somewhere near his head, as if to fend off a blow. He must have heard everything that is going on——Randy's yell, then Ned's hasty footsteps across the hall, followed by the slam of the communications room door. The landing floor is tiled and footsteps come chiming up that stairwell like squeaky church bells. I can hear them now as Ned emerges from the communications room, goes a few steps and halts.

"Harry! Where's Barley?"

"Up here," says Barley quietly over the banister.

"They've given you the thumbs-up!" Ned shouts, jubilant as a schoolboy. "They apologise. I spoke to Bob, I spoke to Clive, I spoke to Haggarty. Goethe's is the most important stuff they've handled for years. Official. They'll go for him a hundred percent. There'll be no turning back any more. You've beaten their whole apparatus."

Ned was used to Barley's distracted ways by then, so he should not have been surprised when Barley gave no sign of having heard him. His gaze was still fixed on the Atlantic. Did he think he saw a small boat founder? Everybody does. Watch the Maine seas for long enough and you see them everywhere, a sail, a hull, now the speck of a survivor's head or hand, ducking under the sea's swell never to resurface. You must go on watching for a long time to know you are looking at ospreys and cormorants going about their hunting.

But Ned in his excitement manages to be wounded. It is one of those rare moments in him when the professional drops his guard and reveals the unfinished man inside.

"You're going back to Moscow, Barley! That's what you wanted, isn't it? To see it through?"

And Barley at last, concerned that he has hurt Ned's feelings: Barley half turning so that Ned can see his smile. "Yes, old boy. Of course it is. Just what I wanted."

Meanwhile it is my turn in the communications room. Randy is beckoning me in.

"Is that you, Palfrey?"

It is I.

"*Langley* are taking over the case," says Clive, as if this were the other part of the great news. "They're giving it a full-facility grading, Palfrey. That's the highest they go," he adds quellingly.

"Oh well. Congratulations," I say and, taking the telephone from my ear, stare at it in disbelief while Clive's drawl continues to ooze out of it like a tap nothing can turn off. "I want you to draw up a document of understanding immediately, Palfrey, and prepare a full-length agreement to cover the usual contingencies. We've got them eating out of our hand, so I expect you to be firm. Firm but fair. We're dealing with very realistic people, Palfrey. Hard-nosed."

More. Still more. And more yet. Langley to take over Barley's pension and resettlement as earnest of their total operational control. Langley to share equally in the running of the source, but to have a casting vote in the event of disagreement.

"They're preparing a full-scale shopping list, Palfrey, a grand slam. They're taking it to State, Defense, the Pentagon and the scientific bodies. All the biggest questions of the day will be canvassed and set down for the Bluebird to respond to. They know the risks but that isn't deterring them. Nothing ventured, nothing gained, they reason. That takes courage."

It is his Despatch Box voice. Clive has India at last. "In the great offence-defence stand-off, Palfrey, nothing exists in a vacuum," he explains loftily, quoting, I had no doubt, what somebody had said to him an hour before. "It's a matter of the finest tuning. Every question is as important as every answer. They know that. They see it clearly. They can pay the source no higher compliment than to prepare a no-holds-barred questionnaire for him. It's a thing they haven't done for many, many years. It breaks precedent. Recent precedent anyway."

"Does Ned know?" I ask when I can get a word in.

"He can't. None of us can. We're talking the highest strategic classifications."

"I meant, does he know you've made them a present of his joe?"

"I want you to come down to Langley immediately and thrash out terms with your opposite numbers here. Randy will arrange transport. Palfrey?"

"Does he know?" I repeat.

Clive makes one of his telephone silences, in which you are supposed to work out all the ways in which you are at fault.

"Ned will be brought up to date when he gets back to London, thank you. That will be quite soon enough. Until then I shall expect you to say nothing. The rôle of the Russia House will be respected. Sheriton values the link. It will even be enlarged in certain ways, perhaps permanently. Ned should be grateful."

The news was nowhere more joyfully received than in the British trade press. *Marriage with a Future*, trumpeted *Booknews* a few weeks later in its trailer for the Moscow book fair. *The long-rumoured engagement between Abercrombie & Blair of Norfolk Street, Strand, and Potomac Traders, Inc., of Boston, Mass., is ON! Seventeen-stone entrepreneur Jack Henziger has finally weighed in beside Barley Scott Blair of A. & B. with a new joint company titled Potomac & Blair, which plans an aggressive campaign in the fast-opening East Bloc markets. "This is a shop window on tomorrow," declares confident Henziger.*

Moscow Book Fair, here they come!

The newsflash was accompanied by a warming photograph of Barley and Jack Henziger shaking hands across a bowl of flowers. The photograph was taken by the Service photographer in the safe house in Knightsbridge. Flowers by Miss Coad.

I met Hannah the day following my return from the island and I assumed we would make love. She looked tall and golden, which is the way she always looks when I have not seen her for a while. A Thursday, so she was taking her fourteen-year-old son Giles to some spurious consultant behind Harley Street. I have never cared for Giles, probably because I know that he was conceived on the rebound, on one of the occasions when I had sent her back to Derek. We sat in our usual evil café drinking rancid tea, while she waited for him to come out, and smoked, a thing I hate. But I wanted her, and she knew it.

"Whereabouts in America?" she said, as if it mattered.

"I don't know. Some island full of ospreys and bad weather."

"I bet they weren't real ospreys."

"They were, actually. They're common there."

And I saw by the strain in her eyes that she wanted me too.

"Anyway, I've got to take Giles home," she said when we had sufficiently read each other's thoughts.

"Put him in a cab," I suggested.

But by then we were opposed to each other once more, and the moment was dead.

13

Katya collected Barley at ten o'clock on the Sunday morning from the forecourt of the immense Mezhdunarodnaya, which was where Henziger had insisted on staying. Westerners know it familiarly as "the Mezh." Both Wicklow and Henziger, seated in the hotel's preposterous Great Hall, contrived to witness their happy reunion and departure.

The day was fine and Barley had started waiting for her early, hovering in the forecourt amid the blind limousines that fetched and disgorged their Third World chieftains in a steady flow. Then at last her red Lada popped up among them like a burst of fun at a funeral, with Anna's white hand streaming out of the rear window like a handkerchief and Sergey, upright as a commissar beside her, clutching his fishing net.

It was important to Barley to notice the children first. He had thought about it and told himself it was what he would do, because nothing was insignificant any more, nothing could be left to chance. Only when he had waved enthusiastically at both of them therefore and pulled a face at Anna through the back window, did he allow himself to peer into the front, where Uncle Matvey sat squarely in the passenger seat, his polished brown face glowing like a chestnut and his sailor's eyes twinkling under the brim of his plaid cap. Sunshine or storm, Matvey had put on his best things to honour the great Englishman: his twill jacket, his best boots and bow tie. The crossed enamelled flags of the Revolution were pinned to his lapel. Matvey lowered his window and Barley reached through it, grasping his hand and yelling "Hullo, *hullo*" at him several times. Only then did he venture to look at Katya. And there was a kind of hiatus as if he had forgotten his lines or his cover story, or simply how beautiful she was, before he hoisted his smile.

But Katya showed no such reticence.

She leapt out of the car. She was wearing badly cut slacks and looked marvellous in them. She rushed round to him beaming with happiness and trust. She yelled "Barley!" And by the time she reached him she had flung her arms so wide that her body was cheerfully and unthinkingly open to him for his embrace——which as a good Russian girl she then decorously curtailed, standing back from him but still holding on to him, examining his face, his hair, his ancient outdoor gear, while she chatted away in a flood of spontaneous goodfellowship.

"It is so *good*, Barley. Really so good to see you!" she was exclaiming. "Welcome to the book fair, welcome to Moscow again. Matvey could not believe it, your phone call from London! 'The English were always our friends,' he said. 'They taught Peter how to sail, and if he had not known how to sail, we would not today have a navy.' He is speaking of Peter the Great, you see. Matvey lives only for Leningrad. Do you not admire Volodya's fine car? I am so grateful he has something he can love at last."

She released him and, like the happy idiot he by now was looking, Barley let out a cry of "God, nearly forgot!" He meant the carrier bags. He had propped them against the wall of the hotel beside the entrance, and by the time he reappeared with them, Matvey was trying to climb out of the car to make room for him in the front, but Barley would have none of it.

"No, no, no, *no!* I'll be absolutely fine with the twins! Bless you all the same, Matvey." Then he threaded and backed his long body into the rear seat as if he were parking an articulated lorry, while he handed round his parcels and the twins giggled at him in awe: this giant Westerner with so many joints and bits left over, who has brought us English chocolates, and Swiss crayons, and drawing books, one each, and the works of Beatrix Potter in English to share, and a beautiful new pipe for Uncle Matvey, which Katya is saying will make him happier than is possible to imagine, with a pouch of English tobacco to smoke in it.

And for Katya everything she could want for the rest of her life—lipsticks and a pullover and scents and a French silk scarf too beautiful to wear.

All this by the time Katya drove out of the Mezh forecourt and bumped on to a pockmarked highway, chatting about the book fair that was opening tomorrow, and steering inaccurately between the flooded craters.

They were heading roughly east. The friendly gold September sun hung ahead of them, making even the Moscow suburbs beautiful. They entered the sad flatland of Moscow's outskirts, with its proprietorless fields, desolate churches and fenced-in transformers. Clusters of old dachas were scattered like ancient beach-huts along the roadside, and their sculptured gables and boxed gardens reminded Barley as always of the English country railway stations of his youth. From his seat in the front, Matvey was poisoning them all with his new pipe and proclaiming his ecstasy through the clouds of smoke. But Katya was too busy pointing out the sights to pay him much attention.

"Over *that* hill lies the so-and-so metal foundry, Barley.

The shabby cement building to your left is a collective farm."

"Great!" said Barley. "Fascinating! What a day, though, wow!"

Anna had emptied her crayons on to her lap and discovered that if she licked the points they left wet trails of paint. Sergey was urging her to put them back in their tin and Barley was trying to keep the peace by drawing animals in her sketch book for her to colour, but Moscow road surfaces are not kind to artists.

"Not *green,* you chump," he told her. "Who ever saw a green cow? Katya, for heaven's sake, your daughter thinks cows are green."

"Oh Anna is *completely* impractical!" Katya cried laughing, and spoke quickly to Anna over her shoulder, who giggled up at Barley.

And all this had to be heard over Matvey's continued monologue and Anna's immense hilarity and Sergey's troubled interjections, not to mention the anguished thunder of the little engine, until nobody could hear anything except themselves. Suddenly they swung off the road, across a grass field and up a hill without even a track to guide them, to huge laughter from the children and from Katya too, while Matvey clutched his hat with one hand, and his pipe with the other.

"You see?" Katya was demanding of Barley above the din, as if she had proved a long-contested point between lovers. "In Russia we may go *exactly* where our fancy takes us, provided we do not trespass into the estates of our millionaires or government officials."

They crested the hill amid more riotous laughter and plunged into a grass dip, then rose again like a brave little boat on a wave to join a farm track that ran beside a stream. The stream entered a birch grove, the track raced beside it.

Katya somehow hauled the car to a halt, heaving on the handbrake as if she were slowing down a sledge. They were alone in Paradise with the stream to dam, and a bank to picnic on, and space to play *lapta* with Sergey's stick and ball from the boot of the car, which required everybody to stand in a ring, and one to bowl and one to bat.

Anna, it quickly became apparent, was frivolous about *lapta*. Her ambition was to get through it with as much laughter as possible, then settle down to lunch and flirt with Barley. But Sergey the soldier was a believer and Matvey the sailor was a zealot. While Katya spread out the picnic, she explained the mystical importance of *lapta* to the development of Western culture.

"Matvey assures me it is the origin of American baseball and your English cricket. He believes it was introduced to you by Russian immigrants. I am sure he also believes that it was invented by Peter the Great."

"If it's true, it's the death of the Empire," said Barley gravely.

Lying in the grass, Matvey is still talking volubly while he puffs at his new pipe. His generous blue eyes, receding into their glorious Leningrad past, are filled with a heroic light. But Katya hears him as if he were a radio that can't be switched off. She picks on the odd point and is deaf to all the rest. Marching across the grass, she climbs into the car and closes the door behind her, to reappear in shorts, carrying the picnic in an oilcloth bag, with sandwiches wrapped in newspaper. She has prepared cold *kotleti* and cold chicken and meat pies. She has salted cucumber and hard-boiled eggs. She has brought bottles of Zhiguli beer, Barley has brought Scotch, with which Matvey fervently toasts some absent monarch, perhaps Peter himself.

Sergey stands on the bank, raking the water with his net. His dream, Katya explains, is to catch a fish and cook it for everyone who depends on him. Anna is drawing. Ostentatiously, leaning away from her work so that others may admire it. She wishes to give Barley a portrait of herself to hang in his room in London.

"She is asking, are you married?" Katya says, yielding to her daughter's importuning.

"No, not at present, but I'm always available."

Anna asks another question but Katya blushes and rebukes her. His loyalist duties completed, Matvey is lying on his back with his cap over his eyes, rattling on about heaven knows what, except that, whatever it is, it is all delightful to him.

"Soon he will describe the siege of Leningrad," Katya calls with a fond smile.

A pause while she glances at Barley. She means, "Now we can talk."

The grey lorry was leaving, and high time too. Barley had been resenting it over her shoulder for quite a while, hoping it was friendly but wishing it would leave them alone. The side windows of its cab were dark with dust. Gratefully he saw it lumber to the road, then lumber out of sight and mind.

"Oh, he is *very* well," Katya was saying. "He wrote me a long letter and everything is excellent with him. He was ill but he is completely recovered, I am sure. He has many matters to discuss with you and he will make a special visit to Moscow during the fair in order to meet you and hear the progress concerning his book. He would like to see some prepared manuscript soon, perhaps only a page. My opinion is that this would be dangerous but he is so impatient. He wants proposals about the title, translations, even illustrations. I think he is becoming a typical dictatorial writer. He will confirm everything very soon and he will also find an apartment where you can meet. He wishes to make all the arrangements himself, can you imagine? I think you have been a very good influence for him."

She was searching in her handbag. A red car had parked on the other side of the birch grove but she seemed oblivious to everything but her own good spirits. "Personally I believe his work will soon be regarded as redundant. With the disarmament talks advancing so rapidly and the new atmosphere of international cooperation, all these terrible things will shortly belong to the past. Naturally the Americans are suspicious of us. Naturally we are suspicious of them. But when we have joined our forces, we can disarm completely and between us prevent all further trouble in the world." It was her didactic voice, brooking no argument.

"How do we prevent all further trouble in the world if we haven't got any arms to prevent it with?" Barley objected, and won a sharp look for his temerity.

"Barley, you are being Western and negative, I think," she retorted as she drew the envelope from her handbag. "It was you, not I, who told Yakov that we required an experiment in human nature."

No stamp, Barley noticed. No postmark. Just "Katya" in Cyrillic, in what looked like Goethe's handwriting, but who could tell? He felt a sudden sense of warning in his head and shoulders, like a poison, or an allergy coming on.

"What's he been recovering from?" he asked.

"Was he nervous when you met him in Leningrad?"

"We both were. It was the weather," Barley replied, still waiting for an answer. He was feeling slightly sick as well. Must be something he had eaten.

"It was because he was ill. Quite soon after your meeting he had a bad collapse and it was so sudden and severe that even his colleagues did not know where he had disappeared to. They had the worst suspicions. A trusted friend told me they feared he might be dead."

"I didn't know he had any trusted friends except you."

"He has appointed me his representative to you. He naturally has other friends for other things." She drew out the letter but did not give it to him.

"That's not quite what you told me before," he said feebly, while he continued to battle with his multiplying symptoms of mistrust.

She was unmoved by his objection. "Why should one tell everything at a first encounter? One has to protect oneself. It is normal."

"I suppose it is," he agreed.

Anna had finished her self-portrait and needed immediate recognition. It showed her picking flowers on a rooftop.

"Superb!" Barley cried. "Tell her I'll hang it above my fireplace, I know just the spot. There's a picture of Anthea skiing on one side, and Hal sailing on the other. Anna goes in the middle."

"She asks how old is Hal?" Katya said.

He really had to think. He had first to remember Hal's birth year, then the year it was now, then laboriously subtract the one from the other while he fought off the singing in his ears. "Ah well now, Hal's twenty-four. But I'm afraid he's made a rather foolish marriage."

Anna was disappointed. She stared reproachfully at them as Katya resumed their conversation.

"As soon as I heard he had disappeared I tried to contact him by all the usual means but I was not successful. I was extremely distressed." She passed him the letter at last, her eyes alight with pleasure and relief. As he took it from her, his hand closed distractedly over hers and she let it. "Then eight days ago, a week ago yesterday which was Saturday, just two days after you telephoned from London, Igor telephoned me at my house. 'I have some medicine for you. Let us have a coffee and I will give it to you.' Medicine is our code for a letter. He meant a letter from Yakov. I was amazed and very happy. It is even years since Yakov has sent me a letter. And such a letter!"

"Who's Igor?" Barley said, speaking rather loudly in order to defeat the uproar inside his head.

There were five pages of it, written on good white unobtainable writing paper, in an orderly, regular script. Barley had not imagined Goethe capable of such a conventional-looking document. She took back her hand, but gently.

"Igor is a friend of Yakov from Leningrad. They studied together."

"Great. What does he do now?"

She was annoyed by his question and impatient to have his good reaction to the letter, even if he could only judge it by appearance. "He is a scientist of some kind with one of the ministries. What does it matter how Igor is employed? Do you wish me to translate it to you or not?"

"What's his other name?"

She told him, and in the midst of his confusion he was exalted by her abrasiveness. We should have had years, he thought, not hours. We should have pulled each other's hair when we were kids. We should have done everything we never did, before it was too late. He held the letter for her and she knelt herself carelessly behind him on the grass, steadying herself with one hand on his shoulder, while with the other she pointed past him at the lines as she translated. He could feel her breasts brushing against his back. He could feel his world steady itself inside him, as the monstrosity of his first suspicions made way for a more analytical frame of mind.

"Here is the address, just a box number, that is normal," she said, her fingertip on the top right corner. "He is in a special hospital, perhaps in a special town. He wrote the letter in bed—you see how well he writes when he is sober?—he gave it to a friend who was on his way to Moscow. The friend gave it to Igor. It is normal. 'My darling Katya,'—that is not exactly how he begins, it is a different endearment, never mind. 'I have been struck down with some variety of hepatitis but illness is very instructive and I am alive.' That is so typical of him, to draw at once the moral lesson." She was pointing again. "This word makes the hepatitis worse. It is 'irritated.' "

"Aggravated," Barley said, quite calmly.

The hand on his shoulder gave him a reproving squeeze. "What does it matter what is the right word? You want me to fetch a dictionary? 'I have had a high temperature and much fantasy—' "

"Hallucination," Barley said.

"The word is *gallutsinatsiya*—" she began furiously.

"Okay, let's stick with that."

" '—but now I am recovered and in two days I shall go to a convalescent unit for a week by the sea.' He does not say which sea, why should he? 'I shall be able to do everything except drink vodka, but that is a bureaucratic limitation which as a good scientist I shall quickly ignore.' Is that not typical also? That after hepatitis he thinks immediately of vodka?"

"Absolutely," Barley agreed, smiling in order to please her—and perhaps to reassure himself.

The lines were dead straight as if written on a ruled page. There was not a single crossing out.

" 'If only all Russians could have hospitals like this, what a healthy nation we would soon become.' He is always the idealist, even when he is ill. 'The nurses are so beautiful and the doctors are young and handsome, it is more a house of love here than a house of sickness.' He says this to make me

jealous. But do you know something? It is most unusual
that he comments on anybody happy. Yakov is a tragedian.
He is even a sceptic. I think they have cured his bad moods
as well. 'Yesterday I took exercise for the first time but I
soon felt exhausted like a child. Afterwards I lay on the
verandah and got quite a suntan before sleeping like an
angel with nothing on my conscience except how badly I
have treated you, always exploiting you.' Now he writes
love talk, I shall not translate it."

"Does he always do that?"

She laughed. "I told you. It is not even normal that he
writes to me, and it is many months, I would say years,
since he spoke of our love, which is now entirely spiritual. I
think the illness has made him a little sentimental, so we
shall forgive him." She turned the page in his hand, and
again their hands met, but Barley's was as cold as winter,
and he was secretly surprised that she did not comment on
it. "Now we come to Mr. Barley. You. He is extremely cautious. He does not mention you by name. At least the illness has not affected his discretion. 'Please tell our good
friend that I shall try my best to see him during his visit,
provided that my recovery continues. He should bring his
materials and I shall try to do the same. I have to deliver a
lecture in Saratov that week'——Igor says that is the military
academy where Yakov always gives a lecture in September,
so many things one learns when somebody is ill——'and I
shall come to Moscow as soon as possible from there. If you
speak to him before I do, please tell him the following. Tell
him to bring all further questions because after this I do not
wish to answer any more questions for the grey men. Tell
him his list should be final and exhaustive.' "

Barley listened in silence to Goethe's further instructions, which were as emphatic as they had been in
Leningrad. And as he listened, the black clouds of his dis-

belief swept together to make a secret dread inside him, and his nausea returned.

A sample page of translation, but in print, please, print is so much more revealing, she was saying on Goethe's behalf.

I wish for an introduction by Professor Killian of Stockholm, please approach him as soon as possible, she was saying.

Have you had further reactions from your intelligentsia? Kindly advise me.

Publishing dates. Goethe had heard that autumn was the best market, but must one really wait a whole year? she asked, for her lover.

The title again. How about *The Biggest Lie in the World?*

The blurb, please let me see a draft. And please send an early copy to Dr. Dagmar Somebody at Stanford and Professor Herman Somebody-else at MIT. . . .

Barley painstakingly wrote all this down in his notebook on a page he headed BOOK FAIR.

"What's in the rest of the letter?" he asked.

She was returning it to its envelope. "I told you. It is love talk. He is at peace with himself and he wishes to resume a full relationship."

"With you."

A pause while her eyes considered him. "Barley, I think you are being a little childish."

"Lovers then?" Barley insisted. "Live happily ever after. Is that it?"

"In the past he was scared of the responsibility. Now he is not. That is what he writes and naturally it is out of the question. What has been has been. It cannot be restored."

"Then why does he write it?" said Barley stubbornly.

"I don't know."

"Do you believe him?"

She was about to be seriously angry with him when she caught something in his expression that was not envy and not hostility but an intense, almost frightening concern for her safety.

"Why should he spin you the talk just because he's ill? He doesn't usually fool around with people's emotions, does he? He prides himself on speaking the truth."

And still his penetrating gaze would not relinquish her or the letter.

"He is lonely," she replied protectively. "He is missing me so he exaggerates. It is normal. Barley, I think you are being a little bit—"

Either she could not find the word, or on second thought she decided against using it, so Barley supplied it for her. "Jealous," he said.

And he managed what he knew she was waiting for. He smiled. He composed a good, sincere smile of disinterested friendship and squeezed her hand and clambered to his feet. "He sounds fantastic," he said. "I'm very happy for him. For his recovery."

And he meant it. Every word. He could hear the true note of conviction in his voice as his eye moved quickly to the parked red car on the other side of the birch grove.

Then to the common delight Barley hurls himself upon the business of becoming a weekend father, a rôle for which his torn life has amply prepared him. Sergey wants him to try his hand at fishing. Anna wants to know why he hasn't brought his swim suit. Matvey has gone to sleep, smiling from the whisky and his memories. Katya stands in the water in her shorts. She looks more beautiful to him than ever before, and more remote. Even collecting rocks to build a dam, she is the most beautiful woman he has ever seen.

Yet nobody ever worked harder on a dam than Barley that afternoon, nobody had a clearer vision of how the waters should be held at bay. He rolls up his stupid grey flannel trousers and soaks himself to the crotch. He heaves sticks and stones till he is half dead, while Anna sits astride his shoulders directing operations. He pleases Sergey with his businesslike approach, and Katya with his romantic flourish. A white car has replaced the red one. A couple sit in it with the doors open, eating whatever they are eating, and at Barley's suggestion the children stand on the hilltop and wave to them, but the couple in the white car don't wave back.

Evening falls and a tang of autumn fires drifts through the dying birch leaves. Moscow is made of wood again, and burning. As they load the car, a pair of wild geese fly over them and they are the last two geese in the world.

On the journey back to the hotel, Anna sleeps on Barley's lap while Matvey chatters and Sergey frowns at the pages of *Squirrel Nutkin* as if they are the Party Manifesto.

"When do you speak to him again?" Barley asks.

"It is arranged," she says enigmatically.

"Did Igor arrange it?"

"Igor arranges nothing. Igor is the messenger."

"The new messenger," he corrects her.

"Igor is an old acquaintance and a new messenger. Why not?"

She glances at him and reads his intention. "You cannot come to the hospital, Barley. It is not safe for you."

"It's not exactly a holiday for you either," he replies.

She knows, he thought. She knows but does not know she knows. She has the symptoms, a part of her has made the diagnosis. But the rest of her refuses to admit there's anything amiss.

The Anglo-American situation room was no longer a shabby basement in Victoria but the radiant pent-house of a smart new baby skyscraper off Grosvenor Square. It styled itself the Inter-Allied Conciliation Group and was guarded by shifts of conciliatory American Marines in military plainclothes. An air of thrilled purpose pervaded it as the expanded team of trim young men and women flitted between clean desks, answered winking telephones, spoke to Langley on secure lines, passed papers, typed at silent keyboards or lounged in attitudes of eager relaxation before the rows of television monitors that had replaced the twin clocks of the old Russia House.

It was a deck on two levels, and Ned and Sheriton were seated side by side on the closed bridge, while below them on the other side of the sound-proofed glass their unequal crews went about their duties. Brock and Emma had one wall, Bob, Johnny and their cohorts the other wall and centre aisle. But all were travelling in the same direction. All wore the same obediently purposeful expressions, faced the same banks of screens that rolled and flickered like stock-exchange quotations as the automatic decodes came in.

"Truck's safely back in dock," said Sheriton as the screens abruptly cleared and flashed the codeword BLACK-JACK.

The truck itself was a miracle of penetration.

Our own truck! In Moscow! Us! In English it would have been a lorry but here it was a truck in deference to the American proprietorship. An enormous separate operation lay behind its acquisition and deployment. It was a Kamaz, dirty grey and very big, one of a fleet of trucks belonging to SOVTRANSAVTO, hence the acronym daubed in Roman letters across its filthy flank. It had been recruited, together with its driver, by the Agency's enormous Munich station during one of the truck's many forays to West Germany to collect luxury commodities for Moscow's privileged few with access to a special distribution store. Everything from

Western shoes to Western tampons to spare parts for Western cars had been shuttled back and forth inside the truck's bowels. As to the driver, he was one of the Long Distance Gunners, as these luckless creatures are known in the Soviet Union—State employees, miserably underpaid, with neither medical nor accident insurance to protect them against misfortune in the West, who even in deepest winter huddle stoically in the lee of their great charges, munching sausage before sharing another night's sleep in their comfortless cabins—but making for themselves in Russia, nevertheless, vast fortunes out of their opportunities in the West.

And now, for yet more immense rewards, this particular Long Distance Gunner had agreed to "lend" his truck to a "Western dealer" here in the very heart of Moscow. And this same dealer, who was one of Cy's own army of *toptuny*, lent it to Cy, who in turn stuffed inside it all kinds of ingeniously portable surveillance and audio equipment, which was then swept away again before the truck was returned through intermediaries to its legal driver.

Nothing of the sort had ever happened before. Our own mobile safe room, in Moscow!

Ned alone found the whole idea unsettling. The Long Distance Gunners worked in pairs, as Ned knew better than anyone. By KGB edict, these pairs were deliberately incompatible, and in many cases each man had a responsibility to report upon the other. But when Ned asked if he could read the operational file, it was denied him under the very laws of security he himself held dear.

But the most impressive piece of Langley's new armoury had still to be unveiled, and once again Ned had not been able to hold out against it. From now onwards, sound tapes in Moscow would be encrypted into random codes and transmitted in digital pulses in one-thousandth of the time that the tapes would take to run if you were listening to them in your drawing room. Yet when the pulses were restored to sound by the receiving station, the Langley wizards insisted, you could never tell the tapes had had such a rough time.

The word WAIT was forming in pretty pyramids. Spying is waiting.

The word SOUND replaced it. Spying is listening.

Ned and Sheriton put on their headsets as Clive and I slipped into the spare seats behind them and put on ours.

Katya sat pensively on her bed staring at the telephone, not wanting it to ring again.

Why do you give your name when none of us give names? she asked him in her mind.

Why do you give mine?

Is that Katya? How are you? This is Igor speaking. Just to tell you I have heard nothing more from him, okay?

Then why do you ring me to tell me nothing?

The usual time, okay? The usual place. No problem. Just like before.

Why do you repeat what needs no repetition, after I have already told you I will be at the hospital at the agreed time?

By then he'll know what his position is, he'll know which plane he can catch, everything. Then you don't have to worry, okay? How about your publisher? Did he show up all right?

"Igor, I do not know which publisher you are referring to."

And she rang off before he could say more.

I am being ungrateful, she told herself. When people are ill it is normal that old friends should rally. And if they promote themselves overnight from casual acquaintance to old friend, and take centre stage when for years they have hardly spoken to you, it is still a sign of loyalty and there is nothing sinister about it, even if only six months ago Yakov declared Igor to be unredeemable—"Igor has continued along the path I left behind," he had remarked after meeting him by chance in the street. "Igor asks too many questions."

Yet here was Igor acting as Yakov's closest friend and putting himself out for him in risky and invaluable ways. *"If you have a letter for Yakov, you have only to give it to me. I have established an excellent line of communication to the sanatorium. I know somebody who makes the journey almost every week,"* he had told her at their last meeting.

"The sanatorium?" she had cried excitedly. "Then where is he? Where is it located?"

But it was as if Igor had not yet thought of the answer to this question, for he had scowled and looked uncomfortable and pleaded State secrecy. Us, State secrecy, when we are flaunting the State's secrets!

I am being unfair to him, she thought. I am starting to see deception everywhere. In Igor, even in Barley.

Barley. She frowned. He had no business to criticise Yakov's declaration of affection. Who does he think he is, this Westerner with his attaching manners and cynical suspicions? Coming so close so quickly, playing God to Matvey and my children?

I shall never trust a man who was brought up without dogma, she told herself severely.

I can love a believer, I can love a heretic, but I cannot love an Englishman.

She switched on her little radio and ran through the shortwave bands, having first put in the earpiece so as not to disturb the twins. But as she listened to the different voices clamouring for her soul—Deutsche Welle, Voice of America, Radio Liberty, Voice of Israel, Voice of God knew whom, each one so cosy, so superior, so compelling—an angry confusion came over her. I'm a Russian! she wanted to shout back at them. Even in tragedy, I dream of a better world than yours!

But *what* tragedy?

The phone was ringing. She grabbed the receiver. But it was only Nasayan, an altered man these days, checking on tomorrow's plans.

"Listen, I am confirming privately that you really wish to be at the October stand tomorrow. Only we must begin early, you see. If you have to get your kids to school or something of that sort, I can easily instruct Yelizavyeta Alexeyevna to come instead of you. It is no hardship. You have only to tell me."

"You are very kind, Grigory Tigranovich, and I appreciate your call. But having spent most of last week helping to put up the exhibits, I should naturally like to be present at the official opening. Matvey can manage very well to see the children off to school."

Thoughtfully, she put the receiver back on its cradle. Nasayan, my God—why do we address each other like characters on the stage? Who do we think is listening to us who requires such rounded sentences? If I can talk to an English stranger as if he is my lover, why can't I talk normally to an Armenian who is my colleague?

He rang, and she knew at once that she had been waiting all this while for his call, because she was already smiling. Unlike Igor, he did not say his name or hers.

"Elope with me," he said.

"Tonight?"

"Horses are saddled, food for three days."

"But are you also sober enough to elope?"

"Amazingly, I am." A pause. "It's not for want of trying but nothing happened. Must be old age."

He sounded sober too. Sober and close.

"But what about the book fair? Are you going to desert it as you deserted the audio fair?"

"To hell with the book fair. We've got to do it before or never. Afterwards we'll be too tired. How are you?"

"Oh, I am furious with you. You have completely bewitched my family, and now they ask only when you will come back with more tobacco and crayons."

Another pause. He was not usually so thoughtful when he was joking.

"That's what I do. I bewitch people, then the moment they're under my spell I cease to feel anything for them."

"But that's terrible!" she cried, deeply shocked. "Barley, what are you telling me?"

"Just repeating the wisdom of an early wife, that's all. She said I had impulses but no feelings and I shouldn't wear a duffle coat in London. Anyone tells you something like that, you believe it for the rest of your life. I've never worn a duffle coat since."

"Barley, that woman—Barley, that was a totally cruel and irresponsible thing for her to say. I am sorry but she is completely wrong. She was provoked, I am sure. But she is wrong."

"She is, is she? So what do I feel? Enlighten me."

She broke out laughing, realising she had walked straight into his trap.

"Barley, you are a very, very bad man. I shall have nothing to do with you."

"Because I don't feel anything?"

"For one thing, you feel protection for people. We all noticed that today, and we were grateful."

"More."

"For another, you feel a sense of honour, I would say. You are decadent, naturally, because you are a Westerner.

That is normal. But you are redeemed because you feel honour."

"Are there any pies left over?"

"You mean you feel hunger too?"

"I want to come and eat them."

"Now?"

"Now."

"That is completely impossible! We are all in bed already and it's nearly midnight."

"Tomorrow."

"Barley, this is too ridiculous. We are about to begin the book fair, both of us have a dozen invitations."

"What time?"

A beautiful silence was settling between them.

"You may come at perhaps-half-past-seven."

"I may be early."

For a long while after that neither of them spoke. But the silence joined them more closely than words could have done. They became two heads on a single pillow, ear to ear. And when he rang off it was not his jokes and self-ironies that stayed with her but the tone of contented sincerity—she would almost say solemnity—that he had seemed unable to keep out of his voice.

He was singing.

Inside his head, and outside it too. In his heart and all over his body at last, Barley Blair was singing.

He was in his big grey bedroom at the gloomy Mezh on the eve of the Moscow book fair, and he was singing "Bless This House" in the recognisable manner of Mahalia Jackson while he pirouetted round the room with a glass of mineral water in his hand, glimpsing his reflection in the immense television screen that was the room's one glory.

Sober.

Hot sober.

Barley Blair.

Alone.

He had drunk nothing. In the safe truck for his debriefing, though he had sweated like a racehorse, nothing. Not even a glass of water while he had regaled Paddy and Cy with a sweetened, unworried version of his day.

At the French publishers' party at the Rossiya with Wicklow, where he had positively shone with confidence, nothing.

At the Swedes' party at the National with Henziger, where he had shone yet more brightly, he had grabbed a glass of Georgian *shampanskoye* in self-protection because Zapadny was so pointedly amazed he was not drinking. But he had contrived to leave it undrunk behind a flower vase. So still nothing.

And at the Doubleday party at the Ukraina with Henziger again, shining like the North Star by now, he had clutched a mineral water with a bit of lemon floating in it to look like gin and tonic.

So nothing. Not out of highmindedness. Not a reformed spirit, God forbid. He had not signed the Pledge or turned over a new leaf. It was merely that he wished nothing to mar the clear-headed, reasoned ecstasy that was collecting in him, this unfamiliar sense of being at dreadful risk and equal to it, of knowing that whatever was happening he had prepared himself for it, and that if nothing was happening he was ready for that too, because his preparedness was an all-round defence with a sacred absolute at its centre.

I have joined the tiny ranks of people who know what they will do first if the ship catches fire in the middle of the night, he thought; and what they will do last, or not do at all. He knew in ordered detail what he considered worth saving and what was unimportant to him. And what was to be shoved aside, stepped over and left for dead.

A great house-cleaning had taken place inside his mind, comprising quite humble details as well as grand themes. Because, as Barley had recently observed, it was in humble detail that grand themes wrought their havoc.

The clarity of his view amazed him. He peered round him, took a turn or two, sang a few bars. He came back to where he was, and knew that nothing had been left out.

Not the momentary inflection of uncertainty in her voice. Or the shadow of doubt flitting across the dark pools of her eyes.

Or Goethe's straight lines of handwriting instead of wild scrawls.

Or Goethe's cumbersome, untypical jokes about bureaucrats and vodka.

Or Goethe's guilty dirge about the way he had treated her, when for twenty years he had treated her however he had damn well felt like, including using her as a throwaway delivery-girl.

Or Goethe's callow promise to make it all up to her in the future, so long as she'll stay in the game for the time being, when it is an article of Goethe's faith that the future no longer interests him, that his whole obsession is with now. "There is only *now!*"

Yet from these spindrift theories that were most likely nothing more than theories, Barley's mind flew effortlessly to the grandest prize of his clarified perception: that in the context of Goethe's notion of what he was achieving, Goethe was *right,* and that for most of his life Goethe had stood on one side of a corrupt and anachronistic equation while Barley in his ignorance had stood on the other.

And that if Barley were ever called upon to choose, he would rather go Goethe's path than Ned's or anybody else's, because his presence would be urgently required in the extreme middle ground of which he had elected himself a citizen.

And that everything that had happened to Barley since Peredelkino had delivered the proof of this. The old isms were dead, the contest between Communism and capitalism had ended in a wet whimper. Its rhetoric had fled underground into the secret chambers of the grey men, who were still dancing away long after the music had ended.

As to his loyalty to his country, Barley saw it only as a question of which England he chose to serve. His last ties to the imperial fantasy were dead. The chauvinist drumbeat revolted him. He would rather be trampled by it than march with it. He knew a better England by far, and it was inside himself.

He lay on his bed, waiting for the fear to seize him, but it wouldn't. Instead, he found himself playing a kind of mental chess, because chess was about possibilities, and it seemed best to contemplate them in tranquillity rather than try and sort through them when the roof was falling in.

Because if Armageddon didn't strike, there was nothing lost. But if Armageddon did, there was much to save.

So Barley began to think. And Barley began to make his preparations with a cool head, exactly as Ned would have advised if Ned were still holding the reins.

He thought till early morning and dozed a bit and when he woke he went on thinking, and by the time he strode cheerfully into breakfast already looking round for the fun of the fair, there was an entire section of his head that was given over full time to thinking what the fools who do it describe as the unthinkable.

14

"Oh come, Ned," said Clive airily, still elated by the wizardry of the transmission. "The Bluebird's been ill before. Several times."

"I know," said Ned distractedly. "I know." And then, "Maybe I don't mind him being ill. Maybe I mind him writing."

Sheriton was listening chin in hand, as he had been listening to the tape. An affinity had grown up between Ned and Sheriton, as in an operation it must. They were handling the transfer of power as if it had happened long ago.

"But my dear man, that's what we all do when we're ill," Clive exclaimed in a misjudged demonstration of human understanding. "We *write* to the whole world!"

It had never occurred to me that Clive was capable of illness, or that he had friends to write to.

"I mind him handing chatty letters to mysterious intermediaries. And I mind him talking about trying to bring more materials for Barley," Ned said. "We know he never normally writes to her. We know he's security conscious to a fault. Suddenly he falls ill and writes her a gushing five-page love letter via Igor. Igor who? Igor when? How?"

"He should have photographed the letter," said Clive,

becoming disapproving of Barley. "Or taken it off her. One or the other."

Ned was too wrapped up in his thoughts to give this suggestion the contempt it deserved.

"How could he? She knows him as a publisher. That's all she knows him as."

"Unless the Bluebird told her otherwise," said Clive.

"He wouldn't," Ned retorted, and returned to his thoughts. "There was a car," he said. "A red car, then a white car. You saw the watch report. The red car went in first, then the white car took over."

"That is pure speculation. On a warm Sunday the whole of Moscow takes to the countryside," said Clive knowledgeably.

He waited for a reaction but in vain, so he returned to the subject of the letter. "*Katya* didn't have any problems with it," he objected. "*Katya*'s not crying foul. She's jumping for joy. If she didn't smell a rat, and Scott Blair didn't, why should *we*—sitting here in London, doing their worrying for them?"

"He asked for the shopping list," said Ned, as if still hearing distant music. "A final and exhaustive list of questions. Why did he do that?"

Sheriton had finally stirred himself. He was flagging Ned down with his big paw. "Ned, Ned, Ned, Ned. Okay? It's Day One again, so we're jumpy. Let's get some sleep."

He stood up. So did Clive and so did I. But Ned stayed doggedly rooted where he was, his hands clasped before him on his desk.

Sheriton spoke down at him. With affection, but with force as well. "Ned, just hear me, Ned, okay? Ned?"

"I'm not deaf."

"No, but you're tired. Ned, if we bad-mouth this operation one more time, it will never come back. We are going with *your* man, the one *you* brought to *us* in order to persuade *us*. We moved hell on earth to get this far. We have the source. We have the appropriation. We have the influential audience. We are within pissing distance of filling gaps in our knowledge that no smart machines, no electronic heavy breathers, no Pentagon Jesuits can get within light-years of. If we keep our nerve, and Barley does, and Bluebird does, we will have landed a bonanza beyond the dreams of the most accomplished fantasists. If we stay in there."

But Sheriton was speaking with too much conviction, and his face, for all its pudgy inscrutability, was betraying an almost desperate need.

"Ned?"

"Hearing you, Russell. Loud and clear."

"Ned, this is no longer a cottage industry, for Christ's sake. We played big, now we have to think big. You don't get bigger than this. Presidential findings are not an invitation to doubt our own good judgment. They are in the way of being orders. Ned, I really think you should get some sleep."

"I don't think I'm tired," said Ned.

"I think you are. I think everyone will say you are. I think they may even say Ned was very bullish for the Bluebird until the big bad American wolf came and took his joe away. Then all of a sudden the Bluebird was a very iffy source. I think people are going to say you are tired as hell."

I glanced at Clive.

Clive too was looking down at Ned, but with eyes so cold they chilled my blood. Time to move you on, they were saying. Time to measure you for the drop.

Both Henziger and Wicklow kept a close eye on Barley that day and reported on him frequently, Henziger to Cy by whatever means they used, Wicklow by way of an irregular to Paddy. Both attested to his high spirits and relaxed manner, and in differing language to his sovereignty. Both described how at breakfast he had enchanted a couple of Finnish publishers who were showing interest in the Trans-Siberian Railway project.

"They were eating out of his hand," said Wicklow, providing an unconsciously comic picture of breakfast, but at the Mezh anything is possible.

Both recorded with amusement Barley's determination to act as their tour-guide when they reached the permanent exhibition site, and how he obliged their taxi to drop them at the end of the grand avenue so that, as first-time pilgrims from the world of capitalism, they could make their approach on foot.

So the two professional spies strolled contentedly through the wet autumn sunshine with their jackets over their shoulders and their joe between them while Barley favoured them with his own eccentric guided tour, extolling the "late Essoldo period" architecture and the "Revolutionary Rococo" gardens. He doted on the immense ornamental pool and its golden fish spewing jets of water at the rumps of fifteen naked golden nymphs, one for each of the Socialist republics. He insisted that they dawdle at the white-pillared love bowers and temples of delight—whose portals, he pointed out, were dedicated not to Venus or Bacchus but to the fallen goddesses of the Soviet economy—coal, steel and even atomic energy, Jack!

"He was witty but he wasn't high," reported Henziger, who had already taken fondly to Barley in Leningrad. "He was damn funny."

And from the temples Barley marched them up the triumphal avenue itself, the Emperor's Ride, perhaps a mile of it and heaven knows how broad, celebrating the

People's Achievements in the Service of Mankind. And surely no vision of popular power was ever portrayed in such despotic images! he proclaimed. Surely no Revolution had so perfectly enshrined everything it had set out to raze to the ground! But by then Barley had to bellow his irreverences over the din of the loudspeakers, which all day long pour floods of self-congratulatory messages on to the heads of the benighted crowds below.

Finally they arrived, as they had to, at the two pavilions housing the fair.

"On my right, the publishers of Peace, Progress and Goodwill," Barley announced, playing the referee at a prize fight. "On my left, the distributors of Fascist imperialist lies, the pornographers, the poisoners of truth. Seconds out. Time."

They showed their passes and walked in.

The exhibition stand of the newly inaugurated and geographically confusing house of Potomac & Blair was a small but satisfactory sensation of the fair. Langley's lovingly created P. & B. symbol shone resplendent between the dowdier displays of Astral Press and Purbeck Media. The stand's interior design, characterised by its Langley architects as tough but tasty, was a model of instant impact. The exhibits—many of them, as is customary, dummies of books still to enter the production line—were prepared with all the attention to detail that intelligence services traditionally bestow on fakes. The only good coffee at the fair was to be found bubbling on an ingenious machine in the rear cubby-hole. There was Langley's own Mary Lou to serve it. For the favoured, there was even a forbidden shot of Scotch to help them through the day—forbidden, indeed, by special edict of the organisers, for even literary reconstruction must be the work of sober men.

And Mary Lou, with her homespun schoolgirl smile and billowing tweed skirt, made a natural product of the nicer side of Madison Avenue. Nobody need ever have guessed she had a little of Langley's thread woven into her as well.

Neither was Wicklow, with his polished patter, anything other than the quick-eyed, upwardly mobile young publisher they make these days.

As to honest Jack Henziger, he was the archetype of the settled buccaneer of the modern American book trade. He made no secret of his antecedents. Pipelines in the Middle East, humanity in Afghanistan, red beans to opium-growing hill-tribes in Thailand—Henziger had sold them all, whatever he had sold for Langley on the side. But publishing was where his heart was, and he was here to prove it.

And Barley seemed to revel in the artifice. He threw himself upon it as if it were his long-lost reality, shaking hands, receiving the congratulations of his competitors and colleagues, until around eleven he professed himself restless and proposed to Wicklow that they tour the lines and take comfort to the troops.

So off they set, Barley bearing in his arms a bunch of white envelopes of which he occasionally pressed one into a chosen hand as he yelled and greeted his way along the packed alleys of visitors and exhibitors.

"Well blow me over, if it isn't Barley Bloody Blair," a familiar voice declared from the centre of a multi-lingual display of illustrated Bibles. "Remember me, do you? Third from the left in the mink jock-strap, back in your humble days?"

"Spikey. They let you in again," said Barley with pleasure, and handed him his envelope.

"It's when they won't let me *out* I'm worried. This your dad, then?"

Barley presented the distinguished editor Wicklow, and Spikey Morgan bestowed a priestly blessing on him with his nicotine-stained fingers.

They pressed on, only to stumble into Dan Zeppelin a few yards later. Dan did not talk. Dan conspired in a gravedigger's murmur, leaning across his counter at you over folded arms.

"So I mean tell me something, Barley. Okay? Are we pioneers or are we the fucking Mitford sisters? So a few unbooks are books this year. So a few unwriters have been sprung from jail. Big deal. I walk into my own stand this morning, there's some asshole pulling the books out of my shelves. 'May I ask you a personal question?' I says. 'What the fuck are you doing with my books?' 'Orders,' he says. Six books, he confiscated. Mary G. Ambleside on fucking *Black Consciousness in Song and Word*. Orders! I mean who are we, Barley? Who are they? What do they think they're restructuring when there was never a structure in the first place? How do you restructure a corpse?"

At Lupus Books they were directed to the coffee room, where our Chairman Himself, the newly knighted Sir Peter Oliphant, had upstaged even the Russians by reserving a table. A handwritten notice in both languages confirmed his triumph. The flags of Britain and the Soviet Union warned off doubters. Flanked by interpreters and high officials, Sir Peter was dilating on the many advantages to the Soviet Union of subsidising his generous purchases from them.

"It's the Earl!" cried Barley, handing him an envelope. "Where's the coronet?"

With scarcely a flicker of his dusty eyelids, the great man continued his dissertation.

At the Israeli stand an armed peace reigned. The dark queue was orderly but mute. Boys in jeans and sneakers lounged against the walls. Lev Abramovitz was white-haired and overpoweringly tall. He had served in the Irish Guards.

"Lev. How's Zion?"

"Maybe we're winning, maybe the happy ending's at the beginning," Lev said, pocketing Barley's envelope.

And from Israel, with Barley leading at a canter, they pounded across the concourse to the Pavilion of Peace, Progress and Goodwill, where there could no longer be any doubt of the massive historical upheaval taking place, or of who was doing the heaving.

Every banner and spare bit of wall screamed the new Gospel. In every stand of every Republic, the thoughts and writings of the no-longer-new prophet, with his birthmark turned away and his jaw raised, were blazoned alongside those of his colourless master, Lenin. At the VAAP stand, where Barley and Wicklow shook a few hands and Barley shed a batch of envelopes, the Leader's speeches, wrapped in shiny covers and rendered into English, French, Spanish and German, made a totally resistible appeal.

"How much more of this shit do we have to take, Barley?" a blond-faced Moscow publisher demanded *sotto voce* as they went by. "When will they start repressing us again to make us comfortable? If our past's a lie, who's to say our future isn't a lie as well?"

They continued along the stands, Barley leading, Barley greeting, Wicklow following.

"Joseph! Great to see you! Envelope for you. Don't eat it all at once."

"Barley! My friend! Didn't they give you my message? Maybe I didn't leave one."

"Yuri. Great to see you! Envelope for you."

"Come and drink tonight, Barley! Sasha is coming, so is Rosa. Rudi's giving a concert tomorrow so he wants to stay sober. You heard about the writers they let out? Listen, it's Potemkin village stuff. They let them out, they give them a few meals, show them off and throw them back inside till next year. Come over here, I got to sell you a couple of books to annoy Zapadny."

At first Wicklow didn't even realise they had arrived at their destination. He saw a Roman standard hung with faded flags and some gold lettering stitched on red bunting. He heard Barley's yell of "Katya, where are you?" But nothing said who owned the stand and probably that was a part of the display that hadn't arrived. He saw the usual unreadable books on agricultural development in the Ukraine and the traditional dances of Georgia expiring on their shelves under the strain of previous exhibitions. He saw the usual half-dozen broad-hipped women standing around as if they were waiting for a train, and a small unshaven fellow clutching his cigarette in front of him like a conjuror's wand, scowling at Barley's nametag.

Nasayan, Wicklow read in return. *Grigory Tigranovich. Senior Editor, October Publishing.*

"You are looking for Miss Katya Orlova, I think," Nasayan told Barley in English, holding his cigarette still higher as if to get a clearer look at his visitor.

"I'll say I am!" Barley replied with enthusiasm, and a couple of the women smiled.

A grin of frightful courtesy had spread over Nasayan's face. With a flourish of his cigarette he stepped aside and Wicklow recognised Katya's back as she talked with two very small Asians whom he took to be Burmese. Then an instinct made her turn and she caught sight of Barley first, then Wicklow, then Barley again, while a splendid smile lit her face.

"Katya. Fantastic," said Barley shyly. "How are the kids? Did they survive?"

"Oh thank you, they are *very* well!"

Watched by Nasayan and his ladies, as well as by Wicklow, Barley handed her an invitation to the great *glasnost* launch party of Potomac & Blair.

"Oh by the way, I may skip some of the gay whirl tonight," Barley remarked as they made their way back to the Western pavilion. "You and Jack and Mary Lou will have to manage on your own. I'm dining with a beautiful lady."

"Anyone we know?" Wicklow asked. They both laughed. It was a sunny day.

She's fine, Barley was thinking contentedly. If something is happening, it hasn't happened to her yet.

How much did we know or guess, any of us, of Barley's feelings towards Katya? In a case so scrupulously monitored and controlled, the question of love received diffident handling.

Wicklow, diligently promiscuous in his own life, was puritanical about Barley's. Perhaps as a young man he still could not take seriously the notion of an older passion. For Wicklow, Barley was merely infatuated, which he usually was anyway. People of Barley's age were not in love.

Henziger, who was Barley's rough contemporary, regarded sex as an unsung perquisite of the secret life, and took it for granted that a square-shooter like Barley would put his body where his duty lay. Like Wicklow, but for different reasons, he found nothing exceptional in Barley's tender feelings towards Katya and operationally much to recommend them.

And in London? There was no sharply defined view. On the island Brady had said a mouthful, but Brady's assault had been repelled and his advice with it.

And Ned? Ned had a wife as soldierly as himself, and as unawakened. Name me a joe in a bad country, Ned liked to say with a rueful smile, who doesn't fall for a pretty face if she's on his side against the world.

And Bob, Sheriton and Johnny seem all to have assumed in different ways that Barley's private life and his appetites generally were of such a seedy complexity that they were best left out of the equation.

And Palfrey, what was old Palfrey thinking—hurrying up to Grosvenor Square in any spare hour and, if he couldn't make it, phoning Ned to ask, "How's the boy?"

Palfrey was thinking about Hannah. The Hannah he had loved and loves still, as only cowards may. The Hannah whose smile was once as warm and deep as Katya's. "You're a good man, Palfrey," she will say with terrible control on the days when she is trying to understand me. "You'll find a way. Maybe not now, but one day." And oh, Palfrey found a way all right! He pleaded the code—that convenient code that rules that a young solicitor caught in adultery is *ipso facto* excluded from doing anything about it. He pleaded children, hers and his—so many people involved, dear. He pleaded marriage, curse him—how will they cope without us, dear, Derek can't even boil an egg? He pleaded the partnership and, when it was dissolved, he buried his stupid head in the sands of the secret desert where no Hannah would ever be able to threaten him again. And he had the nerve to plead duty—the Service would never forgive me a mucky divorce, dear—not its legal adviser, it couldn't.

I was thinking about the island too. About the evening Barley and I had stood on the shingle beach watching the fog-bank roll at us across the grey Atlantic.

"They'd never get her out, would they?" Barley said. "Not if things went wrong."

I didn't answer and I don't think he expected me to, but he was right. She was a thoroughbred Soviet national and she had committed a thoroughbred Soviet crime. She was nowhere near the swappable class.

"Anyway, she'd never leave her children," he said, confirming his own doubts.

We watched the sea for a while, his eyes on Katya and mine on Hannah, who would never leave her children either, but wanted to bring them with her, and make an honest man out of a career-obsessed Chancery Lane hack who was sleeping with his senior partner's wife.

"Raymond Chandler!" Uncle Matvey yelled from his chair, over the clamour of neighbours' television sets.

"Terrific," Barley said.

"Agatha Christie!"

"Ah well, now, *Agatha*."

"Dashiell Hammett! Dorothy Sayers. Josephine Tey."

Barley sat on the sofa where Katya had settled him. The living room was tiny. The span of his arms could have bridged the width of it. A glass-fronted corner cupboard contained the family treasures. Katya had already given him the tour of them. The pottery mugs, made by a friend for her wedding, their medallions portraying the bride and groom. The Leningrad coffee set, no longer complete, that had belonged to the lady in the wood frame on the top shelf. The old sepia photograph of a Tolstoyan couple, the man bearded and resolute in his stiff white collar, the girl in her bonnet and fur muff.

"Matvey is passionate for English detective fiction," Katya called from the kitchen, where she had last things to do.

"Me too," said Barley untruthfully.

"He is telling you it was not permitted under the Czars. They would never have tolerated such an intrusion into their police system. Do you have vodka? No more for Matvey, please. You must take some food. We are not alcoholics like you Westerners. We do not drink without food."

Under the pretext of examining her books, Barley stepped into the tiny passage from where he could see her. Jack London, Hemingway and Joyce, Dreiser and John Fowles. Heine, Remarque and Rilke. The twins were in the bathroom chattering. He gazed at her through the open kitchen door. Her gestures had an air of timeless and deliberate delay. She's become a Russian again, he thought. When something works, she's grateful. When it doesn't work, it's life. From the living room Matvey was still talking gaily.

"What's he saying now?" Barley asked.

"He is talking about the siege."

"I love you."

"The Leningraders refused to accept that they were beaten." She was preparing cakes of liver on rice. Her hands kept still a moment, then went on with their work. "Shostakovich still composed even if the ink froze in his inkwell. The novelists went on writing, you could hear a chapter of a new novel any week if you knew the right cellars to go to."

"I love you," he repeated. "All my failures were preparations for meeting you. Fact."

She breathed out sharply and they both fell silent, for a moment deaf to Matvey's jolly monologue from the sitting room, and to the sounds of splashing from the bathroom.

"What else does he say?" Barley asked.

"Barley——" she protested.

"Please. Tell me what he's saying."

"The Germans were four kilometres from the city on the south side. They covered the outskirts with machine-gun fire and shelled the centre with artillery." She handed him mats and knives and forks and followed him to the living room. "Two hundred and fifty grams of bread for a labourer, others a hundred and twenty-five. Are you really so fascinated by Matvey, or are you pretending to be polite as usual?"

"It's a mature, unselfish, absolute, thrilling love. I've never known anything approaching it. I thought you ought to be the first to know."

Matvey was beaming at Barley in unalloyed adoration. His new English pipe gleamed from his top pocket. Katya held Barley's stare, started to laugh, shook her head, not in negation but in daze. The twins rushed in wearing their dressing-gowns and swung on Barley's hands. Katya settled them to the table and put Matvey at the head. Barley sat beside her while she poured the cabbage soup. With a prodigious show of power Sergey drew the cork from a wine bottle, but Katya would take no more than a half-glass and Matvey was permitted only vodka. Anna broke ranks to fetch a drawing she had made after a visit to the Timiryasev Academy: horses, a real wheatfield, plants that could survive the snow. Matvey was telling the story of the old man in the machine shop across the road, and once more Barley insisted on hearing every word.

"There was an old man Matvey knew, a friend of my father's," Katya said. "He had a machine shop. When he was too weak from starving, he strapped himself to the machinery so that he would not collapse. That was how Matvey and my father found him when he died. Strapped to the machinery. Frozen. Matvey also wishes you to know that he personally wore a luminous badge on his coat"— Matvey was proudly indicating the very spot on his pullover—"so that he didn't knock into his friends in the dark when they took their buckets to fetch water from the Neva. So. That is enough of Leningrad," she said firmly.

"You have been very generous, Barley, as usual. I hope you are sincere."

"I have never been so sincere in my life."

Barley was in the middle of toasting Matvey's health when the telephone started ringing beside the sofa. Katya sprang up but Sergey was ahead of her. He put the receiver to his ear and listened, then replaced it on the cradle with a shake of his head.

"So many misconnections," Katya said, and handed round plates for the liver cakes.

There was only her room. There was only her bed.

The children had gone to their bed and Barley could hear them snuffling in their sleep. Matvey lay on his army bedroll in the living room, already dreaming of Leningrad. Katya sat upright and Barley sat beside her, holding her hand while he watched her face against the uncurtained window.

"I love Matvey too," he said.

She nodded and gave a short laugh. He put his knuckles against her cheek and discovered that she was weeping.

"Just not in the same way I love you," he explained. "I love children, uncles, dogs, cats and musicians. The entire Ark is my personal responsibility. But I love you so profoundly that I am ashamed to be articulate. I would be very grateful if we could find a way to silence me. I look at you, and I am absolutely sick of the sound of my own voice. Do you want that in writing?"

Then with both hands he turned her face to him and kissed her. Then he guided her towards the top of the bed and laid her head on the pillow and kissed her again, first her lips and then her closed wet eyelashes while her arms gathered round his back and drew him down on her. Then she pushed him away from her and sprang up and went to look at the twins before returning. Then she slid the bolt inside her bedroom door.

"If the children come, you must dress and we must be very serious," she warned, kissing him.

"Can I tell them I love you?"

"If you do I shall not interpret."

"Can I tell you?"

"If you are very quiet."

"Will you interpret?"

She was no longer weeping. She was no longer smiling. Black, logical eyes, searching like his own. An embrace without reservation, no hidden codicils, no small print to the agreement.

I had never known Ned in such a mood. He had become the Jonah of his own operation and his rugged stoicism only made his forebodings harder to take. In the situation room he sat at his desk as if he were presiding at a court martial, while Sheriton lolled beside him like an intelligent Teddy bear. And when as a reckless throw I walked him down the road to the Connaught where I occasionally took Hannah and, to ease the waiting, fed him a magical dinner in the Grill, I still could not penetrate the mask of his forbearance.

For the truth was, his pessimism was seriously affecting my own spirits. I was on a see-saw. Clive and Sheriton were up one end, Ned was the dead weight at the other. And since I am no great decision-taker, it was all the more disturbing to watch a man normally so incisive resign himself to ostracism.

"You're seeing ghosts, Ned," I told him with little of Sheriton's conviction. "You've gone far beyond whatever anybody else is thinking. All right, it's not your case any more. That doesn't mean it's a shipwreck. And your credibility is—well, ebbing."

"A final and exhaustive list," Ned said again, as if the phrase had been dinned into him by a hypnotist. "Why final? Why exhaustive? Answer me that. When Barley saw him in Leningrad, he wouldn't even accept our preliminary questionnaire. He threw it back in Barley's face. Now he's asking for the whole shopping list in one go. *Asking* for it. The *final* list. The grand slam. We're to get it all together for the weekend. After that the Bluebird will answer no more questions from the grey men. 'This is your last chance,' he's saying. *Why?*"

"Look at it the other way round a minute," I urged him in a desperate murmur when the wine waiter had brought us a second decanter of priceless claret. "All right. The Bluebird has been turned by the Sovs. He's bad. The Sovs are running him. So why do they close it down? Why not sit back and play us along? *You* wouldn't close it down if you were in their shoes. You wouldn't hand us an ultimatum, create deadlines. Would you?"

His reply put paid to the best and most expensive meal I had ever given a fellow officer in my life.

"I might have to," he said. "If I were Russian."

"Why?"

His words were the more chilling for being spoken with a leaden dispassion. "Because he might not be presentable any more. He might not be able to speak. Or pick up his knife and fork. Or pour salt on his grouse. He might have made a couple of voluntary statements about his charming mistress in Moscow who had no idea, but really no idea, what she was doing. He might have—"

We walked back to Grosvenor Square. Barley had left Katya's apartment at midnight Moscow time and returned to the Mezh, where Henziger had sat up for him in the lobby, ostensibly reading a manuscript.

Barley was in high spirits but had nothing new to

report. Just a family evening, he had told Henziger, but good fun all the same. And the hospital visit still on, he added.

The whole of the next day nothing. A space. Spying is waiting. Spying is worrying yourself sick while you watch Ned sink into a decline. Spying is taking Hannah to your flat in Pimlico between the hours of four and six when she is supposed to be having a German lesson, God knows why. Spying is imitating love, and making sure she's home in time to give dear Derek his dinner.

15

They went in Volodya's car. She had borrowed it for the evening. He was to wait for her outside the Aeroport metro station at nine, and at nine exactly the Lada pulled up precariously beside him.

"You should not have insisted," she said.

The tower blocks glowed above them but in the streets there was already the menacing atmosphere of curfew. Scents of autumn filled the damp night air. A half-moon, draped in shrouds of mist, hung ahead of them. Occasionally their hands brushed. Occasionally their hands grasped each other in a strong embrace. Barley was watching the wing mirror. It was smashed and some of the bits were missing but he could see enough in it to watch the cars that followed without overtaking. Katya turned left but still nothing passed them.

She wasn't speaking so he wasn't either. He wondered how they learned it, where is safe to speak, where isn't. At school? From older girls as they grew up? Or was it your earnest little lecture from the family doctor somewhere round the second year of puberty? "It's time you learned that cars and walls have ears just like people . . ."

They were bumping over a pitted sliproad into a half-finished carpark.

"Imagine you are a doctor," she warned him as they faced each other across the roof of the car. "You must look very strict."

"I'm a doctor," Barley said. Neither of them was joking.

They picked their way between a maze of moonlit puddles to a pathway covered in asbestos awning, leading to double doors and an empty reception desk. He caught the first alarming smells of hospital: disinfectant, floor polish, surgical spirit. At a crisp pace she marched him across a circular hallway of mottled concrete, down a linoleum corridor and past a marble counter staffed by sullen women. A clock said ten-twenty-five. Making a consciously officious gesture, Barley compared it with his watch. The clock was ten minutes slow. The next corridor was lined with figures slumped on kitchen chairs.

The waiting room was a gloomy catacomb supported by immense pillars with a raised platform at one end. At the other, swing doors gave on to the lavatories. Somebody had rigged a temporary light to show the way. By its pale light, Barley could make out empty coat-racks behind a wooden counter, parked stretcher trolleys and, fixed to the nearest pillar, an ancient telephone. A bench stood against the wall. Katya sat on it, so Barley sat beside her.

"He tries always to be punctual. Sometimes he is delayed by the connection," she said.

"Can I speak to him?"

"He would be angry."

"Why?"

"If they hear English on a long-distance line they will immediately pay attention. It is normal."

A man in a head-bandage looking like a blinded soldier from the front wandered into the women's lavatory as two women emerged. They grabbed hold of him and redirected him. Katya unclipped her handbag and took out a note-book and a pen.

He will try at ten-forty, she had said. At ten-forty he will attempt the first connection. He will not speak for long, she had said. To speak too long even between safe tele-phones is unwise.

She stood up and walked to the telephone, ducking like a regular under the cloakroom counter.

Will he tell her he loves her? Barley wondered—"I love you enough to risk your life for me"? Will he give her the love talk he gave her in his letter? Or will he tell her that she is an acceptable price for the cleansing of his uneasy soul?

She was standing sideways to him, gazing keenly through the swing doors. Had she seen something bad? Had she heard something? Or was her mind already far away with Yakov?

It's how she stands when she's waiting for him, he thought—like someone who is prepared to wait all day.

The telephone rang hoarsely, as if it had dust in its lar-ynx. A sixth sense had already guided her towards it, so it had no chance to give a second squawk before she had it in her hand. Barley was only a few feet from her but he was hard put to it to hear her voice above the background clat-ter of the hospital. She had turned away from him, pre-sumably for privacy, and she had boxed her hand over her free ear so that she could hear her lover in the earpiece. Barley could just hear her say "yes" and "yes" again, sub-missively.

Leave her alone! he thought angrily. I've told you before and I'm going to tell you again at the weekend. Leave her alone, keep her out of this. Deal with the grey men or me!

The notebook lay open on a rickety shelf attached to the pillar, the pen on top of it, but she hadn't touched either

one of them. *Yes. Yes. Yes.* I did that on the island. *Yes. Yes. Yes.*
He saw her shoulders rise into her neck and stay there and
her back stretch as if she had taken a deep breath or
enjoyed some pleasurable moment within herself. Her
elbow rose from her side to cram the earpiece more firmly
into her head. *Yes. Yes.* What about *no* for once? *No, I won't
lie down for you!*

Her spare hand had found the pillar and he could see the
fingers part and brace themselves as the tips pressed into
the dark plaster. He saw the back of her hand whiten as it
stiffened, but it didn't move, and suddenly her hand
alarmed him. It had found a climbing hold and was cling-
ing to it for grim life. She was on the cliff face and the fin-
gerhold was all she had between her lover and the abyss.

She turned, the receiver still pressed to her ear, and he
saw her face. Who was she? What had she become? For the
first time since he had met her she was without expression,
and the telephone jammed against her temple was the gun
that somebody was holding there.

She had the hostage stare.

Then her body began sliding down the pillar as if she
couldn't be bothered any more to hold it upright. At first
it was only her knees that gave way, then she crumpled at
the waist as well, but Barley was there to hold her. He
flung one arm around her waist and with the other he
snatched the phone from her. He held it to his ear and
shouted "Goethe!" but all he got was a dialling tone so he
rang off.

It was an odd thing, but Barley had forgotten until now
that he was strong. They started to move but as they did so
she was seized with a violent revulsion against him and
lashed out silently with her clenched fist, cracking him so
hard over the cheekbone that for a moment he saw nothing
but a dazzling light. He grappled her hands to her sides

and held them there while he pulled her under the counter and frogmarched her through the hospital and across the carpark. "She's a disturbed patient," he was explaining in his mind. "A disturbed patient in a doctor's care."

Still holding her, he tipped her handbag on to the roof of the car, found the key, unlocked the passenger door and bundled her inside. Then he ran round to the driver's side in case she had ideas of taking over after all.

"I shall go home," she said.

"I don't know the way."

"Take me home," she repeated.

"I don't know the way, Katya! You'll have to tell me right and left, do you hear?" He grabbed her shoulders. "Sit up. Look out of the window. Where's reverse on this bloody thing?"

He fiddled with the gears. She grabbed the lever and slammed it in reverse, making the gearbox scream.

"Lights," he said.

He had already found them, but he made her turn them on for him, willing her by his anger to respond. As he bumped across the carpark, he had to swerve to avoid an ambulance entering at speed. Mud and water blacked out the windscreen, but there were no wipers because it wasn't raining. Stopping the car, he sprang out and smeared the windscreen halfway clean with his handkerchief, then back into the car.

"Go left," she ordered. "Be quick, please."

"We came the other way before."

"It's one way. Be quick."

Her voice was dead and he couldn't rouse it. He offered her his flask. She pushed it aside. He drove slowly, ignoring her instruction to be quick. Headlights in the driving mirror, not gaining or losing. It's Wicklow, he thought. It's Paddy, Cy, Henziger, Zapadny, the whole Guards

Armoured of them. Her face lit and went out again under the sodium streetlamps but it was lifeless. She was staring into her own head at whatever frightul things she saw in her imagination. Her clenched fist was in her mouth. Its knuckles were wedged between her teeth.

"Do I turn here?" he asked her roughly. And again he shouted at her. "Tell me where to turn, will you?"

She spoke first in Russian, then in English. "Now. Right. Go faster."

Nothing was familiar to him. Every empty street was like the next one and the last one.

"Turn now."

"Left or right?"

"Left!"

She screamed the word at the top of her voice, then screamed it again. After the scream came her tears and they went on coming between choking hopeless sobs. Then gradually the sobs began to falter and by the time he drew up at her apartment block they had ceased. He pulled the handbrake but it was broken. The car was still rolling as she shoved her door open. He reached for her but she was too quick. Somehow she had scrambled on to the pavement and was running across the forecourt with her handbag open, foraging for her keys. A boy in a leather jacket was lounging in the doorway and he appeared to want to block her. But by then Barley was level with her, so the boy leapt aside for them to pass. She wouldn't wait for the lift or perhaps she'd forgotten that there was one. She ran up the stairs and Barley ran after her, past a couple embracing. On the first landing an old man sat drunk in the corner. They climbed and kept climbing. Now it was an old woman who was drunk. Now it was a boy. They climbed so many flights that Barley began to fear she had forgotten which floor she was supposed to live on. Then

suddenly she was turning the locks and they were inside
her apartment again, and Katya was in the twins' room,
kneeling on their bed with her head struck forward and
panting like a desperate swimmer, one arm flung across
the body of each sleeping child.

Once more there was only her bedroom. He led her to
it because even in that tiny space she no longer knew the
way. She sat on the bed unsurely, seeming not to know
how high it was. He sat beside her, staring into her dull
face, watching her eyes close, half open and close again,
not venturing to touch her because she was rigid and
appalled and apart from him. She was clasping her wrist
as if it were broken. She gave a deep sigh. He said her
name but she didn't seem to hear him. He peered round
the room searching. A minuscule worktop was fixed
along one wall, a make-up table and writing desk combined. Tossed among old letters lay a ring-backed writing
block similar to the sort that Goethe used. A framed
Renoir reproduction hung above the bed. He unhooked
it and set it on his lap. The trained spy ripped a page out
of the notebook, laid it on the picture glass, took a pen
from his pocket and wrote.
Tell me.
He put the paper before her and she read it with indif-
ference without relinquishing her wrist. She gave a faint
shrug. Her shoulder was leaning against his, but she was
unaware of it. Her blouse was open and her rich black hair
was tousled from the running. He wrote again, *Tell me,* then
he grabbed her by the shoulders while his eyes implored her
with a desperate love. Then he stabbed his forefinger at the
sheet of paper. He picked up the picture and rammed it
into her lap for her to press on. She stared at the paper and
at *Tell me,* then she gave a long heartbreaking choke and

put her head down until he lost sight of her behind the chaotic curtain of her hair.

They have taken Yakov, she wrote.

He took back the pen.

Who told you?

Yakov, she replied.

What did he say?

He will come to Moscow on Friday. He will meet you at Igor's apartment at eleven o'clock on Friday night. He will bring you more material and answer your questions. Please have a precise list ready. It will be the last time. You should bring him news of publication, dates, details. You should bring good whisky. He loves me.

He grabbed back the pen.

Was it Yakov talking?

She nodded.

Why do you say they've taken him?

He used the wrong name.

What name?

Daniil. It was our rule. Pyotr if he is safe, Daniil if he is taken.

The pen had been passing urgently between them. Now Barley held on to it as he wrote question after question. *He made a mistake*, he wrote.

She shook her head.

He has been ill. He has forgotten your code, he wrote.

She shook her head again.

Has he never got it wrong before? he wrote.

At this she shook her head, took back the pen and wrote in an angry hand. *He called me Mariya. He said, Is that Mariya? Mariya is how I should call myself if there was danger. If I am safe, Alina.*

Write his words.

This is Daniil. Is that Mariya speaking? My lecture was the greatest success of my career. That was a lie.

Why?

He says always, in Russia the only success is not to win. It is a joke we have. He spoke deliberately against our joke. He was telling me we are dead.

Barley went to the window and looked steeply down at the concourse and the street. The whole dark world inside him had fallen into silence. Nothing moved, nothing breathed. But he was prepared. He had been prepared all his life, and never known it. She is Goethe's woman, therefore she is as dead as he is. Not yet, because this far Goethe has protected her with the last bit of courage left in him. But dead as dead can be, any time they care to reach out their long arm and pick her off the tree.

For perhaps an hour he remained there at the window before returning to the bed. She was lying on her side with her eyes open and her knees drawn up. He put his arm round her and drew her into him and he felt her cold body break inside his grasp as she began sobbing with convulsive, soundless heaves, as if she was afraid even to weep within the hearing of the microphones.

He began writing to her again, in bold clear capitals: PAY ATTENTION TO ME.

The screens were rolling every few minutes. Barley has left the Mezh. More. They have arrived at the metro station. More. Have exited (*sic*) the hospital, Katya on Barley's arm. More. Men lie but the computer is infallible. More.

"Why on earth's he driving?" Ned asked sharply as he read this.

Sheriton was too absorbed to reply but Bob was standing behind him and Bob picked up the question.

"Men like to drive women, Ned. The chauvinist age is still upon us."

"Thank you," said Ned politely.

Clive was smiling in approval.

Intermission. The screens slip out of sequence as Anastasia takes back the story. Anastasia is an angry old Latvian of sixty who has been on the Russia House books for twenty years. Anastasia alone has been allowed to cover the vestibule.

The legend speaks:

She made two passes, first to the lavatory, then back to the waiting room.

On her first pass, Barley and Katya were sitting on a bench waiting.

On her second, Barley and Katya were standing beside the telephone and appeared to be embracing. Barley had a hand to her face, Katya also had a hand up, the other hung at her side.

Had Bluebird's call come through by then?

Anastasia didn't know. Though she had stood in her lavatory cubicle listening as hard as she could, she hadn't heard the phone ring. So either the call had failed to come through or it was over by the time she made her second pass.

"Why on earth should he be embracing her?" said Ned.

"Maybe she had a fly in her eye," Sheriton said sourly, still watching the screen.

"He drove," Ned insisted. "He's not allowed to drive over there, but he drove. He let her drive all the way out to the country and back. She drove him to the hospital. Then all of a sudden he takes over the wheel. Why?"

Sheriton put down his pencil and ran his forefinger round the inside of his collar. "So what's the betting, Ned? Did Bluebird make his call or didn't he? Come on."

Ned still had the decency to give the question honest thought. "Presumably he made it. Otherwise they would have gone on waiting."

"Maybe she heard something she didn't like. Some bad news or something," Sheriton suggested.

The screens had gone out, leaving the room sallow.

Sheriton had a separate office done in rosewood and instant art. We decamped to it, poured ourselves coffee, stood about.

"Hell's he doing in her flat for so long?" Ned asked me aside. "All he has to do is get the time and place of the meeting out of her. He could have done that two hours ago."

"Maybe they're having a tender moment," I said.

"I'd feel better if I thought they were."

"Maybe he's buying another hat," said Johnny unpleasantly, overhearing us.

"Geronimo," said Sheriton as the bell rang, and we trooped back to the situation room.

An illuminated street map of the city showed us Katya's apartment marked by a red pinlight. The pick-up point lay three hundred metres east of it, at the south-east corner of two main streets marked green. Barley must now be heading along the south pavement, keeping close to the curb. As he reached the pick-up point, he should affect to slow down as if hunting for a car. The safe car would pull alongside him. Barley had been instructed to give the driver the name of his hotel in a loud voice and negotiate a price with his hands.

At the second roundabout the car would take a side turning and enter a building site where the safe truck was parked without lights, its driver appearing to doze in his cab. If the truck's wing aerial was extended, the car would make a right-hand circle and return to the truck.

If not, abort.

Paddy's report hit the screens at 1 a.m. London time. The tapes were available for us less than an hour later, blasted from the roof of the US Embassy. The report has since been torn to pieces in every conceivable way. For me it remains a model of factual field reporting.

Naturally the writer needs to be known, for every writer under the sun has limitations. Paddy was not a mindreader but he was a lot of other things, a former Gurkha turned special forces man turned intelligence officer, a linguist, a planner and improviser in Ned's favourite mould.

For his Moscow persona, he had put on such a skin of English silliness that the uninitiated made a joke of him when they described him to each other: his long shorts in the summer when he took himself on treks through the Moscow woods; his langlaufing in the winter, when he loaded up his Volvo with ancient skis and bamboo poles and iron rations and finally his own egregious self, clad in a fur cap that looked as though it had been kept over from the Arctic convoys. But it takes a clever man to act the fool and get away with it for long, and Paddy was a clever man, however convenient it later became to take his eccentricities at face value.

Also in controlling his motley of pseudo language students, travel clerks, little traders and third-flag nationals, Paddy was first rate. Ned himself could not have bettered him. He tended them like a canny parish priest, and every one of them in his lonely way rose to him. It was not his fault if the qualities that made men come to him also made him vulnerable to deception.

So to Paddy's report. He was struck first by the precision with which Barley gave his account, and the tape bears him out. Barley's voice is more self-assured than in any previous recording.

Paddy was impressed by Barley's resolve and by his devotion to his mission. He compared the Barley he saw before him in the truck with the Barley he had briefed for his Leningrad run and warmed to the improvement. He was right. Barley was an enlarged and altered man.

Barley's account to Paddy tallied also with every checkable fact at Paddy's disposal, from the pick-up at the metro and the drive to the hospital, to the wait on the bench and the stifled bell. Katya had been standing over the phone when it rang, Barley said. Barley himself had scarcely heard it. Then no wonder Anastasia hadn't heard it either, Paddy reasoned. Katya must have been quick as light to grab that receiver.

The conversation between Katya and the Bluebird had been short, two minutes at most, said Barley. Another neat fit. Goethe was known to be scared of long telephone conversations.

With so much collateral available to him therefore, and with Barley navigating his way through it, how on earth can anybody afterwards maintain that Paddy should have driven Barley straight to the Embassy and shipped him back to London bound and gagged? But of course Clive maintained just that, and he was not the only one.

Thus to the three mysteries that by now were sticking in Ned's throat—the embrace, the drive from the hospital with Barley at the wheel, the two hours they spent together in the flat. For Barley's answers, we must see him as Paddy saw him, bowed over the low light on the table in the truck, his face glistening from the heat. There is the whirr from the bafflers in the background. Both men are wearing earphones, a closed-circuit microphone lies between them. Barley whispers his story, half to the microphone, half to his station chief. Not all Paddy's nights of adventure on the North-West Frontier could have yielded a more dramatic atmosphere.

Cy sits in the shadows in a third pair of earphones. It is Cy's truck but he has orders to let Paddy host the feast.

"Then she goes and gets the wobblies," says Barley, with enough of the man-to-man in his voice to make Paddy smile. "She'd been winding herself up all week for his call and suddenly it was over and she went pop. Probably didn't help her, me being there. Without me around, I reckon she'd have held it back till she got home."

"Probably would at that," Paddy agrees understandingly.

"It was too much for her. Hearing his voice, hearing he'll be in town in a couple of days, her worries about her kids— and about him, and about herself as well—it was just too much for her."

Paddy understood perfectly. He had known emotional women in his day, and was experienced in the sorts of thing they cried over.

From there everything else flowed naturally. The deception became a symphony. Barley had done what he could to comfort her, he said, but she was in bad shape so he put his arm round her and lugged her to the car and drove her home.

In the car she did some more crying but she was on the mend by the time they got to her flat. Barley made her a cup of tea and patted her hand, until he was confident she was able to cope.

"Well done," said Paddy. And if, as he says this, he sounds like a nineteenth-century Indian Army officer congratulating his men after a futile cavalry charge, that is only because he is impressed and his mouth is too near the microphone.

There is lastly Barley's question, which is where Cy came in. With hindsight, no doubt, it sounds like a straight declaration of larcenous intent. But Cy didn't hear it that way and neither did Paddy. Neither, in fact, did anyone in London except Ned, whose impotence was by now unnerving. Ned was becoming the pariah of the situation room.

"Oh yes—that's it—what about the shopping list?" says Barley as he prepares to leave. The question emerges as one of several small administrative worries, not a solo. "When do you get to press the shopping list into my hot little hand?" he asks repetitiously.

"Why?" says Cy from the shadows.

"Well *I* don't know. Shouldn't I bone up on it a bit or something?"

"There's nothing to bone up," says Cy. "It's written questions, yes-or-no answers, and it is positively important that you do not know any part of it, thank you."

"So when do I get it?"

"The shopping list we do as late as possible," says Cy.

Of Cy's own opinion of Barley's state of mind, one nugget is recorded. "With the Brits," he is reported to have said, "you never know what the hell they're thinking anyway."

That night at least, Cy had a certain justice on his side.

"There was no bad news," Ned insisted while Brock played the truck tapes for the third or thirtieth time.

We were back in our own Russia House. We had taken refuge there. It was like the early days all over again. It was dawn, but we were too wakeful to remember sleep.

"There was no *bad* news," Ned repeated. "It was all *good* news. 'I'm well. I'm safe. I gave a great lecture. I'm catching the plane. See you on Friday. I love you.' So she weeps."

"Oh, I don't know," I said, talking against my own mood. "Haven't *you* ever cried when *you* were happy?"

"She weeps so much he has to cart her down the hospital corridor. She weeps so much she can't drive. When they get to her apartment she runs ahead of him to the door as if Barley doesn't exist, because she's so *happy* that the

Bluebird's flying in on time. And he comforts her. For all the good news she's had." Barley's recorded voice had come on again. "And he's calm. Totally calm. Not a worry in the world. 'We're bang on target, Paddy. Everything's fine. That's why she's weeping.' Of course it is."

He sat back and closed his eyes while Barley's trustworthy voice continued to talk to him from the recorder.

"He doesn't belong to us any more," said Ned. "He's gone away."

As also, in a different sense, had Ned. He had launched a great operation. Now all he could do by his own reckoning was watch it hurtle out of control. In my whole life I never saw a man so isolated, with the possible exception of myself.

Spying is waiting.
Spying is worrying.
Spying is being yourself but more so.

The nostrums of the extinct Walter and the living Ned rang in Barley's ears. The apprentice had become heir to the spells of his masters but his magic was more potent than theirs had ever been.

He was on a plateau none of them had ascended. He had the goal, he had the means to reach it and he had what Clive would have called the motivation, which in better mouths was purpose. Everything they had taught him was paying off as he rode calmly into battle to deceive them. But he was not their trickster.

Their flags were nothing to him. They could wave in any wind. But he was not their traitor. He was not his own cause. He knew the battle he had to win and whom he had to win it for. He knew the sacrifice he was prepared to make. He was not their traitor. He was complete.

He did not need their sacred labels and their weakling

systems. He was one man alone but he was greater than the
sum of those who had presumed to take control of him. He
knew them as the worst of all bad weapons, because their
existence justified their targets.

In a gentle way that was not even all that gentle, he had
discovered anger. He could smell its first kindling and hear
the crackle of its brushwood.

There was only now. Goethe was right. There was no
tomorrow because tomorrow was the excuse. There was
now or there was nowhere, and Goethe, even nowhere, was
still right. We must cut down the grey men inside ourselves,
we must burn our grey suits and set our good hearts free,
which is the dream of every decent soul, and even—believe
it or not—of certain grey men too. But how, with what?

Goethe was right, and it was not his fault or Barley's
that each by accident had set the other in motion. With the
radiance of spirit that was rising in him, Barley's sense of
kinship with his unlikely friend was overwhelming. He
brimmed with allegiance to Goethe's frantic dream of
unleashing the forces of sanity and opening the doors on
dirty rooms.

But Barley did not dwell long on Goethe's agony.
Goethe was in hell and very likely Barley would soon be
following him. I'll mourn him when I have the time, he
thought. Until then his business was with the living whom
Goethe had put so shamefully at risk, and in a brave last
gesture had attempted to preserve.

For his immediate business Barley must use the grey
men's wiles. He must be himself but more so than he has
ever been before. He must wait. He must worry. He must
be a man reversed, inwardly reconciled, outwardly unful-
filled. He must live secretly on tiptoe, arch as a cat inside
his head while he acts the Barley Blair they wish to see,
their creature all the way.

Meanwhile the chess-player in him reckons his moves. The slumbering negotiator is becoming unobservably awake. The publisher is achieving what he has never achieved before, he is becoming the cool-headed broker between the necessity and the far vision.

Katya knows, he reasons. *She knows Goethe is caught.*

But they do not know she knows, because she kept her wits about her on the telephone.

And they do not know I know that Katya knows.

In the whole world I am the only person apart from Katya and Goethe who knows that Katya knows.

Katya is still free.

Why?

They have not stolen her children, ransacked her flat, thrown Matvey in the madhouse or displayed any of the delicacy traditionally reserved for Russian ladies playing courier to Soviet defence physicists who have decided to entrust their nation's secrets to a derelict Western publisher.

Why?

I too this far am free. They have not chained my neck to a brick wall.

Why?

Because they do not know we know they know.

So they want more.

They want us, but more than us.

They can wait for us, because they want more.

But what is the more?

What is the clue to their patience?

Everybody talks, Ned had said, stating a fact of life. *With today's methods everybody talks.* He was telling Barley not to try and hold out if he was caught. But Barley was not thinking about himself any more. He was thinking about Katya.

Each night, each day that followed, Barley moved the pieces round in his mind, honing his plan while he waited, as we all did, for Friday's promised meeting with the Bluebird.

At breakfast, Barley punctually on parade, a model publisher and spy. And each day, all day long, the life and soul of the fair.

Goethe. Nothing I can do for you. No power on earth will prise you from their grip.

Katya, still savable. Her children, still savable. Even though everybody talks and Goethe in the end will be no exception.

Myself, unsavable as ever.

Goethe gave me the courage, he thought, as his secret purpose grew in him, *and Katya the love.*

No. Katya gave me both. And gives them to me still.

And the day as quiet as the days before, the screens near-blank, as Barley steers himself methodically towards the evening's grand Potomac & Blair Launch Party in the Spirit of Goodwill and Glasnost, as our flowery invitations have it, printed in triptych with deckle edges on the Service's own printing press not two weeks ago.

And intermittently, with a seeming casualness, Barley assures himself of Katya's continuing welfare. He rings her whenever he can. He chats to her and makes her use the word "convenient" as a safety signal. In return he includes the word "frankly" in his own careless chatter. Nothing heavy; nothing on the matter of love or death or great German poets. Just:

How are you doing?

Is the fair wearing you out, frankly?

How are the twins?

Is Matvey still enjoying his pipe?

Meaning, I love you, and I love you, and I love you, and I love you frankly.

For further assurance regarding her safety, Barley despatches Wicklow to take a passing look at her in the

Socialist pavilion. "She's fine," Wicklow reports with a smile, humouring Barley's nervousness. "She's steady as she goes."

"Thanks," says Barley. "Jolly nice of you, old boy."

The second time, again at Barley's bidding, Henziger himself goes. Perhaps Barley is saving himself for the evening. Or perhaps he does not trust his own emotions. But she is still there, still alive, still breathing, and she has changed into her party frock.

Yet all the while, even driving back early to town in order to be ahead of his guests, Barley continues to muster his private army of alterable and unalterable facts with a clarity that the most trained and compromised lawyer would be proud of.

16

"Gyorgy! Marvellous! Fantastic! Where's Varenka?"

"Barley, my friend, for Christ's sake save us! We don't like the twentieth century any better than you English. Let's run away from it together! We leave tonight, okay? You buy the tickets?"

"Yuri. My God, is this your new wife? Leave him. He's a monster."

"Barley! Listen! Everything is fine! We have no more problems! In the old days we had to assume that everything was a mess! Now we can look in our newspapers and confirm it!"

"Misha! How's the work going? Super!"

"It's war, for Christ's sake, Barley, open war. First we got to hang the old guard, then we got to fight another Stalingrad!"

"Leo! Great to see you! How's Sonya?"

"Barley, pay attention to me! Communism is not a threat! It's a parasite industry that lives off the mistakes of all you stupid assholes in the West!"

The reception was in the mirrored upstairs room of an elderly mid-town hotel. Plainclothes guards stood outside on the pavement. More hovered in the hall and on the staircase and at the entrance to the room.

Potomac & Blair had invited a hundred people. Eight had accepted, nobody had refused, and so far a hundred and fifty had arrived. But until Katya was among them Barley preferred the spaces near the door.

A flock of Western girls swept in, escorted by the usual dubious official interpreters, all men. A portly philosopher who played the clarinet arrived with his newest boyfriend.

"Aleksander! Fantastic! Marvellous!"

A lonely Siberian called Andrey, already drunk, needed to speak to Barley on a matter of vital urgency. "One-party Socialism is a disaster, Barley. It has broken our hearts. Keep your British variety. You will publish my new novel?"

"Well I don't know about that, Andrey," Barley replied cautiously, glancing towards the door. "Our Russian editor admires it but he doesn't see an English market. We're thinking about it."

"You know why I came tonight?" Andrey asked.

"Tell me."

Another jolly group arrived, but still with no Katya among them.

"In order to wear my fine clothes for you. We Russians know each other's tricks too well. We need your Western mirror. You come here, you depart again with our best images reflected in you and we feel noble. If you have published my first novel, it is only logical that you publish my second."

"Not if the first one didn't make any money, it isn't, Andrey," said Barley with rare firmness, and to his relief saw Wicklow slipping towards them across the room.

"You have heard that Anatoly died in prison of a hunger strike in December? After two years of this Great New Russia we are enjoying?" Andrey continued, taking another enormous pull of whisky, supplied courtesy of the American Embassy in support of a more sober Russia.

"Of course we heard about him," Wicklow cut in soothingly. "It was disgusting."

"So why don't you publish my novel?"

Leaving Wicklow to cope, Barley spread his arms and hastened beaming to the door. The superb Natalie of the All-Union State Library of Foreign Literature had arrived, a wise beauty of sixty. They fell into an adoring embrace.

"So whom shall we discuss tonight, Barley? James Joyce or Adrian Mole? Why are you looking so intelligent, suddenly? It is because you have become a capitalist."

A stampede flung half the company to the further end of the room and caused the guards to peer through the doorway in alarm. The roar of conversation dipped and recovered. The buffet had been unveiled.

But still no Katya.

"Today under the *perestroika* it is all much easier," Natalie was saying through her irresistible smile. "Foreign travel is no problem. For example to Bulgaria. All we have to do is describe to our bureaucrats what kind of person we think we are. Naturally the Bulgarians need to know this before we arrive. They **must** be warned what to expect. Are we an intelligent person, medium intelligent or normal intelligent? The Bulgarians need to prepare themselves, perhaps even train themselves a little. Are we calm or excitable, plain-minded or full of imagination? When we have answered these simple questions and a thousand more of the same sort, we may proceed to the more important issues, such as the address and full names of our maternal grandmother, the date of her death and the number of her death certificate and, if they are feeling like it, perhaps also the name of the doctor who signed it. So you may see that our bureaucrats are doing everything possible to introduce the new, relaxed regulations quickly, and send us all abroad on holiday with our children. Barley, whom are you staring round for? Have I lost my looks or are you bored with me already?"

"So what did you tell them?" Barley asked with a laugh, and willed himself to keep his eyes on her.

"Oh, I said I was very intelligent, I was a calm, amusing person and the Bulgarians would be delighted with my company. The bureaucrats are testing our determination, that is all. They hope that if we have to satisfy so many different departments we shall lose courage and decide to stay at home. But it is getting better. Everything is getting a little better. Maybe you don't believe it, but the *perestroika* is not being run for foreigners. It is run for us."

"How is your dog, Barley?" a man's gloomy voice murmured at Barley's side. It was Arkady, unofficial sculptor, with his beautiful unofficial girlfriend.

"I haven't got a dog, Arkady. Why do you ask?"

"Because from this moment it has become safer to discuss one's dog than one's fellow human beings, I would say."

Barley turned his head to follow Arkady's gaze and saw Alik Zapadny standing on the far side of the room in earnest conversation with Katya.

"We Muscovites are talking too dangerously these days," Arkady continued, his eyes still fixed upon Zapadny. "We are becoming careless in our excitement. The informers will have a good harvest this autumn, even if nobody else does. Ask him. He is at the peak of his profession, I would say."

"Alik, you old devil, what are you pestering this poor girl about?" Barley demanded as he embraced Katya first and then Zapadny. "I could see her blushing from across the room. You want to watch him, Katya. His English is almost as good as yours, and he talks it a lot faster. How are you?"

"Oh thank you," she said softly. "I am *very* well."

She was wearing the dress she had worn at their meeting at the Odessa. She was withdrawn but in command of herself. Her face had the battered eagerness of bereavement. Dan Zeppelin and Mary Lou stood with them.

"We were having rather an interesting discussion on human rights, as a matter of fact, Barley," Zapadny explained, waving his glass in a circular gesture round the company as if he were taking a collection. "Weren't we, Mr. Zeppelin? We are always so grateful when Westerners preach to us about how to behave towards our criminals, you see! But then what is the difference, I am asking myself, between a country that locks a few extra people in prison, and a country that leaves its gangsters at large? I think I have just found a negotiating point here for our Soviet leaders, actually. Tomorrow morning we shall announce to the so-called Helsinki Watch Committee that we can have nothing further to do with them until they have put the American Mafia behind bars. How would that be, Mr. Zeppelin? We let ours out, you put yours inside. It's a fair deal, I would say."

"You want the polite answer or the real one?" Dan snapped over Mary Lou's shoulder.

Another polyglot group of guests swept past, followed after a theatrical pause by none other than the great Sir Peter Oliphant himself, surrounded by a retinue of Russian and English bag-carriers. The noise grew, the room filled. Three sickly-looking British correspondents inspected the depleted buffet and departed. Somebody opened the piano and began playing a Ukrainian song. A woman sang well and others joined her.

"No, Barley, I do not know what terrifies you," Katya was replying, to Barley's surprise, so he must have asked her. "I am sure you are very brave, like all English."

In the heat of the room and the swirl of the occasion, his

own excitement had turned suddenly against him. He felt drunk but not from alcohol, for he had been nursing one tired Scotch all evening.

"Maybe there's nothing there," he ventured, addressing not just Katya but a ring of unfamiliar faces. "Out in the woodwork. Talent." Everyone was waiting, Barley too. He was trying to look at all of them while his eyes saw only Katya. What had he been saying? What had they been hearing? Their faces were still turned to him but there was no light in them, not even Katya's; there was only concern. He stumbled on. "We had this vision, all of us, for years, of great Russian artists waiting to be discovered." He faltered. "Well, didn't we? Epic novels, plays? Great painters, banned, working in secrecy? Attics full of wonderful illegal stuff? Musicians the same? We talked about it. Dreamed about it. The secret continuation of the nineteenth century. 'And when the thaw comes, they'll all come out of the ice and dazzle us,' we told each other. So where the hell are they, all these geniuses? What if they froze to death in the ice? Maybe the repression worked. That's all I'm saying."

A spellbound silence followed before Katya came to his aid. "The Russian talent exists and has always existed, Barley, even in the worst times. It cannot be destroyed," she declared with a hint of her old strictness. "Perhaps it will first have to adjust itself to the new circumstances, but soon it will express itself brilliantly. I am sure that is what you wish to say."

Henziger is making his speech. It is a masterpiece of unconscious hypocrisy. "May the pioneering venture of Potomac & Blair provide a modest addition to the great new era of East-West understanding!" he declares, puffed up by his conviction. His voice lifts and with it his glass. He is the honest trader, he is every decent American with his heart in the right place. And no doubt that he is precisely what he thinks he is, for the ham actor in him lies just below the surface. "Let's make each other rich!" he cries, raising his glass still higher. "Let's make each other free! Let's trade together, and let's talk together and let's drink together, and let's make the world a better place. Ladies and gentlemen——to you and to Potomac & Blair and to our mutual profit——and to the *perestroika*——good health! Amen!"

They are yelling for Barley. Spikey Morgan starts it, Yuri and Alik Zapadny take it up, all the old hands who know the game yell, "Barley, Barley!" Soon the whole room is yelling for Barley, some of them without even knowing why, and for a moment none of them sees him anyway. Then suddenly he is standing on the buffet table holding a borrowed saxophone and playing "My Funny Valentine," which he has played at every Moscow book fair since the first, while Jack Henziger accompanies him on the piano in the unmistakable style of Fats Waller.

The guards at the door creep into the room to listen, the guards from the stairs come to the doorway and the guards from the hall come to the stairs as the first notes of Barley's swansong gather clarity and then a splendid power.

"We're going to the new Indian, for Christ's sake," Henziger protests as they stand on the pavement under the stodgy gaze of the *toptuny*. "Bring Katya with you! We've booked a table!"

"Sorry, Jack. We're bespoke. Longstanding date."

Henziger is only putting on a show. "She needs welfaring," Barley has confided to him. "I'm going to take her off and give her a quiet supper somewhere."

But Barley did not take Katya to dinner for their farewell evening, as the irregulars confirmed before they were stood down. And it was Katya, not Barley this time, who did the taking. She took him to the place known to every urban Russian boy and girl from adolescence, and it is to be found at the top of every purpose-built apartment block in every major city. There is not a Russian of Katya's generation who does not count such places among her memories of early love. And such a place was to be found at the top of Katya's staircase also, at the point where the last flight ends and the attics begin, though it was more sought after in winter than in summer because it included the suppurating hot-water tank and steaming black-bandaged pipes.

First it was necessary for her to inspect Matvey and the twins and establish that they were still safe, while Barley stood on the landing and waited for her. Then she led him by the hand up several flights until the last, which was of wood. She had a key and it fitted the rusted steel door that ordered all trespassers to keep their distance. And when she had unlocked it and relocked it, she led him across the rafters to the bit of hard floor where she had prepared a makeshift bed, with a muddied view of the stars through the filthy skylight and the chugging of the pipes and the stench of drying clothes for company.

"The letter you gave to Landau went astray," he said. "It ended up in the hands of our officials. It was the officials who sent me to you. I'm sorry about that."

But there was no more time for either of them to be shocked by anything. He had told her little of his plan and he told her no more now. It was understood between them that she knew too much already. And besides, they had more important matters to discuss, for it was on this night also that Katya told Barley the things that afterwards constituted the rest of his knowledge of her. And she confessed her love for him in terms simple enough to sustain him through the separation they both knew lay ahead of them.

Nevertheless Barley did not outstay his welcome. He did not give the men in the field or the men in London cause to be anxious for him. He was back at the Mezh by midnight, in good time for a last one with the boys.

"Oh, Jack, Alik Zapadny's summoned me to his traditional farewell snoot for old hands tomorrow afternoon," he confided to Henziger over a nightcap in the first-floor bar.

"Want me to come along?" asked Henziger. For like the Russians themselves, Henziger harboured no illusions about Zapadny's regrettable connections.

Barley smiled regretfully. "Your knees aren't brown enough, Jack. It's for us golden oldies from the days when there was no hope."

"What time?" asked Wicklow, ever practical.

"Four o'clock, I think he said. Seems a damned odd time for a drink. Yes, I'm sure he did. Four."

Then he wished them all an affectionate goodnight and rode to Heaven in the lift, which in the Mezh is a glass cage that slides up and down the outside of a steel rod, to the private worry of many honest souls below.

It was lunchtime and after all our sleepless nights and wakeful dawns there was something indecent about a sensation that occurred at lunchtime. But a sensation it was. A hand-carried sensation. A sensation inside a yellow envelope inside a locked steel briefcase. Gaunt Johnny from their London station ran into the situation room with it, having brought it under guard from the Embassy across the square. He ran right through the lower level and up the little staircase to the command area before he realised we had moved to Sheriton's rosewood parlour for our sandwiches and coffee.

He handed it to Sheriton and stood over him like a stage messenger while Sheriton read first the covering letter, which he stuffed into his pocket, then the message itself.

Then he stood over Ned while Ned read the message too. It wasn't till Ned passed it back to me that Johnny seemed to decide he had read it enough times: a signals intercept, transmitted by the Soviet military out of Leningrad, intercepted in Finland by the Americans and decrypted in Virginia by a bank of computers powerful enough to light London for a year.

Leningrad to Moscow, copy to Saratov.

Professor Yakov Savelyev is authorized to take a recreational weekend in Moscow following his lecture to the military academy in Saratov this Friday. Please arrange transport and facilities.

"Well thank you, Mr. Administration Officer, Leningrad," Sheriton murmured.

Ned had taken back the signal and was re-reading it. Of all of us, he seemed to be the only one who was not impressed.

"Is this all they broke?" he asked.

"I don't know, Ned," said Johnny, not bothering to conceal his hostility.

"It says here 'one over one.' What's that supposed to mean? Find out whether it's the only one in the batch. If it isn't, perhaps you'd be good enough to find out what else they picked up on the same trawl that was worth a damn." He waited till Johnny had left the room. "Perfect," he said acidly. "Copybook. My God, you'd think we were dealing with the Germans."

We stood about, nibbling distractedly at our food. Sheriton had shoved his hands into his pockets and turned his back to us while he stared out of the smoked-glass window at the silent traffic. He was wearing a long-haired black cardigan. Through the interior window the rest of us could watch Johnny talking on one of the supposedly safe telephones. He rang off and we watched him come back across the room to us.

"Zero," he announced.

"What's zero?" Ned said.

" 'One over one' means one over one. It's a solo. Nothing either side."

"A fluke then?" Ned suggested.

"A solo," Johnny repeated stubbornly.

Ned swung round to Sheriton, who still had his back to us. "Russell. Read the signs. That intercept is completely on its own. There's nothing anywhere near it and it stinks. They're tossing us a piece of bait."

Now it was Sheriton's turn to make a second study of the sheet. When he finally spoke, he affected a deep weariness and it was clear he was reaching the limits of his tolerance.

"Ned, I am confidently assured by the cryptographers that the intercept came from lowgrade military crap put out on an army squeezebox vintage 1921. Nobody plants deception that way any more. Nobody does those things. It's not the Bluebird that's going off course. It's you."

"Maybe that's *why* they planted it that way! Isn't that what you and I might do? Come in on the blind side?"

"Well, maybe we would at that," Sheriton conceded, as if it scarcely mattered to him. "Once you start thinking that way, it's pretty hard to think any other way."

Clive at his worst. "We can hardly ask Sheriton to break off the operation on the grounds that everything is going *well*, Ned," he said silkily.

"On the grounds of pixie voices," Sheriton corrected him, his temper gathering as he wandered moodily back into the room. "On the grounds that anything going our way is a Kremlin plot, and everything we fuck up is evidence of our integrity. Ned, my Agency damn nearly died

of that ailment. So did you guys. We're not going that
route today. It's my operation and my ass."

"And my joe," said Ned. "We've blown him. And we've
blown the Bluebird."

"Sure, sure," said Sheriton with icy affability. "No question." He glanced unlovingly at Clive. "Mr. Deputy?"

Clive had his own ways of sitting on the fence, and they
were all of them well tried. "Russell—if I may say so—
Ned. I think you are both being slightly egotistical. We are
a service. We live corporate lives. It is our masters, not we
ourselves alone, who have given the Bluebird their blessing.
There is a corporate will here that is bigger than any of us."

Wrong again, I thought. It is smaller than all of us. It is
an insult to the powers of each of us, except perhaps of
Clive, who therefore needs it.

Sheriton turned back to Ned, but still did not raise his
voice. "Ned, do you have any idea what will happen in
Washington and Langley if I abort *now?* Can you imagine
the peals of hyena laughter that will resound across the
Atlantic from Defense, the Pentagon and the neanderthals?
Can you guess what view might be taken of the Bluebird
material until now?" He pointed without apparent rancour
at Johnny, who sat skull-eyed, watching each of them in
turn. "Can you see this guy's report? This Judas? We were
sowing a little moderation around town, remember? Now
you tell me I've got to throw Bluebird to the jackals."

"I'm telling you not to give him the shopping list."

Sheriton inclined his ear as if he were a little deaf. "*Barley*
the shopping list? Or *Bluebird* the shopping list?"

"Neither of them. Abort."

Finally Sheriton became very angry indeed. He had been
winding himself up for this moment, and now it had
arrived. He stood himself before Ned and not two feet from
him, and when he flung up his palms in remonstration he

wrenched half his fluffy cardigan with him so that he resembled an overweight bat in a fury.

"So okay! Here's our worst-case situation. Cooked Ned-style. Okay? We show Bluebird the shopping list and he turns out to be their asset, not ours. Have I considered that possibility? Ned, night and day I have considered little else. If Bluebird is their guy and not ours, if Barley is, if the girl is, if all or any of the players is less than strictly kosher, the shopping list will shine a very bright light up the anal orifice of the United States of America." He began pacing. "It will show the Sovs what has been given away by their own man. So they'll know what we know. Already bad. It will show the Sovs what we *don't* know, and *how* we don't know it. More bad, but there's worse to come. Cleverly analysed, the shopping list can show them the gaps in our intelligence-gathering machinery and, if they're cleverer still, in our own grotesque, fucking ridiculous, incompetent, ludicrously overstocked arsenal. Why? Because in the end we concentrate on what scares us, which is what we can't do and they can. That's the down side. Ned, I have looked at the bank balance. I know the stakes. I know what we can earn ourselves from Bluebird and what he stands to cost us if we screw up. Losing disenchants me. I've seen it done. I am not impressed. If we're wrong, it's shit city. We knew that back on Nowhere Island and we know it a little better now because it's live-ammunition time. But this is *not* the moment to start looking over our shoulders unless we have a cast-iron reason!"

He came back to Ned. "*Bluebird is straight,* Ned! Remember? Your words. I loved you for them! I still do! Bluebird is telling the unpolluted truth as he knows it. And my myopic masters are going to have it shoved up their asses even if it turns their balls to water. Do you read me, Ned? Or have I put you to sleep already?"

But Ned would not rise to Sheriton's black rage. "Don't give it to him, Russell. We've lost him. If you give him anything at all, give him smoke."

"*Smoke?* Play Barley *back,* you mean? Admit the Bluebird's bad? Are you joking? Give me *proof,* Ned! Don't give me *hunches!* Give me fucking *proof!* Everybody in Washington who hasn't got hair between his toes tells me that Bluebird is the Holy Bible, the Talmud and the Koran! Now *you* tell me, give him smoke! You got us into this, Ned! Don't try and jump off the tiger at the first fucking stop!"

Ned pondered this for a while, and Clive pondered Ned. Finally Ned gave a shrug as if to say perhaps it made no difference anyway. Then he returned to his desk where he sat alone seeming to read papers, and I remember wondering suddenly whether he had a Hannah too, whether we all did, some life unled that kept him to the wheel.

Perhaps it was true that VAAP had no small rooms or perhaps Alik Zapadny, after his years in prison, had an understandable aversion to them.

In any case, the room he had singled out for their encounter seemed to Barley big enough for a regimental dance, and the only thing small about it was Zapadny himself, who crouched at one end of a long table like a mouse on a raft, watching his visitor with darting eyes as he ambled down the parquet floor at him, his long arms dangling at his sides, elbows up a little, and an expression on his face such as neither Zapadny nor perhaps anyone else had ever seen in him before: not apologetic, not vague, not wilfully foolish, but of an almost menacing firmness of intention.

Zapadny had arranged some papers before him, and a heap of books beside the papers and a jug of drinking water and two glasses. It was evident that he wished to offer Barley an impression of being discovered in the midst of his duties, rather than facing him in cold blood without props or the protection of his numberless assistants.

"Barley, my dear chap, look here it's most kind of you to call by and say your farewells like this, you must be as busy as I am at this moment, my hat," he began, speaking much too quickly. "I would say that if our publishing industry continues to expand like this, then I see no way out of it, though it is only my personal and unofficial opinion, we shall have to employ a hundred more staff and most likely apply for larger offices also." He hummed and fussed his papers and pulled back a chair in what he imagined to be a gesture of old-style European courtesy. But Barley as usual preferred to stand. "Well it's more than my life is worth to offer you a drink on the premises, when the sun is not even over the yardarm as we say, but I mean do sit down and let us kick a few thoughts around for a few minutes"—raising his eyebrows and looking at his watch—"my God, we should have a month of it, not five days! How is the Trans-Siberian Railway progressing? I mean I see no basic difficulties there, provided our own position is respected, and the rules of fair play are observed by all the contracting parties. Are the Finns being too greedy? Perhaps your Mr. Henziger is being greedy? He is certainly a hard-nosed character, I would say."

He caught Barley's eye again and his discomfort increased. Standing over him, Barley bore no resemblance to a man who wished to discuss the Trans-Siberian Railway.

"I find it actually a little odd that you insisted so dogmatically on speaking to me completely alone, you see," Zapadny continued rather desperately. "After all, this one is fairly and squarely in Mrs. Korneyeva's court. It is she and her staff who are directly responsible for the photographer and all the practical arrangements."

But Barley also had a prepared speech, though it was not marred by any of Zapadny's nervousness. "Alik," he said, still declining to sit down. "Does that telephone work?"

"Of course."

"I need to betray my country and I'm in a hurry. And what I would like you to do is put me in touch with the proper authorities, because there are certain things that have to be hammered out in advance. So don't start telling me you don't know who to get hold of, just do it, or you'll lose a lot of Brownie points with the pigs who think they own you."

It was mid-afternoon but a wintery dusk had settled over London, and Ned's little office in the Russia House was bathed in twilight. He had put his feet on his desk and was sitting back in his chair, eyes closed and a dark whisky at his elbow——not by any means, I quickly realised, his first of the day.

"Is Clive Without India still cloistered with the Whitehall nobles?" he asked me, with a tired levity.

"He's at the American Embassy settling the shopping list."

"I thought no mere Brit was allowed near the shopping list."

"They're talking principle. Sheriton has to sign a declaration appointing Barley an honorary American. Clive has to add a citation."

"Saying what?"

"That he's a man of honour and a fit and proper person."

"Did you draft it for him?"

"Of course."

"Silly fellow," said Ned with an air of dreamy reproof. "They'll hang you." He leaned back and closed his eyes.

"Is the shopping list really worth so much?" I asked. I had a sense, for once, of being more practically disposed than Ned was.

"Oh it's worth everything," Ned replied carelessly. "If any of it's worth anything, that is."

"Do you mind telling me why?"

I had not been admitted to the inmost secrets of the Bluebird material, but I knew that if I ever had been I would not have been able to make head or tail of them. But conscientious Ned had taken himself to night-school. He had sat at the feet of our in-house boffins and lunched our grandest defence scientists at the Athenaeum in order to bone up.

"Interface," he said with contempt. "Mutually assured bedlam. We track their toys. They track ours. We watch each other's archery contests without either of us knowing which targets the other side is aiming at. If they're aiming for London, will they hit Birmingham? What's error? What's deliberate? Who's approaching zero-CEP?" He caught my bewilderment and was pleased with himself. "We watch them lob their ICBMs into the Kamchatka Peninsula. But can they lob them down a Minuteman silo? We don't know and they don't. Because the big stuff on either side has never been tested under war conditions. The test trajectories are not the trajectories they'll use when the fun starts. The earth, God bless her, is not a perfect globe. How can she be at her age? Her density varies. So does the old girl's gravitational pull when things fly over her, like missiles and warheads. Enter bias. Our targeteers try to compensate for it in their calibrations. Goethe tried. They pour in data from earth-watch satellites, and perhaps they succeed better than Goethe did. Perhaps they don't. We won't know till the blessed balloon goes up, and nor will they, because you can only try the real thing once." He stretched luxuriously as if the topic pleased him. "So the camps divide. The hawks cry, 'The Sovs are pinpoint! They can knock the smile off the arse of a fly at ten thousand miles!' And all the doves can reply is '*We* don't know what the Sovs can do, and the Sovs don't know what the Sovs can do. And nobody who doesn't know whether his gun works or not is going to shoot first. It's the uncertainty that keeps us honest,' say the doves. But that is not an argument that satisfies the literal American mind, you see, because the literal American mind does not like to grapple with fuzzy concepts or grand visions. Not at its literal field level. And what Goethe was saying was an even larger heresy. He was saying that the uncertainty was all there was. Which I rather agree with. So the hawks hated him and the doves had a ball and hanged themselves from the chandelier." He drank again. "If Goethe had only backed the pinpoint boys instead, everything would have been fine," he said reprovingly.

"And the shopping list?" I asked him again.

He peered whimsically into his glass. "The targeting of one side, my dear Palfrey, is based on that side's assumptions about the other side. And vice versa. *Ad infinitum.* Do we harden our silos? If the enemy can't hit them, why should we bother? Do we superharden them—even if we know how—at a cost of billions? We're already doing so, as a matter of fact, though it's not much sung about. Or do we protect them imperfectly with SDI at a cost of more billions? Depends what our prejudices are and who signs our pay cheque. Depends whether we're manufacturers or taxpayers. Do we put our rockets on trains or autobahns or park them in country lanes, which happens to be this month's flavour? Or do we say it's all junk anyway, so to hell with it?"

"So is it ending or beginning?" I asked.

He shrugged. "When did it ever end? Turn on your television set, what do you see? The leaders of both sides hugging each other. Tears in their eyes. Looking more like each other every day. *Hooray, it's all over!* Bollocks. Listen to the insiders and you realise the picture hasn't altered by a brush-stroke."

"And if I turn my television off? What will I see then?"

He had ceased to smile. Indeed his good face was more serious than I had ever seen it before, though his anger—if such it was—seemed to be directed at no one but himself.

"You'll see *us*. Hiding behind our grey screens. Telling each other we keep the peace."

17

The elusive truth that Ned was speaking of came out slowly and in a series of distorted perceptions, which is generally the case in our secret overworld.

At 6 p.m. Barley was seen to "exit" the VAAP offices, as our screens now insisted on advising us, and there was a flurry of apprehension that he might be drunk, for Zapadny was a drinking buddy and a farewell vodka with him was likely to be just that. Barley emerged, Zapadny with him. They embraced fulsomely on the doorstep, Zapadny flushed and a little excitable in his movements and Barley rather rigid, hence the watchers' worry that he was drunk, and their rather odd decision to photograph him—as if by freezing the moment they might somehow sober him up. And since this is the last photograph of him on the file, you may imagine how much attention has been paid to it. Barley has Zapadny in his arms, and there is strength to their embrace, at least on Barley's side. In my imagination, if no one else's, it is as if Barley is holding the poor fellow up in order to give him the courage to keep his half of the bargain; as if he is literally breathing courage into him. And the pink is weird. VAAP is a former school on Bolshaya Bronnaya Street in the centre of Moscow. It was built, I guess, at the turn of the century, with large windows and a plaster façade. And this plaster was painted in that year a light pink, which in the photograph is transformed to a flaming orange, presumably by the last rays of a red sun. The entwined men are thus caught in an unholy scarlet halo like a red flash. One of the watchers even gained the entrance hall on the pretext of visiting the cafeteria, and tried to achieve the reverse shot. But a tall man stood in his way, watching the scene on the pavement. Nobody has identified him. At the news-stand, a second man, also tall, is drinking from a mug, but not with much conviction, for his eyes too are turned to the two embracing figures outside.

The watchers took no note of the scores of people who had passed in and out of the VAAP building during the two hours Barley had been in the place—how could they? They had no idea whether the visitors had come to buy copyrights or secrets.

Barley returned to his hotel where he had a drink in the bar with a bunch of publishing cronies, among them Henziger, who was able to confirm, to London's relief, that Barley was not drunk—to the contrary, that he was calm and in thoughtful spirits.

Barley did mention in passing that he was expecting a phone call from one of Zapadny's outriders—"We're still trying to stitch up the Trans-Siberian thing." And at about 7 p.m. he suddenly confessed himself ravenous, so Henziger and Wicklow took him through to the Japanese restaurant, together with a couple of jolly girls from Simon & Schuster whom Wicklow was counting on for light relief to ease Barley's passage to his late-evening rendezvous.

Over dinner Barley sparkled so brightly that the girls tried to persuade him to come back to the National with them, where a party was being thrown by a group of

American publishers. Barley replied that he had a date but might come on afterwards if it didn't run too long.

Exactly at 8 p.m. by Wicklow's watch, Barley was summoned to the telephone and took the call in the restaurant, not five yards from where the party was sitting. Wicklow and Henziger strained, as a matter of routine, to catch his words. Wicklow recalls hearing "That's all that matters to me." Henziger thinks he heard "We've got a deal" but it might have been "*not* a deal" or even "not yet real."

Either way, Barley was cross when he resumed his seat and complained to Henziger that the bastards were still holding out for too much money, which Henziger regarded more as a sign of his internal stress than of any great concern for the Trans-Siberian project.

Quarter of an hour later the phone rang again and Barley returned from his conversation smiling. "We're on," he told Henziger jubilantly. "Sealed, signed and delivered. They never go back on a handshake." At which Henziger and Wicklow broke out clapping and Henziger remarked that "we could do with a few more of *them* in Moscow."

It seems not to have occurred to either man that Barley had never before shown so much enthusiasm for a publishing agreement. But then what were they supposed to be looking for, except the night's great coup?

Barley's dinner conversation was later painstakingly reconstructed, without result. He was talkative but not excitable. His subject was jazz, his idol was Slim Gaillard. The great ones were always outlaws, he maintained. Jazz was nothing if not protest. Even its own rules had to be broken by the real improvisers, he said.

And everyone agreed with him, yes, yes, long live dissent, long live the individual over the grey men! Except nobody saw it that way. And again, why should they?

At 9:10 p.m., with less than two hours to kill, Barley

announced that he would stretch out in his room for a bit, he had letters to write and business to clear up. Both Wicklow and Henziger offered to give him a hand because they had orders not to leave him to himself if they could avoid it. But Barley declined their offers and they could not insist.

So Henziger took up his post in the next-door room and Wicklow placed himself in the lobby while Barley stretched out, though in reality he cannot have stretched out even for a second, for what he accomplished verges on the heroic.

Five letters were traced to this short span, not to mention two telephone calls to England, one to each of his children, both monitored within the United Kingdom and bounced through to Grosvenor Square but neither of operational consequence. Barley was merely concerned to catch up with family news and enquire after his granddaughter, aged four. He insisted she be brought to the telephone, but she was too shy or too tired to talk to him. When his daughter Anthea asked him how his love-life was, he replied "complete," which was held to be an unusual sort of reply, but then the circumstances were not usual.

Ned alone remarked that Barley had said nothing about returning to England the next day, but Ned was by now a voice in the wilderness and Clive was seriously considering taking him off the case altogether.

Barley also wrote two shorter letters, one to Henziger, one to Wicklow. And since they were not tampered with, so far as the laboratories could afterwards determine, and since—even more remarkable—the hotel delivered them to the correct room numbers promptly at eight o'clock next morning, it was assumed that these letters were in some way part of the package that Barley had negotiated while he was inside the VAAP building.

The letters advised the two men that if they left the country quietly that day, taking Mary Lou with them, no harm would come to them. Barley had a warm word for each.

"Wickers, there's a real publisher in you. Go for it!"

And for Henziger, "Jack, I hope this won't mean you take premature retirement in Salt Lake City. Tell them you never trusted me anyway. I didn't trust me, so why should you?"

No homilies, no apt quotations from his large, untidy store. Barley, it seemed, was coping very well without the assistance of other people's wisdom.

At ten o'clock, he left the hotel accompanied by Henziger only, and they had themselves dropped on the northern outskirts of the town where Cy and Paddy were once more waiting in the safe truck. This time Paddy was driving. Henziger sat beside him and Barley got in the back with Cy, slipped off his coat and let Cy put on the microphone harness and give him the latest operational intelligence: that Goethe's plane from Saratov had arrived in Moscow on time, and that a figure answering Goethe's description had been observed entering Igor's apartment block forty minutes ago.

Soon afterwards, lights had come up in the windows of the target flat.

Cy then handed Barley two books, one a paperback copy of *From Here to Eternity* which contained the shopping list, the other a fatter volume, leather bound, which was a concealment device containing a sound-baffler to be activated by pulling open the front cover. Barley had played with one in London and was proficient in its use. His body microphones were tuned to defeat the impulses of the device, but normal wall microphones were not. The disadvantage of the baffler was also known to him. Its presence in the room was detectable. If Igor's flat was microphoned, then the listeners would at once be aware that a baffler was being used. This risk had been passed by both London and Langley as acceptable.

The other risk had not been considered, namely that the device might fall into the hands of the opposition. It was still in the prototype stage and a small fortune and several years of research had been lavished on its development.

At 10:54 p.m., just as Barley was leaving the safe truck, he handed Paddy an envelope and said, "This is for Ned personally in case anything happens to me." Paddy slipped the envelope in his inside jacket pocket. He noticed that it was a fat envelope and, so far as he could see in the half-light, it was not addressed.

The most lively account of Barley's walk to the foot of the apartment block was provided not by the military reportese of Paddy, still less by the Haig-speak of Cy, but in the boisterous tones of his good friend Jack Henziger, who escorted him to the entrance. Barley did not utter, he said. Neither did Jack. They'd no wish to be identified as foreigners.

"We walked alongside of each other out of step," Henziger said. "He has this long step, mine's short. It bothered me we couldn't keep step. The apartment house was one of these brick monsters they have out there with like a mile of concrete around them, and we kept on walking without getting anywhere. It's like one of those dreams, I thought. You keep on running but you don't make any distance. Very hot, the air. Sweaty. I'm sweating, but Barley's cool. He was collected, no question. He looked great. He looked straight into my eyes. He wished me a lot of luck. He was at peace with himself. I felt it."

Shaking hands, Henziger nevertheless had a momentary impression that Barley was angry about something. Perhaps angry against Henziger, for now in the half-dark he seemed determined to avoid Henziger's eye.

"Then I thought, Maybe he's mad at Bluebird for getting him into this. Then I thought, Maybe he's mad at all of us, but too polite to say it. Like he was being very British somehow, very laid back, very understated, keeping it all inside."

Ninety seconds later, as they were preparing to leave, Cy and Paddy saw a silhouette at Igor's window and took it to be Barley's. The right hand was adjusting the top of the curtain, which was the agreed signal to say "All's well." They drove away and left the surveillance of the apartment to the irregulars, who covered each other in shifts all night, but the light in the apartment stayed burning and Barley didn't come out.

One theory out of hundreds is that he never went up to the apartment at all, and that they took him straight through the building and out the other side, and that the figure in the window was one of their own people—for instance, one of the tall men in the photograph taken in the VAAP foyer that afternoon. It never seemed to me to matter, but to the experts for some reason it did. When a problem threatens to engulf you, there's nothing like irrelevant detail to keep your head above water.

Speculation about Barley's disappearance began slowly and built throughout the night. Optimists like Bob, and for a while Sheriton, clung on till dawn and after. Barley and Bluebird had drunk themselves under the table again, they kept insisting in order to keep each other's spirits up. It was Peredelkino all over again—a re-run, no question, they told each other.

Then for a short while they worked up a kidnap theory, until soon after five-thirty in the morning—thanks to the time difference—when Henziger and Wicklow had their letters and Wicklow without further fuss took a cab to the British Embassy, where the Soviet guards at the gate did not obstruct him. The result was a flash signal to Ned, decypher yourself, from Paddy. Meanwhile, Cy was putting through a similar message to Langley, Sheriton and anyone else who was still willing to listen to a man whose Moscow days looked like being over very soon.

Sheriton took the news with his customary phlegm. He read Cy's telegram, he looked around the room and realised that the whole team was watching him—the smart girls, the boys in ties, loyal Bob, ambitious Johnny with his gunman's eyes. And of the Brits, Ned, myself and Brock, for Clive had prudently discovered urgent business elsewhere. There was a lot of the actor in Sheriton, just as there was in Henziger, and he used it now. He stood up, he hauled at his waistband, he massaged his face like a man reckoning he needed a shave.

"Well, boys. Better put the chairs on the tables till next time."

Then he walked over to Ned, who was still sitting at his desk studying Paddy's telegram, and he laid a hand on Ned's shoulder.

"Ned, I owe you dinner some time," he said.

Then he walked over to the door and unhooked his new Burberry and buttoned himself into it and departed, followed after a moment by Bob and Johnny.

Others did not bow out so elegantly, least of all the barons of the twelfth floor.

Once again, a committee of enquiry was formed.

Names should be named. Nobody should be spared. Heads must roll.

The Deputy to chair it, Palfrey to be secretary.

Another purpose of such committees, I discovered, is to impart a sense of ceremony to events that have passed off without any. We were extremely solemn.

The first to be heard, as usual, were the conspiracy theorists, who were recruited in short order from the Foreign

Office, the Defence Ministry and a rather unlovely body called the Informal Consultants, which consisted of industrial and academic scientists who fancied themselves as Sunday spies. These amateur espiocrats commanded huge influence around the Whitehall bazaars, and were heard at inordinate length by the committee. A professor from Edinburgh addressed us for five full pipe-loads and nearly gassed us all, but nobody had the nerve to tell him to put the damn thing out.

The first great question was, what would happen next? Would there be expulsions, a scandal? What would become of our Moscow station? Had any of the irregulars been compromised?

The audio truck, though Soviet property, was an American problem, and its abrupt disappearance caused hushed concern among those who had favoured its use.

The question of who is expelled for what is never a plain one, for heads of station in Moscow, Washington and London are these days declared to their host countries. Nobody in Moscow Centre had any illusions about Paddy's activities, or Cy's. Their cover was not designed to protect them from the opposition, but from the gaze of the real world.

In any case, they were not expelled. Nobody was expelled. Nobody was arrested. The irregulars, who were stood down indefinitely, went peaceably about their cover jobs.

The absence of a retaliatory gesture was quickly seen by Western pundits as vastly significant.

A conciliatory move in the season of *glasnost?*

A clear signal to us that the Bluebird was a gambit to obtain the American shopping list?

Or a less clear signal to us that the Bluebird material was accurate, but too embarrassing to acknowledge?

The battle-lines were set. Somewhat along the principle that Ned had already explained to me, doves and hawks on both sides of the Atlantic once more gleefully parted company.

If the Sovs are sending us a signal that the material is accurate, why then clearly the material is inaccurate, said the hawks.

And vice versa, said the doves.

And vice versa again, said the hawks.

Papers written, feuds waged. Promotions, sackings, pensions, medals, lateral postings and downgradings. But no consensus. Just the usual triumph of the fattest, disguised as rational deduction.

In our committee Ned alone refused to join the dance. He seemed cheerfully determined to accept the blame. "The Bluebird was straight and Barley was straight," he repeated to the committee over and again, without once losing his good humour. "There was no deception by anyone, except where we deceived ourselves. It was we who were crooked. Not the Bluebird."

Soon after he had delivered himself of this judgment, it was agreed he was under mental stress and his attendance was required more sparingly.

Oh, and note was taken. Passively, since active verbs have an unpleasant way of betraying the actor. Very serious note. Taken all over the place.

Note was taken that Ned had failed to advise the twelfth floor of Barley's drunken breakout after his return from Leningrad.

Note was taken that Ned had requisitioned all manner of resources on that same night, for which he had never accounted, among them Ben Lugg and the services of the head listener Mary, who sufficiently overcame her loyalty to a brother officer to give the committee a lurid account of Ned's high-handedness. Demanding illegal taps! Imagine! Faulting telephones! The liberty!

Mary was pensioned off soon after this and now lives in a rage in Malta, where it is feared she is writing her memoirs.

Note was also taken, if regretfully, of the questionable conduct of our Legal Adviser dePalfrey—I even got my "de" back—who had failed to justify his use of the Home Secretary's delegated authority in the full knowledge that this was required of him by the secretly agreed Procedures Governing the Service's Activities as Amended by et cetera, and in accordance with paragraph something of a deniable Home Office protocol.

The heat of battle was, however, taken into account. The Legal Adviser was not pensioned off, neither did he take himself to Malta. But he was not exonerated either. A partial pardon at best. A Legal Adviser should not have been so close to an operation. An inappropriate use of the Legal Adviser's skills. The word "injudicious" was passed around.

It was also noted with regret that the same Legal Adviser had drafted a glowing testimonial of Barley for Clive's signature not forty-eight hours before Barley's disappearance, thus enabling Barley to take possession of the shopping list, though presumably not for long.

In my spare hours, I drew up Ned's terms of severance and thought nervously about my own. Life inside the Service might have its limitations but the thought of life outside it terrified me.

The announcement of Bluebird's passing provided a temporary setback to our committee's deliberations, but it soon recovered. The offending item was a six-line affair in *Pravda*, carefully pitched to be neither too much nor too little, reporting the death after illness of the distinguished physicist Professor Yakov Savelyev of Leningrad and listing his several decorations. He had died of natural causes—the bulletin assured us—soon after delivering an important lecture to the military academy at Saratov.

Ned took the day off when this news reached him, and the day became three days, "a light flu." But the conspiracy theorists had a ball.

Savelyev was not dead.

He had been dead all along, and the version we had dealt with was an impostor.

He was doing what he had always been doing, running the Scientific Disinformation Section of the KGB.

His material was vindicated, was not vindicated.

It was worthless.

It was pure gold.

It was smoke.

It was a truthful message of peace sent to us at immense risk by the moderates inside Moscow's ruling ranks in order to show us that the Soviet nuclear sword had rusted in its scabbard and the Soviet nuclear shield had more holes in it than a colander.

It was a fiendish plot to persuade the American fainthearts to take their fingers off the nuclear trigger.

In short, there was enough for everyone to get his teeth into.

And, because in the symbiotic relationship that exists between belligerent states nothing can take place in the one without setting off a mirror reaction in the other, a counter-industry grew up and the history of the American part in the Bluebird affair was hastily rewritten.

Langley knew all along that the Bluebird was bad, said the counter-industry.

Or that Barley was.

Or that both of them were.

Sheriton and Brady were playing double-double games, said the counter-industry. Their one aim was to plant the smoke convincingly and steal another march on the Russians in the endless struggle for the Margin of Safety.

Sheriton was a genius.

Brady was a genius.

They were all, all geniuses!

Sheriton had scored a brilliant coup. Brady had.

The Agency was staffed by nothing but brilliant strategists who were quite unlike their dismal counterparts in the overt world. God preserve the Agency. Where would we be without it?

As if all this were not enough, new tiers of possibility were added to the old. For example, that Sheriton had been the unwitting instrument of the Pentagon and Defense. It was they who had prepared the phoney shopping list and they who had known all along that the Bluebird was a plant.

And each fresh rumour had to be taken seriously in its turn, even if the only real mystery was who had fabricated it or why. The answer, in many cases, appeared to be Russell Sheriton, who was fighting for his hide.

As to the Bluebird, if he had not died of natural causes, he was certainly doing so now.

Ned alone, returned from his self-imposed vigil, was once more so crass as to speak the likely truth. "The Bluebird was straight and we killed him," he said roundly, at the first meeting he attended. He was not invited to the next one.

And all this while our search for Barley did not let up, even if there were those of us who were glad not to find him. We edged towards him, round him and, too often, away from him. But we were honourable men. We never let up.

But what had Barley traded—and for what?

What were the Russians prepared to buy from him—from Barley, who till now had only needed an expensive lunch, paid for most likely out of his own pocket, to talk himself into an irreversible loss?

He was blown, after all! To smithereens! Already by the time he went to them! And knew it!

What had he got to offer them that they couldn't help themselves to? We are talking after all of torture, of the foulest methods, and registers of agony from which even the return is unimaginable hell. The Russians might be improving their image, but nobody seriously supposed that they were going to abandon overnight methods that had stood them in good stead for thousands of years.

The first and most obvious answer was the shopping list. Barley could tell the Russians baldly he would not obtain it from his masters until he had the necessary assurances. And that he would sooner boil in oil for the rest of his life than fetch the shopping list for free.

And they believed him. They saw that they would have to go without the shopping list if they didn't play his game. And because the grey men of either side are as scared of self-sacrifice as they are of love, the tender sages of the KGB evidently preferred to deal with the part of him they understood, rather than meddle with the part they didn't.

They knew he had the power to refuse them, to say, "*No,* I will not fetch the shopping list. *No,* I will not walk into Igor's apartment until you have given me your more than solemn word."

They knew, when they had listened to him, that he had the strength. And, like us, they were a little embarrassed by it.

And Barley—as he had told Henziger and Wicklow at
dinner—had never met a Russian yet who could give his
solemn word and walk away from it. He was not talking of
politics, of course—just business.

And in return? What did Barley buy with what he sold?

Katya.

Matvey.

The twins.

Not a bad deal. Real people in exchange for unreal arguments.

For himself? Nothing. Nothing that could conceivably
modify the strength of his demand on account of those
whom he had taken into his protection.

And little by little it became clear that Barley for once in
his life had hammered out a first-rate contract. If the
Bluebird was a lost cause, Katya and her children showed
every sign of being a saved one. She remained at October,
she was sighted at the occasional reception, she answered
her telephone at home and at her office. The twins still
went to school and sang the same daft songs. Matvey wandered his amiable ways.

Soon, therefore, another great theory added itself to the
rest. "The Sovs are engaging in an internal cover-up," it
ran. "They do not wish to give currency to Bluebird's reve-
lations of incompetence."

So the needle swung the other way for a while and
Bluebird's material was deemed genuine. But not for long.

"This is what they *want* us to believe!" a man of power
cried.

So the needle swung hastily back to where it was before,
because nobody wants to be made a fool of.

But Barley's deal held. Katya did not lose her privileges,
her red card, her apartment, her job or even, as the months
went by, her looks. At first, it was true, the reports spoke of

the pallor of widowhood, of an unkempt appearance and long absences from work. And clearly nobody had promised Barley that she would not be invited to make a voluntary statement about her relationship with the late Bluebird.

But gradually, after a becoming period of withdrawal, her ebullience reasserted itself and she was seen about.

And of Barley himself?

The trail went hot, then cold, then very cold indeed.

Formal letters of resignation, postmark Lisbon, were received by his aunts within a few days of the book fair and bore the marks of Barley's earlier style—a general weariness of publishing, the industry has outgrown itself, time to turn his hand to other things while he still has a few good years ahead of him.

As to his immediate plans, he proposed "to lose himself for a while" and explore unusual places. So it was clear that he was not in Russia any more.

Seemingly clear, that is.

And after all, he said so himself. So did the pretty girl in the Barry Martin Travel Agency, which has its offices in the Mezhdunarodnaya. Mr. Scott Blair had decided he would fly to Lisbon instead of back to London, she said. A courier from VAAP brought his ticket. She rewrote it and booked him on the Aeroflot direct flight, leaving on the Monday at 1120 hours, arriving Lisbon 1530, stopping Prague.

And somebody used that ticket. A tall man, spoke to nobody, a Barley to the life, or nearly. Tall like the men in the VAAP lobby perhaps, but we checked him anyway. We checked him all along the line and the line only stopped when it reached Tina, Barley's Lisbon housekeeper. Yes, yes! Tina had heard from him, she told Merridew—a nice postcard from Moscow saying he'd met a lady-friend and they were going to take a holiday!

Merridew was profoundly relieved to learn that Barley had not, after all, returned to his patch.

Then over the next months a picture of Barley's after-life began to form before it disappeared again.

A West German drug-smuggler while in detention heard that a man of Barley's description was under interrogation in a prison near Kiev. A cheerful fellow, said the German. Popular with the inmates. Free. Even the guards gave him the odd grudging smile.

An adventurous French motoring couple returning home had been assisted by a "tall friendly Englishman" who spoke some French to them when they were involved in a traffic pile-up with a Soviet limousine near Smolensk. Nobody was hurt. Six foot, brown floppy hair, polite, with a big laugh, and tended by these burly Russians.

And one day near Christmas, not long after Ned had formally handed over the Russia House, a signal came in from Havana reporting a Cuban source to the effect that an Englishman was under special detention at a political jail near Minsk, and that he sang a lot.

Sang? went the outraged signal back. Sang about *what?*

Sang Satchmo, came Havana's reply. Source was a jazz fiend, like the Englishman.

And the text of Barley's letter to Ned?

It remains a small mystery of the affair that it never reached the file, and there is no record of it in the official history of the Bluebird case. I think Ned hung on to it as something he cared about too much to file.

So that should be the end of the story, or rather the story should have no end. Barley, in the judgment of the knowing, was all set to take his place among the other shadows that haunt the darker byways of Moscow society—the trodden-out defectors and spies, the traded ones and the untrusted ones with their pathetic wives and pallid minders, sharing out their dwindling rations of Western treats and Western memories.

He should have been spotted after a few years, accidentally but on purpose, at a party where a lucky British journalist was mysteriously present. And perhaps, if times remained the same, he would be fitted out with some taunting piece of disinformation, or invited to throw a little pepper into the eyes of his former masters.

And indeed that was the very ritual that seemed to be unfolding when a flash telegram from Paddy's successor reported that a tall sandy Englishman had been sighted—not only sighted, heard—playing tenor saxophone at a newly opened club in the old town, one year to the day after his disappearance.

Clive was hauled from his bed, signals flew between London and Langley, the Foreign Office was asked to take a view. They did, and it was unequivocal for once—*not our problem and not yours.* They seemed to feel the Russians were better equipped to muzzle Barley than we were. After all, the Russians had obliged before.

Next day a second telegram arrived, this time from fat Merridew in Lisbon. Barley's housekeeper, Tina, with whom Merridew had reluctantly maintained relations, had been instructed to prepare the flat for the arrival of her master.

But *how* instructed? asked Merridew.

By telephone, she replied, Senhor Barley had telephoned her.

Telephoned you where *from*, you stupid woman?

Tina hadn't asked and Barley hadn't said. Why should she ask where he was, if he was coming to Lisbon any day?

Merridew was appalled. He was not the only one. We advised the Americans, but Langley had suffered a collective loss of memory. They near as nothing asked us, Barley who? There is a public notion that services such as ours take violent retribution against those who have betrayed their secrets. Well, and sometimes it is true, they do—though seldom against people of Barley's class. But in this case it was immediately clear that nobody, and least of all Langley, had any wish to make a shining beacon out of somebody they would greatly prefer to forget. Better to square him, they agreed—and keep the Americans out of it.

I mounted the staircase apprehensively. I had declined the protective services of Brock, and Merridew's half-hearted offer of support. The stairwell was dark and steep and inhospitable, and unpleasantly silent. It was early evening but we knew he was at home. I pressed the bell but did not hear it ring, so I rapped the door with my knuckles. It was a stubby little door, thickly panelled. It reminded me of the boat-house on the island. I heard a step inside and at once stood back, I still don't know quite why, but I suppose it was a kind of fear of animals. Would he be fierce, would he be angry or over-effusive, would he throw me down the stairs or fling his arms round me? I was carrying a briefcase and I remember transferring it to my left hand as if to be ready to protect myself. Though, God knows, I am not a fighting man. I smelt fresh paint. There was no eyehole in the door, and it was flush against its iron lintel. He had no way of knowing who was there before he opened to me. I heard a latch slip. The door swung inward.

"Hullo, Harry," he said.

So I said, "Hullo, Barley." I was wearing a lightweight dark suit, blue in preference to grey. I said, "Hullo, Barley," and waited for him to smile.

He was thinner, he was harder and he was straighter,

with the result that he had become very tall indeed, taller than me by a head. You're a nerveless traveller, I remember thinking as I waited. It was what Hannah in her early days used to say we should both of us learn to become. The old untidy gestures had left him. The discipline of small spaces had done its work. He was trim. He was wearing jeans and an old cricket shirt with the sleeves rolled to the elbow. He had splashes of white paint on his forearms and a smear of it across his forehead. I saw a step-ladder behind him and a half-whited wall, and at the centre of the room heaps of books and gramophone records partly protected with a dustsheet.

"Come for a game of chess, Harry?" he asked, still not smiling.

"If I could just talk to you," I said, as I might have said to Hannah, or anybody else to whom I was proposing a half-measure.

"Officially?"

"Well . . ."

He studied me as if he hadn't heard me, frankly and in his own time, of which he seemed to have a lot—much, I suppose, as one studies cellmates or interrogators in a world where the common courtesies tend to be dispensed with.

But his gaze had nothing downward or shameful in it, nothing of arrogance or shiftiness. It seemed, to the contrary, even clearer than I remembered it, as if it had settled itself permanently in the far regions to which it used occasionally to drift.

"I've got some cold plonk, if that'll do you," he said, and stood back to let me pass him while he watched me, before he closed the door and dropped the latch.

But he still didn't smile. His mood was a mystery to me. I felt I could understand nothing of him unless he chose to tell it me. Put another way, I understood everything about him that was within my grasp to understand. The rest, infinity.

There were dustsheets on the chairs as well but he pulled them off and folded them as if they were his bedding. Prison people, I have noticed over the years, take a long time to shake off their pride.

"What do you want?" he asked, pouring us each a glass from a flagon.

"They've asked me to tidy things up," I said. "Get some answers out of you. Assurances. Give you some in return." I had lost my way. "Whether we can help," I said. "Whether you need things. What we can agree on for the future and so on."

"I've got all the assurances I need, thanks," he said politely, lighting on the one word that seemed to catch his interest. "They'll move at their own pace. I've promised to keep my mouth shut." He smiled at last. "I've followed your advice, Harry. I've become a long-distance lover, like you."

"I was in Moscow," I said, fighting hard to find the flow to our conversation. "I went to the places. Saw the people. Used my own name."

"What is it?" he asked with the same courtliness. "Your name. What is it?"

"Palfrey," I said, leaving out the "de."

He smiled as if in sympathy, or recognition.

"The Service sent me over there to look for you. Unofficially but officially, as it were. Ask the Russians about you. Tidy things up. We thought it was time we found out what had happened to you. See if we could help."

And make sure they were observing the rules, I might have added. That nobody in Moscow was going to rock the boat. No silly leaks or publicity stunts.

"I told you what happened to me," he said.

"You mean in your letters to Wicklow and Henziger and people?"

"Yes."

"Well, naturally we knew the letters had been written under duress, if you wrote them at all. Look at poor Goethe's letter."

"Balls," he said. "I wrote them of my own free will."

I edged a little nearer to my message. And to the brief-case at my side.

"As far as we're concerned, you acted very honourably," I said, drawing out a file and opening it on my lap. "Everybody talks under duress and you were no exception. We're grateful for what you did for us and aware of the cost to you. Professionally and personally. We're concerned that you should have your full measure of compensation. On terms, naturally. The sum could be large."

Where had he learned to watch me like that? To with-hold himself so steadily? To impart tension to others, when he seemed impervious to it himself?

I read him the terms, which were somewhat like Landau's in reverse. To stay out of the United Kingdom, and only to enter with our prior consent. Full and final set-tlement of all claims, his silence in perpetuity expressed *ex abundanti cautela* in half a dozen different ways. And a lot of money to sign here, provided—always and only pro-vided—he kept his mouth shut.

He didn't sign, though. He was already bored. He waved the important pen away.

"What did you do with Walt, by the way? I brought a hat for him. Kind of tea-cosy in tiger stripes. Can't find the damn thing."

"If you send it to me, I'll see he gets it," I said.

He caught my tone and smiled at me sadly. "Poor old Walt. They've given him the push, eh?"

"We peak early in our trade," I said, but I couldn't look him in the eye, so I changed the subject. "I suppose you heard that your aunts have sold out to Lupus Books."

He laughed—not his old wild laughter, it was true, but a free man's laugh, all the same. "Jumbo! The old devil! Conned the Sacred Cow! Trust him!"

But he was at ease with the idea. He seemed to take genuine pleasure in the rightness of it. I am scared, as we all are in my trade, of people of good instinct. But I was able to share vicariously in his repose. He seemed to have developed universal tolerance.

She'll come, he told me as he gazed out at the harbour. They promised that one day she would come.

Not at once, and in their time, not in Barley's. But she would come, he had no doubt. Maybe this year, maybe next, he said. But something inside the mountainous bureaucratic Russian belly would heave and give birth to a mouse of compassion. He had no doubt of it. It would be gradual but it would happen. They had promised him.

"They don't break their promises," he assured me, and in the face of such trust it would have been churlish in me to contradict him. But something else was preventing me from voicing my customary scepticism. It was Hannah again. I felt she was begging me to let him live with his humanity, even if I had destroyed hers. "You think people never change because you don't," she had once said to me. "You only feel safe when you're disenchanted."

I suggested I take him out for food but he seemed not to hear. He was standing at the long window, staring at the harbour lights while I stared at his back. The same pose that he struck when we had first interviewed him here in Lisbon. The same arm holding out his glass. The same pose as on the island when Ned told him he had won. But straighter. Was he talking to me again? I realised he was.

He was watching their ship arrive from Leningrad, he said. He was watching her hurry down the gangway to him with her children at her side. He was sitting with Uncle Matvey under the shade tree in the park below his window, where he had sat with Ned and Walter in the days before his manhood. He was listening to Katya's rendering of Matvey's heroic tales of endurance. He was believing in all the hopes that I had buried with me when I chose the safe bastion of infinite distrust in preference to the dangerous path of love.

I succeeded in persuading him to come to dinner, and as a kindness he let me pay. But I could buy nothing else from him, he signed nothing, he accepted nothing, he wanted nothing, he conceded nothing, he owed nothing and he wished the living lot of us, without anger, to the Devil.

But he had a splendid quiet. He wasn't strident. He was considerate of my feelings, even if he was too courteous to enquire what they were. I had never told him about Hannah, and I knew I never could, because the new Barley would have no patience with my unaltered state.

For the rest, he seemed concerned to make me a gift of his story, so that I would have something to take home to my masters. He brought me back to his flat and insisted I have a nightcap, and that nothing was my fault.

And he talked. For me. For him. Talked and talked. He told me the story as I have tried to tell it to you here, from his side as well as ours. He went on talking till it was light, and when I left at five in the morning, he was wondering whether he might as well finish that bit of wall before turning in. There was a lot to get ready, he explained. Carpets. Curtains. Bookshelves.

"It's going to be all right, Harry," he assured me as he showed me off the premises. "Tell them that."

Spying is waiting.

ALSO BY

JOHN
LE CARRÉ

THE HONOURABLE SCHOOLBOY

SMILEY'S PEOPLE

SINGLE & SINGLE

A PERFECT SPY

TINKER, TAILOR, SOLDIER, SPY

THE LITTLE DRUMMER GIRL

THE NÄIVE AND SENTIMENTAL LOVER

PRAISE FOR *I KNOW WHAT'S BEST FOR YOU*

"A resonant collection that champions reproductive freedoms in the face of widespread opposition... A clarion call for reproductive rights."

—*Kirkus*

"Immersive...a timely and frequently captivating look at a hot-button issue."   —*Publishers Weekly*

"In the urgency of our current moment, it is easy to feel despair, to feel overwhelmed. This multi-genre, creative, striking collection reminds us of the complex and intricate ways that reproductive freedom belongs to all people. This collection also points to many possible forms of resistance, beginning with seeing the autonomy of each person written in the deep intimacy of the body. By continuing to read, to write, and to speak out, we begin to counter the increasing threats to our rights."

—Dana Spiotta, author of *Wayward*

"This book is for anyone whose body has been distrusted, coerced, policed, or violated; and for everyone who cares about the grave threats to bodily autonomy in the twenty-first century. The writers in this collection approach reproductive justice from a range of identities, beliefs, and experiences, and what emerges is a thrillingly personal and political response to the emergency we're in."

—Leni Zumas, author of *Red Clocks*

"An urgent, vital collection of essays and fiction, by turns frank and fierce, beautiful and brave. Such voices, and stories are too often silenced or unspoken; it's a gift to hear them now, and a duty to listen."

—Peter Ho Davies, author of
A Lie Someone Told You About Yourself

I KNOW WHAT'S
BEST FOR YOU

McSWEENEY'S
SAN FRANCISCO

I KNOW WHAT'S BEST FOR YOU

STORIES ON REPRODUCTIVE FREEDOM

Edited by

SHELLY ORIA

With support from The Brigid Alliance

McSWEENEY'S
SAN FRANCISCO

FOREWORD
BY SHELLY ORIA

BOOKS ARE SOULFUL BEINGS that come into our fast world slowly. While they're being written, revised, edited, copyedited, and published, the world around them shape-shifts.

When I began to curate this book at the end of 2019, I would often calm myself down by watching videos of Ruth Bader Ginsburg performing TRX push-ups. *She's well*, the videos would whisper to me, *She's strong. Breathe.* The world, since then, has changed its shape.

A few months earlier, on a sunny Saturday, I met Carol Davis for lunch in Manhattan's West Village. Carol cofounded The Brigid Alliance—a nonprofit that arranges and pays the way for individuals across the country forced to travel for abortion care—and now she was discussing with McSweeney's a potential collaboration: an anthology that would respond to our urgent reproductive freedom crisis. I'd just curated and edited another anthology for McSweeney's, *Indelible in the Hippocampus: Writings from the Me Too Movement*, and Amanda Uhle, McSweeney's publisher, asked if I'd take on this new project, a book she hoped would be similar in format and spirit. I arrived at that lunch thinking I was versed in the topic of reproductive freedom, that I understood our crisis and its circumstances. But as I listened to Carol, I realized the situation was far more dire than I knew.

According to the Center for Reproductive Rights, if *Roe v. Wade* were overturned, twenty-four states could immediately prohibit abortion. When you consider that laws restricting abortion are being enacted at an alarming rate—forty-six laws in eighteen states in the first nine months of 2019 alone—the terror intensifies. And have you heard of fake clinics? According to US reproductive rights organization Reproaction, there are currently about 2,700 anti-abortion centers[1] across the country—more than three times[2] the number of clinics that provide abortion care— many of which masquerade as abortion clinics, so they may promote their agenda in all kinds of effective ways, such as suggesting a woman take time to consider her options and scheduling her next appointment for a date when her pregnancy would be too advanced to terminate legally.

---

1 https://reproaction.org/fakeclinicdatabase/
2 https://unladylike.co/episodes/100/crisis-pregnancy-centers

One could put together a powerful book—ten powerful books—filled with stories of abortion or the lack of access to one in today's America. But I felt drawn to a broader approach and invited writers and artists to respond to any aspect of reproductive freedom with which they connected: miscarriages, fertility, contraception, surrogacy, childfreeness... and, of course, abortion. My experience with *Indelible in the Hippocampus* offered insight that made this wide lens feel essential.

In 2017, when millions of people around the globe were sharing #MeToo stories and I began curating *Indelible in the Hippocampus* for McSweeney's, I sought to make a book that would elevate that movement's message and also address its lack of inclusivity; at the time, the stories of white, straight, beautiful actresses dominated our cultural conversation to the point of distortion (even though a Black woman, Tarana Burke, founded the movement in 2006). Making an inclusive anthology—with voices that spanned backgrounds, races, genders, and ages—became even more important to everyone involved. And when *Indelible* came out, when I discussed it or read from it alongside other writers and activists in different cities around the country, it was, in fact, the book's intersectionality that seemed to draw in most readers.

It was at those same events, listening to womxn share their stories, witnessing mothers and daughters who showed up together—so many mothers and daughters, and seeing them wrecked me like nothing else on that tour—that an even bigger narrative began to crystallize. It seemed clear that every aggression they described lived within a context of oppression. That sexual violence against womxn is one of innumerable mechanisms that ensure womxn hold less power than men.

And yet I operated—and the movement seemed to operate—as though there were a finite number of abusers and, if our society exposed and punished them all, our work would be done.

There is a dotted line connecting the powerful Hollywood producer in his robe to every other man who's abused his power and harmed womxn and their bodies. This isn't to say that these men and their stories are the same. It's to suggest that you can follow that dotted line of oppression to Texas, where a six-week abortion ban just went into effect, forcing any Texas resident who needs an abortion to travel for one—or give birth. And you can follow the line to One First Street in DC, where the heavily conservative Supreme Court will soon be hearing what many view as a test case to overturn *Roe*.

As we continue our cultural conversation on reproductive health, as it perhaps heightens over the coming months and years, my hope is that we fight the terrible symptom while keeping in mind the larger illness that produces it, a system in which certain bodies hold inherent power over other bodies.

It is understandable, of course, that we tend to focus on symptoms of societal illnesses more than we focus on the connections among them; seeing those connections can cause paralyzing despair. But if the goal is to see and insist on that larger context without despairing, then that is where art becomes essential.

The stories in this book—by which I mean the short fiction and personal essays, the poems and plays, the comic and photographs—have not only deepened and changed my understanding of reproductive freedom but managed to do so while making me laugh and making me, somehow, against all odds, optimistic. And no matter what shape the world has taken by the time you hold these stories in your hands, I hope they do the same for you.

I KNOW WHAT'S BEST FOR YOU ALL OVER THE WORLD

THIS BOOK WAS COMPILED in response to the American reproductive freedom crisis, and the voices in it speak to the American experience. To explore aspects of reproductive freedom around the world, an international supplement, *I Know What's Best for You All Over the World*, will launch in digital form and be available as an ebook, free with purchase of this book. As I write these words, I'm editing a short story by a Brazilian writer and personal essays from Poland and China. To read these pieces and others from around the globe, visit *mcsweeneys.net/iknow* and enter the code IKNOW to download the ebook.

HYMN

BY DESIREE COOPER

WITH NOTHING ELSE TO feed him, she pushed the last slice of bread into his baby bird mouth. "Take this, eat." She taught him how to pray as he trembled in the bathtub where the bullets couldn't find him. They said it together every night as they practiced living on their knees: *If I should die before I wake*. He didn't die, such was the shield of her love. She willed it and he thrived, a rose in the desert.

Day by day, she reminded him: "I love you with all my heart, all my mind, all my strength." Blessed are those who are another's joy.

But in the Valley of Shadows, the serpents slithered. Samaritans never stopped to help. Fishes and loaves did not multiply. Suffer, little children. A table was always set for the privilege of the enemy. In the house of many mansions, the rich hoarded their manna.

He wore his coat of color, a gift from his mother. He looked good. *This is my body*. In his pride, he was a target for the rulers of the fish, the fowl, and all other living creatures. They burst into his front door: Render to Caesar, the things that are Caesar's.

They threw her begotten son into the yard, a pig in the dirt. In the doorsill, his mother wept. Giving his last breath back to her, he despaired: *"Why hast thou forsaken me?"*

LET'S JUST BE NORMAL AND HAVE A BABY

BY ALISON ESPACH

MY HUSBAND, TIM, HAS nine months to live, which doesn't upset him as much as you might think. Tim has been dying for years now, and he's become quite good at it. He journals in the morning and then takes long, meaningful walks along the beach. He collects seashells for our kitchen vase and makes elaborate dinners for me when I come home from work, the kind of recipe with over twenty ingredients. He doesn't even want to travel the world anymore—we've already done that. He just wants to be at home with his wife, eating a good meal. And the food Tim cooks is so good—overwhelming, really—that it makes me sleepy. I sit back in my chair and say, "Jesus. What are you trying to do, kill me?"

Tim laughs. "I'll clean," he says. "You go get ready for bed. I'll be up in a minute."

My husband is sweet—too sweet. After being the perfect person all day, he still has the energy to admire me from the bedroom doorway. He stands there longer than he should, just looking at me, and I can't take it anymore, how he tilts his head as if he is trying to get one last look. It makes me feel as if he is already a ghost, watching me get dressed for bed alone.

But of course, he's not a ghost. He's still very much alive, and I don't know why I have to keep reminding myself of this. He walks toward me, puts his hands on my waist. He has nine months to live, which sounds like no time at all when I say it in my head, but like a lot of time when Tim says it. He always says it with such enthusiasm, as if these last nine months will be our finest. As if we'll eat such good food and have such great sex, I won't even notice that he's dying. And for the most part, that is how it's been. We've eaten so much good food and had so much sex that he's actually starting to become a little predictable about it, walking into the bedroom, moving the hair off my shoulder. Saying, "Oh, Lisa," and then kissing me slowly up the spine.

But tonight, I don't feel like it. Tonight, I am not wearing my I-want-to-have-sex-with-my-husband-before-bed outfit. It was a long day at work, and I'm very tired. Not to mention a bit cold. It's January. Every day there's a dry freeze upon our roof, which is why I put on my I-am-very-tired-and-a-bit-cold outfit when dinner is over. Flannels and my old oversized college sweatshirt and the headband I always forget to remove after washing my face.

But my husband doesn't care about my outfit. He probably doesn't even notice. My husband was not raised like me—trained to believe that there are certain blouses that will make men fall in love with you, certain shoes that will help you win cases in the courtroom. My husband does not look for his own power in places outside of himself, in clothing stores and in the dark of our closet, which is something I've always loved about him. How he sat down at the bar on our very first date knowing exactly what he wanted to drink. A gin and tonic. My husband, he's reliable, consistent. The same wonderful man every day. And, time has proven, he will have sex with me in any outfit.

"You look beautiful," he says.

My husband thinks everything is beautiful, even my headband. He's been complimenting me a lot since we got back from the doctor's, for the same reason he's started staring out the window a lot, admiring the trees. He's been investing meaning in meaningless things, like the snow that falls on his open palm and the new calendar he bought from CVS, each month a different Labrador, the kind of dog he always wanted but traveled too much to keep. Normally we spread our calendar flat on the butcher block—but Tim hung this one up. He said he wanted to see each one of his final months on the wall. He wanted to look each day square in the eye.

My husband is all about meaningful eye contact these days. In our bedroom, he turns me around, looks me in the eye, and begins to take off the clothes I just put on, one article at a time, like people do in the movies. I've always liked this, too, how slowly and seriously Tim takes sex, but when I undress him, it doesn't feel the same anymore. It feels cryptic. As if I'm stripping Tim of important layers of Tim, and after, when he's standing before me naked, he keeps looking me in the eye as if he's not undressed, as if I can somehow help him out of his I-am-going-to-die-soon outfit, a long flesh fault running alongside his ear.

"Let's have a baby," Tim says.

"A baby?"

"You know," he says. "The miniature people with no teeth."

I laugh, but only because I'm confused.

"Why would we want to take care of a miniature person with no teeth?"

"Isn't that what married people do?" he asks, smiling. "Or is that just a nasty rumor?"

"Definitely a rumor," I say. "Besides, we don't want that."

"We don't?"

Lately, the cancer in Tim's brain has been messing with his memory. Gives him seizures in the night sometimes. I spend a lot of time holding Tim's hand as he shakes, reminding him of who we are. This is what we do on the nights that we aren't having sex.

"No," I say. "We've never wanted that."

"Are you sure?"

"Yes," I say. "I'm very sure."

Not wanting children was what bonded us on our very first date, when I confessed right away that I didn't want to get married or have kids. That's what it started to feel like in my mid-thirties, a confession, a terrible thing I had to reveal before the drinks arrived, because if I didn't, men would look at me over the perfectly lovely tiramisu and say, "Well, that's too bad," as if I had poisoned it. Sometimes, they got curious. Asked me about my parents and then my ovaries—were they good? Some even tried to argue me out of it—strangers who didn't know me, now suddenly very worried about my being alone one day in a nursing home, dribbling oatmeal down my chin. "Why didn't you tell me this before our date?" one of them even asked, as if I were an imposter. And I was getting very tired of this—these men were wasting my time too. They were never the men I expected them to be. And so when I sat down at the table on my next date, I told Tim right away.

"Just so you know, I don't want to get married, and I don't want kids," I said, and then our margaritas arrived.

Tim leaned forward.

"Good," Tim said. "Because I'm dying, and I can't do any of that."

At first, I didn't believe him. At first, I was just as bad as those men. Tim looked healthy across the table, fresh-faced and flushed, like a man who just walked off of his boat. A man who would live forever. He looked like all he wanted to do was drink his margarita, which was comically large.

"Are you joking?" I asked.

"That's what *I* asked," Tim said. "But the doctor was not joking. Says he's got proof and everything. Scans. X-rays. Blood tests."

I laughed. I knew even then that I would fall in love. That maybe I already was in love. Here was a man who wanted to make me laugh about his own death. A man who accepted us both as we were. A man who wanted to make the best out of the time he had left, which was how I often felt about my life, even though I wasn't sick.

"I've got two years," Tim said. "Maybe three, if I'm good."

I felt I should say something more. Like, *I'm sorry*. Like, *If you're dying, then why on earth are you online dating?* But I held my tongue. I didn't know what it meant to be dying. I hardly even knew what it meant to be online dating. And I hoped that when I died, I could do it like Tim. Go to fine restaurants with strangers and hold up my drink and feel grateful for the margarita.

"To three more beautiful years," he said, raising his glass.

And they really were three beautiful years—the best years of my life. We ate a lot of food. We went on a lot of vacations. And my boss was very understanding. Sentimental ever since a city bus nearly swiped him out of existence, and so when I asked for time off, he said, "Go. Go to France. Go to California. Live your life." And there, wherever we were, it was like something out of a movie, except better, because it was my life, and I got to be the woman standing on the balcony overlooking the ocean with a man I loved. We ate oysters and went bungee jumping. We stayed up all night and talked about who we used to be. He woke me up on the hottest nights, asked me to come swimming with him. Tim was fun. Tim was always standing in a beautiful body of water, asking me to come join him. And I knew that the movies were right: dying really did make people better—something we joked about all the time.

"You would *not* have liked me before I was dying," Tim said in the pool. "Trust me. I was kind of an asshole."

And I believed him. I have finally learned to believe what people tell me about themselves, and over the three years, Tim has told me a lot—those months in college when he maniacally tried to become a professional punter for the Patriots and those women he dated just because they had long blond hair or those jobs he took because they made him a shit ton of money. His last job was his worst—in sales—so why continue? He quit as soon as he was given his death sentence, and he said it felt good, living off his retirement.

"All of a sudden, I'm rich!" he said. "Dying has given me my life back."

I wasn't dying, but I knew what he meant. Work didn't seem that important now that I was in love for the first time in my life, finally and wholly connected to another human being in the way I had always dreamed, and maybe—a therapist suggested—it was *because* he was dying. Because you *know* you can't be together forever.

"Or maybe," I argued, "I'm just in love."

"That's always a possibility," the therapist said, and that was the last time I saw her, because why did I pay some woman to tell me the truth about myself? I already knew the truth about myself. I was in love.

I did not hesitate when Tim proposed in the middle of the night after only a year. I rested my head on his chest. His heartbeat was fine. Loud in my ear. I thought, *Maybe we'll both live forever*. I confess, this is what I secretly believed, as we bought a house near the sea, as we boarded planes for far-off places, as we giggled inside the fancy restaurant after the waiter profusely shamed himself for "accidentally omitting the palate cleanser." We said this to each other for months after, whenever one of us started to get mad at the other: "Is it because I accidentally omitted the palate cleanser?" And we cracked up. And it was nice how the worst of our fights always turned into our favorite jokes. Life was not meant to be taken so seriously. Life was funny. Life was *good*.

This is what I had believed, even as I dressed for the doctor's office in January, as I combed my hair and put on my everybody-is-going-to-be-fine blouse, a bright red thing I wore on days I went to court. I held Tim's sweaty hand, sliding my dry, coarse fingers through his. I was quiet as he was quiet. I put my other hand on his back and made tiny circles like, *It's OK, it's OK. It's OK?*

No.

The oncogene amplification is much greater than previously believed, the doctor said.

At least that's what he sounded like. Then he pushed his glasses further up his nose.

"What does that mean?" I asked.

"Nine months," he said. "Maybe a year."

And I did feel as if it were my fault, like I should be able to do or say something more, the whole way home. But I couldn't. I looked down at my blouse and thought, *My husband is dying. No matter what I wear, my husband is dying. My husband is dying.* That was when I first understood it for real, and now that I understand it, I can't stop seeing it all over his body and his face and in the red scar along his skull. Each night feels like his last, and I'm exhausted by this, all the grief I'm going to feel forever.

"We can't have a baby," I say. "You're dying."

He pulls away from me. He laughs a little.

"Thanks for reminding me," he says.

I am guilty, though I don't know of what. I cover myself at night in old sweatshirts and blankets. I cry sometimes, and this upsets Tim, because Tim just wants to live. Tim just wants to do crazy, miraculous things like be a father.

"At the doctor's, it occurred to me that if you got pregnant now, I could actually *meet* our child before I died," he says. "I just keep thinking about that. Actually getting to hold our baby before I go."

"But I don't understand," I say. I can feel my heart speed

up, the way it does in court when the defense brings out a piece of evidence I'd never reviewed before. When the other side breaks the rules and nobody seems to care but me. "You never wanted to be a father before."

"Death changed me, I guess," he says.

He is joking, but I don't laugh. I am getting tired of joking about his death. At night, when I close my eyes, I can feel all that is about to happen to us, and it feels real. It feels like he is actually changing, like he wants more now than ever before, and he's hurt because I don't. He resents that I am still the same person, getting into bed under sheaths of fabric that signify nothing other than it's bedtime, sleep-time, not sex-with-cancer-husband time.

"Come on," he says. "Let's just have a baby. It'll be fun. The baby will be cute. That's what I always hear about babies."

"It's not that simple."

"People do it all the time," he says. "My father did it, and he was a moron."

"This isn't a joke," I say. "It's my *life*."

"I know," he says. "But it's my life too."

His fingers graze my belly button, the most naked part of my stomach. A hole without a covering. He measures its circumference with his tongue: "A perfect circle," he says. The size of a marble.

"Stop that," I say.

I swat him because I don't like it when he does this. Lately, he's been looking at my body like it's an open field, a place where he can imagine great things for himself. He's been entering me and pulling out later and later, coming all over my chest. After, he looks up at the ceiling. He cries. He goes into the bathroom, takes his medicine for the seizures and the painkillers for the pain, which make him unable to control his speech. He slurs his words, replaces his *t*'s with *p*'s. He asks me what I think it will be like when he's gone, and I don't know what to say.

"Like you're gone, I guess," I say.

And I know this must sound cruel. But I really don't know how else to answer. I can't imagine what something like that will feel like.

In February, there is snow all over the ground, all over the evergreens. On good days, Tim stands tall in the kitchen with a mop in hand and makes jokes I try to appreciate: *dead man mopping*. He writes important things on the new dog calendar, mutual events, things we are going to share together. Brunch at the Potters', Logan's birthday party, Mother coming for dinner. He says, "Why don't we go somewhere warm for a few weeks?"

But I can't. "I have work," I say. I've got meetings. Appointments. Things I must do if I want to continue living for years and years and years. I buy a separate calendar, just for me, a small one with no pictures of anything, just empty pages for all the things that I don't feel right putting on the dog calendar. My dentist appointment, my driver's license renewal. A family reunion a year from now, when I know Tim will be dead. I hide it under the nighttime reading books, the ones with predictable endings that I now have difficulty understanding.

On bad days, his gums bleed on his toothbrush. He has seizures without warning. Drops to the floor and begins to shake, and yet he claims that I am the one who is changing. I am the one who takes B6 supplements, folic acid, and buys aluminum-free deodorant. I am the one who worries about things that are meaningless to Tim now, like tartar buildup. One night, he watches me save a Word document titled "Ten-year Financial Plan" on the computer and looks like he's about to throw up right there on the monitor. I shut down the computer, go into the bathroom, put on my headband, and scrub my face with a coarse washcloth, and he just watches from behind as I scrub and scrub and scrub the dead skin off my face, and I can finally breathe again.

"Stop," he says.

"Stop *what*?"

He holds up my secret calendar.

"Stop hiding things from me," Tim says. "What *is* this?"

"A calendar."

"We already have a calendar."

"But this one is for different stuff."

"For your secret life."

"My appointments. My boring life."

"Your continuing life."

"Yes, to help manage my continuing life," I say. "God, Tim, be reasonable. It's just a calendar."

"No, *you* be reasonable," he says. "You don't have to hide this from me. You need to treat me like the man I always was."

So I say, "Fine, why are you snooping in my things?"

And he says, "I didn't realize you had your things and I had my things. I thought this was *our* bedroom."

He goes to take a shower, which is rare for him. Showers are tiring. He can't even hold his hands up over his head long enough to wash his hair before they go numb. But he needs to cool off, he says. And after, he has cooled off.

"Lithsen," Tim says. "Listen. The point is, I'm running out of pime."

"I know."

He turns to me, caresses my face.

"You're so beautiful," he says.

This is when I start to cry.

At breakfast, Tim's speech is restored, like someone hit him in the head and shook him back into being himself.

Tim likes his tea with cream and his eggs undercooked. I get out the frying pan, rub the butter over the surface, and say "Mm-hmm?" every time I think he has spoken. But he's not speaking. He says, "I didn't say anything."

Tim sits back in his wooden chair, barely sips his tea.

"It's funny to think that my cancer cells are killing me right now," he says. "As I sit here sipping tea, they're killing me."

"Maybe not," I say.

The doctor said it was important to visualize things. Good things. And maybe that's what the baby is all about. Maybe the baby is just a fantasy, a carrot in the distance that will keep Tim walking.

"What do you think they are doing then?" he asks.

"Could be watching a film," I say.

"Maybe," he says. "But it's a little early in the morning for a movie."

"You think our cells know that it's early in the morning?"

"Of course they do," Tim says.

I go to work. I don't know what Tim does all day. For weeks, I don't ask.

In March, the snow melts and Tim is still full of energy. Tim is planting violas all around our yard. They make our house look so alive that I question the doctor's specific knowledge.

"Did he make any sense to you?" I ask. "I'm thinking now that he made no sense. Do you think he knows everything there is to know?"

"Irrelevant," Tim says. "There's no point to the experimental surgery."

"Are you sure there's no point to it though?"

"Yes," he says. "A million times, over and over again, I'm uncomfortable with the idea that, in order to continue living, I'd have to do it as a guinea pig."

"Well, I'm uncomfortable with the idea that, in order for you to continue dying, you will have to die."

"We've been over this, Lisa. This is my decision."

It was true. We had gone over this. Just like we had gone over the decision about the baby.

"Don't expect me to change my decisions then," I said.

"I'm tired," he says. "I'm getting tired. I don't want to fight."

"Of course."

We stir our tea. Rather, I stir the tea because Tim doesn't want tea, but I know he wants a mug with a spoonful of sugar and a drip of cream in case he changes his mind about wanting tea. Though he doesn't. He has reached a certain irreversible point, reclined in his chair. Steadfast about dying the way he wants to die.

I can't help myself.

"The point of living longer is to stay with me," I say.

"You won't want me like that," he says.

"Of course I will."

He laughs.

"You don't even want me now."

"That's not true," I say.

But it must be true, because we haven't had sex for nearly three weeks. I look at the dog calendar, as if the dogs somehow know this too. But the black dog of March is silent, sitting in a wicker box surrounded by daisies.

In April, Tim's mother comes for dinner often. She is surprisingly pleasant until she has three glasses of wine and starts saying terrible things to me in the kitchen as we clean. She says, "A baby might be nice." She says, "Won't it be a little piece of him?" She says, "This is my only son." She says, "You know, I didn't even want Tim, but now look at me. Now look at how upset I am."

I can see how upset she is. There are tears running down her face, ruining her face, every time she leaves our house.

"We agreed we didn't want kids," I say.

"What's *wrong* with you?" she asks. "You sound like a lawyer."

"I am a lawyer," I say.

His mother always forgets this, a fact her brain won't process, the way I always forget when she's coming over for dinner. But I won't explain myself. There is nothing wrong with me. I am perfectly healthy. That's what the doctor told me at my last physical.

"You're cold," Tim's mother says. "I told Tim that years ago. I said, 'That woman is cold.'"

"Good thing I'm not a blanket then," I say.

After she leaves, we usually talk about her, go through a highlight reel of all the tiny ways she offended us. This used to be one of Tim's favorite things to do after she left—"I can't believe she said that to you," he would say—because he has always struggled with his mother. She was tough. But one night, after she leaves, we don't talk about her. He turns from me in bed. He brings the covers up to his chin.

"I'm cold," he says, shivering. He becomes so quiet, I can't tell if he's sleeping.

"Tim," I say. "Tim, Tim, Tim?"

But he doesn't answer. And I know that this is what it will feel like once he's dead.

In May, I start thinking about Tim's death so much, I'm sometimes surprised he's still here, underneath our bedspread, something I can still collect in my hands. It's surprising to see the muscles in his forearm, the blood pulsating at his neck.

"There are just so many things left to do," Tim says.

"Like what?"

"I still have to climb Mount Everest," he says.

"Of course. I mean, most people still have to do that."

"I still have to run a marathon."

"Overrated," I say.

"I still have to have a son and teach him how to throw a baseball."

"But what if your son hates baseball?"

"Then I'd teach him how to hold a tennis racket," he says. "And if he didn't want to do that, I'd buy him a dictionary and we'd start memorizing all the words from A to Z. And he would say, Dad, why is the bogeyman in the dictionary, you swore he wasn't weal. And I would pat his head, and say, Goodnight, I wove you, I wove you, I wove you. I would wove him so much."

This is what happens when we don't fall asleep before midnight.

In June, the dog sits next to a bike, curiously sniffing a black rubber tire. Tim is slowly sagging in his chair, and I'm unable to discern whether the wooden legs are the chair's or Tim's. I'm making eggs on the stove, trying to decide if this is the beginning of my life or the end of my life, when Tim clears his throat. Tim has an important announcement.

"This is my last calendar," Tim says.

Tim speaks like the last of something is just as noteworthy as the first. That all moments in life deserve their own cataloguing: baby's last step, baby's last outfit, baby's last word, baby's last breath.

"Isn't that weird?" he says. "You never think you'd know something so stupid so concretely. This is the last calendar I will ever own."

"Tim, please," I say.

"I will never own another calendar."

"It's breakfast," I say. "It's too early to be macabre."

He picks up his fork, stabs it in the yellow egg. "What if it were dinner?"

"I don't know."

"What's the difference between dinner and breakfast?"

"Is this another joke?"

"No."

"Then, I guess, the amount of marinara sauce."

"Let's go for a walk," he says.

"Are you feeling OK?"

"Yes. It's only breakfast. I'm fine."

"But it's raining. Don't you want to stay inside?"

"Lisa, I'm the one who is dying; don't you forget that."

"Like I'd forget."

"Got to keep my figure," he says. "How else will I pick up women poolside in heaven? There will be a pool; you know that, right?"

I know. I know all about this magical place that I dreamt up for him in the late hours when Tim got scared.

"It will be clean without chlorine, and you won't have to take a shower first," I say.

"So warm, I won't even have to dry off after," he says.

But now it's not a joke. Now, I know he is punishing me, letting me know that there will be women in heaven who will want to have his baby. He does not smile anymore, and his collarbone sits starkly across his neck like a thick, metal chain. I throw the runny egg in the garbage and do what my friends and family suggested: whatever he wants.

"Let's go for a walk," I say.

I take his hands, and his knuckles are sharp blades against my skin. And maybe it's really true. Maybe there will be women in heaven, just waiting to have his baby. Maybe these are things he believes now.

What will you name your baby? I want to ask, but I don't.

I put on my fun-outdoors-activity outfit and am silent

at the risk of making too many jokes that are not mine to make so early in the beautiful day.

In July, the dog is brown, upright, a broad chest on a pedestal. At dinner, Tim is hunched over like a defeated human, slurping in a single spaghetti noodle. I am in my work-to-dinner outfit: a red camisole with pearl buttons and chapped lips that are so inarticulate, everything they do and say feels like a stale performance of someone's past.

"What do you think the problem is?" he asks, wiping the marinara sauce off his chin.

"I think it's the sauce," I say. "Too much onion powder."

"I mean, why don't you want kids?"

"Oh, this again," I say. He says nothing. "I just don't."

Never once did he ask me to explain it before. He just understood it was something I didn't want. He understood that not having a baby was sort of like never coloring my hair red. There's nothing wrong with anybody coloring their hair red. It looks really nice on some people. But it's just not my hair color, and nobody ever expects it to be. Nobody comes up to me and says, "Why don't you want your hair to be red, what is wrong with you?" as if that were the only suitable option.

"Maybe we could go to a therapist," he says. "Figure it out."

"I think we have bigger problems," I say.

These are some of our recent problems: the seizures Tim is having in the middle of the day. The medicine he takes that makes him go to the bathroom several times during the night and the way he looks at me after he wets himself in bed. The way he begs me not to feel sorry for him: "Please, I am nobody's victim. Please just treat me like the man I always was." So I put a bucket by our bed. I say, "OK, fine." I say, "Maybe if you start making it to the bucket, we can sell all your urine to science and go on a nice vacation."

"That'd be nice," he says. "Maybe Paris."

But we don't go anywhere. We are patient inside. We are still and complacent inside. We eat when we need food, we nod our heads when we seek affirmation, and we say things we swear we both mean.

"Cremate me," Tim says.

"You want to be turned into ash?" I ask.

"I want you to roll me up and smoke me like a joint."

"That's seriously what you want?"

"I don't know. I'm too relaxed to know anything for sure," Tim says.

Yet, he draws conclusions anyway. He says things like, "Dying now is probably just like dying later." And "What do you think it will feel like? Like going to take your next breath and you just can't find it, or are you already so dead by the time you die, you can only watch it from above the ceiling fan of the hospital room?"

I'm not sure.

"I don't think there are ceiling fans in hospitals," I say, and he laughs so hard. He turns to me.

"Thank you for making me laugh." He runs his hands along my body, to show me how grateful he is.

"Lisa," he says.

These days, Tim is more dead than alive, and it feels cruel and unusual to refuse him things he wants. But I am still tired, the way I used to always be tired before, when I didn't get a good night's sleep. It felt OK not to have sex with Tim then. Tim had a few more years. But now that Tim has weeks—a month maybe—he looks at me like all he needs is my body, and I feel more and more obliged to give it to him, as if it is a life raft. We kiss until he pulls away. He always has to pee, just before sex.

"I'll be right back," he says.

He gets up and out of the bed, runs to the toilet, and flushes every time.

"You don't have to flush every time you pee," I say.

"It's rude not to," he says and climbs back under the covers. "I may be dying, but I still have manners."

"I guess that's something."

He holds my face. "Look at me," he says. "You're never looking at me anymore."

"What?" I ask. "What do you want?"

"I really want a baby," he says.

He clarifies. "Let's just make a baby," he says. "Let's just be normal and have a baby."

I do not look at him. I stare past his face like the bedpost will do something miraculous any minute now. I close my eyes. I am going to scream, and then I remember: he'll be dead soon.

"Tim," I say. "You're *dying*."

"Exactly," he says. "And aren't you scared you'll be alone?"

"I'll be alone," I say. "Even with a child."

But Tim doesn't understand this. Tim says, "But you won't be. You'll have the child."

"The child will make it worse."

"How could the child make it worse? It's a child."

Exactly. It's a child. And the child will need things. And I do not want daily reminders of Tim that need to regularly eat. I do not want to look at something that is almost Tim, once-was Tim, who stands two feet tall at my knees and asks me to cut the crusts off the turkey sandwich, because I'll say, "Tim, I don't understand. You always liked the crust."

"You're so beautiful," he says.

Tim strips off my I-am-not-ready-for-this outfit, and my skin is tight against his flesh. He sweats, and, with every drop of perspiration, I sink into the bed. I feel farther and farther from him, as if he is evaporating above me. With every drop of his head against my shoulder, he says, "It's like my body is yours," and I say, "No, no, my body is yours." And doesn't that make you angry? Sometimes, my body feels just like your body. But I know it's not. Because, Tim, at your funeral, I will stand out in the rain just looking for you. I will feel the droplets against my skin. I will wonder: Tim, do you still know what water is? I will return home, and there, the dogs will be asking for you. Wondering where you went. And it will feel as if time has stopped, and yet the dogs will look at me each month, with their little noses. They will say, Tim, Tim, Tim, why don't you come outside and throw the ball for us?

"Tim!" I yell, as he collapses over me.

"I'm sorry," Tim says.

Tim couldn't control himself. Tim doesn't understand what just happened. Tim didn't mean to.

I run to the bathroom. I feel my husband leaking out of me, down my leg. And sometimes, even though he's dying, I hate him. Sometimes, I think, *It will be just fine if he dies. I will be just fine.*

"Did you do that on purpose?" I ask.

"No," he says. "That was an accident. You really think I would do that on purpose?"

But I don't know. I just don't know.

The next day, I go to the pharmacy alone. I swallow the pill in the parking lot of CVS without water. It sticks in my throat, and I wonder if all the choices I have ever made have been a mistake. I wonder if I am a terrible person for denying my husband his only dying wish. I wonder what we would name our baby. Would it be Karl, like his father? Susan, like his mother? And then I turn on the car and I swallow again, because there will be no Karl or Susan.

There will be only me, and I will be a new woman, the kind who has buried her husband.

After, I don't go home right away. I feel an urge to meet this woman. I am intrigued by her and all that she will suddenly know and feel. So I go to the mall and search for a black dress because that is what she will need to wear when her husband is dead. I need only one, but I end up buying five of them because I can't bring myself to try them on at the store. The mall is too cold. I watch in disbelief as the cashier scans them like they are regular dresses.

"My husband is dead," I say, to try out the words.

"I'm so sorry to hear that," she says, and it is disappointing, how anticlimactic it all will be.

At home, Tim is watching TV, but he is unimpressed by drama too. He says watching people on TV is like watching aliens complain about life on earth. He shuts the TV off, and I consider trying on the dresses for him because that is what he would have asked me to do when he first started dying. He would have wanted a private funeral fashion show just for him. He would have said, "*That's* what you're wearing to my funeral?" and we would have laughed. But he is different now, slowly sinking into the earth with each passing day, and I am not. I hide the dresses deep in the closet, and we don't speak for days. I worry that we'll never speak again, that maybe this is how he will die—quietly, alone in the corner, both of us angry. Until one night at dinner, Tim looks up over his plate and says, "Is it because I omitted the palate cleanser?"

I laugh. But I don't know what to say.

"You know, they say lack of communication is the number one reason for the death of a marriage," Tim says, and I say, "Are you joking?"

Tim doesn't know. He rubs his chin.

"My mouth feels funny," Tim says.

"What do you mean?" I ask.

"Something is not right," he says. "My mouth is not right."

He stands up. But then he is on the floor again, seizing. I hold his hand, as he says, "Just talk me through this," and I do. His eyelids flutter, and he goes somewhere I cannot follow. I tell him things I've been meaning to tell him. The dinner was delicious, I say. The shrimp were just right. And the violas you planted. They look beautiful. Finally, when he comes to, he says, "I'm OK, I'm OK."

I keep looking at him all night, expecting him not to be OK.

"Stop looking at me like that," he says.

"I can't," I say.

"Then get into bed with me," he says. "And stare at the wall. Pity that instead."

Tim is OK, Tim is OK. Tim is in our bed. I press my ear to his heart for evidence, and there it is. The drumbeat of his life. He runs his hands through my hair. He can't believe how long it's gotten. He can't believe how my hair will continue to grow for years after he's gone, like the violas outside the window. Sometimes, he confesses, the thought makes him angry. But that night, the thought makes him happy. It makes him want to plant more things before he goes.

"Maybe we can plant a few trees this weekend," I say.

"Yes, let's do that this weekend," he says.

I fall asleep quickly thinking about our trees and the nice weekend ahead of us. But later, I dream about Tim dying. I dream about the paramedics breaking into our bedroom like a SWAT team, searching for his body, and I'm confused, because Tim is not dead yet. I point to my husband in bed as proof, but they say, "Nobody is there." They say, "Mrs., Ma'am, excuse me," like this is a formal occasion. They say, "Your husband is already in the bag."

And I just look at them, as if they are the ones betraying me. I say, "This is my house! This is my husband. This is my life." But they don't care. They don't apologize. They are just doing their jobs. They pick up the bag. They are a distant chorus of "Mrs., Ma'am, excuse me, please step away from the body," and so I wake.

After, I don't know what to do with myself. Tim is still alive, still asleep. I walk into our closet, and I run my hand along the seams of all the my-husband-is-dead dresses. I try each one of them on, stare at myself in the mirror until I see that my husband is right—my hair really has gotten long, and I wonder how long it will become by the time I am old. I close my eyes and imagine my hair all the way down past my feet and into the ground. I imagine it hardening and thickening like a root, keeping me sturdy and strong, the way I felt at the very beginning, when I was lifting up my glass to toast to something.

¥360/$360

BY KIM GEK LIN SHORT

¥360

SOCIAL MAINTENANCE FEE, ONE CHILD CHINA, 1987

THE PEOPLE DON'T ASK Real Momma when she expects. In Zhōngguó she won't straddle her bike with corpse. The crud on her ankles the fat footprints in the road. It's a long walk to not be a momma. The people don't ask Real Momma *do you need the toilet*. Corpse pose in her drawstring pants. Over-quota oozing a just-born mud. The people don't pick the river bottom from her hair. The two banana-shaped bends with feet: the people don't pick the toes tied with tubers. It is invisible. The people don't give Real Momma a barf bag. When the second is born a girl when the third is born a girl. She barfs where the bank was cut. The people don't ask Real Momma what sex she sank in the pond. Hēiháizi sex: a black weed. The people don't throw a party. The sound of the people not throwing a party. She hears it the whole walk back.

$360

COST OF ABORTION, PRO-X AMERICA, 1987

THE PEOPLE ASK AMERICAN Momma when she expects. In the parking lot a one-piece population plugs the path. The dirt on those not-orthopedic boots. It's a long walk to not be a momma. The people prod American Momma *where do you kneel*. Buckle up tight in that forgiveness-asking spot. Kudos on your elastic pants. The people pour American Momma bona fide wash. A cleanup gush for grand old constipation. Kudos on squeaking your shit. The people rate American Momma her top two names. Blur of boots on *Nothing But*. Stirrups chafing *If I Did*. The people chide American Momma a chant to make war of. Kudos on your super crampy curse. The people taunt American Momma *what will you wipe*. 1) A high hide pastel paint. 2) A menstrual pang. The people wipe her body. The squeak of the people wiping her body. She hears it the whole walk there.

PROGRESSION

BY SAÏD SAYRAFIEZADEH

THE NEWS THAT THE State of Virginia has, as of January 2020, finally become the thirty-eighth state to ratify the Equal Rights Amendment unfortunately arrives—at least for my mother and me—far too late. No doubt my mother, who is eighty-six years old and suffering from dementia, will be unable to recall that cold winter morning in 1976, when the two of us woke before dawn to travel to Richmond, Virginia, by Greyhound bus, along with fellow members of the Pittsburgh branch of the Socialist Workers Party. I was seven years old then and en route to yet another demonstration for the ERA, which, by this time, had been thoroughly impressed upon me by my mother as one of the great and attainable social changes that could actually happen in my lifetime (workers revolution being another).

The ride from Pittsburgh to Richmond took nearly six hours, and the combination of the cold winter air, the stale heat blowing through the vents, the uncomfortable seats, and the incessant forward motion along highways caused me, midway through our journey, to vomit into an empty soda cup held in front of my mouth by my mother. But once in Richmond, my health and mood lifted, and we were joined by more protesters—mostly women—including members from other Socialist Workers Party branches around the country. Together, we listened optimistically to speaker after speaker—also mostly women—as they exhorted Virginia to join the thirty-five states that had already ratified the ERA. There was no time to waste, of course, since a deadline—seemingly arbitrary—had been established: if thirty-eight states had not ratified the ERA by March 22, 1979 (thus making it a constitutional amendment), everything would be lost, and we would revert back to zero with nothing to show for our efforts.

Richmond was as cold as Pittsburgh and got colder as the day went on, and when the last speaker had finished, all five hundred of us marched through the frigid air toward the statehouse, chanting and holding our banners aloft, passing shoppers and office workers who stopped to stare at us as if we were a circus come to town. I felt the familiar sensation that I always felt when I was at a protest, that of being on display, like a monkey led through the streets for townspeople to gape at. There was a woman leading the throng and chanting through her bullhorn, "Hey, hey, what do you say? Ratify the ERA!" Hopeful voices rose up in unison, and my mother joined the chorus, her voice sounding exceptionally slight and frail in the wide open air of the city. I shouted along, because to remain silent would have made me conspicuous in the eyes of both the bystanders and the people with whom I was marching.

"What do we want?" the bullhorn asked.

"The ERA!" I screamed.

"When do we want it?" the bullhorn asked.

"Now!" I screamed.

There was comfort in being among five hundred other like-minded people who were able to see the problem outlined before us and understand that there was a clear remedy for it. And as I marched and shouted, I began to feel that we were the ones who were inside, and those who stood idly on the sidewalks with their bags and their brief-cases were lost on the outside. They were the circus and I had come to watch *them*.

When we finally arrived at the Virginia statehouse, a few more women took the microphone to again make our demands known to anyone who might be listening. Behind them was a well-scrubbed flight of stairs ascending toward a gigantic white building surrounded by impassive columns. "The seat of ruling-class power," my mother told me. Its grand, imperial architecture had a sobering effect on the day's events, putting into perspective what the odds really were. By late afternoon the protest was over, and with the winter sun beginning to set, my mother and I boarded the Greyhound bus and rode the six hours back to Pittsburgh where—amid childlike thoughts of having, through our efforts that day, actually won the ERA—I fell asleep in mother's lap.

ANTI-FAIRY TALES FROM THE FEMININE BOOK OF FUCK THIS

BY KATE TARKER

CASTING NOTE:
IMAGINE THE CHARACTERS LOOK JUST LIKE YOU.
THEN READ AGAIN AND IMAGINE THEY DON'T.

CHAPTER TWENTY-SEVEN.

A new Wife, late twenties, rummages frantically in her tote bag. Her Husband, same age, is under the covers trying to block out the light.

WIFE

Honey? You asleep?

HUSBAND

Mmm.

WIFE

Can you help me? I can't find my rights.

HUSBAND

Huh?

WIFE

My reproductive—they've gotta be here somewhere.

HUSBAND

They're not with the essential documents?

WIFE

You didn't see 'em, did you? Lying around?

HUSBAND

Honestly, I don't think about them all that much, since
you're on the ring.

WIFE

Shit.

HUSBAND

I'm sure they're here somewhere. Don't freak out.

She empties out drawers. Pulls heavy coats and boxes out of the closet. He sits up, more awake.

HUSBAND

Sweetie?

She stubs her toe. Screams.

She turns on all the lights in the apartment and walks to the front door. She opens the door and tests the lock. He walks over to her.

WIFE

Does this look broken? The door?

HUSBAND

Nothing else is missing. Why would someone break in just

to take this from you?

WIFE

I don't know, man, you tell me.

She walks to the center of the living room and puts her hands on her hips. She pulls off all her clothes, piece by piece. After each one, she pats her soft flesh down.

Pat pat pat pat pat pat pat.

Pat pat pat pat pat pat pat.

Nothing there.

Nothing.

He walks up to her. Reaches out. Gently touches her shoulder blade. She swings around, furious.

HUSBAND

Honey?

WIFE

WHERE ARE MY RIGHTS.

HUSBAND

I don't know! OK? I'm sorry! But also, it's two in the morning— and we both have work tomorrow— and neither one of us is much of a rock star without sleep—

WIFE

I had them last month, swear to God.

HUSBAND

You're not pregnant. Right? We can look again after breakfast.

WIFE

If I can't say no, how can I ever mean yes? I'm so young. I want my career to launch. I want to go to Istanbul. I want to learn how to fly a plane. I want to do amazing things ... for people I'm not related to. I want my whole life to unfold.

HUSBAND

Honey. Deep breath. It can't all disappear overnight.

She closes her eyes. Breathes.

WIFE

I hate having to worry how to hold on to more agency than a toddler gets.

HUSBAND

We're safe here. It's not like this is Texas. Or Ohio / Georgia / Missouri / Alabama / Iowa / Kansas / Kentucky / Pennsylvania / Illinois / Rhode Island / Louisiana / Oregon / Utah / Florida / Delaware / West Virginia / Oklahoma / Tennessee / Utah / Montana / North Carolina / Michigan / North Dakota / Mississippi / Indiana / South Dakota / Wisconsin / Massachusetts / Maryland / New Jersey / New Mexico / New York. There's a reason we left the Lone Star State.

WIFE

Did you just say New York?

HUSBAND

Yeah. Why?
... Oh.

WIFE

No. No no no no no no NO NO NO NO NO NO NO NO.

She sits down on the floor, at a total loss.

He sits down, too.

HUSBAND

We'll figure this out.

WIFE

With what? Magic?

CHAPTER THIRTY-FIVE

Inside a beat-up minivan. Mom drums lightly on her steering wheel to some punk rock.

Daughter, restless and speckled in mud, bops around in the back seat.

> MOM

How was practice?

> DAUGHTER

Good. I kicked total ass.

> MOM

Of course you did. That's 'cause you're awesome. Don't kick the back seat.

Daughter keeps kicking the back seat, like a metronome. Mom ignores this. Eventually, Daughter gets bored and looks out the window. They pass by strip malls, endless strip malls.

DAUGHTER

Mom. Are you sure you're thirty-five?

MOM

Pretty sure. Why?

DAUGHTER

'Cause I'm seven.

MOM

You working on your math?

DAUGHTER

Didn't you have me at twenty-six?

MOM

Mm-hmm. Same age Nana was when she had me.

DAUGHTER

Twenty-six plus seven is thirty-three.

MOM

That's right! And that makes you seven.

DAUGHTER

Um. Mom? That makes me *nine*.

MOM

This discussion's over.

DAUGHTER

Are you really that bad at math?

MOM

I froze you at seven.

DAUGHTER

You did *what*?

MOM

For me, life got rough after seven. So I try to cap you around that age.

Mom looks at her kid through the rearview mirror. At her joyfully messy hair. At her half-painted rainbow nails. At her intelligence.

MOM

I hate this. But I think the time has come. For the talk.

Daughter locks deeply skeptical eyes with her.

MOM

Honey. You know how you had an imaginary friend when you were three?

DAUGHTER

Yeah ...

MOM

Well, sweetie. You're *Mommy's* imaginary friend.

DAUGHTER

What the FUCK?

MOM

You love soccer and french fries and the names of presidents. You're active and lots of fun. You love bad words and so do I.

DAUGHTER

So the other girls on the soccer team ... ?

MOM

Ah ...

DAUGHTER

Madison? Taylor? REAGAN??

MOM

Figments, decorative flair. Total bullshit.

DAUGHTER

What about the minivan?! Don't tell me you made up the Toyota?!

MOM

I'm so bad at imagining what this life would be like, all I can conjure up is this stale midwestern fantasy ... Ooh look, an Arby's!

DAUGHTER

BUT I LOVE THIS MINIVAN. THIS MINIVAN IS

COVERED IN MY MUD AND FOOD AND SWEAT.

Mom sees an animal on the road and panics. She swerves. Misses it, just barely.

> DAUGHTER

Omigod.

> MOM

I don't actually know how to drive. Never got my license. But don't worry.

They continue on, in tense silence.

The landscape gets more rural. They pass by cows and rolling fields.

> DAUGHTER

This is so humiliating. You're never gonna have me, are you?

> MOM

Yeah ... I love kids ... but realistically, I don't know how that would be possible.

DAUGHTER

Oh come on!

MOM

I'm not exactly rolling in dough. At some point, you have to cut your losses. For sanity's sake.

DAUGHTER

If you really wanted me, you'd find a way to pay for me.

MOM

With what? Magic?

Daughter covers her ears and screams.

MOM

Look. This is not that big of a deal. You *might* still happen. And even if you don't ... you know, it's really cool and unprecedented that I get to be an ordinary person, passing through. Nothing more, nothing less. Enjoying my brief time out here.

DAUGHTER

I hate you and I hope you die.

Mom lights a cigarette. Inhales the harshness. Breathes it out.

MOM

Do you want a puff?
I'm a nonsmoker. But my mom smokes. Your Nana.

DAUGHTER

Yeah, I *know.*

Mom takes one more drag.

MOM

Pretty sure she smoked when she was pregnant with me.

She flicks the cigarette out her window.

MOM

The real bummer is, your dad would be a truly awesome—

Daughter swings the car door open. Mom slams on the breaks.

MOM

Hey. Stop.

DAUGHTER

Give me one good reason to stay.

MOM

You don't know what it's like. Being childless.

MOM

Sometimes ... I can really psych myself up. Convince myself I'm a person. But other times ... I don't actually believe I'm worth anything. Or deserve anything.

Unless I have *you.*

There are some shit days, where the only way I can make myself brush my hair or go outside or do my work is by imagining I'm doing it for you. It's fucked up, I know, but ...

Please.

DAUGHTER

Pussy.

MOM

Cunt.

DAUGHTER

Bitch.

MOM

Pootang.

Daughter scowls, but pulls the door shut and snaps her seat belt back in place.

MOM

We can stop for a milk shake, 'k? On the way home.

DAUGHTER

Where do you actually live?

MOM

In a big, big city.

DAUGHTER

I wanna know about your real life.

MOM

I'll tell you. When you're older.

DAUGHTER

Bitch.

Mom laughs. Daughter smiles.

Mom drives deeper into the dark and cranks up the music.

CHAPTER SIXTY-EIGHT

A beautiful blue-sky day. Tourists huddle around their Guide, a woman in her late sixties.

GUIDE

Thank you all for signing up for this nature walk through the Norman Bird Sanctuary! I am a retiree, and a volunteer, and I love birds. Together, we'll pass through diverse habitats and sumptuous ridge vistas, overlooking the gorgeous ocean. Then we'll meander through my pain, exasperation, and rage, and finish up right back here at 583 Third Beach Road in Middletown, Rhode Island.

A TOURIST

How long is the tour?

GUIDE

Estimated round-trip walking time, twenty minutes.

They begin their walk.

GUIDE

I'm your guide, or, if you prefer, your guide-ess. I used to think it was dumb to mark gender with the ending of a word. *Especially* when talking about professions. Actor. Actress. President. Vice-Presidentress. But the older I get, the more I understand feminine endings and their purpose. It's to help women understand their career will likely start out strong, but over time, mysteriously arc back down, whimper, and disintegrate.

She pulls out her binoculars and scans the treetops.

GUIDE

I think it's a heads-up, and a heads-up is an act of kindness. Now, the secret to birding is simple and plain. Use a mnemonic.

THE INDIGO BUNTING

Fire, fire! Where, where? Here, here! See it, see it!

GUIDE

Hear that? That's the indigo bunting. Reminding you that the elemental safeguards of your selfhood are disappearing all around you. Sex ed. Birth control. Abortion. All roasting in the blinding flames of a pseudo-religious barbecue.

THE BARRED OWL

Who cooks for you, who cooks for you all?

GUIDE

Mmm. That's the barred owl. Demanding money and respect, after centuries of underpaid and unpaid labor. Labor forced, and labor stolen. Scrubbing and stirring, all for someone else's gain.

WHITE-EYED VIREO

Spit, and see if I care, spit.

GUIDE

I love that sweet songbird! The white-eyed vireo doesn't give a rat's ass. Remember her call, ladies, when someone labels you a slut online. In my case, it's usually when I disagree with people, politely, about horticulture.

BROWN THRASHER

Drop it, drop it, cover it up.

GUIDE

That's the brown thrasher, singing a song for the worst

of days. She reminds us of the self-obliterating but essential tactics that many people are forced to employ, just to survive.

THE MEADOWLARK

But I do love you. But I do love you.

GUIDE

Ah. The lovely meadowlark. Voicing a painful truth. I love you, but I need you to stop killing me. This one's *such* a popular tune. Sung by all genders, races, ages, and up and down the income ladder. In my family, the women tend to sing it to their men. It was passed down from my grandmother, to my mother, to my child.

They keep walking, for a beat.

GUIDE

He only threw me down the stairs once. My dad. But that was enough to make me miscarry.

A TOURIST

Why didn't you stop him?

GUIDE

With what? Magic?

The Guide looks sharply at the Tourist, then turns back to scanning the trees.

GUIDE

I think that's why I love the great outdoors. I can't stand being inside a house.

A minute or so passes. Then she hears it.

THE HERMIT THRUSH

Where are you? And here I am. Why don't you come to me? Here I am, right near you.

GUIDE

Oh! That's my favorite! The hermit—

She turns to her crowd but realizes they've disappeared.

A beat.

GUIDE

Where are you? And here I am. Why don't you come to me? Here I am, right near you.

She waits for her tourists to reappear.

Where are you? And here I am. Why don't you come to me? Here I am, right near you.

She walks off-path and sits down by the seesawing waves.

GUIDE

Keep singing. Keep singing ...

PROTEST

BY R.O. KWON

JOHN LEAL TOLD US we'd have to attend a protest in Manhattan, a pro-life march. It's taking place this Saturday morning, he said. I know it's not much notice, but Christ is asking us to be with Him. John Leal outlined a plan he'd established, with local churches, to drive to New York with people, supplies, and then he swept into one of his wild soliloquies, telling us again about the time he'd helped a desperate girl in the North Korean gulag abort a half-foreign child. Though he saved the girl's life, he still wept if he thought about the fetus he pulled out, its recognizable fist.

It was close to midnight when I walked home with Phoebe. The night was mild. She was quiet; I held her hand. I'd fallen behind with studying, and I was tired. I hadn't slept; I wished to be home. I'd have proposed calling a taxi, but, the previous evening, I'd discovered I didn't have my half of the month's rent. I was still working a partial load at Michelangelo's, a few night shifts each week. I'd been offered a follow-up research position, a role extending the last project; I turned it down, since I had no time. I suggested a fellow Phi Epsilon. Short of options, I had to activate a credit card I'd once received, unsolicited, in the mail. I didn't want the debt. I'd learned what harm a credit habit might inflict. I'd kept the card just in case, for emergencies, positive I wouldn't use it. But then, last night, I'd pulled a label off the plastic, the adhesive giving up its hold with sickening ease: like mother, like son.

What's more, if I went to the march, I'd have to switch Saturday's shift for a less profitable slot. More cash lost. The trip would involve spending, too. I wanted to quiz Phoebe as to what she thought of it. By the time I joined Jejah, John Leal's group, they'd stopped picketing Phipps clinic; why, she hadn't known. She'd never protested the clinic, she'd said, but she believed, as I did, that abortions should remain legal. I didn't think she could have changed her mind. We waited at the light. Instead, while a flesh-pink neon sign, Tivoli, fizzed behind us, I asked about the first gulag story he'd told. The pregnant girl, I said. Lina. Mina. She was kicked in the stomach. You told me about it: she died, then trailed him. Is this one girl?

I saw a taxi turning, its sign lit. No, they couldn't be, Phoebe said, at last.

I flagged down the cab. In silence, we rode home. I've examined this night, Phoebe. I've rethought what I said to you, and I'm still sure of this much: I kept quiet a long time, then I asked a single question.

*   *   *

We followed him as he pushed a path into the waiting crowd. The protest hadn't started yet, but wind rippled plastic-sheathed signs. Sunlit fetuses swung up, down, while flags flicked like striped tongues. John Leal halted; he spun, abrupt, and doubled back. I thought he'd tell us we'd taken a wrong turn. Instead, he butted his face up to mine, so close I felt his breath.

Will, he said. Oh, Will. He'd learned, he said, that I was full of questions. So, I was confused about his time in the gulag—which, all right, it had been a bewildering time for him, as well. Given I hadn't lived through it, how much more so for me. But why hadn't I brought my questions to him? It grieved him that I could still be this prideful. Think, he said, of John the Baptist telling us he couldn't touch the latchet of his Lord's shoes. I still hadn't learned how to be a disciple. It was high time I did. If, that is, I had it in me. I should kneel, he said.

He handed me a thin rag; he told me to wipe the others' shoes, then his feet. I cleaned each muddied shoe. Melted ice soaked cold into my jeans. I held his foot, working the rag through his toes. Flecks of tissue gleamed, like nacre, in the cracked skin. I was trying to think. His time in the gulag, he'd said. It was what I'd asked Phoebe. The question about Mina, but we'd been walking home. We'd left John Leal at his house. If he hadn't, how'd he—

I glanced at Phoebe, but she looked down. She'd turned red. Phoebe didn't blush often. If she did, the cause tended to be physical. She'd had too much alcohol, or it was hot. Phoebe hadn't been drinking, though. It was a cold morning. Each breath showed white. I wouldn't have believed it possible, but she still couldn't look at me. She'd gone to him with what I'd said.

*   *   *

It was past the time the march should have begun, and people were losing patience. I'll give it five minutes, then I'm calling it quits, a man said. Placards leaned against a building wall. I saw John Leal talking to people I didn't recognize. With a nod, he stepped on an upended crate. His mouth moved. In that hubbub, I couldn't pick out his words. Phoebe apologized again, tearful. It's all right, I said, but she had more she wanted to explain. It's fine, I said. Hoping she'd calm down, I kissed Phoebe's head. I was intent on listening to John Leal's speech: I was curious what his effect would be with this large an audience, if they'd respond as we did. He lifted his head, pitching his voice.

... hands splashed with blood, he said. We're all here this Saturday morning, and I know I don't need to tell you the truth that an unborn child has a heartbeat before it's a month old. I don't have to tell you that, within the first three months of fetal life, a human infant's strong enough to grip a hand. But I'm not sure if it's done much good, all this truth. What point it's had, if you and I aren't saving lives.

Wind gusted, flapping nylon jackets. Instead of trying to talk across the noise, he held up his palm, indicating he'd wait. More people turned in his direction.

The Lord is calling us, he said. But we've failed, you and I, in following Him. We're living in a time of great evil. Rivers of blood, replenished with children's bodies, are flooding this nation, and we've let the blood spill. If we are lukewarm, the Lord has said, He will spit us out of His mouth. I'll ask you what I've asked myself, late at night, as I wait upon His Spirit: if the likes of you and I won't be radical for God, who will?

While he talked, his voice had risen. He finished with a shout, then he fell silent. The crowd around us was hushed, listening. Raising his head, he asked if he could get an amen. Several people replied; he asked again. This time, the amens belled toward him. I felt my ears ring. Yes, Lord, he said. Oh, Lord, I beg, be here with us. He called out the opening line of a hymn, one I recognized, and the crowd sang it back to him. Phoebe joined in, hands folded. She rocked back and forth, eyes closed, and I thought of the night we'd met, how she'd danced until she gasped for breath, holding the thick hair in a ponytail. It was damp at the tips. Sweat trickled down her slim throat. Phoebe's rolling hips parodied that night; so, too, the rapt, upheld face. The other night, she'd told me, as she apologized, that he'd asked how I was doing with Jejah. He'd spoken with love, she said, and she'd responded in kind, without thinking. I'm not upset with you, I said. I wasn't: she didn't have to apologize. I felt a long confusion lifting. If anything, I should be grateful. For some time, I'd also failed to think.

The crowd kept singing. I watched, alone. It was a horde, and they all had what I lacked. In what He's credited to have said, the Lord is explicit. He insists on full, absolute devotion, nothing less. John Leal had that part right. But from the start, I'd obeyed His call. I'd pledged my life to Him, intending to serve Him with all I had, if to no avail, which left me believing God had to be nothing, a fiction; that, or He didn't want me.

Fifteen minutes, a man said. The crowd shifted forward. I put a hand in my pocket, and I felt a twist of plastic wrap I'd forgotten bringing. It was a small bundle of prescribed sedatives, pills I'd grabbed at the last minute

because Phoebe and I planned to stay in the city that night.
I had enough trouble sleeping that I relied on these pills,
the bottle's festive castanet rattle a promise, preludial to
rest. Though I hadn't tried taking them except at night,
before I went to bed, the pills also tranquilized. I could use
a little extra calm, I thought. I opened the cellophane. To
rush the effect, I chewed the pills.

*   *   *

The march began. We'd been asked to walk in silence.
Phoebe stayed close to me, a light hand at my back. The
first time we showered in a shared stall, she'd pointed out
the indent of my spine. This, she said. Here. She'd traced
the rill, following the line down to my ass. I hadn't conceived, before then, of having a back worth noticing: now
I did, the skin gilded with Phoebe's sight.

This situation, well, it was a crisis. The girl I loved
was in a cult—and that's what it is, I thought, a cult. It
was a problem, but I'd solve it, because I was intelligent.
The sun's heat intensified. Disquiet thawed until, tran-
quil, awash, I almost sympathized with these people. If
I were convinced that abortion killed, I, too, might think

I had to stop the licit holocaust. It wasn't so long ago that I'd believed as they did. In fact, I pitied them. Goodwill toward all, I thought. While driving down from Noxhurst, I'd asked Phoebe, at last, if she agreed with the protest's object, having abortions outlawed. It isn't what I want to think, she'd said, but a fetus has a pulse within a month of fertilization. It's alive.

We marched awhile before the pill's effect changed shape. I'd been watching protest signs bob past, marveling at bloodied photos, when a fetus jumped down. Others followed, flailing. Infant fists lifted; placentas writhed like tails, trailing dots of blood. One fell inches from my foot. I squatted, and I picked it up to prevent its being trampled. It was small, not quite spanning my hand, so I retrieved a second twisting fetus, then a third. Phoebe crouched down with me. What's wrong? she whispered.

I asked if she'd give me the handbag; instead, she asked what I was doing. With my chin, I motioned toward my little charges, but I'd lost them. I looked around. White orthopedic shoes flitted past. She nudged me, repeating what she'd said. But they'd vanished. I'd imagined the field of fetal children. The first time I filled the sleeping pill prescription, a pharmacist had cautioned me about potential side effects. Mild hallucinations, he'd said. This wasn't mild, though. I'd have to tell the pharmacist. Phoebe asked if I was hurt, so attentive it brought tears to my eyes. I'd taken a sedative, I explained. It was the pill I used to sleep, except, this time, I'd stayed awake. It had, perhaps, gotten a bit strong.

Stand up, she said, rising.

I tried; I couldn't. She helped me to my feet. The flesh of my arm bulged around Phoebe's tight grip. She released me, and kept marching. I focused on each step: left, then right. The next time I glanced up, John Leal was walking next to Phoebe. His hip grazed her side, so I tapped his arm. I have a question, I told him.

Not now, Will.

I—

We'll talk after this.

No, I said. This isn't a request. I want to talk.

His head tilted, as if to see me in a different light. He glinted at the edges, protean, slipping. I had to grab him while I still could. Pin him down until he'd admit to his shape-shifting lies. He rubbed his face. I can't help you, Will, he said. I've tried, but I don't have the time. To be honest, I've lost interest.

Before I could think of how I'd respond, Phoebe pulled me back. Soon, we'd left the protest behind. We stood out on the street, hailing taxis. Lines of cars sped past, cutting long scars in the slush. The cabs were all occupied. I'd forgotten where I'd parked. I watched the sidewalk flecks, blotted gum. The harsh dazzle of pitted ice. Wind stirred the trash. In a lost, past life, I'd fancied these to be coded messages, dispatches from a loving Lord. Each detail flashed with divine relevance, but it was a false hope. What I had instead was this: salted bitumen, an oil-stained plastic bag. I should give it more attention, not less. I swayed, trying to understand.

With a brush of kidskin, Phoebe put my hand to a lamppost. Hold this, she said. I'll be back in an instant. She crossed the plain of ice until I couldn't be sure which of the distant backs was hers. Folios of newsprint drifted. Close by, a girl in bright lipstick fiddled with a bike's chain. She jumped on its seat; she lurched left, raincoat flaring out. The thin form grew a sail, a pale nephilim wing. I thought she'd fall, but she pinged the bike bell, then swept down the street.

Will, Phoebe called, leaning out from an idling cab. She took me to the station, waiting until the first train that would go north to Noxhurst. Once it pulled in, she talked the attendant into letting her on without a ticket. He doesn't feel well, and I'm not staying, she explained, giving him her smile.

Here, she said, pushing my seat into a recline. I tried to apologize, but she said she had to get back to the protest. She set my phone's alarm to ring before my stop.

What about the apartment? I asked, remembering. Your friend's place.

Oh, that, she said.

She took out her phone. I was about to say I could wait in the apartment until the protest finished, but she said, still looking at the phone, I'm staying the night. From the train, I watched Phoebe go, striding fast, horizontal. I'd have left the train, chased Phoebe down, if I'd been less to blame. The train slid into the afternoon, and I slept until the Noxhurst station.

*   *   *

Up through the next morning, in spite of what she'd said, I still thought Phoebe would come back Saturday night. But I woke Sunday to find she wasn't home. She also hadn't returned my calls. I should have studied; I opened a book, stared at it as long as I could, then poured a drink. I sat in the apartment through morning: I took a bus to Michelangelo's. Though I didn't have a shift, I helped at the front until I noticed a five-top littered with used plates. I carried them back to the kitchen, spilling pesto on my shirt. I dropped a knife. I took the table's busboy out back, and I yelled at him. I asked what the fuck he'd been thinking. Looking down, he muttered that it wasn't his table. It's Gil's, he said, his childish face bagged with fatigue. I excused him. I left, riding the bus home again.

The sun went down, and I called Phoebe. I left a short message asking if she'd let me know she was all right. Relying on the principle that almost nothing happens as I think it will, I started ticking through possible disasters. What I predicted, I'd forestall. I sat at the kitchen table. Each time I emptied a glass, I poured the next drink. It was 3:10 in the morning when the front door swung open. She stood in the hall, half-dissolved in porch light. Easing the lock into its slot, she set down a bag. She turned. Oh, she said, startled. It's you. What are you doing?

I closed the laptop, and, with it, all the light I'd had. I'd been searching traffic-accident reports. She flicked on the hall lamp. I saw Phoebe take in the gin bottle, the knit hat I still hadn't removed. Will, she said. I told you I was staying the night.

I didn't know when you'd be home. I kept calling.

My phone died, she said. I didn't notice it until a minute ago.

Hope rose, then fell. While she hung her coat and pashmina, I took a long, sustaining swig of tonic-splashed gin. The plaid skirt twitched on Phoebe's thighs, brass buttons gleaming. The phone had tolled through its full five rings before it prompted me to leave a message, which meant it had been on. If it hadn't, the phone would have shunted me to Phoebe's voicemail with just one ring. No, each time I called, the phone had vibrated. She'd pulled it out, seen *Will*, and put it back in the bag. I was able to see what she'd done, in such detail that I knew it had to be true. When I could, I asked how she'd gotten home.

I drove, she said. I, well, John Leal did. I was too tired. I'll make tea. Do you want anything?

Getting up, I went to the sink. I'll do it, she said, but she hesitated, then sat. I filled the kettle. From the cupboard, I took down the aged puerh I'd bought in Beijing's tea bazaar, a labyrinth I'd spent hours roving, intent on finding what she'd like best. It's the king of teas, the merchant had explained, pouring me a sample cup. Unable to decide, I'd tried so much tea I'd had to piss outside, behind the building. I broke off a piece. I crumbled it into the mesh basket. Puerh leaves unfurled, like relaxing fists.

You should have something, she said.

I don't want tea.

I'll bet you haven't eaten.

I hadn't, I realized. In a panic, I'd failed to eat since morning. She could tell, by looking at me, if I needed to eat. I took Phoebe the cup. She leaned into my side. With an arm swathed in cashmere, the soft fibers prickling, she pulled me close. My breathing slowed. Once, not long ago, she'd pointed to a picture on a friend's wall, a child with his arms flung out. Posed like a kite, she'd said. A kite, I repeated, the word unrolling a tableau of blanched sand. Heat. Light. Surfboards gliding, iridescent; swimmers beaded with sea foam. Harlequin kites spooled high, lolloping toward the sun. In that childhood photo, I couldn't avoid noticing a crucifixion pose, while she saw—a kite. I'd loved Phoebe's pagan mind, unpolluted with His blood. Phoebe, forgive me, I should have said, help me, but then she shifted to drink the puerh. Let go, I moved to sit at the table, a tall vase of white phlox dividing us. She inhaled steam. Wire hangers, I said.

What?

Bleach, I said. For millennia, women have tried to induce home abortions. They've drunk bleach, hot lye—even the Bible gives tips about this. Quinine. Hippocrates advises a prostitute to jump up and down. I told Phoebe about a high-school friend, Stu, who'd punched his knocked-up girlfriend in the stomach until she fainted. She asked to be kicked down the stairs. He'd done it, blinded with tears. The abortion she wanted was too expensive, and she had Baptist parents she couldn't tell. Once, a local wit, calling in to a radio show, was asked to explain what people did for fun in Carmenita, California. Get pregnant, he said. The kind of people she, Phoebe, knew would always be able to obtain abortions, while fifteen-year-old children in towns like mine spewed—*what?*

Phoebe shook, laughing. No, it's just, Will, you researched this. The quinine. You looked it up, getting all these points in line.

Tell me why you picked Christians, I said.

Excuse me?

You chose the one set of beliefs I wasn't going to be

able to stand. I'm asking if it was on purpose, if it's something I did.

I can't fight tonight, she said. She pushed away the tea. It sloshed in the cup, without spilling. I'm so tired. I don't know what's happened, why you've turned against Jejah, but please, let's go to bed. We'll argue in the morning, if you like.

I looked in the news, I said. From the spring before last, in Yanji, China. I searched headlines. John Leal's a U.S. citizen. If he'd been abducted by North Korean agents, his organization would have reported it. It would be a big fucking deal. "Edwards student missing, presumed kidnapped." But there's nothing, Phoebe. I couldn't find a single mention of him.

Will—

I think he's lying.

Well, I don't.

If you were taking up, oh, Buddhism, I wouldn't mind. If you'd decided to collect old coins—

Oh, she said, leaning back. Old coins. Will, if that's what you want, I'll be less of a hobbyist. I have to stop living in sin. No, let me finish. I've waited for God to hand me a revelation, but I don't think that's how He loves us. Hold on.

This isn't about you, Will. I've given it a lot of thought. If I did what people here do—if I chased high-paid jobs, and I wrote fifteen-page papers on Milton, I have no idea who that would help. But if I could find out what I am. If I have a soul. I've thought about what St. Augustine said, that we have to beg the Lord to know Him. It wasn't until the 18th century that the Church established belief as a precondition of Christian faith—if I act as though I believe, maybe I'll also experience the divine. If I don't, I'll have tried. Isn't that what you did?

She reached across the table, waiting for me to admit that yes, I had. But I was also picturing the two of them in the car's claustral space: a private, long drive, the partial curtain of Phoebe's hair swinging. She laughed, ignoring phone calls. He'd have instructed Phoebe about what to tell me, tonight. It was central to his appeal that he liked giving orders. Is this his idea? I asked.

No.

Did he stay with you last night?

It wasn't, she said. He did, but it's not—

So, let's be honest. This isn't about being a born-again virgin for Christ. It's about you, the wide-eyed acolyte, fucking the guru.

Will, you don't mean this.

Sure, I do. It's what people do in cults like Jejah. You do realize, of course, that it's a cult. That's what's changed, if you're wondering. I wasn't sure, at first, but it's the truth. He's a low-rent Jesus freak with Franciscan affectations. So, how does it work: do you take turns, fucking him, or is it one big orgy, just a giant Christ-loving pile? I wish you'd told me, though. I'd have joined you—

She pushed the cup off the table. A wet stain swelled across the floorboards, broken glass glittering. I'll get it, I said.

Don't, she said, crying. I went to find the broom. When I returned, she was still at the table. I brushed glass into the dustpan, but the bristles proved too coarse. I wetted paper towels. I daubed up what I could. With each pass, I folded the towels in half until the square was too small to use. A glint caught my eye: a piece had fallen on Phoebe's foot, between the fine-boned toes. I picked it off; she shied.

It was glass, I said.

I don't care.

She went into the bedroom. The slam rattled the toaster oven; its lid fell open. I thought of the short-lived ruckus, years ago, when a Carmenita high-school kid, Jim, had sighted Christ's face in a slice of burned toast. Local papers published photos of the miracle bread, His face almost visible. While, at the time, I credited the apparition, I'd also felt the insult. I believed, of course, that household theophanies took place, visions of the Son of Man spotted in pieces of foil, paint blotches. Spitz dogs' assholes. Crocks of jam. Burned-toast Jesus, though, had shown up less than a mile from where I lived. So, what had moved the Lord to neglect me? Instead, He'd picked this kid, a once-a-month Christian: Jim Struth, who didn't love Him, not as I did. A twinge alerted me to a piece of glass in my thumb. I finished wiping the spill, then I went to the sink to pinch it out.

THERE IS NOTHING VERY WRONG WITH ME

BY ONNESHA ROYCHOUDHURI

THERE ARE BOXES OF medications and syringes beside me—evidence of the hormones I paid over $2,000 for that I will begin injecting myself with in a few days. The goal is to have a batch of my thirty-seven-year-old eggs harvested from my ovaries so that they can be frozen in time as I continue to age. All this so that, someday in the near future, I might choose to thaw and fertilize one, implanting a youthful-ish embryo in my wizened uterus.

I did not anticipate going through such a procedure. A year ago, I was planning on having children with my partner. "This is the kind of day we'll tell our grandchildren about," he once told me over a romantic dinner—a dinner we shared after spending the day hiking together with our dog. It was the kind of wholesome scene I had spent most of my life feeling on the outside of. Finally, I thought, I had arrived.

But a few weeks after that dinner, he decided he was no longer interested in having grandchildren, children—or anything, really—with me. After collecting his belongings from our shared home, here is one thing he was still interested in: the toll money he said I owed him from that time he drove me to the airport to visit my dying grandmother.

This happened suddenly enough that, two weeks after the change in household (and, for the record, my repayment in full for those E-ZPass tolls), I found myself in a paper gown at my gynecologist's office, keeping an appointment I'd scheduled months prior to verify that my parts were in good working order. I had a history of suspicious ovarian cysts, and the plan was for me to get the green light before my partner and I could move forward with making a baby.

Now, of course, the conversation had shifted. I matter-of-factly asked what my options were when it came to my fertility. "You do not have a partner?" my doctor asked, a hint of confusion in her voice as she looked down at my chart.

*   *   *

Sometimes, I make a joke. It goes like this: "I forgot I had a body!" I say this upon remembering to move my limbs after spending too many hours staring at a computer screen or reading a book on the couch, my dog a furry barnacle at my side.

"I forgot I had a body!" I say it when someone asks what happened to my knee, my shin, my arm—the bruises or cuts evidence of how easily I lose awareness of my body as it sideswipes bookcases, tables, air-conditioning units.

I forgot I had a body is probably also what I thought when I was twenty-two and had just started working as a journalist in an office where our fifty-something-year-old boss liked to dole out backrubs and tried to get the younger female employees to talk about our sex lives. Back then, I hid my body by wearing—I still cringe to recall it—baggy, drawstring pants to the office, often paired with shirts pulled from the leisure and pajama racks of stores.

I like to be comfortable, I rationalized. I don't remember how I squared that with the fact that I would duck into the bathroom at the end of the workday, changing into a more formfitting set of clothes before going to my second job.

*   *   *

Midday, the pastel-colored truck is parked at the corner of 24th and Broadway. Given the crowd, it would be easy to mistake it for an optimally positioned ice cream truck, except the phrases "Your fertility, understood" and "Own your future" are emblazoned on its side. As is an image of a blond woman in her twenties, looking self-assured in sunglasses. Huddled around the truck is a crowd of women who look like variations on this theme.

I am clearly the oldest—and brownest—woman in this gaggle. We've all signed up to get a free blood test done to measure our levels of anti-Müllerian hormone (AMH)—a shorthand for understanding how many eggs we have left on tap.

I contemplate leaving before it's my turn. I feel out of place and not just for the obvious reasons. The reality is:

I have never been dead set on having children—even less so, my own biological children. I'd always figured that if I ever got the hankering and was too old to crank out one of my own, I'd adopt. In fact, I thought this might be preferable. *Less wear and tear! There are so many children who need homes!*

That was before I watched friends go through the adoption process. Suddenly that helium-light *I'll just adopt!* mentality got weighed down with details: up to $40 thousand in costs, the training sessions, the home visits—all part of the exhausting process of being scrutinized and assessed. How to convince bureaucratic entities that I would make a suitable parent, even as I work to convince myself?

As a single woman and freelance writer in her late thirties, I cannot afford the process and likely wouldn't be a top choice for adoption agencies. The more I explored my options, the more I realized how limited they were— limited by my relationship status, limited by my socio- economic status, and increasingly limited by the banal yet merciless progression of time.

The fertility truck experience is over quickly. A woman collects a vial of blood, and I duck out with a wad of cotton taped in the crook of my right elbow. A week later, I get the news that I have the AMH of a twenty-seven-year-old. I celebrate by drinking a margarita and smoking a cigarette on my stoop.

*   *   *

It strikes me only now—a year later—that, at the same time that I was nursing a decimated heart, barely capable of eating or sleeping, I was also proactively and efficiently shuttling myself to a variety of doctors' appointments and a mobile clinic in order to assess my fertility.

Maybe a better way to put it is this: I knew I had a body, but it felt separate from me. Its realities and potential composed a *situation,* and I was trying to manage it.

"Own your future," while a phrase clearly targeted more for high-achieving millennials, hit home: The future I thought I had been building, one I even had the gall to believe I'd arrived at, was suddenly in shambles. The prospect that I might have any control at all appealed to me with the same seduction an infomercial offers an insomniac.

*　　*　　*

In truth, my body has long felt like an unmanageable situation. When I grew breasts, I became two people: the one who was me and the one to whom men responded. It was as though my new flesh-suit came delivered to me without the requisite script for flirtation and harassment that I seemed to need. I was often left wondering what my line was.

My first period ushered in my introduction to some of the worst pain of my life. As a teenager, while on a jog, I was immobilized by it, throwing up in a grassy island in the middle of a parking lot near my house. Enough time passed that my mother wondered what had happened to me. Her car pulled up next to where I was curled in a ball—less than a quarter mile from home.

When she learned what was going on, her panic quickly transitioned into compassionate camaraderie. It was time to swap war stories, and my mother filled me in on the debilitating pain she experienced like clockwork during her early fertile years.

I had entered the sisterhood, a welcoming coven that stretches back to Eve. There, in its muscular embrace,

I was made to understand that a woman in pain was, well, a woman.

Think of a toddler who falls but only starts to cry when they see concern in their parents' eyes. Which is to say: we calibrate our experiences of pain or danger to what we see reflected back to us.

There was nothing wrong with me. What I was experiencing was, apparently, normal.

*   *   *

I was in high school when my best friend took me to our local Planned Parenthood. I told the doctor I didn't want to use hormonal birth control if I could help it. That I was in a monogamous relationship and wanted to learn about my options. The doctor nodded along as though listening, checked her watch, and then immediately wrote me a prescription for hormonal birth control.

The story I told myself was that the doctor was the expert. What she gave me must be the best choice for me. It was easier to accept this story than the alternative: That what I wanted didn't matter.

It took nearly a decade for me to try again. This time, my

gynecologist listened. I got a copper IUD—the only highly effective, nonhormonal, and non-barrier contraceptive on the market. I tried to adjust—popping ibuprofen like candy and bleeding through my pants everywhere from the lawn of McCarren Park to the produce aisle of Associated Foods.

I was told to give it time. Many women experience increased pain and bleeding. *But how much pain is too much pain?* I searched for data to compare. I sought an expert's response that could tell me how I was supposed to feel. It didn't seem like enough to simply say: *This is too much pain for my body.*

When I finally gave in and had the IUD removed a year later, I felt immediate physical relief, combined with a sense of disappointment in myself.

*   *   *

The *actual* worst pain of my life comes later. At first, the gynecologist I see after an episode of collapsing and throwing up on a sidewalk in Manhattan seems unconcerned. "Maybe you just have gas," she suggests. "But to set your mind at ease," she tells me, "I'll send you to get an ultrasound."

I get a call a few hours after the ultrasound. The gyne-cologist tells me to avoid exercising or "you know, making any sudden movements." I have an eleven-centimeter cyst engulfing my ovary, the weight of it periodically twisting the ovary inside my body.

I see a series of specialists. I lose count of the number of vials of blood drawn. There is evidence the cyst could be cancerous, yet the panoply of doctors I visit seems fix-ated on a different concern. "Don't worry," I'm told again and again. "You can still have a baby with one ovary." I had never once said anything to any of them about wanting to have a baby.

Should I be more concerned about wanting a baby? I wondered.

I'm slated to have surgery in a week, but I'm told to go to the ER if I experience serious pain again. The surgery might not be able to wait. A couple days later, I get out of bed in the morning and fall on all fours. I do not know what to do. *Is the pain even that bad?* I can't move or think, but I also do not want to be dramatic. I call my mother. "On a scale from one to ten, how much pain are you in?" she asks. "Eleven," I say without pausing. This comes as news to me. "Go to the ER," my mother tells me.

In the ER, the admitting doctor asks me, "How many children do you have?" The pain that periodically robs me of language subsides long enough for me to ask, "Don't you mean 'Do you have any children?'" "Yes," he says impatiently.

Thankfully, I do not have cancer. After the surgery, still drugged but mercifully pain-free for the first time in weeks, I am a font of strange phrases. "Thank you for your fine craftsmanship," I tell my surgeon. He laughs and tells me I have one ovary left.

I can still have a baby.

*   *   *

The truth is that I've never been one to ooh and aah over tiny humans. The word "fascinating" comes more quickly to my tongue than "adorable"—watching them take in the world, wondering what they make of it, how they navigate all the stimuli.

The clearest awareness that I wanted a child came not after spending time with a friend's baby or daydreaming with past partners about the children we might have together. It was after teaching a storytelling workshop to teenage girls in a Brooklyn high school.

Over the course of eight weeks, I worked with them as they crafted stories from their lives—stories of heartbreak and navigating family traumas. They were—as all stories from teenage girls are—about coming into your own. Learning who you are and aren't, what you're willing and unwilling to accept.

Watching my students navigate their strength and vulnerability awakened something fierce in me. I was watching them teeter as they walked that tricky line: demanding the world see them for who they were, while, at the same time, desperately seeking approval.

Perhaps a simpler way of putting it: I saw myself in their stories and in that teetering. I wanted to hold them close to protect them; I wanted to push them out into the world armed with a kind of confidence I've only been able to achieve through messy grappling, struggle, and failure— the kind of confidence I continue to perform in the hopes that it will someday come more naturally.

*　　*　　*

By the time I'm ready to pull the trigger on freezing my eggs, I live in a new city and need a new gynecologist. I've learned a few things from my past medical mishaps and insensitive doctors, so I send an email to a few new friends: "Who knows a good gynecologist?"

The doctor is kind without being patronizing. She asks why I'm freezing my eggs, and I tell her I know, at my age, the quality of my eggs is rapidly declining, and I don't have a partner. I don't tell her the rest because I don't yet have words for it: How my partner's sudden departure gave me clarity. How, in as much as could be possible, I no longer wanted my desire for a child to be dependent on someone else. How I was starting to realize that I was not only strong enough to take care of myself but had enough love and fortitude to take care of someone else too.

I don't need to have children. I'm not sure I want children. The language of wants and needs here is tricky. As a writer who came of age in an industry that obligates you to work at least two jobs at a time, often without health insurance, I never had the consistent resources and support it takes to truly envision a sustainable reality with a child.

Now that I'm at a point in my career where I *can* start to envision such a thing, I realize that many of the stories I told myself about my own wants and needs were restricted by what was actually feasible given my socio-economic realities. In a country marked by massive individual debt, inequality, and a profound lack of support and safety nets for women, what does "choice" actually mean?

For too long, I let these limitations masquerade in the language of my own desires.

"You've still got time," the gynecologist says, raising her eyebrows. "You could meet someone tomorrow." "I could meet someone never," I reply, laughing, though it doesn't feel much like a joke. She continues with her rundown of questions. "Any history of sexual assault or abuse?" "No," I reply.

She speaks to me like an equal, though she's wearing proper clothes, while I float in an oversized paper gown that crinkles raucously as I scoot myself to the end of the exam table. My heels—I know the routine by now—find their way into the hard, plastic stirrups. The doctor narrates what she will be doing. "You're going to feel my hand on your inner thigh," she says, as I feel her hand on my inner thigh.

Then she pauses. "And there's nothing I should know about your history—sexual assault or abuse or anything else—before we keep going?" I can feel the "no" rising in me like a reflex.

Only, the way she's asked me twice—broadening it to "anything else" throws me. There's a silence in the room.

"No," I tell her. But back in my car in the parking lot, I sit there, gripping the wheel and staring at my hands.

*   *   *

Here's an anything else: The last time my ex-partner ever touched me. It was after an argument, over the course of which I felt so profoundly misunderstood, I had stopped speaking and started crying. I hated that I was crying, so I went into the bedroom and put my face in a pillow.

A little while later, he came into the room and tried to hold me. "I don't even know why I'm still crying," I said to him. "You just needed to let it out," he said dismissively, though not unkindly.

I was on my stomach, and he began to massage my shoulders, my back. Then, his hand was in my pants. It felt all wrong, but I wanted it to be right. "This feels wrong," I said. The words sounded too severe to me. I tried to soften them. "We haven't even kissed," I offered. What I meant was: "Why won't you look at me?"

He found my face, briefly kissed me, then went back to what he was doing to my body. The whole time he fucked me with his hand, he was leaning over me while I was on my stomach, face against the bed. "Your poor body," he said, now pressing himself against me. "It needed that."

I was still crying. It still felt wrong. But he was telling me with a tone of certainty what my body needed. After a lifetime of experience in just that, I was inclined to believe him.

*   *   *

In many ways, he seemed kind. He talked about nonviolent communication and came to political protests with me. Most mornings, he cooked me breakfast. Still, I experienced my first panic attack after an argument we had about our future together. I had located a problem: His actions didn't seem to be aligning with his words. He located a different problem: Why was I so untrusting?

Later, I talked to him about the panic attack. How strange it was to experience what felt like my body telling my mind something, when I was so used to my brain running the show. He nodded compassionately and said, "Are you sure that was your *first* panic attack? Are you sure it's never happened before?"

And even though I was sure, I thought maybe he knew something I didn't. About my own life and my own body.

"Are you sure?" he asked again a few days later.

And again.

Until I wasn't so sure.

*   *   *

I've had a number of interactions with obviously unkind men, but they have been easier for me to navigate. It's the seemingly kind ones that disarm me and haunt me most.

When I started dating again, I told the kind man I went home with after a few dates—a man who had expressed appreciation for what a clear communicator I was—that I wanted to be physical with him but did not yet want to have sex. He kissed me, thanked me for being direct, and said that sounded just fine. That did not stop him from, less than an hour later, reaching for a condom as though it was inevitable that we would have sex. "Oh, damn," he said, groping around the drawer of his nightstand. "The condoms are in the bathroom."

For a moment, I wondered whether I had said I didn't want to have sex out loud. *Had I just meant to say it but forgotten to?* For a moment, I was about to just go along with it, by which I mean his version of reality and what should come next.

What I'm trying to say is that it is sometimes easier to pretend that what someone else presumes to know about your body, wants with or for your body, is exactly what you want.

It can be easier than having to reckon with the reality that you live in a world where what you say about your own body does not matter.

You pretend their stories are yours until you end up in the parking lot of your new gynecologist, weeping into your steering wheel. You weep because you realize that the phrase "sexual assault" has always sounded cartoonish and utterly inapplicable to your life experiences. But maybe only because, at some point, you stopped believing your body was truly your own.

You need a different phrase. One that captures the things you have done with and to your body—the things that you have allowed to be done to it—because you assumed someone else probably knew better.

The space between what others desired for your body and what you desired for your own became ambiguous enough that, if asked to draw a line, you would try and fail and have to try again.

And then you realize you're talking about yourself in the second person.

*   *   *

To allow a child to grow inside of my body terrifies me. I am not afraid of the biology of it. I am not afraid of the pain. What I worry about most is that the autonomy that I have struggled to achieve—the quiet battles waged every day over my sense of ownership of my own body—will suddenly be erased. I worry that the fragile boundaries I have erected will come tumbling down in an instant.

Will there be room for me to experience being a parent in a way that feels like I'm starting a conversation instead of entering a centuries-old argument? Will I even be aware of the ways in which I make my desires and needs smaller—not simply to accommodate my child but to accommodate society's script for motherhood?

I want to trust that merely going about *being* on one's own terms is not a position that must be defended. I want to trust that I won't have to make myself any smaller than I already have.

I do not trust this.

*   *   *

During the heyday of the #MeToo movement, I was one of a group of women who came forward about our old boss's inappropriate behavior.

In a *This American Life* episode, we shared our stories of minimizing, denying, avoiding, or pushing back against his systematic harassment. It was only through being interviewed by the reporter and reconnecting with my coworkers—some of whom I hadn't seen in almost fifteen years—that I recognized how systematic the harassment was. It was only after hearing another coworker tell me she tried to wear baggy clothes to avoid attention from our boss that I recognized I had been doing the very same thing.

A few months after the episode aired, a well-respected film director expressed interest in producing a TV series inspired by our stories. We were offered a modest sum in exchange for the rights to use these stories.

And that is how I am able to almost-just-barely cover the cost of the fertility drugs that I will soon inject into my body and the procedure I will undergo to extract and freeze some of my eggs.

Which is to say that enduring an abusive and sexist workplace is what made it possible for me to bring a child into this world.

Win?

*   *   *

As I stare at this armada of fertility drugs and the syringes I will use to deliver them, I realize I can no longer glibly say, "I forgot I had a body." It has been through too much for that. I want to stay in it. I want to own everything I am choosing to do with it. I want to listen better to what it tries to tell me—through its panic attacks and restlessness, its aches and premonitions.

When I imagine my child, I imagine the art and work

of seeing them as they are and as they are becoming. In other words: the art and work of stripping myself of the expectations and projections the world has drummed into me and would have me drum into my child.

I want to throw elbows and stomp earth to create space for them to learn themselves and their mind without the demands and assumptions of others weighing so heavily.

What I want is—simply, impossibly—for my child to know their body by their own measure.

I realize that this is likely what my own mother hoped for too—a knowledge that humbles in its inevitability: I will fail. But I still want to try.

I'm trying.

LABOR
AND OTHER POEMS

BY AMA CODJOE

LABOR

MANHATTAN, NY

The Upper West Side brims
with Black women heaving Bugaboo
strollers as if maneuvering horseless plows.
I'm walking up Broadway with a white friend
whose mother's food stamps we used,
as kids, to buy sour straws, barbecue
chips, and frosted pints of Cherry Garcia.
While we zigzag between pedestrians,

she argues that there may be as many
white working-class nannies steering
double-wide strollers as Black.
It's hard to tell, she insists,
whether the white women caring
for white babies are laborers
or mothers. I know we use
the same word to describe work
and the work of giving birth.
Still, I'm tempted to call her bluff.
Today, I do not want children.
I recall instances when I've been mistaken
for mother. Like last May, when a man
clutching a fistful of blush roses
wished me Happy Mother's Day.
Or in a muggy subway car,
as the child beside me rested his head
on my arm. A nearby passenger's eyes
softened at our portrait.
I claimed the sleeping child then,
briefly, I claimed him.
More than once, I've held tightly
the hands of my twin nephews,

who could be confused
for each other—or as mine.
Together, we've waited near
the chasm of the street—gust of cars
stealing their reflections. I've spent hours,
brief minutes, tending to children

I in no way labored for—and then,
with some relief, I have let them go.

MY NOTHINGS

You, who have bowed your head, shed
another season of antlers at my feet, for years

you fall asleep to the lullabies of dolls,
cotton-stuffed and frayed, ears damp with sleep

and saliva, scalps knotted with yarn, milk-breath,
and yawns. Birth is a torn ticket stub, a sugar

cone wrapped in a paper sleeve, the blackest
ice. It has been called irretrievable, a foreign

coin, the moon's slip, showing, a pair
of new shoes rubbing raw your heel.

I lose the back of my earring and bend
the metal in such a way as to keep it

fastened to me. In the universe where we are
strangers, you kick with fury, impatient

as grass. I have eaten all your names.
In this garden, you are blue ink, baseball cap,

wishbone, pulled teeth, wet sand, hourglass.
There are locks of your hair in the robin's nest

and clogging the shower drain. You, who are
covered in feathers, who have witnessed birth

give birth to death and watched death suck
her purple nipple. You long for a mother

like death's mother, want to nurse until drunk
you dream of minnows swimming

through your ears—their iridescence causing
you to blink, your arms twitching.

Even while you sleep I feed you.

MY NOTHINGS

You don't dress your mouth
in my blouse. My body crinkled

like a denim dress pinned
to a clothesline. I'd be lying if I said

there's no wind here, no sun shaping
me 'til I'm filled by a body or falling

from a hanger. There's nothing tragic
except what you know of light.

What you might show of sadness.
You want to be folded: for two long sleeves

to meet kissing-like. To be finished
with me in this particular way.

You want to be caught like birthday cake
scooped from the linoleum floor

and spilled like a bank of pennies
or silt. This is the part where you

have to say it because
I'm a coward—though I'd kill

the daddy longlegs and let you
sleep on my pillow for hours, my hair

in your mouth, could my voice soothe
all I can't say.

MY NOTHINGS

1.
Son and daughter peer through the mirror
not above my bed, trying to find
a language. What look is on their faces,

one asks. Terror, says one. Pleasure,
the other answers. Look at him move
as if inside her there's something

he can barely touch. Look how he tries
over and over. How he becomes
a horse beneath her: his eyes large

marbles on the sides of his face.
Only now does she strip completely.
Our father is a racehorse. Our mother possesses

the spine of a fish. Look at her swim
though nowhere is water. Her nipples
are coins the size of our mouths.

2.
When we move as if underwater,
a scent rises off our bodies as steam.
Our bodies are bodies
of water. Look how we spill over
and again.

3.
Some children wear the birthmark
of never being conceived. Call it
a single thorn in a bramble or the shape
of a torn leaf or the triangular beak
of a mistle thrush snatching
a blackberry from a tangle of thorns.

4.
Dear children, go along
skipping stones and asking for more.
Go ahead nursing and dying,
arguing over who gets
the front seat. Do you have

to be born to die? The promises
I make falter in the current
between us. Is there a ship
besides the body to lull you?

5.
I have tried to strike
the dampest match.

6.
A horse's height is measured in hands.
The body is smudged by a thousand fingerprints.

 Sons and daughters,
  show me your hands.

I'll scrub them with a sliver of silver soap.
We'll wash our hands of it good.

CURSE OF
THE SPIDER WOMAN

BY RIVA LEHRER

WHEN I WAS BORN, IN 1958, doctors were just beginning to learn how to close the neural tube defect known as spina bifida, in which the casing around the spinal cord does not fuse all the way. I spent the first two years of my life at Children's Hospital and then returned again and again for more surgeries and an endless whirlwind of tests, infections, and emergencies. The doctor who saved my life all those dozens of times was a young, soap-opera-handsome surgeon named Lester Martin.

He was my hero —actually, one of my two heroes. The

other was Carole Sue Horwitz Lehrer, otherwise known as Mom. Carole had worked as a medical researcher (for Dr. Warkany, whose specialization was fetal birth defects!), an experience that gave her the determination not to institutionalize me, as parents were told to when I was a child.

How lucky I was to have two heroes.

*   *   *

When you grow up disabled, you are acutely aware that you are different. Normal is a mysterious *something* that you are not. Still, it's not until puberty that you discover just how different you are. Perhaps you grew up assuming that you were indeed a girl or a boy, told that you're a girl or a boy, but as you swing toward adulthood, disability claims your gender too. Many of the things that entitle you to masculinity (strength, speed, sportiness, the credible determination to be an astronaut) or femininity (bodily attractiveness, the aspiration to be a movie star, the desire to have children) might be denied to you if your body/mind doesn't do those things or your society won't let you. When you don't fit the mold of Man or Woman, neither do you fit as Mother or Father. We imagine children as little copies of their parents; society makes it perfectly, lucidly, spectacularly clear that it does not welcome reproduction if it results in even more undesirable bodies.

For me, gender training abruptly stopped. Dolls and dresses didn't mean anything; my cousins and friends began their preparation for their female futures, for marriage and children. It was no mystery that I was being left behind.

At least, that's what it was like to be a crip kid in 1972.

*   *   *

I was fourteen, and most of the girls I knew had already begun their periods, but not me. I was beginning to doubt it would ever happen. Then, the summer before I started high school, I was babysitting, and as my charges paddled around the JCC kiddie pool, I glanced down at my swimsuit bottom and saw a crimson stream snaking down my leg. I thought I was having a medical emergency, so of course I screamed, which meant that the entire pool now noticed the deranged and bleeding girl. A nice woman lent me her beach towel and asked if it was my first time, then put a quarter in the Kotex machine on the bathroom wall and went to call my mother. I spent the weekend curled up in Crampville under rotating heating pads.

Still, I was ecstatic. I would start high school as an Official Girl. If pain was the price to pay for Girlhood, fine. I was fertile. My body had a future. It had a purpose.

Within months, menstruation began to mow me down like a bright-red Sherman tank.

The pain stopped letting up between cycles. My aunts said that some women just had really bad periods and to get used to it. I should have been taken to a gynecologist; instead, my pediatrician sent me to a psychiatrist who asked if I had those cramps when I fought with my mother. "*No,*" I said, "I have them during *my period.*" (*You idiot.*)

I didn't understand. Mom had always taken my smallest pains straight to the doctor. Her level of over-reaction tended toward the positively operatic. Why was *this* pain being treated like a figment of my imagination?

*　　*　　*

November of my sophomore year, I was doodling lions in the margin of my American History textbook when a grenade went off in my belly. I lurched out to the hallway and fell over on the carpet, cheek pressed against a thousand muddy sneaker prints. Two teachers hoisted me to the nurse's office, called an ambulance, and then called my mother.

Sirens. Curious faces. A bitter wind sliding around the stretcher. Mom and Grandma met me in the Children's Hospital ER, where I was given a whomp-load of painkillers. I dimly registered the X-rays, the excruciating pelvic exam, the doctors mumbling in the hall.

Mom roused me at five a.m.—had she ever left?—and said I had a hemorrhaging uterine cyst the size of a grapefruit. (Universal law decrees that tumors and cysts must be golf balls or grapefruit.) Orderlies were on their way to take me to the OR, where Dr. Martin would perform an emergency hysterectomy. Not the usual surgery for a fifteen-year-old; even the nurses were a little nonplussed when they came in my room. When I asked them to explain what was about to happen, their eyes slid away.

I woke up with a wide, flat smile of an incision just above my pubic bone, and the sensation that I'd been set upon by sadistic plumbers.

Eventually the anesthesia receded, and the questions began to arrive. I knew what a hysterectomy was and what it meant for normal women. I had no idea what it meant for me.

I would discover what my hysterectomy meant for Mom.

A couple days after surgery, we were sitting around my hospital room waiting for the lunch trays, when she asked, "Are you glad you won't have periods anymore?"

I hadn't thought that far ahead. There were bandages on my abdomen and giant pads between my legs. I was still the Vesuvius of menstruation. "Yeah, I guess. But Dr. Martin said that I kept my ovaries. Won't I feel something?"

"You might get a little moody. But you're a teenager, so moody is pretty much your job description. A lot of women would give big money not to have cramps every month."

"An operation isn't a whole lot easier, Mom."

"Maybe not." She sighed and covered my hand. This was her sign that she was about to be Deeply Serious. Hoo boy.

"I know this was scary, honey, but it was all for the best. If you hadn't had your uterus out now, you'd be stuck doing it down the line. Your spine isn't able to withstand a full-term pregnancy. If you ever did get pregnant, you'd have to make a terrible decision. Now it's out of your hands. This was a blessing in disguise."

Fury shrapneled my brain. What. The. Hell. I'd *had* to have that fucking *emergency* operation because nobody—including *her*—believed that my period was more painful than it should have been! And she'd always said that men wouldn't be interested in me. Was she saying I would have gotten—jeez!—*offers*?

Mom had been told to abort her last pregnancy—the baby that would become my little brother—in order to save her spine following botched disc surgery. Mom had toughed it out, hadn't she? She'd carried Markie to term, and she was still alive. Still walking. Was I that much worse off?

No one had ever asked me if I wanted to have children. Our relatives asked my girl cousins if they had crushes on boys. Did Diane and Leah and Ellen and Betsy want to go shopping for dresses? Who was taking them to prom? Oh, a boyfriend! How nice!

But no one asked me.

Mom went on, unaware of my rage. "I've been so worried that you'd meet a boy one day, and he'd put you in terrible danger. Even though most men aren't attracted to handicapped girls. I was afraid you'd be forced to make some terrible decisions. Now, though, I think we're in the clear."

It wasn't like this was the first time she'd delivered her "Don't get your hopes up" speech. I'd always thought, secretly, that I *would* find someone someday who would want to marry me—though I'd have settled for someone to take me to the prom. But now, it seemed, she was right: I was a null set. A nothing.

And at the end of all this "kindness," she *smiled*. My mother smiled.

My last morning in the hospital, I caught Dr. Martin's sleeve as he turned to go.

"Could you wait a minute? There's stuff I don't understand." There was no one else I could ask, and it wasn't as if a question about surgery would bother him. He was a *doctor*.

I took a shaky breath. "Um, Dr. Martin. Does having a hysterectomy mean ... that ... I can never have sex? Does it mean I'll never feel anything if I do?" I had a creeping notion that the hysterectomy had paralyzed my orgasm nerves—whatever they were called.

He froze. My idol, my hero—my own Rabbi Loew—said, "Riva, I thought you were a *nice* girl. I cannot believe my ears! Promise me I'll never hear anything like that from you ever again." He stood balanced on the balls of his feet, a granite slab from his back-combed hairline to the soles of his polished shoes.

Or maybe it was me who froze, as Dr. Lester Martin walked out.

*   *   *

I had never talked to anyone about sex. For crip kids, *sex* was the forbidden word, as unmentionable as a demon's name in a Black Forest fairy tale. What little I knew had been gleaned from illicit peeks at the sexually dimorphic pages of my father's *Playboy* magazines and my mother's *True Confessions*. Mom had explained the biomechanics during a hideously embarrassing talk years ago, but I understood little about desire itself, how it fed the fires of adulthood.

At fifteen, I had no idea that there was history and context to my surgery. That there was a history of involuntary sterilization of disabled women. I didn't know of Carrie

Buck, the most famous example, plaintiff in the Supreme Court case *Buck v. Bell*. Carrie Elizabeth Buck was a poor girl from Charlottesville, Virginia, who was raped and impregnated by a member of her foster family when she was seventeen. That family avoided prosecution by committing Carrie Buck to the Virginia State Colony for Epileptics and the Feebleminded, where she was declared incompetent to raise her baby.

While in the Virginia State Colony, Buck was sterilized against her will under the Racial Integrity Law of 1924, a eugenics program carried out by the state of Virginia. Buck's mother, Emma, had already been committed to the colony for "feeblemindedness" and being "sexually promiscuous," often a code word for denoting an "uncontrollable" female. Later, Carrie's younger sister Doris was also sterilized using similar justifications. Carrie's daughter, Vivian, was labeled feebleminded and died at age eight.

There is evidence that none of the Bucks qualified for these spurious "diagnoses"; researchers have cited sources indicating that the Bucks were all of normal intelligence. This is *not* to say that, if they'd had intellectual disabilities, any of this would have been morally or ethically justified. Nevertheless, Justice Oliver Wendell Holmes Jr. in ruling against Carrie in *Buck v. Bell*, pronounced the famous verdict: "Three generations of imbeciles are enough."

The Buck case may be the most infamous, but it is only one of thousands of stories of disabled women being sterilized against their will—and often without their knowledge—throughout the twentieth century and into the twenty-first. Most were—or are—poor; many were women of color; but any woman was at risk of being committed by her family and subjected to this atrocity. This included women who went to public health clinics or were considered "inappropriate" mothers—for any reason whatsoever.

These days, debate continues over whether to sterilize people born with developmental disabilities on the assumption that they'd be incompetent parents. Deaf, blind, and paraplegic people are frequently treated as having no right to reproduction.

Few Americans realize that the eugenics movement began in the United States and not in Germany. The Nazis ran with it, but eugenics began as a lethal export from the Home of the Free. If you can prevent disabled people from having children, it's step two in making sure we cease to exist—right after aborting us to make sure we never exist in the first place.

I do not equate my situation with that of Carrie Buck's—but it's not unconnected either. If my fertility had been valued, perhaps I would have been taken seriously when I complained of pelvic pain. Instead, I had to begin hemorrhaging before anyone examined me. Mom and my doctors thought—not without reason—that pregnancy could lead to severe pain, increased impairment, even death. They'd never given me a choice regarding any surgery I'd ever had, so I suppose it didn't even occur to them to consider the existence of choice, especially once the catastrophe began.

I don't know whether anything could have been done to preserve my fertility, or whether pregnancy would have been as dangerous as my mother claimed, but I do know that her reaction, and that of Dr. Martin, speaks to a long-held societal dread of disabled people making more disabled people. I know that no one, back then, expressed a single word of sorrow at the loss of my ability to procreate.

Carrie Buck's family was trying to hide a rape and subsequent "illegitimate" child by arranging for her to be institutionalized. They were able to do so because people of her time—and for decades since—believed that institutions were the appropriate places for disabled people, and especially disabled women. The Bucks hid behind the warped beliefs of a hundred years ago. No doubt that many families who similarly "put away" their members saw confinement as a kindness, a way to protect parents, siblings, spouses from a world that hated and feared them. Yet who among us would call those families "heroic" for their actions?

The 1970s saw the nascent rise of Disability Rights, but these concepts had yet to filter down to Cincinnati, Ohio. For most of my life, I have borne a hot stone of rage against my mother and Dr. Martin, but now I consider that they were also entombed in a society that tried to prevent disabled children from making more disabled children. They chose to treat me like a child so as to keep me a child, in order that I remain unwounded by rejection. Ignorant of the labyrinth of love. Can I fault them for not being the visionaries I required?

My heroes carved me with their words and their knives. I am a Golem, a living, if incomplete, being. I am still learning how to cut and sew myself into my own shape of monster.

MONSTERS WE CREATE
A SCI-FI FRONTERA FEMMETASIA FABLE

BY GEORGINA ESCOBAR

An excerpt from a play co-created with students at the University of Texas at El Paso in the fall semester of 2019.

THE YEAR IS 2030, and the world has been turned upside down. "The Big Sink"—a climate event in which the seawater levels rose to cover parts of the US (New York, Florida, Delaware, California, parts of Louisiana, Texas, and Alabama)—has forced millions of people to seek refuge in the deserts of the Southwest. The scarcity of resources quickly leads to a war that targets migrant women and their reproductive freedoms.

The repression of reproductive freedom has focused on places along the border; one such place is called Sun

Town. The implementation of the Malthusian law, a new legislation for population control, leads to the creation of Sterilization Camps ("Stamps") for immigrants along the border—constructed to process the population-control-driven sterilization of migrant women. Among other things, the law has launched the New Armed Forces Unit (NAFU), a division set to protect the Stamps.

Darkness.

An eerie sound, like dripping water.

Lights rise on Old Radford House.

FERNANDEZ, J. / FJ (F) 20–30s. A Mexican immigrant. Recently escaped the Stamps where she's been detained for two years. Born to the name Jimena, she has decided to adopt the name reflected on her camp uniform. She recounts a story to ROMAN.

Figures of DOCTORS in plague doctor masks enter and surround her.

ROMAN, (M) 20–30s. Born and raised in the high deserts, he has an honest connection to nature and the natural world but finds comfort in routine. Recently served as an employee for the Stamps. He watches the following, silently.

FERNANDEZ, J.

Once upon a time, there was a prominent border town that was the only one to survive years of scarcity-driven wars. Driven out of the coasts by the Big Sink, millions of people sought refuge in the high deserts. Passage City, or Sun Town, became the hub for Sacrificial Camps. Scamps.

ROMAN SCOFFS.
(*defending her story*)

I'll have to change the name of course. Make it a metaphor. People don't actually have the ear for truth anymore. They just want stories ... just fake-ass stories ...

FJ wears a vacant expression. She's taken away by a distant memory and into:

INTERCOM (VO)

Fernandez, J.— Lot 26. Report to room 99 to begin the gifting process.

FERNANDEZ, J.
(*touches her stomach; to herself*)

Maybe it won't work ... maybe there's still hope ...
Suddenly: NONAME appears behind FJ. It is a creature bigger than a human, daunting, haunting, and grotesque. It looks like the desert wilderness—prickly, dry, and unforgiving—and it uses the language of symbols, which sounds, to humans, like the phrase: "Why?"

FERNANDEZ, J.

... and then you think the unthinkable.
Is that a—(*monster?*)
She calls him over, he responds with:

NONAME

Why ... ?
NONAME runs menacingly to FJ with a scalpel.

FERNANDEZ, J.

Please, don't.
NONAME stands behind FJ and takes her hand to the scalpel. It teaches her how to aim to kill, where to slice— NONAME represents the wilderness in all women whose reproductive freedom is threatened.

FERNANDEZ, J. (CONT'D)

I ... I can't.

NONAME

Why ... ?

They share a moment. FJ studies NONAME with care. It roughly pushes her away.

INTERCOM (VO)

Fernandez, J.—Lot 26. Room 99 to begin the gifting process.

Suddenly we launch into—The Sterilization Dance—*DOCTORS in plague masks engage in a highly stylized sterilization/hysterectomy procedure.*

They RETRIEVE something. The sounds are disturbing. They expand, colonizing what little remains of the untainted air.

What the doctors REMOVE suddenly transforms into a person, a "could-have-been."

This is MAYBEE (F)—one whose language is akin to musical notation, one whose body and movements are elevated to the dignity of signs, the mysterious, and the unconquerable wild.

MAYBEE gasps for air, as if she's been underwater for too long. She is confused and out of sorts, then turns around slowly to see the scene. She sees what could have been her mother, FJ, defeated.

NONAME enters, unseen; it slides the scalpel toward MAYBEE. She picks it up, and, as if given permission to engage her inner truth, she stabs the DOCTORS, sinking the scalpel straight into each of their jugulars. Her killing is satisfying; she slices through centuries of reproductive inequities and other abuses against women. It is guttural but beautiful, vicious but choreographed. MAYBEE's attack is every woman's release.

Suddenly—

Lights shift, and we are back at the Old Radford House. ROMAN stands behind FJ as she finishes reenacting the story, then:

ROMAN

Really?

FERNANDEZ, J.

What "really"?

ROMAN

Suddenly this girl just ... slays the doctors?

FERNANDEZ, J.

That's the part that pulls you out of it? Not the actual sterilization? Typical.

ROMAN

I think there's a danger in fantasizing the—

FERNANDEZ, J.

It's all in the telling. It's how we *say* certain things. It's how we *word them*. Stories are wild things, once they are free, no one knows what they will do.

ROMAN

But naming her "Maybee"?

FERNANDEZ, J.

Maybee takes a scalpel from a monster in order to destroy what separated her from her mother? It's perfect.

ROMAN

It's on the nose.

FERNANDEZ, J.

Roman, look, just. Look. Just. Worry about transmitting the story, OK? We're all depending on this transmission. If the Last Call doesn't go out, and we're trapped here, or if it does, and we're trapped here—

ROMAN

We'll be caught by NAFU. I got it.

FERNANDEZ, J.

Exactly.

ROMAN

(*a bit of a mumble*)
Story's a bit ...

FERNANDEZ, J.

Fix that radio. Leave the writing to me. We're transmitting the Last Call, for god's sake. It's gotta mean something.

ROMAN

Yes, yes.

FERNANDEZ, J.

Are you with me on this?

ROMAN

Sure. But. It's just.

FERNANDEZ, J.

Say it.

ROMAN

A new episode? Ten years later?

FERNANDEZ, J.

It's never too late to do what's right.

ROMAN

We need to leave. Now.

FERNANDEZ, J.

We need to give others hope.

ROMAN

The story just doesn't make sense. What's the point?
Everyone knows what's happening around here—

FERNANDEZ, J.

And yet they look away. Why?

ROMAN

I just don't get it.

FERNANDEZ, J.

It's not for you to get. The ones who get it will get it. It's
a metaphor and—

ROMAN

It's predictable.

FERNANDEZ, J.

Predicta—you want to know what's predictable? Men. Afraid of women. Controlling our bodies. Sterilization camps. People treating—who treat the—people who treat *migrants* like the goddamn plague. People who, like you, do *nothing* ... in the face of—

ROMAN	FERNANDEZ, J.
I do nothing "in the face of"?	Nothing!
Now wait a minute,	Because it was more
that's not fair	comfortable to
I didn't do *nothing*!	—NO, you did nothing!

FERNANDEZ, J.

Predictable!

ROMAN

(*correcting her*)
Immigrant.

FERNANDEZ, J.

What?

ROMAN

The word you're looking for is "immigrant," not "migrant."

FERNANDEZ, J.

Are you fucking kidding me right now?

ROMAN

(*shrugs*)

FERNANDEZ, J.

Migrant. Migrants move. Like birds. To find better conditions for survival. You think I wanted to come to this piece of shit country? I didn't have a choice.

ROMAN

But you stayed in this piece of shit country, that's the difference: migrants keep moving; immigrants stay—

FERNANDEZ, J.

Fuck you, Roman.

ROMAN

It's just a fact, not an attack. Immigrant's not a dirty

word—it's natural. Migrant and immigrant species have meant the survival of *many* of those species. Take tumbleweeds.

FERNANDEZ, J.

Whatever ...

ROMAN

I'm not negating your experience, Jimena.

FERNANDEZ, J.

Don't call me that.

ROMAN

That's your name.

FERNANDEZ, J.

Not anymore. (*She signals to the patch on her jumpsuit, which spells her last name. Below it, a mountain range and a yellow five-point star: the emblem of El Paso, Texas.*) Jimena is dead. Jimena was taken from me. Did you know a woman's name is born in the womb? My mother named me while I was still connected to her. That was my name.

Fed to me by her, like nutrients.... I don't have that name anymore. I don't have that right. And maybe, if you call me by my new name, you'll remember that. (*beat*) It's Fernandez, J. Get it right. It's who they made me. This is who I am now.

STEEL WOMB

BY CARRIE BORNSTEIN

I USED TO JOKE that I should have someone else's baby.

Pregnancy just seemed to *work* for me. I was lucky to conceive on the first try with each of my three kids and never had a miscarriage. I liked birth and hospitals and the way I'd take extra good care of myself throughout the process. Despite (or maybe *because of*?) my insecurities in just about every area of life, I knew pregnancy was my strong suit. The thing about babies, though, is that they grow into kids. The very last thing I wanted was another kid.

One day on a long car trip to visit family, I joked again and decided to look it up online. Do people really do that, I wondered? At 37 I figured I was probably too old. It turned out that, yes, people really do that. And that no, I was not too old.

Something inside me clicked.

Two days later I called my obstetrician. She explained the process and said I'd make an excellent candidate for surrogacy. We'd just need to make sure I wasn't matched with a couple who had the same antibodies I developed upon giving birth to my second child, since that would lead to a toxic environment for the baby. It's rare but could happen if I was matched with the wrong couple. Thankfully, it was something we could easily screen for.

My husband wasn't enthusiastic about the idea. To Jamie, pregnancy meant me lying on the couch surrendered to first-trimester nausea and exhaustion while he put the kids to bed. It was the inevitable spill I'd take on the sidewalk, landing me in the hospital under observation for twenty-four hours just to make sure the baby was OK. It was all those doctor appointments on top of the overload of running a nonprofit, and how my body would get torn apart by it all.

Sure, he was right, but pregnancy ... pregnancy also meant poking the elbow of a fetus inside only to feel it jab right back at me as if to say hello. It meant unlimited milkshakes, second dinner, and cute maternity clothes with the greatest accessory ever sitting right there at my midsection. And while my own path to parenthood couldn't have been easier, I knew there were single people of all genders and gay couples desperate to have a baby who couldn't produce one on their own. I knew couples who struggled for years trying to become pregnant only to have blood slay their budding hope again and again and again. I thought about the woman who carried an uncomplicated pregnancy for months before delivering a baby who had already died inside her. My heart hurt for them all. How could I *not* have someone else's baby?

People sometimes assume that surrogates are just after money. Though it wasn't my primary motivation, the thought of boosting our bank account certainly didn't hurt. With Jamie and I working in nonprofits and trying to send our kids to private school, we didn't exactly have much savings. With a little extra cash, maybe we could put some money away for college. Or even take a vacation.

I had never known anyone who had been, or had even

used, a surrogate, so I sought out someone with firsthand experience. Shira and I met in a bar one night, and she shared, teary-eyed, the medical condition that meant she'd never carry a pregnancy to term. She told me about how badly she wanted to become a mom and the gestational carrier who delivered her three sons. I cried with this stranger over white wine sangria and became even more resolute in my decision. I went home and poured my heart out in an application to the agency she used. Two days later, I was rejected.

The agency said they appreciated my time and attention to detail in completing the application, but they would not be able to proceed due to my Factor V Leiden gene mutation, which could lead to an elevated risk of blood clotting following delivery. I protested, letting them know that I'd never had a blood clot and that mine was actually one of the more minor versions of the mutation, but they were unconvinced. Later that day I got my period. I felt like I had a shadow of a glimpse into the painful world of infertility from which I'd been sheltered.

Researching more, I learned that others with my exact condition had gone on to successful surrogacy. I found a new agency, asked upfront about the issue, and after an application, reference checks, and multiple interviews with their staff, including an in-home screening, they told me about a couple who might be a match. Five months after that first Google search, I opened my email to find the subject line: "Introducing Hannah and Michael!"

I stared at my inbox. There they were. Real people with photos and a story and a message saying they couldn't put into words how lucky they felt to have found me.

The agency arranged a video introduction among the four of us—an awkward supervised double date of sorts, where we tried to determine in the course of an hour whether or not to intertwine our lives forever. Hannah followed up by email, gushing with gratitude. "I feel so happy and hopeful again," she said. "I will never be able to thank you enough for giving us the baby we dreamed of." My husband looked at me and said, "I love you." The hypothetical "someone else's baby" was now "Hannah and Michael's baby," and he was hooked.

We both underwent psychological screenings, and I obtained medical clearance after going over the details of my case with the fertility clinic. I had weekly phone calls with lawyers. We signed a sixty-four-page contract that outlined everything from how many embryos we'd transfer to who would be in the delivery room to how much extra compensation I'd receive should my reproductive organs not survive the ride. I told my children, my parents, and my community that there was a couple across the ocean who'd tried for seven years to have a baby but couldn't. I have a uterus sitting within me, I said, collecting dust.

Our nine-year-old tried to wrap her head around me birthing a baby who wouldn't be related to us. We talked about embryos and gestation. She was fascinated but confused. I bought a children's book about surrogacy, which, in her words, "cleared up a lot of things." We shared the news with our seven-year-old son who replied, "Cool," and walked away. Our four-year-old just wanted to know how the baby would get into me, how it would come out of me, and whether he could see the little hole in my body where all that magic happened. (Nope.)

For three and a half months, I stuck myself with needles the length of a yardstick. In the belly. In the ass. I injected myself with hormones 129 times over the course of 104 days.

In January 2017, Jamie and I took the day off from work. We traveled from Massachusetts to an office building in Connecticut, where, up the stairs and down the hall,

I entered a fertility clinic to get knocked up with someone else's baby. We sat in the waiting room across from two men giddy with chatter next to their surrogate. I deduced from their small talk that she had traveled in from Florida. I was dying to make conversation but restrained myself. Who was this woman, and what was her story? Were we in the same surrogate Facebook group? Maybe if I listened closer, I could catch her name? The doctor came out to let us know there was some kind of trouble thawing the frozen embryo, so we should go out to lunch and come back in an hour. We returned to find the giddy men and Florida woman in the parking lot, now frenzied with excitement, waving ultrasound photos in the air. "Good luck!" we shouted at one another.

Out in the world, the term "pussy grabbing" was suddenly everywhere, with women's lives and bodies dismissed and denigrated at nearly every turn. I recalled the teenaged boy who told eight-year-old me to call him when I turned eighteen. I remembered the high school physics teacher who stood over us girls during tests, left hand on right shoulder, looking down (our shirts?) as he suggested we try again on questions we had gotten wrong. Going along with it stamped my ticket to a good grade for the year. On social media, women everywhere displayed their courage. Too scared to muster anything but a simple #MeToo, I found agency in the power of my uterus.

Bladder full and intended parents on Skype, I listened to Hannah chitchat through nervous tension as Michael silently tapped his leg. I asked for a moment of privacy to collect my thoughts and move forward with intention. Alone with Jamie as we held each other, I swore I'd nurture that embryo's growth for the nine months it would be in my care, after which I'd return it to its parents in the form of a baby. I prayed for patience throughout my journey and blessings that I'd help create a healthy child who would go on to join a family. We gathered around the ultrasound screen as a fertilized embryo traveled through a long white catheter to find a comfortable spot in my womb.

Two days later, our country inaugurated the pussy grabber in chief.

We wouldn't know for another twelve days that, in fact, the transfer had worked. Through the heartbreak of Hillary Clinton's defeat, the Women's March on Washington, and an all-encompassing fear for the future, I thought, If this pregnancy can survive the stress and toxicity around me, this kid is destined for greatness.

Another month went by before I learned that something had gone terribly wrong. The fertility clinic originally told me that the antibody screens were all clear; they were not. In fact, they had never even reviewed my medical records. They ordered the wrong tests and misread the results. And the only reason I discovered this is because I reviewed the charts myself before passing them back to my doctor. I was ten weeks pregnant when my newly assigned maternal fetal medicine specialist confirmed that this fetus living inside me should never have been put there in the first place.

My doctors verified the antibodies in question were present in both egg and sperm. I went from the magic of a perfect beating heart on the ultrasound screen to the dread of carrying a "very high-risk" pregnancy. My blood could attack the baby's, leading to it becoming so anemic that it could require blood transfusions. In utero. Under epidural. Every two weeks.

I should prepare myself, the doctors said, for the possibility of an emergency C-section at as early as thirty-three weeks, after which the baby would likely require another blood transfusion. Or two. Hopefully it wouldn't sustain brain damage as a result.

I was scared. Scared about the impact on my body and my life. I was scared of trying to run an organization and mother three children while potentially needing to drop everything every two weeks without notice, month after month. I was scared of epidurals. And I was disgusted by my selfish worrying; after all, Hannah and Michael were the ones whose baby was in danger.

I agonized that my experience would turn people off to surrogacy when I'd wanted to destigmatize the process. Maybe I should have kept my mouth shut about it all.

I was also furious, because the clinic whose job it was to ensure safety failed to do so and because the agency coordinating the surrogacy went into legal mode to protect itself, abandoning the support it'd promised me. And I was irate watching Hannah and Michael ecstatic at the news that their baby could survive, never seeming to consider the quality of her future life, or what it meant for me and my body and my emotional well-being. I felt like a robot uterus at the whim of others' mercy. I felt like a woman subject to others' control and power.

All the joy vanished. My pregnancy felt—and became—toxic.

Weeks passed as the baby grew from the size of a fig

to a plum to a mango; that cutesy way to describe fetal growth now also tracked my growing anxiety. Was this all really worth it to two people trying to become parents? Plenty of people would terminate with this level of risk. Didn't they even want to consider the possibility?

In Massachusetts, a pregnancy can be ended until twenty-three weeks and six days' gestation. Every doctor I faced asked whether I planned to exercise my right to choose. I told them about page twenty of my Gestational Carrier Agreement, where I'd initialed a paragraph attesting to comply with the intended parents' decision regarding termination. No matter that these private contracts had never been tested in court; I'd agreed to waive my right.

The high-risk doctor called me a saint. Would he have done so if he knew I sat on the toilet wondering why so many miscarry easily while my uterus resembled steel? I prayed that the bleeding might begin soon.

*   *   *

That embryo is a healthy toddler now. My potentially devastating pregnancy turned out to be uneventful—the double-edged sword of accessing top medical care means that, like Eve and Adam, our eyes were opened to a world we never would have known existed otherwise.

Eleanor arrived in the world just shy of thirty-nine weeks' gestation after I labored through the night, pushing for a total of ten minutes. I got to watch a woman become a mother. Hannah moved from cutting the umbilical cord to gently kiss my head. I got to watch a man become a father, a floppy newborn resting on his naked chest.

When I had been ready to give up, they persisted with optimism. I'd almost forgotten about the strength they knew I had within me the whole time.

I get pictures of Eleanor from time to time, mostly around holidays and birthdays. I helped to create a family. I helped to create a child who in no way resembles me, but who would not have existed without me. Staring at her soft skin I see a little girl who, against the odds, kept on going to make her way into the world. I know that, just by the simple fact of being alive, she's developing her own steel core.

Four years later, I still can't feel my upper thighs from the needles that grazed the sciatic nerve leading from the injection sites. I'm told the numbness will go away eventually, but it's the numbness that helps me remember. I'd still do it all over again, if I could choose.

MAHEOV

BY TOMMY ORANGE

MARTIN WAS A MIRACLE baby like Jesus. His parents named him god but they hid it in the middle with purposeful inexactitude. Also he was a twin and they both would have had the middle name god, but Martin's brother died when their mom was having them. All he ended up being called was: the one they lost. They had medically sterilized Martin's mom, which means they tied her tubes was how she told him. Which was how he was a miracle baby, and maybe even twice over because of what happened to the one they lost.

Martin's family is Cheyenne, Cheyenne and Arapaho enrolled, but Southern Cheyenne through and through. To further keep Martin from the embarrassment of having god as a middle name, his parents named him Maheov instead of Maheo—the Cheyenne word for god. *Maheov* was the Cheyenne word for the color orange, which was different from the Cheyenne word for the fruit. *Maheov* was really just the Cheyenne words *red* and *yellow* put together into one word, just like the colors red and yellow together made orange. The secret about them meaning god for him and not the color orange was kept like the secret about his mom being medically sterilized to stop the spread of their kind, their kind of people, that's actually what the Cheyenne word for themselves meant, going way back, according to Martin's dad and a book he made Martin read over and over, written by their relative Henrietta Mann about the history of Cheyenne experience in education systems which was really just about the only history book about their kind of people written by one of them. Martin homeschooled his whole life on account of his parents not believing in what they were doing in the schools, what they were teaching and how they were teaching it, especially regarding the history of

Native people in this country, and most especially regarding Cheyennes.

Homeschooling was hard, and meant Martin didn't have friends like he could only imagine he would have had being in school together all the time and having private jokes and games between classes and knowing just how other kids ran when they were scared of being tagged or what they smelled like at the end of the day or how they might make fun of any of his names the way he'd seen in movies kids make fun of names so much in school. The only time his parents ever used Maheov was if he was in trouble and when that was the case it was Martin Maheov, his first and middle names together calling him into the kitchen or the living room whenever he did something they said he shouldn't or didn't do something they said he should.

The only way Martin had friends was from going to Native American Church meetings on the weekends, which meant driving up north an hour and staying up late with kids he might never see again while their parents ate peyote and prayed all night to Maheo or whatever other names for god they might have used depending on where they came from. Actually there tended to be a lot of Jewish hippies and in that case it was *haShem*, which wasn't their name for god but just meant the Name; and then of course there was Jesus or whomever non-Jewish white hippies prayed to, the Universe or whatever. Mostly playing with the kids he played with meant playing video games or telling scary stories or listening to the big boom of the kettle drum from inside the house wondering how their parents could stay up and sing and pray for so long when they were kids and could barely make it past 2:00 a.m. with soda and video games and on this one night a joint. This was the first time Martin smoked anything more than a cigarette, and while he was nervous, it felt natural, to be trying drugs out, like the beginning, because knowing your parents did drugs regularly, and having it be a part of their religion, did something to the way Martin thought about that joint when it was passed to him. All of which ended up making what ended up happening this one night even crazier than it already was.

They were asking one another about their respective middle names because they were bored and it was super late and there was nothing else to talk about. These kids' names were Seth and Micah, with middle names like Jacob and maybe Esau, which seemed normal enough, but not more normal than Martin. When it came to his middle name, he could have stopped at it being the color orange in Cheyenne or the colors red and orange put together in Cheyenne but it was late and they'd smoked that joint and you want to have something to talk about in these kinds of situations so he told them his mom wasn't supposed to be able to have babies after being medically sterilized, and that he was a miracle baby like Jesus.

"What's *sterilized* mean? I thought it was like, for strength, like for muscles and sports or whatever," Micah said.

"He said *sterilized*, not *steroidized*," Seth said, glaring. The glow from his phone on Micah's face meant he was looking up what *sterilized* meant.

"Wait, so they gave you the middle name god because your mom got sterilized but then had you anyway, even though she wasn't supposed to be able to have babies?" Seth asked.

"It's stupid. I don't actually know what the chances are that sterilization doesn't work. Anyway, doesn't Jesus mean like a whole different thing for you guys, like for Jewish people?"

"Jesus is cool," Seth said, "but he's not like, our guy."

"You know all those ideas about genocide and sterilization Nazis used on Jews they got from what the US did to Native Americans?" Micah said, looking at his phone.

"I homeschooled and both my parents are Native, so like, yeah," Martin said.

"Who do you think the American version of Hitler would be if you had to name one guy?" Seth asked. Martin was about to say Andrew Jackson when he heard yelling outside the window. It was the first time he'd gotten high, and the first time his middle name being god came up with anyone outside of his family, but what made the night memorable was what they watched below—one of the hippies came running out fully on fire and screaming. Martin's dad was trying to put him out with a blanket but he kept yelling that it was god. That it was all god. And it went on like that for he doesn't remember how long, but it seemed like forever, the hippie yelling that all of it was god, Martin's dad trying to put him out with the blanket.

On the way home the next day his dad told him they found out the guy had taken acid before the meeting. That he wouldn't be welcomed back into ceremony. When Martin asked if he'd be OK, neither of his parents answered. So he asked his mom how they could do that kind of medical procedure on her without her saying it was OK. There was a long silence, at first probably because it seemed to have come out of nowhere, and then because it was the kind of question that required more than an answer could give. The sound of the road seemed like it was blaring, like music Martin wanted to be able to turn down, like sometimes how they'd play peyote music too loud in the car on the way back from meetings. Martin wondered if the loudness had something to do with the joint, with being high, with having been high, which made him wonder how long it lasted, its possible residual effects, and then he wondered if different kinds of drugs reacted to each other so like the high of being high from weed and the high of being high or having been high from peyote would those two things together do something else? There clearly was something more still happening to his thinking, he was thinking when his mom finally answered his question.

"White people been thinking they were the better people all along and that progress and civilization means making more of themselves in the world, and making sure less like us make it through. You can see it in movies and books and in every way we never get to be seen the way we really are. And then what little of us gets allowed through is always the same dumb thing," his mom said.

"But they really didn't tell you they were doing it, the sterilization?"

"You found a way through. That's what matters. That we keep making our way through."

"Are Jewish people white?" Martin asked. His mom looked at his dad, then back at him in the rearview mirror with a kind of pained squint Martin couldn't decipher, then back to his dad in this like "aren't you gonna say something" kind of way.

"It's not that all white people are bad," his dad said.

"But are they white?" Martin asked.

"Jesus wasn't white, and he was Jewish," his mom said.

"Why was that guy on fire saying it's all god?" Martin asked. And then, before they could answer, he thought about if he was high and also maybe their highs were reacting to his high. What did any of that mean and was it OK? He knew he was acting different, asking more than he normally did, this time in the car would usually have meant them singing along to their peyote tapes, Martin staring out the window at the way back home, but he couldn't help the way he was thinking and especially help that he kept wanting to ask these questions. "Why are drugs like acid bad and peyote's like, spiritual, or like medicine or whatever?"

"Most drugs aren't inherently bad, it's the way people use them. The kinds of people they already are can come out on drugs in ways that can be bad, can hurt people," his dad said.

"I smoked weed last night," Martin said, not right away feeling nervous about it, which felt weird, and then when no one said anything for a while he did get nervous, and the loud road blared again. Martin knew his question was being weighed against their use of peyote, and what happened with the crazy hippie on fire, and his confession about smoking weed. He also knew that now they knew about him acting different than normal, asking these questions, and he wished he hadn't told them about getting high, because it might diminish their sincerity, make them act like oh this is just a part of the kid getting high for the first time, instead of taking his questions seriously, which, he felt, he didn't have more serious questions than these.

"Did you like it?" his mom asked.

"It was OK, until that guy came out of the teepee on fire. I mean we laughed hella hard together, me and Seth and Micah, we cracked up pretty hard for a while because it was so crazy. Then after seeing dad trying to calm him down and put him out, it stopped being funny and got hella sad. I had told them about being named Maheov and, like, the miracle baby thing, you being medically sterilized, we'd just started talking about it all before the guy came out of the teepee on fire, so then that was like, hanging over me, and they both said they were going to bed kind of suddenly, and I was high and couldn't sleep and felt really scared about a lot of things I can't remember anymore. I'm not trying to smoke weed again any time soon if that's what you're worried about."

Martin's mom and dad both laughed. And he laughed with them. But then it was just like that night when Micah and Seth went to bed. It didn't feel like there was anything to say, or like nothing more could be said about what they were talking about. The road got loud again. Then his parents turned their peyote music up too loud. And the years after that felt blurry to him, like that was the beginning of the end of something in him that he can't remember. They didn't bring him to meetings anymore after that. Then they divorced and his dad moved back to Oklahoma. It was pretty sudden but afterward and especially looking back somehow felt inevitable. About a year after the divorce his mom had a meeting for him, for the family, and Martin ended up at that same house with Seth and Micah in the meeting with them. He was pretty scared to take the medicine. To do drugs like that. But he was with his mom and it felt like she really needed him to be doing that with her. Martin caught eyes with Micah and Seth when the effects of the medicine first started coming on. He almost lost it, almost laughed about the hippie on fire. Later in the night he heard his mom praying about their kind of people, about his dad back in Oklahoma; she was asking god to do what needed to be done to make things as they should be, which to Martin felt almost like saying nothing to god, like saying god do your thing.

But later that night, or early the next morning, he got it. Even about what that hippie could have been thinking, staring into that fire, everything god, and he thanked everything he felt god to be in that moment like he'd never said thank you to anyone. He got way down in his prayer, bent over on his knees. He thanked the journey through tubal ligation and twin sibling death to get to where he could be alive thinking about it all, thanking it all. Martin understood the wisdom that made it medicine, and how stupid he'd probably always be after moving away from that singular moment of understanding and gratitude, which created something in him that he would chase the rest of his life, which wasn't a bad thing to chase, but it sure did end up hurting to hunger for.

WHAT CAN I DO FOR YOU?

YAEL R. SHINAR

A scary, hard thing—
try to make sense of it—
Like knitting a life preserver
from wool
under a wave—
Who can do that?
An anesthetic numbs the senses,
slows the brain signals
until there's no perceivable
or conceivable sense—

This I offer
to displace pain, for a moment,
—suffering, too.
If making sense
of things
is how you deal,
What can I do
for you?

~

Let me, rather than torment you with significance, just
tell you the story.

~

She thought she had a dead baby.
The ob-gyns saw an ultrasound
showing "intrauterine products of conception, consistent with ten weeks of growth,"
but without a "fetal pole," a bright white stripe
on the screen, suggesting ongoing development, visible
before a heartbeat
flickers. The suggestion was absent.
After her baby died, she waited a while before coming
in for a D&C, dilation and curettage,
which sometimes terminates a pregnancy

and sometimes clears an already dead one.

It's therapeutic.

She did come, eventually. She was interviewed and examined by the nurses and ob-gyns, who consulted Anesthesiology for procedural sedation. That was me, Anesthesiology.

~

She sits sideways in a yellow recliner, shoulder buried in the seat back, knees curled to her chest, feet flexed against the armrest. A grown woman, not tall, and a little thinner than anyone would want to be. The chair is too big for her, it holds her like a cave holds a cub without its mama bear.

She stares at a man's face on her phone screen. She doesn't look up when I enter; she doesn't look up when I sit. Their gazes knit some intimacy, preserved from my sense in their silence. Her skin is the color of milky coffee, her nails are filed and smooth. Her braids are bound in a tight, low bun. She's radiant, like a Dove beauty ad.

~

When was the last time you had anything to eat?
I don't know, she says.
Are you allergic to anything?
Why are you wasting my time with these questions,

I just want to get this done.

She's still video chatting with the man.

Who is that?

 I want him on the phone. Why are you wasting my time?

We like to have privacy during some portions of the interview.

 She hangs up.

OK, when was the last time you had something to eat?

 Monday.

It's Thursday today.

You're not buying my lunch, are you?

I'm sorry. I cough into my elbow to hide the tears in my eyes.

It was December 2019,

when a cough was less threatening

than a white woman's pity.

With sedation, you'll be asleep and you won't feel pain.

You'll be conscious, but you won't remember anything.

Most people choose sedation. The other option is a spinal.

We inject numbing medication through a small needle in your low back.

You'll be numb from the waist down, but you'll be awake,

and you'll remember everything. Most people want to be asleep.

I don't want any of that.

Why don't we sign the consent for sedation anyway, in case you change your mind?

Why are you wasting my time? She signs.

~

Pain relief often means loss of agency for the person being relieved. Many analgesics blunt the cognition necessary for reliable decision making, safe operation of machinery. Spinal injections of numbing medications make it impossible to jump and to run.

~

She walks back to the OR with an IV in her wrist, a bag of crystalloid fluid in her hand, connecting tubing slack at her side.

At the OR door she stops and bends her head to the nurse,

who covers her hair in a polypropylene blue bouffant and swings open the door.

She sits on the table,

lies back on the table,
like a blanket unfurling inside a wave.

I guide her head to a pillow, center her shoulders and hips on the table. I hang the fluid on a pole. I Velcro a blood pressure cuff around her bicep. I wrap a sticker around her nail bed to monitor oxygen in her blood. I stick EKG stickers to her chest and snap the EKG wires in place, laying them around her head, framing her face, like a disposable halo. My vials are spiked and locked, my syringes labeled and capped. No anesthesia, no analgesia, no friend   in sight.

The ob-gyns position her legs like fine fibers through a great loom.

~

How are you?
            I'm fine.
They begin. She speaks.
There's something in my hole!
A speculum, I say.
There's something in my hole!
Do you want pain medication?
No!
Ow! What is that pressure in my hole?!

A speculum and forceps. Do you want to hold my hand?
She squeezes my gloved hand.
Ow!
I remove my blue nitrile gloves and hold her bare hand
in my bare hand.
Her grip softens, like I've been a guardrail transformed
into a friend.
The more it hurts, the more she talks.
~
She says,
Will I be able to eat after this?
Do you order from the cafeteria directly to your room?
Can my friend come into my room after?
Will I be able to hold my baby?
I see blank stares from the ob-gyns.
They look to the nurse.
I can do that, the nurse says.
I say,
Yes,
you will be able to hold your baby.
Ow! There's something in my hole!
*Is that why you want to be awake, to make sure you get
a chance to hold your baby?*

Yes.

If I can promise that you will get to hold your baby,
would you want some pain medicine and some medicine
to make you sleepy?

Yes.

I promise.

Put me to sleep.

Propofol 150 micrograms per kilogram per minute.

~

In a *dilation and curettage*, ob-gyns dilate the cervix, scrape tissue from the uterus, suction it into a specimen cup through a woven filter in the center. Sometimes the tissue is sent to pathology for analysis, other times it goes to medical waste. Today the nurse scrapes it from the filter with a sterile spoon, transfers it into a simple sterile cup. Ten-week products of conception look like a handful of blood mixed with frayed cotton and fat. We have told her to expect this.

The nurse swaddles the plastic cup in a baby blanket and tucks it under our sleeping patient's arm. I turn off sedation.

~

Where's my baby?

In your arms, I say.
She closes her eyes,
and we wheel her to recovery.

~

Her friend is there. He looks up from the menu, nods
to me, turns to her. She is sleeping. He watches her sleep,
holds her bare hand in his bare hand,   says nothing.

~

What is the difference, while the heart beats, between
sadness and injury?
Once the heart stops, there is this difference
Sadness pulses
and we have stillness
How we wish for sadness—
How we wish to hold
a baby
and that hope is stronger
than pain
Pain
is sometimes
so strong,
you take a risk,
rely on others—

God they better come through
God they better come through
God they better come through

Details regarding time, place, medical care, and patient characteristics have been changed to protect patient privacy.

PANDEMIC

The abortionist from the coast
flew inland once a week
to offer care
where no one else
cared.
When the pandemic hit, she
cut maternity leave short and drove
8 hours each way
with the nursling.
Lives, she said,
are at stake.

JOURNAL OF MY BIRTH

RACHEL ELIZA GRIFFITHS

1

I HAVE THE RIGHT to make all potential and impossible images of myself.

In spite of this truth, there are voices beneath my skin that say otherwise.

2

Journal of My Birth confronts ubiquitous voices that silently assert privilege against women: through law, by negligence and dismissal. How a woman's body is policed with the agendas of everyone but the woman herself. And, of course, what happens when a woman explicitly, by implication, accepts that agenda.

The ways through which language and image collaborate on these ideas is ever complicated by the politics of—and, perhaps, shame in—the reader.

3

To feel unsafe in a photograph reveals a self-policing that is dangerous.

4

As a Black Queer survivor, and fluent as both a writer and a visual artist, I am wrecked by the process of these photographs.

I am challenging established languages and institutional narratives, mythologies, whether in text or imagery, that make me feel that these portraits—and thus, my body—are *wrong*.

I am reminded of the physicality of each portrait and that it was never "easy" for me to spread, to open my body.

Show and Tell Them Nothing, a voice said.

5

During college, I remember escorting several friends to clinics to have abortions. I remember getting money out of my checking account. I remember that sometimes a friend accepted the money but then never spoke to me again. I remember how a friend tried to continue our friendship after the visit to the clinic but confessed that the sight of me reminded her of what she had done. None of those girls are my friends now, yet they remain vivid to me. I think of them and hope they are safe and living lives they have chosen for themselves.

I remember how those times felt for us—forbidden and fatal.

No matter how much solidarity I offered, things were complicated for each of us. Womanhood was not a monolithic landscape. Our choices lived in a nuanced language that did not speak to, or for, us equally. In spite of our shared experiences, we also confronted issues that often tangled strands of desire and violence. There was power and danger in speaking out or saying nothing.

I was aware of the intricate system that engulfed us before birth. We were overpowered psychologically, physically, and socially by America's brute lineage of shame, racism, classism, and economic control. I was too young and powerless to articulate how fully our bodies were enslaved to ideologies that robbed our right to freedom.

This control of our bodies extended to laws created by men and even—as those men claimed—by God.

6

Before my mother gave birth to me, she was pregnant with a girl she would have named Ashley. In Washington, DC, in the 1970s, my mother's Black body was irrelevant to nearly everyone.

When my mother told her white, male doctor, over and over, that something was wrong, he refused to listen and forced her to carry the child. My mother would go on to birth a dead infant. Her grief over the loss of this baby girl never healed. Her suspicions against medical doctors—and their dismissal of her existence—would prove true time and time again. She spoke bitterly to me about the history of modern-day eugenics and its relationship to Black women.

When I was old enough to understand medical prejudice against Black women's bodies, I watched doctors and nurses handle my mother's body roughly in my presence, or worse, refuse to touch or treat her.

Years later, after my mother's death, my own health exploded, in part due to depression, grief, trauma, and my struggle to gain some kind of footing in a world that discouraged my complex identity.

This struggle also happened in the examining room of my gynecologist. One rainy afternoon as I waited to have a sonogram, I looked over at the screen and noticed that my name was misspelled and my birth date wrong.

According to the "facts" of my own medical records, I was an entirely different woman.

When my doctor, a youngish white woman, came to examine me, I asked her whether there was anything I could do—without endangering my body—to keep the option of pregnancy. She snorted involuntarily and tried to apologize as she giggled. Staring at her, my legs open, I asked her why she thought my question was funny.

To excuse her laughter, she asked me if I was still alone

(I had recently divorced). She glanced at my file, then asked if I was also still an artist. As she indicated that I could close my legs and sit up, the paper crinkled loudly beneath me.

7

In 2015, I created one of the first images of *Journal of My Birth* during a stay at a well-known colony for artists and writers in upstate New York. The residency coincided with the one-year anniversary of my mother's death.

The feeling of my motherlessness haunted my language, and I turned, for strength and counsel, to a lineage of women artists, living and dead, some of whom were non-mothers, some of whom refused the binary argument that choosing to have children threatened the integrity of art making.

Meanwhile, lucid dreams invaded my body. My body was altered, literally, and I experienced intense sensitivity to everything, including my past. I found myself returning to the mental state of the much younger girl I had been when I survived multiple sexual assaults.

During different sessions of the project, I realized that

the voice that afflicted me the most was the voice of my mother, who would have hated these photographs. She would have called them out immediately as nasty or worse: *weird white girl shit.*

Though I was alone while I made the self-portraits, there was always an invisible theater, an unseen jury. It took time for me to confront the voices of shame that insisted I had no right to expose myself, to be vulnerable, to question the highly complex relationships between women, labor, and reproduction.

What became clear was my inherent self-love and my defiance. My refusal to accept fear or to back down from seeing a new aspect of myself. The freedom we collectively deserve as women and creators. Our existence—as creative and maternal forces—is never illegitimate, is never wrong or powerless, and is certainly something we ourselves *must* own and defend.

8

I hope that I have left enough space in *Journal of My Birth* for myself—as artist—and for you—as audience—to breathe. I have faith that we will both look and be seen.

Thus, it is possible for us to reject and to resist any effort—by our government or ourselves—to take away our right to love our bodies and to create whatever forms of life we choose to live.

Journal of My Birth offers an elemental frame and perspective of who I am becoming as much as how I came to be. These self-portraits I have created for myself, of my body, live in me like new life.

IT BEGAN
IN ANOTHER LAND

BY HANNAH LILLITH ASSADI AND SHELLY ORIA

MAY 2020

MY DEAR HANNAH,

I just returned from my daily walk—which I took earlier than usual, since the heavy rains have rendered all breaks between pours opportunities to be seized—and midwalk, the gentle drizzle grew stronger, and before I knew it, I was soaked, and my mask was soaked too. My mask is a thin beanie hat that I rescued from the back of my closet where it shared box space with too-tight jeans and skirts, items intended for Goodwill. I connect the beanie to my face with rubber bands each time, giving it a new life I doubt it expected. I did order a pretty one online—a fancy mask, I almost wrote—but it's not yet arrived. For now the gray little hat is a loyal friend, and the time we spend together in the outside world—air, Hannah! I've never had such strong feelings about air!—is in many ways the highlight of my day in this quarantined time.

Remember I wrote to you from my upstate retreat in early March, trying to finalize our wine date? And you had to say you weren't going to socialize for a while now? Of course you weren't. Of course we weren't. But I did not yet understand. And in that exchange you told me you were pregnant! So I'm writing, perhaps it's obvious, because I want you to write back.

My days are filled with stories of abortion. Poems about the often-hushed trials of motherhood, plays about the complexities of childfreeness, essays about the fight for reproductive freedom in 2020 America land in my inbox, which then marks them with a star. I try to engage with a few stars every day. To compile this type of anthology, I learned with *Indelible*, one must submerge in pain, learn to breathe in its waters. You hope to emerge with some insight. To be honest, some days you hope simply to emerge. And as I work on this book, you've been on my mind so often since you shared your news. What on planet Earth has it been like to grow a human inside you in this time of a global plague? I cannot imagine. I want to hear about your experience, and not the way I might in a text message, but the way we wrote to each other for two years not that long ago, a book's worth of letters, which is to say the way we write to each other when we take the time and care.

This memory has been persistent: at the little wine bar on Smith Street, after long hours of writing at the café across the street, we drank and drank because the lovely Frenchman who owns the place kept pouring, and the Gouda wasn't absorbing the liquid fast enough, and so we were pretty buzzed when you asked if I'd made a choice to not be a mother. I think I just nodded; language is so often inadequate. I think I stared at the whiskey bottles on the shelf behind the bar, their distorted reflection in that cloudy mirror. Was there one moment, you asked, when you ... knew?

The way I remember that night: I never answered your question. We talked about the ambiguousness you felt at the idea of motherhood, at the notion of bringing life into our troubled world. Now I want to ask you the same question: Was there a moment in which your uncertainty lifted? A moment when you knew you wanted to be a mother? But this letter is also my way of responding to that question, or at least searching for a response.

About four years ago, back home in Tel Aviv for the summer, I went to a party and ran into someone I disliked in high school. Like so many other Israeli women, she was a mother of three. Like most Israelis, when she encountered adults who weren't parents, she could only understand their existence through the frame of problem or tragedy. And so in her way, when she asked when I was planning to have kids—unaware of the bluntness of her question, blind to her own aggression in a way that sadly, tragically, defines my homeland—she was practicing kindness. She offered a view of me as a woman who's decided to wait until the last biologically possible moment to become a mother: a woman making a peculiar, risky, or ill-advised choice but not a tragic figure. And when she asked me this question, I smiled and said: Never. We all have teenagers hiding inside us, don't we, waiting for the right combination to unlock their spite, their taste for shock. At least I do. In that crowded apartment in the south of Tel Aviv, I didn't mean what I said; I might as well have slapped her or flashed her; the moment was nothing more than an effort to stun and express rage. But in the days that followed, my body felt light. And so when I was asked again—as you well know, I come from a culture that reveres procreation and disregards boundaries, so the question is common—I again said, Never. I still thought I was lying.

The answer to your question may be that there was never one moment in which I chose childfreeness but rather a near-infinite assembly of moments in which I learned time and again what I'd known for many years.

Another such moment—now dreamlike in texture, shrouded in psyche-fog—happened months after my ex-husband and I moved to New York. A condom broke. Naively, we went to the Rite Aid at the end of our block in Hell's Kitchen. This was 2003, and I remember my shock when I learned that in America I couldn't buy a morning-after pill over the counter. We had no health insurance. When my period was late—my period had never been late—I called my Israeli gynecologist back home as if he could perform an abortion over the phone, or confirm that I needed one. A missing piece in my memory: I don't remember buying or taking a pregnancy test. What I remember is that my husband did some research and told me about an organization called Planned Parenthood. I remember thinking it was a funny name, imagining large conference rooms where people gathered to debate, perhaps drawing graphs or making vision boards, planning their parenthood. And I remember heading to a clinic in Chelsea with my husband, and that it was so cold that day; I remember what it felt like to live in a body that grew up in Middle East weather and had not yet adjusted to East Coast winters. The line was long—we could see it from a distance, snaking around part of the block—and we looked at each other in terror; my husband was even more sensitive to the sting of Manhattan's cold winds. I'm almost positive that in the end we waited less than five minutes, but I'm not sure why or how. And I'm almost positive the waiting room walls were green and that my husband made a joke about it, because waiting rooms in Tel Aviv were never green. Everything was new back then. I don't think I laughed.

The next piece in this memory is a nurse telling me my period was likely late because of my anxiety over the broken condom; I was not pregnant. Does it make sense, Hannah, that I found this out right away? It seems that back in the early aughts, so little ever happened right away.

(Lately—perhaps this is evident—I've been questioning the stories my memory tells me; most of us see ourselves as reliable narrators of our own past, but isn't that just a choice we make because the alternative is too scary?)

This memory, accurate or flawed, is another moment I think of when I consider my choice to be childfree: the nurse's soft voice, a pause in which I took in her words, and then something, maybe relief, moving through me fast, its very end the tip of a knife. It is a painful thing, learning that you don't want the thing you've been told your whole life defines womanhood, even humanity.

Here's one more: a few years ago I got a bad Pap smear and needed a colposcopy. Many years a New York resident at that point, I still felt so overwhelmed by the American healthcare system, which I found not only insanely expensive but also impossibly unnavigable; I decided to get the procedure done in Tel Aviv. My girlfriend at the time, facing childhood trauma that had resurfaced, was in bad shape, and we ended up talking on Skype the whole night before my appointment—her from our Bed-Stuy apartment, me whispering from a tiny room adjacent to my parents' bedroom. For long hours I tried and failed to help her hold memories of violence and violation.

When I arrived at my gynecologist's clinic early the next morning—the same doctor I called all those years ago and many times since, a man who'd been my gynecologist since I was a teenager—I was exhausted, and he seemed no less exhausted, and angry. I didn't know why he was angry, and I still don't, but as he inserted into me something that looked and pinched like tweezers and began to manipulate the tool inside me, as the pain worsened and I looked away, trying to leave my body, he told me this was my fault. I thought I'd misheard him at first, but the pain made speech impossible so I didn't ask or say anything, and he went on: this was my fault because years before I'd refused to take the HPV vaccine. Now I could be sick, and it could have been prevented. Did I think I knew better than him? Didn't I regret now that I discounted his advice? I finally managed a Stop talking please. He did. Minutes later I was sobbing in my mother's arms in the elevator. When she said, That painful, hah? I think I said, He yelled at me. I was a child again in that moment.

Writing to you now, I thought this memory came up since it's a gynecological intervention that felt emotionally unsafe, or perhaps because I retreated to a childlike state in response. But in fact I think the emotional core of this memory, its connection to my childfreeness, is rooted in the night before. Part of me believes I took in my girlfriend's trauma in a way that I shouldn't have—a way that certainly didn't help her, and left me exposed. I do not mean to absolve my doctor's behavior or blame myself, but I know the energetic force field within which I walk this world, and I know it was missing that morning. It disappeared in my attempt to disappear my girlfriend's horrific pain. I do that sometimes in love, and not only in romantic love; I have done this multiple times with my sister, whom I helped raise. Which is to say, I see now that this story came up because it's an extreme example of what I always feared when I imagined motherhood: a loss of self both inevitable and dangerous.

There are so many other such moments I could tell you about, Hannah, each highlighting different aspects of my choice. Some involve other painful experiences, sure, but not all: I have memories of happiness and achievement and lightness that feel tied to the freedom I've decided not to forgo. It's this part of the answer that seems to attract the most vitriol, isn't it? If a woman decides to not become a mother, the very least she can do for society is apologize for her decision and suffer as a result. So absurd, considering that, in the way we are currently living, our planet has about six billion people more than it can support.

I could say much more about childfreeness in the context of climate change, of course, but I won't: I know we share this concern for the future, but I also imagine it's the last thing pregnant you wants to contemplate. I will say that climate concerns don't make me self-righteous: I don't presume my choice in any way morally superior to anyone else's. We all know so little in the end. I want everyone to make the procreative choices they deem right, or the ones to which they feel drawn. And I want to live in a world that shows me the same generosity.

As I imagine you reading this letter, I want to say one more thing: I think this pandemic is our little planet's way of fighting for its life. This isn't a "silver lining" for me; it isn't an attempt to make meaning of the unfathomable suffering.... It's simply what I believe is happening, and it was one of my first thoughts when the virus began to spread. My attachment to this narrative isn't profound; this narrative, at its core, is the story of the future, of the next generation. While calamity can certainly arrive in our lifetime—and arguably already has—the question of its timeline, its progression to the point of no return, is the one that would keep me up at night as a parent. And if the planet succeeds, even in just a tiny, tiny way, that could mean additional years of life, of quality life. I'm rooting for the earth, for the possibility of this catastrophe teaching us to live more sustainably, for new and renewed horizons.

LOVE,
SHELLY

JUNE 2020

DEAR SHELLY,

It is almost painful now to recall that night at Big Tiny with you—any night in a bar with anyone for that matter—and despite however many glasses of wine we had had at that point, I do now vividly remember asking you about motherhood (a question to which at that point I had no answer myself). We didn't linger on it, as you've recalled, and I've since wanted to know what was happening beneath your eyes. It is a question I ask often lately of other women as I stare down the prospect of motherhood myself. Having read your letter, I am grateful to be privy to your years' long epiphany on the subject. But before I respond to your moving account of abstaining from it, I just want to pause for a second on this pandemic, on all that we have lost, on New York City bars for one: the beating heart of life here, their noise, their coziness, the way their windows would fog up in stormy weather. We took them for granted, didn't we? Now that natural New Yorkese—"Let's meet for a drink"—will never sound as simple.

It was all so terrifyingly quiet for months around here. During the peak of the virus's passage through the city, I would stand before my bedroom shutters and watch the traffic lights cycle between red and yellow and green, a drama staged for only me. There were no cars, no passersby. On one night only, a stranger in a building across the street blasted Nina Simone until five or six in the morning. And in the middle of this concert, playing seemingly for no one, I began to wonder if I was only hallucinating this wild violation of sound. If I in fact desired it and manifested it. The city had otherwise been taken by ghosts. In front of that same building now, for the past few nights, rosary candles have been lit. I know many of my neighbors. I've lived on this block for seven years. But I don't know a single soul, living or dead, in that building.

Now as I write to you, mere weeks later, the city has recovered its capacity for making noise, and with a vengeance. That cemetery quiet that characterized the city's spring has unfolded into a summer of protest, police sirens, circling helicopters, and explosions of defiant fireworks, which surround our building in a soundtrack reminiscent of both war and celebration. All of this quiet, and then all of this uproar, have been somewhat more difficult to abide in the absence of my usual coping mechanisms— cigarettes and wine. Every night I go to sleep, praying for my baby girl's safe arrival in the face of all the tumult that has characterized her journey in. I speak to her already as someone in the room with me. But is she? It feels, sometimes, as if she is no more real than a ghost. I can feel her crawling against my skin, learning the limits of the little planet she has lived in these last seven months, and yet I cannot see her.

The experts say that by now my daughter should be dreaming her own dreams, and I have to wonder what her brain makes of this mad world so far. The helicopters now are perched just overhead. If some tragic flaw were to befall their machinery, they would fall into my apartment, this one I love so much, this one I can't seem to bring myself to want to leave despite all that has befallen the city of late (the one abandoned daily by more and more friends). The one in which she was conjured into this world and in which, inshallah, she will be born. Through me, has she already seen all these fireworks exploding over our sleeping heads?

To answer your question directly, the truth is, I think I only really "knew" I wanted to be a mother very recently, and it is a knowledge that still does not come untethered from doubt. My first pregnancy, a year ago, ended in miscarriage. And it was only in its wake, tragically, that I knew

I had actually wanted that fetus to become a baby, that I wanted to be its mother.

So, the story begins there, in that small death I suffered on hands and knees on the floor of my parents' bathroom while visiting for a lamb dinner. My cousin was in New York to visit. I had not seen him since my grandmother's funeral two decades earlier. In fact, I had no memory of him. Instead, as we passed the rice, I kept recalling my tayta's face postmortem, there in that room where the women of the family washed her body in the Muslim fashion. She seemed to be smiling. Just after we had finished dinner, I excused myself to the bathroom. The blood began as a trickle.

It's interesting you remember the green of the Planned Parenthood waiting room, because ever since this particular night, the wallpaper in my parents' bathroom is pink in my memory. But I fact checked myself recently, and no, the wallpaper is white.

Anyhow, there was no pain, only blood, and then all there was, was pain. After not smoking for an entire month, I thought a cigarette might save my life. It wouldn't. Locked in that bathroom wailing, I asked for a book to read. My mother brought me *Salt Houses* by my friend, the Palestinian author, Hala Alyan. Later, it struck me as not a little ironic that her gorgeous opening pages, in a book generally about our people's exile, were also about a character's fertility and frequent miscarriages. But there in that not pink, pink bathroom, reading was not possible; neither was thought. All I could hope for was that time might remain passing. And I confess, there was a sliver of a moment between the blood, the contractions, when I felt as you had in that Planned Parenthood waiting room— simple relief.

The next day, my midwife sent me to the closest (and cheapest) clinic she could find. It was in Bay Ridge, and the medical staff were all Arabs. The nurse—who performed the ultrasound and found no heartbeat where there had been one only a week earlier, who found nothing on the screen but blood—said simply: *You passed it, habibti.* The confirmation of my loss followed by that word, *habibti,* that word in my father's tongue, both broke my heart and saved it. We went to the ocean after we left that office. The rest of whoever that baby of mine might have been passed into the Atlantic. That night, I had a glass of wine and a cigarette. The wine tasted like rubbing alcohol. The cigarette was just fine. Whatever relief I might have temporarily felt in having averted the prospect of motherhood morphed quickly and violently into a wave of unimaginable loss that no amount of substance could deaden.

The story began there but did not end there. In Paris, days after a countrywide strike was announced in December (an almost adorable premonition to the chaos that would envelop the rest of the world months later), there was a pregnancy test tucked in my purse, reading *enceinte,* which I had taken just before being caught in a subway tunnel in a car so packed it made the New York City rush hour (of old) look idyllic. People were screaming in French. The lights turned off. Finally, when the train began to move again, at the next station, there was a stampede of incoming passengers. I felt I might forget how to breathe, and if I forgot how to breathe, my fetus, all too soon, would meet the fate of my last.

In New York City, shortly thereafter, out of the precarious first trimester and into the safer second, our hometown, our streets, became the world's epicenter of COVID-19. When I walked outside, it was with a debilitating fear of every passerby. There were times, too, beneath my mask, I felt I could not breathe, that I was not breathing correctly, that if I did not remove it for a gasp of oxygen, I would pass out, and if I did remove it for a gasp of oxygen, I would fall ill. And either way, my baby would never dream as I pray she dreams right now, quietly in her sea.

And then, at the onset of my third trimester, at the end of May, George Floyd was murdered by asphyxiation.

I could breathe the whole time.

Shelly, it's a fucked, fucked world. Logically, it makes more sense to me to not want motherhood than to want it. So why do we keep bringing life here? Why am I? I don't know if I can answer. Is it the mammal in me that unconsciously desires the line to go on? The Palestinian in me who feels the weight of the broken generations that preceded me, their lost home and shattered dreams? By the woman in me who lost her virginity in rape and wants my maidenhood over and done for good? Or is it the writer in me who just wants my story to live on? Children cannot forget their parents. Children are cursed by their parents. And the curse goes on. We call this curse love, when perhaps it is only a story of survival.

How is it I can long for her to join me in this ugly, sad climate bereaved world of injustice and poverty and pillage and plague? In your letter, I hear you justifying your decision because, at least historically, it is the road less taken. And yet, lately I feel that I will need to spend all the days for the rest of my life justifying my decision to bring my baby, this innocent soul, *here*.

But maybe the real answer, for me, is also one just simply of wanting to know the outer reaches of love. The world is fucked, but this gentle sway in the breeze, the music even of this summer, helicopters and rage and sirens, the superficial breath beneath the fabric of a mask, a sudden sun shower are also laced with love. Perhaps the answer is that I can still see the beauty in us, and all around us, and I want it to go on and on and on.

As I get closer to motherhood, there is nothing I fear more than that which troubled you so in taking on your girlfriend's trauma, in loving too hard—self-effacement. But will I want to trade whatever disappears of me for what was? I won't know the answer, Shelly, until I'm on the other side of this strangest and most sacrificial exercise in love.

Last night I dreamt I was engaged in a strange game, one I kept losing. Part of the reason I could not win was that I was so distracted by a rainbow in the near distance. I wonder if, though by now my daughter dreams her own dreams, she could also see that rainbow.

I think you are in Israel already. Lately, I've been thinking to myself, I just want to go home. But where is that? Is it waiting for me in a town in the hills overlooking the Galilee? The one my father left so long ago? Or is it here, beneath these helicopters, these fireworks, these turbulent, rainbow-colored dreams?

YOURS WITH LOVE,

HANNAH

NOT ANYONE'S HERO

BY KHADIJAH QUEEN

WHEN I FOUND OUT I was pregnant, I didn't want to tell anyone. Not my mother, not my sister, not any of my friends, and certainly not anyone at my command. I'd taken the test in my boyfriend's bathroom. He didn't come home from the club that night. He didn't answer any of my pages. At dawn I finally had to leave his place to report to the ship for duty, and, as I started my car, he pulled up to the house in the passenger side of a nondescript green coupe that wasn't his; some girl in a ratty weave was driving. He got out as I drove off, cursing him out while he laughed and said she was his friend Mario's girl, that he'd been with Mario and them all night. I wasn't hearing it. He chased my car as I drove away, but he was still drunk enough and his pants were baggy enough to trip him up. I don't know how I got through the day—probably as quietly as I could and as snippily as I could get away with. What the hell was I going to do? I went to talk to the elder sailor in our berthing, a first-class we called by her rank— EN1, short for first-class engineman.

She could read the emotions on my face when I said I needed to talk. There was zero privacy on the ship; she had to kick Garcia out of her little office and shut the porthole, not leave it open like we were supposed to. I sat down in the metal chair bolted to the deck in front of her desk, and she looked at me with those red-rimmed, hawklike eyes of hers that reminded me of my uncles in Michigan who drank from flasks all day. She was a mother figure to us, but her hardness was undeniable, too, with that deep smoker's voice that carried through the berthing when she was ordering us to make our racks. "So what you wanna do, Queen," she stated more than asked. I looked at my hands, at the bulkhead, the overhead—anywhere but directly at her face. "I know a place you can go to take care of it, if you want to stay in," she said matter-of-factly. I knew I could do that if I wanted, that I probably should—if I wanted to stay in the Navy. "Nobody would have to know. You could do it on a Friday when you don't have duty and be back to work on Monday. I could go with you," she offered, unsmiling. I don't think EN1 ever smiled, even when she was laughing. "We would sure hate to see you go."

I was quiet for a while, weighing my options. I hated to disappoint her, and I wanted her to know that I was listening. I wished she (or anyone) would give me a reason to think I could continue on in the service, to have any hope that things would get better for me. As one of only thirty women on board a ship of 330 personnel, I endured daily harassment about what I wore, guys I dated, where I spent my time off-duty, the novels I read. I witnessed secondhand the comments made about other female sailors, gossip about who was sleeping with whom, who *would* sleep with whom. The guys liked to complain about women sailors, but they gossiped more than any gaggle of housewives I'd ever seen. And their behavior? Consistently heinous.

On our last underway port visit, one of the officers got in trouble for having sex onstage with a stripper. That was the talk of the boat, and led my direct superiors to a confession about a "souvenir" they'd kept from the last overseas deployment—one of them reached into an old leather backpack that hung on a hook in Sonar 1 and pulled out a pink lace thong. Raucous laughter, salacious hooting, and a game of catch ensued. The guys tossed that stripper's panties back and forth over our heads— the only three women in the division, who happened to be on duty—while we sat at our workstations. "You're not gonna tell on us, are ya, Queen?" one of the southern STG2s drawled. I just rolled my eyes and tried to keep my head down, study the maintenance manuals, mind my own business. But all the bullshit and ignorance and attempts at control wore on me. When I wouldn't date the Puerto Rican sonarman my supervisors had approved for me, they gave me the shit jobs, like tying the ship to the pier and tossing the tobacco slop bucket—I did not smoke or chew—and assigned me the worst middle-of-the-night watch every single underway. I felt harried, sleep deprived, and unsupported. "I hate to leave the ship too," I said to EN1 quietly, "but I think I have to."

Just the other day, the first-class in our division told me I'd have to wait for the next cycle of surface warfare quals, which would set me back for promotion—no reason given. That felt like the last straw, and the more I thought about it, the more convinced I became there was no place in the Navy for me, despite EN1's comment that they'd hate to lose me.

"You got anybody to help you, your mom or some-body?" She already knew who the father was—all the Black people on the boat did. There weren't that many of us, so we kept few secrets. Resisting the urge to touch my fluttering belly, I looked her in the eye. "My mother."

I took a deep breath, pondering abortion. "I can't kill it, EN1," I said softly. That was the truth too—more than I wanted to admit. I could feel this growing life and held on to it like it would save me.

EN1 looked at me for what felt like a long time. She let out a weary sigh. "Well," she said, rising from her chair, "good luck. I can't say I'm not surprised, and I can't say I'm not disappointed. I'll do my best to keep you off the hard jobs in the meantime."

I thanked her and went about my day. I still didn't know what to tell my boyfriend. I didn't want anything to do with him anymore. Could I raise a child on my own? I had no idea. I felt like I didn't know anything, like

I was slipping away. I left the ship that night after working hours, threw a few things into my duffel bag, put on my civvies, and drove around base until I couldn't stand the motion. I drove until I reached the Atlantic, as close as I could get without driving into it; the reflected lights from the city shimmered in waves that failed to lull me, so I started to count them. I kept the car running, thinking that maybe I actually *could* drive into it, gun the gas until the pier disappeared under the wheels and gravity made descent fast, inevitable. I could disappear into the black, and no one would know. Except, right at that moment, someone on watch pulled up, shining their lights into my Ford Escort.

"Hey, how's it going?" the guard asked, feigning nonchalance. I can't remember if he stood next to my window with a flashlight or if his vehicle's headlights formed the harsh, bright circles invading the darkness.

I kept quiet. I think I managed to lift one corner of my lips in acknowledgment, but all of my effort was focused on not crying, on counting those infinite waves, each moonlit curve racing toward the shoreline with the night breeze.

"You're not thinking of going out there, are you?" he asked gently, with a smile. I still couldn't speak. He asked me what my command was. I managed to name a carrier on the opposite end of the pier, far away from where my actual ship was moored. He asked for my ID, but I shook my head. His mouth set in a straight line, but he didn't get belligerent. His voice was gentle, his manner oddly comforting for a man in camos armed with a 9mm.

"Stay right there, OK?"

I nodded. "I'm all right," I managed. As soon as he got back into his car to call for assistance and closed the door, I panicked. If he saw my license plate, he would be able to find my name and figure out my real command, then tell them I was a suicide risk, and I'd be *fucked*. Panic gave me some energy. Shaking, I backed away from the pier and raced toward the gate leading off base. This was before security got ridiculous—before the war started. I got out of there without any trouble and found the nearest motel. I paid for a night with my last forty dollars, took my mostly empty duffel into the room, and stripped down to my T-shirt and skivvies. I drank water and ate Cheez-Its and watched TV and wept. Then something funny and classic came on—*The Golden Girls* or *Good Times*, I think—and I started laughing so loudly that my motel room wall got a few pounds from next door. I turned it down from cackle to giggle, still munching stale snacks. I didn't know what else to do; I didn't know what I *wanted* to do. But I knew I needed to ask for leave, so I could figure things out. I had something like three weeks on the books, but I wouldn't get that. No one got more than a week unless somebody was dead or dying. Instead, I asked for three days. We weren't going underway, and it wasn't that busy.

My supervisors gave me a hard fucking time, of course. They wanted to know why I wanted leave, where I planned to go, tried to make me justify the trip by telling them my personal business. But I told them to mind their own; I knew the official rules said no specifics were required, so I used the language of those rules in my replies. I evaded their prying, and finally the leave got approved late in the week. I drove north, all the way from Virginia to Michigan in one day, to see my mother.

When I got there, I did what I usually did on leave: slept for twelve hours after the grace of eating my mom's food. She'd made all my favorites: richly seasoned baked chicken, mashed potatoes and gravy, greens, cornbread, fresh lemonade with lemons she'd squeezed by hand on that old plastic juicer. The next morning, Mom woke me before dawn and sat on my bed in her housecoat and headscarf, the smell of turkey bacon wafting in from the kitchen turning my stomach a little.

"I had a dream," she said. "You pregnant, ain't you." A statement, just like EN1. I nodded, my face buried in the pillow, trying not to burst into tears. I could feel my body expanding. I felt out of control. I sat up, ran my hands through my super-short curls, and let out an impatient breath, willing myself to get it together.

"You gon' need some help, girl," my mom said. I nodded.

"You would have to come to Virginia," I said.

"All right," she said, without even a hint of pause. And that was that. I drove back to base the next day, eleven hours straight on the open road to think and scream and cry and laugh, to sip vanilla shakes from Rally's, to listen to mixtapes—rapping and singing along with Method Man and Redman and Mary J. Blige—and to wonder what the fuck I was going to do with a baby.

The day after I made the decision to continue my pregnancy, my supervisor—let's call him STG2, for second-class sonar technician—pulled me from watch. The way he did it was secretive; I thought I was in trouble again or that he'd found out somehow. But as we leaned against the bulkhead in the passageway, he said I was finally going to get off of the torpedo magazine station and join *his* workstation group, the coveted Sonar 1.

Ha! Decent working hours and actually getting to do what we trained for in A school. He also said that he would support me in going to officer school, if I still wanted to go. After a shocked silence, I laughed bitterly in an attempt not to cry, my heart racing. I took a few breaths, then, inexplicably, laughed again. I laughed so hard, holding my stomach, that he had to ask me what was wrong. All these months, I thought, I'd been hazed and treated like trash. Was all the shit I went through some twisted kind of test? I looked at him again and howled until I lost my breath. What a waste of time and energy. I felt like I'd escaped some kind of funhouse made of inverted perceptions and fake obstacles. In hindsight, it could also just be that Navy life didn't suit me, and the fates decided to take one more dig before I left. The first classes also could've recognized that I'd checked out and were making a last-ditch effort to pull me back on board. But, at the time, it felt like cruel irony—that I'd gotten in my own way by getting pregnant.

In the split second between the end of my laughter and the start of my confession—and it did feel like a confession, like I had done something wrong—I considered what it might be like to take the route offered to me by STG2. I saw EN1's face, remembered her voice offering advice. She'd had a kid when she was younger, too, and didn't think she'd make more than chief because of it, if that. She believed it had set her back on the timeline and in the eyes of the men in charge of promotion. Did I want a career in the military? Or did I want to take my chances on education and motherhood?

Every now and then I think about how quickly my world shifted in that split second. I think about the strength of my desire to live, to nurture life—mine and the one growing inside me. What kind of life I wanted for myself. I didn't want to kill anything, and I didn't want to die young. If that makes me a coward, so be it. In that moment, though, it took courage to look STG2 in the eye and say I was pregnant, that I was keeping the baby. I wanted to join the other two pregnant women leaving the ship. I told him the father was a civilian and that I was engaged; I wanted them to leave me the hell alone, so I couldn't name the real father.

I would need all the tenacity I had to spend the two months it took to process me over to shore duty and endure the hostility, scorn, bullying, and gleeful disappointment of my shipboard colleagues. I performed my daily work routines and didn't kill myself or anybody else. I ate well and did my job; I refused harmful assignments; I kept up with my watch duties and cleaning rotation. I wore the untucked shirt of the pregnancy uniform they forced me to wear even when I didn't show, but I kept the same walk, my head up and stride tight, and refused to wear the shame they heaped on me. I'd recognized the double standard early on. I'd noticed the men being encouraged to fuck and flirt and the women being locked down by doubt and harm and constant harassment. I didn't know until later, though—until October 12, 2000, when the ship was bombed in Yemen—that my decision saved my life.

The rules say that women serving on board ships can stay until their twentieth week. I don't remember exactly how far along I was, but I found out about my pregnancy and was off the ship before I even started to show. I remember one woman from the *Cole*, a third-class petty officer I ran into at chow during a mess cranking break, long before I left. I tried to make small talk, but she didn't like me either, and barely maintained a sense of politeness. She was the other beautiful one aboard ship, light-skinned and large-breasted with "good hair," as the men liked to describe her, and they also liked to compare us. During that lunch I learned she'd had an infant two weeks before she'd gotten to the *Cole*. She petitioned for longer leave, since the rules say a woman can extend her PRD—projected rotation date—if she takes the full year of leave from deployment postpartum, but was refused, and she couldn't afford not to deploy. She was a boatswain's mate, and they live at sea. Not to mention the needs of the Navy and all. The rules say neither retention nor separation are guarantees once you fall pregnant; the rules say the needs of the Navy determine your fate. Perhaps *fate* is too strong a word. The needs of the Navy determine whether or not you continue in service, whether or not your request to stay on or to leave is granted.

Stay or leave. It does indeed feel like a very fated choice in the moment, even if you *are* sure about your decision, and I certainly don't want to diminish the importance or intensity of that choice-making. But I wish I could've told myself then that life would eventually be so much more than that choice, or the Navy's decision. I wish I could tell myself: the odds against me, and other servicewomen, existed in fact, not in any paranoid fantasy stoked by gaslighting. I did tell myself, over and over, not to let the disdain of others define me. That defiance helped me and my child manage to survive. Not without scars, pain, hardship—and perhaps our lives as a result are not noteworthy in any public sense, because our difficulties were so private, even when externally imposed. We do have our lives, however. Perhaps it is selfish to believe they are worth having, whether the Navy believes that or not.

The BM3 looked at me in the eye that day, as my time on the ship drew to a close, her face screwed up with disgust. "I left my son when he was two weeks old," she said. "He's with my mother back home. Good luck with *your* decision."

A couple of months after I left the ship, about six months into the pregnancy, my son's father drove us to New York. I'd had morning sickness all day for most of those first two trimesters. He drove fast, did not slow into turns, did not care when I told him he was making me sick. I was trapped in speed, the freeway's bumps and curves, my body forcibly whipped along with the machine as my insides resisted. I craved gentleness, needed soothing, but received only more aggression. Did he turn the music up, smile as I kept one arm on the tan leather dash of his souped-up green Nissan, the other arm gripping the door, desperate for stasis? Yes, and the music vibrated, deep bass—reggae always—his window down to add freeway noise to the mix. I held it all in my body. Nausea and discomfort accumulated in my muscles. He didn't stop until we arrived at our destination, ignoring my shock and distress. Still—as I discovered that day, and again two years later when I finally left him—the protective impulse I felt for my child remained fiercely intact. When doubt, insecurity, or shame interfered, I returned to and relied on that fierce protectiveness to sustain us.

When I got out of the Navy, when people asked if I was married, I learned to say yes, I had been married and divorced, and I didn't give a year for my discharge. I learned to evade because people would do calculations and see that I got pregnant while on the ship, and that led to a slew of other personal questions, investigative probing that led to shit I didn't want to talk about. Not only that, they would have personal information that was none of their business, so I just started saying I was in for five years during the '90s and left it at that.

I learned especially never to reveal to fellow veterans that I'd had a child on active duty, because they were the worst, but even strangers curled their lips and made *hmph* sounds: couldn't help themselves. People think they know something about you with that revelation. They make nasty judgments that haven't a damn thing to do with who you are. Even though I always fought back, it still made me judge myself for a long time, made me feel disappointed that I didn't "hold out," whatever the fuck that meant, that I didn't choose a military career—or, perhaps, my country?—over my own flesh and blood. A simple question— Are/Were you married?—led to a cascade of revelation that left me feeling more like Hester Prynne than a veteran, however undistinguished my service. While I knew I did the best I could, the looks on people's faces—pity, disdain, dismissal—filled me alternately with grief and rage, feelings I did not have time for. I had a kid to raise and a degree to finish, and I felt determined that nobody's prejudices would stop me.

I didn't really start telling people that I'd had a child on active duty until he was nearly grown. I am not ashamed of myself as a solo parent, nor am I ashamed of my son— think of it! A child as shame? Ridiculous—and I am not ashamed that I raised him on my own. In fact, I am proud that I kept him fed, housed, nurtured, alive, and thriving creatively all this time. I kept myself alive, too, and I did not need a man to do that. I learned to draw strength from the very thing I was taught by social response that I should hide—my own self, as a woman, a working mother. Now that my son is grown, I know how much fortitude it took to accomplish what I have in this life so far. I am definitely scarred, but not anywhere close to broken. My home, likewise, is not broken, either—never was. It is whole. We are a family.

THE BABIES

BY KRISTEN ARNETT

SHAUNA HID THE PREGNANCY test in a jar of peanut butter. She'd thought all afternoon about the perfect place to stash it and had already considered and rejected other likely locations: taped inside a pizza box (pepperoni spelling out BABY in the oily cheese), stuffed into the base of a succulent they'd picked up a few weeks ago at the farmer's market. She had even briefly contemplated shoving it inside Julie's pillowcase before deciding she probably shouldn't put something she'd peed on where her wife rested her face each night.

And then she'd seen the jar of Jif in the pantry.

It was an inspired choice. Julie loved scarfing down a piece of peanut butter toast when she came home from work; she ate it after stopping at the gym most days, miles on the treadmill even though they had one in their own house, sitting dusty in the back bedroom. And Shauna would say, *Don't eat that, I'm making dinner*, and Julie would reply, *I'll still be hungry, it's an appetizer*, and then they'd both sigh but smile, too, because it was comfortable and nice to truly understand another person.

She knew it was a little gross to put pee inside food, but the idea felt inspired, so she wrapped the pregnancy test in a plastic baggie before shoving it inside the jar. Then she'd set it back inside the cabinet and poured herself a glass of Gatorade, watching the hands of the clock move, slowly, slowly, slower; the hands crept along, waiting for her wife to come home.

They had been trying to conceive for almost three years. They'd tried things the traditional way (well, the "traditional way" when it came to lesbians) and turkey basted Shauna with their good friend Roger's sperm. When that hadn't worked, they began fertility treatments. Julie was eight years older than Shauna, so it was the natural choice to have Shauna carry the baby. Shauna hadn't been sure how she felt about adding a kid to the mix, but she loved her wife, and she thought it would probably all work out just fine.

She sipped her Gatorade and grimaced. Shauna hated sports drinks and really wanted a Diet Coke, but they'd cut out caffeine six months earlier after the doctor said maybe it was preventing her from getting pregnant. Julie had done her part; the egg retrieval, which hadn't been exactly a cakewalk, and Shauna knew she needed to kick it into high gear. So, no more coffee. No ibuprofen. No alcohol. And, worst of all, no Diet Coke, which Shauna loved, a drink she'd been obsessed with since middle school.

"You're disgusting," Shauna told the blue liquid, but she chugged it anyway because she was thirsty and babies needed hydration. Dandelion, their overweight tabby, jumped up on the counter and begged for scratches while she choked it down. Sometimes it felt like she was trying to grow a plant in her belly. Though it wasn't even that easy to keep a plant alive, Shauna knew. So far, every succulent they'd brought home had turned yellow and gooey. *You're smothering them*, Julie told her, over and over again, but Shauna just wanted to make sure they got the proper amount of care.

Julie got home an hour later, and Shauna could not figure out what to do with her hands. They were flapping around like restless birds. She was bad at lying. Julie always knew when she was hiding something. She put a pot of water on the stove and acted like she was trying to cook spaghetti. How big is the baby at this moment, she wondered. Bigger than a pencil eraser? A lima bean? Her wife threw her gym bag onto the counter, and Shauna picked it up and took out the sweaty socks and shorts and sports bra and threw them into the hamper in the laundry room.

"Let's go out to eat, I'm starving," Julie said. She ran her hands through her short, dark hair. Her cheeks were all pink from the heat. Her wife had never looked better than she did in that three-second span, flicking up her hair until she looked like a goofy little porcupine. That is the mother of my child, Shauna thought. The parent of our kid. We're going to have a baby with spiky porcupine hair. A Julie-Shauna baby.

"Why don't you have a quick snack," Shauna replied.

Julie got out the peanut butter and slapped a loaf of bread on the counter. She was aggravated, Shauna could tell, but her wife wouldn't ever say anything about it. She pushed conflict down until it rested like an ulcer in her guts. Her wife was a marketing manager for a chain of local coffee shops. She spent most of her time being "on" for her clients and for her coworkers. When she got home, she deflated, got soft or testy, depending on the day and her mood, and most of the time needed at least an hour before she could hold a conversation. Shauna's father had been that way too. It had been especially bad when her mother had been going through her miscarriages. There had been multiple. Stop thinking about that, this is a happy day, she reminded herself.

Julie was hunting around for something to spread the peanut butter. Shauna handed her a butter knife and a small plate. "Just a paper towel," Julie said, and then she unscrewed the lid to the jar and saw the pregnancy test.

When she pulled it free, it made a wild suction sound, obscene like flatulence, and they both laughed hysterically. "Oh my god," Julie said. They screamed, and then they hugged. Julie put her hands on Shauna's belly, as if she could maybe feel something in there, and they laughed again because there was peanut butter on everything, peanut butter on their hands and clothes, peanut butter on the counter, peanut butter all over the pregnancy test. Dandelion began licking peanut butter off of the counter top. The peanut butter dotted above her lip and gave her a mustache, which made them laugh even harder.

They washed their hands, changed, and went out for a celebratory dinner. It was a beautiful night, an inky sky full of bright stars, and Shauna felt full with love. The wind whipped through the palm trees outside their house, and on the drive over to the restaurant, Shauna held her wife's hand and let the other one flip through the air outside the car window.

"I think, if it's a boy, we should name them Cameron," Julie said.

"If it's a girl, we should name them Cameron," Shauna replied, and then they both smiled at how easy it was to please each other. At the restaurant they shared two plates—chicken parm for Julie and the scallops for Shauna—and the bread rolls were hot, and they both kept looking at Shauna's belly like it held all the answers to every mystery in the universe.

Shauna felt a bubble pop in her stomach. Too much food, she thought, and then: This is what it will be like when I'm finally able to feel the baby. She grabbed one of her wife's hands. Wiped a bit of sauce from Julie's chin with the other. Our baby, she amended in her head.

They set up appointments with the obstetrician and went to all of them together. Three months in, and they'd done all the things they were supposed to do: taking the prenatal vitamins, drinking plenty of water, keeping up routine exercise with nightly walks around the neighborhood. They joined Facebook mommy groups that offered up time-saving tips and tricks and looked up the best crib to buy, found the top-rated strollers. They sat down with both sets of parents and told them. Everyone was excited. Thrilled. Something to look forward to: the first little one in either of their families since the cousins had moved into their cranky teen years. Shauna's mom bought a tiny floral swimsuit that came with a pink hula skirt. "We don't know it's a girl," Shauna said, but her mother said it didn't matter, she was just so excited that she couldn't help herself. She had to buy it.

"It's so important to enjoy these things," her mother said, and she looked so unbearably sad that Shauna hugged her and changed the subject. She knew her mother had struggled with fertility issues. It wasn't something they had to discuss.

Who cares about a hula skirt anyway, she thought. A boy baby could wear it just as easily as a girl.

Shauna looked at herself naked every day and marveled at the changes. The swollen breasts, full of blue veins, milky light under the skin. Nipples darkened. Her hair grew long—from the vitamins and all the water—but also from the baby. It didn't feel like feeding another life; it was sharing an energy source. She felt charged up, a living battery pack placed inside her. It was like a grow light had been aimed at her; she was the plant: flourishing, thriving, blooming.

Julie told her she looked beautiful, and for once, she actually believed it. They had sex morning and night, sometimes even in the afternoons, if her wife could catch a long enough lunch break. They hadn't had so much sex since before they were married.

I am in love, and I am alive, Shauna thought, her wife's tongue flicking warm between her legs, her skin smooth and on fire, the whole of her burning from the inside out.

Julie painted the baby's room. Shauna worried about the fumes, so she watched from the backyard while her wife coated the wall in the palest green. "Green is soothing," Julie said, and they wanted the baby to be soothed. Shauna could have told her that if a baby didn't want to be soothed it wouldn't matter—that if a baby wanted to cry, it would cry all it wanted, paint color be damned—but her wife was determined to do everything exactly right. Shauna had grown up around babies: a younger sister and a bunch of cousins dumped at her parents' house on the weekends, but Julie had been an only child. Julie's parents hadn't wanted to have a bunch of kids. Not like her mother, who'd envisioned a houseful of them, and tried and tried and failed until she'd finally had her hysterectomy. Six or seven, at least, she always said, but there had only been Shauna and her sister.

They assembled the crib: white. Put together the mobile: tiny blue elephants. Read books about pregnancy, about the first year of life postpartum, about what to do with a whiny toddler, about how to talk to your kids about gun violence and strangers and the mechanics of sex.

"What if we can't explain how to use a urinal?" Julie asked. They were lying in bed, each of them reading a copy of a different parenting book. There were stacks of them around the house. Shauna used to read entertainment magazines; now she read articles about the importance of making your own organic baby food.

"We'll be fine," Shauna said. "My little cousin didn't

even want to use the urinal, and he had a dad to show him. Let kids decide what they want."

She thought it was cute that her wife would be so nervous about a child standing up to pee when they didn't even have legs that could support them yet. Couldn't walk or talk. Couldn't even breathe or see or hear. Babies didn't even have kneecaps, they'd learned; babies grow them later on. And when Shauna read that, she realized she knew absolutely nothing about the human body, aside from living inside one for thirty years. She'd had a nightmare afterward: a vision of a lifeless baby inside her, swirling around with no legs.

Julie set down her book and then turned off the lights. She placed a soft hand on Shauna's breast. Everything felt more tender and alive. Budding.

"Touch me more," Shauna said, and Julie did.

They drove in together for their first ultrasound, Julie calling out of work for the morning. They kept calling the pregnancy "theirs," even though Shauna was the one carrying the baby. It would normally have bothered her to hear a husband say something like that, but Shauna liked the combination of the two of them as a single "they." It made her feel like Julie was carrying the baby too. The baby was Julie's egg, after all. Shauna's body was housing it, helping it grow, keeping it safe. Her body wasn't just her own; it was a cocoon. It was an Easy-Bake Oven.

Shauna got onto the table and sat with her elastic-waisted pants pulled down over her stomach. The paper gown crinkled over her top. She held hands with her wife while they waited for the technician to come in and start the ultrasound machine.

"I'm going to ask if they'll give us two printouts," Julie said, smoothing her palm over the paper. It separated, showing a sliver of pale belly. "That way I can take a copy to work for my desk."

"Don't make me cry," Shauna said.

"Everything makes you cry now," Julie replied. That was true enough; Shauna was already tearing up. She used a corner of the paper gown to swipe at her eyes. It ripped a little in her hands, the wet part disintegrating.

The technician came in, said good morning, and booted up the machine. Shauna made sure the gown was smoothed down again and then smiled at Julie, who was nervously plucking at the strap of her purse.

"What's wrong?" Shauna whispered, and Julie told her that she was worried she wouldn't recognize her kid, which made Shauna laugh until she almost peed herself. That was the thing about her body now; it was home to somebody else, too, which meant that she could never predict what would happen with it.

"This will be a little cold," the technician said and squeezed a glob of clear gunk onto Shauna's belly. It *was* cold, actually almost freezing, and she jumped a little, especially when the woman smeared the wand around in it. It felt weird and tickly, and she bit her lip to keep from laughing again. All of a sudden, everything seemed hysterical.

The technician poked more. Julie asked if they could get a second printout of the sonogram. "For my work desk," she explained, but Shauna saw that the technician wasn't paying attention. Her face scared Shauna, so instead of the woman's face, she looked at the part in her hair. It was severe, dark, and lined with silver, sprinkled with a bit of dandruff.

Like snow settling on an evening field, Shauna thought, though she had never seen snow before in person, because she'd grown up in Orlando, only on TV and in movies and pictures, and then the technician set down the wand and told them that she was going to go grab the doctor.

Everything happened too fast after that. Or it was too slow. Shauna couldn't be sure. Her internal clock was winding in extraordinary ways, and there was no way to tell what anyone was saying or doing or how much time had actually passed. There they were in the room with the technician, and then with the doctor, and then all of them crying; wait, except her wife and the technician; wait, was the doctor crying? Maybe it had only been Shauna, though that couldn't have been right—they'd passed the receptionist on their way out, and her wife had gone up to make their follow-up appointment to plan what to do next (but what could they even do, what was there to do when everything had stopped)—and the receptionist had looked at Shauna with such pity in her eyes, hadn't there been tears there too? It was so hard to see. A room full of lights blinding her, smeary with water, like rain on a windshield at night hit by the force of oncoming headlights. Then they were outside, they were in their car. Julie was driving them. Julie always drove them. Home then, but they just sat in the car. Sat with the car ticking and hissing as it cooled down in the driveway.

"What ..." Julie said, and then she just stopped. Her hands clutched the steering wheel. Both of them were still buckled into their seats. The garage door hadn't been opened. There was a potato vine growing up the side, disappearing into the crack at the top.

Shauna studiously avoided putting her hands anywhere near her belly. She didn't know what would happen if she touched herself there, but she worried that it might break her. Nothing good can come from touching because there is nothing in there at all, she thought, and then she was crying again.

The tears roused Julie, who helped her out of the car and inside. Shauna didn't want to be home—didn't want to be anywhere near the room they'd prepared. The life they now lived was out of sync with everything they'd carefully planned. *This life is a parallel universe*, she decided. Her real life was back in the doctor's office with that technician; she was getting a scan—two scans printed out after, one for her wife's desk at her job—and watching her baby's heart beat quick as a hummingbird's.

Shauna sat on the couch, and Julie brought her a glass filled with water and crushed ice, topped with a lemon wedge. Shauna stared at it, not able to bring it to her lips. This was a thing that her wife had done for her since the pregnancy—try to get her to drink more water, hydrate herself better, by bringing her a special kind. But she wasn't pregnant anymore, was she? So Julie wouldn't need to bring her fancy drinks. She wouldn't need any special treatment.

"I still want to take care of you," Julie said, and Shauna realized she'd verbalized all those thoughts aloud.

"I want a Diet Coke. I can have one now," Shauna said, and then she put a hand to her belly, finally, and burst into tears again.

She lay down on the couch, and her wife left the room, something to do with work, although Shauna had stopped listening. How could your life be doubled for months and then suddenly halved without your consent?

She spent the next few days lying on that same couch in a variety of positions as time crawled toward whatever came next. Because there would have to be a next, and it would not be anything good. The pregnancy had been far enough along that her body wouldn't naturally expel anything in a timely manner; she would need assistance, a professional. That much she remembered from that horrible day at the doctor's office.

Julie set up the appointment. Before they'd gotten married, she'd been in a long-term relationship with her college boyfriend, and she'd gotten pregnant with him once, and they'd had it "taken care of." That's what Julie had said, the exact language she used when she'd told Shauna about it, but that wasn't the language she used now. Not with their situation. Julie talked around it: said she would "look into it," that she'd "handle everything," that there was "nothing to worry about." Julie claimed, "We will get through it together."

And even though Shauna hadn't disliked that "we" before—had loved it, really—she now found herself bristling every time it was used. Because it wasn't really the same, was it? Julie wasn't the one who had to go through a procedure. She wasn't the one who'd have to let a stranger invade her body. To let that person excavate the life she'd been growing. It was only Shauna, and she would go through it alone, regardless of how many times her wife talked about their shared grief. The physical pain of it would be hers alone to bear.

On the morning of the appointment, they climbed into the car. It sat in the same spot they'd left it after the ultrasound, baking out in the middle of the driveway. It was hot inside the car, even though it was still morning. Early enough that the sun was still climbing melon-coral over the brushy heads of the oaks. Shauna was sweating profusely from the heat and from anxiety; a drip of it slid down her cheek and landed on the front of her sleep shirt. She hadn't bothered changing. The doctor had told her to "wear something comfortable," and what Shauna had wanted to say was that nothing felt comfortable, that the only comfortable thing would be to go to sleep for a while.

Julie leaned over and wiped the sweaty residue from her upper lip with her thumb. It was a thing she'd done a million times before, a sweet touch from her wife who loved every part of her occasionally messy body, but now the touch felt offensive. She managed to sit through it without wincing, but her skin crawled. It wasn't just her wife, she understood that. Julie was going through her own grieving process. The baby had been hers too. It had been her egg. Her child. But Shauna couldn't get herself to hold her wife's grief as well as her own; there just wasn't room for it. She didn't want to be touched by anyone. Because the only person she wanted to be able to touch her was the one who could not, would not ever. The one who would be taken.

It isn't fair, she thought. It isn't goddamn fair. But fair didn't matter when it came to bodies or anything in life, she knew; it was something that she'd told her younger sister all the time. Growing up, she'd been the one to have to tell her about things. All the bad shit of life that happened whether you wanted it or not. When their family dog had to be put to sleep, who'd had to hold her sister as she wept? Shauna, of course. Shauna smoothing back her little sister's tangled hair as she wept and called for Muffin, the golden retriever who'd slept in her bed every night. There was no Shauna to sweep back her own hair in this scenario. She was regressing, curling up into herself, wanting to be inside her own belly. If she were inside her own stomach, in her own womb, she could still hold that snuffed light.

The trip was farther than Shauna had anticipated. A forty-minute drive to get to a clinic. There were fewer places that operated locally now, Julie told her after she'd made the call. It was harder and harder for anyone to even get to a Planned Parenthood, much less one of these particular places that dealt with later-stage pregnancies. Shauna tuned out the rest of the conversation. She didn't care where they were going. She just wanted it over. Done.

They turned the corner and saw a crowd of people collected outside a squat concrete building.

"Oh no," her wife said, and Shauna was about to ask what was wrong, but then she saw the signs. There were about twenty people milling around outside the clinic. What shocked Shauna the most was how wildly they varied in age. Some of them were around her and Julie's age, sure, but there were others who were much older. Grandmother types who looked like they should be at a church bake sale. And kids. There were little kids weaving between the adults' legs. One little girl with a fountain of hair sprouting from the top of her head couldn't have been more than three years old. She toddled around like she'd just recently learned to walk.

"They'll have people to help us," Julie said, and Shauna realized they were going to have to go inside past all these people. The people looked angry, even from far away. They were going to yell at her, and she was going to have to hear them. On this day, she would be forced to deal with people who didn't care that she was in pain.

"Let's get it over with," she said, because she couldn't bear to think of leaving and coming back, not again, even though her wife said they absolutely could if she was worried about their safety.

They strode across the parking lot, fingers laced together, and then came the droning hum of all those voices raised at once. "Don't look at them," her wife said, but Shauna couldn't help herself. There were all those signs, the ones with pictures of dead babies on them. Bloody, some of them. Others just piles of what looked like loose meat. Red and sticky.

That's what is inside of me, Shauna thought, and then a couple of women from the clinic bracketed them and moved them through the tunnel of protesters. It's a blessing I can't make out what most of them are saying, she decided. They were so loud, all at once, that it just became a swell like the buzz of hornets. There were a few individual words that came through, though: murderer, killer. But otherwise, the shouts were only noise.

They'd almost reached the door when someone shoved a child into their path. It was the little girl with the ponytail. Her eyes were opened wide and full of tears. She looks petrified, Shauna decided. The kind of fear that little kids always get on their faces when something is happening with adults that they can't understand. A woman, possibly her mother, grasped her under her arms and shoved her forcefully in Shauna's face.

"How could you do this to a child?" The woman held the girl up higher. Shauna saw that she was wearing a T-shirt with a little spray of tulips over the pocket. It read "funshine" in cursive script. She remembered the little swimsuit her mother had bought her unborn child, the one with the tiny hula skirt. She realized her child would never get to wear it.

The woman shook her daughter a little for emphasis, and the girl's ponytail bobbled, a little spray of hair, that silky toddler stuff that lasts only the first few years of life.

"My baby is already dead," Shauna replied, and the woman reeled back, snatching her child to her chest. As if Shauna might infect her.

Then the helpers opened the doors, and they swept inside the lobby. The door closed behind them and the sound vacuumed out. No noise. Barely a hum. So quiet, it was like there was no one there at all.

"I'm ready," Shauna announced, and they took her to the back.

THE FIG QUEEN

BY SALLY WEN MAO

A WOMAN WANTED TO become small. So she shrank, smaller and smaller still, until she was small enough to fit into the calyx of the foxglove she'd planted last winter. Her garden was now a jungle, a hemisphere, and the bees had transformed into helicopters overnight. They welcomed her as her neighbors; they offered her honey. The neighbor's fig tree grew wild over her fence, and soon figs were falling from the branches, their purpled flesh an endless feast.

The woman was finally living a life of abundance, because she was small, because she did not take up space.

She missed nothing from her old life. She did not miss the drudgery, the neuroses, the loneliness of the past. She settled into her newfound wonder, feeding on nectar that tasted like marzipan apples, relaxing from the perch of her foxglove, taking in the view of the garden that was her kingdom—all that she'd planted, all that blossomed from tiny seeds she'd once held in her hands.

Eventually she realized that someone else was now living her life. Someone else was making appointments, going to work, going on dates, going to therapy, picking up groceries, cooking, making calls for her. Someone else was watering the plants and flowers in her garden, someone with her exact physical appearance. A doppelganger—or a replacement? At first, she felt indignant, pacing around in her calyx. She was anxious that this imposter would ruin the life that was hers, the life that she'd grown from the ground up. She paced and paced and waited every night for this alien version of her to come home, at first afraid that this replacement's personality change would render her unrecognizable to her friends, her coworkers, and her family. Lurking beneath this fear, she was also worried that none of them would recognize her transformation at all, and her disappearance would go unnoticed.

Months went by, and she realized that this imposter was not ruining her life. In fact, this imposter was living her life much better than she had. This imposter was getting a promotion and arguing for a salary she would've never thought to ask for. This imposter was booking a trip to Lisbon, where she'd wanted to go since she read Pessoa's *Book of Disquiet* in college. This imposter was making new friends and reconnecting with old ones and hosting dinner parties where she successfully mixed these two groups. This imposter was always the brightest person in the room, cracking jokes that made everyone laugh. This imposter was always laughing off the "nihao"s and "konichiwa"s from men on the street because she didn't take things so *seriously*. This imposter was going out until 4:00 a.m. on the weekends, plopping down on the bed wearing short skirts and leather jackets she could never afford, that she believed she could never pull off. This imposter found a lover who took her on ski trips and to family functions, and the imposter would be gone for days at a time, busy with her newfound life.

She'd never hosted dinner parties. She'd never taken trips. She'd never had a boyfriend. Suddenly, she was getting anxious again, anxious that she had not adequately lived her life, and now she had given it up to a doppelganger who was going to enjoy all the things she hadn't, that she'd always wanted. One day, the imposter brought home the lover, and she watched them from the perch of her petal—herself, on her bed, making love to a stranger. Hold on, though—she looked closer, and realized it wasn't a stranger at all, but the man who, just the year before, had broken her heart. Left her by the curbside in front of a bodega, left her crying into her iced coffee, the ashes of her cigarette dusting her bare knees. The man had said he wasn't looking for a relationship, that he didn't like her like that, even though they slept together a few times; he wanted her for sex; he was sorry. This man had never taken her outside of his apartment, let alone to Thanksgiving with his family upstate. She had not met a single one of his friends.

And now there he was, not just making love to this imposter but also whispering sweet words, whispering how much he wanted to show her off to his friends, to go to Europe with her, all the words she'd fantasized before, uncannily—eerily—coming to life. She watched them for the rest of the night. For the first time since her transformation, she wanted to be noticed—she shouted for them, she waved at them, but they could not see or hear her. She was a voyeur spying on her own existence. She began to understand that this was her worst fear coming true. That perhaps, just perhaps something essential inside her was rotten—something that was primevally hers, fixed and unsalvageable. It caused people like this lover, and all her former lovers, to abandon her. But when somebody else occupied her body, this didn't happen. And just like that, she heard herself climax. A hot hiss of breath escaping from a throat that looked just like hers.

Last year when she was still "seeing" that man on and off, they had been careless and drunk one night, and the next morning she was so hungover that she forgot to buy Plan B. Soon after, he ghosted her. It was incremental: at first, he would not respond to her texts until two or three in the morning. Then he stopped responding at all. This should have been the first sign that she was better off without him, but in those weeks of silence, the woman felt as if her body was decomposing. It must have been the oxytocin, she rationalized—it was just chemicals tying her to this man, nothing more.

When she missed her period that month, she was still in a haze, barely eating or sleeping, and didn't notice at first. But after several more weeks passed, she decided to go to her gynecologist, who administered a pregnancy test. *Positive.* Before she imagined an actual child, she imagined the child's potential trauma: born into a world where even the love between one's parents could not exist. She thought back to her own parents, who were silent for most of their marriage; she couldn't tell if it was out of habit or bottled-up resentment. She felt as if her own body was mocking her with its fertility. If this love was going to be barren, then why didn't her uterus get the memo?

She went home and watered her foxgloves, her dahlias, her camellias. Then she sat on her plastic chair and wept. She suddenly craved bruised fruit. The tree from the neighbor's yard dangled its branches over the fence, swarming with black stony figs, fat and ripe.

For the first time, she noticed the swarm of insects by the fig tree. They were tiny fig wasps, though she didn't know it at the time—she thought they looked like gnats or mosquitoes. Concerned, she consulted her hardcover book about gardening and insects and came across the entry on fig wasps. A fig, it turns out, is not a fruit but an inflorescence, a cluster of tiny flowers that needed special wasp pollination. The pregnant female wasp finds the tiny ostiole, or hole, at the bottom of the fig and crawls inside with the intention of laying eggs. As she lays her eggs, she also pollinates the florets.

She learned two facts about fig wasps that stunned her so much she underlined them in her book. The first was that, in the process of trying to squeeze through that impossibly narrow portal of the fig, the pregnant female wasp loses her antennae and her wings. The second was that, once she crawls inside, she lays her eggs and dies. The fig's enzymes slowly consume her, digesting her body until she becomes a part of its seeds and flesh.

The woman had eaten so many of these figs, and it had never occurred to her that tiny wasps could be living and dying inside them. In the summer, she would sometimes go for days without eating anything else. They reminded her also of her lover, who loved figs.

Later that night, she called him, wanting to inform him about the test. She had never called him before. When he answered, they had a casual yet flirtatious conversation that gave her hope, and she could not bring herself to tell him and ruin the mood. "How have you been?" he asked, finally. "Sorry I lost touch; I've been so busy, you know."

After hanging up, she made an appointment at the clinic for the following Tuesday. She thought about asking him to go with her, but she didn't want to put pressure on him or inconvenience him. He didn't want anything serious, he had told her; her pregnancy was definitely a serious matter.

Nevertheless, when he started texting her again, her body felt light, the lightest it'd been in weeks, and she felt herself sucked back into this airtight ostiole of romantic desire. They started talking more regularly and met up a few more times over the course of a few months before the incident at the curb by the bodega. By then, she had already gone to the clinic, where her doctor informed her that she was seven weeks along and gave her a box containing two pills.

After taking the first pill, she bled profusely, her body cramping. She spent hours on the toilet every day, passively bleeding, and wondered if this was just all life was, all she was meant to do: bleed, bleed, bleed. Blood would flow out of her until she ran out. No pads, tampons, or diva cups stanched the flow. A gloom like a decomposing wasp rustled inside of her, and the rot felt familiar, the rot felt true. She imagined herself suspended in a fig's red flesh, bleeding all over its flowers.

The next evening, he came over and as usual she fed him the figs from her neighbor's tree. His favorite thing about figs, he told her, was that they had no pits. How easy it was to just swallow them whole.

They sat together in silence, watching the sunset from her street-level window. When he reached for her, a small noise escaped her throat, a yelp. She hid her body from him, suddenly protective of it. Nausea and lightheadedness wracked her, and she made up an excuse to go to the bathroom and vomit.

He didn't ask her what was wrong. Instead, he turned on the television and flipped through the channels, pretending like nothing was happening. She actually felt relieved at his lack of curiosity, because she wouldn't know how to explain without telling him the truth. Finding nothing of interest on TV, he left soon after.

Summer molted into fall, and she grew bored of her smallness. Around this time, the imposter was on her vacation to Europe. Imagining the terracotta rooftops of that city she'd never seen, Lisbon, the deep blue of the Tagus River, she felt an intense longing.

The woman wished to take back what she had said about wanting to be small. She grew bored of the smell of flowers and the taste of nectar, figs, and honey and began wanting human pleasures again. The view from the foxglove began to madden her, fill her with despair. All she did with her time was survey the fig tree. The female wasps kept digging and dying, digging and dying. She witnessed one female after another attempt to wrangle their bodies through the tiny holes at the bottoms of figs. The ones who succeeded sawed their own wings off. Like cellophane or parachutes, pieces of wing fell from the sky.

Then she noticed that there were new tenants living in the figs. Newborn female wasps were leaving—the daughters of the wasps that had died. They'd hatched inside the fig, already orphaned, already ready to embark on the journey of finding another fig tree. The skin of the figs on the branches began to break, and the newly minted female wasps were liberated.

That's when the woman considered: perhaps she, too, could leave? Perhaps she could also journey to an unknown fig tree, escape this life once and for all. By this point, she had learned to communicate with the bees and other insects that frequented this garden. She asked them to relay her message to the fig queen, who had just emerged from the plumpest fig on the farthest corner of the branch.

Word got back to her that the queen had agreed. The woman found herself swooning: *Oh.* Emerging from her fig womb, the queen was unrivaled in her majesty, wearing a gown of pollen that resembled intricate lace. The queen's brown body was decked in a sleek armor resembling patent leather, and her silky wings fanned out, a holographic vision catching every errant ray.

Soon the queen descended down onto her foxglove, and the woman climbed on, holding on to her thorax. The queen's body was sticky with nectar, and the pollen felt fluffy, like hairy flesh—the woman grew drowsy, but she didn't want to sleep. They were flying up in the air, and she saw her garden grow smaller and smaller, and yet it was very much unlike being on a plane—no glass or metal separated her from the wind, which could not hurt her. From her vantage point, she saw the corner store. She saw her neighbors sitting on the stoop eating their figs. She saw the park where she used to lie out in the grassy knoll alone. She saw the botanical garden where the peonies and wisteria still budded, their petals all sprayed with rat repellent. She saw the statue of the weeping girl near the algae-green pond. She saw the fish market, with its display of striped sea bass, golden pompano, red snapper. She even saw the bodega where she got dumped, and it looked marvelous with its display of bounties.

She was amazed. The journey to another fig tree felt like the farthest she'd ever traveled in her life, even though it had to be no more than a few hundred yards. When they eventually reached their destination, she almost threw up, her wonder mutating into dread. As she was dropped onto the branch of a new tree, she pleaded to the queen not to let her go. She didn't want her majesty to die so young. When she saw that the ostiole of the new fig was already open, she screamed at the queen not to rip off her wings. Instead of waiting on the branch witnessing the horror, she found herself running, climbing over onto the queen's antenna, lunging herself into the red fragrant flesh of the fig. She would use her own body as a shield to save the queen. She would pollinate the fig herself.

Then, as if the fig was listening to her, the hole closed up once she climbed inside. Whole gardens of florets, pale and vulnerable, waited for her. In this red fig womb, suddenly she was more exhausted than she had been all her life. Too tired to remember anything about herself, too tired to save herself from being digested. Deeper and deeper she crawled into the fig, following its perfumed trail. It turned out that the fig, ever the hospitable host, was expecting her and had already made a bed for her. She climbed as far as she could, the pollen falling off of her, and curled into a ball on the soft pink bed.

In the red fig womb, she became an amorphous thing, a zygote, a fetus; she was breaking down. A fugue state, where life and death had no language, the ending was a beginning was an ending, and she felt her own nonexistence like a warm airless room, a sauna. Her naked flesh in that air of fever vapor. Her lovely bloodless flesh in a sauna and then a clinic room, bent against the metal speculum. Her bathroom where she took that pill. The blood stains on the toilet seat, on the bathroom floor. In her bleeding, she had spared someone from existence. She thought of her mother, who mentioned once off handedly that she had three abortions before finally choosing to have her. The one-child act in China made her mother anxious about her body, its fickle patterns of creation. In the end, she finally had her daughter and the trouble with daughters was that they, too, would eventually bleed. Without bleeding, who was she? Who was her mother?

In the kingdom of fig wasps, there were no queens. Every female wasp who made the journey of breaking her body was a queen—their coronation was death and decomposition. The imposter living her life was not an imposter but just another version of herself, a self that was not broken, a self that did not believe she was broken—this woman had been sleeping inside her, underneath her pain, all this time, but she did not recognize her. In her fig womb, the city of Lisbon materialized. A chill fall breeze blew through the open door leading to the balcony. The suitcases were packed. A note taped on top. *Goodbye. We'll meet again soon.*

Underneath the handwriting was a printed quote from Pessoa: "In everything I judge to be sleep there is always another noise heralding the end of everything, the wind in the dark and, if I listen harder, the sound of my own lungs and heart."

Even if it meant death, the woman couldn't think of a better way to go—the juices and the fragrance of inflorescence lulled her, and somehow, she heard music. When she was ready to die, she fell asleep.

She opened her eyes, and she was back in her bed, covered in sweat. The alarm rang next to her. With wonder and relief, she felt a foreign yet familiar heaviness in every limb—how much effort was required just to arch the spine, to reach her arm out and hit the snooze button! The unsung effort the neck expended just to hold her head up!

Every part of her, from her soles to her scalp, felt sore with muscle and bone. Even so, she had a newfound respect for this body, its dance with gravity. An hour went by before she could will herself to get up.

She cautiously stepped onto her kitchen tile, afraid that she would crack it with the weight of her foot. Then she walked outside onto her patio, her garden. She watered her foxglove, her oxalis, her camellias. She picked up some figs that had fallen onto the ground.

Then she opened her laptop and checked her inbox and noticed it was full of emails from people she didn't know. Strangers, new friends, some whose names she recognized from the dinner parties. And many, many emails from that ex-lover. His latest email was sent at 11:00 a.m. "Where are you??" was the subject line. The message was blank. She rolled her eyes. Oh, so *now* he was looking for her? She clicked through the rest of the increasingly frantic emails he had sent, and gathered that she—no, her imposter— had been in Lisbon with him and disappeared from their room that morning while he was out for a run. She checked the inbox history: according to the receipts from Tripadvisor, they had booked a beautiful hotel with a balcony overlooking the river. It dawned on her that now that she was back in her full-sized body, the imposter might have vanished. She wondered if she should reply, if she should book a flight. She could arrive at their hotel by the next bright morning, and he would be so relieved to see her again he wouldn't even notice that she was different—if she was even different at all.

It had been her dream—to travel with this man. It had been her dream that he'd come back. For so many nights last year, the moment she closed her eyes, she relived the way he touched her, where he put his hands, what he whispered as she slept—surprisingly tender things that had confused her; she relived the nightmare of iced coffee and cigarettes and the bodega. Sometimes she imagined an alternative fantasy where she chose not to take the pill. What then? Perhaps they would have been a family. She knew full well the impossibility of these fantasies, and yet there was safety in that certainty, in knowing it would never happen.

But that moment had passed, and now she found herself feeling something she didn't expect: amusement, even satisfaction, that she was not going to Lisbon, not for this man, no. She was amused that he was so confused about her whereabouts, that he probably at that moment felt abandoned by her, disoriented in a foreign country and suddenly alone. But she owed him no explanations about where or who she was. Today, tomorrow, she would go to the botanical gardens, a ten-minute walk, smell the rat-repellent fragrance of wisteria and peonies, record their names. She would revisit the places she saw from the air on her journey—the neighbor's stoop, the corner store, the pond, the weeping girl, the fish market, and maybe even the bodega.

Before she left her apartment, she gathered and washed some figs in a bowl. Then she drew a bath and soaked for a while, eating the figs one by one, swallowing even the hard stems. The steam and water loosened her tense muscles, and her aches started to vanish. She scrubbed herself until the dead skin fell off, and underneath, she was new.

TWO POEMS

BY MARY JO BANG

A QUESTION

What if it's true, that we only live once,
and if so, who are you to tell me how.
I've let you live freely, let you be yourself.
Not once did I say *stupid-ass prick hypocrite*

and yet, you, you would take from me
what you want, try to control everything
about me. Take the accidents of nature,
a weed gone wild in the night, take that

and use it to say you are better at seeing
what is good for me and for the wide world.
Oh, please, we are animals and only if you
can agree on that can we actually speak.

I do not need you and yet you seem to need
to harness me to matters I cannot fathom
being mother to. See how that works out.
You won't notice the outcome. You'll be

thinking of yourself and admiring the ass
of another woman while your wife's knitting
a gift for your throat. That tool you use to
tell us who you are and what we have to be.

A SET SKETCHED
BY LIGHT AND SOUND

Outside, there's barking. The radio's on
loud but no one is talking. The long day
is darkening. Two silver stars are parking
at the curb, a long silent line. Reading

Charles Lamb, on the truth: *They do not so*
properly affirm, as annunciate it. Like an angel,
I wondered? Like a Gabriel telling a girl
the facts of life: You spread your legs

and yes, just like that— A sudden baby
crying behind the face of a girl staring
at the treetops outside the clerestory
windows of a church of one. The rain

comes in around the frames, a thin trickle
that makes the concrete go gray. A bell
sounding, fine-tuned to a storm. A bell, or
even better, a siren. An alarm that tells

of the need to absent yourself, to lie down
and behave as if you have no agency,
snug against the wall. The path formed
by the water is a line that holds the brain

hostage as it goes on being one detail,
becoming one more in a body of minutiae,
one end ending then, another years later
in a new now: listening to the outside

come in through the window. Between
time one and time two, a chasm opens:
into that, you sweep the sounds. That,
in turn, turns off the harsh light falling on

the event. The curtain over who you were.
You, as everything that happened to you.
You, that time, being told what to do.

WOMEN LIKE ME

BY ERIN WILLIAMS WITH KATE NOVOTNY

My doula had short, curly hair the color of soil, doughy skin, and a backpack full of worksheets and contracts for me to sign. We sat at the kitchen table.

WE DON'T CALL IT A BIRTH PLAN, BECAUSE PLANS OFTEN CHANGE. SO LET'S TALK ABOUT YOUR BIRTH WISHES.

A vaginal birth. Soft music, maybe classical. I could become the kind of person who appreciated that. I'd labor in water but give birth on land, specifically inside a hospital, just in case. My partner would be there. He'd grown a mustache for the occasion of the first few pictures. I wanted to be able to walk around while I labored, not lie in bed surrounded by machines. I'd bring a birthing ball. When it was all over, I wanted a large cheese pizza.

DO YOU WANT AN EPIDURAL?

PROBABLY. MAYBE NOT. I DON'T KNOW. I MIGHT.

A LOT OF WOMEN ASK FOR EPIDURALS IN THE MOMENT BUT DON'T ACTUALLY WANT THEM. MANY OF MY CLIENTS DEVELOP CODE WORDS THAT ARE USED ONLY WHEN THEY'RE REALLY SERIOUS ABOUT GETTING THE EPIDURAL.

OK.

DO YOU WANT TO PICK A CODE WORD?

SURE. HOW ABOUT "SPAGHETTI."

GREAT. SO IF YOU SAY, "I WANT AN EPIDURAL," I'll ASK THEM NOT TO GIVE IT TO YOU. BUT IF YOU SAY, "I WANT AN EPIDURAL SPAGHETTI," THEN YOU'LL GET THE EPIDURAL. DOES THAT MAKE SENSE?

YES.

She made a list in her notebook. She explained more about what her role would be as my doula. She'd be available anytime by phone or email. I could ask questions as my pregnancy continued. She'd help me labor virtually, and then in-person when the contractions got close enough. She'd be there at the hospital: advocate, masseuse, cheerleader, expert, ice chip aficionado, spaghetti whisperer.

She took a thick stack of contracts out of her backpack. $1,000 now, $1,000 after the birth. Without hesitation, I signed.

A full week after my due date, the landscape outside thick with snow, I drove to a local mall to walk the retail legs that stretched from the fountain at its center. I called my midwife crying.

A few days later, the baby was still stubbornly in place. With my midwife's blessing, I made an appointment at the hospital for the following evening. I signed the paperwork and donned the gown.

They put medicine in my cervix to ripen it, a white speck smaller than the head of a pin. I labored in a bathtub in the corner of my private room. I labored in the bed. I watched a Keira Knightley movie. I played Candy Crush. I got more medicine. I listened to classical music. I said "spaghetti." I got Pitocin to speed up my lagging contractions. The epidural wore off. I screamed. I got more spaghetti. 51 hours after my arrival at the hospital, they wheeled me into the operating room. My arms were splayed out on either side of me, shaking. They put a curtain up so I couldn't watch them saw me in half like a magician's assistant. They held her gunky, red cheek up to mine.

It wasn't until my belly was sliced open that I understood that, despite my wishes and plans and classical music and doula and midwife, I was completely out of control. Swirling inside of complicated organ and hormonal systems that prestigious specialists only vaguely understand, the soup of neurotransmitter and substance and structure (ovary, fallopian tube, uterus, cervix, vagina), the false promise of control breaks down.

It was only then that I realized I was at the complete mercy of this hospital, these tired nurses and doctors and the relentless beeping apparatus that promised I was okay.

For many Women Like Me*, this is the first time our fate rests in the hands of an institution. We do not have control. Lucky for us, it's a system that's been fundamentally designed and funded to protect our lives.

That is power.

I was scared of losing control, and I did lose it, but I was safe. I had my giant purple plastic birthing ball, my iPad, my little jacuzzi to labor in. Eventually I went home (with a fat, healthy baby) and wrote a blog post about how traumatizing it all was.

blogs.com/alabaster_mama_drama

hi readers!

so sorry for my long absence... y

birth to a small mammal...

*I am excluding non-binary and trans birthing people from this call-out, though some participate in and enjoy varying degrees of privilege. When I say "Women Like Me," I am referring to gendernormative white women, particularly the ones who have a purchase history at goop.com (guilty).

Women Like Me— we love our control. When coronavirus hit and some state governors began denying birth doulas "essential worker" status, petitions sprang up, flooding with the signatures of thousands of women demanding reproductive justice.* Politicians responded swiftly, backtracking bans. We needed our comfort, the gentle reassurance of an experienced person hired to assuage every fear and massage every ache.

*During the height of the coronavirus outbreak in NYC, Efe Osaren spoke out on social media about the problem of a Black doula traveling through a city during a pandemic to support her white birth client without adequate personal protective equipment (PPE).

The grease that makes all these wheels turn is white supremacy. It's the power that made governors change their mandates. It's what all but guaranteed the safety of me and my baby.

Research shows that Black birthing people are 3-4 times more likely to die, and in certain geographic areas 12 times more likely to die, than white birthing people. Most of these deaths are considered preventable.

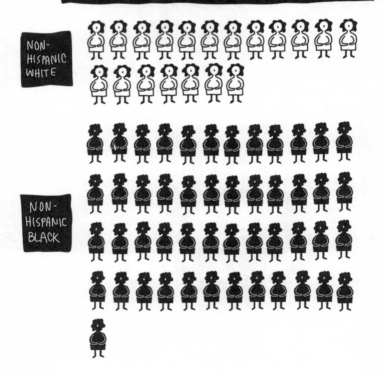

MATERNAL DEATHS PER 100,000 LIVE BIRTHS IN 2016

NON-HISPANIC WHITE

NON-HISPANIC BLACK

Confronting the abysmal statistics about Black maternal mortality requires that Women Like Me think a little harder about what reproductive justice means. Many Women Like Me have never been denied access to birth control. We live in places where abortion access is not hindered by complicated state laws or geography. We might have health insurance. We've never been arrested (okay except that one time- spring break!- but there were almost no consequences).

Women Like Me might be aware of their white privilege, but not the grave depths of it. We go swimming in the ocean but stick to the shore. We tend to ignore the fact that even if we suited up and went out far enough, rented one of those submarine pods that can withstand metric tons of pressure, we would never reach the bottom.

BUT WE CANNOT CLAIM TO CARE ABOUT REPRODUCTIVE JUSTICE UNTIL WE UNDERSTAND AND TAKE ACTION AGAINST OUR COMPLICITY IN WHITE SUPREMACY.

When birth control became legal in the United States with the 1965 ruling of Griswold vs. Connecticut, it did not impact all women equally. While white reproduction was and is considered by many to be an act of individual fulfillment and happiness, Black reproduction is plagued with stereotypes of Black degeneracy, from Reagan's "welfare queens" to crack babies. As Black activist and academic Angela Davis wrote about birth control, "What was demanded as a 'right' for the privileged came to be interpreted as a 'duty' for the poor."* She's referring to the racist and neo-Malthusian ideas that have spawned the nonconsensual sterilization of Black women since the Civil War.

In North Carolina in the 1930's and 1940's, nearly 8,000 "mentally deficient" people were forcibly sterilized. About 65% were Black, though Blacks comprised around ⅓ of the state population. These attempts curb "illegitimate" Black births and trim the welfare rolls also prevented more Black children from entering desegregated schools in the 1950s.*

BLACK   WHITE

TOTAL STERILIZATIONS

It did not end there. In 1973, Mary Alice and Minnie Relf, poor, Black, mentally-disabled sisters living in Alabama, were sterilized. They were 12 and 14 years old.

Their mother, who was illiterate, signed an "X" on a piece of paper she thought authorized birth control shots. They were both wheeled into the operating room and surgically sterilized.*

*See Angela Davis, "Racism, Birth Control, and Reproductive Rights"

In white minds, Black reproductive choices are choices. In white minds, risky prenatal behaviors stereotypically associated with Black mothers, like crack-smoking or landing a prison sentence, are their own fault. They have little to do with who we are: the privileged majority, who are bolstered by a foundation of history, policy, and invented notions of racial supremacy. Just 30 years ago, Charleston, South Carolina, started jailing pregnant women who tested positive for smoking crack. Some women were forced to finish out their last weeks of pregnancy inside a prison cell, others had their legs and arms shackled to hospital beds with iron cuffs. All of their babies were taken. Of the nearly 50 women arrested, chained, and imprisoned, all were Black but one.* We called that a choice.

* See Killing the Black Body by Dorothy Roberts

While mainstream reproductive rights agendas have focused mainly on abortion access, they have largely ignored other harmful racist policies that mainly impact Black, Indigenous, and people of color. There's not one reproductive "choice"– to have or not have an abortion. Reproductive health policy operates along a spectrum and spans an entire human life.

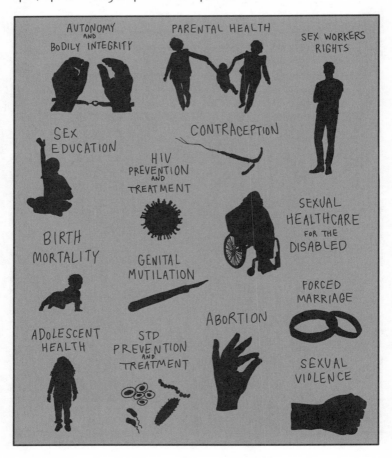

In Reproductive Justice in the Twenty-First Century, Loretta J Ross and Rickie Solinger argue that "choice" implies that reproduction is an individual decision outside of social structures, which doesn't recognize the complexity of these decisions. Disadvantaged people who get pregnant are labeled bad choice makers. Good choice makers embody popular notions of femininity: they are white, financially secure, partnered.*

INDIVIDUAL FULFILLMENT	DEGENERACY
FAMILY PLANNING CHOICE MARRIED HOME BIRTH FERTILITY BOY MOM! WINE SCREEN TIME SOCCER MOM STABLE HELICOPTER PARENTING GENDER REVEAL PARTY STAY-AT-HOME MOM	JEZEBEL UNWANTED PREGNANCY UNWED CRACK BABY LAZY CRIMINAL MEAN ADDICT STOIC SINGLE MOM ANGRY WELFARE QUEEN TEEN MOM SELFISH UNEMPLOYED

---

* See "Reproductive Justice in the Twenty-First Century" by Loretta J Ross and Rickie Solinger

Racism impacts the scope of choices people are allowed to make at all points throughout their lives, from where they live and what they do all the way up to and beyond birth. There is no reproductive justice without social justice. The reproductive privileges that Women Like Me enjoy depend on the reproductive castigation of other women. We celebrate the small wins that exacerbate their oppression.*

For example, pro-choice white women have fought to make voluntary sterilization procedures like tubal ligation or hysterectomies easier to obtain, viewing barriers to access as anti-choice. These measures are in direct opposition to the interests of Black and Indigenous women, who have long suffered involuntary sterilization by a structurally-racist healthcare system that makes these procedures too easy to perform and too difficult to litigate.**

*2005 Asian Communities for Reproductive Justice via Loretta J Ross
** Dorothy Roberts, Killing the Black Body

IT IS MY SPECIFIC NEED FOR ACCESS AND CONTROL THAT ENDANGERS BLACK LIVES.

THE WEAPONIZATION OF WHITE FEMININITY IS A DAILY THREAT TO BLACK, INDIGENOUS, AND PEOPLE OF COLOR.*

*See Rachel Cargle's, "Dear White Women" available at www.rachelcargle.com

Reproductive justice is fundamentally a question of human rights. It's a function of geography, class, gender, ability, race, sexuality, and immigration status, all of which are built on the foundation of white supremacy.

The 50 years following the legalization of abortion have been characterized by prohibitive legislation and continued social stigma. Racist and classist ideas and harmful stereotypes have helped to decimate the social programs that support reproductive labor.

The rate at which Black mothers and babies die preventable deaths is not a curiosity or an anomaly. It's the result of a culture that ruthlessly and systematically devalues Black lives.

The medicalization of birth and the field of gynecology owe themselves to the Black women whose bodies were sliced open without their consent so that white women and babies could live.*

There is no reproductive justice without recognition of and reparations to the Black women who have suffered and died for generations within the arms of the American healthcare system.

The reproductive choices I've made throughout my life— occasionally so privileged that they're goofily code-named after Italian specialty dishes— must be understood for what they are and have always been: white supremacy.

Reproductive advantages for white women continue to occur at the expense of Black lives. Women Like Me must reconcile the truth of our past and our present. We must honor the Black women whose lives were taken so that our babies could be born, pink and screaming. We must devote our continuing fight for reproductive justice to the sanctity and safety of Black lives.

---

*See Medical Bondage: Race, Gender, and the Origins of American Gynecology by Deirdre Cooper Owens

THEIR LIVES WERE SACRIFICED SO THAT
WE COULD SURVIVE.

MY NIECES

BY DEB OLIN UNFERTH

I LOVE MY NIECES. I have three in descending size, each radiant and perfect in their unique ways: one throwing the blankets over the railing, another running down the hallway in a mad glee, the eldest playing "cat." Look at them out in the backyard, flipping around on the various apparatuses their father banged together for them. Of course I feel fiercely protective of them. I tape their scrawled drawings to my refrigerator with satisfaction. I will buy them some piece of plastic if they want it, buy them all the crappy pieces of plastic there are! They must go to the best schools, have the best tutors, travel the world. Just getting a niece into a good kindergarten is such a battle these days. My sister must fight, fight, fight—I'll help, leave them my money when I die—must lift them, walk in her gym shoes over whatever is beneath. The nieces want a rainbow Jell-O? Grind up the bones so that my nieces may get their cool colorful treat. Look at these videos of their school performances—singing songs, leaping around a wooden stage. I watch with pride, joy! Other kids are there, too, but I barely see them. Other kids are mere decorative streamers beside the stars of the show, my blood, *my nieces.*

It's so weird. I become *literally blind* to other children when my nieces are there. Only if another kid topples off the stage or vomits or performs an extraordinary feat will I be dragged away. I am transfixed by the powerful pull of relation: I, who decided early on that I never wanted children, partly for the very reason that I did not want to be indifferent to all but what I called my own.

If there are no nieces on the stage? Just strangers' children on, say, YouTube? Then I do see them. I linger on this one's awkward dance, this one waving to the audience, that one's pout. Each child is fragile, funny, shining. My mind builds their stories. They all become my nieces.

That woman in a mask in the post office, that man moving a cart down the street, they are my nieces. And the nonhuman animals, they are my nieces. The fish are my nieces, and they do feel pain. The animals in the zoo, nieces. And the massive shrinking insect population. I have so many nieces. The old, old trees are my nieces, and they talk to one another through their secret underground pathways. I sit on my porch and feel the press and pull, the pulse of my nieces, in the air and the damp ground, the lizards and squirrels, the waving weeds, the plants I planted and the ones I did not. I feel their familiar ways, their link to me, the connection between us (not so far away on the tree). But the most destructive nieces of all, the ones who will suck it all up, trample it all down, throw it in the garbage to float out to sea? My nieces. And me, of course.

I think about terms like "selfless motherhood" and "parental sacrifice." I understand what it is to love a child so much that you feel yourself becoming a better person just by looking at them. You'll forgo any pleasure, any need. To release ego for love—what a relief, what a revelation. It's a miracle. You can finally look away from yourself and *love*. I understand the temptation to interpret this as selflessness.

And yet, we know how sticky the ego is. It doesn't evaporate that easily. It *transfers*. Parenthood can be a brilliant, incontestable excuse for capitalist conquest, dynastic rule, for taking more than our share and believing it is an act of selfless love. As far as I'm concerned, the burden of proof is on the child bearer.

Sure, I know I'm not perfect either. I'm not fooling anyone with my vegan entrée, my rescue dog, my reusable bags, my Prius—but, hey, at least I don't have *kids*.

Ah, humans. We root for them, but should we? Look at all we've done. If only we didn't exist as individuals, it would be easy to dismiss us as a blight to scour out. If only we didn't exist as masses, it would be easy to love us one by one. We are an endless contradiction, two things at once at all times. Infestation. Miracle. (Especially my nieces.)

I write this in April 2020, in the early days of the pandemic. I've been watching clips of the empty cities, of elephants emerging from the forests of Thailand, of the smog lifting and revealing ancient green mountains in the distance. There are more birds out this spring, more crickets, because humans have finally *shut the fuck up*. A planet with less us. A portent of the future, perhaps. A promise, a warning, a window, a door? I hope so. But by the time this essay appears, it will likely be nostalgia, a pause before we went back to the churning destruction in the name of our nieces.

THEY JUST MIGHT BE SEEN

BY DONNETTA LAVINIA GRAYS

THEY SIT ON THE *edge of the stage. Pregnant belly peeking through an open Carhartt jacket.*

They speak directly to the audience. The others (their parents, their coach, and their lover) take up space in isolated light behind them.

Time: They are here in the present. Their parents, their coach, and their lover are in a time before and a time after.

Place: Just outside of a shotgun house. A rural town. Too far away for anyone to care.

PART ONE: THEN

THEM

A boy's body ain't supposed to feel full like this.

Their Parents

MA

That sound like a name that do something?

PA

Autumn? If you mean like fall, then, yeah. Fall do something. Spring a season and a verb too.

MA

Autumn Janeé Crowder. I wanna see it in stone. On a building. Does it sound like it would be on a building?

PA

Like a courthouse?

MA

Library. Research wing of a hospital. Some college somewhere.

PA

Maybe she get a first word in. Get her to crawling real good. Walk a little bit. Then we'll see.

THEM

A boy's words supposed to say things that ain't got feelings in 'em. His walk supposed to tell other folks *how* to feel. A little scared maybe.

Their Coach

COACH

Decrease the carbs. Six months and we get five seconds off your time. I want you fast. I want you lean.

THEM

A boy's body ain't supposed to whip through the air like nothing.

Their Lover

LOVER

You—you put words in my mouth, and they live in there like bar soap. How is it you punishing me, and you the one spit razors? Make me out to be the enemy all you want. But this ain't some "It's not you, it's me" shit. This is all you, baby. ALL you.

THEM

A boy's heart ain't supposed to break.

(*Pause*) A boy's body ain't supposed to feel full like this. I press my hands down the sides of my hips. I press my hands down the sides of my hips. Sand them down. My hands are rough now. I've been working out. Made my own gym out back when I was fifteen. Cinder blocks. Bags of feed. Now I have free weights in the carport. Makes my hands rough, so I take 'em and sand them hips down with 'em. Breasts. They get sanded too. Sand down that full. Blow the sawdust from the palms of my hands into folks' eyes so they have to squint.

  Like looking into light.

PART TWO: NOW

Their Parents

MA

That sound like a name that do something?

PA

Cyrus. If you mean like the sun, then, yeah. Sun do something. Got a whole mess of stuff in the sky do some shining.

MA

Cyrus Janeé ... Cyrus James. Cyrus *James* Crowder. I wanna see it in stone. On a building. Does it sound like it would be on a building?

PA

Like a courthouse?

MA

Library. Research wing of a hospital. Some college somewhere.

PA

Maybe they get a word in. See what walking is ... then we'll see.

THEM

A boy's walk supposed to have a way 'bout it that nobody questions.

Their Coach

COACH

Increase the protein. Six months and we get ten more pounds on you. I want you to take a hit, but I want you to give one too.

THEM

A boy's body supposed to be able to take a hit.

Their Lover

LOVER

You—you put words in my ear, and they live in there like music. How is it that I thought I was singing to you, and you the one hit the high note? Make me out to be a partner. 'Cause this ain't some "It's not you, it's me" shit. If you push me away, it's all you, baby. ALL you.

THEM

A boy's mouth could pour poetry down his lover's neck. Stroke the back of a head while looking into his eyes. See the face of God.

(*Pause*) Make a boy's body get full ... like this. (*Caresses their belly*) With life.

(*Smiles*) And, not after a life. But, within a life continued. Full.

Fingertips run down the sides of my hips. Fingertips run down the sides of my hips. Graze them. Praise them a little. My hands are rough. I've been working out. Made my own gym out back when I was fifteen. Cinder blocks. Bags of feed. Now we have free weights outside on the carport. Makes a boy's hands rough. So, I take my fingertips and graze them hips like a box full of sepia-toned photographs reclaimed from a high shelf. Memories resting like daydreams on broad shoulders. Memories etching shadowed definition into biceps. And I praise them all. Scars across my chest. Each one an affirmation. They get praised too. Make a joyful keloid noise!

I run my fingers across 'em as a sculptor would a fine

piece of wood. Blow the shavings from the palms of my hands into folks' eyes so they have to squint.

Like looking into light.

COMPLIANCE: A GUIDE

BY CADE LEEBRON

1. When I was sixteen, I was having sex with my then-boyfriend and the condom broke. I remember hearing a noise, like a popped balloon, but I was a teenager and new to sex and didn't know what had happened until after. He called his mom, she was out of town; she told us to find a pharmacy the next morning and get the morning-after pill. It sounded like a simple thing to do.

2. The next morning, I left early, nobody else in my house was awake. I left a note on the kitchen table, saying

I'd gone out for breakfast with a friend. First we went to a pharmacy, where they told us that they couldn't do anything for us. Then we went to a hospital, where they said the same thing. I don't remember how we found the clinic with the disapproving male doctor, only that by the time we got there, it felt like we'd been walking around our city all day.

3. The doctor said we had to have a parent present, no not my boyfriend's mom, my mom. I called her and asked her to come to the clinic. She met us there.

4. I didn't want to tell her, not because she wasn't *cool* but because she was *my mother*, and sex is complicated and because above all else, I felt that my sex life was private and not her business, not anyone's business but mine. I still feel that way—not just about myself but about the sex lives of young women, that young women are entitled to our bodies and our pleasure. That we, too, are entitled to our protection and our reproductive rights.

5. Before the disapproving doctor gave me the pill, he

asked me in front of both my boyfriend and my mom if really, no really, the condom had actually broken or if there had been no condom at all. He could have asked me alone or before my mother arrived. He chose to wait for the moment when he had the largest audience.

6. When he finally handed over the pill, he told me to eat carbs with it. I went to my boyfriend's house and took the pill and ate an entire sleeve of Chips Ahoy.

*   *   *

1. When I was in my early twenties and in my creative writing MFA program, people would occasionally say things to me about how my work was too political and not quite nonfiction. They would say the typical things: *You cannot write the universal; you cannot write for other people; you have to only write your specific story, other people will connect to that story, and that is how you will achieve universality.*

2. I then parroted these lessons to my undergraduate

students because I thought they were correct, because I thought this was nonfiction craft.

3.   I think now that this is a form of oppression. People in power don't want stories of groups of marginalized people. For example, they would rather that women did not write about what it is to be a woman in a country that is hostile to women. They would rather that we wrote individual stories that feel anecdotal and dismissible. You start to notice this in things like Title IX cases on university campuses. They act like every rape is a completely unique situation instead of acknowledging that rape is a huge problem on college campuses, instead of creating a viable system to deal with another existing system—the system of violence. They act shocked to hear that every single rape has occurred. And then, with every single rape, they want to reinvent the wheel of response.

4.   But in my MFA program I thought, OK, yes, if I try to speak to a group experience, I am perhaps appropriating from others in my group. If, as a disabled bisexual woman, as a queer woman who has survived rape,

I try to write about being a part of any of these groups or intersections of groups—disabled people, queer people, women, queer women, disabled women, survivors of rape, disabled survivors of rape, queer survivors of rape, queer disabled people—I will be telling a story I do not fully know. I cannot hope to speak for anyone else because I cannot see inside their brains. Stories I have been told by friends or acquaintances are the nonfiction equivalent of hearsay. They can't enter the room. I have to speak as though my story is happening inside a bubble, untouched by the experiences of others and unrelated to those experiences, no matter how similar they might be.

5. I cannot see inside anyone else's brain. It is important to not appropriate. What is also important is that we have to speak truth to power and that we are allowed to extrapolate from our own experiences and the experiences of our friends. We are allowed to notice the trends we are experiencing—rape culture, misogyny, etc.—the trends that we are a part of. Being alive is a kind of research. We don't have to wait for the scholars and the scientific studies to say something about

what it's like to live in certain kinds of bodies in the world.

*   *   *

1. When I was sixteen, after the incident with the condom and the disapproving doctor, my mom took me to a gynecologist to get birth control. I don't remember the conversations we had prior to this appointment, but I do remember that my mom was trying to be both supportive and protective.

2. In the exam room, just me and a doctor, the doctor brandished the wand for a transvaginal ultrasound. It looked huge. I didn't want her to touch me with it. She told me she needed to perform the ultrasound in order to prescribe birth control. (False.) She told me if I said no, she would go into the waiting room and tell my mom I wasn't cooperating. (Humiliating.) She said if I'd had sex before, the ultrasound wouldn't hurt at all. (False.)

3. The pressure to be a compliant patient is like nothing else I know in this world. In no other situation in

my personal life does *compliance* sound like the thing I should be aiming for.

4. I allowed her to perform the transvaginal ultrasound, and then she prescribed birth control pills, and then I took those pills, unquestioningly or something close to it, compliantly, for six years.

*   *   *

1. As an adult person, I have two packs of the morning-after pill in my desk drawer. I ordered them online, where they are much cheaper than in pharmacies. Of course, most people who need the morning-after pill can't wait days for an online delivery.

2. Once, at a friend's wedding in my early twenties, I had sex with a man whom I'd met that night and the condom broke and I wasn't on birth control at the time so I found a pharmacy the next day and then texted with my friends about it, laughing.

3. Then he and I went on a few dates and had sex again,

and again the condom broke and when he offered to pay for morning-after pill round two, I said yes.

4. I texted my friends about it again and we thought it was funny. Like, how does that happen twice with one person? This man and I laughed about it, too, like we laughed together about writers on the internet and the bottle of Fireball he had in his apartment. Acquiring the morning-after pill as an adult in a different city could be no big deal because nobody was saying no, telling me to call my mom. The thing that worried me the most was letting a man pay for my contraception—I prefer to give a man, any man, no reason to feel like I owe him.

* * *

1. I get so tired of women who need to express that they are *on their grown woman shit*. I get so tired of women who put other women below them based on age or experience or aesthetic or sexuality. I love my Glossier stickers on my cheap laptop, my thrift store clothes, my millennial pink, my emojis, my Instagram persona, and my Urban Decay eye shadow. Babe, I am still on

my teenage girl shit. You know what is glorious? Teenage girl shit. What makes a grown woman different
from a teenage girl? Not much. We have so many of the
same concerns, we as grown women just have slightly
fewer limitations, slightly fewer people saying they are
allowed to know our business by law.

2. Not: fewer people trying to say they deserve to know
    our business. Just: slightly fewer people who are legally
    allowed into our private lives.

3. How many times have I tried to write about teenage
    girl shit? Oh, and don't I know the things that are said
    about it. *This is melodrama. You're a teenage girl and
    nobody will want to know about your life. The stories
    you want to tell are not important. Grow up.*

4. And then: *You're not a teenage girl anymore and so you
    can no longer tell these stories. You have found a way
    to appropriate your own story! Congratulations. Find
    something new to talk about.* Babe, I am still on my
    teenage girl shit, and these are still the stories I want to
    tell. When we are teenage girls, we are told to shut up

because we are kids and our stories aren't important. Meanwhile, we are going through many of the same trials grown women go through, just with even less agency. When we grow up and are no longer teenage girls, we are told that we can no longer tell those stories, we have aged out of them.

5.   And so who is telling the stories of teenage girl shit?

*   *   *

1.   For a few years, in my early and then mid-twenties, I took a break from the pill. It was increasing the frequency of my migraines, and various doctors didn't listen to me when I said that to them.

2.   So I just stopped taking it and used other methods of contraception.

3.   Then I missed the ease and control of the pill and found a doctor who listened to me about my migraines and prescribed a different pill, which I started taking, and which did not cause additional migraines.

4. Then yet another doctor told me I was being irresponsible by taking the pill that didn't give me migraines, because it was slightly less effective than other birth control pills. So I made another appointment with, yes, another brand-new doctor to discuss options.

5. This doctor was puzzled. She sat me down in a little exam room and listened to the story of me and birth control pills. She said, "So this pill works for you, and you like it, but another doctor made you feel bad for taking it?"

6. Yes.

7. Almost every story I know about contraception is a story about shame, a story about compromise and compliance.

8. Many of these stories are stories in which I am made to do something unnecessarily unpleasant in order to acquire necessary contraception. Make my mom hear about a broken condom or make me undergo an unnecessary transvaginal ultrasound or make me pay $50 for a morning-after pill at a pharmacy or make me

take a daily pill that gives me migraines even though there's a better option.

9. It is in situations like this where the phrase *pink tax* comes to mind because I don't know what else to call this because *pink tax* is not quite what I mean and feels inadequate.

10. *Misogyny* but let's not argue.

*   *   *

1. At a certain point in my life, many of my doctors stopped talking to me about how to prevent a pregnancy and instead started talking about how to cultivate one. This wasn't based on anything I said about wanting or not wanting to have kids. If they asked me about kids, I mostly expressed ambivalence or said things like *Not in the next ten years. Not in the next five years. Not right now.*

2. It seemed to be based on a mental timetable they had laid out for female patients and neglected to confirm

with the specific person sitting in front of them. Perhaps a switch flips when a patient hits age twenty-four and *pregnancy* comes out of the *to prevent* category and lands on the *to do* list. Less consequence or source of shame and more biological imperative.

3. At one appointment with a neurologist, he spent most of our time together discussing how I would be able to safely get pregnant, given my disability and long list of medications. We would need to make sure I was off of X medication for a certain amount of time, and Y medication as well, whereas Z medication might be safe for a hypothetical baby. We were negotiating the health of a fantasy—not mine, his. And yet the health of the fantasy was prioritized over the health of me, my health; I was the patient he was supposed to be seeing.

4. This was not a plan I'd asked him to help me make. There were other questions, unrelated to babies or pregnancy, that I'd wanted to address and which we simply did not get to.

5. After, my primary care doctor was looking at the

neurologist's notes in my chart and seemed surprised—she knew I was on birth control and not planning on having children anytime in the near future, yet all of his notes regarded planning for a pregnancy. Why was that? I couldn't explain it to her.

6. Of course, many disabled women have the opposite problem. Doctors with all their bad ideas—eugenics masquerading as genetics—often discourage disabled people from having children.

7. I have lost track of the number of times I have wound up in the ER with symptoms of my disability that could overlap with symptoms of a pregnancy; I have lost track of the number of time that ER doctors have insisted it could be a pregnancy instead, despite my existing diagnoses and my existing birth control pills; I have lost track of the number of times these doctors have said, *Let's run some tests,* and then used my blood to run a pregnancy test without my knowledge or consent. I do know that every time, the test has come back negative, and they have told me the result as though it was an answer to a question I asked.

8. I haven't ever asked a doctor in an ER, *Am I pregnant?* I haven't ever asked a doctor outside of an ER, *Can you help me plan for a pregnancy?*

9. My disability is invisible and so my doctors sometimes tell me that I am *very healthy*, even while staring directly at test results and diagnoses that suggest the opposite. My doctors sometimes spend our limited time together talking about a pregnancy plan that I don't need instead of the symptoms that affect me daily. My doctors can be quite concerned about which of my necessary medications would harm a fetus that does not yet exist.

*   *   *

1. When I was seventeen I had a friend who was assaulted and needed the morning-after pill. We went to the pharmacy and she used her fake ID to get the morning-after pill so they didn't call her mom.

2. I remember thinking, *Oh, that's very smart, I should have done that.* My personal instruction manual had missed a step.

3. We as a group of teenage girls sat around trying to puzzle through the directions. Mostly what we wanted to know was if she could have a beer with her pill. I remember that we were horrified by what had happened, that we were trying to be supportive, that we sat around and laughed with her about the fake ID and the pill and the beer and about how bullshit the whole thing was.

4. Do you get me when I tell you that this is not a story about shame? This is not a story that requires contraception to be a learning moment.

5. But maybe this is also not my story to tell or maybe she would tell it differently. Let me try again.

6. Any instruction manual or guide ends when you either complete the task or choose to do something different.

7. When I was eighteen and in college, I was the friend who was assaulted and I don't even remember if I got the morning-after pill. I was mostly alone. People had started saying things like *Get over it* and *Grow up*.

8. When I was twenty-two and in my MFA program, I was again the friend who was assaulted and I did get the morning-after pill and I had some friends who were supportive, don't get me wrong, but again people—other women, mostly—said things to me like *Get over it* and *Grow up* and *Well, what* he *said was*—

9. If this is grown woman shit, you can keep it.

*   *   *

1. I want to stay in the space where we are seventeen and sitting at a table together, drinking beer and puzzling over the instructions for the morning-after pill, and we have no desire to grow up or to be older because why would we want that.

2. Or: in bed with my then-boyfriend the night of the popped balloon condom. I remember the room being gray and his bed being gray and the light being gray and how he held me was warm and close and I remember the worry in his face. The worry he probably saw

reflected back at him. The way that many stories of contraception, the ones that end in shame and pain, started with pleasure.

3. Can we stay there?

4. Oh, and don't I know what someone could say, online or in an MFA program or when reading this at home. *Your question is naive. Grow up.* Hold on. I don't want to grow up, if by *Grow up* you mean *Accept this bullshit.* I want to imagine something different. I don't think sex between men and women and its linked fear of pregnancy—danger of pregnancy, potential consequence or joy or accident of pregnancy, prevention of pregnancy—I don't think these things must necessarily lead us to shame.

*　　*　　*

1. I am trying to imagine a future without it. I wonder if you can come there with me. I think what a lot of us want from sex is pleasure and we accept the shame as a consequence of getting something that we wanted. I am not

supposed to say *we,* I know. I am supposed to tell a single story of *I* and I am not supposed to extrapolate.

*   *   *

1. Any instruction manual or guide ends when you either complete the task or choose to do something different.

*   *   *

1. Sometimes extrapolation is a way of connecting. I imagine that sometimes we are alike, you and I. We want pleasure. We take shame in trade. We accept that birth control requires prescriptions and that prescriptions require obedience and compliance and behaving a certain way for doctors. We accept that seeing a doctor requires health insurance and that health insurance comes from private companies and costs money and that not all of us are eligible for it. We accept a system of life because we stumbled into it; it was fully grown and we were just teenage girls and who were we to argue. We talked back but we got shouted down and then we became, instead, compliant. Or anyway: that

was me. After a lot of shame and shouting I became, for a while, quiet and compliant. If you would like me to tell a single and unconnected personal story without extrapolation, here is part of it.

*   *   *

1. But remember how it was, when we were *we* and when we were young and daring? Before we got divide-and-conquered out into single stories. When we talked back. When we were on our teenage girl shit, when we took the morning-after pill with whole sleeves of Chips Ahoy, with plastic cups of beer, with friends. When we put glitter on our eyelids and pulled fake IDs out of our purses, when we walked into the darkness of a weekend night in an excited way instead of afraid all the time, when the risk of our own little crimes didn't even enter our calculations. Oh, and don't I know, how the young are naive and how sometimes their consequences catch up with them. But don't I also know the willingness to dream, and to imagine, and to defy.

DIVORCEDLY

BY TIPHANIE YANIQUE

WANT

1.

Now

This thing is about desire. I know because I've had a worry of want all my life. I'm a feast of want. I wanted a professorship. I wanted marriage. I wanted children. The want wouldn't let up. I had a kid but wanted another. I had a husband but wanted a better one. I became a professor but was on contract. I wanted tenure. Inside of my want was already an "I can get." There is a privilege to my desire. I've been privileged in this way.

It's disgusting. But I don't want the boy to feel ashamed of his desire.

So, I'm sitting here on this donut with my butt sinking into the hole. This is the opposite of sexy. Or maybe it's a little sexy because my nether regions are just hanging out there feeling unencumbered. But who knows this? No one. Who is looking? Josie is looking. That's me. I'm Josie. I'm the only one looking.

What I am looking at is this white woman, her mouth opens and closes and opens and opens. She makes delicious sounds, like she has just been given a German chocolate cake, and there is nothing she has ever wanted more than a slice of chocolate cake. Her mouth is wet and opens and closes and opens like she's getting a forkful of that so sweet dark cake every second. And yes, she is beautiful. And sexy. The sexy part is clear for all to see, because the woman is indeed having sex. She is beautiful while having sex, which is a sign that she is a professional.

Josie, think something academic and smart. This is what I tell myself, because I'm a professor, and when needed I can get professorial with myself. But nothing smart is alighting. I try to think about what I am thinking, because being meta is usually some kind of smart. I am thinking that this, what I am watching, is not acting. It's faking. There's a difference. My ex-husband always said I thought too much, even though he was also a professor. I would say, "Thinking is what adults *do*." But right now all this adulting is making my mouth taste nasty.

How did the boy understand these things he saw? I can go an entire session of sex with my eyes closed, and that's how I prefer it. Oh, Josie, I think. And then I think, When will I ever have sex again?

The boy doesn't understand that porn is basically Disney for sex. Because the woman's legs are really shiny. The boy was probably thinking that those legs could hold him in an octopus grip, so that now the boy will never eat calamari again without getting a woody.

There goes the woman's mouth opening. And the man? He is all appendages. Now the man puts his brown thumb into the woman's open, red mouth. And the woman sucks the man's thumb like she is a baby and his thumb was her own mama's nipple. It's an artful hunger, or it's a hunger of artifice. I can see the woman's whole body—her beautiful, made-up face. Her ass is taut, but she's not tense, she's just twenty-something and she's taut because of that twenty-something-ness. Her breasts make no sense. They are too large and hard to be comfortable. My own set are small and soft—I've breastfed four children. But this woman's look so sturdy they must be uncomfortable to carry around, discomforting to touch. The man, actually, hasn't yet touched them at all. Touching or not touching; this is the kind of thing that gets put into a legal contract.

Instead of touching her breasts, the man grabs the woman's waist and pulls her body right onto his body. The camera goes in close, and it looks like the woman's vagina is a ravenous, unlipsticked mouth sucking the man's penis. The camera pulls back out and the woman's actual face looks—what the hell—like she might cry. Like she'd been crying already. The good kind of crying. Like, the-sex-is-so-good-I'm-falling-in-love-right-now kind of crying. Which makes no sense. Because that would mean that this woman is really acting, or that she is maybe even feeling something real. Like emotion. Which is particularly disturbing because another man ends up in the middle of them. I know this because the video was at the threesome when I caught it.

This is my child's laptop. My youngest. The only boy. I have no idea how to wipe his computer clean. I have no idea how to make sure that tomorrow at 9:00 a.m., when he logs into his Google classroom, this video won't pop up, like it did this morning. I'm watching it now because I want to know what he knows. It's 11:57 p.m., and I am so tired that I start to cry, but I keep watching the two people doing so many things, and they are doing them so hard and so well.

2.
That Morning

OK, Josie. You remember how your mother used to tell you she had a sixth sense? Or that she had eyes in the back of her head? And remember how, when you were a kid, you thought that it might be fucking true, because *how on earth* did she know all that she knew. Right, Josie? You remember when you got wise and realized that it wasn't magic Mom had, just wisdom, just her own memory of childhood? And then you knew your mother was no better, no different than you. Just older. Remember? Josie?

Well, get yourself, together Professor Baker. Fact is, you had no clue. Because something completely unconsidered—let's call it what it is, a mother's intuition—led you to your son's room this morning. He's in the middle of a school homeroom meetup/hangout/whatever, which means you have a break from him, and there is no reason at all for you to go into his damn room. The email the teacher sent even said something like that—that this is independent work. You read that email. You read all the damn emails. Because that is how you are, Josie. You have integrity, and as an educator yourself, you respect his teacher. He is being teacher supervised right then, albeit through a screen.

But when you walk into that boy's room, you stand over him and you notice first that he has muted himself. Because anyone, the teacher and all the students, can clearly hear, or *would have* been able to clearly hear, the sounds coming from the video in the pop-up window that emphatically is *not* part of your son's homeroom meetup/hangout/whatever session. The boy—your boy—is not engaged with the larger part of his screen, now featuring a video on Representative John Lewis; his teacher and his fellow students' faces in little squares to the right—some kids looking at their screens, some eating, some intermittently punching away a younger sibling, some nothing more than an empty chair; the teacher smiling as though her face is frozen, which maybe it is. And there is your son's face, looking as though he is looking at the screen, but not blinking, and with his eyes averted just a little. Your son is so transfixed by the actions in the small video, small though it may be, that he doesn't even slam his laptop closed when you enter his room. He just looks up slowly when you stand over him, your own mouth covered, his own mouth open and his eyes dry. This is your son, remember. With eyes red like he hasn't blinked in twenty-two minutes, which is how long the video has been going. You, his mother, simply lift the laptop off of his lap, where his pants are tented.

To anyone looking at you, you are totally calm; you are calmness itself. But inside, your heart is literally hurting, it's beating so damn hard. Each of your other three children have computers too. You turn out of your children's room and walk up quietly behind the girls, huddled at the dining table. Your daughters don't turn to look at you. They are doing the same homework, even though they are not triplets and are not, any of them, in the same grade. The middle school has just one curriculum for sixth and seventh and eighth—which is bullshit, but you are so grateful for this bullshit. All of their laptops are open, but they are crowded around the middle of them, as they do. The computer is reading to them, like they are pre-schoolers. It is the story of a princess who wants badly to sleep but can't because of pee underneath her bed. Or a pea underneath her bed. You suddenly don't know the difference.

You don't speak to the baby—who is not a baby, the boy—until hours later, after the girls have set the table for dinner.

You'd wanted to stop at the girls.

You'd wanted to stop at two, to be honest. But your husband had wanted a third. That one broke you. And then your husband had wanted a son. Your *ex*-husband. And that boy broke you for good, in all the ways.

When your boy comes to the dining table this evening, his face, brown as it is, is aflame. His eyes are narrowed and his jaw is clenched. "What is your problem?" asks one of the girls—the middle one who feels some kinship to her brother because she is sure she is the only one of you who wanted him. "*You* are my problem," he yells back. "You, all of you!" Which you gather he'd been wanting to say for a while, because this is the kind of elegant retort your son can't normally muster off the cuff. You alone are his mother and so you alone know that he is embarrassed, maybe scared that he might be in trouble because of the video. Or maybe scared that his sisters might know about the video. Well, it's not fear exactly but something more refined: shame. But your baby boy has one of those faces Black boys too often have in this country, one that looks more grown up than it should. He doesn't look scared. He looks scary.

3.
Back to Now

I had picked up the laptops three weeks ago when the schools in Atlanta went virtual. Then, the computers had seemed like lifelines. Thank God I'd chosen the good school district over my ex's demands that the kids and I move to a more affordable area. He didn't want his child support payment going up. He never said that exactly, but I was married to him for over a decade. And now? Oh, vindication, because since the pandemic canceled school, every single child in our district had the tech they needed by the end of week one of online schooling. New York, where the kids' dad lived, had still been *in* school then. But

Atlanta was already good to go. "You are taking my Black son to the racist deep South?!" my ex had shouted on the phone. But Atlanta was more prepared than anywhere for a health pandemic, perhaps because they'd been having a racial one for a century. Well, whatever it takes.

But this? Porn on a school-issued laptop? Didn't they put protections on these things? Shouldn't this never ever *ever* happen? Even if my boy had looked up "sex with a woman," the computer should have known to decline! Forbid! But instead, this school-issued device served my boy a threesome with a white woman and two Black men. My Black boy. My boy, who is ten and tall and strong for his age. Ten! And Black boys are always being made to think that their sexual prowess is what they have to offer. Even the overattention given to them for sports and dance is about sex, all about the idea that Black men were made for studding, as they had been during slavery. I have my doctorate in exactly this sort of thing. And here is the local elementary school making it too easy for my boy to slide right into the stud-slave stereotype. And ten! He is only ten.

His father is back in New York, probably watching porn all day and night, now that he's in quarantine. He lives in

New Rochelle, which is the center of it all, it seems. He'd probably seen this exact video. He'd watched so much ugly porn when we were going through the divorce, like how people bury their sorrows in drink.

4.
Back in the Day

Let's go back. Back to when Josie was a married woman. When she had it all, everything she wanted. A tenure-track job, three beautiful, healthy brown children. A husband who was six foot two and recently named Professor of the Year for Excellent Teaching—which for Josie translated into a husband with whom she could wear stilettos and talk nerdy. A dream. But let's go to a room. A small sterile room.

The room was not Dr. Josephine Baker's office. It was not her classroom. Either of those rooms would have made her an authority. Her office had her degrees in wood on the wall, and her awards in glass on the shelves, and a stack of playing cards featuring Black feminist icons in varnished card-stock paper on her desk. There was always an orchid on her filing cabinet. Sometimes it was yellow, sometimes it was purple—her sorority colors. Whenever an orchid stopped blooming, she would throw it away and get another. Her office smelled like the spray she used—something citrus or coconut to remind her of home. Even though the island where she was from didn't smell like oranges, and coconuts don't really have a smell until they are in your mouth. It was only that Josie had been trained by colonialism to think that the Caribbean smelled like fruit. In reality, her island smelled like the sea, but that couldn't be replicated.

If the room had been her classroom, it would have smelled of chalk. And of student sweat. And of Dr. Baker's perfume, which was a scent her husband had picked out for her when they were just married and had only a bit of money—mostly her money, which is how it had been then when he was in graduate school, but it was theirs because they were married. Her last name was also their name—because they were married—even though Josephine Baker was a peculiar name for a Black feminist literary scholar. Her husband, who was a sociologist, loved it, adored it, thought it was awesome and said so often. And Josie wanted to be the best wife. And so, she had taken

Baker on with gusto. I'm Josephine Baker, she would say. Josephine Baker, PhD. In her classroom, she wrote it on the board at the start of every single class.

In those rooms, Dr. Baker might say, "Stop. Take a second and think through what you are saying. Are you really making an argument *against* Dionne Brand here in Intro to Feminist Literary Studies? Are you really trying to be against being against language? You might consider that you are using this language, and it is failing you right now." Or she might say, "Just spit it out. I'm not going to change your grade, kid. I have a line of students outside for office hours. I don't keep tissues in my office for these kinds of emotions." Yes, student sweat was the smell.

But this room was not those rooms. This room was a medical examination room, and Josie was not the authority here.

"Just tell me what I need to do. Please." That was Josie in this room.

Josie was using words like "please," and also, she was asking someone else to tell her what to do. She was thinking about her thinking, which was her go-to meta thing when she couldn't think straight. So in her head now she was all: Why did they call this thing she was lying on a table? Why don't they call it a desk? Was the patient there to be eaten like food? Was medicine really about consumption? But out loud, she was: "Please, help me."

It was just Josie and this white woman in the room. The white woman wasn't wearing a white coat. The woman wasn't even a doctor exactly, but a nurse practitioner, which is always what Josie chose if she had the choice. Josie believed any woman's medical provider should be as witchy as possible, and that meant an NP would do. Her daughters—and she had three of them—saw this same woman. The woman, Nurse Misty, knew Josie. Knew Josie literally inside and out.

"Well. We caught it early. So you have lots of options." The nurse practitioner looked at Josephine and waited for a response. Josie looked back. The NP's face was unmoving. There was a game here. The nurse was a white woman. In America at that time—and before that time and now and perhaps forever more—a white woman knew when to whisper and when to holler, when to get her way and how. This white woman was using her white woman power for good: she knew what Josie wanted. And she knew she had to give it to Josie in a way that Josie could accept.

"Well. Dr. Baker. There is Mifeprex and Misoprostol.

That's the abortion pill. You have another week or so if that is how we decide to go. After that, the options narrow." The nurse practitioner looked at Josie straight between the eyes, like she was taking aim. "After that, we are looking at a D and E. Surgery. They'll put you under, so you won't feel it. We don't do that here."

Josie became more still and more quiet. Nurse Misty proffered a box of tissue, which at least got our girl Josie to move. Josie wiped her eyes, she wiped her nose. She felt great sympathy for her students now. After this day, she'll go out and buy a six-pack of tissues to keep under her desk. She's had so many white women cry in her office. Cry because Christina Sharpe made them cry. Because Hadiya Sewer made them cry. Because Claudia Rankine made them cry. Because the C- that Dr. Baker gave them made them cry. In a college classroom, Black women just seemed to make white women cry. But out in the real world, it was the other way around. Such as in this room, the real world of a medical office. Nurse Misty was making Dr. Baker cry.

"Dr. Baker?" said the nurse, insisting, Josie knew, on Josie's title because she wanted to remind Josie, remind this woman on her table, that this was *her* decision to make. And that she, Josie, was fully capable of making such a decision.

"The morning-after pill?" Josie asked now, because that was the only thing she knew about it. She was beyond the shame of admitting that she—who professed over such things as women's bodies as metaphor for landscape, and illness in girl characters as existential trial—did not know what in the hell Misoprostol was. But every twelve-year-old female American had heard of the morning-after pill. In college, Josie had marched for the right to whisper "morning-after pill" into the huge rubbery ear of a kind but grumpy pharmacist. Josie had marched in a NOW parade to fight for—what legislation? No one who was there could remember, years later. But everyone who was there remembered Josie's T-shirt; some of them even imagined they'd worn the same T-shirt, but we know that it had only been Josie. "I have had an abortion," it read. Big and bright and red like period blood on a white T-shirt, even though it wasn't true. Josie had never had an abortion, then or since. At this point in the story, she'd had three pregnancies, never had a miscarriage. She'd wanted every baby she ever had.

She'd had every baby she ever wanted.

"You're too far along for the morning-after pill," said the nurse.

Fuck. Fuck. Fuck ... fuck. Josie didn't have language, and language was her thing. Josie was feeling things that made no sense, in that they all made sense but were contradictory. She felt things such as, You can't have another baby, Josie. And, But wouldn't it be nice for you to meet this person, since he or she is already on the way? Out loud Josie said something that had no place for doubt: "I already have three children."

"You already have three children," Nurse Misty said flatly. Nurse Misty, Josie noted again, was white. And Josie was thankful for the ignorance and bliss of that whiteness. An older Black nurse here in Westchester, New York, may have called Josie "ma'am." An older Black nurse in Westchester, New York, might have made clear the thing that Josie also knew: that a married, educated woman like Dr. Baker was just the kind of Black woman Black people in America needed to be procreating. This nurse, for her part, had never forgotten that Josie was Black, which is why she kept calling her Dr.

"I'm a professor," Josie said.

"You are a professor," said the nurse, because she knew.

"I need to finish my book and get tenure."

"You need to finish your book and get tenure."

"And the last pregnancy nearly broke me."

"*Did* break you," corrected the nurse.

5.

Back Before That Even

Nurse Practitioner Misty had been there. Had held Josie's hand, had told Josie that, yes, it was going to hurt more than the previous two deliveries combined. That the epidural wouldn't get to the bone, that the anesthesia was unfortunate because now it meant Josie's legs were numb and so Josie couldn't even use them to brace herself. "Dr. Baker, the pain is going to define pain from here on," the NP had said. "But you will live." And then, "And the baby will live." The two MDs and Josie's own husband were down between Josie's legs. The nurse was up by Josie's head.

Within minutes, her husband was grinning and taking photos and cutting the cord. But first, before all that, Josie's pelvic bone had snapped in two. Stars had burst in her head like fireworks, and blood filled her mouth like she had gulped it from a lake of blood. She didn't hear her daughter's screaming, because that newborn girl didn't scream. Josie wouldn't have known either way; her own shrieks came from her chest and had nothing to do with her, except that they were all she could hear. Her husband had looked at her like she was evil, something straight from hell. Something he had to protect himself and his baby daughter from. Then he had turned from her to cut the cord.

Three months later Josie was sitting on a panty full of ice and in front of a divorce lawyer, the newborn baby nursing at her breast. Josie kept that attorney a secret between her and the baby. "I just want to get information," Josie had said to the woman across the desk. "You'll be back," said the attorney. "Most men ain't shit. And they only get worse when their wives have children."

6.
Back to: Back in the Day

Let's get back to that room. The room of nightmares. The room that Josie will return to again in her mind, in her sleep, in her prayers. "My body can't do that again," Josie said now to Nurse Misty. Josie realized she was crying again because the nurse was offering her the tissue again. This tissue wasn't the tough hospital kind. It was thick and unsanitary in its plushness. Josie took note. She would always and forever have the plush kind in her own office, for her own students.

The nurse pursed her lips. The nurse had an opinion that she herself didn't approve of, but she was a good nurse and so did not keep the information back: "Your body actually can do it again, Dr. Baker. But I would not recommend it. It is not recommended."

Which was unfortunate, we know. Because that equivocation would make it too hard and too easy for Josie. Nurse Misty could see it in Dr. Baker's face. The nurse tried again. She smiled now, which meant things were getting serious.

"Dr. Baker, how long were you in the wheelchair?"

"Just a month or so." The "just" was so ridiculous, even Josie smiled.

She'd had two small children and a newborn. Her husband, who was already senior faculty, was on paternity leave too. Their university was generous and progressive.

He was working on an article for the *Journal of the Association of Sociology Scholars* (*Journal of ASS*). Josephine was working on learning how to walk again. She would interrupt her husband's writing and thinking to ask him to put something on a plate for her, so she could eat. It was hard to make a sandwich from the wheelchair. When her favorite cousin, Denise, called to check on her, Josie said, "He is always so helpful. He makes me lunch. He brings the baby to me so I can nurse." Josie would smile at her husband with the phone in the crook of her shoulder. The baby in her arms. He would meet her eyes and smile back, as if he believed what she was saying. Then, one day when she got off the phone, he'd asked: "Do you really think you need that wheelchair? Or do you just like being able to tell your friends that I serve you?" And he hadn't been smiling.

"Dr. Baker. How long did you use the walker?" asked the nurse now. The nurse practitioner and the PhD had only been together in this room for minutes, but it felt like hours, hours, hours. Josie's new life would begin in this room. And end. The walker? The walker was still in their apartment two years later, in the closet where her husband wouldn't have to see it. Often, when he left before her, she would call her eldest daughter to pull the walker out so Josie could navigate the apartment more easily. The eldest was only nine then, but the child never told her father that she did this for her mother. Now, in this room, Josie did not answer the nurse.

"Misty. Just tell me, please. What would it be like this time?"

"Dr. Baker. Your recovery time would be longer. You would have trouble walking, maybe for years. Maybe for always. You'll be needing cortisone shots when you hit your fifties and your natural estrogen starts to drop—"

"Shots in my pussy?"

"Yes, Dr. Baker. Shots in your pubic symphysis. They help."

"Until they don't," said Josie, because Josie's mother had taken cortisone before the cancer. It helped until it didn't. And then, well, there was her mother's cancer.

"Correct, Dr. Baker. The cortisone shots won't keep the pain away forever."

"I don't want another baby." Which was the most true reason, and the one that Josie had to wait until the end to get to.

"You don't have to have another baby."

"But I have to talk with my husband."

Nurse Misty faltered for the first time. Her brows went up, and her back went straight. The nurse nodded. It was over.

7.

Back in the Day, a few weeks later

Here's the thing. Josie's husband had wanted a boy so badly. The man, let's recall, was smart and charming—won a teaching award for how besotted his students could be. His campaign for the baby was clever and cruel: He picked up his nephew "for hoops," even though he had never done that before. He went over to a male grad student's apartment to watch a sports event. Again, something he had never done. "Just guy time." That was Tuesday and Wednesday. On Thursday, during family dinner, he asked the girls if they wanted another sibling. "A brother would be cool," their second daughter said and looked at her father for approval. "Gross," said their eldest. "A brother *would* be cool," her husband said and looked at his wife. The littlest girl was little and said nothing. On Friday,

Josie's husband reinstated date night, though they'd given that up since the most recent baby was born, and walking out and about had been an uneasy thing.

Over unagi and edamame, the man made his case clear: "I know this is your decision, but it's also *our* decision," and "We can do this," though they knew, and the waiter knew, and anyone of us who has ever made it to adulthood knew, that the "we" actually meant just Josie and that no one, not even the witch Nurse Misty, really knew what might happen. They didn't know if this was even the hoped-for boy. On Saturday, Josie's husband took the girls out for ice cream with the littlest—and he never took the littlest—"Giving you some *you* time." Though all Josie did in the empty house was clean and cry. Then on Sunday, they all went to church. As they always did.

The pastor was gifted and obscenely handsome. His wife was the choir director, but the pastor controlled the all-woman choir as though they were each his own woman and they knew him intimately. The women stood and shouted and trilled and moaned based entirely on the movement of the pastor's fingers. His sermon was called "Black Life Matters," which he announced at the start, making everyone, Dr. Baker included, nod. Some of the more Pentecostal among them made loud affirming noises. Some waved their hands. The pastor repeated the phrase again and again, "Black Life Matters," winding through police brutality and school justice and prison reform, and then, finally, he began to manipulate the phrase. "Black Men Matter. Black Boys Matter. Black Babies Matter."

Dr. Baker is a literature professor, after all, so she could see where the language was going. She looked over at her husband, his guilty face locked onto the pastor. Before the pastor could say, "All Black Life Matters," Josie was getting second person with herself. Stand up, Josie, she commanded herself. Walk out, Josie. She walked out of the sanctuary as the pastor shouted to her back, "We know how hard this is for our Black mothers, we respect your choice as a woman ... but as a church community, we need our Black boys to come into this world. *They* take them out, *we* can't take them out too."

When Josie stood, her daughters followed her instinctually, but her husband stayed in the pew. "Black Unborn Life Matters!" yelled the pastor, and the choir started screaming. Josie stayed downstairs in the church's fellowship hall until it was time for church to let out. The girls ran circles around the huge open space, while Josie waited and stared into another space inside of herself. It never dawned on Josie to command herself to leave her husband there at church. That would come later.

The next day was Monday, and Josie went back to the doctor. She hadn't made an appointment, and so Nurse Misty wasn't available. "I just want to know the gender," she said, her professor voice stern. "Probably too soon to tell if it's wiener or bun," but they let a tech hook her up anyway. "Hot dog," said the tech. Josie didn't tell her husband that she would keep the baby. But he knew. He'd known all along.

Josie was in the wheelchair, again, before the baby was even born. She had the boy. And then she rolled herself into the divorce attorney's office three months after he was born. She'd left him with a nanny, because she couldn't maneuver the wheelchair and nurse him at the same time.

She would never make tenure because she would never finish her book. She would never be rid of her ex's stupid name because it was on all of her published papers—which is all she would ever have to show she earned her profession. Josephine Baker, PhD.

8.

Back to Now

So I'm still here now waiting for the part where the woman has a big Black dick in her mouth and another big Black dick in her ass. But the other man hasn't even arrived on the scene yet, and it is already fourteen minutes in. It is a long video. The boy, my boy, must have thought of the first man as a big, muscular version of himself. I wonder if it scared him when another man entered. Who would he imagine that man to be? The beautiful, sexy woman never seems to de-slick, even when she gets two dicks going at her. This is why men don't understand that it takes actual creativity to keep a woman going. I'm watching this and I'm embarrassed. But not for the reason another version of me would think. I'm embarrassed because I've never been in a threesome. Never even seen one. I'm waiting for that part because that is where the video was when I walked in on my boy.

My ex-husband had suggested that—a threesome. "As a way," he said, "to save our marriage." I mean. Men. I told him I didn't know a Black man who would do that, even though I knew my husband wasn't suggesting a threesome with another man. That would mean something for *me*, and my ex-husband never thought that way, never thought about what I might want.

And so here we are now. My own son, my baby, has discovered his own simple, stupid, selfish dick. And that women's bodies are there to selflessly take said dick. Or dicks.

And now my bedroom door is opening. "Mom," says my son's baby voice from the shadows. He is speaking numbly and flatly because that is how he gets when he is overtired. "I'm sorry, Mom," he says. "The video just popped up and I couldn't look away." He is awake even though it's tomorrow. I can't see him, but I've heard his voice begin to change, and I've been seeing him learn to change it, to manipulate his voice in order to manipulate other people. Me, especially. "Mom?"

I look at the time on the screen again and then realize that my screen is still open, and the video is still on. It hasn't gotten to the point where the second man joins them. I realize, shamefully, wantingly, that this is what I have been waiting for. I close my computer slowly so it seems like there is nothing there to see. "It's OK," I finally say to this boy, who is my boy, even though nothing is OK. The world is being sickened with a virus. My children haven't spoken to their father in weeks. They haven't seen him in months. The boy steps into my room, as if my OK is consent. And here he is. My son. The baby. "Baby" is what I used to call my husband before this boy was born.

My ten-year-old's little muscled chest is bare. He has a towel around his waist. His whole body is wet; his hair, which is fluffy because barbers are closed since covid, is dripping. He's been in the shower. I've been watching this video so intently that I hadn't even heard the shower going. The one shower in this house of six. No, not six. Five. "Fuck," I say. Which I have never before said in front of my children. I am an English professor, an adjunct, but still. I tell my children that language matters. "Fuck, fuck, fuck," I say again. My son's face is alarmed, which makes him look scared, and—to someone else, someone not his mother—scary. The medical donut I'm sitting on shifts and makes a farting noise, which makes my son smile. His face relaxes now.

"Mommy," he says, less babyish now. "I keep seeing it in my head. And now"—he points to his crotch—"my penis is so hard, it hurts."

"Stop touching it!" I say, like a curse. I look down at my computer again to make sure it's closed.

"But I'm not touching it. It's doing it all by itself." He is whining manipulatively again. Or maybe this is all just really awful and worth the whine. None of us has been within six feet of a person who doesn't live in this house for almost a month now. It's been lonely, and maybe sex is the most opposite of lonely.

Right now, I wish I was still married. I could have checked out on this long ago. Told his father that this was some boy business, so the two of you take care of it. But I am a single mother. And COVID-19 is killing people. And my family, every family in America, is quarantined for their own safety. And there is no man to come over and have a face-to-face, man-to-man with my boy. I can't even call my ex-husband; he would blame the school district and me for choosing it. And here is my son, who is only ten, discovering desire for the first time. And he is scared and ashamed. And I am too.

And it is just us here in this room.

"Let's get you a glass of milk," I say. "And then you can read a book out loud to me." I ease myself out of the bed. The donut farts and farts, and we snicker together. I take my tiny geisha steps to the kitchen.

My son pours us each a glass, because, yes, he is ten, but

he is thoughtful. I look through the freezer for the frozen chocolate cake I bought weeks ago. I push aside frozen fish fingers and frozen peas and frozen broccoli. I can't find that chocolate cake, or any chocolate cake, though I can see the rich, black color in my mind. I give up looking for it but can't stop wanting it. Instead, I find us something to read.

My son and I meet back in my bedroom. I've found a graphic novel for ages eight to twelve. Pictures, but not porn—perfect. We've read it before, but the jokes still land. My son laughs until he forgets his near-pubescent body. He snorts milk through his nose. His body is a boy's body, and at this moment, his body has nothing to do with sex. His body is about laughter and milk snort. I yelp, but I don't care that he gets milk all over my sheets. "Sshhh!" we both say to each other and then cover our mouths. We hear one of the girls tossing in the room next door. I take over the reading, and we read the book until the book is almost done. I don't finish because he's fallen asleep, his warm body against mine, a milk mustache on his innocent face. I look at him for a while. I feel in love.

The donut beneath my butt is flaccid, the air gone from it. I tug myself off the bed. I put my arms beneath my boy's body. I brace myself. Then I lift him.

My physiatrist says I should not be carrying anything heavier than a textbook, and my son—my baby—he is tall and strong for his age. But I am still taller and stronger. When I lift him, I feel the lightning of pain from my groin to my ass and hips, like someone scraped a knife from one crack to the other. I lurch but I don't drop my boy. My mouth fills with spit, and it tastes thick with milk. I think of the chocolate cake, and I remember that I had never bought a chocolate cake at all. I say in my mind, Josie, this is the last time you will carry your boy. He is too old for this. You are too broken for this. I want to cry, commanding myself this way. But instead, I say, "Don't cry, Josie," out loud, though in a whisper. I think of the ice on my pubic bone.

I carry my boy down the hallway, taking my steps easy so the pain doesn't shoot, just sits. He is so limp and so heavy in sleep. The bedroom door is open. In the darkness of his room, I stand over his bed and wonder how I am going to lower him down. How am I going to lean over and not drop him and not break myself? It's me or him.

But I'm a mother, and so of course I choose to not wake him. Ice after, I say into the room of my mind. The image of the ice is delicious. I slowly lean over the bed.

I am doing this so slowly; so slowly I can feel my muscles shivering. I feel hot. I feel sweat. I bend my knees, lean my butt back—but still the pain.

When my boy's head finally kisses the pillow, my legs buckle, but I manage to get him gently onto the mattress before I sink to my knees. The pain in my pubis is now also in my armpits, and in my ass crack, and in that little dip at the back of my skull, but I don't make a sound. I stay there, kneeling, for a few minutes, waiting for the floor to stop spinning. Waiting for the feeling that I just broke my body to stop being the primary feeling. I listen to the girls' sleeping breaths from around the room, because they all four share this room. Because I can't afford a three bedroom in this school district. I try to still the space between my legs, the space where I made these children, but it feels like someone touched a torch to me there, and I am still on fire. I think of the walker in my closet. I need it, but it's where I need to go, back in my bedroom. I think of ice, and my mouth wets.

"Josie," I have asked myself many times before, "do you regret your boy?" No, I don't regret my child. I would die for this boy, easily. This boy has almost killed me already, and still, I would choose him over me again and again. "But,

Josie," I have asked myself, "do you regret keeping the pregnancy that turned out to bear this boy?" Yes. Absolutely. "Do you regret marrying his father?" Yes, Josie, I do. Every day. The regret is even in my dreams. "And, Josie, if you could go back in time and choose to never marry their father, would you have chosen against that man, even though it would mean never having had *these* children, Josie, your children?" Yes, Josie. I want another version of my life. One where I have just two children. Or maybe just three. I want tenure at a respectable institution. I want my dissertation turned into a book. Don't we all know, girl. "We know that what you really want, Josie, is a husband who loved you enough to choose your body over this boy's body." Yes. And also, I want ice.

My mouth waters. Yes, I want ice so badly. And so I start to stand. Carefully, so carefully. When I stand, I look down at my baby boy, and I see that he is awake. Wide awake. He'd never been asleep at all. His eyes are open, staring, wanting all of me just for himself. Josie? Josie?

CLIMATE PRIMER FOR BABIES

BY DEBORAH LANDAU

1. *A melt in the cryosphere*
Reincarnation appeals to babies.
They might come back thousands of years after
the trash and plunder
(such *tristesse*!)
to feel our great regret.
The babies are singing to keep it from happening.
They think there's a way outta here.
Evening comes on.

2. *Acid oceans*

Dear babies, we're sorry.

Some curse we brought upon yourselves.

The lake dried up we find less and less shade

for your days yet still sperm forth.

Fish in shortish supply plums in short supply—air.

From womb to tomb to womb in loop-the-loop, and how
    we clung to it.

Milk for everyone meat for everyone gas for everyone
    water and heat and air

the planet grown dystopian crepuscular—

and why did we prick forth a child.

3. *Wildfires*

If we'd known the fate of babies would we have moth-
    ered them?

It's cringeworthy.

Babies, we're ashamed. What the fuck.

Day then night, then another blazing irradiated day.

The roly-poly babies grow frantic.

In their eyes you can see they might be giving up.

They're writing our postscript.

This is not what they'd been promised.

Ah! They start to cry.

4. *Smog*
Another smoky morning. Are we all that matters?
This has gone too far.
We fucked up the curriculum
and now the babies will pay
> *damned the planet they'll inherit*
> *damned the planet they'll*
> *damned the planet*
> *damned*

They wait in our apocalypse box.
There's no way out.

5. *Hostile habitats*
What good are father and mother now?
We can mr and mrs all night but the comfort is slight.
We try to sleep but don't have much expertise at it,
crushed in bed we search each other
for some alternative, swelling for a while
with the plumpest most syrupy distraction
until there's some marveling at the world, the stroke and
    colors of it.

Such flush intensifies the reddened place we make our
    days.
In our blazing hands break all the apple trees.

6. *Weeds, diseases, pests*
These are the babies of mourning.
Levity as a liquor of sorts a songbird in the hedge
    blooming
calm of vanilla entering the bloodstream lithing down
    the ribs.
A boom on the skyline and the babies are in a rhythmic
    kind
of extinction—above the city an illumination.
Meanwhile at crib level at the height of their height they
    are still
amusing themselves with a groove and a hoot
their bodies a sampling a song more and more unfun
yet with a spunk for living still they are hungry
and we are three times a day.

7. *Mass extinctions*
We couldn't master ourselves.
We kept asking for it, asking for it—

the climate emergent and feral following its own
    chemistry
our chemistry was anxiety our prison self-inflicted
the city stops the day fills with cups and cups of smoke
we knew it was coming knew it would come
a library of irradiated air flooding aglow
and strolling velvets us all onward into summer fire.

---

3 Note: *Heading titles are taken from* "How Climate Change Plunders the Planet," Environmental Defense Fund, https://www.edf.org/climate/how-climate-change-plunders-planet.

SCARLET LETTER

BY SARAH GERARD

MY HUSBAND WAS UNEMPLOYED, and I'd been working for two months at a magazine where I stared into a computer screen all day for a near-minimum-wage salary. I confirmed I was pregnant in the bathroom of The Grey Dog on Mulberry Street, the day after I found out my first book would be published, after months of rejection. I was twenty-eight.

I'd been married three tumultuous years. I was dreaming of an exit I wouldn't find for another three. Our marriage from the start was ill conceived—we were young and impulsive. We were living in a tiny studio apartment the size of a prison cell. We called my parents from my husband's car, parked across the street from our marriage counselor's office, to ask them for five hundred dollars.

I called in sick the day I took the second pill. I'd taken the first one the day before and had carried my dead fetus for twenty-four hours. I lay crying in the bathtub with my husband, blood snaking through the water around us, dying it pink, waves breaking through my abdomen.

My grief seemed to stand in opposition to my politics. It was dark and overwhelming, my uterus a cavern. I bled for weeks. I was alone in my body, preoccupied with my perceived debt to my mother's generation for the sacrifices and stands they'd made that had won me freedom from unplanned parenthood. Admitting I was in pain was an unspeakable secret, something I could never reveal, even to myself.

The persistent cultural stigma around reproductive freedom denied me the right to grieve properly, so my anger and sorrow spilled out everywhere. Each successive failure to write about it only underlined its banality. I shoehorned it into the first paragraph of a book review, only to have the editor who had solicited me turn it down. "I had an abortion too," she told me, "but it's really nobody's business."

I'd hoped to give my trauma at least some use. I grappled with the undramatic nature of it: I had not been raped, I was not a teenager, I was not homeless, I was not even single. At the time, I believed that I needed a justification. I don't. Neither do you. I was forced to admit that my story was unremarkable—as it should be.

I have never wanted to be pregnant. Some women find the experience of bodily transformation fascinating; I do not. I felt as if my body had been stolen from me. I've had a conflicted relationship with my body since childhood; I struggle with gender and food. It's taken me a long time to learn to nourish rather than to punish, to understand my body's needs and prioritize them. For these reasons, and others ethical and political, I would prefer to, and I will, become a parent through other means.

It's my choice. I don't need to tell you an abortion was right for me; it's right for one in four American women. I don't need to tell you what happens to women who are denied the right to a safe abortion, or what happens to their children—how often they fall through the cracks of a fractured system, how they suffer—how we, spiritually, as a human race, suffer with them—or how easy it is to find the data of desperation that follows unplanned pregnancies in the public costs of unemployment, government assistance, emergency room visits, domestic violence, hunger, and foster care. I don't need to tell you that the rate of abortions drops with greater access to contraception. That, if I'd had access years ago, I wouldn't be writing this. I don't need to convince you.

CHRISTIANS IN THE CATACOMBS

BY KIRSTIN VALDEZ QUADE

SOMETIMES, EVEN FIVE YEARS later, after all that happened, Lauren dreams that she is back in Cavalry Youth Group, playing Bible games. Regardless of how uneventful these dreams are—and they're almost always uneventful, with an intense dream-focus on logistics and turn-taking—Lauren wakes in the dark with her heart pounding. Tonight, in the dream, they are playing Biblical Charades, and Lauren is watching Shannon Williams enact something incomprehensible, waving her arms like an octopus. Lauren is trying to concentrate, when her eyes fly open.

Terror courses through her, and she listens in the dark, wondering if whatever woke her was inside or outside the dream. The apartment is quiet. In the vents, the air conditioner labors. Lauren switches on the bedside lamp, listens hard for a noise from the hall, switches off the lamp. Still, she has a sense of a malicious presence breathing in the room. She wraps the blanket tightly around her, despite the fact that it is too hot. Her heart thrashes, the blood loud in her ear.

In life, the games were an embarrassing affair. There was the self-conscious reluctance to participate, countered by the reluctance to let down sad, goofy, enthusiastic Pastor Kevin, and then there was always the moment at the end, when Pastor Kevin gave his earnest, long-winded explanation of the lesson behind whatever stupid game they'd been forced to play. Christians in the Catacombs, for example, was just Sardines, but it was a lesson in Christian persecution, which was a big thing even today. They had to learn about how in the olden times the Christians all crammed into the grave niches in the catacombs to hide from the Romans and, what, slept there? Like Japanese businessmen in those capsule hotels? Lauren thought it was gross, pretending to sleep among dead people, but she did enjoy folding herself into the utility closet beside Chris Macomb. They barely had a chance to whisper *hello* before geeky Sam Pinto found them and squeezed in, too, plucking at his braces in the dark. Lauren could smell Chris Macomb's powerful deodorant, and she felt his leg against her own.

Bible Verse Pictograms, Balloons of Faith, sometimes just plain old tag. The game Lauren liked best was Guess the Baby, which wasn't actually a game and just happened once, when everyone brought in a baby picture, and Pastor Kevin stuck them on the wall, and you had to guess who was who. The lesson was about how a person can grow closer to Jesus over time. Lauren enjoyed these glimpses into people's pasts, into their home lives, liked seeing whose mothers dressed them like little Edwardian lords and whose mothers photographed them drool-bellied in saggy diapers. Lauren had chosen the picture her mother kept on her bureau, when she was a fat-cheeked one-year-old gazing seriously out from under the big bow stuck atop her bald head.

"You're cute," Chris Macomb said, tapping the bow.

"Thanks," said Lauren. She pointed to the big-headed blond toddler in a baseball jersey. "You too." Even as a baby, his dimples were as deep as the tufting on a couch.

She didn't have a crush on Chris Macomb per se— all things considered, she was more into Patrick Diaz at school, who was a senior on the soccer team and whose calves she couldn't help staring at. But she thought Chris Macomb might like her, and she liked that. Pastor Kevin, hovering, cast Lauren a warm smile, telegraphing his approval, and Lauren blushed.

Back then, at sixteen, Lauren was a good girl. A good enough girl. She went to church with her parents and little sisters, attended youth group each Wednesday night. At the snack table, she almost always skipped the Safeway cookies and stuck to Diet Coke and carrot sticks. If temptation was especially strong, she had her cinnamon gum. Her grades were high, she ran track—she was especially good at the 400 meter—she volunteered every Tuesday afternoon to read with third graders at a poor school in South Tucson. She loved her tutoring job, loved little Jackson, who, every few minutes would stand and announce, "Time for the wiggle dance!" and shake himself vigorously, then sit, ready once again to frown at the words. She planned to go to community college first, then transfer to the U of A. She'd major in elementary education and help other little kids find strategies to make their way through the school day.

She definitely had her crap together, but that didn't mean she was uptight. She posted sexy selfies, blowing kisses at the mirror, one tank top strap slipping down a shoulder; she went to parties in the foothills and demurred when offered weed or cigarettes. She'd had a boyfriend the year before, and she'd given him hand jobs and let herself be fingered.

One evening, after a rousing game of In the Lion's Den, Chris Macomb placed a plastic cup of Diet Coke on Lauren's desk, then nudged her, indicating her journaling Bible with his chin. "Nice," he said. She shrugged. She was proud of her work: her tidy, cheerful handwriting, which could be its own font, her doodles and painstakingly drawn borders. She never used a highlighter, but instead underlined passages with a ruler and a gel pen, according to a color-coded system. Chris's own Bible was filled with blank margins, except for a few notes scrawled in ballpoint when Pastor Kevin put things on the board to copy down.

Chris tapped the page, where she'd written Psalm 119:105 in an outline of a lightbulb, with gold wavering lines emanating from the words. *Your word is a lamp to guide my feet and a light for my path.* She loved those words, had also copied them out on a piece of cardstock she stuck over her desk. It filled her with calm, the idea that a word could be a lamp guiding her on, and all she had to do was attend and follow that bobbing light through the dark. She'd thought, then, that that lamp would always be there, urging her along. "That must've taken a long time," Chris Macomb said. "What do you do if you mess up? Like, do you ever spell something wrong?"

Lauren's face heated with the pleasure of his attention. "Usually I trace it in pencil first, but not always."

She set her mouth carefully. Lauren was the kind of person for whom looking hot was within the realm of possibility but also a major effort. She had to watch how she smiled, because if she smiled big, too much of her gums showed. Her hair was thin and not blond enough. She rinsed it with lemon juice and chamomile, blew it out, sprayed it to give it volume and shine. She almost wished she was less attractive, like Shannon Williams, because then she could just give up and not worry about it.

"Do you want to go see *Frozen IV* with me?" he asked then, and she said yes, even though she wasn't that interested in him, because she thought it was cute. After all, he was a good guy, liked by teachers and parents and Pastor Kevin. His voice wavered when it was his turn to say what made him blessed, and he always said something sweet, like, "I'm blessed to have such a loving cat." And how many guys wanted to see *Frozen IV*? He paid for her ticket and her Diet Coke and her popcorn (no butter).

After, in the movie theater parking lot, the lights of the mall dim behind them, he'd opened the back door. "Get in," he urged, with those deep dimples, and she'd tipped her head, giggled uncertainly, aware of how she must look to him. She wished she'd reapplied gloss; her lips were dry and stinging a bit from the salt in the popcorn.

She'd been fine with the kissing—into it, even—and didn't mind when he unhooked her bra beneath her shirt. She didn't love when he kneaded her breasts so hard and was almost relieved when he left them alone to work his hand into the waistband of her jeans. She was more surprised when he yanked them down without unzipping them, the denim scraping her hips.

"Thank you for the movie," she said after, when he pulled up in front of her house, and she slid out of the car with relief. She wished he'd drive away, but he waited for her to unlock her front door and go inside.

Lauren watched herself in the mirror on the bathroom door from her perch on the toilet as she gently dabbed between her legs. Her mascara had blurred around her eyes. Her face looked patchy and pale. The pimple on her chin had swelled instead of settling, and foundation was caked around it, dry and cracked. If she held her own gaze, though, she steadied herself, and she didn't think about the thin, bright blood between her legs, which was less than she'd expected. It hurt down there, and so did her throat. "You like this," Chris Macomb had said, and though she kicked and wriggled at first, once he leaned into her windpipe, she stopped struggling and just began to pray.

On television, girls went to the police, and then an investigation began, and the girls were ridiculed at school and online and more often than not they killed themselves, leaving behind a note that broke everyone's hearts.

The missed period wasn't a concern, not at first. She was never regular, and even less during track season. But three weeks passed, then six, and once the fear popped into her mind, the knowledge was lodged in its entirety.

There were no legal abortions anymore, not in Arizona, a change that Lauren herself played a part in, with all her

Right to Life campaigning, the picketing outside clinics. Her signs are still in her parents' basement, with the pictures of bloodied babies ripped with hooks from wombs.

She'd heard, of course, about coat hangers. But the coat hangers in her house were plastic, except two, which were wood. She took a wooden spoon from the snowman canister on the counter that her mother made in a tole-painting class, and, back in her bedroom, inserted it experimentally into her vagina. But the handle was only an inch or so deep before she stopped, heart pounding. She was afraid of Hell, yes, but also afraid of the pain and blood. And what if the baby came out mangled and crying? What would Lauren do then? She extracted the spoon, dragged up her underwear and yoga pants, lay panting on the carpet. The spoon was discolored, stained from some long-ago tomato sauce, and it smelled like garlic. Lauren sat up and vomited into the trash can by her desk.

The pregnancy was hard: she was nauseated well into the third trimester. She remembered her biology class, learning that the baby functions as a kind of parasite, leaching the nutrients from the bloodstream, the minerals from the bone. Soon she felt him move in her, this baby, this person, this soul rammed into her by Chris Macomb.

When she told Chris Macomb, in the parking lot after the last youth group meeting she'd ever attend, he said, "Sucks," but he looked so entirely blanched and terrified that she almost pitied him. She'd been afraid that he might apologize and beg her forgiveness. She'd been afraid he'd insist on marrying her. But his terror calmed her, and she turned away, feeling competent, adult, superior.

"How could you do this to yourself?" her mother asked, her eyes shining with tears. "What about college? Marriage? You had so much going for you." Seeing her mother's distress, Lauren couldn't tell her how it had happened. She said simply that the father wasn't going to be involved, and her mother swallowed and nodded. Her parents helped her, though, helped her find an apartment and to arrange for day care, and Lauren graduated from high school and found a job as a receptionist at a day spa on Speedway.

Now Nathan is four years old. His face has narrowed from the face of a baby into the face of a child. Nathan resembles the picture on the classroom wall when they played Guess the Baby: the same curly sandy hair and brown eyes, the same deep dimples, but he doesn't smile much.

Lauren has, mostly, grown out of the little cruelties. When he was a baby, for example, she might take away the bottle before he was done. Or scrub his bottom too harshly. Or wait to pick him up when he cried for her, distressed. *Go away, go away,* she'd chant quietly as she held him, and he sucked industriously at his bottle, gazing calmly up into her face.

She no longer fantasizes about leaving him—in the car on the hot day, behind a scalding dumpster—but in the beginning, the fantasies were so constant that she, in essence, inoculated herself from ever actually accidentally leaving him. She cannot love this child, but she loves him anyway.

At school, apparently, Nathan has antics: impersonations of elephants, funny voices he pulls out. "Oh, he's a real ham," one of the preschool teachers tells her, and Lauren doesn't know what she means. He's not a ham at home. At home he's serious and considerate, bringing her pictures he's drawn of the two of them standing together outside various structures: houses and castles and tree forts. Always, the two of them are holding hands and Lauren is smiling hugely. He must have heard about breakfast in bed at school—from a picture book?—because for a week he brings her crackers and apples on a tray in the morning, until she tells him not to.

Each time he performs one of these little services, she thanks him and makes herself hug him, but it's creepy, isn't it? A kid being so solicitous? She can't help but think of Chris Macomb bringing her cups of soda at youth group. "You like Diet, right?"

Yesterday, when she went to pick up Nathan from day care, she watched him chase a girl across the playground. The girl fell, and Nathan skidded to a stop beside her, lunged down. He stretched over the girl, their bodies close, and bile rose in Lauren's throat.

Then he extended his hand, pulled the girl up. "It's OK," he said, inspecting the sand pressed into her knees, brushing them off gently. He peered at the sand that came off into his hand.

Lauren gripped the monkey bars. How could she think she could pursue elementary education? She thought sourly of little Jackson and his wiggle dance.

Sometimes, in the dream, Nathan is there with her at Cavalry Youth Group. They are playing Christians in the Catacombs. She and Nathan are hiding in the utility closet, which is also the linen closet at her parents' house.

Outside, steps are coming closer, and the smell of death is thick around them. She tries to push him beneath the pillows to save him from the Romans, and she knows she is pushing the pillow too hard into his face. But each time Nathan slips out and eyes her grimly. "Here I am," he says.

But this is not the dream that woke her tonight. Tonight, the dream that woke her was Biblical Charades. Nothing scary happened, nothing happened at all, just Shannon Williams waving her arms wildly around her head. Burning bush?

Lauren plumps her pillow, moves to the cooler side of the bed, and arranges herself beneath the sheet. She closes her eyes and breathes slowly, counting in and out.

Her mind is still alert; if there was a sound to hear, she'd hear it. But there is nothing, except, perhaps, the faintest shift in the pressure of the air. She opens her eyes.

Her son is standing above her, his pale face looming over her in the dark.

Lauren opens her mouth to scream but can't, as if a hand were on her windpipe, and the scream dilates inside her.

"Mommy," he whispers. "I need you."

WE BLED ALL WINTER

BY SHELLY ORIA

I

WE BLED THAT WHOLE winter. I fell in the snow once, carrying groceries, and when I rose I watched the white beneath me swallow up some red, making a light pink stain. You could see sprinkles of street dirt if you looked hard. It was beautiful in the way anything can be beautiful.

My girlfriend hacked the neighbors' internet searching for answers. How much bleeding was normal when terminating a pregnancy—I didn't listen well when we left the clinic, but more than a few days seemed excessive— and was there any precedent to her sympathy bleeding?

"Sympathy bleeding" was what we called it, what we guessed was happening. The internet said what the internet always said: most likely we both had cancer. When Jasmin returned from the backyard—leaning against the fence, we could often catch the stolen signal—she seemed exhausted. *It's over*, she said, *we're dying*. She was joking, but I could see the fear. I chuckled, to remind her we were fierce. *Oh*, she said, *also we should see our doctor right away*. The internet always assumed everyone had a doctor.

I appreciated my girlfriend's blood at first, this physical proof of her worry, then resented it because it felt like her body was mimicking mine. Maybe I just wanted sole ownership of my one trauma; back home, where my girlfriend's people are oppressed by mine, my girlfriend suffered multiple unfathomable traumas. She watched military bulldozers mangle her Nablus childhood home, then grind the parts down to dust and debris, and she told that story like it was nothing, because there was so much worse. She didn't share those horrors with me often, but sometimes she tried. I never knew how to love her right in those moments.

Some days that winter, the blood felt contained, subtle, an afterthought. On those days we pretended nothing was wrong. Other days we'd wake to soaked bedsheets, color anything that hosted our lower bodies for more than a moment. I'd put a soft hand over my girlfriend's because her face looked like she was ready to take some sort of action; I feared the moment when she'd try and fail. She felt protective, and responsible for getting me here—she came first, found a restaurant that would hire us both off books, asked me to join—so I knew she'd do anything. A willingness to do anything when nothing is possible can be dangerous. This was a country preoccupied with the notion of citizenship, a country in which health was costly and the cost of money high. I knew these things only from watching movies and the news, but my girlfriend had lived here before; she warned me that we would be on the wrong side of so much, on the wrong side of safety. I heard what she never said too: she was used to hardship, but I might crumble. My hand on her hand was saying I wasn't crumbling. It was saying, "Let's wait it out. The bleeding may still get better. It may one day pass."

Despite the freezing cold, my girlfriend would spend stretches of time in the backyard asking the internet all our questions, because our phones were shit and hardly worked inside. Or our plan was shit, because we were broke, and reception was shit, because we had to leave the city when we quit our job; here in the boonies we could crash for free, but there weren't many cell towers. (*We're not in the boonies*, my girlfriend would say, half amused, half annoyed; *there are houses on both sides of this house.* My girlfriend often corrected me about terms people used in this country. *Then what do you call it when there's more trees than people and you can't get online?* I'd ask. *A sign that you've taken some wrong turns*, my girlfriend would say.) She'd come back to me with answers to random questions, with guesses as to what might be going on with our bodies, with tips for our situation. *Meat!* she declared once; *balancing our hemoglobin levels is key.*

One thing I learned that winter is that everything I'd thought about blood was wrong. Bleeding is strength. A bleeding body is a strong body: it is unafraid to give itself to the earth. It is unafraid to grow frail. There is no greater strength than the lack of fear at the prospect of weakness.

Before that winter, I never considered myself strong. I considered my girlfriend strong, maybe the strongest person I'd ever met. And when, soon after I arrived in this country, things got tense at the restaurant where we worked, because she and Ohad, the owner, openly disliked each other, I thought the tension could be explained by their shared exceptional strength; in my experience, remarkably strong people rarely got along. *You don't mean strong, you mean charismatic*, Jasmin said when I tried to sell her on this theory. *No no no*, I said, mostly because the conversation suddenly felt like a trap; if I admitted I found Ohad charismatic, some questions might follow. It took me a while, likely longer than it should have, to face the real reason for this trouble: the attention Ohad was paying me.

When my girlfriend's cousin—whose basement we were staying in—learned about our situation, he began checking on us every few days, though we all knew that really he was only checking up on Jasmin. He wouldn't come in, always talked to us from the doorstep; I suspected he wanted to keep his distance from me. So when Jasmin was out getting his car oil changed and he knocked on our door, I assumed it was some kind of mix-up. But when I opened, he came in, sat down at the kitchen table—our basement was its own small apartment—and gestured for me to do the same. When he mentioned Ohad's name my face must have lost some of its color, which had a yellow hue these days to begin with; he moved a glass of water that was on the table in my direction. When I did nothing he said *Drink* in a way that told me no matter how bad or frail I looked, we were having this conversation. Apparently, because we were hard to reach, Ohad had been writing to me and getting no response; he ended up tracking down and calling my girlfriend's cousin, who, because he was smart and knew he should update me on this in private, was tasked with curating a situation in which my girlfriend would be absent. We sold sandwiches at a local shop in the mornings, but other than that we rarely left the house.

This Ohad is your boss, he said, *yours and Sabrin's?* No one ever called my girlfriend Sabrin except her family. *Yes*, I said, *former boss. He thinks you are carrying his child*, he said. *Yes*, I said. *He is married?* he said, and I couldn't tell if it was in fact another question, but I nodded. *You must tell him*, he said, and I was quiet, because I didn't want to tell Ohad anything. I'd told him too much already. But I never said I was keeping the baby; that assumption was a choice he made. There's a difference between lying to someone and letting them believe a lie. *Does Sabrin know about this ... connection?* the cousin asked. *Yes*, I said. (And no, I thought.) Anyone in the history of people talking to each other who gave a straightforward answer to a loaded question was lying. *OK*, he said, *good*. I looked at the floor to avoid his eyes because I didn't agree that anything about this was good. I could feel him searching for my eyes. Finally he said, *You know we can't have trouble, yes?* And here I looked up because he was our host and he was trying to make sure I wouldn't put him at risk. I said, *Of course*. He said, *This man, I know this kind of man*. I understood what he meant: Ohad was someone used to getting his way in life. Whatever he needed that made him call, he wouldn't go away until his need was satisfied.

What my girlfriend's cousin meant by *trouble* was that he faced imprisonment or even death on the other side of the ocean; he could never risk giving someone like Ohad reason to make a call and report us. And while for me and my girlfriend, something like, say, a trip to the emergency room could end in a detention center, the real danger in that for us was losing each other. Back home, politics and our families and decades of conflict and oppression meant that we could never be together. I was the most likely to avoid deportation—I had the fairest skin and better paperwork—and maybe that's why I thought the loss of our love was the greatest danger, because I was advantaged not only in this way but also in terms of the reality that awaited me overseas. My girlfriend and I both repeated our line many times—our greatest risk was losing our relationship—but perhaps this was a half-truth. Perhaps she never wanted to name her misfortune or my privilege. Perhaps we both clung, each for her reasons, to this semblance of equality afforded us as foreigners in this country. In the kitchen, when my girlfriend's cousin held my eye, he was forcing me to admit this half-truth. *I understand*, I said. *I will talk to him.* I looked at my feet. *You can use the landline upstairs*, he said. I felt my eyes welling up at this kindness, though it's possible this was his way of making sure I called. Still, he was the only family member of my girlfriend's who I'd ever met, maybe the only one I'd ever meet, and I felt in that moment that he was choosing to see me as his own blood instead of someone whose people oppressed his people. *Thank you*, I said, and heard the emotion in my own voice, which embarrassed me. Neither of us moved or said anything for a moment, and it suddenly occurred to me he might mean for us to head upstairs now. *I'll talk to Jas first*, I said. He nodded but I still corrected myself. *Sabrin*.

*   *   *

When my girlfriend returned, she made some joke about her cousin babying his car—the last oil change hadn't been too long ago—and when I said *yeah* she squinted her whole face at me, because my girlfriend's intuition was her superpower. *Something happen?* she asked. I needed a minute—a day, a week, a lifetime—to think things through before we talked, but I wasn't going to get that time. I felt scared, the kind of fear that alters your body temperature. My fear was: I'd mention Ohad's name and my girlfriend's blood would boil and she wouldn't listen, wouldn't hear me. My fear was: I'd mention Ohad's name and my girlfriend would listen too well, would hear and see not so much what I was sharing, but what I was hiding. My fear was that my girlfriend would leave me.

You could say that I slept with my boss; in most ways that matter, you'd not be wrong. You could say that I flirted with him first—teased him, as he said that night, *You've been teasing me for months, now suddenly you're a deer in headlights?*—and you could say that I let my attraction to him live in me and that at times it showed. It drove Jasmin mad, but she never confronted me. A cultural difference?

I'd have yelled, thrown plates at the walls of our city apartment. But she did nothing; "you mean he's charismatic" was as close as she got to a confrontation that whole time. You could say that I cheated on my girlfriend; you could say to me: whatever happened the night you got pregnant, whatever you claim Ohad did to you, you still cheated on Jasmin with him, several times, weeks before that night. You'd not be wrong, or not exactly wrong, by which I mean that's what Jasmin would've said if she'd known everything. But all she knew was the night of the assault, not the nights that came before, and anyway I'd never dare say to her face that those nights hadn't been sex, because that is some straight-people bullshit. One thing about lesbian sex is that it redefines pleasure, and in redefining pleasure, it robs you of the simplistic hetero line between touch and sex. So if you described the closeness during shifts— soft palm lingering on a shoulder, just making sure the other person heard that table five asked for their check; fingers touching fingers, just pointing to an appetizer's code on a screen—and how those touches between Ohad and me intensified slowly but also fast, if you described how he shoved his tongue into my mouth one night and I nearly gagged, the smell of sardines in my nose and my butt pushed against the spare fridge in the back, and if you then described how I did the same to him the next night, pushed something into his face that you could call my tongue but I would call violence, and he let me, and he was soft with me then while I remained hard. If you described how I came that night, how Ohad made me come—or maybe it's more accurate to say I used a man's knee to make myself come and it just so happened his name was Ohad and he was my boss—if you described it, and how the smell of sardines felt different then, the way a strong orgasm can alter your sensory field. If you described all that a hundred times, if you yelled and screamed, if you looked at me with pain, disappointment, disgust—do you really imagine you'd be doing anything to me that I've not been doing to myself? What I've realized is that I don't know how to measure betrayal. I meant for less of it and ended up with more. In men's brains there's a chronology of progression to touch; Ohad came to work that night— our first overlap since I rubbed myself against his knee— knowing what would happen at the end of the shift. And because there was no question in his mind, he asked me nothing. He pulled up my skirt, pulled down my panties, put himself into me, somehow all in one shocking motion.

It didn't feel like another body had entered mine; it felt like a brick was shoved into me and broke my insides. I don't think I said no or stop; I didn't say anything, I don't think, and I didn't move.

I shook him off of me in the end, after he was done. That moment haunts me, the motion my muscles proved capable of after all.

This was all on my face now, which I knew because I could see Jasmin's angst, a particular kind of worry she'd developed for me in recent weeks. We were sitting on the bed but far enough from each other that she could lean in my direction and still not reach me. *Hey*, she said, her upper body bent toward me, her eyes trying to meet mine. *Flashbacks?* I nodded. *He called*, I said, and her face froze. *Who called?* she asked though she knew, and I didn't want to say his name so I just waited. *Why would he*—she started to ask and I said, *Jas, before we left the city I told him I was pregnant. I'm sorry I kept this from you.* I felt very light, saying these nothing words, and I could feel my body wanting to leave my body, to levitate and watch these two women from above. Are they going to have the kind of fight that changes what they see when they look at each other? I moved to the edge of the bed so I could feel the floor under my feet. Jasmin was asking questions like When did this happen? and I told her the truth—when I went to get our last paychecks, which I was supposed to get from our friend a block away from the restaurant, but our friend was late. Or maybe I was early. Jasmin frowned at this. But how could I explain to her: back then my brain kept suggesting that in fact nothing bad had happened, that the way I described that night to Jasmin had been an exaggeration, a lie I told so my girlfriend wouldn't say I cheated. What's the big deal, to that girl, in going to the restaurant? If he'd be there, then he'd be there. And he was there, of course. His eyes widened at the sight of me at the door; immediately he gave a quick look around and signaled for me to follow him to the back. And I did. I followed him to that small room. I followed him although my legs started shaking, making their point that this was a bad idea. I think he asked why we quit and I made a face. He said something like *She pissed?* because what he thought had happened was that I told Jasmin he and I hooked up and she flipped. My life through his eyes was a whole other life. And maybe that's why I needed to say that none of this was chill, to say You harmed me, to say Harm has consequences, motherfucker. So I said, *Ohad, I'm pregnant.*

On the bed now, I could see my girlfriend's face working to accept my choices, to swallow her anger. *I'm going to call from upstairs tomorrow*, I said. *You don't owe him an update*, she said, her jaw so clenched the air of her words was struggling to come out, *you don't owe him shit. It's what your cousin wants me to do*, I said, which was the truth but still felt like a lie. *Fine*, Jasmin said and got up, about to leave the room. I grabbed her hand. *Jas*, I said. *I just need a minute*, she said.

On the phone Ohad's voice sounded familiar but warm, concerned, an uncle version of the man I knew. I didn't focus on my feet; I didn't will my body to stay in my body. It took me a while to tell him I was no longer pregnant and in that time I learned the reason for the call. The reason for the call was that Ohad wanted me to give him the child—instead of giving it up for adoption, which is what he believed I was doing. *Is that crazy*, he asked, *am I crazy?* He never waited for me to answer. He talked about his wife a lot—she was an activist, an environmentalist. I vaguely knew these things but said nothing; I'm not sure I even hmmed, but Ohad was never the kind of man who needed the sound of his own voice reinforced. Bringing a child into our ailing world, he explained, stood against everything his wife believed in—the surplus of human life was already in the billions, more than our planet could withstand, all that. *But this*, he said, *this is different. This baby is already on its way. It's my only chance at a biological child in this life*. He actually thought I'd feel bad for him—I could hear the expectation in his voice. And maybe I did feel bad, guilty, even. I've known men like him my whole life; they believe so honestly in their entitlement, it's near impossible to talk to them without believing it too. Eventually I couldn't handle the sales pitch—he and his wife would take care of all expenses, set us back up in the city, Jasmin and I could be involved in the child's life if we wished—and I said, *There's no baby, Ohad*. The silence that followed felt explosive. I heard myself say *I lost it* and another silence followed. Then he began to cry.

When I came back down Jasmin was in the kitchen and everything smelled like fried onion and sumac. *How'd it go?* she asked with her back to me, cooking. *Fine?* I said. *Tell me,* she said. Her voice was cheerful. Everything felt wrong but I understood we were pretending this was no big deal and I wanted to contribute. *Not much to tell*, I said. *Now he knows*. I shrugged, though she couldn't see. *Took a while, though*, my girlfriend said. I shrugged again. *I got into the whole fake clinic story,* I said, which was true—at the end of our call I told Ohad the story of how Jasmin and I made an appointment first with an abortion clinic that turned out to be a creepy anti-abortion center. They read to us from the bible and kept referring to us as friends no matter what we said. It probably took us longer than it should have to realize we were in the wrong place—across the street from the actual clinic, in a building that looked identical. I'd told Ohad this story like a funny anecdote. I mentioned their sign, which read "Plan Your Parenthood." *Why would you tell him that story?* Jasmin asked, and she turned around then with such sharpness that she knocked a jar of olive oil off the counter. It shattered with a spectacular sound, the promise of tiny shards for weeks. I got up to help her clean but Jasmin's arm stretched out to stop me, and I paused, still by the table. *What's the point of you getting in this mess*, she said, but she didn't move. We looked at each other. *He was crying*, I said. *I didn't know how to get him to stop crying. Also I accidentally said it was a miscarriage, sort of, and didn't know how to correct myself.* My girlfriend's face asked if I was joking and my face said nope, totally serious. She shook her head, and now I couldn't read her face; in a way, it was all so ridiculous and Jasmin often found absurdity hilarious. A part of me imagined she might laugh now, that we might laugh together. But she said, *So you lied to him before you told him the truth.* I said, *Not exactly.* I don't think she heard me. She said, *And that horrible place ... we lost a crucial week thanks to them, we were both so upset. How's that a joke?* I said, *We made it in time.* I tried to smile. Yes, everything could have been much worse only a day later, the second trimester cutoff, but I was trying to remind Jasmin that didn't happen. *Not the point,* she said. She looked at me and her eyes welled up; I walked into the puddle of oil and I didn't slip and I hugged her and she let me.

About a week later, Jasmin pulled me to her one morning when I was barely awake. I remember this moment well, the careful sun in the window, the lavender smell of Jasmin's skin, her eyes shining the way they did when she wanted me. But soon she froze, pulled her hand from inside me and I felt my confusion physically, acutely. *You've stopped bleeding too,* she said, and I realized she was right, I hadn't bled in maybe a few days, but her tone and her face made me want to deny it. *I hadn't noticed but yeah*, I said, *I guess you're right*, and I sounded like I was lying though why would I? *It's so weird*, Jasmin said, shaking her head gently, *I haven't bled since ... last week*. *OK*, I said. *Since he first called*, she said. *OK*, I said again. *I don't see the connection?* I said. *Yeah*, she said and rolled onto her back. We lay there like that for some moments; I was looking at her and she was looking at the ceiling. *Did he really assault you?* she asked after a while. *What?* I said. A thousand needles poked my skin. She looked at me. *I have to ask,* she said. *He did*, I said. *OK*, she said, *OK. I'm sorry.* We looked at each other and I know we both saw it, that fork in the road. One path was our future, as silly or sentimental as it might sound—I saw in that moment the future Jasmin and I could have, a future in which maybe the world was burning but we escaped all the fires together. *It wasn't the first time, though*, she said, *that night*. I felt my eyes blinking more than they should. *Right,* I said. *Right*, she said, and her voice sounded different. *You know I knew, right?* she said, *You must have known. I didn't know*, I said. She went back to looking at the ceiling. *I feel like I've known from the start and also like I haven't believed it until this moment,* she said. Then she said, *Or maybe until he called.* We kept lying there for what seemed like a couple of years. I tried to speak many times—to explain, to apologize—but whenever my breathing changed, organized itself toward speech, Jasmin said, *Don't. Please don't. Not now.* I wanted to pee, wanted to get us both some water, but I was scared to leave the bed. I was guarding us somehow, guarding her state of mind. *I've never lost it on you this whole time,* she said, *never showed you real anger. And I appreciate that,* I said, which sounded both dumb and condescending. Jasmin gave a bitter chuckle. *I'm saying ... it's a problem,* she said. I didn't know what to say. She sat up then, one sudden movement, and it made me dizzy. I sat up too. She said, *I've been talking to someone. A ... healer, sort of. A shaman, you could say, but Muslim.* I asked, *How? When?* The least relevant questions, but my brain wanted the practical details in that moment—how Jasmin could hide conversations from me in these tight quarters we shared. *Outside,* she said, and I understood this to mean when she was out there in the cold getting online, or rather sometimes when I thought that's what she was doing. *My cousin wanted someone to help me,* she said, *he worried*. I waited for more until she said, *The shaman told me to watch the blood. He said I'd stop bleeding when my soul got strong enough*. I couldn't name what it was in her words that felt ominous. *So we're stronger now*, I said, *that's good*. Jasmin looked at me. *You feel stronger?* she asked. She didn't say "strong enough to be on your own" but that's what I saw in her eyes. *I don't know*, I said, *maybe not*. She leaned over and kissed my forehead. Then she held my face. *I could kill him with my bare hands for what he did to you*, she said, *but who's going to kill you for what you did to me?* She let go of my face. I started to say those things are not the same but I stopped mid-sentence. *I can't force myself to forgive*, Jasmin said, *I think that's what my body has been showing me*. I said, *I don't see how the blood*—but Jasmin interrupted. *You keep thinking of us as one,* she said, *but we are two separate bodies*. I wanted to ask if this was more wisdom from the shaman—I couldn't bear this moment, couldn't bear my own need—but I kept my words in my mouth. *We are*, I said instead. *We are two separate bodies.*

II

In the dream I come clean and Katerin laughs. I say *I slept with someone*, or I say *I need to tell you something* and right away she knows. We jump in the ocean and swim or sometimes we're at a birthday party and she feeds me cake. It is silly to her, my confession. Katerin's mother is French—Katerin herself grew up outside Paris until age nine—and I don't think it's bad to say the French are more open as a people, sexually speaking. The two times I met Katerin's mother she touched my face in a way that felt more oomph than mother-in-law, looked me up and down, said, *Ah, Ohad*, in a way that let the sound of the *D* linger and circle, *Ohadddu*. No one had ever pronounced my name this way. So is it crazy to think the daughter of this woman might consider extramarital sex part of life? I brought it up once or twice—monogamy, fidelity—around the time we got engaged, but Katerin pretended not to hear. This is a skill she has, a necessary skill if one works at trying to save the earth; my wife never gets bogged down by the prospect of future disasters.

My own mother, who I support but don't talk to much, is Israeli, and I only mention it because so is the girl—the one who seduced me. Years ago I dealt with severe depression and while therapy never helped, I've done enough of it to know that if I had a therapist that's where he'd go: *Ah, Israeli, didn't you say your mother was Israeli?* I can see Katerin raising one eyebrow, the way her face calls bullshit. *She* seduced *you?* And I'm not an idiot, I wouldn't put it this way to my wife, but it is the truth. So what does this Israeli connection mean—that I let myself get seduced because of the girl's hard Rs, her aggressive nature, her mannerisms that felt familiar? I don't think so. I've never fetishized my mother's homeland like some Jews I know. Perhaps—and I'm not usually a spiritual person—that night was fated.

The only bad versions of my dream are the ones in which I reveal the reason for my confession, the ones in which I ask Katerin if she'd be open to us raising this child. *Ah, she is pregnant, the girl*, she says, and suddenly her eyes are vacant. Then she usually shoots me or stabs me. She still laughs first—in all the versions of this dream she laughs at the news—but sometimes the next thing she does is inflict violence on me. I look at my sternum where the bullet hit or the knife turned and I wait for the blood. There's often a pause, a moment when I wonder if I misunderstood; maybe she didn't really fire the gun, maybe the tip of the knife never broke skin, because where's the blood? And then I wake up.

Katerin gets out of bed every morning to fight what is arguably a lost cause, though you wouldn't get her to admit this truth, the inevitability of ecological collapse—not without putting some hard liquor in her. She fights with spreadsheets and slides, apps and softwares that synthesize information, an infinite number of index cards; the organization she works for coordinates the efforts of climate activists worldwide. It is offensive to my wife that people still procreate.

I've begun to work late and then later; when I get home, no matter the time, I grab my gym bag and head out. *I'm going to cancel your membership*, Katerin says one night when I get into bed in the almost-morning, *sign you up someplace that isn't open around the clock*. She smiles when she says this, pulls me to her, half asleep; the threat is my wife's way of flirting, of saying she misses me. And I want to let my muscles relax into her, I want to cancel the gym membership myself, cancel it a million times. I want to come home earlier, I want to be able to look at my wife without looking away, which is all to say I want to forget that I ever fucked up. And I know I can do that, if only I let go of this fantasy of becoming a father. Let the girl raise the child or, more likely, give it up for adoption, which is what she hinted when she told me she was pregnant. I don't judge her; she's undocumented, no money, no family here. I get the impression her family back home isn't the kind that embraces a knocked-up girl. And maybe she wouldn't want to go home anyway; I've known a lot of undocumented workers over the years, as anyone does in my field, and most of them would never leave this country. I don't judge them, either—after all, my own mother was an immigrant, my wife was an immigrant, both of them legal and lucky, but still, I have compassion for that type of hardship. Yet it's the truth: the ones who aren't so lucky, who aren't so legal, like the girl—in most cases you'd have to point a weapon to their skull to get these folks to board a plane headed the wrong way. And you could say it's a beautiful thing, that tenacity. Or you could call them all parasites. By nature, I tend to see both points of view in most situations.

For long weeks now, that's what I've been trying to do: force my brain to see the other point of view in my personal situation. It's best for everyone involved—certainly Katerin, but also the girl, maybe even the kid—that I let this go. And the girl, she's sensible. If she feels she can raise the child, I'm sure she will. If she'll need money, she'll reach out, and I'll help. For moments here and there, I think: nothing more to it. Why complicate everything? Then I imagine a tiny infant, and when I say "imagine" what I mean is that I see him, the baby, my son. He has the girl's blue eyes but the rest of his face—the forehead that takes up just a bit too much space, the strong cheekbones—looks like me, or really, like my father. Whenever I try to let this whole thing go, I see him, and my body heats up. How can I abandon my child? But I'd not only be telling my wife that I cheated; I'd be making a request that feels like a bigger betrayal than my night with the girl—which wasn't a full night, of course, barely an hour, pressed against the bar after closing, an exchange so fast and undignified it's astonishing that it managed to originate a life.

Tuesday after the gym, I hit the shower, it's probably three in the morning, and I don't hear the bathroom door open, so when Katerin moves the shower curtain to join me, I jump. *Scoot*, she says, her usually mild accent sexier, thicker, as it always is when she's not fully awake. Under the stream of water my wife looks at me, her eyes big and full of feeling—so much so that I wonder if I'd misjudged, perhaps she hadn't been asleep. *What's been going on, Ohad?* I bite my lip not to cry and she touches that lip with her thumb. *What is it?* I look at the tile, look at my wife, the tile, her face. *You'll leave me*, I say. *You slept with someone*, she says. She keeps her eyes on me; somehow she knows to expect more. And somehow when I tell her—the pregnancy, my fantasy—she seems relieved. *You are not in love with this woman?* she asks, and I make a strange sound, a hybrid of a laugh and a snort, perhaps mixed with water drops, and Katerin can see, and I can see that she sees, how little this part of the story matters. She straddles me, my wife, and again I almost cry, this time in relief, but I've never been good that way in water and eventually we move to the bedroom, both of us dripping. Katerin throws her large towel on top of the sheets, then pushes me onto the towel. It's been a while since our sex has been aggressive like that—I realize while it's happening just how polite we've been with each other's bodies lately—and it feels at once hopeful and ominous. Throughout, she avoids my mouth. I spoon her afterward, looking for the right way to ask, but no good words exist for this question, and Katerin's breathing starts to slow into sleep, so I just say it. *Are you open, then? To the baby thing?* I can feel my wife's body freeze in my arms, her breathing jolted, but she doesn't say no. She doesn't say anything. *It would be like adopting*, I say, *no human added to planet earth who wasn't coming anyway*. Katerin is still silent, and I start to say something about what it would mean to me, having a biological child, but she interrupts me. *Talk to her*, she says. *And if she agrees?* I say. I see the back of my wife's head move ever so slightly, a weak, hesitant nod.

On the phone the girl sounds like a different person from the Israeli server I remember, and this new person is pissed. It occurs to me that she might have feelings for me, that she may have been disappointed that I wasn't interested in more, which never crossed my mind before; she had a girlfriend, a Palestinian who also worked for me, and the two of them seemed in love, or at least absorbed in the kind of tension and drama most lesbians who ever worked for me seemed to favor. I assumed she flirted with me to make her girlfriend jealous, which certainly worked—the way that Palestinian used to look at me made me under-stand that sometimes "death stare" isn't a metaphor; I could see my mortality reflected in her eyes. And it was a shame, too, because she and I used to be buddies before she asked me to hire her "partner." I remember telling her not to use that word with me; *partner is the person who co-owns your business with you*, I said. *Is that who she is to you?* I could tell she wanted to punch me right then, but she was asking for a favor so what was she going to do? And there was something about this moment—I didn't tell her I was joking, that I'd meant to be playful. *It can mean romantic partner*, she said, because that's how she was— she wouldn't punch me, but she wouldn't take bullshit, either—and I said, *After twenty years maybe*. We stared at each other and she could tell what was coming. *How long you two been together?* I asked. She kept staring at me, said nothing. *You got a year?* I asked. She nodded, said, *Almost. Sure*, I said, *I'll hire your* girlfriend. I winked at her but she didn't wink back. What the hell was her name?

I recalibrate, on the phone, realizing I may have broken the girl's heart, or at least her pride. *It feels good to hear your voice*, I say. *Yeah*, she says. *Are you ... mad at me?* I ask. *How did you even find me here?* she asks in response.

She sounds truly bewildered by this, so I say *I have my ways*. I suppose she forgot she gave this relative's number to several servers at the restaurant. *How've you been feeling?* I ask her and then add, *physically*. *Not great, actually,* she says, and while I know it's common for women to feel crummy during pregnancy, there's something about the way she says it that gets my digestive tract going the wrong way, sending acid all the way up. Part of this is audible, so I say, *Excuse me*, pause for a beat to get my bearings—or perhaps it's courage I'm waiting for—and get to it, plunge into a long monologue, a speech in which I beg her to trust me with our child instead of some stranger. I don't totally know what I'm saying—she gives so little in return, it's hard to know what might be working or when to course-correct. I make promises I'm not sure I can keep—I'll buy them a house—and say she can be as involved or not as she'd wish, a prospect I have no idea if Katerin would consider reasonable or a dealbreaker. This goes on for a while, and I'm exhausted, and the sound of my own voice is unbearable, but I know, somehow I know, that what's truly unbearable is yet to come, that what's truly unbearable will enter this space the moment I finally shut up, so I don't, I keep going, keep talking, and finally she interrupts me, saying my name more than once just to stop the word flood, saying, *Ohad ohad ohad, stop. There's no baby*, she says.

What matters after that? That I think for a split second she means there was never a baby, that she lied, then realize my mistake? That after long minutes of comforting her for miscarrying, when she tells me a strange and elaborate story about her and Jasmine—that's the Palestinian's name, of course—finding themselves in a clinic that wasn't a real clinic, and that word, clinic, reverberates, I finally get what actually happened? Does that matter? For a moment I'm so hot with rage that I start to sweat—that she killed my unborn child, that she didn't think to talk to me—but my anger dies down as fast as it rose, giving room for what I truly feel, this dense dark sadness. So little matters. I say something ridiculous to the girl before we get off the phone; though she ruined everything, in this moment I feel she is the only person who shares my grief, and I tell her to let me know if she ever needs money, if she ever needs anything. And instead of thanking me she says a ridiculous thing back. *Trying to pay off your guilt?* she says. It's a crazy thing to suggest, of course—neither of us meant for her to get pregnant, and she's the one who intervened instead of letting our mistake turn into something beautiful. *My guilt?* I say, and wonder if she's faulting me for not pulling out early enough, but does it matter? *Be well*, I say.

It is absurd that my wife holds me in her arms when I hang up the phone with the girl I cheated on her with, but she does: she sees the look on my face and she comes over to the couch, sits by my side, and hugs me. *I don't deserve your sympathy*, I say into Katerin's neck, *I'm such an asshole. What does it say about me that I married an asshole?* Katerin asks.

Later I try to tell her more, though she's asked no questions. I feel the need to hear myself say the word *abortion*, relay everything I just learned, so my brain can begin to accept this new reality. My wife is on her laptop, working, but she nods at me. *I'm listening*, she says when I pause. But the only moment she really listens is when I mention that place that masqueraded as a clinic. Katerin stops typing. *It's a huge issue, these fake clinics*, she says in her activist voice. *Do you know about this? These "Crisis Pregnancy Centers" are popping up all over the place, misleading women into believing they have more time than they do to get an abortion, scaring women with false medical information* ... I tune out while Katerin goes on like that for a while, as she does about anything she deems an injustice. *They mostly go after uneducated women and women with no means—you said your friend's an immigrant?* My *friend*. I'm not sure how to respond to this question. *Well, in this case nothing happened*, I say. *They figured it out, she and her girlfriend, and they left. Caused a scene on their way out from what I understand*. I know I'm being foolish but it feels like Katerin is taking their side over mine. *Good for them*, she says. *Good for them for not letting those assholes get away with their bullshit*.

In bed that night I kiss my wife's shoulder, let my hand slide down. Her ass is cold though the room is warm. *I just started bleeding*, Katerin says, as if we haven't fucked a million times before when she was on her period. I pull my hand out of her underwear. *I love you*, I say.

When I wake up in the morning everything is foggy and my temples are throbbing. I recognize the sensations right away though I haven't felt them in years. There's no getting out of this bed. My first thought is that Katerin has never seen me like that; hearing about depression and seeing someone in this state are two very different things. I send some emails and make a few calls while my voice is recognizable—my chef, a bartender I've been meaning to make my AGM for a while now, my former office manager who could take over payroll for a stretch as a favor.

For days, there's a fresh cup of tea by my bed whenever I open my eyes, sometimes a tray of food, and occasionally Katerin herself, looking at me with what seems a mix of pity and rage. *I'm not dying*, I tell her. *Could have fooled me*, she says. *I'll be OK*, I tell her another time, *it'll pass*. I pull the blanket and it hits the mug by my side; the sound of it breaking is ten times louder in my head than it probably is outside of it. *Sorry*, I mutter, and Katerin picks up the big pieces with her hands, places them back on my nightstand. I want to tell her she shouldn't do that, she could cut herself, but instead I close my eyes. *What are you taking*, she asks, *that you can sleep this much?* When I don't answer, she says, *Don't give into this, Ohad. I know what I can handle in life*, I tell my wife, *and I know what I can't handle*. It's a nonanswer meant to convey that she should let me weather this the only way I know how, but that's not what she hears. I see her chest rise, then fall. *And not getting to be a dad, that's more than you can handle in this life*, she says, *that's what you're saying*. My brain is the weight of my whole body and Katerin's voice is muffled.

I manage to say, *That's not what I said*, and I can't tell if I'm lying. I also can't tell what my wife is thinking, where the conversation is going. She nods a few times, keeps nodding, seems in conversation with herself; it's dizzying and I have to look away. *You're suffering*, my wife says. I look at her again now and her eyes are wet. She leans over, kisses my cheek. *I don't want you to suffer*, she says, *no, of course I don't want you to suffer*. I squint, a habitual response to confusion, but it hurts now. *What are you saying?* I ask my wife. If I didn't know better, I'd think she's hinting she might change her mind about children. *I'm saying we have some work to do as a couple*, she says, *and maybe we need some help*. I wait for more because I can see there is more. *I want to make this marriage work*, Katerin says, *and clearly that would require compromise from both of us. Some adjustments. Of expectations.* I stare at her. *That's all I've got*, she says. *But are you saying*, I start to ask, and she puts a finger to my mouth. Her finger smells nice, a mix of her aloe body lotion and some fruit she must have just sliced—a pear, I think. My mouth, on the other hand, probably smells like death; it tastes like cement. But still I open it to suck on her finger, a fast movement that surprises her and surprises me too. Perhaps something is shifting in me. I let go of my wife's finger. *How did I get so lucky?* I ask her. She shakes her head. *I'm not making any assumptions*, I say, *I'm really not, I get it. But I'm the luckiest guy, that's all.* My wife smiles at me, but her smile seems a bit sad, or maybe I'm imagining. *Yeah,* she says. *Some people are born lucky.*

III

I'm bad at quoting scripture like I am bad at quoting anything, because the letters dance for me when I most need them to be still. Marjorie tells me to memorize, tells me not reading well is no excuse, she's not very good at reading either, she says, but she doesn't let it get in the way of the Work, does she? All due respect to Marjorie, I don't think I let anything get in the way of anything else; there is more than one and also more than two ways of doing our Work. Also Marjorie is lying: she has a master's degree. She got this master's degree by being bad at reading? I don't think so. But I don't say any of this to Marjorie, because she runs the Center and I'm just a volunteer. I am part of a program where if I'm good at my job, I'm supposed to get hired in the end, but how do you prove you're good at your job if your Center manager says otherwise? Also, there's no point in arguing. I know the Bible says not to argue for nothing; I don't need to quote anything to know what's right. So instead of talking back I make my voice small and say to Marjorie, *Unfortunately my brain won't do that either,* meaning memorize. Maybe it's not that I make my voice small so much as it is my voice making itself small. This is a thing that happens in my throat sometimes. It's pitiful but also effective; Marjorie feels bad for me when I get like that, says, *It's OK, just find other ways to Connect.* Connecting is our goal: when you Connect, you just see in the eyes of the woman that the baby will be safe. Quoting scripture is just one way we're taught to Connect, and of course it's only effective with women of faith, but the thing about people like Marjorie is that they imagine faith in every pair of eyes. Marjorie grew up in the South, where, from what I understand, most people hold the Lord in their heart, and she only moved here when the Center opened last summer, so in my opinion she just doesn't get it: majority of women around here, you quote scripture to them, they sprint for the door. Or they stare at you and *Is this a real clinic?* is suddenly all over their face, and you better say something quick before they ask a question that's tricky to answer. It's all so delicate. If they ask, I never say yes, because that would be illegal and here at the Center, we never break the law; I just nod and say, "You're in the right place, honey," or I say, "You are exactly where you should be."

Marjorie and I have had a version of our exchange more times than I can count; the problem is that I don't Connect to enough women, and ironically, this is because I *do* connect—I listen to their stories and I feel their pain and sometimes I forget the protocols. I just tell them I can see their heart is good, that I know they'll make the right decision. By right decision of course I mean keep the baby, but how would they know what I mean is Marjorie's point, are they mind readers? If a woman leaves without signing her Pregnancy Verification Form and without making a future appointment with us, then we have failed to Connect. Today's talking-to starts the same as always, but then it turns, or maybe it's different all along and it just takes me a moment to notice. Marjorie says the same things, I say the same things, but when my voice gets small she doesn't tell me to try better next time; instead, she gives me a look that I would describe as hard. A hard look. We're at the staff kitchenette, which is such a narrow space that we're forced to stand closer than we otherwise would, so Marjorie might as well be holding a magnifying glass; there's no way I'd be able to hide the emotion I feel in my stomach once it makes its way to my face. I nod at her, maybe too many times, mumble, *Got it, no problem*, and sneak out, beeline to the bathroom so I can let the tears out. *Stop by my office at the end of your shift*, Marjorie says to my back.

Whatever our disagreements, until today I always felt like Marjorie rooted for me to improve. I told her more than once she reminds me of my sister Alice—Alice who I call my older sister when talking to other people because blood shouldn't dictate who you call family, Alice who's often so hard on me that it can seem cruel. But it's a compliment to Marjorie when I say this, because I know, have always known with Alice, that everything she does and says to me comes from love. I moved in with Alice to save money when I joined the volunteer program and overall I would say it was a very good decision. But more often than not I come home to Alice telling me I didn't do this or that: if I cleaned the dishes good enough, I forgot to pick up radishes at the store like she asked, or maybe I made fish for dinner and how could I forget she's allergic? She's right most the time—my mind just isn't home these days. The thing about the Center is you never really finish a shift; the shift finishes you. It stays with you. The women that seek our help—and the men that sometimes accompany them, the occasional children, those sweet innocent faces—how can those interactions just ... evaporate? How can anyone hold all this pain and helplessness and then let it all go when they exit the Center's front door? Not dream about it at night? I guess some people pull that off, all in a day's work, and if you ask Marjorie, they have it right, they will last longer. The head-shakers—whatever a woman shares with them, they shake their head, say *that's too bad*—the ones always calling the women "lost sheep" and "misguided souls," especially the women that don't Connect. I shouldn't speak ill; everyone at the Center means to offer solace. But let's just say it's not been easy to make friends. And the person waiting for me when I come out of the bathroom, she's one of the headshakers, one of many Advocates and Counselors who I know roll their eyes behind my back. I take too much time with each case, lose too many, a sappy, not-too-bright volunteer. And coming out of the bathroom with a wet face plays right into that story; I'd have taken better care at the sink if I anticipated this moment. *Hey*, Talma says, *I saw you talked to Marjorie?* If she saw, why is she here asking me about it, I think but don't say. Instead I nod. We start walking the long corridor that leads to the exam rooms but Talma is being very slow. *What did you tell her?* she asks, and I search her face for the parts I must be missing, because why on earth is it Talma's business? *It's my neck on the line here as much as yours*, she says, and I say, *Talma, I have no clue what you're talking about*, and she says, *So she hasn't told you? I'm so confused. I'm confused too*, I say, and for a moment we stop our slow walk and stare at each other. *You remember those women that attacked me*, she says and looks in the general direction of the waiting area where one day earlier this winter a woman—Iranian, I think she was— pushed Talma away from her pregnant friend. Talma's elbow somehow landed on a window and broke it, though I believed the rumor that Talma elbowed that window, a way to make herself the aggrieved party in the incident. For days later she cared for her bloody wound in common areas so we'd all see. I was right there—Talma and I were both assigned the case—but as Alice would say, I always miss the most important parts. I must have been talking to the pregnant woman, because I knew we were about to lose her and I did my best to Connect in the last moment or two. *I can tell you're very strong*, I told her, *your strength will see you through this challenge, you'd make a wonderful mother*. Then we both jumped at the sound of glass breaking and someone, maybe Talma, shrieking. *I remember*, I tell Talma. *Well, they're threatening to sue. And you know how Marjorie resolves these situations*. I didn't know, but I could guess; legal challenges are bad for the Center, so of course Marjorie would try to appease anyone who had an issue. *We're both done if you ask me*, Talma says. *But you're the one who had the conflict*, I say. *We both had a conflict*, Talma says slowly, *and we were both assigned the case, together. OK*, I say. We're standing by exam room one now, a closed door. *Well, that's the answer to my question*, Talma says, and I say, *You haven't asked me anything.* She says, *Clearly you don't have my back.* I think for a moment. *If I say that escalation was both our fault, then we're both fired. How would that help you?* I ask. *For you this isn't an actual job*, she says. *And even if it was, you don't have kids at home that depend on your salary. But you do whatever you think is right.*

I can't concentrate on much after that, and waiting till the end of my shift seems unbearable. I walk over to

Marjorie's office and tap my fingers on her half-open door.
She looks up from her desk, seems surprised to see me. I
suppose I've never stopped by her office spontaneously
before. Or maybe she sees something in my face that surprises her; maybe I still look like someone who just wept
quietly in a stall. *Talma talked to you*, she says, and now
I'm the one surprised. Marjorie points at one of the chairs
across from her and I come in, close the door, sit down.
Look, she says, *I'm no dummy, I know your ways and
I know Talma's and there's no way that incident was your
fault.* My body should relax to hear this, but it doesn't;
my muscles are a knot and my breath still shallow. *But you
understand, don't you?* Marjorie asks. I give a faint nod,
though I don't really know what I just claimed to understand. *I can't afford to lose Talma; she's very experienced,
very skilled. And to this woman—it's not like she knows
who's who. I tell her the worker on the case has been fired
for cause, she goes away. Or at least that's my hope.* I stare
at a plant behind Marjorie. It looks thirsty, unhealthy. I
try to think fast. *If she doesn't know*, I say, *can't you just
... tell her you fired me?* Marjorie chuckles. *I know the
type, believe me—she's trouble, if I lied to her it would
backfire. And thou shalt not bear false witness*, she adds

quickly. Something isn't adding up in my brain, but I'm not sure how to ask if illegal immigrants can sue. *The Iranian woman*, I say, *is trouble? Or the Jewish one?* Marjorie seems confused. *You must be thinking of a different escalation*, she says. *This woman is just a little bit French. No no*, I say, *I have the right incident—when Talma broke the window. It was two friends, one of them Arab and I think the pregnant one a Jew, illegals. Not French.* I can tell Marjorie is losing patience with me. *Look*, she says, *the details don't really matter, OK? I looked up the name she gave me, and we have a case number for it and an escalation note, so this isn't a mix-up. And I think you know I wouldn't do this if I didn't have to, right? But we can't afford a lawsuit or bad publicity. This woman just won some big case against several* states, *something about deforestation. Trust me, anyone who uses words like* deforestation *is bad news.* Marjorie chuckles at this but it sounds forced. When I don't chuckle back, she says, *If I didn't know the difference between a nothing call and the kind of person who's out for blood I wouldn't be running the Center.* She looks at me and I can tell she's sorry. *Think of it as saving the Center!* she says, her voice an octave too high for the circumstances. I nod. *I'm truly not sure this would even work,* she says. *The incident might only be an excuse for her to sue, try to get us on something.* This only makes me feel worse, that maybe she's letting me go for nothing. *Could I come back if that happened?* I ask, and Marjorie looks at me like she does whenever my voice gets small, though my throat isn't doing anything weird. She smiles. *Let's pray,* she says, *for the good of the Center, that this problem goes away.* I want to ask her if it's because I don't quote scripture, because I don't Connect enough—I want to know if this would still happen if I was better at my job—but Marjorie seems ready to end our meeting. She smiles at me again. She says, *This is unfortunate.* Something about her smile, something about that word, *unfortunate,* makes me want to scream, and for a quick moment I think I might. I'd use bad language, say this is bullshit, tell Marjorie she's talking like this is out of her hands, some unavoidable evil, what a freaking joke. She's *choosing* to ruin my life, and just as easily she could make a different choice. But I look at Marjorie's eyes, and there is nothing there for me, and I know the Bible says to refrain from anger, so I refrain. *Yes,* I say. *It's unfortunate. Very unfortunate.* I keep sitting there, though I know Marjorie wants me to leave. Perhaps eventually I'd be forced to leave. But for now, I avoid

Marjorie's eyes, relax my muscles, and stay in the chair. My body is grounded. My spirit is calm. And in this moment it turns out that I can quote after all. I hear myself say to Marjorie, *The Lord will fight for you. You have only to be silent.* Marjorie smiles at me but she seems concerned. It's clear that she's not listening properly, or mishearing my intention, so I repeat. My voice is quiet but steady, a confident whisper. *You have only to be silent.*

ABOUT THE BRIGID ALLIANCE
BY CAROL DAVIS

A COUPLE OF YEARS ago I had the crazy idea to ask Amanda Uhle if McSweeney's would consider putting together an anthology about reproductive freedom. As a cofounder of The Brigid Alliance, a nonprofit travel service for abortion seekers, I have long known about the alarming divide between the constitutional right to have an abortion and the ability to access one. Abortion access was something my generation held as sacrosanct in the years after *Roe v. Wade* became part of the collective psyche. Before *Roe*, I knew of several young women who had to resort to unsafe, secretive, and humiliating measures to have abortions. The women I knew carried deep emotional scars, and I still hold the memory of their stories in mind, which is one of the central forces behind this anthology. As you have no doubt felt in the stories you've just read, the power of narrative is profound.

There was a time when I believed the stories about abortion access had been relegated to the past. I was dead wrong. Abortion remains limited or simply unavailable in many parts of the country. Clinics are forced to operate under restrictive and often arbitrary law or forced to close because they cannot afford to meet the same medical standards mandated for hospitals. The remaining operational clinics are often several states away, forcing many individuals to seek care far from home, *if* they are able to afford the cost of travel. And that is often a big *if.* Despite the fact that abortion is still legal in all fifty states, misinformation campaigns and restrictive state laws work to diminish hard-won protections. Women and girls as young as ten years old are forced to travel hundreds of miles to access care or are forced to have a child. The heavy burden, both financial and emotional, often falls upon those already living below the poverty line, and who already struggle to maintain healthy, dignified, and productive lives for themselves and their families. These restrictions serve no one, but rather collude with existing structures of injustice and fuel a furious acceleration to what the U.N. Human Rights Council considers a severe human rights crisis.

The Brigid Alliance grew out of sleepless, adrenalin-addled nights, where the only antidote to the political shambles wrought by a morally vacant administration was to imagine a way forward, to imagine a country that normalized abortion as medical care and offered protections for everyone who needed them. Until that time, The Brigid Alliance would offer those protections. Since August 2018, The Brigid Alliance has arranged and paid for travel support for nearly 2,200 women and girls. Support begins with the first telephone conversation and continues throughout the journey, until the client returns home safely. Our intake coordinators speak to each client with patience, thoughtfulness, and compassion, arranging every detail, whether straightforward or complex. We customize each itinerary to meet the individual needs of the traveler: round-trip airfare, train or bus tickets, a hotel room, childcare, cash for meals, taxis, or a new set of tires for a client's car. The guiding light is our pledge to close the gap to access. In this way, The Brigid Alliance makes choice possible.

While the new administration offers some hope for reproductive freedom, it cannot undo the years of legislation—driven by anti-choice and right-wing fundamentalists, who have worked steadily to enshrine systemic misogyny, racism, and bigotry—which forms the basis of most anti-abortion regulation. And as legal cases work their way through to the Supreme Court, the ultra-conservative majority of justices will no doubt overturn *Roe v. Wade*, or render it meaningless. This past year, as communities around the country were swept under by COVID-19, these hardened biases were especially heinous, as some state representatives used the pandemic to restrict abortion access even further.

My hope is that the narratives in this beautifully orchestrated anthology will open our minds and our hearts, to continue a dialogue about the realities and experiences of abortion access. The collective voice herein speaks to our shared humanity; the power of narrative has the power to unite. Until the political and social systems reflect the same humanity and respect for all lives, The Brigid Alliance will work to mitigate the obstacles to abortion access.

SHELLY ORIA is the author of *New York 1, Tel Aviv 0* (FSG, 2014) and the editor of *Indelible in the Hippocampus: Writings from the Me Too Movement* (McSweeney's, 2019). In 2017, *CLEAN*, a digital novella Oria was commissioned by McSweeney's and WeTransfer to coauthor, received two Lovie Awards from the International Academy of Digital Arts and Sciences. Oria's fiction has appeared in the *Paris Review* and on *Selected Shorts* at Symphony Space, received a number of awards, and been translated into several languages. Oria lives in Brooklyn, New York, where she has a private practice as a life and creativity coach. Her website is www.shellyoria.com.

KRISTEN ARNETT is a queer Florida writer. Her recent novels include *With Teeth*, published by Riverhead Books in June 2021, and *Mostly Dead Things* (Tin House Books, 2019), which was a *New York Times* bestseller and a finalist for the Lambda Literary Award in Lesbian Fiction.

HANNAH LILLITH ASSADI teaches fiction at the Columbia University School of the Arts. Her first novel, *Sonora*

(Soho Press, 2017), received a Rosenthal Family Foundation Award in Literature from the American Academy of Arts and Letters and was a finalist for the PEN / Robert W. Bingham Prize for Debut Fiction. In 2018, she was named a National Book Foundation 5 Under 35 honoree. Her second novel, *The Stars Are Not Yet Bells*, is forthcoming from Riverhead. She lives with her family in Brooklyn, New York.

CARRIE BORNSTEIN lives in Sharon, Massachusetts, with her husband, Jamie, and their three children, three chickens, two guinea pigs, and one dog. In 2017 she served as a gestational carrier for a couple overseas and blogged about her journey at theresnoiinuterus.wordpress.com. She is currently the CEO of Mayyim Hayyim Living Waters Community Mikveh and Education Center, a twenty-first-century creation, rooted in ancient tradition and reinvented to serve the Jewish community of today.

AMA CODJOE is the author of *Bluest Nude*, forthcoming from Milkweed Editions in fall 2022, and *Blood of the Air* (Northwestern University Press, 2020), winner of the Drinking Gourd Chapbook Poetry Prize. Among other honors, Codjoe has received fellowships from Cave Canem Foundation, the National Endowment for the Arts, the New York State Council on the Arts / New York Foundation for the Arts, and the Jerome Foundation.

DESIREE COOPER is a former attorney, Pulitzer Prize–nominated journalist, and 2015 Kresge Artist Fellow. The former communications director for Planned Parenthood of Michigan won the 2014 N.O.W. Harriet Tubman Community Service Award. In 2018, she released a short film, *The Choice*, which has medaled in film festivals from Berlin to California. The author of the award-winning collection of flash fiction, *Know the Mother* (Wayne State University Press, 2016), she is also a contributor to the seminal anthology *Choice Words: Writers on Abortion* (Haymarket Books, 2020).

GEORGINA ESCOBAR is a queer Mexican playwright and maker of sci-femme narratives, ultra-humanistic mythos, and *frontera*-funk stories. A MacDowell Fellow, Djerassi Resident Artist, and recipient of the Kennedy Center Darrell Ayers Playwriting Award, her work has made the Kilroys List, National Music Theater Conference (Eugene

O'Neill Theater Center), The Mix, and 50PP and been seen or workshopped at INTAR, Clubbed Thumb, Lincoln Center, Milagro, Aurora Theatre, Bushwick Starr, and Two Rivers, among others.

ALISON ESPACH is the author of the novels *The Adults* (Scribner, 2011)—a *New York Times'* Editor's Choice, and a Barnes and Noble Discover Pick of the Month—and *Notes on Your Sudden Disappearance*, forthcoming from Henry Holt & Company in 2022. Her short story series *In-Depth Market Research Interviews with Dead People* is an Audible Original, and her other work has appeared in *McSweeney's*, *Vogue*, *Joyland*, *Salon*, and other places. Currently, she teaches creative writing at Providence College in Rhode Island.

SARAH GERARD is the author of the essay collection *Sunshine State* (Harper Perennial, 2017) and the novels *Binary Star* (Two Dollar Radio, 2015) and *True Love* (Harper, 2021). She lives in Denver, Colorado, with her partner, the writer Patrick Cottrell. Her website is sarah-gerard.com.

DONNETTA LAVINIA GRAYS is a Brooklyn-based playwright-actor from Columbia, South Carolina. Her plays include *Where We Stand* (Lucille Lortel, The Drama League, and AUDELCO Award Nominee), *Last Night and the Night Before*, *Laid to Rest*, and *The Review or How to Eat Your Opposition*. She has received the Whiting Award in Drama, Helen Merrill Playwright Award, NTC's Barrie and Bernice Stavis Playwright Award, Lilly Award, and Todd McNerney National Playwriting Award and is the inaugural recipient of the Doric Wilson Independent Playwright Award.

RACHEL ELIZA GRIFFITHS is a poet, photographer, and novelist. Her hybrid collection of poetry and photography, *Seeing the Body* (W. W. Norton, 2020), was selected as the winner of the 2021 Paterson Poetry Prize. Griffiths's visual and literary work has appeared widely, including in the *New Yorker*, the *Paris Review*, the *New York Times*, and *Guernica*. She is the recipient of fellowships, including from Cave Canem, the Robert Rauschenberg Foundation, and Yaddo. She lives in New York City.

R.O. KWON's nationally bestselling first novel, *The Incendiaries*, is published by Riverhead, and it is being translated into seven languages. Named a best book of the year by over forty publications, *The Incendiaries* received the Housatonic Book Award and was a finalist or nominated for seven other prizes, including the National Book Critics Circle First Book Award. Kwon and Garth Greenwell co-edited the nationally bestselling *Kink*, an anthology published by Simon & Schuster.

DEBORAH LANDAU is the author of four books of poetry: *Soft Targets* (winner of The Believer Book Award), *The Uses of the Body*, *The Last Usable Hour*, and *Orchidelirium*, which won the Robert Dana Anhinga Prize for Poetry. Her poems have appeared recently in the *New Yorker*, the *Paris Review*, *Poetry*, *American Poetry Review*, the *New York Times*, and *The Best American Poetry*, and she was a 2016 Guggenheim Fellow. She is a professor and director of the Creative Writing Program at New York University and lives in Brooklyn with her family.

CADE LEEBRON is a disabled writer. Her work has appeared in the *New York Times*, *Electric Literature*, and elsewhere. She exists online at www.mslifeisbestlife.com and on Twitter @CadeyLadey.

RIVA LEHRER is an artist, writer, and curator who focuses on the socially challenged body. She is best known for representations of people whose physical embodiment, sexuality, or gender identity have long been stigmatized. Lehrer's memoir, *Golem Girl*, was published by the One World imprint of Penguin Random House in 2020, won the 2020 Barbellion Prize for Literature, was a finalist for the National Book Critics Circle Award, and was shortlisted for the Chicago Review of Books 2020 Award.

SALLY WEN MAO is the author of two collections of poetry, *Oculus* (Graywolf Press, 2019), a finalist for the Los Angeles Times Book Prize, and *Mad Honey Symposium* (Alice James Books, 2014). The recipient of a Pushcart Prize and a National Endowment for the Arts grant, she was recently a Cullman Fellow at the New York Public Library, a Jenny McKean Moore Writer-in-Washington at the George Washington University, and a Shearing Fellow at the Black Mountain Institute. Her poetry and prose have appeared in *The Best American Poetry*, the *Paris Review*, *Tin House*, *Poetry*, *Harper's Bazaar*, the *Kenyon Review*, the *Georgia Review*, *Guernica*, and *A*

Public Space, among others. She is a Kundiman Fellow in fiction and poetry.

KATE NOVOTNY has served birthing people as a birth doula since 2004 and as a perinatal nurse since 2007. She has cared for birthing families across the United States and in Central America. She is passionate about confronting trauma in birthing families and their caregivers. She has hosted the Taproot Doula Project since 2013, to dispel stigmas around our birthing bodies and amplify the need for funding of Black and Indigenous birth workers, as they reclaim ancestral birth wisdom.

TOMMY ORANGE's debut novel, *There There*, was a *New York Times* bestseller, won the 2018 PEN America Hemingway Award, and was a finalist for the Pulitzer Prize in fiction. Orange is an enrolled member of the Cheyenne and Arapaho Tribes of Oklahoma. He was born and raised in Oakland, California.

KHADIJAH QUEEN, PhD, is the author of six books, including *I'm So Fine: A List of Famous Men & What I Had On* (YesYes Books, 2017), praised in *O Magazine*, the *New*

Yorker, *Rain Taxi*, the *Los Angeles Review*, and elsewhere as "quietly devastating" and "a portrait of defiance that turns the male gaze inside out." She teaches creative writing at Virginia Tech.

ONNESHA ROYCHOUDHURI is a writer, storyteller, and educator. Her work has appeared in outlets such as *Rolling Stone*, *This American Life*, the *Kenyon Review*, *n+1*, *Virginia Quarterly Review*, the *Boston Review*, the *Nation*, *Salon*, and *Mother Jones*. She is the author of *The Marginalized Majority: Claiming Our Power in a Post-Truth America*, named one of the best books of 2018 by *Kirkus Reviews*.

SAÏD SAYRAFIEZADEH is the author, most recently, of the story collection *American Estrangement* as well as the memoir *When Skateboards Will Be Free* and the story collection *Brief Encounters with the Enemy*. His work has appeared in the *New Yorker*, the *Paris Review*, *Granta*, and *The Best American Short Stories*. He is the recipient of a Whiting Writers' Award for nonfiction and a Cullman Center for Scholars and Writers' fiction fellowship. He teaches creative writing at New York University and Hunter College.

YAEL R. SHINAR is a physician and poet.

KIM GEK LIN SHORT is the author of the lyric novels *The Bugging Watch & Other Exhibits* and *China Cowboy*, both from Tarpaulin Sky Press. Her story in prose poems "Run (Rope-a-Dope)" was exhibited at the Magic Child Repository at Gallery Z, and her chapbook *The Residents* was published by Chicago's Dancing Girl Press. Her work appears in anthologies such as *Electric Gurlesque, The &NOW Awards, Forgotten Philadelphia,* and *Narrative (Dis)Continuities* and in literary magazines such as the *American Poetry Review, Fence,* and *PEN America.*

KATE TARKER is an American playwright and artist who grew up in Germany. Plays include *THUNDERBODIES* (Soho Rep.), *Dionysus Was Such a Nice Man* (The Wilma, FoolsFURY), and *Laura and the Sea* (Rivendell Theatre Ensemble). She is the recipient of a Jerome Fellowship, The Vineyard's Paula Vogel Playwriting Award, and Theater Masters' Visionary Playwright Award. Kate holds commissions from Soho Rep. and Playwrights Horizons and has been published in the *Paris Review.* She holds an MFA from Yale.

DEB OLIN UNFERTH is the author of six books, most recently, the novel *Barn 8*.

KIRSTIN VALDEZ QUADE is the author of *The Five Wounds* and *Night at the Fiestas*, winner of the National Book Critics Circle's John Leonard Prize. She has received a 5 Under 35 award from the National Book Foundation, a Rome Prize, a Stegner Fellowship, and the Rona Jaffe Foundation Writers' Award. Her work has appeared in the *New Yorker*, the *New York Times*, *The Best American Short Stories*, *The O. Henry Prize Stories*, and elsewhere. She teaches at Princeton University.

ERIN WILLIAMS is a comics artist interested in graphic medicine and social justice. She is the author of *Commute: An Illustrated Memoir of Female Shame* and the illustrator of the *Big Activity Book* series. She has ten-plus years' experience in data analysis and scientific research. Her work has been featured in *MoMA Magazine*, the *Believer*, *Salon*, *BuzzFeed*, and several academic journals. She lives in New York with her family

TIPHANIE YANIQUE is a novelist, poet, essayist, and short

story writer. Her writing has won the Bocas Award for Caribbean Fiction, the Boston Review Prize in Fiction, a Rona Jaffe Foundation Writers' Award, a Pushcart Prize, a Fulbright Scholarship, and an Academy of American Poets Prize. She has been listed by the *Boston Globe* as one of the sixteen cultural figures to watch out for, and her writing has been published in the *New York Times*, *Best African American Fiction (Bantam, 2009)*, the *Wall Street Journal*, *American Short Fiction*, and other places. She lives in Atlanta and is a professor at Emory University.

TO ANYONE WHO'S EVER fought for reproductive rights and justice—in the courts, in the streets, in clinics and hospitals, in public and in private, where activism can at times be most bruising: I am grateful for your courage. This book is for you.

RBG, I imagine that even in the afterlife your schedule is jam-packed, so you might not get a chance to read this book; please know it was compiled with eternal gratitude to you and for you.

Thank you, Carol Davis, for imagining this anthology into being. And thank you for the work that you do every day. A simple statement of fact: this world is a better place thanks to you and everyone else at the Brigid Alliance.

Amanda Uhle, on my last count you were doing the work of eighty-seven people and managing to be in 3.5 places on average in any given moment. Working as closely with you as I have these past couple of years, I assumed I'd uncover the secret to your superhuman juggling, but the more I see, the more perplexed I feel. Thank you for always being so present, for supporting every idea I've had along the way, and for being the absolute best person to work with.

Amy Sumerton, I must have done something right in another life and working with you on this book has been my reward. There's no other explanation I can think of. Thank you.

To all the contributors: thank you for your unrelenting honesty, thank you for the rewrites and the heart you put into them, thank you for trusting me with your stories.

There are spaces in this world that attract and create magic, and McSweeney's is one such space. Sunra Thompson, thank you for your artistry and for caring as much as you do. Dan Weiss, a man who knows every bookseller on planet Earth, thank you for your expertise and for your kindness. Raj Tawney, thank you for your faith in this book and for being someone who always says yes. Kitania Folk, once upon a time I felt so overwhelmed by this project that I almost cried, and you put everything into a color-coded spreadsheet that had a thousand tabs and still somehow seemed friendly, and just like that, I could breathe again. You are missed. I'm equally indebted to Eric Cromie, Claire Boyle, Alvaro Villanueva, Conor O'Brien (who spots every errant comma), and to every single person at McSweeney's.

Chesley Hicks, it is a lucky manuscript that gets to be scanned by your keen eye. Thank you.

Diana Spechler, thank you for the title of this book (and for the title of the previous book) (and for so much else).

Elizabeth Reichert: it is one of the worst versions of me, the one you deal with. "We Bled All Winter," perhaps more than anything I've ever written, would not have come into this world (and certainly not in time) without your steady hand, your steady heart. Thank you always and forever.

For research guidance and resources, my thanks to the good people at the Center for Reproductive Rights. Additional thanks to *Reproductive Justice: An Introduction* by Loretta J. Ross and Rickie Solinger. And for help with my research for "We Bled All Winter," many thanks to Ricky J. Duarte, Jessica Burch Rothacker, and Jordan A. Rothacker.

Working on a project of this nature, and during a global plague at that, has been *an experience*. Thank you for holding it all with me: Courtney Zoffness, Galit Lotan, Maya Michaeli, Diana Spechler, Kerry Carnahan, Georgia Wall, Alison Espach, Michal Engelberg (I should write your name three times), Jill Jarvis, Tali Herskowitz,

Robert Lopez, and Sally Franson. Much love and gratitude also to all Orias and Friedmans in California and to Hossannah Asuncion, Nelly Reifler, Julie Stevenson, Lynn Melnick, T Kira Madden, Annie Levy, Tamar Feldman, Quito Ziegler, Karen Kubey, Abigail Ulman, Lucy Ives, Gretchen Jones, Karissa Chen, Agnes Borinsky, and the one-and-only Emily Bell. Special thanks to Noah for that rare and exacting type of support, special thanks to Justine for everything that you are.

PJ Mark, thank you for your generosity, thank you for that one call in particular when I was freaking out, thank you for always knowing all the things. I'm especially grateful to you—and to Ian Bonaparte, Paul Lucas, and others at Janklow & Nesbit—for helping me with initial outreach. Special thanks to Lizz Winstead for invaluable early feedback.

Leni Zumas, Peter Ho Davies, Lauren Groff, Nick Flynn, Ottessa Moshfegh, Elif Batuman, Dana Spiotta, Victor LaValle, Marisa Siegel, Raluca Albu: the support you offered this book has meant more to me than you know. Thank you.

People all over the world—quite literally—have shown me and this project incredible generosity by helping me find writers and translators in more than fifteen countries for the online international supplement to this book. *I Know What's Best For You All Over the World* will launch on the McSweeney's website in April 2022 thanks to Mikkel Rosengaard, Danai Sioziou, Birna Anna Bjornsdottir, Nana Nkweti, Dzekashu MacViban, Jolanta Rozylo, Ronnie Beck, Zeela Kotler Hadari, Yochai Maital, Asaad Zoabi, Rasha Khayat, Erin Williams, Rachel Eliza Griffiths, Marcela Lanius, Jeremy Tiang, and Brian Zittel.

For ten weeks during the scary and difficult 2020, I got to work on this book from an apartment in Tel Aviv that overlooked the sea, a place where from the balcony you could smell the salt. My deepest thanks to the Glasenberg family for that generosity. And much gratitude to Art Omi for putting together a Covid-safe residency in those pre-vaccine days—no small logistical feat—and for inviting me.

To my parents and my sister, the three pillars of any strength and courage I possess, thank you for your fierceness and thank you for your love.

Your purchase of this book entitles you to the supplement, *I Know What's Best For You All Over the World*, for free. To check out stories, essays, poems, photographs, and more, created by writers and artists from around the globe exploring aspects of reproductive freedom in their locale, visit *mcsweeneys.net/iknow* and enter the code IKNOW to download the ebook.